Linguistics at Work
A Reader of Applications

Dallin D. Oaks

Linguistics at Work
A Reader of Applications

Dallin D. Oaks
Brigham Young University

HEINLE & HEINLE

TM

THOMSON LEARNING

For more information, contact Heinle & Heinle Publishers Cambridge, MA 02142, or electronically at
http://www.thomson.com

Thomson Learning Europe
Berkshire House 168-173
High Holborn
London, WC1V 7AA, England

Thomson Learning Editores
Campos Eliseos 385, Piso 7
Col. Polanco
11560 México D.F. México

Thomas Nelson Australia
102 Dodds Street
South Melbourne 3205
Victoria, Australia

Thomson Learning Asia
221 Henderson Road
#05-10 Henderson Building
Singapore 0315

Nelson Canada
1120 Birchmount Road
Scarborough, Ontario
Canada M1K 5G4

Thomson Learning Japan
Hirakawacho Kyowa Building, 3F
2-2-1 Hirakawacho
Chiyoda-ku, Tokyo 102, Japan

Thomson Learning GmbH
Königswinterer Strasse 418
53227 Bonn, Germany

Thomson Learning Southern Africa
Building 18, Constantia Park
240 Old Pretoria Road
Halfway House, 1685 South Africa

ISBN 0-155-03532-0

The Adaptable Courseware Program consists of products and additions to existing Heinle & Heinle
Publishing Company products that are produced from camera-ready copy. Peer review, class testing, and
accuracy are primarily the responsibility of the author(s).

Preface

One of the most frequently asked questions in the introductory linguistics classroom is what someone might do with linguistic information and theory. This book is designed to illustrate the broad use and application of linguistic knowledge in a variety of fields. *Linguistics at Work* reinforces linguistic concepts that students learn in an introductory linguistics course from a new angle, showing applications of linguistics that students might not otherwise consider.

This linguistics reader is different from other readers currently available both in its conception and its scope. While some current anthologies provide further readings on linguistic theory, they are not designed to show a broad spectrum of application. This limitation also occurs in language-based readers for composition courses that focus on general language issues such as language prejudice or semantic connotation. In contrast, *Linguistics at Work* presents readings that demonstrate the significance of a range of linguistic applications and provide an interesting, varied, and valuable resource for an introductory linguistics or language course.

The title of this reader refers to "applications" of linguistics rather than "applied" linguistics. This usage is quite deliberate. The purpose of this reader could be misunderstood if the term "applied linguistics" were used because often the term "applied linguistics" is a synonym for teaching English as a second language or for foreign language instruction. This reader is intended to include many more uses than those involved in the pedagogy of language; for example, it shows how people use linguistic knowledge and expertise in such areas as law (serving as expert witnesses or consultants in court cases), in the film industry (creating an artificial but realistic language for a major motion picture), or in business (analyzing male and female speech patterns to provide more equity in workplace conditions).

Linguistics at Work is divided into nine chapters, each containing a group of articles related to one of the following areas of application: 1) Linguistics and Law; 2) Linguistics, Medicine, and Therapy; 3) Linguistics, Business, and the Workplace; 4) Linguistics and Issues of Gender, Race, and Culture; 5) Linguistics, Education, and Social Policy; 6) Linguistics and Composition; 7) Linguistics and Literary Analysis; 8) Linguistics and Translation; and 9) Linguistics and Language Instruction. Also included is an alternate contents, which is divided according to linguistic disciplines. The alternate contents will help a teacher who might want to assign readings that deal with phonetics and phonology, for example. In the case of an article that involves more than one linguistic discipline, the alternate contents will identify other linguistic disciplines that are also significantly represented within the article.

The reader contains articles by prominent linguists and professionals in other fields or disciplines who are applying or reporting on the importance of linguistic methods or scholarship to their own work. Such articles show the importance of linguistics and reinforce the idea that the material students encounter in their linguistics course could be of importance to them in whatever field they may enter.

Features have been included in this reader that make it accessible and useful to students and teachers: an alternate contents, chapter introductions, headnotes introducing each of the articles, discussion questions following each article, additional activities and paper topics at the end of each chapter, and a glossary that defines linguistic terms from the readings when those terms are not already explained or illustrated. The discussion questions are divided between those that merely check comprehension by eliciting particular facts or summaries of parts of an article, and those that require more analysis or personal reaction to what has been read. The additional activities and paper topics are intended to involve students in trying out some applications themselves.

This reader benefitted from suggestions and assistance I received from a number of individuals. I wish to acknowledge my editors at Harcourt Brace, particularly Michael A. Rosenberg, Tia Black, and Denise Netardus.

Some of my students and colleagues also provided comments and assistance. Among my students, I wish to mention the help I received from Wendy Baker and David S. Pace. Among the colleagues who provided useful help and suggestions, I wish to thank Royal Skousen, William Eggington, Cheryl Brown, Melvin Luthy, Robert Blair, Susie Preston, Jo Calabio, Sharon Boyle, Don Norton, and Joyce Baggerly. Cynthia Hallen deserves particular thanks for preparing the glossary for this reader, and Paul Baltes was especially helpful with some timely advice and assistance.

I also wish to acknowledge the numerous suggestions I received at various stages from the following reviewers: Catherine Ball, Georgetown University; Dawn Bates, Arizona State University; Marianna DiPaolo, University of Utah; Robert Doak, Wingate College; Connie Eble, University of North Carolina; Patrick Farrell, University of California, Davis; John Hagge, Iowa State University; Barbara Lafford, Arizona State University; Joan Livingston-Webber, University of Nebraska, Omaha; Rae Moses, Northwestern University; Anna Theresa Perez-Leroux, Pennsylvania State University; James Tollefson, University of Washington; and Robert Trammel, Florida Atlantic University.

Finally, I wish to thank my wife Marleen for her patience and assistance throughout this project.

Contents

Chapter 5   Linguistics, Education, and Social Policy   333

Chapter 6   Linguistics and Composition   450

Chapter 7   Linguistics and Literary Analysis   524

Chapter 8   Linguistics and Translation   595

Chapter 9   Linguistics and Language Instruction   662

Alternate Contents

(Listed by Linguistic Disciplines)*

Phonetics and Phonology

Morphology

Syntax

---

*Some articles represent more than one linguistic discipline. Such additional disciplines are noted in parentheses.

Semantics and Pragmatics (Includes Discourse Analysis)

Language Varieties (Issues of Style, Register, Contrastive Rhetoric etc.)

Language Varieties (Regional and Social Dialects)

Linguistics and Law

In this chapter you will read about some applications of linguistics to the legal profession. A major contribution of linguistics to law consists of ongoing research that provides new insights into important language behavior. But the contribution of linguistics to law is more than just the production of scholarly research available to the legal profession. In fact, as this chapter will show, it is becoming more common for court cases to involve expert testimony by linguists who draw on their specific areas of expertise. This chapter contains articles that will help provide some ideas about how the fields of phonetics, phonology, morphology, syntax, semantics, and language varieties are relevant to the legal profession.

In the first article, "Language and Memories in the Judicial System," Elizabeth F. Loftus demonstrates how the phrasing and choice of words in questions to witnesses can actually cause those witnesses to subsequently recall an event differently. This possibility has significant implications for the kinds of questions that are directed toward witnesses after an event and raises important issues about the reliability of witnesses.

Roger W. Shuy shows the kind of linguistic analysis that can be used to answer questions that might otherwise remain unanswered. In his article "Language Evidence in Distinguishing Pilot Error from Product Liability," he describes his role in a court case that questioned whether faulty mechanical equipment was responsible for impairing a pilot's ability and causing a fatal crash. Shuy's analysis of black box recordings with regard to pronunciation, syntax, and discourse features helped clear an airplane engine manufacturer.

In "Forensic Analysis of Personal Written Texts: A Case Study," Robert Eagleson outlines the role of linguistic analysis in the outcome of a legal investigation into the case of a man suspected of murdering his wife. After she had been missing for a while, the suspect produced a letter he claimed was typed by his wife that explained she was running away with another man. Linguistic examination of that letter, as well as others previously written by the suspect and his wife, eventually pointed conclusively to the suspect as the real author of the letter in question. He later confessed to killing his wife and authoring the false letter.

William Labov is well known for his work with dialects. In his article "The Judicial Testing of Linguistic Theory," he discusses his experiences with several court cases in which he and colleagues provided important linguistic testimony. In one case he provided phonological and dialectal evidence that helped to acquit a man who had been accused of phoning in a bomb threat to an airline.

In "*Mc-:* Meaning in the Marketplace," Genine Lentine and Roger W. Shuy explain their involvement as consultants in a trademark infringement case between McDonald's and McSleep Inns over the morpheme "Mc." In this article, it becomes clear that the study of morphology can have important applications in the real world.

The articles in this chapter represent a fraction of the possible applications of linguistics to law. Linguists have looked at other areas such as translation in the courtroom (see Susan Berk-Seligson's article in Chapter 8), semantics involved in the interpretation of legal documents and laws, and the significance of instructions given to jury members.

An awareness of linguistic methods and research is important to members of the legal profession. Attorneys can enhance their effectiveness by being aware of various kinds of linguistic research and by determining which of their own cases would benefit from an examination of such research. This may also lead them to consult experts in specific linguistic fields.

Language and Memories in the Judicial System

Elizabeth F. Loftus

Over the years, many experiments have been conducted that explore and clarify how language interacts with our brain. In the following article, Professor Elizabeth F. Loftus, well known for her work in memory and linguistics, reports on the results of some fascinating experiments about the effect that seemingly insignificant differences in the wording of a question can have on people. Her article discusses how the connotation of a particular word or the presupposition contained within an utterance may influence the testimony of a witness. Loftus shows that not only can the phrasing of a question bias an answer, but such phrasing may even change a person's existing memory of an event. Such information has serious implications for the credibility we attach to eyewitness accounts.

A trial lawyer once asked me whether social scientists had written any books on how to ask questions in court. Did anything exist, he wondered, which would help him better phrase his questions in order to accomplish desired ends? If a linguist and a psychologist set out, independently, to write such a book, similar "advice" might be offered, but different reasons for that advice would be advanced. The linguist might draw upon his knowledge of the structure of language, whereas the psychologist would bring to bear empirical evidence on the behavior of people. Which set of reasons would be right?

Through examples I provide in this paper, I argue that both the linguist's understanding of the structure of language and the psychologist's appreciation for human behavior are useful for understanding how language and behavior interact with one another.

One arena in which human language and memory interact is our judicial system. For example, when a crime or accident occurs, a witness to the event may be asked to answer questions about what he has seen. As I show, extremely subtle changes in the wording of those questions can have a substantial effect on the answers given. Furthermore, one question can influence the answer to a totally different question asked at some later time. Apparently, questions asked immediately after an event can introduce new—not necessarily correct—information, which is then added to the memorial representation of the event, thereby causing its alteration. Many of these effects are predicted by standard linguistic analyses, and thus provide empirical support for these analyses.

3

Questions and Answers

Articles: *The* versus *A*

Experimental Results   In an experiment, subjects viewed a film of an automobile accident and then answered questions about events that did and did not occur in the film. For some of the questions, the English article *the* (the definite article) was used, as in "Did you see the broken headlight?" For other questions, the article *a* (the indefinite article) was used, resulting in questions like "Did you see a broken headlight?" Questions using *the* produced fewer "don't know" responses and more false recognition of events that had not occurred in the film than did questions using *a* (Loftus and Zanni 1975). A similar result was observed when four-year-old children were interrogated about the contents of filmed commercials that had been presented a few moments earlier. "Did you see *the. . .* ?" produced more false recognitions of objects that did not actually exist. Since the children rarely produced a "don't know" response, the effects of the two articles on "don't know" frequency could not be determined (Dale, Loftus, and Rathbun 1977).

Linguistic Analysis   What is the difference between *the* and *a*, and why should use of these articles produce differential responding from a person who has witnessed some event? Language users "understand" that the definite article *the* typically precedes a noun whose referent is presumed to exist by both speaker and hearer, while use of the indefinite article *a* makes no such presumption (Anderson and Bower 1973, Brown 1973, Chafe 1972, Maratosos 1971, Osgood 1971). More specifically, Chafe (1972:56) has said that the definite article is used where: (a) the speaker knows about a certain item; (b) he assumes that the hearer also has such knowledge; and (c) he assumes that the hearer knows that he is presently talking about this item. For example, if a student were walking by, and I noticed that the student was frowning, I might say "The student is angry." In using the definite article, I indicate that I have some particular student in mind, and I have some reason to think that my listener knows which student I am talking about.

   When experimental subjects are asked questions about an accident they have witnessed, knowledge about the use of *the* versus *a* comes into play. The question "Did you see a broken headlight?" implicitly asks two questions: (1) was there a broken headlight? and (2) if there was, did you see it?

   If a subject decides that the answer to the first question is "yes," he can then focus on whether or not he saw it (Question 2) and make his decision. Because a filmed accident occurs in the space of seconds, it is nearly impossible to be certain of Question 1, and thus it is likely that the subject will respond "don't know" much of the time. In contrast, the question "Did you see the broken headlight?" can be translated into the nearly equivalent

"There was a broken headlight. Did you happen to see it?" Question 1 need not be answered, for its answer is effectively "yes." The subject needs only to answer Question 2 and decide whether he saw the headlight. According to this analysis, fewer "don't know" responses would be expected. Furthermore, if a subject's recollections tend to conform to what he believes actually did occur, then the definite article may lead to a greater "recognition" of events, even when they never, in fact, occurred.

Quantifiers: *Some* versus *Any*

Experimental Results   Ninety-four students viewed a film of an automobile accident and then answered 16 questions about events that did and did not occur in the film. Half of the questions pertained to items that did occur and half to items that did not. Half of the subjects were queried with the quantifier *some,* as in "Did you see some people watching the accident?" The other half were queried with *any,* as in "Did you see any people watching the accident?"

Table 1 presents the percentage of "yes," "no," and "I don't know" responses for both the *some* and *any* subjects. Whether an item occurred or not, subjects interrogated with *some* were more likely to respond "yes." To test statistically for the difference between interrogation with *some* and with *any,* two percentages of "yes" responses were calculated for each of the 16 questions. When the item was actually present, seven out of eight yielded more "yes" responses with *some* rather than with *any* ($p < .05$, by sign test). When the item was not present, all eight questions produced more "yes" responses with *some* ($p < .01$).

Linguistic Analysis   Why should the use of *some* versus *any* produce different answers to questions in which these words are included? Quantifiers such as *some* and *any* alternate in declarative and negative sentences. Thus, we might say "I saw some broken glass" or "I did not see any broken glass." For questions, however, it has been argued that *any* is the preferred form, but that *some* is frequent and appears to convey a different expectation (Bolinger 1960).

Table 1   Percentage of "Yes," "No," and "I Don't Know" Responses to Items That Were Present and Not Present in the Film.

RESPONSE	PRESENT			NOT PRESENT	
	SOME	ANY		SOME	ANY
Yes	68	59		29	21
No	22	33		66	72
I don't know	10	8		5	7

In questions, *some* conveys a stronger expectation of a positive response than the corresponding *any* question (Lakoff 1969). For example, compare "Who wants some beans?" to "Who wants any beans?" According to Lakoff's analysis, these two questions differ in meaning, although their surface differences are minimal. "Who wants some beans?" is an invitation to have some beans; the speaker assumes that someone will want them. "Who wants any beans?," when spoken by the person offering the beans, assumes that it is unlikely anyone will want them. In other words, "the first of these questions, then, assumes a 'yes' answer; . . . The second assumes either a negative answer, or makes no assumption" (Lakoff 1969:610).

These linguistic intuitions received further support from a demonstration reported by Livant (n.d.), who simply asked adults to judge whether a speaker expected a "yes" or "no" response to questions using *some* and *any*. Livant found a greater tendency for people to expect "yes" for *some* than *any*. Eyewitnesses who answer questions about their experiences can apparently sense these expectations, and their responses are accordingly affected.

Tag Questions

Experimental Results One hundred and forty subjects participated in an experiment in which they watched a short film, and then answered questions about it. Two versions of the film were prepared; they were identical except that one contained a bicycle parked along the side of a road whereas the other did not. One critical question was embedded in a list of 10 questions. For half of the subjects, the critical question asked "Did you see a bicycle?," whereas for the remaining subjects it asked "You did see a bicycle, didn't you?" The nine filler questions were designed to conceal the true purpose of the experiment. Table 2 presents the percentage of "yes" responses for both the ordinary and the tag questions. Whether the bicycle was present or absent, subjects interrogated with a tag question were more likely to report that they had seen the bicycle. Statistical tests for the differences between two proportions confirmed that tag questions produced more "yes" responses than ordinary questions, both when the bicycle was present ($z = 1.99$, $p < .05$) and when it was not ($z = 2.10$, $p < .05$).

Table 2 Percentage of Subjects Who Reported That They Had Seen a Bicycle When It Was Present and When It Was Not.

PRESENT		NOT PRESENT	
ORDINARY QUESTION	TAG QUESTION	ORDINARY QUESTION	TAG QUESTION
51	74	12	33

A final group of 25 subjects viewed the version of the film containing the bicycle, and then read a description of the film, ostensibly written by a policeman who had viewed it. In this description, a statement was made asserting the presence of a bicycle by the side of the road. A few minutes later, the subjects were given a questionnaire containing 10 questions, one of which was "Did you see a bicycle?" Twenty-one subjects (84%) claimed that they had.

Linguistic Analysis   A tag question is appended to a declarative statement, as in "The light was green, wasn't it?" Typically, a tag serves as a request for confirmation of the declarative. In Brown's words (1973:408): "The peculiar beauty of the English tag question is that it is semantically rather trifling, a request for confirmation, and it has such simple equivalents as *huh?* and *right?*" In fact, these simple tags are acquired very early by children, at about the time they use two-word utterances. Thus, while there are cases in which tag questions do not solicit confirmation (e.g., Jackendoff's 1972 example: "Max certainly has finished eating dinner, hasn't he?," said with the falling intonation of a rhetorical question), for the most part they do ask for agreement.

   Parenthetically, tag questions provide an area in which the usual distinction between linguistic competence and linguistic performance becomes quite blurred (Brown and Hanlon 1970). The argument is as follows. The tag question *Wasn't it* would follow a declarative sentence such as *The light was green*. The speaker knows that not any tag will do: *Didn't it?*, *Isn't it?*, and *Won't it?* will simply not work. Thus, the speaker must have created the appropriate tag, probably by operating on the antecedent (in this case by interrogation and negation and cutting off the predicate after *was*). To accomplish this correctly involves knowing a good deal about the structure of the tag that would be formally represented in its derivation. In short, in the case of tag questions, "*performance* comes more than ordinarily close to *competence*" (Brown and Hanlon 1970:156).

   Lakoff (1972) distinguishes tag questions from ordinary statements. Whereas a true normal statement demands agreement or acquiescence from the hearer, the tag merely asks for agreement, leaving open the possibility that it will not be received. Thus a tag takes an intermediate place between a statement and a question. The statement assumes that the hearer will agree, the question leaves the response of the hearer up to him, but a tag implies that while the speaker expects a particular response, the hearer may not provide it. The effect of the tag, then, "is to soften the declaration from an expression of certainty, demanding belief, to an expression of likelihood, merely requesting it" (Lakoff 1972:918).

   In the previous experiment, three conditions were used which can be compared to those discussed by Lakoff. When the bicycle was present, subjects were exposed to a normal statement asserting its existence, a tag question requesting agreement with its existence, or an ordinary question leaving the subjects free to decide about its existence. The percentage of subjects claiming to have seen the bicycle varied predictably with these three conditions. Analogous results occurred when the bicycle was not present. Thus, a person who is queried about his recollections regarding an object, be it present or not, apparently senses the expectations of the asker, and obligingly fulfills them.

One Question Influences Another   The previous examples show that the wording of questions asked of a witness can have a substantial effect on the answers given. Further, many of these effects would be predicted from standard linguistic analyses. In fact, the writings of linguists provided the impetus for many of the previous experimental designs.

The questions used to interrogate a witness can also influence the answers to different questions asked, often considerably later. That is to say, one question can influence the answer to another. After describing some previously published and some new experimental data illustrating this point, I discuss the thesis that questions asked about an event shortly after it occurs may supplement or distort a witness's memory for that event.

Presuppositions

Experimental Results   In this section, I briefly describe two experiments concerning the effect of the wording of a question on the answers to other questions asked some time afterward. In both experiments, subjects viewed a film of a traffic accident. Viewing of the film was followed by initial questions which contained a presupposition that was either true or false. A subsequent question, asked some time later, inquired as to whether the subject had seen the presupposed objects (Loftus 1975).

In the first of these studies, subjects were asked "How fast was (the) car going when it ran the stop sign?" when a stop sign actually did exist. A few minutes later, they were asked whether they had seen a stop sign for the car in question. Compared to a control group whose initial question had not presupposed the existence of a stop sign, the "stop sign" subjects were significantly more likely to report that they had seen the presupposed object.

What about false presuppositions? In one experiment, subjects saw a film of an accident and were asked the key question "How fast was the white sports car going when it passed the barn while traveling along the country road?" No barn actually existed. One week later, these subjects returned and answered a new set of questions, including "Did you see a barn?" Compared to a control group whose initial questionnaire had not mentioned a barn, these "barn" subjects were much more likely to report that they had seen the nonexistent barn.

Linguistic Analysis   Philosophers and linguists interested in the field of semantics have extensively discussed "presupposition." One view of presupposition was put forth by Strawson (1952): A statement presupposes X if X is a necessary condition for the truth or falsity of the statement. For example, "The car was speeding when it passed the stop sign" presupposes the existence of a stop sign. The presupposition is a necessary condition for the truth or falsity of the statement. Put another way, it is a condition that must be satisfied for the sincere use of the statement (Karttunen 1973).

The term "pragmatic presupposition" has been used to refer to a condition necessary for a statement to be appropriate in a given context (Bates 1976). Since these will vary according to the context in which the statement is made, they cannot be defined by reference to the statement alone. Although presuppositions are usually discussed in terms of the statements that include them, it is obvious that questions can contain presuppositions as well. Thus "How fast was the car going when it ran the stop sign?" also presupposes the existence of a stop sign.

In a normal conversation, most hearers will make the assumption that what is being communicated is true and most speakers assume that hearers will believe what is said (Grice 1968). Given these rules of conversation, it is to be expected that persons who are exposed to questions containing presuppositions will tend to believe those presuppositions. If people have a tendency to report that they have seen objects which they "know" to exist, then presuppositions—be they true or false—should augment this tendency since they effectively tell the hearer that certain objects did exist.

Why Questions

Experimental Results   Seventy-four experimental subjects were shown a series of 30 color slides depicting successive stages in an auto-pedestrian accident. The auto was a red Datsun seen traveling along a side street toward an intersection. The Datsun turns right and knocks down a pedestrian who is crossing at the crosswalk. Because the event happens so quickly, it is impossible to tell where the pedestrian was looking just before stepping into the crosswalk.

Immediately after viewing the slides, the subjects answered a series of five questions. The critical question asked half of the subjects "Why didn't the pedestrian look when he crossed the street?," whereas the other half were asked "Why did the pedestrian look when he crossed the street?" To the first question, subjects typically said something like "He was talking to his friend," whereas to the latter question they replied "To see if any cars were coming."

Three days later, the subjects returned for a new set of questions. The critical question asked whether the subject had seen the pedestrian looking in the direction of the cars before crossing the street. Subjects who had been queried with "Why did . . .?" tended to report that they had seen the pedestrian looking in the direction of the cars; those queried with "Why didn't . . .?" were more likely to report that the pedestrian failed to look.

Linguistic Analysis   *Why* questions typically contain presuppositions. Thus "Why is the concert being held in the auditorium?" presupposes that there is a concert being held in the auditorium (Lawler 1971). "Why did Lucy bring the dessert?" presupposes that Lucy brought the dessert (Miller and Johnson-Laird 1976).

Compare "Why didn't the pedestrian look when he crossed the street?" with "Why did the pedestrian look when he crossed the street?" The former question presupposes the pedestrian did not look, whereas the latter presupposes that he did. As we have seen, when a question presupposes the existence of some object, and now the occurrence of some event, the likelihood is increased that people will think that they actually perceived that object or event.

Verbs of Contact

Experimental Results   Loftus and Palmer (1974) found that subjects seeing films of accidents estimated the speed of the colliding cars to be faster if questioned with "About how fast were the cars going when they smashed into each other?" than if the same question were asked with *collided, bumped, contacted,* or *hit* in place of *smashed.* For example, those queried with *smashed* estimated that the cars were traveling 40.8 miles per hour on the average, while those queried with *hit* estimated 34.0 miles per hour.

A second experiment involved presenting subjects with filmed accidents and, as before, interrogating them about vehicular speed using either *smashed* or *hit.* One week later, these subjects returned and, without viewing the film again, answered a new series of questions about the accident. The critical question was "Did you see any broken glass?" There was no broken glass in the accident, but since broken glass is commensurate with a high-speed accident, it was expected that subjects who had been asked the *smashed* question might more often say "yes" to this critical question. This prediction was confirmed: those subjects who were asked the question with *smashed* were more likely to say "yes" to the question "Did you see any broken glass?" than the subjects who had been queried with *hit.*

Loftus and Palmer (1974) proposed that when a person sees a complex event such as an automobile accident, he first forms some representation of the accident he has witnessed. An investigator then, while asking "About how fast were the cars going when they smashed into each other?," supplies a piece of new information, namely, that the cars did indeed smash into each other. When the new information is integrated into the old representation, the witness will have a memory of an accident that was more severe than, in fact, it was. Since broken glass is typically associated with severe accidents, the subject is more likely to think that broken glass was present.

Linguistic Analysis   As Fillmore (1971) has noted, not all contact verbs mean the same thing. For example, the verbs *hit* and *smashed* involve specification of differential rates of movement. Furthermore, the two verbs involve differential specification of the likely consequences of the events to which they refer. The impact of an accident is apparently gentler for *hit* than for *smashed*. Thus it would be predicted that people who are asked the question "About how fast were the cars going when they smashed into each other?," would produce higher estimates of speed than those asked the same question with the verb *smashed* replaced by *hit*. Furthermore, the consequences of an accident labeled *smashed* would be more severe than the consequences of one labeled *hit*. Broken glass is more likely in the former case.

Language and Memory   When a person witnesses some event, he must comprehend it, and his memory for the event is a natural by-product of the process of comprehension. In order to comprehend any event, various aspects of the input must be interpreted. An interpretation is a relatively complete version, only part of which is based upon the environmental input that gave rise to it. Another part is based on prior memory or pre-existing knowledge, and a third part is inference. The inferences that are generated are likely aspects of the situation which have not actually been observed. We store in memory not the environmental input itself, nor even a copy or a partial copy, but the interpretation that we gave to the input when we experienced it.

New information to which a witness is exposed can become integrated into the existing memorial representation of an event, thereby causing it to be supplemented or altered. Thus if a witness is told that the pedestrian did not look before crossing the street, or that the traffic light was green, these facts can become incorporated into his memory. Soon facts that were acquired during the process of perception and "facts" that were supplied subsequent to the event may become indistinguishable.

Information need not be directly asserted in order to be accepted. As we have seen, it can also be introduced in the form of a tag question, as in "The light was green, wasn't it?" It can be presented as a *why* question, as in "Why didn't the pedestrian look when he crossed the street?" Its introduction can be subtle, as in the use of particular words which are known to induce people to make inferences. The inferences are made by the witness, and then believed as if they were actually experienced. Thus if an investigator uses the word *seize* rather than *take*, his hearer will probably infer that a great deal of intensity was involved in the taking, and may recall things as being more intense than they were. Should the witness later find out that the taking was very gentle, he may accuse the investigator of misleading him. But he cannot accuse him of lying.

As I read the works of modern linguists, experiments come to mind that beg to be conducted. For example, would Fillmore's (1971) intuitions regarding certain motion verbs be supported empirically? That is to say, relative to *slide* the verb *scuttle* is supposed to suggest movement across a surface that is more interrupted. If we asked an eyewitness "How far did the car scuttle before stopping?" would his answer be different from the witness who was asked "How far did the car slide?" Similarly, is "Did the robber *leap* to his escape?" functionally different from "Did the robber *jump* to his escape?"

Consider "Did you see the man *strolling* (*walking, running*) from the scene of the accident?," using verbs discussed by Miller (1972). Would one verb cause the man to be remembered as having moved more rapidly?

Compare *accuse* versus *criticize*. It has been argued (Fillenbaum and Rapoport 1971) that *accuse* is used in a situation which is unquestionably bad, and the speaker wants to claim that a certain person is responsible. *Criticize* is used when a certain person is definitely responsible and the speaker wants to claim that the situation was bad. Would eyewitnesses to a crime who were subsequently told that "Mr. Smith accused Mr. Jones of the embezzlement" be likely to recall the incident differently from the witness who heard that "Mr. Smith criticized Mr. Jones for the embezzlement"?

Indeed the possibilities are unlimited for the study of how words actually function when they are comprehended by the average human being. The variation in a single word spoken to a witness to some event can fairly dramatically affect that witness's recollection of the event. This phenomenon provides yet another compelling demonstration of the strong interdependence between language and memory.

References

Anderson, J. R., and G. H. Bower. 1973. Human associative memory. Washington, D.C.: V. H. Winston.

Bates, E. 1976. Pragmatics and sociolinguistics in child language. In: Language deficiency in children: Selected readings. Edited by E. Morehead and A. Morehead. Baltimore: University Park Press.

Bolinger, D. L. 1960. Linguistic science and linguistic engineering. Word 16.374–391.

Brown, R. 1973. A first language: The early stages. Cambridge, Mass.: Harvard University Press.

Brown, R., and C. Hanlon. 1970. Derivational complexity and order of acquisition in child speech. In: Cognition and the development of language. Edited by J. R. Hays. New York: Wiley. (Reprinted in: Brown, Roger. 1970. Psycholinguistics: Selected papers by Roger Brown. New York: Free Press.)

Chafe, W. L. 1972. Discourse structure and human knowledge. In: Language comprehension and the acquisition of knowledge. Edited by J. B. Carroll and R. R. Freedle. Washington, D.C.: V. H. Winston.

Dale, P. S., E. F. Loftus, and L. Rathbun. 1978. The influence of the form of the question on the eyewitness testimony of preschool children. Journal of Psycholinguistic Research 7.269–277.

Fillenbaum, S., and A. Rapoport. 1971. Structures in the subjective lexicon. New York: Academic Press.

Fillmore, C. J. 1971. Types of lexical information. In: Semantics: An interdisciplinary reader in philosophy, linguistics, and psychology. Edited by D. D. Steinberg and L. A. Jakobovits. Cambridge, England: The University Press.

Grice, H. P. 1968. The logic of conversation. Unpublished MS. Philosophy Department, University of California, Berkeley.

Jackendoff, R. S. 1972. Semantic interpretation in generative grammar. Cambridge, Mass.: MIT Press.

Karttunen, L. 1973. Presuppositions of compound sentences. Linguistic Inquiry 4.169–193.

Lakoff, R. 1969. Some reasons why there can't be any *some–any* rule. Language 45.608–615.

Lakoff, R. 1972. Language in context. Language 48.907–927.

Lawler, J. M. 1971. *Any* questions? In: Papers from the Seventh Regional Meeting of the Chicago Linguistic Society. Chicago: Chicago Linguistic Society.

Livant, W. P. n.d. Sentences with kernels? A study of a family of questions. Unpublished MS.

Loftus, E. F. 1975. Leading questions and the eyewitness report. Cognitive Psychology 7.560–572.

Loftus, E. F., and J. C. Palmer. 1974. Reconstruction of automobile destruction: An example of interaction between language and memory. Journal of Verbal Learning and Verbal Behavior 13.585–589.

Loftus, E. F., and G. Zanni. 1975. Eyewitness testimony: The influence of the wording of a question. Bulletin of the Psychonomic Society 5.86–88.

Maratsos, M. P. 1971. The use of definite and indefinite reference in young children. Unpublished Ph.D. dissertation. Harvard University.

Miller, G. A. 1972. English verbs of motion: A case study in semantics and lexical memory. In: Coding processes in human memory. Edited by A. W. Melton and E. Martin. Washington, D.C.: V. H. Winston.

Miller, G. A., and P. N. Johnson-Laird. 1976. Language and perception. Cambridge, Mass.: Belknap.

Osgood, C. E. 1971. Where do sentences come from? In: Semantics: An interdisciplinary reader in philosophy, linguistics, and psychology. Edited by D. D. Steinberg and L. A. Jakobovits. Cambridge, England: The University Press.

Strawson, P. F. 1952. Introduction to logical theory. London: Methuen.

Content Questions

1. In relation to the use of articles, how was the experiment set up to ensure that witnesses to the accident had seen the same event from the same direction?

2. What is the difference between what is implied with a definite or indefinite article?

3. Which quantifier is more closely associated with negative statements?

4. What do the experiments with articles, quantifiers, and tag questions show about the effect that seemingly unimportant differences in the wording of a question have on a witness's response?

5. In the experiment about presuppositions, what was significant about the fact that the witnesses reported having seen a barn?

6. Which type of question does Loftus indicate usually involves a presupposition?

7. What role can the semantic connotations of certain words used in questioning have in the subsequent memories of an individual about an event?

Questions for Analysis and Discussion

1. What subtle influence can the use of definite articles have in the answers to questions posed to a witness in a court case?

2. Some people assume that the study of grammar is only to help someone use "correct" forms. In light of this article, how might a knowledge of grammar help an attorney as he or she argues a case?

3. Besides the bias that can be introduced during a trial through questions containing false presuppositions, how might the use of presuppositions in a question-and-answer session prior to the trial actually affect the memory of witnesses when they later testify in court?

4. Loftus reports on the effect a word such as *smash* can have on leading to an inference. She also mentions the similar potential of other words such as *seize, scuttle, leap, stroll,* and *accuse.* What other examples can you provide that might contain a particular bias? Explain your choices.

5. How reliable do you think eyewitness accounts are? Can they always be trusted? What factors should be considered in relation to eyewitness testimony?

6. The research reported in this article involves linguistics, psychology, and law. What are some of the benefits of cross-disciplinary approaches to problem solving?

Language Evidence in Distinguishing Pilot Error from Product Liability

Roger W. Shuy

Roger Shuy is a linguistics professor at Georgetown University who has published extensively on various applications of linguistics to law. In the following article, which originally appeared in the *International Journal of the Sociology of Language,* he shows how useful discourse analysis can be in answering questions about communicative events. Shuy describes how the outcome of a liability case was influenced by his expert testimony and analysis. Shuy analyzed the recorded conversation that took place between a pilot and control tower personnel prior to a fatal airplane crash. Critical to the case was a theory that the crash might have been caused by a toxic leak from the engine, which could have entered the cabin and affected the pilot's performance. Shuy analyzed the voice tapes to see whether such a theory was supported by the evidence. In this article you should note how many linguistic disciplines and approaches are used to analyze the pilot's responses.

In 1980 a small Lear jet crashed while attempting to land in a thunderstorm in Louisiana. The pilot and the four passengers were killed. Over a period of years, the insurer settled the claims of the families of the deceased but was not satisfied that the accident was caused by pilot error, as the FAA had concluded. Although nothing in the wreckage provided clues to anything but pilot error, the insurance company developed the theory that the engine of the plane had malfunctioned in a subtle way, causing a substance called trimethylol propane phosphate (TMPP), a toxic gas, to leak into the cabin and impair the judgment and actions of the pilot. The plane crashed considerably off course, supporting this theory.

Five years later, the insurance company brought a civil suit against both the manufacturer of the engine and the builder of the plane itself. After a series of lengthy hearings, depositions, and motions, the attorneys for the defendants got the idea that tangible evidence as to whether or not the pilot had been impaired or overcome by TMPP was the tape recording of his communications with various ground-control centers from the time of his takeoff to his crash landing. In the spring of 1987 I was asked to listen to these tape recordings and to determine whether or not the pilot's language provided any clues to his alertness and competence.

The duration of the flight was some three hours and three minutes. There was no copilot so all air transmissions were indisputably those of the

15

pilot. Most of the work of flying a plane, and therefore most of the talk with the tower, takes place at the beginning of a flight (on the ground and on takeoff) and at the end of a flight (while landing and on the ground). As the plane passes over various parts of the country, its monitoring is switched to local control towers, usually near large urban areas such as Chicago, Kansas City, or Memphis. When such switching takes place, a new tower voice can be heard and various ritualized acknowledgments and identifications must be made.

For listeners not versed in the specialized style of air-to-ground communication, understanding can be difficult. The question, then, of what might be considered normal and acceptable must be addressed within the boundaries of this specialized communication style.

I began my analysis with the hypothesis that potential disturbances in the pilot's language caused by ingestion of a toxic gas such as TMPP would be reflected in aberrations in syntax, pronunciation, conversational cooperation, speech acts, and pauses. When the case went to trial, I gave testimony in these areas.

A serious problem for my hypothesis was that relatively little is actually known about TMPP. My first step was to determine whether or not any research had been done on the effects of TMPP on human speech. Various library searches through MEDLINE and TOXLINE revealed that documented research had never been carried out on animals with a brain stem. Only mice and rabbits had been used in experiments, and these studies pointed out that massive doses of TMPP caused erratic behavior in these animals. I also learned that TMPP is in a class of bicyclophosphates that are GABA inhibitors. TMPP is a relative of TCP, a common additive to oil used in automobiles. GABA inhibition is a common effect, for example, of Huntington's disease, and it affects speech severely. But to know how TMPP affects speech, one would need, minimally, research on primates or other animals with brain stems. Such studies would need to show that ingestion of TMPP affects the cerebellum, the motor pathways in the brain stem, the basal ganglia, or the descending pyramid tract and the motor cortex. If the effect of TMPP was on other parts of the cerebral cortex, there would be no language effect or disarthria. In such cases the effect would be more like aphasia. The question of whether or not the pilot's judgment could be impaired independent of his language production was, therefore, not answerable from current knowledge and research. If the chemical has a selective effect and is not focused on the motor system, a potential argument could be made that the pilot's error in judgment was not related to language at all.

As is often the case, this lack of knowledge could cut both ways. To this point we had no real evidence that TMPP was even ingested by the pilot. It was only a theory. But if TMPP had been ingested, we cannot know whether language would be affected since it is not known whether judgment can be affected independent of language production. Those who believe that language is the first thing to go base their belief on theory. On the other hand, those who hold the modularity belief, that judgment is independent of language, also have no research evidence to support their position. At this point I discussed the question with several neurolinguists, who expressed the belief that the modularity theory was wrong and that the ingestion of drugs, alcohol, and foreign toxic or semitoxic substances does indeed affect language first, independent of other effects on judgment.

In summary, we were faced with a most peculiar trial setting. The plaintiff had no physical evidence that TMPP caused the accident and the defense had no research evidence to know what possible effect TMPP might have on a human being. But if the plaintiff could argue from theory, there is nothing to prevent the defense from countering with its own theory. The test would be which theory would be most convincing.

When I was finally called as an expert witness, I explained the five types of linguistic analysis I carried out on the tape-recorded pilot-and-ground communication. I then divided the flight into three time segments. The first segment began on the ground in Chicago and continued through takeoff and until ground and air communication subsided, some 18 minutes altogether. The second segment began when ground and air communication resumed as the flight was monitored by the Kansas City and Memphis towers, some eighty minutes. The third segment began as the flight approached its destination and was monitored by the New Orleans area towers, some 27 minutes altogether. It was necessary to compare the pilot's speech at various points throughout the flight. Individual transmissions could have been compared but for the purposes of this trial, such analysis would have been far too detailed and time consuming, if not tedious. Instead I chose to focus on three time periods of the flight that, although not equal in duration, were roughly equal in quantity of speech. In any case, the plaintiff's theory was that the TMPP began to leak into the cabin during the flight. If there was a substantive change in pilot behavior during the flight even the plaintiff would agree that the pilot's behavior was normal at the onset of the flight.

With these three time frames established, I began my analysis of the language used by the pilot, beginning with syntax. The following is the substance of my testimony at the trial. Naturally this testimony was produced as a series of discrete questions posed by the attorney and not as an uninterrupted exposition as reported here. But the content and the basic sequence were the same.

1. Syntax

For the benefit of the jury, I explained that syntax is, quite simply, the structure of sentences. All languages have rules of syntax. For example, the basic minimum of a sentence is a predicate. This can be a verb or a verb phrase. In addition, most sentences contain physical subjects, although the subject can be omitted physically if it is expected to be "understood" by the listener. Thus the sentence, "Gonna get a new car," can be understood to mean "I'm gonna get a new car" in most contexts, if the information is appropriate for a statement (falling intonation on the last word).

If a person's language were being affected by an external substance, such as gas or alcohol, some aberration in syntax might be expected.

Syntax is also affected by ritualized language expectations (Brown and Yule 1984). Thus certain topics, participants, and settings influence language structure through acceptable norms of practice. That is, CB operators have known conventions of speech that are acceptable and expected in their communications. Physicians in the hospital context, talking with other medical personnel, engage in a kind of language shorthand that is, for them, in that context, predictable and efficient. Likewise, pilot/ground communications have taken on conventions of speech appropriate to that context.

In order to determine the structure of syntactic patterns of air-to-ground communication, I analyzed transcripts of many such communications. This structure is relatively simple. It contains certain obligatory segments and other optional ones. The options are dependent on conditions dictated by conventional air/ground communication practice. These optional and obligatory structures can be described in a number of ways, depending on which theory of grammar one is using. For simplicity of representation and visual clarity, I determined that the most efficient grammatical theory to describe and display this structure to a jury is tagmemic grammar (Cook 1978). Tagmemic grammar visualizes language as a linear clause series of slots and fillers. The slots have obligatory or optional syntax categories. The fillers are the semantically variable ways to fill or occupy these slots.

Analyzing the syntactic structure of the pilot's speech throughout the flight in question, the following tagmemic structure slots are realized. Obligatory slots are marked +. Optional slots are marked ±:

$\pm$ Acknowledge $\pm$ Identify $\pm$ Closing + Subject + Predicate
$\pm$ (+ Subject + Predicate ∞)

This formula states that the utterance may begin with an acknowledgment of the preceding statement, such as "Okay," but that this slot is *not* obligatory in all utterances. This is also true of the Identify slot, and the Closing slot. They may be present, but optionally so. It is obligatory, however, to realize a subject slot and a predicate slot. There is no option here. The formula then contains a parenthesis that includes a second subject slot and predicate slot (followed by a symbol for infinity). This part of the formula indicates only that any amount of sentence compounding can take place. Such compounding usually takes place with an *and* joining the two elements, as in

Subject	Predicate		Subject	Predicate
We	are refuelled	*(and)*	we	are ready to go.

In principle, there is no limit to the number of compound clauses that can be added to a sentence. Thus, the symbol of infinity in the formula.

With this linear syntactic formula in mind, I examined all utterances made by the pilot at the beginning of the flight in Chicago (approximately 14:13 hours to 14:31 hours), at the middle of the flight in Kansas City and Memphis (approximately 14:31 hours to 15:51 hours), and at the end of the flight in New Orleans (approximately 16:49 hours to 17:16 hours). I compared the syntactic structures of the beginning portion with those of the middle and the end portions. I found no difference in syntax structure, no aberration, and, therefore, no indication of any external effect that a substance such as toxic fumes, gas, or particulates might be able to produce.

A comparison of the recorded talk involving the pilot in the first 18 minutes with the middle 80 minutes and the last 27 minutes evidences no instances of ungrammatical structures. The tagmemic formula described above is followed with appropriate, not inappropriate, optional variants. There are no unusual slot reversals or other indications of external effects on the pilot's speech. One might hypothesize that under the effect of external substances such as toxic fumes, gas, or particulates, the pilot might delete more subject realizations, uttering sentences without physical subjects (what might be called "understood" subjects). But this is not the case. He does produce two sentences with "understood" (but not uttered) subjects out of nine subject–predicate pairs at the end of the flight. But he also produces three out of nine sentences with "understood" (and not uttered) subjects in the first part of the flight. During midflight, the pilot produces the largest frequency of "understood" subjects, ten out of 13. If this were evidence of an external influence on his speech, it is extremely odd that his ratio of "understood" subjects returns at the end of the flight to a ratio parallel to that of the flight's beginning (see Appendix).

Sentence Complexity

Likewise it might be hypothesized that a pilot's ability to produce more complex sentence structures would decrease under the influence of an external substance such as toxic fumes, gas, or particulates. Again, the pilot's speech shows no sign of such influence. Three of his 18 utterances in the first segment of the flight contain compound clauses (16%). In midflight, the ratio of sentence complexity reduces to slightly over 6 percent (one out of 17 utterances). In the last flight segment, however, the ratio increases to 13 percent, with two compound sentences out of 16, even in the midst of attempting to land his plane.

Word Frequency

Perhaps the simplest measure of syntax is that of number of words per sentence, or word frequency. A natural hypothesis would be that a pilot suffering from the influence of an external substance such as toxic fumes, gas, or particulates would produce significantly fewer words per sentence. Again, the most frequent and common evidence of cognitive impairment would be reflected in language. In the three segments of the flight, however, we see no significant diminution of word frequency, despite the fact that in the last segment the pilot is obviously doing considerably more work than he had had to do since he took off. These ratios are as follows:

	UTTERANCES	WORDS	RATIO
Beginning	18	162	9.00
Middle	19	157	8.27
End	16	124	7.75

Although the ratio of the first segment is slightly higher than the others, it should be pointed out that part of this segment was on the ground, during which the pilot uttered his longest sentences, one reaching 36 words in length.

2. Speech-Act Analysis

Speech acts are, essentially, the way people use language to get things done. Some linguists state that the basic unit of human communication is not the word, the sentence, or the sound, but rather the production of the utterance in the performance of illocutionary acts (Searle 1969). Such acts include making statements, asking questions, giving orders, apologizing, advising, threatening, and so on. The analysis of language using the speech act as a unit of measurement provides a profile of language not observable in more traditional analyses that focus on the forms, or structures, of words, clauses, or sentences. Speech acts come closer to intentional meaning, and, although it is never possible to determine the exact intention of a person, the analysis of speech acts reveals strong clues to intention simply by the way that person uses the forms of language to create a speech act. Likewise, comparison of a person's speech acts at one point in time with the same person's speech acts at another point in time reveals differences or similarities of intentions across the two time periods.

There were nine speech-act types used by the pilot in the utterances analyzed. There are many other speech acts available in the English language as a whole that were not used (such as denying, complaining, offering opinions, threatening, advising, etc.).

Among the speech acts used by the pilot, certain ones are more formulaic, such as greeting, thanking, and closing. Others give more evidence of the cognitive, rather than social, engagement of the pilot. Reporting facts, such as locating altitude or flight course, are fairly ritualized in air/ground communication. Failure to report facts, when appropriate, would be evidence of lack of cognitive engagement and might be interpreted as being the result of the influence of some external substance on the speaker. There is no substantive change in the pilot's ratio of the speech act of reporting facts throughout the flight. Nor does he report facts inappropriately (out of sequence, for example).

Other speech acts evidencing cognitive engagement include replying to questions, acknowledging instructions, requesting information, and correcting the errors of the other person. These speech acts cannot be accomplished effectively by a person who is cognitively disabled. During the last portion of the flight, the pilot accomplishes all of these speech acts and, therefore, displays evidence of normal cognitive engagement. The following chart displays the pilot's speech acts during the three parts of the flight:

SPEECH ACT	14:13 TO 14:31 BEGINNING OF FLIGHT	14:31 TO 15:51 MIDDLE OF FLIGHT	16:49 TO 17:16 END OF FLIGHT
Report fact	4	9	7
Greeting	1	1	1
Reply to question	1	0	1
Repeat information	1	0	0
Acknowledge instructions	12	4	7
Request information	1	2	1
Thanking	1	0	0
Closing	3	4	2
Correct other person	0	0	1
Totals	24	20	20

3. Pause-Filler Analysis

Pause fillers are used by virtually everybody in speech. They are usually realized by "uh," "er," or "um." Pause fillers are defined as speech sounds that have no dictionary meaning and that are used to fill silences for a number of purposes (Levinson 1983). The most common purpose is to let the listener know that you have the floor and that you are about to talk or that you are not finished yet and will continue to talk very soon. In one sense, they protect the speaker against interruption. Pause fillers require no interpretation of word meaning. They convey only social or interactional meaning. Sometimes pause fillers also signal that the speaker cannot make up his or her mind about what to say, that he or she is groping for the right word, or that the speaker is very concerned about the effect of what he or she might say on the listener. Whatever the reason for the use of pause fillers, however, one thing is certain: they must be used at the proper points in the conversation. One appropriate point is at the beginning of an utterance, before the first semantic word (noun or verb) is spoken. Another proper place is between clauses or phrases. Still another appropriate place is before a word that should come naturally but, for some reason, is difficult to utter or think of. Pause fillers occur most frequently when the speaker has many things on his or her mind or is trying to talk while doing something else at the same time. They are also more frequent in long and complex sentences than in short and more formulaic ones.

The pilot produces a total of 15 pause fillers in the conversations analyzed, as follows:

TAPE SEGMENT	TOTAL WORDS	TOTAL PAUSE FILLERS	RATIO
Beginning: 14:13 to 14:31	162	7	1:27.0
Middle: 14:31 to 15:51	157	5	1:31.4
End: 16:49 to 17:16	124	3	1:41.3

There are two types of pause fillers used by the pilot. That is, the context in which the pause filler was uttered gives indication of two distinct functions of the filler, "uh." One pause-filler type is found at the beginning of an utterance and signals the meaning of "attention please, I'm about to talk." The other pause-filler type is a pause relating to uncertainty of what is to be said next. These occur in utterance-medial position, after the speaker has already said one or more words. The following chart displays all of the pause fillers by these two types:

TAPE SEGMENT	PAUSE FILLERS: ATTENTION TYPE	UNCERTAINTY TYPE
Beginning: 14:13 to 14:31	2	5
Middle: 14:31 to 15:51	3	0
End: 16:49 to 17:16	5	0

The significance of the above distribution is as follows. All of the pause fillers signifying uncertainty occur at the beginning of the flight. Four of the five, in fact, occur while the plane is still on the ground. The pilot is confused about whether he is going to land at Moisant or Lakefront, and he begins his repetition of the tower's lengthy flight instructions with an "uh." During the middle and end portions of the flight, however, the pilot uses pause fillers only for attention-getting sounds that precede his utterances.

If the pilot were being influenced by an external substance such as toxic fumes, gas, or particulates, one might predict an increase in the ratio of the uncertainty type of pause fillers. Cognitive confusion, disorientation, or a diminution of the essential thought processes might well be expected to be revealed in the pilot's subconscious use of pause-filler utterances. The pilot's own language, however, shows no evidence of this.

4. Pronunciation Analysis

Although the effect of toxic fumes, gas, or particulates on the production of speech sounds in humans is unknown, we might hypothesize that it would have some effect, possibly similar to that of alcohol. With the latter, the speech sounds most readily influenced are the fricative sounds, particularly the sounds of words containing the "s" and "z" sound, since these involve minute tongue-muscle movement toward the front of the mouth (the tongue tip is curled upward at the side edges beneath the alveolar ridge while air is expelled over the top of the tongue, producing a friction noise as it passes between the alveolar ridge and the tongue itself). The same effect might be expected on the "sh" sounds (where the tongue position is similar to that of the "s" and "z" sounds, but the side edges of the tongue are flattened instead of curled upward, producing even more friction sounds). Likewise, the "th" sounds also might be expected to be affected (the tongue tip is just behind the upper front teeth instead of at the alveolar ridge). These relatively minute tongue-placement differences are normal for speakers with no external influence from substances such as alcohol. When certain amounts of alcohol are consumed, however, the tongue becomes less able to produce the minute changes and the sounds become interchanged, giving the effect of slurred speech.

To test the hypothesis that an external substance, such as toxic fumes, gas, or particulates, might produce a similar effect on the pilot's speech, I compared the production of all these fricative speech sounds in the recorded portions of the pilot's speech at the beginning, middle, and end of the flight, as follows:

SOUND	/s/	/z/	/sh/	/θ/	/ð/	/ks/	/ts/
Words used	Houston	zero	Mitsubishi	three	the	taxi	Mitsubishi
	six	Kansas		think	that's	expect	
	Moisant	is			they	six	
	see	thousand			that		
	Kansas						

	seventy	that's	its	frequency	Memphis	City
Beginning: 14:13 to 14:31						
17	9	3	2	3	14	3
Middle: 14:31 to 15:51						
20	6	6	2	3	13	7
End: 16:49 to 17:16						
11	9	9	1	0	18	8
Total 48	24	18	5	6	45	18
Produced normally (%)						
100	100	100	100	100	100	100

There was no diminution of the pilot's ability to produce these fricativized sounds from the beginning to the end of the flight. There is no phonetic support for any hypothesis in which it may be claimed that an external substance had any effect on the speech of the pilot in this flight.

5. Conversational-Cooperation Analysis

Conversation does not normally consist of a succession of disconnected remarks. Talk is a characteristically cooperative effort and each participant recognizes, to some extent, a common purpose or set of purposes; otherwise the event would not be a conversation at all. The general principle that participants expect each other to observe is that their conversational contributions be in accord with the accepted purpose or direction of the talk exchange. This is called the "cooperative principle" (Grice 1975). There are four maxims of the cooperative principle—the rational rules that allow us to make sense out of that which other people communicate to us:

1. *Quantity.* Make your contribution as informative as required; no more, no less.
2. *Relevance.* Make your information relate directly to the topic. Be relevant.
3. *Sincerity.* Do not say what you believe to be false.
4. *Manner.* Avoid obscurity and ambiguity. Be orderly.

Adhering to these maxims yields results in accord with the cooperative principle. Openly flouting these maxims leads to confusion, to lack of comprehension, or even to outrage.

Since this structure of a conversation exists, one can use the maxims as a touchstone for the conversations between the pilot and various ground-control centers. If the pilot had suffered exposure to an external substance such as toxic fumes, gas, particulates, or alcohol, we can hypothesize that such an effect would diminish his ability to engage in a cooperative conversation. We might expect him to lack informativeness, relevance, sincerity, or clarity.

There is no evidence in the tape-recorded conversation of this pilot that his abilities to carry on a cooperative conversation were diminished. Although only a specialist in air traffic could testify as to whether or not all communications from the pilot were neither more nor less informative than they needed to be, the tape recording reveals no evidence of complaint from the ground personnel about the degree of informativeness the pilot provided. We can, therefore, assess his language as informative enough. Likewise, there was no complaint or hint of discomfort in the communications from ground-control personnel that the pilot was irrelevant, insincere, or ambiguous. The best tests of the maxims of cooperative conversation are the responses of the listeners. They treat the pilot's reports of readiness, destination, movement, and flight level as though they were relevant, informative, sincere, and clear. The pilot asks two questions on these tapes. To Palwaukee Control, while waiting to take off, he asks, "Did they find out what the hold is yet?" Palwaukee's response is prompt and courteous. The second question was asked to Moisant ATC, as he was preparing to land: "What altitude did you want me at?" Moisant then repeats what was said in a previous 38-word utterance containing seven propositions. Neither response yielded any hint that ground personnel considered the pilot uncooperative or disoriented.

Finally, at Lakefront Local Control, the pilot says, "We're in the approach." Lakefront control, possibly confused by the fact that the plane ahead of him had requested to go back up and not try to land, confuses our plane, referred to as Mike Alpha, with the preceding aircraft, called Six Golf Hotel, and asks, "Six Golf Hotel, you're on the approach now?" Mike Alpha responds, "No. Mitsubishi nine six two Mike Alpha. We're on the approach." Lakefront LC then gives a weather report and asks Mike Alpha, already on the approach, to report Alger for him. (Alger is a specified point in the landing approach.) Mike Alpha responds, "Okay, Mike Alpha," and is not heard from again. Even with the pilot's difficulty in making Lakefront hear him (Lakefront LC had asked him to "try again" to call them), even after Lakefront LC had misidentified his call as that of Six Golf Hotel, even after the pilot had indicated that he was on the approach already, the pilot does not vacate the cooperative principle. There is no evidence of any external substance that might have caused his language to be affected.

Conclusion

Cognitive impairment, such as confusion or disorientation, is normally realized first in one's speech. In fact, most psychologists use a person's speech as evidence of cognition of any kind. Virtually all measures of cognition used by the field of education are discovered through language. Tests of all types ask people from school age on up to use language to answer questions posed in language. Evidence of cognitive impairment analyzed by neuroscientists is primarily that of the language used by patients or subjects of experiments.

If there were any signal of diminution of the thought processes of the pilot of Mitsubishi 962 Mike Alpha, it should be evident in his use of language. Analysis of his use of syntax, speech acts, pause fillers, pronunciation, and conversational cooperativeness reveals no meaningful change from the beginning to the end of the flight and no meaningful difference from what might be expected of any pilot engaging in such conversation. There is, therefore, no evidence of any influence on his language such as might be produced by an external substance such as gas, toxic fumes, or particulates.

Naturally, this was not the only testimony offered in this case, but upon completion of the trial I was told that this testimony was crucial in the jury's verdict, that pilot error was, indeed, the cause of the crash and that the plaintiff's theory of the pilot's ingestion of TMPP caused by engine malfunction was unfounded.

Appendix

Table 1. Syntactic Structure of Pilot's Sentences, 14:13 to 14:31, Beginning of Flight

SENTENCE NUMBER	±ACKNOWLEDGE	±IDENTIFY	±CLOSING	+SUBJECT	+PREDICATE	±(+SUBJECT	+PREDICATE)
1	x	x		x	x	x	x
2	x						
3	x			x	x	x	x
4				x	x		
5		x		x	x		
6	x	x					
7		x		x	x	x	x
8		x	x				
9	x	x		(x)	x		
10	x	x	x	(x)	x		
11	x			x	x		
12	x	x	x				
13		x					
14		x		(x)	x		
15	x	x(unint.)					
16	x	x					
17	x	x					
18		x					
Totals	11	14	3	9(3)	9	3	3

Table 2. Syntactic Structure of Pilot's Sentences, 14:31 to 15:51, Middle of Flight

SENTENCE NUMBER	±ACKNOWLEDGE	±IDENTIFY	±CLOSING	+SUBJECT	+PREDICATE	±(+SUBJECT	+PREDICATE)
1	x	x		(x)	x		
2	x	x					
3	x			x	x		
4		x					
5		x		x	x	(x)	x
6	(unint.)						
7		x	x				
8	x	x		(x)	x		
9		x	x				
10	x	x		(x)	x		
11		x					
12	x	x		(x)	x		
13		x	x				
14	x	x		(x)	x		
15	x	x		(x)	x		
16	x	x		x	x		
17		x		(x)	x		
18	x	x		(x)	x		
19		x	x				
Totals	10	17	4	12(9)	12	1	1

Table 3. Syntactic Structure of Pilot's Sentences, 16:49 to 17:16, End of Flight

SENTENCE NUMBER	±ACKNOWLEDGE	±IDENTIFY	±CLOSING	+SUBJECT	+PREDICATE	±(+SUBJECT	+PREDICATE)
1	x	x		(x)	x		
2	x	x	x				
3	x	x		(x)	x		
4	x	x		x	x		
5	x	x	x				
6	x	x		x	x	x	x
7	x	x					
8		x		x	x		
9	x	x		x	x	x	x
10	x			x	x		
11	x	(unint.)					
12	x	x					
13	x	x					
14		x		x	x		
15		x		x	x		
16	x	x					
Totals	13	14	2	9(2)	9	2	2

References

Brown, G.; and Yule, G. (1984). *Discourse Analysis.* Cambridge: Cambridge University Press.

Cook, W. A. (1978). *Introduction to Tagmemic Analysis.* Washington, D.C.: Georgetown University Press.

Grice, H. P. (1975). Logic and conversation. In *Syntax and Semantics 3: Speech Acts.* P. Cole and J. Morgan (eds.). New York: Academic Press.

Levinson, S. (1983). *Pragmatics.* Cambridge: Cambridge University Press.

Searle, J. R. (1969). *Speech Acts.* Cambridge: Cambridge University Press.

Content Questions

1. Why was an assessment of the pilot's speech relevant to determining the liability of the engine manufacturer?

2. What did Shuy do to determine what normal syntactic patterns of communication would be for air-to-ground speech? What did Shuy discover about the use of "understood subjects" at the beginning and end of the flight?

3. What are some of the types of speech acts that Shuy examined?

4. What are pause fillers? What are they used for?

5. Where are the so-called appropriate places syntactically for pause fillers to occur?

6. At what point in the flight did the pause-filler type indicating uncertainty occur? Why was this significant to the case?

7. Which natural class of sounds did Shuy expect would have been influenced if the pilot had absorbed toxic gas? Did these sounds show any such influence?

8. What are the four maxims connected with the cooperative principle?

Questions for Analysis and Discussion

1. Author Roger Shuy acknowledges that speech conventions may vary according to the setting, topic, and participants. Why would these factors have to be considered when assessing impaired speech?

2. With regard to the place of articulation of fricatives, why might they be more likely to be affected than stops when someone's speech has been influenced by chemicals?

3. Shuy makes a critical assumption about the relevance of previous research to the case he served on. Do you think his assumption was appropriate? Why or why not?

4. What was significant about the pilot's use of pause fillers as it relates to whether the pilot was impaired?

5. What role did the cooperative principle play in the analysis of the pilot's speech?

Forensic Analysis of Personal Written Texts: A Case Study

Robert Eagleson

When people write, they often leave clues to their own identity. This is the case not only with handwriting but also with published documents that might seem to leave no personal trace. As the article below explains, this occurs because people form habits in the way they express themselves. One field that examines the habits that vary from one individual to another is stylometry. Individuals involved in this field often use sophisticated linguistic methods combined with statistical processing of data. In literary studies, wordprint analysis has been used to answer questions about the disputed authorship of various texts. This type of analysis has been applied in determining the authorship of some of the Federalist papers as well as some writing attributed to Shakespeare. But wordprint analysis also has applications in legal settings when the authorship of an important document is in doubt. In the article below, Robert Eagleson, formerly of the University of Sydney and currently a language consultant, describes such a situation. While the document in question did not require some of the more complex wordprint analyses that are applied in some cases, it is a good illustration of some personal features that can be compared.

Introduction

The Case

In 1981, a Sydney husband was arrested on a charge of homicide. When originally interviewed by the police, he had produced a six-page letter which he claimed had been written by his wife as a farewell to the children. Among other things the letter explained that the wife was leaving home to live with another man elsewhere. As the police could not find the wife's body, the authenticity of the letter became critical. Although the police were suspicious, any possibility of arguing for its genuineness would have seriously undermined the other evidence.

Because the letter had been typed on the family typewriter, and because the husband insisted that the wife had written it, the likely authorship was reduced to either the wife or the husband. As the letter was completely typewritten without even a signature, it could not be subjected to the usual handwriting tests. However, the police were able to obtain a reasonable amount of material that had been written by both the husband and the wife in the months preceding the event. It became a question of comparing the disputed letter with other writings of the husband and wife to see which one was the likely author.

Texts

The texts available for investigation were:

F	(the "farewell" letter in dispute): 2551 words—all typewritten.
H	(a letter and other writings of the husband): 3725 words—all typewritten.
W	(a letter and other writings of the wife): 3294 words—all handwritten.

H and W especially were fairly comparable in size. Moreover, they were similar in level of formality. Though the size of each was not large, this quantity was balanced by the fact that at least two of the sets had quite distinctive characteristics in context-independent, objective elements of language, and in particular by the fact that certain divergent forms arose in relatively large numbers. The range of the types of dissimilarity that could be found and the persistent uniformity in the results of their application offset any theoretical reservations that might have been felt about the size of the sample texts—they had qualities which established their adequacy. Examples drawn from these texts are referenced as follows: (W14.4)—meaning line 4 of page 14 of the wife's material.

Procedures

The procedures start from the premise that writers have many constant features in their practice springing from ingrained habits of using language, so that the writings of one author will resemble each other in numerous ways. These are features which are not affected by variations in subject matter or "field," such as the vocabulary differences produced by a shift from law to cricket. Nor are they features that are affected by variations in formality or "tenor": grammatical and lexical choices will alter as we move from a casual to a formal situation. In comparing two texts we look for those features which are largely independent of context and which are likely to occur no matter what the writer is discussing and no matter what the circumstances. These context-independent linguistic characteristics are also objective, yielding to verification by anyone subjecting the material to scrutiny. They do not depend on personal interpretation to produce results.

More often than not, the difference between authors is a matter of the frequency with which a linguistic form is used rather than its absolute use or non-use in one of the authors. We look at the rate at which an author uses certain forms which are common to several pieces of writing. The assumption is that the rate of frequency for the occurrence of the selected forms is fairly constant in the texts of the one writer (see Smith, 1994). Any fluctuations should have an explanation. Major categories for analysis are: syntactic structure, morphological inflections, vocabulary, spelling and punctuation.

It is essential that the agreement should involve several features and not just one or two items, and several instances of each feature. The greater the number of features and the more the features belong to different categories, the stronger the case for shared authorship. At the same time we seek to show that the unattested document disagrees with other documents in the same features and, possibly, in other points. In effect we work in two directions: to establish significant similarities with certain known sources and significant dissimilarities with others. Such procedures are well established: see particularly Ellegård (1962), Svartvik (1968), and Michaelson et al. (1978a, b). These procedures have been applied by the author and others in disputes over the reliability of police records of interview (police "verbals") in recent years.

The Evidence   ·

Spelling

Errors in Individual Words   The proportion of spelling errors in individual words, excluding faulty capitalisation, in the three sets was: F(1.7%), H(2.5%) and W(0.3%). The farewell letter and the husband's documents were much closer in the rate of spelling error; the wife's documents were markedly different. The authors of F and H are comparatively weak spellers, the author of W a reasonable one.

Even more telling, the F and H shared the same spelling mistakes, while W avoided them for example:

F	H	W
assult, assullt	assult (twice), assulted (twice)	assault
carring	carring (twice)	carrying
thier	thier	their
treat	treat (twice), treaten	threatened

F and H also had difficulty with derived forms of *sex,* whereas W coped successfully, for example, F:"sex's remarks" (for "sexist"); H: "sex intercourse" (for "sexual"); and W: "sexually molest." Again, F and W conflicted in the spelling of some words which did not occur in H:

F	W
eet (twice)	etc
Ughily (three times)	ugly (six times)

This series offered additional, separate confirmation that the writers F and W differed in spelling practice. "Ugly" was particularly convincing as it could not be attributed to a typing error.

Capitals with Common Nouns H showed a strong tendency to spell a common noun with a capital where normal practice expects a small letter. The practice was less frequent in F, though the number of instances in this letter might be reduced because it was typewritten. W very rarely committed this fault. There were some interesting contrasts:

F	H	W
Mother	Mother	mother
Old	Old	old
Solicitor	Solicitor	solicitor
You	You	you

As well, F and H were inconsistent in their behaviour here. *Mother, old,* and *you,* etc., were sometimes spelt with a capital and sometimes with a small letter. W maintained a consistency.

Small Letters with Proper Nouns The farewell letter (F) was inconsistent in its practice of spelling proper nouns. It has such pairs as:

Billy:	Henry:	Olga:	Pam:	Vicki:
billy:	henry:	olga:	pam:	vicki

It also has "jim" (four times) but "Don," "Fred," "Ian." H has a similar inconsistency with such pairs as:

Chris:	God:	Joan:	Tommy
chris:	god:	joan:	tom

It also has "pam" (twice) but "Don," "Vicki," and "green" but "Valley." W did not show this trait, always spelling proper names used as nouns with a capital. There was one instance of a small letter in place of an unexpected capital, but then the item was being used as a modifier: "the irish joke" (W14.4).

Intrusive Apostrophe   In both F and H there were several occurrences of an apostrophe in noun, pronoun and verb endings where it is not normally required, for example:

F	H
(making me) offer's	(the poor little) kid's
(Beautiful) baby's	(my) trouble's
(it) hurts	(kids) saving's
(he) put's	(the only) one's
(he) want's	he's (fault)
wors't	(of) her's
wor'st	

There were no instances of this intrusive apostrophe in W. In quoting her husband, the wife inserted an apostrophe in the non-standard *you's*, but this could be rather a recognition of the irregularity of the form, just as many write "the 3 R's." The apostrophe here is certainly not of the same type as the intrusive ones found in F and H.

Grammatical Morphology

The Verb: Present Tense Inflection   Both F and H were erratic in the use of the s inflection in the environment of the third person present singular, and there were several instances of omissions. There were none in W. The facts were:

F	H	W
–	believe	–
get	–	–
–	give	–
keep	–	–
–	think	–
want	want (4 times)	–

The Verb: Past Tense Forms   There were many instances of the use of the regular weak past tense ending in "-ed," in all three sets of documents. In F and H, however, it was also often omitted. There were some seven instances in F, and in H thirty-seven failures to attach the morpheme. Parallel examples are:

F6.4	He would get upset with them because they *believe* me.
H6.11	I never really *believe* her.
F6.2	He *threaten* me.
H12.6	She had a knife and *threaten* during argument.

W was quite accurate in the use of the past tense morphemes. With verbs which indicate the past tense through internal changes rather than the addition of an inflection, F and H showed a similar fluctuation in practice, choosing non-standard forms as frequently as standard ones:

F	H
come (1 out of 3)	come (2/6)
done (2/2)	done (2/3)
–	keep (1/1)
seen (1/2)	seen (5/7)
–	sware (1/1)

That is, F and H used the non-standard forms more frequently than the standard.

In W, there were only two instances of non-standard forms: *come* and *swang*. Both occur only once each, and the one instance of "come" has to be set against fourteen occurrences of the standard form "came," and *swang* is matched by one occurrence of "swung." That is, the non-standard forms must be regarded as random instances in W, a possible slip or error, whereas they have a more regular status in F and H. In the expression of the past tense, then, F and H had a strong non-standard component both in regular and irregular verbs, whereas W was definitely standard, with only two non-standard occurrences and those in irregular verbs.

Syntax

Sentence Structure In F many independent sentences were not clearly separated. Instead they were run together without any marking of their division with a full stop and a capital letter, for example, "since his accident at work he's slowed down before that he wanted it everynight always woke up with a horn everymorning ready to go for it again" (F3.13–15). A full stop would have been in order after "down," and "before" should have begun with a capital letter. A similar arrangement might have applied after "everynight."

Alternatively, a comma was found inserted in place of the required full stop, for example, "Alan look after helen, when she has the baby, look after it be proud of it like I am of you, never bad talk or run it down" (F1.14–15). A full stop, for example, would have been in place after "helen," with "when" being spelt with a capital letter.

The same weakness in sentence control characterised H, but did not appear in W. The total numbers of errors in sentence-division were: F(80), H(142), and W(4). The correlation between F and H is strong enough to point to a close similarity in linguistic practice. The correlation between F and W on the other hand appears quite weak.

In this part of the investigation two criteria were used to establish the division between sentences: the presence of a full stop at the end of one and the presence of a capital letter at the beginning of the next. I have left out of consideration those instances in which the writers failed to insert a full stop but commenced a segment, which was legitimately a fresh sentence, with a capital letter. It seemed reasonable to regard the capital letter as sufficient recognition of sentence division; for example, "he would keep saying he wanted to go to Noosa Heads, just because you were there I was suppose to keep dropping my pants till he decided to take me, when tommy . . ." (F2.2–3); and "the Oldman will look after the children He loves you very much" (F6.27). The details of such instances, with absence of stop but with presence of capital, were: F(6), H(44) and W(19).

The reasonable exclusion of these figures did not in any way affect the conclusion reached on control of sentence structure. Even if they had been included in the earlier totals, they would not have materially altered the strong correlation between F and H, and the distinction between them on the one hand, and W on the other.

Disrupted Structures   In the farewell letter (F) there are nine instances of what might be termed disrupted structures, that is, sentences in which a structural element had been omitted. Six of these involved the word "to": "got you . . . paint" (F2.28); "whether . . . start" (F4.1); and "try . . . help" (F6.28). One involves the omission of "of": "hundreds . . . dollars" (F2.18).

There is nothing difficult about the types of structures involved in these examples. On the contrary they are straightforward and fairly frequent. Moreover, the words "of" and "to" are simple and well known. Their use is almost automatic, and their absence could not be attributed to some stylistic intricacy in the pattern. Their relatively small number might lead to them being regarded as slips.

The same disrupted patterns, however, occurred in the husband's writing (H), though with greater frequency. There were forty-seven instances of the pattern with "to" missing, and fourteen of those with "of" missing.

Punctuation

Comma: Omission at End of Clauses   In F the practice of inserting a comma between clauses within sentences was not always followed, for example, "Ian Henry to halfdrunk knocking at your door at all hours of the night trying to climb on top of you, telling me how beautiful I was wants his daughter to look . . ." (F2.10–11). A comma would have been in order both after "night" and after "was." H exhibited the same type of omission but to a considerably greater degree, but this feature was almost absent in W. The details were: F(20), H(62), and W(5). For the document to share the feature in equal strength, taking F as the base, the figures should have read: F(20), H(29), and W(26). F and H clearly had much more in common than either of them had with W.

Comma: Omission in Series   A comma between items in a series was regularly omitted in F; for example, "Meg Ruth Barbara Myself and others" (F2.23). The same sort of omission occurred in H. Moreover, the proportion of occurrences in F and H was the same. The feature never occurred in W. The details were: F(14), H(22), and W(0).

Asides   There were three occasions in which asides were indicated by the use of brackets or dashes in F. One was: "he would run out and buy something to try to get me to love him, (poor old fool)" (F6.14). On the other hand, there were twelve occasions in which the asides were not marked. On three other occasions commas were used in place of brackets or dashes. On four other occasions brackets were used incorrectly. H also failed to signal asides appropriately on twelve occasions. W, however, was always accurate in this area.

Full-Stops: Influence on Spelling   Punctuation has an influence on spelling inasmuch as a full-stop at the end of one sentence leads to the word beginning the next sentence being spelt with a capital letter, even though elsewhere the word would be spelt with a small letter. In F there were fifty-eight occasions a small letter appeared instead; for example, "and what I have to offer them. you my babe . . ." (F3.5). In H there were seventy-one full-stops; twenty-two of them were followed by a small letter. In W in all 225 occasions where a full-stop occurred at the end of a sentence, the opening word of the next sentence began with a capital letter. The details were: F(15), H(23), and W(0). The accuracy of W in this matter is as significant, when compared with F and H, as is the fairly high correlation between F and H.

Findings

There were many significant differences between the language of the farewell letter and the language of the wife's documents. These had nothing to do with extraneous matters, such as variation in subject-matter or in level of formality, but reflected instead a marked divergence in underlying linguistic practice. The clear conclusion on the basis of this evidence was that the wife—the author of the documents labelled W—was not the author of the farewell letter.

On the other hand, there were many strong similarities between the language of the farewell letter and the language of the texts composed by the husband. The high correlation between the two indicated a strong probability that the husband was the author of the farewell letter. There was definitely nothing in F that would be inconsistent with his normal linguistic practice. On the contrary, the large degree of comparability pointed in his direction.

Equally to the point, it was not possible to find a feature in which F and W agreed to the exclusion of H. Where F and W agreed, for example in the order of subject and predicator or the forms of personal pronouns, so also did H. It was only F and H that matched up to the exclusion of W. Indeed, the style of writing in W stood apart quite dramatically from that of F and H, mainly because of the good control of sentence structure. The sentences in W were well constructed and properly delimited. Even when the wife was presenting notes, and so used truncated sequences, she observed the normal conventions for sentence construction. In addition to this feature, which has already been commented on in above (Syntax: Sentence Structure), there were such other niceties unique to W as:

1. The marking of a special word with inverted commas, e.g. "He 'rasberried' in my face" (W12.22) and "snarling" (W14.12).
2. Varied sentence openings, e.g. "Upon arriving home my husband . . ." (W16.5).
3. The exploitations of a wide range of punctuation marks. Not only did W have the full-stop and question-mark, but it alone employed the exclamation mark and quotation marks.

Not only did W not share many features with F and H, it was uniquely different from them in others. Table 1 summarises the findings of the linguistic investigation at points of significant comparison between F and W, and F and H.

This table demonstrates clearly that the language of the farewell letter was inconsistent with the language of the wife and that it was not reasonable to consider her as its author. The table also forcefully demonstrates that if only one of two persons was the writer of the farewell letter, then on the basis of the evidence coming from the investigation of the language it was legitimate to conclude with a high level of probability that the author of the texts, (H), was also the author of the farewell letter.

Table 1   Summary of Comparison of Three Sets of Documents

	H	F	W
1. SPELLING			
1.1 Errors in individual words	+	+	−
1.2 Capitals with common nouns	+	+	−
1.3 Small letters with proper nouns	+	+	−
1.4 Intrusive apostrophe	+	+	−
2. GRAMMATICAL MORPHOLOGY			
2.1 The verb: present tense	+	+	−
2.2 The verb: past tense	+	+	−
3. SYNTAX			
3.1 Sentence structure	+	+	−
3.2 Disrupted structures	+	+	−
4. PUNCTUATION			
4.1 Comma: with clauses	+	+	−
4.2 Comma: in series	+	+	−
4.3 Asides	+	+	−
4.4 Capitals after full-stops	+	+	−

Notes: + = possession of a shared feature; − = absence of shared features.

Postscript

The husband pleaded his innocence at the committal proceedings and continued to affirm that the wife had written F. The linguistic evidence was subject to extensive cross-examination. After being committed for trial, the husband changed his plea to one of manslaughter for which he was subsequently found guilty. He admitted to writing the farewell letter F.

References

Ellegård, A. (1962) *A Statistical Method for Determining Authorship: the Junius Letters, 1769–1772.* Gottenburg: Gottenburg Studies in English.

Michaelson, S., Morton, A. Q. and Hamilton-Smith, N. (1978a) *To Couple is the Custom.* Edinburgh: Department of Computer Science, University of Edinburgh.

Michaelson, S., Morton, A. Q. and Hamilton-Smith, N. (1978b) *Justice for Helander.* Edinburgh: Department of Computer Science, University of Edinburgh.

Smith, W. (1994) Computers, statistics and disputed authorship. In John Gibbons (ed.) *Language and the Law.* London: Longman, pp. 374–413.

Svartvik, J. (1968) *The Evans Statement: a Case for Forensic Linguistics.* Gottenburg: Gottenburg Studies in English.

Content Questions

1. Describe the setting of the case. What was the situation and available evidence that led investigators to select the texts that they did for comparison?

2. Describe the kinds of evidence that were compared among the documents.

3. What kinds of similarities and differences existed among the three sets of writing?

Questions for Analysis and Discussion

1. Sociolinguistic research has noted the tendency for women to be more concerned with being "correct" in their choice of linguistic forms. How would the investigation in this police case have been different if the husband had used more "correct" forms?

2. Assume a slightly different scenario in which it did occur to the husband that the false letter he composed was going to be examined carefully. Given his apparent lack of sophistication with language, are there any differences between his writing and his wife's that he might not be aware of and might still include in his letter? If so, what might those differences be?

3. An examination of the wife's writing did show one occurrence of the nonstandard form "swang." How might you account for such a usage by an individual who normally uses standard speech? Are there any verb forms you are unsure about in our language?

4. If you were a jury member considering a case such as this, would you find the presentation of such evidence about the differences in the sets of documents and what those differences indicate about the probable authorship to be convincing evidence? Why or why not?

The Judicial Testing of Linguistic Theory

William Labov

The kind of linguistic analysis appropriate to a case depends on the nature of the problem. Some techniques or disciplines in linguistics are more appropriate to a given issue than others. In the following article, William Labov, a linguistics professor at the University of Pennsylvania and well known for his work in dialects, reports on his involvement along with other linguists in several legal cases. In two cases that involve the readability of a document, syntactic analysis was of great importance. In the third case, the Prinzivalli case, conclusions based on phonetics, phonology, and sociolinguistics became critical to the trial's outcome. Paul Prinzivalli was accused of phoning in a bomb threat to an airline. As Labov examined the linguistic data related to the case, he became convinced that Prinzivalli was innocent. This article examines the linguistic evidence that helped to acquit the defendant.

Among the evidence discussed in relation to the Prinzivalli case is the use of acoustical analysis. Acoustic phonetics rarely gets much, if any, attention in introductory linguistics courses, but its findings can be significant. In this article you may not understand every detail as it relates to acoustics, but watch for the significance of acoustic phonetics in addition to phonology and sociolinguistics as they relate to the case.

In linguistics, as in many other academic disciplines, we tend to think of theories as internal products, most properly used and evaluated by the scholars who produced them. The general public can hardly be expected to judge the rightness or the value of these theories, without knowing the linguistic data they are based on or the methods used to construct them. We tend to think, moreover, that people involved in everyday affairs are strongly biased by their immediate needs and interests, so that they are not likely to weigh the correctness of scientific theories with the objectivity that is called for. On the other hand, those who work in isolation from political and practical concerns are thought to be more objective in their approach to research and knowledge. It is not uncommon for scholars to assert with pride that they are interested in knowledge for its own sake, and not for any practical application it might have.

In harmony with this academic view, professors have warned their students of the bad consequences of efforts to apply their theories to the pressing issues of the larger social world. It is not hard to demonstrate that in the course of popularization, scientific ideas are often weakened and distorted. Students learn that losses in scientific accuracy and objectivity will more than cancel out any gains that might result from their engagement in the social struggle.

In the presentation here, I will not try to estimate the fairness of this portrait of the academic world, nor its freedom from the bias of partisan politics. Most readers have ample experience of their own to judge the matter. I will be looking at the other side of the coin. I will be dealing with situations where linguistic data, theory, and conclusions are presented in a forum far removed from the academic scene, where lawyers and judges work to resolve questions of fact that have important consequences in the world at large. It will appear that objectivity is highly prized in these judicial contexts, perhaps more highly prized than in the laboratory or the classroom.

The course of this discussion will involve us in the familiar problems of the relations between theory and practice, theory and data, theory and facts. Within the academic framework, facts are valued to the extent that they serve a theory, and only to that extent. Academic linguists see themselves engaged in the business of producing theories: theories are the major product and end-result of their activity. It seems to me that there is something backwards in this view, and we should seriously consider whether it might be reversed.

The discussion to follow will consider three cases where linguistic testimony played an important part in a judicial decision. They cover only a small fraction of the range of issues on language and the law that have been brought to linguists' attention in recent years. In these three cases, linguistic data and theory were introduced to support an expert opinion on the facts of the matter under consideration.

It is true enough that almost all linguistic testimony comes in the form of expert opinion, with a system of advocacy where one can expect to find an opposing expert opinion. This can happen in civil suits, automobile accidents, or criminal cases of various kinds. But in the cases I will report here, there is a more serious issue of taking sides on matters of right and wrong. In each of these cases, the facts are part of a larger situation involving justice and injustice, and the linguistic testimony has been used in the search for justice—at least as the linguist sees it.

The U.S. Steel Case

In the 1960s the American steel industry was the focus of a number of federal actions to eliminate practices that discriminated against minorities and women. One of these class action suits was located in Pittsburgh, on behalf of black steel workers in that city. The linguistic issues concerned the fairness of a legal notice that informed the steel workers that they would have to give up their claims in the local suit to accept a partial settlement of a national suit.

The Pittsburgh case was rooted in the history of black steel workers over the previous two decades. Blacks had come from the South to work in the steel industries of Chicago, Gary, Cleveland, and Pittsburgh during the war years and after. Some had been brought as strike breakers, but almost all had come as lower-paid workers, in janitorial and furnace-type jobs that were considered less desirable and paid less than others. A complex system of tracking made it difficult for them to move upward, since if they moved to a better-paying track they would lose the seniority they had gained in the lower-paying one.

In the late 1960s a number of federal suits were brought under Title VII of the Civil Rights Act of 1964, to correct such practices and establish equal pay for blacks and whites, men and women. The Equal Employment Opportunity Commission and the legislation that established it made possible the creation of class action suits, where a single attorney could obtain corrective action for a very large number of clients. One such suit was brought on a national basis against the nine major steel corporations, and settled by a consent decree under federal judge Pointer in Birmingham in 1974. A certain amount of money was to be paid to black and women steel workers as compensation for the lower salaries they had received, and corrective action was to be taken to eliminate many of the practices considered unfair by the courts (though the steel industries never admitted that they had discriminated).[1]

In Pittsburgh, attorney Bernard Marcus had worked over many years to establish a class action suit representing some 600 black steel workers at the local Homestead works against U.S. Steel and the union. He hoped this suit would bring considerably more profit to the steel workers than the national settlement was likely to do.[2] He had experienced many difficulties in getting the class action established, and had carried an appeal as far as the Supreme Court to obtain permission to communicate with his clients. He had joined forces with the NAACP Legal Defense Fund to pursue the case. The linguistic issue arose at a moment where it seemed that new action by all the other parties involved might reduce the class he was representing to almost nil.

An "Audit and Review Committee," representing the steel union, the companies, and the government, was about to send out checks in settlement of the national case. To accept the check, local steel workers would have to give up their claim in the local case. Marcus felt that the letter the

---

[1]Consent decrees I and II issued by Judge Sam C. Pointer, Jr. on April 12, 1974, signed by representatives of the Department of Justice, the Department of Labor, the Equal Employment Opportunity Commission, Armco Steel, Bethlehem Steel, Jones & Laughlin, National Steel, Republic Steel, U.S. Steel, Wheeling-Pittsburgh Steel, Youngstown Sheet & Tube, and the United Steelworkers of America. It included provisions for back pay, goals, and timetables for hiring, promoting, transferring, and training minorities and women.

[2]Jimmie L. Rodgers and John A. Turner vs. United States Steel Corp., Local 1397, AFL-CIO and United Steelworkers of America, AFL-CIO, Civil Action 71-793 in the U.S. District Court for the Western District of Pennsylvania.

committee was sending out explaining the issues, along with the legal notice of waiver, was biased in favor of accepting the check and against continuing the local case.[3]

In the fall of 1975, Marcus called me and asked me if I could, as a linguist, examine the letter for objectivity and comprehensibility. I assembled
a group of four who might be able to throw light on the matter. Two
would be concerned with the comprehensibility of the document. Mort Botel of the University of Pennsylvania Graduate School of Education was
one of the country's leading experts on readability, and the author of one
of the widely used indices of readability. Jeff van den Broek (1977) was
then engaged in a dissertation on sociolinguistic variation in syntactic complexity in the Flemish of Maaseik, and had done extensive work on measures of syntactic complexity.[4] Two would be concerned with possible bias
in the document. Anthony Kroch's dissertation (1979) dealt with the semantics of quantifier scope,[5] and he examined the text for semantic bias of
quantifiers and other grammatical features. My own contribution centered
on the empirical question as to whether the formulations of the letter actually did produce a semantic bias in those who had to make the decision.

The notice was a 12-page document, under the authorship of the joint
committee representing the steel companies, the steelworkers' union, and
the government agency. It introduced the consent decree and the local case
(the *Rodgers* case), and notified readers that they were members of both
classes. It urged the steel workers to read the notice carefully, and to get
help if they did not understand it. It explained the relations of the two
cases, and the consequences of signing the waiver or not signing it. The last
page was the legal notice of waiver itself, which was one long sentence in
technical legal language. This sentence was also to be printed in small type
on the back of the check to be signed.

Our group testified in Pittsburgh February 17–18, 1976, before Judge
Hubert Teitelbaum in a hearing on the comprehensibility and objectivity of
this notice of rights. Botel was qualified as an expert on readability, and
made a strongly favorable impression on the judge. We presented the data
on readability by half-pages of the letter, as shown in Figure 1. At the top
of the diagram are some general titles that give some idea of the content of
the pages concerned.

The vertical axis on the left shows the Botel readability measure, based
on word-frequency as registered in the Lorge-Thorndike list. The measure
is in terms of grade-level: it can be seen to vary widely from one section of
the document to the other. The index falls to a low level—that is, readability is high—in the section on "How to get information," which begins:

---

[3]Notice of rights to back pay under Consent Decree I U.S. et al. v. Allegheny Ludlum Industries, Inc. et al., Basic Steel Industry Audit and Review Committee.

[4]See Van den Broek 1977 for other uses of these measures.

[5]Kroch 1972 deals with the semantics of time adverbials such as *at least,* and Kroch 1979 is
concerned with the semantics of quantifiers such as *any.*

(1) You should read this letter carefully. If you have any questions which are not answered by this letter, representatives of the Implementation Committee at your plant will be available to answer such questions at the times and place shown on the sheet which you have received along with this letter.

The grade level index is also quite low in the discussion of possible outcomes, where on page 3.1c we read:

(2) Whichever of the parties in *Rodgers* (either plaintiffs or the defendants) are successful, the unsuccessful parties would be entitled to appeal to a Court of appeals and possibly could appeal to the United States Supreme Court. Such appeals could result in affirmance or reversal of any judgment entered by the District court. Accordingly, it is likely that it will be at least several years even after trial of this case before it is finally known whether plaintiffs or the plaintiff class will receive any back pay or injunctive relief in the *Rodgers* case. Consequently, it is unlikely that there would be any final resolution of the *Rodgers* case, including appeals, before 1979.

On the other hand, the grade level is quite high, and readability low, when the notice deals directly with the Rodgers case, as on p. 3.1b:

(3) The *Rodgers* plaintiffs seek an injunction prohibiting defendant Company and defendant Unions from continuing such alleged discriminatory policies or practices, as well as back pay, punitive damages, attorneys' fees, and any other relief which the District Court may deem appropriate.

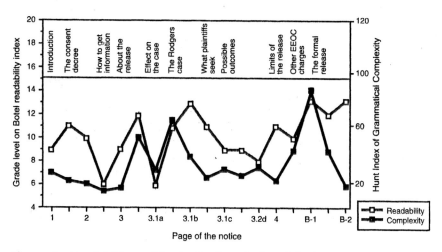

Figure 1 **Readability and Syntactic Complexity of the Notice**

Van den Broek had also examined the text with eight different measures of syntactic complexity, which were all highly correlated. He selected the Hunt Measure for display in court, based on the mean length of T-Units (independent clauses and all clauses dependent on them). It is superimposed on the readability measure in Figure 1, using the vertical index on the right, to show that in general, there is a good agreement between the two measures. The sections that show the lowest grade levels for readability also show the lowest syntactic complexity, and vice versa. Both measures reach a climax with the formal release, which begins with the sentence:

> (4) I, the undersigned, acknowledge receipt of the gross sum shown on the face of this check, in consideration of which I irrevocably and unconditionally release United States Steel Corporation, the United Steelworkers of America, the past and present parents, subsidiaries, divisions, offices, directors, agents, local unions, members, employees, successors and assigns of either of them (severally and collectively "Releasees") jointly and individually, from any and all claims known or unknown which I, my heirs, successors and assigns have or may have against Releasees and any and all liability which Releasees may have to me or them: (1) resulting from any actual or alleged violations occurring on or before April 12, 1974, based upon race, color, sex or national origin, of any federal, state or local equal employment opportunity laws, ordinances, regulations, orders, the duty of fair representation or other applicable constitutional or statutory provisions, orders or regulations; and/or (2) resulting at any time from the continued effects of any such violations by Releasees of any such laws, etc.

The readability and complexity measures diverge at the end of the release, where the language shows complex arrangements of fairly ordinary words as in

> (5) This release is the sole and entire agreement between me and Releasees and there are no other written or oral agreements regarding the subject matter hereof.

Kroch was qualified as an expert in linguistics, and testified on the semantic bias introduced by words like EVEN, AT LEAST, and ANY. He explained to the court that in passages like (2), it was always possible to characterize a length of time by either a least lower bound—WILL BE AT LEAST THREE YEARS—or a most upper bound—WILL BE FINISHED IN LESS THAN FOUR YEARS, and the consistent choice of the former showed a clear bias. He showed that EVEN and ANY introduce further bias toward the writer's point of view that no progress toward the resolution of the case is likely. The multiplication of these presuppositions and negative implications all led to the idea that one should accept the offer and abandon further action.

Judge Teitelbaum carefully followed Kroch's testimony on what the sources of bias were and how they might be eliminated. Here, for example, is an extract from Kroch's discussion of the third sentence in (2) above, as he applies arguments based on Gricean implicatures and his own work on the semantics of time adverbials:

> (6) KROCH: Beginning with the words "Accordingly, it is likely that it will be at least several years even after trial of this case before it is finally known whether plaintiffs or the plaintiff class will receive any back pay. . . ." When you indicate only the lower bounds of a time period and not the upper bounds there is a strong suggestion by the reader that it may well drag on indefinitely. Now, I understand that lawyers want to be careful not to make promises that they can't fulfill and that things often go on longer than you might think. However, this document is addressed to laymen who will read it as ordinary English. They won't read these qualifications as being particularly lawyers' qualifications; they will read them as ordinary English and a speaker of ordinary English at least assumes that when a phrase like "at least" is used that the author is using it because he cannot say something more clear and helpful to him. That, on the other hand, it could have said something like, "It is likely that within three or so years this case will be settled." Now, that is slanted the other way . . .
>
> THE COURT: Would it be perfectly unslanted if it said, "You should be advised that it may be three years before this matter is settled." Is that in the middle?
>
> KROCH: Well, frankly, I would take that as in the middle, but whether it is perfectly unbiased is not a question that I can judge immediately.

Throughout the trial, the courtroom was quite full, and several benches were occupied by steel workers from the Homestead plant. We noticed that they paid a great deal of attention to Kroch's testimony, and enjoyed particularly his exchanges with the judge and the defense attorneys.

My own testimony had two parts. One concerned the distribution of elements with semantic bias as against the distribution of readability and complexity. Figure 2 shows the biasing elements that we identified by the half-page, against the background established by Figure 1. It is immediately evident that these biasing elements—ANY, EVEN, AT LEAST, etc.—were not scattered randomly throughout the text. Instead, they are concentrated at just those points where the text is simplest: first, in the section on "How

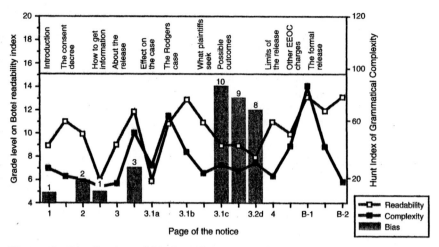

Figure 2   **Distribution of Biasing Elements in the Notice**

to get information," and then in "Possible outcomes." Our answer to both questions: "is the letter comprehensible? is it objective?" were therefore "Yes." But where the document was comprehensible, it was not objective; and where it was objective, it was not comprehensible. We need not think of such a distribution of bias as the result of deliberate manipulation. Where the authors of the letter tried most earnestly to simplify their language and help the reader decide what to do, they naturally introduced their own way of looking at things—that the Pittsburgh steel workers should take the money and run.

So far, our testimony rested in part on accepted techniques of measurement, in part on linguistic theory, and in part on the specific organization of the document. We emphasized the negative implications of ANY in passages like (2). ANY is a negative polarity element and demands negative contexts in sentences like "I (don't) think anything about it." There is a further implication that the occurrence of ANY in neutral contexts strengthens negative interpretations of the existential situation. In (2) the repeated use of this quantifier leads to the implication that even if a judgment is arrived at, there may not be any parties found injured; and even if parties are found to be injured, there may not be any pay awarded. The weakest point in the expert testimony was that our view of semantic bias rested on the linguists' interpretations and any agreement we could elicit from the judge. It was evident that the judge felt that he was as competent as anyone else to interpret the meanings of the words. He was more impressed by the objective measures of readability than by the linguists' analyses of semantic bias. I therefore introduced the results of an experiment designed to determine if the negative implications of ANY were sufficient to influence readers' judgments in a material way.

In this type of field experiment, a situation is constructed where the word or form in question is embedded in an ambiguous sentence, almost evenly balanced by the context. The listener's interpretation is preserved for several more sentences, while he or she discusses the situation. Here, I approached residents of Mantua, a black area of Philadelphia, with a request for help on a case being developed by the NAACP Legal Defense Fund:

(7) This is about a guy in Pittsburgh. He worked for U.S. Steel, for quite a few years. There was a group that was suing the steel companies for back pay, on account of discrimination in hiring policies, so that there were a lot of black people who were earning less money for a long time. So one day he got a letter from the company with a check for $700. If he signed the check within 30 days, he could cash it; but he had to sign a release, giving up any claim or connection with this suit for back pay. He had to figure out what were the chances: if there was a good chance of collecting on the suit, to let the check go; if the chances weren't so good, to cash the check and forget about the back pay. So he went to a lawyer. And the lawyer told him *there was no question about his getting any back pay.* Now how would you deal with that? would you take his advice?

The semantic question revolves around the interpretation of the italicized clause, which was alternatively delivered in two forms to subjects:

(8a) there was no question about his getting any back pay.
(8b) there was no question about his getting the back pay.

Answers to the questions did not always reveal the interpretations made by listeners, but in 16 out of 22 cases, there was a clear indication as to whether people thought the advice was positive—that he would get the back pay, and he should wait for it; or negative—that he would not get the back pay, and should not wait. The effect of *any* was clear:

Table 1.   Negative Implications of ANY vs. THE in U.S. Steel Experiment

Interpretation of lawyer's statement on chances of suit	*any* back pay	*the* back pay
positive	2	8
negative	5	1
undetermined	4	4
	11	11

Probability by Fisher's Exact Test, p = .036

This result supports our analysis of the negative implications of ANY in these contexts: the use of ANY can effectively alter listeners' interpretation of a situation and their probable course of action.

The Outcome

The judge was at first favorably inclined toward our testimony, and in fact asked Mort Botel if he would act as AMICUS CURIAE and rewrite the notice:

> (9) THE COURT: Do you want to do something for history and do it
>   in this case?
>   BOTEL: Well, I agree with Mr. Marcus when he said before that
>   this is worth doing.
>   THE COURT: Doctor, it is only worth doing as far as I am con-
>   cerned if it is done by the experts totally independent of
>   counsel and without the interjection of any legal concepts
>   in it, but really stating what is there.

Unfortunately, the judge was not willing to accept the delay that Botel estimated would be necessary to produce a revised notice in truly neutral and readable form. He did ask for a brief on the law concerning the responsibility to communicate to the public, and found none. The judge finally decided to rewrite the notice himself, taking officially into account the existence of these biasing elements. Actually, he changed it very little, and we can consider the case lost.

Judge Teitelbaum ruled against the plaintiffs, arguing that "any benefits which might theoretically be gained by such a revision are far outweighed by the detriments that would attend a lengthy delay."[6] Nevertheless, he entered into the opinion the following appreciation of the new issues raised:

> (10) In support of their position, plaintiffs have offered the testimony of
>   various experts in the fields of linguistics and (for want of a better
>   term), "readability." I have listened attentively to that testimony and,
>   candidly, cannot say that I find it to be utterly devoid of merit. In-
>   deed, I am inclined to believe that the general question of the "read-
>   ability" level of class and other legal notices is one which might well
>   require serious judicial consideration at an appropriate time.

He added in a footnote that neither the parties nor the Court had been able to find a case which addresses the "readability" level argument advanced by plaintiffs.

Though the U.S. Steel case was not won, it introduced into federal courts the issue of the responsibility of the judicial system to communicate

---

[6]Opinion of March 8, 1976, in the case of Rodgers v. United States Steel Corp., No. 71-793.

its instructions clearly to the public that must act on them. Since that time, considerable progress has been made in that respect. My own participation in this case convinced me that the federal courts did offer a forum that would attend to and assess objective evidence on these issues.

The "Thornfare" Case

In 1982, Wendell Harris and I used similar methods to develop testimony in federal court on the "Thornfare" legislation, which involved a parallel challenge to the objectivity and comprehensibility of a legal notice. Letters were being sent out to 80,000 welfare recipients notifying them that they would get assistance for no more than 90 days a year, since they had been reclassified as "transitionally needy." We were able to support a legal challenge to this letter by Community Legal Services of Philadelphia. Research in the community by Harris and myself was introduced in court to show that the letter was a biased guide to action: whereas the legislature had provided eight different grounds for appealing such a reclassification, the letter led readers to believe that there were no such grounds.[7]

On December 24th, Judge Norma Shapiro enjoined the state from further terminations, and ordered that a new letter be sent out which was more objective and comprehensible. While fewer than one out of 50 people had appealed the first wave of 17,000 letters, one out of seven appealed the second letter. Stronger legal challenges were made to the Thornfare legislation in the months that followed, and this may be considered only a successful delaying action. But as one attorney put it, "we helped quite a few people get through the winter."

The Prinzivalli Case

In October 1984 I received two tape recordings from attorney Ronald Ziff of Los Angeles. The first tape contained excerpts from a series of telephoned bomb threats made to Pan American Airlines at the Los Angeles Airport. They included such phrases as:

(11) . . . uh, it's gonna be planted on that plane by [a minority] Communist group and I hope you die on it. It's gonna be a bomb, a nuclear bomb that's gonna be able to kill you and everybody on that plane, and I hope you know it by now.

(12) . . . there's gonna be a bomb going off on the flight to L.A. It's in their luggage. Yes, and I hope you die with it and I hope you're on that.

---

[7]Labov and Harris 1983 provides a more complete report on this case.

(13) It's like gonna be a big shoot out tonight up in the air when that plane takes off. On 815 there's gonna be a big shoot out tonight up there.

(14) At eleven when it takes off at 11:15 tonight we're gonna shoot it down. They will shoot it down up in the air after it takes off for tonight.

The second tape had recordings of Paul Prinzivalli speaking the same words. He had been accused of making these telephone calls and was awaiting trial under a series of felony charges. The recording was made by Sandra Disner of the UCLA Phonetics Lab, who with Peter Ladefoged was working for the defense, particularly on voice-print identification data that showed that the two recordings had different voice qualities. They had referred Ziff to me because the defendant was from the New York metropolitan area of Long Island, and apparently people thought that the bomb threat caller was also from New York. I was asked to contribute my knowledge of the New York City dialect to bear on the case.

As soon as I played the tapes I was sure that Prinzivalli was innocent. He obviously was a New Yorker: every detail of his speech fitted the New York City pattern. But it was equally clear that the bomb threat caller was from Eastern New England. In any phrase, one could hear the distinctive features of the Boston area. Every phonetician familiar with the area who heard the tapes came to the same conclusion within a sentence or two, and non-phoneticians who knew the Boston area had the same reaction. In the course of my work for the case, I made recordings of several Bostonians; they all recognized the bomb threat caller as coming from their area without any question.

There was therefore no doubt about the guilt or innocence of Prinzivalli. The problem was how to convey this linguistic knowledge to a judge in the Los Angeles area who, like many other West Coast people involved, heard the two speech patterns as very similar. One could of course testify on the basis of an expert phonetician's opinion that the two dialects were different. But it seemed to me that unless that opinion could be supported by objective evidence that would bring home the reality of the situation to others, there was a serious danger that an innocent person would be convicted of a major crime, with a heavy prison sentence. It is well known that Americans are not sensitive to dialect differences, and from the standpoint of the West Coast, the difference between New York and Boston is hardly noticeable. The differences might appear great to a phonetician attuned to sound patterns, but not necessarily to an untrained listener raised on the West Coast.

Until I arrived in Los Angeles, I knew nothing more about the case than what was on the tapes, and that this was evidence being used to accuse a man of felony charges carrying heavy prison sentences. Here I will present the background facts that were given me after the trial: some have been reported in recent newspaper accounts.

The defendant was a cargo handler for Pan American, the airline involved. He was said to have a grudge against the airlines, because of their handling of shift schedules, among other things, and had been heard to say that he would "get even" with the company. Several executives of Pan American thought the bomb threat calls sounded like Prinzivalli, though others who had worked closely with him thought they did not. He was arrested and released on bail. The bomb threats continued and his bail was increased to $50,000 which he couldn't raise. When he was returned to jail, the bomb threat calls stopped. A month later the district attorney offered to release Prinzivalli on time served if he would plead guilty to three felony counts. He refused, and spent the next eight months in the Los Angeles County jail, awaiting trial.

To prepare for the trial, I first made detailed phonetic transcriptions of the two sets of recordings. I then made instrumental measurements of the formant positions, using the linear predictive coding algorithm at the Linguistics Laboratory of the University of Pennsylvania, and the various charting programs which we use for displaying vowel systems. I did all of this measurement myself, though the other phoneticians at the laboratory—Franz Seitz, Sharon Ash and David Graff—all contributed their critical thinking to the investigation. Since I was to present the testimony, it was important that I be able to answer for the continuity of the data and the procedures used throughout by personal knowledge.

I also made recordings of several Bostonians speaking the same words, and was able to confirm the similarity of the Boston pattern to the phonetic features of the tape. Several new and remarkable characteristics of the Boston dialect appeared in these investigations, which I did not introduce into the testimony, but do lend further certainty to our conclusions.

The trial was held in Los Angeles on the week of May 6th, without a jury, before Judge Gordon Ringer.[8] The defense had been willing to wait for an opening in Ringer's calendar, since they shared the general high opinion of his intelligence and ability. The prosecution presented evidence from ticket-reservation clerks who had given descriptions of the bomb threat voice at the time, from executives at Pan American who believed that the voice on the recorded bomb threat calls was Prinzivalli's, and evidence that he was a disgruntled employee.

The defense began with efforts to introduce evidence from voice-print identification by Disner and Ladefoged. Although Ladefoged opposed the free use of voice-prints to identify voices as the same, he has since con-

---

[8]The account of the trial that I will present below is limited to my own testimony, the preparation for it, and information I received from the defense attorneys on what happened immediately after. There was other important testimony that I did not hear, in particular the statements of Disner and Ladefoged, since I was not allowed to be in the courtroom while they were testifying.

cluded that voice-print identification is more evidentiary than we had thought, and can be used to argue that two voices are different. Disner's analysis showed that the individual voices on the tapes had different qualities. However, there was considerable legal argument on the admissibility and reliability of voice-print identification.

I testified on Friday May 10th. I was qualified as an expert on linguistics on the basis of my phonetic studies of New York City and other areas, of sound changes in progress and dialect diversity in the United States. The testimony was divided into four parts: auditory comparison of the dialect features; differences in phonological structure; relation to established knowledge of the dialect areas; and instrumental measurements of the vowel systems. As an expert witness, my role was to present an opinion, along with an account of the various steps that I had taken to reach that opinion, and the evidence that was the basis of it. But my aim was to present that evidence clearly enough so that Prinzivalli's innocence would appear to the judge as a matter of fact, rather than a matter of opinion.

In the first part, I played the tape recordings submitted to show the steps I had gone through to form an opinion. The most effective instrument here was the Nagra DSM loudspeaker, which projected to the four corners of the courtroom a clear and flat reproduction of the voices. Several people who had thought the voices sounded similar were suddenly struck with the differences that they now heard when the sound was projected through the Nagra.

I first called attention to the contrast in the pronunciation of the words BOMB and OFF in the phrase, AND A BOMB GOING OFF, as spoken by the bomb threat caller and the defendant, and displayed the IPA transcriptions of Figure 3.

I also prepared a third tape with copies of the words BOMB and OFF in close juxtaposition, as spoken by the bomb threat caller and the defendant, so that it would be immediately apparent that the vowel quality of BOMB and OFF was the same for the bomb threat caller, but different for the defendant. All of the tokens of short *o* and long open *o* words spoken by the bomb threat caller are low back-rounded vowels. But the defendant shows the characteristic New York City distinction between low central /a/ in POSITIVE, lower back /ah/ in BOMB, and the high, over-rounded and ingliding /oh/ in OFF.

The second part of my testimony introduced the theoretical basis of the argument: the concepts of phoneme, phonemic inventory, and phonemic merger. The notion of word class and phonemic identity are difficult

Figure 3 IPA Transcriptions of the Bomb Threat Caller and the Defendant's Pronunciations of BOMB and OFF.

Bomb Threat	deˇz gənə bi ə bɔᶛm goɨn ɒf ɒn ðə fla˂ɪt tu ɛl eⁱ
Defendant	dɛˆz gɔnə bi ə bɒm goɪŋ oᵊf ɑn ðə flaɪt tu˂ ɛl ɛˆⁱ

enough to establish among linguists, but much more so for the nonlinguist who thinks about language in terms of words and sounds rather than structure. The major emphasis was put on the merger of COT and CAUGHT in the Eastern New England area (as in Pittsburgh and throughout the Western United States), and on the structural difference between dialects that make such a distinction and those that don't. I also drew attention to some diagnostic phonetic features in the tape recordings, such as the tense front vowel in AIR as spoken by the bomb threat caller, with a following /j/: [ejə].

At this point the judge remarked that the tape of the bomb threat caller did sound to him like Robert Kennedy. But for reasons to appear later, it was important to draw attention away from such direct impressions, and focus instead on abstract structural features of the two recordings. In addition to the merger in the low back vowels, the bomb threat caller showed a consistently fronted nucleus of /ay/ in DIE and FIVE. It was evident that this nucleus was structurally identified with short /a/, while the defendant's New York City pattern showed the expected coincidence of the nucleus of /ay/ with the low central vowel /ah/ of ON.

Most significant was the vowel in THAT in the phrase, "I hope you're on that" in (12) above. In New York City, this is always and absolutely a lax /æ/, and never shows the tensed and fronted phoneme /æh/. But in Eastern New England, THAT can have the tensed, raised and fronted vowel, at roughly the same position as New York City THERE. In fact, the sentence "I hope you're on that" was mistranscribed in the text originally submitted to the court as "I hope you're on there." Most people still heard it as "there" until I replayed it through the Nagra loudspeaker and pointed out the unreleased /t/ at the end which was clearly audible. Such a pronunciation of THAT is not a real possibility for a New Yorker: of the thousands of short A words measured in our New York City studies, not one ever showed tensed /æh/ or /eh/ before voiceless stops.

The third part of my testimony introduced evidence from American dialectology, to show that the phonological differences between Eastern New England and New York City were established facts in linguistic scholarship. A copy of Kurath and McDavid's *The Pronunciation of English in the Atlantic States* (1961) was introduced into evidence, and the following data was displayed from the table of low back phonemes of each dialect region (p. 12):

Table 2 **Low Back Vowel Phonemes in ENE and NYC**

WORD CLASS	EASTERN NEW ENGLAND	NEW YORK CITY
cot, crop, stock, etc.	ɒ	ɑ
loss, frost, off, etc.	ɒ	ɔ
law, salt, talk, hawk, etc.	ɒ	ɔ

The first column shows for Eastern New England a single phoneme for three word classes: short *o* words ending in voiced stops, which are low central unrounded in New York City, and short *o* words ending in voiceless fricatives, which merge in New York City with the third class of original long open *o* words in the phoneme /ɔ/.

I added to this evidence the figures from my own study, "The three dialects of English" (Labov in press), which include the distribution of the COT-CAUGHT merger for the United States as a whole. These data are drawn from a 1966 study of the speech of long-distance telephone operators, and include information on the perception of speech as well as production.[9] They show the merger located in Eastern New England, an expanding area around Western Pennsylvania, Canada, and most of the western United States. There is no sign of this merger in the New York region or the surrounding mid-Atlantic states.

The last part of the testimony introduced instrumental measurements of the vowel systems of the bomb threat caller and the defendant, providing confirmation of the auditory impressions and the structural analyses.

The vowel system of the bomb threat caller is shown in Figure 4a. This is a two-formant chart, with the first formant on the vertical axis, and the logarithm of the second formant—approximating the perceptual relations—on the horizontal axis. Though we had measured the entire trajectory, and had evidence on differences in trajectories, the patterns appear most clearly in the distribution of vowel nuclei, as shown by the single point for each word selected to represent the nucleus in a systematic way.

Figure 4b showed a comparable analysis for the defendant. To support such displays, it was necessary to present to the court the theoretical concept of formant, and its relation to vowel quality, with some of the limitations involved. It was also necessary to explain the differences between linear predictive coding analysis of the digital signal and spectrographic analysis, which had become involved with the problem of the admissibility of voiceprint evidence. Since we had not used spectrographic techniques in our analysis of the vowel system, our evidence was free of the legal challenges that had been made to voice-print evidence, which uses the electro-mechanical spectrograph.

The significant features of Figures 4a and 4b were presented through a series of simpler displays. Figure 5a showed the single low-back phoneme of the bomb threat caller, with the vowels of BOMB, OFF, ON, POSITIVE and COMMUNIST all in the same low-back range.

---

[9]In this study, operators were asked for the telephone number of a Mr. [hərɪ hak], spoken with a low front central vowel. Operators from a one-phoneme area first looked up the spelling H-A-W-K, since it is more common than H-O-C-K. In the course of the discussion that followed, they also gave their own pronunciations of these two words, as well as COT and CAUGHT, reacted to my own two-phoneme pronunciation, and were led to give some information on their own geographical background. Though the mechanization and centralization of telephone information makes it impossible to pursue this approach, it gave a fairly fine-grained view of the status of the merger at that time.

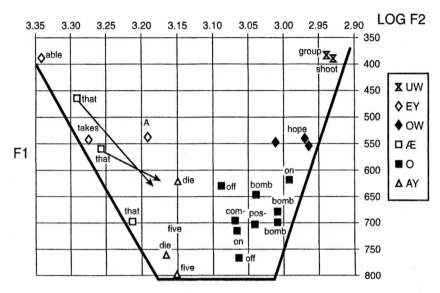

Figure 4a   **Vowel System of the Bomb Threat Caller**

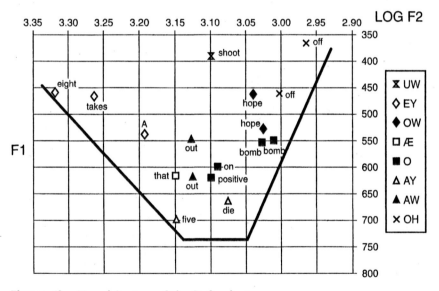

Figure 4b   **Vowel System of the Defendant**

Figure 5b showed the corresponding data for the defendant, with the three distinct phonemes characteristic of the New York City system. Most short *o* words like ON, POSITIVE and COMMUNIST have a low central vowel that is represented by the phoneme /a/. A small number of short *o* words are lengthened and backed, and join other long *a* words like FATHER in the phoneme /ah/: BOMB is a member of this class (Cohen 1970).

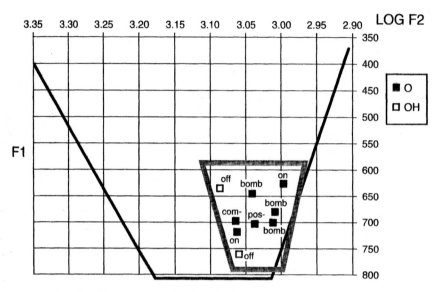

Figure 5a   /o/ Phoneme of the Bomb Threat Caller

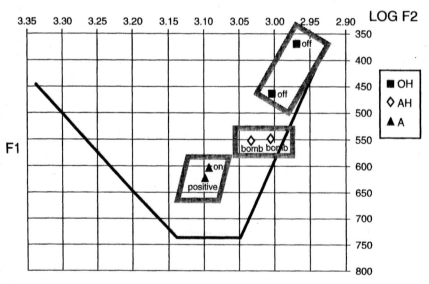

Figure 5b   /a,ah, oh/ Phonemes of the Defendant

Figures 6a and 6b dealt with the fronting of /ay/ which marks the Eastern New England dialect; in this system, the nucleus of /ay/ is identified with the nucleus of the /ah/ phoneme that merges traditional long *a* words like FATHER and HALF with words where post-vocalic /r/ is vocalized as in CAR and MARKET. In all of these words, the /a/ nucleus is fronted and shows

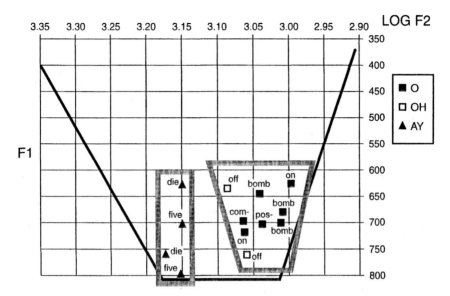

Figure 6a Low Front /ay/ of the Bomb Threat Caller

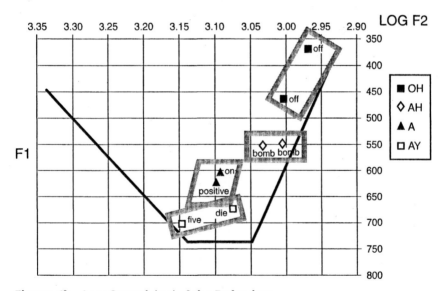

Figure 6b Low Central /ay/ of the Defendant

a good margin of security separating it from the low back phoneme that merges /o/ and /oh/. The only representatives of these two fronted phonemes in the bomb threat calls are the /ay/ words. Figure 6a showed the consistent fronting of /ay/ in the bomb threat calls. The comparable Figure 6b showed the situation for the defendant: here /ay/ ranges across the bottom of the vowel system, and the nucleus is not separated from the /a/ phoneme in ON, POSITIVE and COMMUNIST.

At this point it was not necessary to introduce more diagrams or explain the implications of the instrumental data in greater detail. The judge intervened to interpret the diagrams himself, since he saw clearly the relation between the previous testimony and the instrumental display.

I concluded my testimony by stating that all of the linguistic features found in the bomb threat call could be identified with the linguistic features of the Eastern New England dialect, and that the defendant's speech consistently showed the features of the New York City dialect. In answer to the defense attorney's final question, I stated that the two recordings were spoken by different people.

Judge Ringer then asked the defendant to rise and recite the pledge of allegiance to the flag: "I pledge allegiance to the flag of the United States of America and to the Republic for which it stands, one nation, indivisible, with liberty and justice for all." The defendant did so, and the judge asked me if I could point out any relevant dialect characteristics in what he had just said. I was able to indicate a number of defining features of the New York City dialect including the high back ingliding /oh/ in ALL, the tensed /æh/ in STAND, and in particular the tensed /æh/ in FLAG. New York City has tense /æh/ before all voiced stops, including /g/. Other Mid-Atlantic dialects have the phonemic split between lax /æ/ and tense /æh/, but none of them have tense /æh/ before /g/. As one passes from New York to Philadelphia, the first sub-class to drop out of the tense category is short *a* the words before /g/: FLAG, BAG, RAG, etc. This confirmed the previous testimony that Prinzivalli's speech showed the specific and consistent features of the New York City dialect.

The prosecution asked only a few questions on cross-examination. Most of the questions concerned the identification of individuals, and whether I could say if a given speech sample belonged to a given person. In response I tried to point out that I had no expertise in the identification of individuals, but that my knowledge concerned speech communities. Though sociolinguistic studies have found from the outset that communities were more consistent objects of description than individuals, there are limits on the range of variation for any individual who belongs to that community.

The question that naturally followed was whether an individual New Yorker could imitate a Boston dialect—whether Prinzivalli could have disguised himself as a Bostonian. My reply was that when people imitate or acquire other dialects, they focus on the socially relevant features: the marked words and sounds, but not on the phonological structures. I was able to cite Payne's work in King of Prussia (1980), which shows that all children acquire the low level sound rules of the Philadelphia area in a few years, but only those with parents raised in Philadelphia reproduce the phonological distribution of Philadelphia lax /æ/ and tense /æh/. If it could be shown that the defendant had had a long familiarity with the Boston dialect, and a great talent for imitation, then one couldn't rule out the possibility that he had done a perfect reproduction of the Boston system. But if so, he would have accomplished a feat that had not yet been reported for anyone else.[10]

On the following Monday morning, Judge Ringer called the attorneys to the bench and asked them if they wanted to continue the case. Since the prosecuting attorney did not consent to dismiss the charges, additional testimony was submitted on voice-print identification. The following morning the prosecuting attorney summarized his case. When the defense attorney rose to present his final argument, Judge Ringer said that there was no need for him to do so. He acquitted the defendant, finding on the basis of the linguistic testimony evidence of a reasonable doubt that Prinzivalli had committed the crime. In discussion in chambers and to the press, he stressed the clarity and objectivity of the linguistic evidence, a point on which all the attorneys agreed.

Prinzivalli was offered his job back at Pan American, on condition that he did not sue for damages or back pay. He filed suit for damages; the case has not yet been resolved, but he has been reinstated at Pan American and is now working in Long Island. In a letter of thanks to me he said that he had waited 15 months for someone to separate fact from fiction, and when he heard it done in the courtroom he was much moved.

Conclusion

These three cases are taken from a larger set where linguistic evidence was used to testify in the search for a just interpretation of the facts of the matter. I have chosen them to illustrate the possibilities open to a science of linguistics which draws on observation and experiment to establish its conclusions. All our efforts were not equally successful. But in each case, the objectivity of this approach to linguistics was favorably received by those who are quite removed from the academic issues that determine success or failure within our field.

I have been struck by the intense interest of both attorneys and judges in the objectivity and reliability of evidence. In our legal system it is assumed that there will be advocates and experts on each side. It is assumed that each side will use every rhetorical device to strengthen its case. There

---

[10]A current case in Southern New Jersey involves a parallel problem of identifying the voice of a recorded threat with the voice of a particular person. Here the specific characteristics of the Philadelphia dialect have been useful in arguing that the defendant did not make the call attributed to him. In preparing testimony for this case, Sharon Ash of Penn Linguistics Laboratory carried out experiments to determine whether people trying to disguise their voices altered the phonological features of their dialects. She found that subjects changed many aspects of their speech in attempting to disguise their voices, but the specific phonology of Philadelphia became more prominent.

is no claim for impartiality in argument. Therefore all the more value is put on the solidity and objectivity of evidence that is inserted into this system of advocacy, which creates belief and justifies decisions in the face of contending parties. It has been pointed out to me that judges in particular are grateful for evidence that allows them to decide a case with confidence, and commit themselves to sleep at night without wondering if they have sentenced an innocent person to jail or let a criminal go free.

The bridge between the facts of a case and the conclusion cannot be made without the help of linguistic theory. No web of inferences and deductions can be made without general principles that rest on a long history of observation and testing. Here I have illustrated the application of the theory of negative polarity, and the association of negative polarity with distinctive meaning. I have also dealt with the theory of the phoneme, intimately connected with the fundamental concept of the arbitrary character of the linguistic sign.

When we contrast linguistic theory with linguistic practice, we usually conjure up a theory that builds models out of introspective judgments, extracting principles that are remote from observation and experiment. This is not the kind of theory I have in mind when I search for a way to establish the facts of a matter I am involved in. It is hard to imagine that a concept like subjacency or the Empty Category Principle would be used in court to decide a question of fact.

We are, of course, interested in theories of the greatest generality. But are these theories the end-product of linguistic activity? Do we gather facts to serve the theory, or do we create theories to resolve questions about the real world? I would challenge the common understanding of our academic linguistics that we are in the business of producing theories: that linguistic theories are our major product. I find such a notion utterly wrong.

A sober look at the world around us shows that matters of importance are matters of fact. There are some very large matters of fact: the origin of the universe, the direction of continental drift, the evolution of the human species. There are also specific matters of fact: the innocence or guilt of a particular individual. These are the questions to answer if we would achieve our fullest potential as thinking beings.

General theory is useful, and the more general the theory the more useful it is, just as any tool is more useful if it can be used for more jobs. But it is still the application of the theory that determines its value. A very general theory can be thought of as a missile that attains considerable altitude, and so it has much greater range than other missiles. But the value of any missile depends on whether it hits the target.

References

Cohen, Paul. 1970. The tensing and raising of short [a] in the metropolitan area of New York City. Columbia University Master's Essay.

Kurath, Hans & Raven I. McDavid, Jr. 1961. The pronunciation of English in the Atlantic states. Ann Arbor: University of Michigan Press.

Kroch, Anthony. 1972. Lexical and inferred meanings for some time adverbs. Quarterly progress reports of the Research Laboratory of Electronics of MIT: 104.19–23.

Kroch, Anthony. 1979. The semantics of scope in English. New York: Garland Publishing Co.

Labov, William. In press. The three dialects of English. Quantitative analyses of sound change in progress, ed. by P. Eckert. New York: Academic Press.

Labov, William and Wendell Harris. 1983. Linguistic evidence in the Thornfare Case. Ms.

Payne, Arvilla. 1980. Factors controlling the acquisition of the Philadelphia dialect by out-of-state children. Locating language in time and space, ed. by W. Labov, 143–178. New York: Academic Press.

Van den Broek, Jeff. 1977. Class differences in syntactic complexity in the Flemish town of Maaseik. Language in Society 6.149–182.

Content Questions

1. Based on readability tests, in the U.S. Steel case, which parts of the notice appeared to be harder to read? Which parts were easier?

2. How did the differences in readability relate to the goal desired by those who prepared the notice?

3. What kind of bias was contained in the notice with the use of the words *any* and *at least?*

4. In the Prinzivalli case, which dialect area did the caller's pronunciation appear to match? What about Prinzivalli's pronunciation?

5. Labov indicates that as soon as he heard the tapes of the bomb threat and of Prinzivalli, he knew that Prinzivalli was innocent. But what did Labov indicate would be the problem in the case?

6. What were the four principal parts of Labov's testimony in the case?

7. Contrast Prinzivalli's pronunciation of *bomb* and *off* with the caller's pronunciation.

8. To what extent did Labov think it was possible for someone to imitate the dialect of another region?

9. What effect did the linguistic evidence have in the judge's decision in the Prinzivalli case?

Questions for Analysis and Discussion

1. The Prinzivalli case shows how working in one discipline in linguistics might also require knowledge in another discipline. Based on what Labov

describes about his work in the Prinzivalli case, how important is a knowledge of phonetics and phonology to someone working in dialectology? What kinds of limitations could a person without such knowledge have when working with dialects? Explain.

2. From a linguistic standpoint, how would the fact that the trial in the Prinzivalli case would be held in the western United States before a judge who spoke a West Coast dialect make the preparation of the case more difficult?

3. What role did phonetic transcription play in this trial?

4. This article also includes charts made from high-tech machinery providing acoustic evidence. Most introductory linguistics courses spend little time, if any, dealing with acoustic phonetics, but from observing these charts and reflecting on how such data is compiled, what advantages do you think such an analysis could have in a courtroom setting?

5. When the judge asked the defendant to recite the pledge of allegiance and the defendant pronounced the word *flag* with a tense /æh/ before /g/, why was that significant in relation to the case? Explain this with regard to a phonological rule mentioned in the article and the likelihood of a person being able to imitate even the phonology of a different dialect.

Mc-: Meaning in the Marketplace

Genine Lentine and Roger W. Shuy

The meaning of individual words is at the heart of legal interpretation.
But as the following article illustrates, an even more basic level of meaning
can acquire importance in legal settings. In the following article, which
first appeared in the journal *American Speech,* Genine Lentine and Roger
W. Shuy show the importance of a morphological analysis they performed
in connection with a trademark infringement suit.

The lexicon of the English language, or of any language for that matter, responds to constant cultural changes, both subtle and conspicuous. Forces
such as technology can add lexical entries with each new advance. Marketing also influences the lexicon when brand names become generic expressions or "normal, everyday names for things" (Cruse 1986, 146); such
generic terms then require a specifying modifier for clarity of reference. Expressions like *Panasonic Walkman* and such questions as *What brand of
Xerox machine do you have?* do not sound anomalous because the nouns
in those expressions have become generic through popular usage (though
these trademarks themselves remain vigilantly protected against commercial use). A strong market presence can, in this way, actually introduce new
terms into the lexicon. Moreover, the process is not confined to semantic
change. Witness, for example, the phonologically deviant (for English) yet
common pronunciation of the brand name *Nike* as [nayki]. In no other
word in English do the the letters *ike* signal the pronunciation that they do
in this word, and yet most American English speakers pronounce the name
as it is shown here. Through constant exposure, advertisers thus teach the
speech community not only WHAT they want a morpheme or phrase to
mean but HOW it should sound.

Corporations do not necessarily mind when their mark becomes a
household word—no doubt some cheer! However, when another corporation moves in on their lexical territory by using either the mark or something close to it, they allege TRADEMARK INFRINGEMENT. This paper
describes our contribution to a million-dollar trademark infringement suit
involving Quality Inns International (QI) and the McDonald's Corporation. At the request of a Washington, DC, law firm,[1] we performed an in-
ductive analysis, based on newspaper and magazine citations, of the place

---

[1] We were engaged by Laurence R. Hefter and Robert Litowitz of the firm of Finnegan, Henderson, Farabow, Garrett, and Dunner.

of the *Mc-* formative in the English language. We found that it acts much like a derivational affix, except that, unlike most affixes in this category, it has several senses. More importantly, we found that while large corporations can have great power in generating raw material for lexical change, and while they can prevent other corporations from using specific words in specific ways, they have little effect on stopping the machinery of semantic change once it has begun to operate within the language of everyday spoken and written discourse.

The background of the case is as follows. In the fall of 1987, QI announced plans for a new chain of low-priced hotels to complement their other market categories. They announced that they would call this chain *McSleep Inns;* by 1990, QI planned to open about 200 McSleep franchises. However, only three days after the initial announcement, McDonald's Corporation sent QI a letter, alleging trademark infringement and demanding that QI not use the *McSleep* name. QI responded by seeking a declaratory legal judgment that the mark does not infringe upon any federally registered trademarks, that it does not allege false description or origin, and that it does not infringe upon or violate any common-law rights that McDonald's might have. Preliminary maneuverings lasted for a year, culminating in a seven-day trial in July of 1988 before United States District Judge Paul V. Niemeyer in Baltimore, Maryland. In the end, Judge Niemeyer ruled that QI could not use the prefix in the name of their proposed hotel chain.

Explaining their choice of the name *McSleep* in deposition testimony, QI expressed the belief that the name would project, among other things, an image of thrift and cleanliness. Drawing upon stereotypes of the Scottish character, the president of QI, Robert C. Hazard, said in deposition, "You have got an idea of affordable and you have got an idea that Scots are consistently thrifty, I think they are clean, you know, they are not—like other people—they're considered to be consistently clean, thrifty people."

In a previous, unrelated case, McDonald's had successfully sued "McBagel's," a small restaurant in New York City; the judge ruled that using *Mc-* in combination with a generic food noun did indeed constitute infringement. The use of *Mc-* with a generic term not related to food, however, was not tested. QI's suit against McDonald's asserted that QI had a right to use the name in a non-food industry context, as McSleep Inns were not to contain restaurants. McDonald's claimed to the contrary that, although it does not own the trademark *Mc-* by itself, it owns a FAMILY of such marks which deserve special trademark protection. They claimed that because McDonald's marks are formulated by combining the *Mc-* or *Mac-* prefix with a generic word to form a "fanciful," "arbitrary" trademark or service mark, they are marks that describe nothing in particular and thus need have no inherent link to the goods or services with which they are linked. The key here is that the marks are formed by combination, and it is that formula for combination that has protection.

Another basic issue in the case was whether or not people would think *McSleep Inns* were somehow related to McDonald's. McDonald's contended that the name *McSleep Inn* was likely to cause confusion and that QI had deliberately selected the word *McSleep* to trade on McDonald's reputation and goodwill. They sought to establish that QI could benefit a great deal from "trading" on the McDonald's name, citing such evidence as that the recognition of Ronald McDonald by children age two to eight was 100%, comparable only to their recognition of Santa Claus.

Precedents with respect to the issue of "confusion" are many. For example, the marks for Notre Dame University and Notre Dame cheese were allowed to coexist, as were the marks for Bulova watches and Bulova shoes and for Alligator raincoats and Alligator shoes. Because these marks occur in widely divergent fields, the public presumably would not make a necessary connection between the two corporate entities. In some cases, however, as Judge Niemeyer points out in his published opinion (1988, 29), "a close affinity of markets for two different products or services can create in the public perception a belief or expectation that one would be expected to go into the other." An important legal principle known as the Aunt Jemima Doctrine concerns related but noncompetitive markets. In this 1917 case, Aunt Jemima Mills Pancake Batter held the trademark, against which the proposed Aunt Jemima Syrup was found to infringe, not only because syrup and flour are both food products but also because they are commonly used together. This doctrine was important to the case at hand: although *McSleep* and *McDonald's* are not in competing areas, there is thought to be a logical connection between the food industry and the lodging industry.

Also central to this case was the issue of generic labels. When a trademark becomes so strong that it becomes the generic label for goods or services associated with another corporation, the owners of the trademark can still protect the mark from corporate use, but they have little influence over its use in everyday language. In some cases, we have lost sight of the original corporate source for certain terms because the owner of the marks surrendered the rights to that mark. Examples of these terms are *aspirin, cellophane,* and *escalator.* While this type of generic term is not uncommon, there are also nouns which became generic while the corporation was still protecting its trademark. For example, despite the Xerox Corporation's attempts to encourage speakers into using *photocopy* as a verb instead of *xerox,* the latter can still be heard in offices across America. Similarly, while the Kimberly Clark corporation still owns the trademark *Kleenex,* many people always ask for a *kleenex* when they need a tissue of any type. The list goes on and on, with examples such as *Q-Tip, Cuisinart,* and *Thermos.*

Mc- shows an unusual mixture of both popular and corporate use. Trademark cases often involve the use of a protected lexical item, in most cases a word or phrase, by one company in a way that allegedly causes confusion with or dilution of another company's mark. One recent example of this is with Toyota's new line of Lexus cars. The Mead Corporation sued Toyota in order to protect their on-line search network called Lexis from trademark dilution. This was fairly straightforward because most English speakers do not frequently use the word *Lexis*. Most speakers could not even produce a definition for *lexis;* its primary dictionary meaning is strongly related to Mead's trademarked name. The case of *Mc-*, however, is not so one-dimensional. To begin with, *Mc-* is not a word at all, nor even a single free morpheme. Rather, it functions as a derivational prefix—a very productive prefix, as we will show below, one that speakers of American English across the country regularly hear, read, and use.

In court, McDonald's suggested that they were themselves responsible for the productivity of the *Mc-* morpheme—indeed, they had even overtly pursued an advertising campaign to that end. Roy T. Bergold, Jr, vice president of advertising for McDonald's, described a campaign in which Ronald McDonald was shown teaching children to put the prefix before many different words, creating *McFries, McShakes,* and *McBest.* The purpose of these commercials was, Bergold said, to create a *McLanguage* specifically associated with McDonald's.

QI made four main arguments in presenting their case that McDonald's cannot claim ownership over every formative of *Mc-* plus a generic word. The first was that there was no likelihood of confusion between *McSleep* and *McDonald's.* The second was that the uses were not competitive: McDonald's marks have been developed in the fast-food business and do not preclude the use of *McSleep Inn* in the lodging business. The third defense involved the fact of extensive third-party uses; having allowed or acquiesced to the extensive use by third parties of a proliferation of words formulated by combining *Mc-* with a generic word, McDonald's should be denied the right to preclude the use of *McSleep Inn,* QI argued. Although there were many such third-party uses listed in the trademark register, rules of evidence permitted QI's attorneys to include only those names for which there was concrete evidence of commercial use. The attorneys found such evidence in telephone directories, credit reports, and newspaper references. They also made phone calls and visited the businesses for purposes of verification. In these names, we find examples mainly of the Scottish association (as in *McDivot's* and *McGruff* the crime dog) and of the sense of "basic, convenient, standardized, inexpensive," as in *McLube* automobile service, *McThrift Inn,* and *McMaids* (see the appendix below for the published sources for all cited forms).

The fourth argument was the one for which our testimony was used. QI maintained that *Mc-* has become generic: it has entered into the English language with a recognized meaning of its own. To determine whether or not this argument could be supported within the field of linguistics, we proposed the following analytical procedure and methodology, which served as the basis for testimony.

We surveyed, with the use of a computer search system called Nexis and a national clipping service, a wide sample of sources, looking for words containing the *Mc-* prefix. The data were newspaper and magazine citations collected primarily between March and July 1988. The sources represented a wide range of speech communities within the United States. The sample consisted of about 150 articles in which writers used the prefix *Mc-* with a descriptive or generic term. Our sample included such national magazines as *Forbes, Time,* and *Working Woman,* major newspapers such as the *Los Angeles Times* and the *Washington Post* and local papers such as the *Maple Heights Press,* and technical publications such as *Rubber and Plastics News.* Shuy explained (in his testimony to the court, 1988) the rationale for our choice of a database:

> I wanted a body of data because I did not want to rely upon my own intuitions. I wanted to have an empirical base from which to do the analysis. One can in analysis of any kind sit and think about it and say here's what I know to be true because I am a native speaker of this language and here is how it works, and I know. Or, you can do experiments by, say, bringing people into a laboratory, sitting them down and asking them questions. Or, one can do empirical studies with actually existing natural events, in this case, articles in magazines. . . . Here we have a body of citations and evidence from all over the country and in which the people who wrote it didn't know that they were going to be looked at with this case in mind.

Our goal was to discover inductively how writers, and therefore (with proper respect for the differences between speaking and writing) speakers, use and understand the *Mc-* morpheme. At no point in the trial did we dispute that the *Mc-* prefix has a strong association with McDonald's. We acknowledged this obvious use of the prefix and focused our attention on tracking its spread into other analogous domains. The 94 articles accumulated for our research were gathered together as a two-volume exhibit; excluded from the exhibit were all articles that were specifically about McDonald's restaurants and/or specific McDonald's products.[2]

The range of citations was surprisingly broad. We found an abundance of evidence for the productivity of the morpheme *Mc-.* Writers attached the prefix to words referring to everything from tune-ups to major surgery. We even found examples in which one use would spawn a subsequent use, for example in the case of *McPaper* giving rise to *McTelecast.*

We analyzed each of the 94 citations, drawing from context the senses of the prefix. From this, we produced a rough list of properties associated with the use of *Mc-* and found that *Mc-* had seven distinct senses or functions and that the cues within the articles made clear which senses were

---

[2]In some of the exhibited stories there was an occasional mention of McDonald's as an illustration of some other point, but by no means as the main focus of the articles.

intended. Each of the 94 articles fell into one of the seven meaning categories. The seven categories thus grew out of our reading the articles; that is, we did not set up categories and then read the articles to find examples. We found that the prefix was combined mainly with generic nouns, and in some cases with proper nouns, adjectives, adverbs, and verbs. In testimony, illustrative articles were discussed for each of the seven categories of meaning. Following are the senses and functions of *Mc-* that we found represented in the sample:

1. Ethnic associations (includes surnames)
2. Alliterative patternings arising from a proper name
3. Acronyms
4. Products of the McDonald's Corporation
5. Macintosh computer products or related businesses
6. Parodies of a fast-food product or service
7. The meaning "basic, convenient, inexpensive, standardized."

What started out as a simple patronymic prefix has undergone processes of lexical shift, lexical narrowing, and lexical generalization. While the meanings and functions may have been largely set in motion by McDonald's, they now often refer to generalized concepts such as "speed," "efficiency," and "consistency."

The first category, ETHNIC ASSOCIATIONS, included examples in which the prefix was used in order to reinforce a reference to either Scotland or Ireland, especially citations in which the authors made references to thriftiness and other stereotypical attributes associated with the Scottish. Mencken (1963, 388–89) notes that nearly all the words and phrases in English which are based on *Scotch* embody references to the traditional frugality of the Scots, for example, *Scotch Coffee* "hot water flavored with burnt biscuit"; *to play the Scotch organ* "put money in a cash register"; and *Scotch pint* "two-quart bottle." Thus, most of these references were in some way connected with thriftiness. A slightly different example was a crossword puzzle in the *Washington Post Magazine* entitled *McPuzzle.* The theme clues included "Kilted Mystery Writer," "Kilted Gunshot Victim," and "Kilted Racket man." Clearly, the creator of the puzzle was inviting us to make the connection between kilts and Scotland. Another example was an advertisement which drew upon the association with Irish surnames. It read, "McSure it gets there o'ernight," and included such stereotypical tokens of Irishness as the four-leaf clover and the word *blarney.*

The next category, ALLITERATIVE PATTERNINGS ARISING FROM A PROPER NAME, was unlike the other categories in that it was based more on form than on content. In this category, the *Mc-* was not semantically connected in any way to the topic of the article, but rather appeared to have been added for the sheer fun of the repetitive pattern. Examples of this are "McVeto McKernan," "McLish—it rhymes with McDish," and "Jim

McMyth" (to refer to Jim McMahon). One article was entitled, "Parents Aided in the 'Mc' of Time." It was about a series of events all involving names beginning with *Mc-*: in Macomb, a town in McDonough County, Illinois, an officer named McBride delivered a baby for a couple named McGrew on St. Patrick's Day (the latter an ethnic reference to things Irish). In these examples there are no clues in the articles that any of the authors is attributing any specific qualities to the noun; rather, the prefix is used playfully in each case—for aesthetic purposes, much in the same way that children play with patterned code languages (Crystal 1987, 58).

The third category, ACRONYMS, was a straightforward one in that it involved the use of initials of the title for something. We had only two examples in this category: *McDap,* which stood for "Mason County Drug Abuse Program," and *McRIDES,* in which the *Mc-* was derived from *Morris County.*

As explained earlier, we did not analyze the articles contained in the fourth category, which were specifically about McDonald's and their products. The fifth category was an obvious one: MACINTOSH COMPUTER PRODUCTS OR RELATED BUSINESSES. These uses were not considered relevant to the *McSleep* case for two reasons. First, McDonald's and Macintosh had apparently ironed out their differences over these names. More importantly, the spelling usually associated with Macintosh computers is *Mac-,* not *Mc-* (although the pronunciation and stress are sometimes the same).

In sorting out the articles, we found that often writers would, in talking about a product or service, create an imaginary set of details about that product or service, making it seem like a fast-food restaurant. This led to the sixth category, PARODIES OF A FAST-FOOD PRODUCT OR SERVICE. The key factor in putting articles into this rather than the final category (described below) is that, in these articles, the author describes something hypothetical or fanciful. For example, in the article "*McSoup* Stirs Dreams of Kitchen Glory," the author, Patti McDonald, dreams of having a soup restaurant:

> "How about McSoup?" I said proudly.... "We could even name our restaurant McDonald's and who knows, some day we could even open a chain of them." My husband babbled something about worried about some kind of McSuit if we did such a thing but I didn't understand what he was talking about.... I seem to be on my way to McRiches.... I will be in my kitchen, making McSoup and dreaming about my pending empire.

In this article, modals such as *could,* the future tense in "I will be in my kitchen," and the author "dreaming" about her "pending" empire all indicate a hypothetical, fanciful concept. In another article, which described the growing popularity of squid, the author said, "Squid McNuggets may be a long way off, but the ugly mollusks are finding their way onto the dinner plates of more and more Americans." This brief reference again indicates a future, hypothetical event.

Another article in this category exaggerated the array of services available to residents of Marin County, California. It reads,

> After paying Bobby Divot a half a hundred for his sage advice, I decided to look for a quick fix for the problems in my upper works. This being Marin County, I didn't know whether to try "Gurus R Me," "Marin County Computerized Psychic Matching Service and Burrito Take Out" or "McMeditation—Over 5,000,000 Mantras Served."

In this example, again, the author uses the *Mc-* prefix to evoke an image of a restaurant or service that would be on a mass-market scale and that would have a "quick-fix" approach. The ridiculous nature of the other names in the list cue the reader to the author's satirical intent.

There was relatively little debate about the first six categories. At issue, and central to the lawsuit, was category seven: THE MEANING "BASIC, CONVENIENT, INEXPENSIVE, STANDARDIZED." Our contention was that not one of the 56 articles presented in this category was specifically about McDonald's or even about hamburgers. Instead, the attachment of the prefix suggested to the reader that the product or service described had the attributes "basic, convenient, inexpensive, standardized." Not all 56 of the articles implied all four of these meanings, but most implied at least three of them.

In arriving at the wording of definition seven, we grouped together related common key words and phrases from the articles and found terms that could subsume the groups. Words and phrases such as *lacks prestige, everyday, lowbrow,* and *simple* mapped onto the concept "BASIC."

The heading CONVENIENT was suggested by such attributive words as *highly advertised, franchised, easy access, quick, self-service,* and *handy location.* Terms such as *lacks prestige* and *lowbrow* suggested the term INEXPENSIVE. The heading STANDARDIZED had many hyponyms, including *assembly-line precision, high volume, reduces choices, mass merchandising, standardized, state-of-the-art marketing,* and *prepackaged.*

An article that typifies this sense of *Mc-* appeared in *Forbes* magazine. It was called "McArt" and contains phrases such as "mass market art" indicating basic convenience. From the words "mass marketing," "galleries open seven days a week," and "chains," we arrived at a sense of convenience and standardization. These references to the product labelled "McArt" in the article's title tell us essentially what the writer intended when the word *art* was prefixed with *Mc-.*

Another of the articles we cited was called "McLaw: Lawyering for the Masses" (it appeared in *The California Lawyer*). The author describes the easily accessible and inexpensive basic legal services that are cropping up increasingly across the country. Expressions such as "near-omnipresence," "franchise legal clinics," "serving the masses," "everyday legal problems," and "drive-in windows" occur frequently throughout the article. The word *McLaw* appears five times. There is no mention of McDonald's and no direct or indirect reference to hamburgers. It is clear that all four of the characteristics of this final category are described in this article: "basic," "standard," "inexpensive," and "convenient." *Near omnipresence* and *drive-in windows* indicate "convenience." The article notes that these clinics serve the masses and that consultation fees are $20 to $25, indicating that they are "inexpensive." *Everyday legal problems* and *franchised legal clinics* map on to both "standardized" and "basic." Another line from the article suggesting "basic" is "McLaw attorneys lack the prestige, comforts, and salary that come with other types of private practice." Clearly, it is the productive morpheme *Mc-* that is imparting these senses, for if we remove the *Mc-*, leaving *Law attorneys lack the prestige, comforts . . .*, the sentence makes no sense. In linguistic terms, the pair of sentences is a sort of MINIMAL PAIR in that the presence or absence of only one element, *Mc-,* creates a contrast in meaning.

Similarly, an article called *McMiz* about the marketing of the musical *Les Miserables* also used *Mc-* in this way. The following paragraph is revealing in that the author lumps all fast food restaurants together, indicating a generalization of the prefix:

> Maybe it's unfair to link the epic (and epically expensive) "Les Miserables" with fast food. But it's not an entirely unapt allusion, either. Producer Cameron Mackintosh and his organization have perfected elaborate and elegantly aggressive marketing, merchandising and standardized production techniques that the burger giants might envy.

Significantly, the author refers to "fast food" and "the burger giants" rather than specifically to McDonald's, thus suggesting that the comparison is being made to the whole category of large fast-food corporations. The comparison is further broadened when the author comments that the productions are "multiplying like Mrs. Field's cookie boutiques at an unprecedented speed,"—interesting because again *Mc-* is being used to refer to the larger phenomenon of fast food, not just specifically to McDonald's.

Many other references suggest this more general use of the prefix. For example, in an article about the newspaper *USA Today,* Marti Ahern says, "Some call it McPaper—fast news for the fast-food generation." Another article about *USA Today* discusses the editor John Neuharth's decision to print as the lead story the report of death of Princess Grace of Monaco instead of one about the assassination of a Lebanese president-elect. Neuharth was faulted for this by editors at the more established papers, who then dubbed the paper *McPaper.* Clearly what was operating here was not a direct comparison to McDonald's, but rather a more abstract connection of the similar properties of "giving the people what they want."

Similarly, Erma Bombeck used the prefix in its mass-market, "panderous" sense when she referred to "McStory on the paper's front page" in a column she wrote about the media's preoccupation with the wardrobes of Nancy Reagan and Raisa Gorbachev. In this article, she talked of reading a "McStory," without making any mention even of fast food, much less McDonald's. Furthermore, she does not even use quotes around the expression, suggesting that she does not feel obliged to alert the reader to an unusual word or to an unusual use of an ordinary word.

Conclusion

Based upon our analysis, then, we found that the prefix *Mc-* acts like any ambiguous lexical item, in that a reader or hearer must rely on context to determine which of the possible senses the author is intending. At trial, we emphasized the point that meaning is flexible, determined by context. We used the example of the polysemous/ambiguous word *green,* which has a number of related and distinct senses. We argued that when a word is ambiguous, placing it within a specific context often disambiguates it. For example, *green* in the sentence *Give me the green* has a very different sense if the sentence is uttered by one speaker holding the other at gunpoint than it does when uttered by an artist gesturing to his assistant. Sometimes we have to look no further than the sentence itself to conclude which sense of an ambiguous word is intended, as in the sentence *The new cowhand was still a little green,* in which the words *new* and *still* cue us that the intended sense is most likely "inexperienced." In a sentence such as *The young sailor was green,* however, we entertain two possible senses, "seasick" and "inexperienced." In such a case, the hearer or reader would look for evidence elsewhere in the context to determine which sense is intended.

We argued that with the prefix *Mc-* there were several factors suggesting that a person reading the prefix in many of these articles could dismiss the possible association with McDonald's. Placing the prefix in the context of hotel marketing—in other words, situating an abstract *Mc-* name within an actual usage situation unrelated to fast food—it becomes unlikely that one would immediately associate *Mc-* with McDonald's. We argued that the entire package of *McSleep* marketing materials provided contextual cues to the consumer in a manner that is analogous to the way in which words in a sentence or utterance provide cues to the reader or hearer. The samples of marketing materials for the hotel chain routinely included the QI four-chain logo, firmly contextualizing it within that corporation rather than within McDonald's. Additionally, the logo was to include a stylized setting sun, an element common to all of QI's logos. The franchisees were also to be required to display the legend "by QI" underneath the McSleep Inn logo on their main exterior signs. Again, the combination of these elements would draw the viewer's attention from the McDonald's association, much as we would rule out the prototypical sense of "green color" in the sentence *The girl went green at the thought of drinking sour milk,* even though it may be true that the primary sense of "green" referring to the color gives rise to the metaphorical extension of it to the sense of "nauseated." That is, we quickly move from the literal level, when it is apparent that that level is not relevant, and seek a metaphorical meaning. This metaphorical process is what we found overwhelmingly in the citations using *Mc-*.

Independent of the analysis we performed for QI, McDonald's Corporation enlisted the advertising firm of Leo Burnett to conduct a survey of the public's perception of the *Mc-* formative. Because their study was not based on actual usage data, but rather on a survey taken at a McDonald's office location, we felt that their results revealed a marked bias, which is reflected in the following definitions taken from their results. One description of the meaning read "a kid's product . . . a product children will like better because it's associated with McDonald's." Another meaning presented in the Leo Burnett survey is "reliable, at a good price." Still another was "prepackaged, consistent, fast, and easy." The most negative of the definitions provided in the study was "processed, simplified, has the punch taken out of it." Their study further acknowledged that ten to twenty percent of the people surveyed had an even more negative view, saying that *Mc-* connotes "junk food, processed, not real, pre-made, uniform, cheap, bland, a gimmick, etcetera." Still, their optimistic view of the prefix's connotations is best represented by a quote taken from one of their own documents: "By virtue of extensive advertising and sales effort and expense and maintenance of the highest standards of quality and service by McDonald's, 'McDonald's' and its 'Mc' formative marks have come to be so distinctive and well recognized that the vast majority of consumers upon seeing the marks identify them with McDonald's."

Throughout the case we conceded McDonald's Corporation's original association with the prefix; our results differ from those of the Leo Burnett survey in that we noted the relatively tiny degree to which writers still make that association explicit. Furthermore, we found that its use is today predominantly pejorative. Writers in our corpus used the prefix in such a way that suggested that the prefix has come into its own, with any metaphorical connection to McDonald's fading very fast. It is the sheer market presence of McDonald's that keeps the name and all it stands for current in our consciousness; however, it appears that the prefix has broken loose from those associations and has taken on a life of its own, with the senses intact, but with the original literal connotation becoming considerably less strong. Based upon the evidence of what we found in the citations, we argued that the prefix is at an intermediary phase in its history. It has taken on associations from McDonald's, but it is proceeding to shed those associations and keep the abstract senses that have evolved.

The question of why this prefix has such a strong attraction for speakers and writers remains. One explanation is that it exerts a purely aesthetic appeal in cases where the speaker is clearly doing it for the fun of it, as in the case of "McVeto McKernan." In a similar way, the attorneys' support staff during the case called their office the *McCommand Center*. Judge Niemeyer himself glibly expressed the hope in his published opinion that he would not be considered a *McJudge*. The main appeal of *Mc-*, however, lies in the fact that the prefix has an undeniable economy, a property fundamental to linguistic codes. Just as it is more elegant to say *zipper* than to say *hookless fastening device*, it is easier to say *McSurgery* than to say, periphrastically, *standardized, assembly-line surgery*. To attribute recognized and accepted general characteristics to an otherwise neutral word, people have learned, simply attach *Mc-* to it. Whether the connotation is pejorative or ameliorative is conditioned by the appropriateness to the enterprise of the implied concepts; clearly, a *McLube* should be a fast and efficient place to get one's automobile serviced, but the prospect of going under the knife of a *McSurgeon* is rather daunting.

In the two years since the case, we have continued to see and hear many words formed with this prefix. Writers and speakers continue to get more creative with its use; in cases such as *McPinion, McNificent,* and *Mc-Stake* it is even being used as a lexical root. The data we analyzed and the citations we continue to see demonstrate that while McDonald's can be effective in preventing commercial use of the prefix, the two injunctions against its commercial use have done very little to stall its rapid expansion into the popular lexicon.

Appendix

List of Citations for *Mc-* and *Mac-*

1. Ethnic Associations (Includes Surnames)
McDuff   1. Computer discount store with a Scottish motif   *Computer & Software News* 7 Dec 1987; 2. Local police search dog   *Western Real Estate News* 20 Nov 1987, Waukesha, WI *Freeman* 2 Mar 1988

McGruff   Public service mascot for crime prevention, dressed as a bloodhound in a trenchcoat   Louisville, KY *Courier-Journal* 8 Apr 1988, *Jersey Journal*

McNificent, McSure   Overnight mail advertisement using a leprechaun and a four-leaf clover   *USA Today* 17 Mar 1989

McPuzzle   Crossword puzzle with clues pertaining to Scotland   *Washington Post Magazine* 17 Apr 1988

MacThrift   Budget office supply store with a Scottish motif   Greensboro *News & Record* 28 Feb 1988

McThrift Motor Inn   Budget motel with a Scottish motif   Norfolk, VA *Ledger-Star* 17 Feb 1989

2. Alliterative Patternings Based on a Proper Name
McAuto   Subsidiary of the McDonnell-Douglas Corporation   *Capital District Business Review* 11 Apr 1988

McBooks   Bookstore named after its owners, McCarthy and McGovern   DeWitt, NY *Business Journal* Feb 1988

McCrazy   Tennis player John McEnroe, known for wild fits of anger   *Sports Illustrated* 16 Aug 1986

McDance   Collaborative work involving musician Bobby McFerrin   Ogden, UT *Standard Examiner* [n.d.] Apr 1988

McLish—it rhymes with McDish   Female body-builder, Rachel McLish   *Los Angeles Times* 26 Jun 1987

Air McMail   Football coach David McWilliams   AP Sep 1986

Jim McMyth   Football player Jim McMahon   *Washington Post* 15 Jan 1988

Spuds McPuppies   Miniature bull terrier puppies named after Budweiser mascot Spuds McKenzie   [source omitted]

McSpeedport   Racetrack in McKeesport, PA   *Pittsburgh Press* 6 Mar 1988

Quick Thaw McStraw   Milkshake named after the Hanna-Barbera animated character, Quick Draw   McGraw Phoenix, AZ *Republic* [n.d.]

Mc of Time   Police officer named McBride, who delivered a baby for a couple named McGrew in McDonough County in the town of Macomb   Taunton, MA *Gazette* 22 Mar 1988

McVeto McKernan   Name given to Maine governor John McKernan by protesting union workers   Bangor, ME *News* 27 Feb 1988; Portland, ME *Press Herald* 12 Feb 1988; Augusta, ME *Kennebec Journal* 23 Feb 1988

3. Acronyms
McDap   Mason County Drug Abuse Program   *USA Today* 2 Mar 1988

McRIDES   Morris County RIDES, a ride-sharing program   *Mt. Olive Chronicle* 18 Feb 1988; Morristown, NJ *Daily Record* 6 Feb 1988

4. Products of the McDonald's Corporation [not analyzed in this study]

5. Macintosh Computer Products or Related Businesses
McBike   Electronically controlled exercise bicycle   Midland, MI *News* 17 Dec 1988

McConsociates, Inc.   Computer consulting firm   Beverly, MA *Times* 14 Mar 1988

McTek   Computer discount store specializing in Macintosh products   *Micro Cornucopia* Feb 1988

McToy   Computer accessory for accelerating processing time   *Incider* [n.d.]

6. Parodies of a Fast-Food Product or Service
McChowMein   Hypothetical name for a Chinese fast-food restaurant   Philadelphia *Inquirer* 22 Feb 1988

McFido's   Hypothetical name for an actual restaurant for dogs   Chicago *Herald* 9 May 1988

McFoam   Burger boxes in a science fiction film parody, *The Attack of the Burger Pods*   Minneapolis *Star Tribune* 5 May 1988

McMeditation   Hypothetical fast-service meditation center   Pacific *Sun* 29 Jan 1988

McMania   Hypothetical drive-through therapy clinic   Gastonia, NC *Gazette* [n.d.]

Lamb McNuggets   What the author of the article imagines that an animated wolf should eat   *Comic Buyer's Guide* 2 May 1988

McPaper McNuggets   Detroit *News* 16 Feb 1988

News McNuggets   *AOPA Pilot* Jan 1988

Squid McNuggets   Hypothetical squid tidbits   Bremerton, WA *Sun* [n.d.]

McShaft   Hypothetical fast-service drive shaft mechanics shop   Santa Ana, CA *Register* 8 Feb 1988

Sausage McSouffle   Chicago *Sun-Times* 4 Feb 1988

McSoup   Hypothetical soup restaurant empire name   Ansonia, CT *Sentinel* 20 Nov 1987

7. The Meaning "Basic, Convenient, Inexpensive, Standardized"

McAmerica   *American Politics*   Jan 1988

McArt   "mass market art"   *Forbes* 7 Mar 1988

McBimbo   *American Politics* Jan 1988

McBook   "A book so slender and so filled with fast-food humor that his [Cosby's] detractors have called it McBook."   Los Angeles *Times* 25 Sep 1987

McCaviar   "It's for people who like caviar, but don't want to go broke eating it."   *Crain's* 27 Jun 1988

McChekhov   "makes fast food from the great Russian writer Anton Chekhov's short stories . . . not so much based on his stories, . . . but looted from them."   Baltimore *Sun* 23 Dec 1987

McChic   *American Politics* Jan 1988

McCinema   "quick fix films, hastily written, overly sentimental, contrived and silly."   North Kingstown, RI *Standard-Times* [n.d.]

McDigest   "a daily digest of news, polls, punditry, & gossip."   *Regardie's* Apr 1988

McDome   "a multipurpose stadium."   St. Louis *Construction News & Review* Nov 1987

McDrive-thru   "retreat to the nearest McDrive-thru."   Toledo, OH *Blade* 21 Feb 1988

McDuck's   Used in a cartoon showing an employer arranging to "cater" the company Christmas party at a drive-in window with the name McDuck's on the menu.   *Rubber & Plastics News* 14 Dec 1987

McEverything   "This is the era of instant gratification, of pop tops, quick wash, fast fix, frozen foods, McEverything."   Fort Myers, FL *News-Press* 17 Feb 1988

McEconomics Economic policies of the Ronald Reagan administration   *American Politics* Jan 1988

McFashion   "kids are drawn by smaller 'express' stores the same way they're attracted to fast food."   *Entrepreneur* Mar 1988

McFood "It's a push-button, do-it–yourself, convenience-oriented world. . . . We can zap a lean cuisine in the micro, or order McFood from a drive-in McSpeaker." Burlington, NJ County *Times* 10 Apr 1988

McFuneral "The industry even has its own 'McFuneral' in Service Corp. International of Texas, which . . . now owns and operates more than 300 cemeteries and more than 600 funeral homes nationwide." *Puget Sound Business Journal* 7 Mar 1988

McGlobe "People shouldn't travel halfway around the world only to find the same hamburger joints they've got back home. . . . We are on the brink of becoming McGlobe." Charleston, WV *Mail* 11 Mar 1988

McGod The God of TV evangelists *American Politics* Jan 1988

McHairpiece "The Aderans Co. [a hairpiece marketer] plans to create a vast franchise network throughout this country beginning this spring." Hagerstown, MD *Herald* [n.d.]

McHealth Care "large for-profit hospital and HMO chains have earned the industry epithet 'McHealth Care.' " UPI 5 Sep 1986

McHistory "In its fast food vending of McHistory" Butte, MT *Standard* [n.d.]

McJobs "They are McJobs that are low-paying and require little if any skill." Hillsbory, OH *Press Gazette* 7 Apr 1988

McJournaled "If the very subject that should have been treated thoughtfully is McJournaled, abbreviated to the trivial, . . . then isn't the editor saying to the reader that it really isn't worth his or her attention?" *Folio* Dec 1987

McLaw "The near omnipresence . . . and the homogeneity of their 340 offices have prompted pundits to dub the franchise phenomenon 'McLaw' suggesting that legal advice is dispensed through drive-in windows." *California Lawyer* Dec 1987

McLife Results of genetic engineering *American Politics* Jan 1988

McLifestyle "What we need and have come to expect in this, our McLifestyle is speed. Speed and easy access." Lewiston-Auburn, ME *Sun-Journal* 7 Feb 1988

McLube "Little drive-in shops offering a 10-minute oil change and chassis lubrication are about to become a supercharged market." Augusta, ME *Kennebec Journal* [n.d.] Feb 1988

McLunch "Cheap, filling, and child-friendly meals." Columbia, MD *Flier* 11 Feb 1988

McMail "If the U.S. Postal Service were sold today to a private business we'd see changes overnight. The first thing we would notice is that U.S. Post Offices would be replaced by 'McMail.' " Centerville, OH *Times* 28 Mar 1988

McMaids [source omitted]

McMarines *American Politics* Jan 1988

McMarketing "creative, successful marketing and advertising strategies should be available as quickly—and be priced as inexpensively—as high-volume, fast-food lunch options. . . . Naturally this type of venture would emphasize speed and low price, rather than good quality." Bradenton, FL *Herald* 4 Apr 1988

McMedia   ". . . education delivered via the mass media of cable TV, videocassettes, and radio." [source omitted]

McMedicine   "Its critics sometimes refer to it as 'McMedicine,' but proponents of primary care medical centers growing in number say they fill a community's need for prompt and inexpensive care for minor problems."   Maple Heights, OH *Press* 18 Feb 1988

McMed Students   UPI 5 Sep 1986

McMiz   "elaborate and elegantly aggressive marketing, merchandising and standardized production techniques that the burger giants might envy."   *Washington Post* 3 Jul 1988

McMoral Majority   *American Politics* Jan 1988

McMovie   ". . . like fast food, it satisfies the appetite and tastes good. . . . a film hallmarked by a monumental vacuity; a central impoverishment of means, ends and ideology which cuts across genre."   *Psychiatric News* Apr 1988

McMovies   "instant videos of both the NY Giants & Denver Broncos"   Denver *Post* [n.d.]

McMovie, TV   "Flat and naggingly ersatz, the film proves roughly as memorable as a fast-food restaurant. It's another TV McMovie"   *Washington Post* 29 Apr 1988

McNews   "McNews, a mere tidbit of information, . . ."   Columbus, OH *Dispatch* 24 Apr 1988

McNewspaper   Champaign-Urbana, IL *News-Gazette* 8 Apr 1988

McOffice Supply   ". . . fears the existence of a 'McOffice Supply' dealership, if dealers do not create an individuality for their customers."   *American Office Dealer,* southwestern ed. Apr 1988

McOil Change   *Forbes* 11 Aug 1986

McPaper   "fast news for the fast-food generation"   *Phoenix Business Journal* [n.d.], "you could sell a whole lot of papers and make a whole lot of money" Grand Island, NE *Independent* [n.d.]; see also quote S.V. MCTELECAST

McPaper Caper   Reference to the development of the newspaper *USA Today* York, PA *Dispatch* 29 Jan 1988

McParticles   "A truly American sport. Participants motor through 24 fast-food windows, gulping down burgers, fries, fish sandwiches and various McParticles en route."   Framingham, MA Middlesex *News* 22 Feb 1988

McPost Office   "What we really need is a McPost Office. . . . Anyone who has ever been to the post office knows how poor the service can be."   Elgin, IL *Courier News* 21 Jan 1988

McPrisons   "Prison franchises: another alternative to prison overcrowding." [source omitted]

McProgram   The television equivalent of the newspaper, *USA Today.*   Albany, NY *Knickerbocker News* 4 Mar 1988

McRather   "Like its print model, the *USA Today* TV show will be a fast-paced potpourri of news and features, divided into four sections, money, sports, life and USA"   *Time* 11 Apr 1988

McRead(s) "Three 'McReads' just right for an airport layover or the beach." *Christian Science Monitor* 29 Jul 1986

McRobot *Newsweek* 28 Mar 1988

McService *American Politics* Jan 1988

McShopping "The impersonal McShopping of the giant, corporate-owned malls is here to stay." Syracuse, NY *Herald Journal* 1 Feb 1988

McSimplification *American Politics* Jan 1988

McSouth *American Politics* Jan 1988

McSpeaker see quote s.v. MCFOOD Burlington, NJ County *Times* 10 Apr 1988

McStory "I read a McStory on the paper's front page that detailed what the American public needed to know were the real differences between Russia and America: Raisa Gorbachev uses Henna Hair Dye ... Nancy Reagan ... uses Clairol Chestnut and Moonlight Blond highlights" Dubois, PA *Courier-Express* 9 Jan 1988

McSurgery "An increase in the number of surgical procedures that can be done without overnight hospital stays has been predicted because of the approval of a new anesthesia" Asbury Park, NJ *Press* 27 Dec 1987

McSuperpowers *American Politics* Jan 1988

McSweater "The main goal [of Benetton] was to make garments that could be fashionable but at the same time on an industrial scale so everyone could buy them." *Working Woman* May 1986

McTax Chain "the seasonal storefront tax preparers." *Working Woman* Mar 1988

McTelevangelism *American Politics* Jan 1988

McPaper Epithet for the newspaper *USA Today* *Christian Science Monitor* 1 Dec 1987, *American Politics* Jan 1988

McPreachers *American Politics* Jan 1988

McTelecast "I know people call the newspaper 'McPaper.' I have no problem with them calling the television version 'McTelecast.' The paper is a quick read; we will be a quick watch." *Christian Science Monitor* 1 Dec 1987

McTelevision Detroit *News* 7 Apr 1988

McTrash *American Politics* Jan 1988

McVideo Champaign-Urbana, IL *News-Gazette* 8 Apr 1988

McYear Headline for an article reviewing major news stories for the year 1987 "a fast-food, service-with-a smile, prefabricated, standardized, marketing-dominated [nightmare]." *American Politics* Jan 1988 (The article contains 23 different terms using the *Mc*-prefix.)

McZippy Burger West Covina, CA *Highlander* [n.d.]

References

Cruse, D. Alan. 1986. *Lexical Semantics,* New York: Cambridge UP.

Crystal, David. 1987. *The Cambridge Encyclopedia of Language.* New York: Cambridge UP.

Mencken, H. L. 1963. *The American Language*. Abridged ed. Ed. Raven I. Mc-David, Jr. New York: Knopf.

Niemeyer, Paul V. 1988. Opinion. *Quality Inns International v. McDonald's Corporation*. Civil No. PN-87–2606. U.S. District Court, District of MD.

Shuy, Roger W. 1988. Testimony. *Quality Inns International v. McDonald's Corporation*. Civil No. PN-87–2606. U.S. District Court, District of MD.

Content Questions

1. What do the authors indicate is unusual about the pronunciation of *Nike?*

2. Briefly describe the setting of the trademark infringement suit described in this article. What had happened to promote a lawsuit, and what was at stake?

3. What is the "Aunt Jemima Doctrine" and how does it relate to this case?

4. What examples does the article provide of trademark names that have entered common usage as generic names?

5. The authors point out that the morpheme *Mc-* acts like a derivational prefix, but it differs from some derivational prefixes because it is so "productive." What does that mean?

6. What issue of the case were the expert-witness linguists called in to address?

7. What are the seven categories of meaning that the authors found through the data they examined?

Questions for Analysis and Discussion

1. Why was it so important to the case to show whether the morpheme *Mc-* had become generic?

2. According to Lentine and Shuy, McDonald's claimed that it had been responsible for making the morpheme productive and that McDonald's had even taught children how to combine the morpheme into many words. What is the potential danger of such a strategy in relation to maintaining trademark control of a particular morpheme?

3. Compare the methodology of Lentine and Shuy in collecting samples of actual usage with the methodology of the advertising firm that conducted a survey. Aside from the issue about where that survey was conducted, which methodology would you think is more reliable for showing the meaning of

a morpheme? How reliable are speakers' intuitions about their own language?

4. The authors contrast the examples of *McLube* and *McSurgeon* to show the importance of context for our reaction toward the morpheme *Mc-*. Examine section 7 of the article's appendix. What other contrasts could you make?

5. What does a lawsuit, such as the type represented in this article, say about the reality of morphemes rather than words as the minimal unit of meaning in a language?

Additional Activities and Paper Topics

1. Research some of the material that has been written about prejudice against a particular ethnic or racial group. Examine also the relationship between particular "accents" and negative stereotypes. Report on your information and speculate on the subtle influence that linguistic prejudice could have in law enforcement or legal settings. (**Phonetics & Phonology**)

2. Prepare a list of a number of products whose brand names you suspect have come to be used as the general name for that type of product. Then prepare a survey with questions to test people's usage of items on your list. For example, on your survey you might ask, "What do people need to take when they have a headache?" Survey a group of people and report on your results. Comment also on what your results might suggest about the degree of control that a particular company has on its product's name. (**Morphology & Semantics**)

3. Try your hand at comparing and contrasting the writing style (not handwriting) of two individuals from whom you have received correspondence. Make sure that you are comparing two similar types of correspondence. Don't compare, for example, a formal letter from one person and an informal written greeting from another. Report any differences you note between the two sets of writing samples and explain which features seem to be characteristic of each set. On the basis of what you have noted, comment on what features you would look for in an anonymously authored writing sample if you knew that it had come from one of those two individuals and you had to determine which person had authored the writing sample. You may also choose to represent some of your observations with a binary chart as Eagleson did in his article. (**Morphology & Syntax**)

4. Watch court TV or attend an actual criminal trial when the closing arguments are given. Listen carefully to the language used by both the defense and prosecuting attorneys. Note any uses of language that seem biased to you, such as the use of semantically marked terms, presuppositions, and the like. (You may want to review some of Elizabeth Loftus's studies mentioned in her article for some ideas of the kinds of things to listen for.) Report any interesting results. (**Semantics & Pragmatics**)

5. Look at the four maxims representing the "cooperative principle" as listed in Shuy's article. These maxims, from H. P. Grice's work, can be discussed in relation to legal settings. Discuss these maxims in terms of the expectations we have for witnesses in court cases. Comment also on the consequences that follow for a violation of each of these maxims. (**Semantics & Pragmatics**)

6. Design and conduct a language experiment with a similar research design to one of those conducted by Loftus, though with a much smaller

number of individuals. Report on your results. Remember as you report your results to accurately assess how reliable your research was, what kinds of problems you encountered, how many individuals were involved, and what kinds of conclusions are or are not merited on the basis of how carefully you set up and conducted the experiment and how large the sample of individuals was that you tested. (**Psycholinguistics, Semantics, & Pragmatics**)

Linguistics, Medicine, and Therapy

This chapter considers some of the applications of linguistics to improved medical care or more effective therapy. While only a few examples of application can be represented here, these applications illustrate some of the kinds of problems that linguistic study can address for people involved in medical or therapeutic contexts, whether as medical personnel, therapists, patients, or even as concerned parents who observe developments in their children's speech.

One important application relates to the study of communication strategies among caregivers and their patients. Breakdowns in communication can have serious consequences in the medical profession, because it is through language, for example, that a doctor acquires much of the necessary information he or she may need in making a proper diagnosis and treatment. And it is through language that instructions must be given to those who will be performing that treatment, including the patients themselves. As linguists study language and discourse in greater detail, they may help in identifying how breakdowns in communication occur and how these problems might best be addressed. The first article in this chapter relates to the understanding of different languages or language varieties in medical settings. This article, "Communication Barriers in Medical Settings: Hispanics in the United States" by Ozzie F. Díaz-Duque, looks at the importance of informed and competent translators in medical settings. Díaz-Duque illustrates, for example, how a translator must be informed about medical expectations related to an individual's cultural background, differences in vocabulary usage according to dialect, and appropriate decision making by the translator with regard to register.

In another article, "Doctor Talk/Patient Talk: How Treatment Decisions Are Negotiated in Doctor–Patient Communication," Sue Fisher describes some startling findings from research she conducted into the discourse between doctors and patients. Fisher followed the cases of twenty-one women who had been referred to two different clinics for diagnoses and treatment. Fisher shows how seemingly small differences in discourse between the doctor and patient could lead to radically different treatment. Her research has serious implications for how doctors and patients communicate with each other.

On a different topic, Janet Romich's article, "Understanding Basic Medical Terminology," briefly illustrates the morphology of medical terms, providing some abbreviated lists of medical suffixes, prefixes, and roots, as well as a couple of examples of morphological rules for combining these forms. Learning some basics of medical terminology could be useful not only for medical personnel, but also for their patients, especially if those patients want to do more extended reading on medical topics. The morphological approach to learning medical terms can be helpful for someone who must learn many vocabulary terms. But that type of approach must be used cautiously since the meaning that results from the combination of a given set of morphemes is not always transparent or predictable. Still, many students have learned medical terms through a consideration of their individual morphemes; this approach is easier than a rote memorization of terms that takes no account of recurring morphemes.

Speech pathology is another field in which linguistics has significant contributions to make. While many of us might consider the applications of phonetics and phonology to speech pathology, the relevance of linguistics to speech pathology is much broader than just the perception, production, and distribution of sounds. Language abnormalities manifest themselves in a variety of ways whether with children or adults. In "Facilitating Grammatical Development: The Contribution of Pragmatics," Laurence B. Leonard and Marc E. Fey describe the relationship between pragmatics and syntax in the context of abnormal language development in children. The authors also show how a speech pathologist can apply such pragmatic and syntactic knowledge in clinical practice.

The final article of the chapter, "The Acquisition of Language" by Breyne Arlene Moskowitz, discusses some of what is known about how normally developing children acquire language. This knowledge can be useful as a point of comparison with children who demonstrate a contrasting pattern of development.

Communication Barriers
in Medical Settings:
Hispanics in the United States

Ozzie F. Díaz-Duque

In a medical setting doctors rely on their patients to provide them with important information for making informed decisions on the proper diagnosis and treatment of various ailments. In some cross-linguistic situations, however, a patient must communicate through an interpreter. In these cases, the interpreter's role is vital to the well-being of the patient. In this article, which originally appeared in the *International Journal of the Sociology of Language,* Ozzie F. Díaz-Duque, of the University of Iowa, explains some important considerations regarding the necessary preparation and responsibilities of a medical interpreter. Although the article deals specifically with medical interpreters who work with Spanish speakers, the principles outlined in the article are more broadly applicable.

The success of health care delivery depends greatly upon open channels of communication between the health care provider and the patient. Language and cultural barriers undermine the effectiveness of health care, compounding the communication difficulties already existing in medical settings among people who share a language and culture.

Medical interpreters may be in a position of great power since they manipulate and process vital information between two or more parties who are in unequal positions of power. Patients may feel socially, professionally, and psychologically inferior to the physician. In addition, depending upon the physician for healing, patients are obliged to place their trust in the interpreter's ability to faithfully express their concerns.

Various health care providers around the United States have begun to address the complex issues of language, culture, and effective communication (see for example González-Lee and Simon 1987; Grasska and McFarland 1982; Meleis and Jonsen 1983; Putsch 1985). In addition, federally funded institutions have addressed the needs of multilingual/multicultural communities through the concept of accessibility, based on Title VI of the Civil Rights Acts of 1964 in conjunction with Section 504 of the Rehabilitation Act of 1973 (Putsch 1985). Accessibility of services includes hiring interpreters for patients who do not speak English or who are hearing impaired and communicate through sign language. The quality and operational management of these programs varies widely. Most hospitals serving a multicultural/multilingual population depend upon bilingual staff, other patients, and relatives to communicate with monolingual patients. Few hospitals in the United States have well established professionally staffed interpreting services.

This paper identifies some of the linguistic and cultural barriers encountered in a large medical setting and offers some solutions to overcome those barriers. The emphasis is placed upon the Hispanic patient; and the issues addressed are sociolinguistic barriers in cross-cultural communication, differences in ethnomedical systems, beliefs, and expectations, and technical aspects of interpreting in the medical setting.

The Setting and Methodology

The flow of patients requiring special communication services in the University of Iowa Hospitals and Clinics is sufficiently large and varied to demand a professionally staffed system. The hospital complex, the largest university owned teaching hospital in the United States, serves a metropolitan population of 75,000 as well as patients from 50 states and over 25 foreign countries. The majority of monolingual Spanish speakers who request services come from surrounding communities and other cities in the states where there are pockets of Hispanic populations. Many of these Hispanic communities are spatially and culturally isolated (González and Wherritt forthcoming). The daily population of 1,000 inpatients and 1,100 outpatients includes non-English speakers, deaf and blind/deaf patients, and bilingual patients whose command of English may not include health or medical related vocabulary. The medical center is staffed by 1,100 physicians and dentists and over 8,500 health care professionals.

A small percentage of the staff is bilingual, and attempts are made to refer patients to physicians who are able to communicate in the patient's native language, although this rarely occurs. The situation is further complicated by the number of interactions between patients and health support personnel which may include the hospital switchboard, scheduling, registration and insurance clerks, receptionists, nurses, technicians, social workers, and pharmacists.

Interpreting and translation services are provided through the Department of Social Services. The staff includes two full-time interpreters of Spanish and one part-time interpreter/translator of Spanish and American Sign Language. In order to facilitate communication with speakers of other languages, the medical center has created a Language Bank which includes 70 freelance interpreters in 25 languages. Since its inception in 1975, the Interpreting and Translation Service has met the needs of thousands of patients.

During the past 15 years, the author has interpreted for Hispanic patients and has gathered a series of tape recordings from interviews conducted with these patients at the University of Iowa Hospitals and Clinics.

Based on the author's experience and data, some problems of medical interpretation are outlined in this paper and a set of preliminary solutions is offered.

Institutional Response

A widespread misconception exists that bilingualism automatically qualifies a person to interpret in any setting. Few health professionals and their patients are aware of the complexities involved in interpreting or translating from one language into another (Díaz-Duque 1982: 1380). As a result, health professionals may recruit the patient's family, friends, and even other patients to interpret. Friends and relatives usually do not have a health care background and, therefore, lack appropriate health care terminology. In addition, they are not familiar with hospital policies, procedures, and routines. Ethical principles, such as the right to confidentiality, may be violated by the use of nonprofessional interpreters.

Good translations are based on a thorough knowledge of both the language and the culture of the patient, since communication barriers can arise from either source (Meleis and Jonsen 1983: 890–893). All parties involved in an interpreting setting imbue their interactions with their own cultural values and beliefs. These values may include conflicting perspectives on health, origins of diseases, healing, treatment, and the expected role of both the patient and the healer.

Most health care institutions in the United States have not dealt adequately with the complex issues of cross-cultural communication. During the past 15 years, some progress has been made through legal actions based on reimbursement guidelines set forth by the Refugee Assistance Program (Social Security Administration 1979, 1980) and Medicare's Provision of Bilingual Services (1979), as well as through legislation discussed above. Federally funded institutions are now required by law to provide services to users in their dominant language. Although these measures have improved accessibility for the monolingual patient, little has been done to standardize and regulate the training and hiring of qualified medical interpreters. Government sponsored programs and materials are available, but these efforts have barely begun to address the problems of cross-cultural health care of multilingual/multicultural populations in the United States (USDA/USDHHS 1986: 22–25).

Sociolinguistic Barriers: Interpreters, Hispanic Patients, and Health Care Providers

Culturally linked verbal and nonverbal nuances play roles in communication. For example, all languages have several registers or modes of expression, such as formal, polite, informal, and intimate. The interpreter must be able to determine the patient's register and communicate at that level. There are vital reasons for maintaining such accuracy. One important one is that patients may withdraw from the communication process if given the impression that their speech is socially inferior to that of the interpreter or the health care provider. Furthermore, miscommunication with the physician might occur if the interpreter selects a more formal register than that of the patient. For example, the phrase *Tengo una bola en el tragadero* can be processed in a high register as "I have an esophageal growth." Such polishing distorts the patient's perception of his or her physical condition. It also gives the physician the impression that the patient has a good command of medical terminology. This type of polishing results in a cognitive incongruence which will affect physician/patient rapport and, ultimately, treatment and patient compliance. Translation should remain as faithful as possible to register. It is vital for ethical and professional reasons that the patient's perception of the medical problem, state of mind, educational background, self-image, and attitudes toward health and practitioner be conveyed accurately.

A flowery or anecdotal style is characteristic of the discourse of some Hispanics. The busy professional, looking for short, succinct answers, may be dismayed or irritated by the amount of anecdotal information which some Hispanic patients provide. For example, a patient answering the question, "How long have you had problems with your joints?" provided the following answer:

> *Pos, fíjese, he tenido esta punzadita aquí, en los cuardriles, que a veces me sube hasta la mera paleta o se me corre hasta el pescuezo; esto lo tengo desde que visité a mi cuñada en West Liberty. Estábamos allá, en las labores, con los tomates, por dos meses, creo que cerca de Illinois, no sé bien dónde; y así, doblada todo el santá día, con el mayordomo encima de una, y mi cuñada, la pobre, con trastornos de mujer, batallando con lo suyo también. En fin, fuimos al médico las dos, allá el del rancho, pero aquí me tiene, en las mismas. ¿Qué le parece esto doctor?*

> "Well, you see, I've had this stabbing pain here, by the hips, which sometimes goes right up the shoulder blade, or goes up to the neck; I've had this since I visited my sister-in-law in West Liberty. We were there, working in the fields with the tomato crop for two months, I think it was near Illinois, I don't know exactly where; so there I was, bending over all day long, with the foreman on my back, and my sister-in-law, the poor thing, with female problems, dealing with her own misery, too. At any rate, both of us went to the doctor over there at the ranch, but here I am, still the same. What do you think of this, doctor?"

The interpreter must decide whether to interpret accurately or to summarize, selecting only facts which seem pertinent. In the University of Iowa setting, at times, the seemingly irrelevant material has contained key details in the patient's medical history, and anecdotal presentations have served to alleviate nervousness felt by patients in relaying information to the physician. Some patients feel more comfortable if the attention is deflected from the medical problem or the presentation of the symptoms. Cultural factors may also play a role in what seems to be the patient's verbal meanderings.

In any case, the interpreter is in no position to edit any of the client's utterances. To avoid potential problems in the flow of dialogue, it is the responsibility of the interpreter to explain his or her role at the onset of the interview and to encourage both clients to take control of the situation, interject comments, or ask for explanations.

Hispanics in the United States also speak different varieties of Spanish. The use of an unfamiliar regional variety by an interpreter may confuse the communication or the situation. Parts of the body, physiological functions, symptoms, and food items present the most common problems in this respect. A term used for a food item by one Hispanic group may refer to a specific body part in another; other terms have various meanings within particular subgroups. The confusion may result in amusing or embarrassing situations, or it may have life threatening consequences. For example, a Chilean patient in the maternity ward startled a Cuban-born interpreter by exclaiming with agitation: *Pero-¿cuándo me van a traer la guagua? ¡La he estado esperando toda la mañana!* The interpreter understood this as, "When are they going to bring me the bus? I've been waiting for it all morning!," not realizing that *guagua* is a Chilean regionalism for "baby." While humorous and without negative repercussions, this exchange illustrates a common misunderstanding among speakers of different varieties of Spanish. A similar problem arises with the translation of "constipation." For some Spanish speakers, *constipación* refers to nasal congestion, not intestinal constipation. The alert interpreter should be aware of regional variants and use appropriate equivalents or seek clarification for such pitfall terms.

It is also important to allow for the lack of linguistic equivalents and different degrees of comprehension between persons of different cultures. For instance, Spanish-speaking patients with little or no formal education consistently confuse neurological problems with nervous problems since, for many Hispanics, the terms *problemas de nervios* "problems of the nerves" refers to mental health. Therefore, some neurological conditions such as "stroke" or "seizure" are variably understood.

Interpreters must also be aware of the varied English language proficiency of Hispanics. Often patients learn the meaning of a word or phrase in one context and apply it to others indiscriminately. Thus, one patient who was told that she was "to be discharged" the next day, understood this as "you will develop a discharge tomorrow"!

Many Hispanic patients have limited vocabulary and little understanding of register in such subjects as body parts, sexuality, or reproduction.

Often, the patient's lexical repertoire is inadequate for expressing functions such as elimination and menstruation. Many Hispanic women who have come to the University of Iowa Hospitals and Clinics have never given names (certainly none which they would consider socially or medically acceptable) to body parts (pelvis, vagina, clitoris, for example) or aspects of sexual response (foreplay, lubrication, masturbation, or orgasm). Whether this absence of vocabulary is due to cultural taboos, the patient's education, or both, the interpreter must transmit messages accurately and clearly while maintaining decorum and diplomacy in subjects which the client considers indelicate or taboo. Even under the best circumstances, the patient may still give the wrong answer or no answer, or simply succumb to embarrassment.

Nonverbal cues of Spanish monolingual patients are often equally misleading. For example, Hispanic patients with limited understanding of English often nod in agreement in the presence of a physician. This 'nodding syndrome' is usually the result of fear, embarrassment, or lack of understanding. Health care professionals and medical interpreters need to be aware of such phenomena since many of the questions asked are of a yes/no variety: "Are you allergic to any medicines?", "Have you noticed any blood in your stools?", or "Are you feeling pain now?", to name only a few.

The interpreter serves as the communicative link between the patient and the health professional. We have seen how difficult it is to accurately communicate the patients' message to the health care provider. On the other hand, it is just as difficult to communicate the health professionals' message to the patient. Health professionals speak a language of their own, and often this jargon is not decoded for the patient. If it is suggested that the interpreter adhere to the patient's register, similarly it might be argued that the interpreter also translate the physician's register. A client may not understand a semantically faithful translation which includes medical jargon, yet paraphrases or elaborations by the interpreter present other communicative problems. The interpreter may indeed not be qualified to illustrate or expand upon what is said by a professional in a different field.

In order to overcome the sociolinguistic barriers discussed above, a skilled and experienced bilingual and bicultural interpreter must be utilized. This person must have a command of standard and nonstandard Spanish, as well as varieties spoken in the United States and in different monolingual settings. In addition, the interpreter must have thorough knowledge of health terminology and be familiar with the health care field.

In the psychiatric setting, accurate communication is particularly important. Hispanics underutilize psychiatric services. This underutilization results, in part, because few Hispanic health care professionals exist in this field and even fewer Anglo Spanish-speaking practitioners are available (Torrey 1972). In addition, Hispanics fail to seek out psychiatrists and psychotherapists because their understanding of the origin and treatment of mental illnesses and conditions differs greatly from that of mainstream psychiatric practice. Contemporary psychiatry has no tradition for dealing with such conditions as *susto* "magical fright," *mal de ojo* "evil eye," or *mal puesto* "casting evil spirits."

Because of the intimate nature of psychiatric consultation, even the most qualified interpreter may prove to be intrusive. Many psychological problems stem from deep personal turmoil; a third party who controls communication undoubtedly intrudes upon this delicate setting. Psychiatric patients may express themselves in an abstract emotive manner, typical of persons undergoing personal distress. In some cases, patients may be in a hallucinatory state which may be reflected in incoherent or incongruent utterances or behaviors. The interpreter needs to be particularly insightful in these kinds of settings.

A Mexican American migrant worker told the therapist (via the author, who was interpreting) that he felt *como un jitomate reject por el mayordomo*. The translation offered was "I feel like a tomato rejected by the foreman." Knowing the patient's background, the therapist was able to unearth various reasons for the patient's attitude. An inexperienced interpreter might not have given appropriate translations for regionalisms such as *jitomate* or *mayordomo* or recognized code switching in the use of "reject." It has been recommended that therapists rely on interpreters who are of the same cultural background as the patient (USDA/USDHHS 1986: 11). However, this assumption is not always valid, since the interpreter may overidentify with the client and tamper with utterances in order to make what may seem to be necessary cultural adjustments (Putsch 1985: 3346).

Differences in Ethnomedical Systems

In addition to linguistic barriers, differences in ethnomedical systems and beliefs may pose insurmountable problems in communication. For example, language problems are often related to the health professional's unfamiliarity with folk medicine practices and related vocabulary. The Hispanic patient who may have total or partial faith in folk healing practices can and often does seek help from modern orthodox practitioners. The patient may lack confidence in physicians who often dismiss folk medicine as nonsensical and unscientific. The monolingual patient expects the interpreter to provide a cultural and linguistic bridge providing rapport on both linguistic and cultural levels. However, even bicultural interpreters may have difficulty in identifying and accurately translating terms used in folk healing. Folk healing involves ritual, secrecy, and jargon; and folk healers, like their medical counterparts, use specialized language that the patient may not fully understand. As a result, patients become poor historians of their ailments and subsequent treatment.

The interpreter may be challenged in translating such terms as *mal de ojo* "evil eye," *aire* "air malady," *susto* "magical fright," *caída de la mollera* "fallen fontanel," and *empacho* "stomach illness." Even if a translation is offered, the average physician will not know the etiology or symptoms of the above terms. Therefore, the physician may be unprepared or unable to provide the appropriate treatment.

Some Hispanics feel that health is directly related to nature, the weather, the environment, the time of day, work, their circle of friends, family, spirituality, or material status. This philosophy may startle some medical practitioners in the United States. Such discomfort on the part of medical personnel may result in inadequate health services. Yet, Hispanics who have received health care from a folk healer know that these healers would never isolate the patient's symptoms from the social environment. The patient may lose confidence in a health care practitioner who demands concrete answers void of sociocultural content.

The efficacy of the interpreter will be impaired if sociocultural understanding of the different ethnomedical systems is lacking. For example, an elderly patient who was having an extensive medical workup for gastrointestinal maladies expected immediate diagnosis and results from her physician. When she asked her physician when she would get her medications and go home, the interpreter told her without processing her question that "He [the physician] is not like your *curandera* back home, he needs to do real tests and diagnose you properly." This patient's expectations were based on previous experiences in folk medicine where healers diagnose problems rapidly, without the aid of technology, and offer an immediate treatment or cure. The interpreter's intervention prevented the physician from knowing the patient's expectations of his professional services and violated the patient's right of expression and accessibility.

Conclusion and Guidelines

Misunderstanding occurs in the medical setting even when the participants speak the same language. This problem is compounded by the participation of the interpreter. This paper has shown that interpreters must be sensitive to sociolinguistic and sociocultural differences between patients and health care providers. The interpreter must be faithful to the patient's register and language variety. At the same time, the interpreter must be familiar with the patient's ethnomedical system. Good medical interpreters must also be faithful to the sociolinguistic variants and the messages of the health care providers, at the same time that they must be knowledgeable about traditional medicine in the United States.

These are the guidelines that health care professionals working with non-English-speaking or limited-English-speaking Hispanic patients must follow:

1. Familiarize themselves with ethnomedical systems of the patients.
2. Use professional interpreters, rather than family members or other patients, in order to communicate with patients.
3. Refrain from transmitting or receiving vital communication from patients unless they have adequate sociolinguistic and sociocultural knowledge of their clients.
4. Translate all educational, medical, and legal documents such as operation consent forms.
5. Create a library of health education materials written in Spanish in a comprehensible style.

Professional medical interpreters, on the other hand, must follow these guidelines:

1. Establish ground rules at the onset of exchanges for both patient and health care provider.
2. Address the clients directly by name.
3. Be alert for verbal and nonverbal cues.
4. Refrain from making aside comments, either to the patient or to the health care provider.
5. Translate in a consecutive mode, processing manageable units of utterances.
6. Avoid simultaneous or summary methods of interpreting.
7. Reassure patients and respect their rights of confidentiality and privacy.

As the English-only movement attempts to restrict public services in Spanish in the United States, it is important to recognize the difficulties inherent in medical interpretation and to plan for more efficient services for non-English-speaking Hispanics. Health care professionals, short of becoming bilingual, need to learn about popular beliefs, folk medicine, and the variety of sociocultural barriers which interfere with the competent delivery of health care. Ideally, health care professionals would receive cross cultural training during their schooling. In addition, they would be taught Spanish if they were to work in areas with large Hispanic populations. Some programs in the United States have begun to address this need (González-Lee and Simon 1987: 502–504). At the same time, efforts must be made to educate Hispanic clients about health care practices in the United States in order to demystify medicine, physicians, and medical technology. The goal of proper medical interpretation should be to bring this medical world closer to all people in a language they understand.

References

Díaz-Duque, Ozzie F. (1982). Overcoming the language barrier: advice from an interpreter. *American Journal of Nursing* 82(9), 1380–1382.

González, Nora, and Wherritt, Irene (forthcoming). Spanish language use in West Liberty, Iowa: a pilot study. In *Spanish in the United States: Mexican and Puerto Rican Varieties,* J. Bergen (ed.). Washington, D.C.: Georgetown University Press.

González-Lee, Teresa, and Simon, Harold J. (1987). Teaching Spanish and cross cultural sensitivity to medical students. *Western Journal of Medicine* 146, 502–504.

Grasska, Merry Ann, and McFarland, Teresa (1982). Overcoming the language barrier: problems and solutions. *American Journal of Nursing* 82(9), 1376–1379.

Meleis, A. I., and Jonsen, A. R. (1983). Ethical crisis and cultural differences. *Western Journal of Medicine* 138, 889–893.

Putsch, Robert W. (1985). Cross-cultural communication: the case of interpreters in health care. *Journal of the American Medical Association* 254(23), 3344–3348.

Torrey, Edwin F. (1972). *The Mind Game: Witch Doctors and Psychiatrists.* New York: Emerson Hall.

United States Department of Agriculture/United States Department of Health and Human Services (1986). *Cross Cultural Counseling: A Guide for Nutrition and Health Counselors.* FNS-250. Alexandria, Va.: United States Department of Agriculture/United States Department of Health and Human Services.

Content Questions

1. Besides a knowledge of the languages with which he or she is working, what kinds of knowledge are important for a medical interpreter?

2. Why is a knowledge of register so important for translators working between languages? What kinds of false expectations could a translator create between two parties through a failure to take register into account?

3. What does the author suggest that an interpreter explain to the clients before beginning to interpret in a medical setting?

4. What example does Díaz-Duque provide to show that different regional varieties can cause problems even among native speakers of that language?

5. What does it mean to say that an interpreter must be aware of the ethnomedical system of the patient?

6. What do the two sets of guidelines at the end of the article relate to?

Questions for Analysis and Discussion

1. If you were going to translate for someone or if what you were saying or writing were going to be translated, what might you want to clarify beforehand with the parties involved as it relates to register?

2. How important is it for a translator to take varying dialects into account? Within a medical context, what serious consequences could a faulty translation between a doctor and patient have on diagnosis and treatment?

3. How would you respond if you were a medical interpreter who has been told by medical personnel that your services were not needed with a non-native speaker? If you knew their conclusion was based on the fact that the non-native speaker had nodded to statements about diagnosis and treatment, what might you warn the medical personnel about?

4. Imagine yourself as a medical interpreter. Why would you want to follow the instruction to "avoid simultaneous or summary methods of interpreting"?

Doctor Talk/Patient Talk: How Treatment Decisions Are Negotiated in Doctor–Patient Communication

Sue Fisher

Sue Fisher is a sociology professor whose research includes language and health issues. In this article, she calls attention to some possible linguistic and social factors that might contribute to an inappropriately high number of hysterectomies being performed on women. Fisher analyzes some of the discourse that occurs within the consultation between the doctor and patient and reveals some startling patterns that should prompt medical personnel to seriously reevaluate the extent to which they might allow linguistic and other social factors to affect the type of treatment they recommend. It should also cause all of us to consider the importance of our own communication with health-care professionals.

Hysterectomies are performed at a higher rate than any other surgical procedure. The National Center for Health Statistics estimates that 794,000 women had hysterectomies in 1976, which represents a 15% increase over the three previous years. In 1976, 10 out of every 1,000 women underwent this surgery. At the current rate, the Center notes, more than half the women in the U.S. will have their uteruses removed before they are 65 years old (National Center for Health Statistics 1976).

The increase in hysterectomies is a major problem. A 1976 congressional subcommittee estimated that in 1974, there were 2.4 million unnecessary surgeries at a high cost to the American public. The costs were more than monetary. Unnecessary surgery caused 11,900 deaths in 1975 ("Cost and Quality of Health Care" 1976). The death rate for hysterectomies is higher than the reported death rate for uterine/cervical cancer (Larned 1977). The American Cancer Society estimates that of the 46,000 cases of uterine or cervical cancer reported every year, 12,000 are fatal (Virginia Health Bulletin 1977). For hysterectomies, the fatality rate is 1,000 out of every one million. In addition the Cancer Society claims that the majority of these cancer deaths could be prevented with regular Pap smears and gynecological examinations (Larned 1977; Virginia Health Bulletin 1977).

Yet, these figures do not represent the psychosocial costs of hysterectomies. A 1973 English study found that within three years of having hysterectomies, one-third of the women studied were treated for depression (Caress 1977). Psychiatrists agree that a hysterectomy can often damage a woman's sense of identity. Larned reports Dr. Peter Barglow's findings that

> the hysterectomy is clearly and immediately visualized [by the patient] as an irreversible drastic procedure which removes an organ with high value in the ego's image of the body, as well as with considerable conscious value in the woman's sense of self and identity. Surely, the loss of an organ whose presence was reaffirmed monthly cannot be so easily denied. (Larned 1977:206)

Physicians believe that with adequate counseling, "well-adjusted" women can cope with hysterectomies (Larned 1977).

How are treatment decisions negotiated in practitioner–patient communication? How is the exchange of information in medical interviews organized, and how does that organization produce and constrain the negotiation of treatment decisions? Given the asymmetry inherent in the doctor–patient relationship, medical practitioners not only have technical skills and medical knowledge that patients lack, but they also have the potential to control patients' access to and understanding of the information on which they will make their treatment decisions. This power imbalance increases when practitioners, especially residents, perceive patients as poor and powerless.

This discussion shows how medical practitioners act as gatekeepers, providing options to some that are denied to others. It suggests that medical interviews are social events in which the asymmetry in the practitioner–patient relationship combines with the practical concerns each brings to the examining room or consulting office, which influences therapeutic discourse and the treatment decisions.

The Background Context

The research discussed here was done in a university teaching hospital. Like most teaching hospitals, the delivery of health care was organized into inpatient and outpatient services. The outpatient services were further divided into two clinical systems. These clinical systems were organized around medical specialties. My research was done in a paired set of clinics in the Department of Reproductive Medicine and the specialty of oncology (cancer).

Because of the organization and staffing of each clinic, I have called them the Faculty Clinic and the Community Clinic. The Faculty Clinic was staffed by professors of reproductive oncology and, for the most part, accepted patients referred by other medical practitioners in the community. The Community Clinic was staffed by residents under the supervision of staff physicians and primarily accepted patients referred by social agencies or other clinics in the hospital's system of community clinics.

Over the course of a nearly two-year period, I followed 21 women with abnormal Pap smears referred to, diagnosed, and treated in the Faculty and Community Clinics. I found, among other things, that women with abnormal Pap smears referred to the Community Clinic were more likely to receive nonconservative treatment (i.e., to have hysterectomies) than were women referred to the Faculty Clinic (see Fisher 1979a).

The sample population was assembled largely for practical reasons. My entry into the hospital had been gained with the help of a staff physician who was a gynecological oncologist. As a consequence, the population was defined as women with cancerous or precancerous problems in their reproductive systems.

As I was interested in patients' careers as well as the negotiation of treatment decisions, I followed patients longitudinally through the diagnosis/treatment/recovery process. Doctor–patient interactions were captured on audiotape. Early in my involvement with patients, I found that I was not prepared to deal with death on a daily basis; thus, no patients with invasive disease were part of the sample population.

To document the organization of doctor–patient communication, I spent nearly two years as a participant–observer. For the first 13 months, I conducted informal interviews with staff physicians, attending physicians, residents, medical students, nursing staff, and other support personnel. I attended lectures for residents, read patients' files, observed in consulting offices and examining rooms, and visited patients in the hospital to talk informally about what they were feeling. For the next eight months, I audiotaped the exchange of information between practitioners and patients.

The analysis in this chapter is drawn from verbatim transcripts of audiotaped practitioner–patient communication, information gathered from medical files, and other ethnographic materials. My background knowledge grew from impromptu interviews with practitioners and was heightened by attending lectures with residents, studying the residents' training manual, and reading appropriate sections of their gynecological textbooks.

To display how medical decisions were negotiated in practitioner-patient communications. I extended the analysis beyond the linguistic boundaries of the transcripts and blended verbatim linguistic data with more impressionistic ethnographic data. Neither practitioners nor patients say aloud all that contributes to their decision making.

For example, patients rarely say aloud that they do not trust their medical practitioners or that they suspect them of trying to manipulate the situation. Similarly, neither staff doctors nor residents say aloud that a patient looks like a poor woman, or that she talks like an uneducated woman. They do not say that how patients talk, look, or dress leads them to believe that the patients are not responsible and will not return for necessary follow-up care. They do not say that these factors contribute to their recommending a less conservative treatment. Neither doctors nor residents say aloud that a particular patient has all of the children she needs or should have because she is on welfare and cannot afford the children she already has. They do not say that hairy underarms and legs, asking too many questions or being too quiet, acting too passive or too aggressive, or wanting children (or more children) contributes to the treatment they recommend. Residents do not say aloud that they need surgery experience or that a particular patient is a good candidate for a hysterectomy (even though a hysterectomy is not absolutely necessary on medical grounds). Although not said aloud, my observations suggest that these factors (and others like them) contribute to the negotiation of treatment decisions.

The Medical Context

Women with abnormal Pap smears provided an ideal population to study the negotiation of differential decision making. Pap smears are preventive health measures. They are recommended for most women once a year as a screen for cervical cancer.

The results of Pap smears traditionally come in five classes. Class 1 is normal, and class 5 is the most abnormal and may indicate invasive disease. Classes 2, 3, and 4 represent a gray area between normal cells and invasive disease. They often indicate dysplasia, or abnormal changes in cells that, although not cancerous, may be precursors to cervical cancer.

Pap smears in the gray area give medical practitioners the widest latitude in their decision making. When a Pap smear is abnormal, the medical task is to ensure that the whole area of abnormal cells can be visualized to rule out the possibility of invasive disease. Once the extent of the lesion and the degree of abnormality have been determined, treatment decisions are based on two separate but interrelated goals: (*a*) to protect the patient from developing more extensive disease (cancer), and (*b*) to preserve, where possible, the patient's reproductive functions.

During my study, I observed three treatment options routinely used to treat women with Pap smears in the range between normal and invasive disease: cryosurgery (freezing), cone biopsy or conization, and hysterectomy.

Cryosurgery is an office procedure that retains a woman's reproductive capacity. Cone biopsy or conization is a hospital procedure done under anesthetic. A thin, cone-shaped slice is cored out of the endocervical canal and examined. Cone biopsies can be either diagnostic or therapeutic. If the upper limits of the cone sample are free of abnormal cells, then this diagnostic procedure becomes an effective therapeutic one. It threatens, but does not terminate, reproductive capacity and has been demonstrated to be as effective in treating dysplasia as has the hysterectomy. Hysterectomy is the surgical removal of the uterus.

The manual prepared for residents further stipulates how treatment decisions are to be made. It says that when the limits of the lesion are seen and there is no evidence of invasive disease, treatment should be based on the patient's wish. If she wishes to retain her reproductive capacity, conservative measures like cryosurgery may be used. If she requests sterilization, hysterectomy is the treatment of choice. According to the manual, hysterectomies are indicated only when conservative techniques fail, when there is evidence of invasive disease, or when a patient requests a hysterectomy for sterilization.

These seem rather clear criteria for medical decision making. Yet, based on my observations, treatment decisions are not as clear as they seem. On purely medical grounds, it is hard to explain why no patients in the Faculty Clinic received hysterectomies. Or, even though there was no evidence of invasive disease, why 7 out of 13 women in the Community Clinic were given hysterectomies.

Given the parameters just outlined, we could speculate that perhaps the women in the Community Clinic requested hysterectomies for sterilization. However, I was in the examining room while treatment decisions were reached; and during the two years of my research, these patients never requested sterilization.

The Social Context

If treatment decisions are not made on medical grounds alone, how, then, are they made? Much of the literature of medical sociology (cf. Ehrenreich and Ehrenreich 1970; Freidson 1970; Mechanic 1968; Navarro 1973; Stevens 1966; Waitzkin and Waterman 1974) suggests that medical decisions are made using social criteria.

Still, the medical decisions made in the study cannot be justified solely on social grounds. Social criteria like referral patterns, organization of the setting, and such demographic factors as age, ethnicity, number of children, and social class did not completely account for the distribution of treatment decisions. When social criteria were considered, a trend emerged. Young, Caucasian, single or divorced women with few or no children who are referred by private physicians or social agencies to the Faculty Clinic are more likely to receive conservative treatment. Older, Mexican, or Mexican-American women, married or divorced with multiple children, referred from within the system of Community Clinics or by social agencies to the Community Clinic are more likely to receive less conservative treatment (i.e., to receive hysterectomies).

These social factors are important, yet they are not explanatory. An analysis of the medical and social factors that underlie treatment decisions focuses on the product of a decision. Once products, or treatment decisions, are tabulated and grouped together, all instances of a given treatment are treated the same. This kind of analysis leaves several questions unexplored. Chief among them are as follows: How do practitioners and patients gather information from each other to reach decisions? What input do practitioners and patients make into the decision-making process? Given the practitioners' specialized medical knowledge and technical skill and the asymmetry inherent in the relationship, how do practitioners decide what treatment to recommend? Once they have decided, how do they convey that information to patients, and what are the consequences, in terms of treatment outcomes, of how information is exchanged?

These questions shift the focus from an exclusive concern with products to an analysis of process as it occurs in organization contexts. It displays treatment decisions as produced and constrained by the exchange of information in medical interviews.

The Analytic Context

When listening to conversation, one is impressed with the variety of ways that information is exchanged. When analyzing discourse, one is equally impressed with its organized character. Theory and research in several disciplines suggest that language is a social production in which different linguistic arrangements are visible in different situations and in which there is a relationship between the words spoken, the actions performed, and the structure of talk. More recently, language has been analyzed as discourse— a naturally occurring, locally organized, social production.

Hymes (1962) states that one of the goals of an "ethnography of speaking" is to capture naturally occurring talk, do a detailed analysis of it, and display it as socially produced. The sociolinguistic concepts of "communicative competence" and its methodological counterpart, an "ethnography of speaking" (Hymes 1962, 1972, 1974), have been the foundation of many studies that examine the properties of natural language use (cf. Bernstein 1971; Ervin-Tripp and Mitchell-Kernan 1977; Halliday and Hasan 1976; Labov 1972; Philips 1972; Shatz 1975; Shatz and Gelman 1973; Shuy 1983).

Labov and Fanshel (1977) demonstrate Hymes's (1962) claim that discourse is a social or speech event organized around an exchange of information. As a speech event, therapeutic discourse is a routinized form of behavior with well-defined boundaries. It is an interview structured by who initiates the event and who is helped by it.

Labov and Fanshel found the speech event in therapeutic discourse to be asymmetrical. The participant who initiates the event and is helped by it (the client/patient) is in a subordinate position. In addition, they demonstrated that the asymmetry is socially produced and structures the exchange of information between participants.

The asymmetry Labov and Fanshel discuss is similar to Waitzkin and Waterman's (1974) "competence gap." Waitzkin and Waterman claim that socioeconomic factors cause doctors and patients to enter a therapeutic interview with different resources. This produces an inherent asymmetry, which affects health care delivery.

In a discussion of medical interviews, Shuy (1982) suggests that a great deal hinges on small features of the interview that are normally taken for granted by medical practitioners and only recently have come under investigation by social scientists. He points out that medical interviews are like other conversations in that they are structured, predictable, and organized around topics. He also demonstrates that medical interviews are different from normal conversation.

In normal conversation, there is an expectation of balanced participation. Participants talk, introduce topics, and respond to topics in about the same quantities. Not so in medical interviews. Shuy further claims that the differences in medical interviews have an impact on patient's participation and understanding. Others also have argued that how information is exchanged has an impact on how it is understood (cf. Chafe 1976; Cicourel 1974, 1975; Keenan and Schieffelin 1976; Kuno 1976).

The Decision-Making Context: The Medical Interview

An analysis of the practitioner–patient communication through which treatment decisions are negotiated provides information not available when only the medical and social criteria underlying medical decision making are considered. These criteria are, in many ways, external and constraining "social facts" that produce and inhibit the decision-making process. Yet, treatment decisions are also affected by the participants' interactional activities and, as such, are socially produced in the setting. An analysis of the strategic use of language in medical interviews displays how treatment decisions are accomplished within the contextural framework provided by medical and social factors.

Medical interviews are social events oriented toward the specific end of a treatment decision. In this event, practitioners have, and use, quite a wide latitude of choice in recommending treatment options. In analyzing how language is strategically used to accomplish treatment decisions, I do not intend to characterize the field of medicine as a whole or to praise or criticize particular medical practitioners. Rather, it is my intention to demonstrate that medical practitioners and patients have different practical concerns that organize how they exchange information. This organization has consequences in terms of the decisions reached.

Patients enter medical interactions from a position of relative weakness. For example, they have an abnormal Pap smear and feel threatened by the possibility of a cancer-related medical problem. They enter unfamiliar surroundings in which all of the other participants seem to share a common language. This language is, for the most part, unintelligible and frightening to them.

Medical practitioners, on the other hand, are in their "home court" in the medical setting. They understand and have some control over the workings of the hospital and clinic bureaucracies. The special medical jargon is their professional lexicon. They have knowledge and skills that are usually mysterious to patients. It is from this position of relative strength that practitioners greet patients and the medical interview begins.

Medical practitioners, in addition, are very busy. Their time is budgeted and oriented toward making a diagnosis and recommending treatments. For practitioners, the diagnostic/treatment process is a general concern. Their focus is on how, within certain parameters, to treat a specific medical problem. The patient is one among many with similar problems.

For residents, the diagnostic/treatment process includes an additional concern. They need surgical experience if they are to become competent practitioners. This creates a dual focus for them: (*a*) providing adequate medical care, and (*b*) producing maximum opportunities for surgery experience.

In addition, medical practitioners are not as able to separate themselves from death as I had been. The relationship between abnormal Pap smears, cancer, and the kind of death most cancer causes may contribute to the practitioners' treatment recommendations. This may be especially true when they treat lower-class, minority women, who practitioners may view as immature, irresponsible, and unlikely to return for the necessary follow-up care.

The practical concerns are not the same for patients. Patients are not interested in making a diagnosis. They cannot recommend treatments, do not need surgery experience, and have not faced death on a daily basis. Their time is not measured into equal increments to be divided among a maximum number of patients. For patients, the focus is on the meaning of their medical problem and how it will affect their everyday lives. Time is measured as time away from school, job, or family; time until they find out the results of laboratory tests or treatments to be recommended; time as a bomb ticking away precious moments before the suspected cancer explodes and takes over their lives. Patients are interested in finding out what their abnormal Pap smears mean, whether they indicate cancer, and what needs to be done. They are afraid of the unknown, worried about the possibility of having cancer, and fearful that their lives, reproductive capacities, and value as women may be at risk (Fisher 1979b).

Both the practitioner and patient have information that is necessary to the decision-making process of the other. To gain access to this information, they exchange information organized around topics by requesting and providing information to each other. During the exchange, language functions strategically to move the decision-making process closer to a treatment decision. On some occasions, requests for information function as "questioning strategies." Both the practitioner and patient request specific information and provide access to less specific information. For example the question, "What did Karen tell you about your Pap smear?" is a request for specific information. It is also a way to gain less specific information about the woman's competence as a patient.

Both practitioners and patients use questioning strategies. They are used by medical practitioners during talk about reproduction to gain access to information that only patients can supply. Patients use questioning strategies during talk about treatment options to gather information about the necessity of a recommended treatment. When used by residents and staff physicians, they are used differently and these differences impact upon the decision-making process.

On other occasions, information is provided in ways that function as "presentational" and "persuasional" strategies. Both strategies are negotiating mechanisms. They provide information while *suggesting* or *specifying* how the information should be understood.

Presentational strategies are "soft sells." They provide information while *suggesting* how patients should make sense out of it. For example, a practitioner would say, "We usually treat this by freezing." This presentation provides the patient with information about a treatment option while suggesting that it is the "usual" or "normal" way to treat her condition.

Persuasional strategies are harder sells. They provide information while *specifying* how it should be understood. For example, a practitioner might say, "What you should do if you don't want any more children is have a hysterectomy. No more uterus, no more cancer, no more babies, no more birth control, and no more periods." This presentation provides the patient with information about what treatment she should have while specifying why she should have it (no more uterus, no more cancer, etc.).

Only practitioners use presentational and persuasional strategies. And, again, the strategies are used differently by residents and staff physicians. They are used when talking about cancer and treatment options to provide information about what treatment decision the patient should make.

Questioning, presentational, and persuasional strategies are interactional mechanisms that accomplish treatment decisions. They are the strategies through which the information necessary to negotiate treatment decisions is exchanged.

The Communication Context: Negotiation Mechanisms

An analysis of the strategic use of language suggests that practitioners have power that patients lack, a power manifested and reflected in how practitioners present information to patients. Although patients do not have the same kind of power practitioners do, they too have input into the decision-making process. They can ask questions that can redirect talk about treatment options and that can affect how the treatment decision is reached.

The discussion of how language is strategically used takes the analysis beyond the linguistic bounds of the transcript and embeds it in its ethnographic context. A comparison across settings, participants, and treatment decisions provides a view of how treatment decisions are negotiated and accomplished in the situated actions of the participants and in specific organizational contexts.

Medical Practitioners' Use of Questioning Strategies

Questioning strategies provide a slot for patients to display their competence.[1] Marrianna, for example, was diagnosed and treated in the Faculty Clinic. She was a 21-year-old Anglo woman; a student at a local university; had never married; and had been pregnant once and had had an abortion. She was referred to the junior oncologist in the Faculty Clinic by a women's health care specialist. A routine Pap smear taken in this clinic was returned with the notation that it contained abnormal cells; and because of the professional relationship between the women's health care specialist and the new doctor in the hospital (the junior staff oncologist), she was referred to the Faculty Clinic.

On her first visit, the doctor twice requested information in a strategic manner. He said, "Now did Karen explain to you the abnormal, what this abnormal Pap smear business is?"

The patient answered. "She [the women's health care specialist] explained that the cells looked abnormal . . . the cells are in a dysplastic condition."

The doctor continued by asking, "Dysplasia, what's your understanding of that?"

To which she responded, "Well, what's anyone's understanding of it? They're abnormal and you don't know why and they don't know if it leads to cancer."

In both of these requests for information, Marrianna responded by providing the information requested, and in so doing, presented herself as a competent young woman.

In the next case, the same doctor asked similar questions, but the patient did not display herself as competent. The patient, Anelen, was a 30-year-old Anglo woman. She had been married once, divorced, been pregnant once, and given the child up for adoption. She was referred by the same women's health care specialist.

---

[1] In this discussion *competence* is not intended to index the patient's overall ability, but rather it indexes the patient's ability to display herself as appropriate within the doctor's medical framework.

During the interview the doctor asked a question that functioned strategically. He said, "Do you know that the Pap smear, do you understand what the Pap smear means? What it does?"

The patient responded by saying, "Uhmm, Karen explained a little, but I'm not sure of the possibilities. I don't even know what all those are but she told me not to worry yet."

Anelen's response neither provided the information requested nor made her appear as a competent woman. To be sure that Anelen had the necessary information to understand her medical problem and reach a decision, the doctor followed this exchange by providing information about her Pap smear and about the diagnostic and therapeutic procedures used to manage it.

In the third example, no slot was provided for the patient to display her competence. Marvi, a 23-year-old Mexican-American woman, was married, the mother of three small children, and was referred to the Community Clinic from the Primary Care Clinic where a postpartum checkup and routine Pap smear disclosed abnormal cervical cells. At the time of Marvi's visit to the Community Clinic, she was pregnant with an unwanted pregnancy, which led to an abortion. Although this was her first abortion, it was not the first time her birth control had failed. Given these factors, it is not surprising that the practitioner had recommended a hysterectomy. What is more surprising is that she did not have a hysterectomy. Marvi is the only woman in the sample population with multiple children who was treated with cryosurgery.

The bureaucratic organization of the Community Clinic contributed to Marvi's treatment with cryosurgery. At the Community Clinic, Marvi was discouraged from having a tubal ligation for sterilization. Instead, a hysterectomy was recommended to treat her medical problem and for sterilization. When the patient was referred to another clinic for abortion counseling, that clinic did not discourage a tubal ligation. Marvi, then, had an abortion and a tubal. When she returned to the Community Clinic, there were no longer any medical grounds on which a hysterectomy could be performed, and so she was treated with cryosurgery.

The exchange of information in Marvi's case took place differently from the exchange in Marrianna and Anelen's case. Marrianna and Anelen were treated in the Faculty Clinic by a professor of medicine—a staff physician. In each case, the physician asked questions that functioned strategically. These questions provided a slot into which patients could respond—displaying their competence in the process.

On the other hand, Marvi was treated in the Community Clinic by a resident who did not use questions in a strategic manner. Thus, Marvi did not have an opportunity to show herself to be a competent patient. When the resident questioned her, he used very specific questions about her birth control practices. Because she had come to the clinic with an unwanted pregnancy, it was quite clear that Marvi had not been a competent user of birth control. It is interesting to speculate on why the resident did not use more general questions, which might have allowed Marvi to display her competence as a patient. I suspect that he had already judged her to be incompetent on grounds that are not displayed in the verbal communication between them. These assumptions structured the exchange of information that followed and had an impact on the treatment recommended.

Patient's Use of Questioning Strategies

Patients also ask questions. They ask them in response to information provided by medical professionals during a discussion of treatment options. When asked by patients, questions have the potential to change the direction of the treatment decision, as shown in the following examples.

When Anelen returned to the Faculty Clinic to discuss the results of her tests and make a treatment decision, she asked a question during a discussion of treatment options. On her previous visit Anelen provided the information that she did not want to have any more children. The doctor responded by recommending a hysterectomy as a permanent method of sterilization and to treat her abnormal Pap smear.

On the second visit, the exchange opened with a discussion that reviews what had transpired on the previous visit and during a previous phone conversation. The doctor reminded Anelen that he has recommended a hysterectomy, and Anelen asked a question that redirected the talk about treatment options and affected the final treatment. She said "Have a hysterectomy and that, I'm that, if there's an alternative. I'm terrified of operations." The doctor responded, "Uh, okay, well, there certainly is an alternative, yeah, we can treat this by just freezing it here in the office and that usually will take care of it about 90% of the time." The discussion of options and the treatment performed was redirected after the patient raised a question. She was treated with cryosurgery.

The next patient, Lucy, was diagnosed and treated in the Faculty Clinic after being referred from a social agency staffed by native Spanish-speaking workers. Lucy was a 42-year-old, bilingual, Mexican-American woman. She was married and had three children. Her diagnosis and treatment in the Faculty Clinic was related to her being a poor, bilingual Mexican-American woman, and to my participation as both a researcher and translator.

The patient had a medical problem for which she went to her private physician. He recommended surgery, and she did not have the money to pay for it. In her search for less expensive medical care, a friend referred her to the outreach clinic staffed by native Spanish-speakers. At the clinic, Lucy received advice about how to apply for MediCal (the California equivalent of Medicaid) and was referred to the junior staff oncologist at the Faculty Clinic.

When the doctor and patient met to discuss treatment options, he informed her that the extent of her lesion had not been visualized, told her that she needed to have a conization biopsy as the next diagnostic step, and talked about a hysterectomy. Lucy was concerned about how she would pay for hospital care and confused by the letter she had received from MediCal. She asked the doctor to clarify the letter and he was unable to do so (which does not speak well for MediCal's style of communication).

To provide the information Lucy requested, the doctor called the billing office. While he was on the phone, Lucy turned to me and asked, in Spanish, if the doctor had said he was going to take out her uterus. I explained, in Spanish, the difference between conization biopsy and hysterectomy and confirmed that the doctor had been talking about removing her uterus. She asked if that would be necessary and I suggested that she ask the doctor.

Two things particularly struck me about our exchange. First, because Lucy spoke English so well, both the doctor and I assumed she understood it equally well. She did not. After reviewing the transcript, I was not surprised. When talking about treatments, the doctor had used several words interchangeably: *womb, uterus, cervix,* and *hysterectomy.* I was also struck by the consequences of our exchange. At the next opportunity, which occurred during a discussion of treatment options, the patient requested information that functioned strategically, changed the direction of the discussion of options, and affected the treatment performed.

While talking about how long the patient would have to be in the hospital, the doctor explained that the longer stay was because they would be taking out her uterus. The patient then asked, "Is that necessary?" The doctor responded, "Well, it isn't absolutely necessary; it may or may not be...." For much of the remaining exchange of information, the doctor worked to move the patient toward a treatment decision of hysterectomy. In each instance, the patient responded by asking if it was necessary or by saying that if it was not necessary, she did not want it. She was treated with a conization biopsy.

Another patient, Pat, asked questions, but did not change the direction of the discussion of options or the treatment performed. Pat, a 32-year-old Anglo woman, had been married, divorced, pregnant five times, and had three children. Although she was an American citizen, she married and had lived most of her adult life in Ireland. Her children still lived there with their father. When she returned to the Community Clinic to discuss her treatment options, she was told that the extent of the lesion had not been visualized, asked if she wanted more children, and told that a conization biopsy followed by a hysterectomy was the best treatment for her.

During the discussion of treatment options and in response to information that the resident was presenting, she made a request for information, a request that functioned strategically. She said,

Well, for this way now would you say, for instance, you're talking about there could be surgery, if, uh, there is an advancement of cancer there, a sign of cancer. Well, also the fact that you asked me did I want any more children, there's another way of doing it too, but it also means that it could travel, is that it, the cancer could spread, say for instance, if I don't have a hysterectomy, is that the idea?

The doctor responded, "Well, if you have cancer, then it has to be treated because it can spread, right?" The talk about treatment options did not change the direction of the discussion of options or the treatment performed. This patient was treated with a vaginal hysterectomy.

The communication in this case between practitioner and patient is different from that with the two previous patients (Anelen and Lucy). Pat is the only patient who added information to the "facts" provided by the medical practitioner. She added the notion that cancer could spread if not treated with a hysterectomy. It was this information the resident picked up and used to justify his treatment recommendation. Pat's question is also not as clear or as strong as those used by the other two patients. She did not ask if there were alternatives or if a hysterectomy was necessary. In addition, she asked two questions during the same utterance. The resident avoided discussing alternatives entirely. And he answered only part of the second question. He did not address whether the abnormal cells would spread if she did not have a hysterectomy. Instead, he answered a hypothetical question that she had not really asked. He answered the question, If it is cancer, would it spread without a hysterectomy? He did not tell her that if she did not have cancer, there were other alternatives.

In Anelen's, Lucy's, and Pat's cases the medical professional's presentation of information provided a slot into which the patient could request information that functioned strategically. In each case, the medical professional's response to the question was different. In addition, the medical professionals themselves elicited information from patients differently in each case. With Anelen, the doctor asked questions to request specific information and to provide a slot for her to display her competence. In response, she neither provided the information he asked for nor displayed her competence. In Lucy and Pat's cases, no questions were asked. Neither patient was given an opportunity to display her understanding of her medical problem or her competence as a patient.

It is interesting to speculate why Lucy and Pat were not given the opportunity to display their competence, as Anelen was; or why neither Lucy not Anelen were given a hysterectomy, as Pat was. On closer inspection, Lucy shares features with both Anelen and Pat. Although Lucy and Anelen were both treated in the Faculty Clinic by the same staff physician, their referral patterns had been quite different. Anelen had been referred by a women's health care specialist with whom she had a long-standing relationship. This relationship provided an outside advocate who could hold the medical practitioner in the hospital accountable. Neither Lucy nor Pat had an outside advocate. Lucy had been referred from an outreach clinic staffed by native Spanish-speakers, and Pat had been referred from within the system of community clinics. In each case, neither the interest of the referring medical practitioner nor the organization of the bureaucracy provided the kind of support Anelen had developed with the women's health care specialist.

It seems reasonable to speculate that both Lucy and Pat were judged as less powerful than Anelen on grounds that are not immediately apparent in their verbal communication. This judgment structured the exchange of information between practitioner and patient and had an impact on the treatment decision reached. Although in each case the medical practitioner provided a slot for the patient to request information that functioned strategically, he responded to the questions patients inserted into these slots differently.

At first glance, then, it would be reasonable to assume that Lucy and Pat, denied the opportunity to display their competence and perceived as less powerful, would be treated with hysterectomies and Anelen would not. My observations suggest two reasons this was not the outcome. First, Lucy was treated in the Faculty Clinic by a staff physician and Pat was treated in the Community Clinic by a resident. Staff physicians do not have the same "need" to perform hysterectomies as do residents, who must have the surgical experience to become fully qualified doctors. Second, Lucy, unlike Pat, used a strong questioning strategy and kept returning to it each time the doctor suggested a hysterectomy. Pat used a weaker questioning strategy and did not return to it, even when her questions were not fully answered. Thus, Pat's impact on the decision-making process was weak, and she was treated with a hysterectomy.

Medical Practitioners' Use of Presentational and Persuasional Strategies

Although both practitioners and patients ask questions, doctors do so during exchanges of general information to gather the details of patients' reproductive history and desire. Patients, by contrast, ask questions during discussions about treatment options. In addition, there are differences in how medical practitioners present information to patients when discussing cancer and treatment options. They use presentational and persuasional strategies to provide patients with the information necessary to reach treatment decisions and with ways of understanding or making sense out of that information.

In each of the previous three cases, the medical professional's response to patients' questions provided specific information and suggested how that information should be understood. In Anelen's case, the doctor responded by saying, "There certainly is an alternative . . ." and by providing the information that cryosurgery is an alternative that is 90% effective. He provided specific information, and by the tone of his presentation, made the choice of cryosurgery perfectly acceptable.

In Lucy's case, the doctor responded by saying, "Well, it isn't absolutely necessary. . . ." The statement that "it isn't absolutely necessary" frames the medical information to suggest a preference: Although a hysterectomy is not absolutely necessary, it certainly is preferable.

In Pat's case, the resident avoided directly answering the patient's question. By answering only a small part of what was asked, he suggested that the answer to the whole was contained within the part; that is, that a hysterectomy was a necessary procedure.

In Anelen's, Lucy's, and Pat's cases the medical practitioners used presentational strategies to suggest how information should be understood. In the next case, information is presented in a way that does more than suggest how to make sense out of it. Persuasional strategies are used to specify the grounds on which understanding is to be based. In presenting the options to Marvi the resident said the following:

> What I was going to tell you is that there are two ways this can be treated. Okay? One is for dysplasia that we could do a hysterectomy and just remove the uterus. That means no more babies in the future and so you know, as a form of contraception also, okay? The second is to freeze the cervix and then follow you with the understanding that that should cure it, but that you need to be followed in the future and that you could have children in the future if that's what your plans include.

The resident presented information about a hysterectomy as the means to have no more babies and as a method of contraception. To a woman who is pregnant with an unwanted pregnancy and who has had repeated birth control failures, this is a particularly persuasive presentation. He continues by saying that she could be treated by freezing the cervix but she could still have children and would have to be followed. Again, a very persuasive presentation. This is a poor woman who does not want more children and does not have either the time or the money to return to the hospital for frequent follow-up care. In addition, the resident presented the hysterectomy option first, and then presented cryosurgery as an option. This order suggested that the less conservative treatment (hysterectomy) was somehow preferable. Later in the exchange, the resident summed up his position using another persuasional strategy. He said, "Absent uterus, no periods, no cancer, no babies."

Similarly, in Pat's case, when the resident presented her with an informed consent form to sign, he said,

> Even though with this form that I have before me that the government requires you to sign, it's a request for a hysterectomy for sterilization, even

though it says here that you have no problems which require a hysterectomy and we know that you do, the hospital and state require me to ask you to sign this so that you understand that what we're talking about is permanent sterilization with no possibilities of future pregnancies.

This, again, is a particularly persuasive presentation. The patient in no way requested a hysterectomy for sterilization. She had been referred to the clinic with a class 5 Pap smear. During a discussion about treatment options, a hysterectomy was recommended as the most appropriate treatment. The grounds for this recommendation were specified as follows: "It [cancer] could come back," and "... for somebody your age, that's had your family, you're sure that you don't want children, I'd recommend a hysterectomy." To a woman who has had a class 5 Pap smear and is already afraid that she has a life-threatening medical problem, this is a particularly persuasive presentation. It heightens the emotional impact of the abnormal Pap smear by stressing that "it" could come back. The "it" being referred to is, of course, cancer. In addition, it is the resident, not the patient, who links the need for a hysterectomy with the patient's age, her childbearing history, and her lack of desire for additional children. To a woman who lived many of her childbearing years in a Catholic country and has had three children and two abortions, this again is a very persuasive presentation.

The persuasive overtones were strengthened when the resident gave her the informed consent to sign and told her that although the form said that she had no problems requiring a hysterectomy, "We know that you do." He brings all of the authority of his medical role to bear in this statement. As a man, as a medical practitioner, and as her physician, he is telling her what to do and implying dire consequences if she does not comply.

There is an additional issue involved in this presentation. The resident told the patient what he was required to by law and then suggested that she ignore it. This amplifies the power and authority of his medical role and his use of it to manipulate her decision-making process. One might ask, What kind of informed consent procedure does this represent?

Accomplishing the Treatment Event

Caress (1975, 1977) suggests several reasons for the explosion of hysterectomies in recent years. First, she argues, gynecologists and obstetricians are surgeons. As the birth rate continues to level out, these doctors face reduced opportunities to practice their surgical skills. Second, many physicians have united their professional skills and their political ideals. As a result, poor, minority women are bearing the brunt of unnecessary hysterectomies. Finally, she claims, hysterectomies are good money makers.

Other reasons for increased hysterectomies have also been discussed. Once reproduction is over, many doctors agree that the uterus is a useless organ. John Morris, M.D., told a congressional subcommittee that, "An arm is a useful structure. Breasts have cosmetic advantages. However, there are certain organs that are absolutely useless. One such is your appendix, another is the uterus after childbearing" ("Important Cost and Quality Issues" 1977:354).

The uterus, seen as a useless organ past childbearing, is also depicted as a potentially dangerous organ. As Dr. R.C. Wright wrote in a 1969 issue of *Obstetrics and Gynecology:* "The uterus has but one function: reproduction. After the last planned pregnancy the uterus becomes a useless, bleeding, symptom-producing, potentially cancer-bearing organ and therefore should be removed" (Larned 1977:199).

Ninety-seven per cent of all gynecologists in the U.S. are men. As men, to some extent their attitudes toward women reflect current views of women in society (Larned 1977). As Scully and Bart (1973) point out, these attitudes are magnified and reinforced in medical school. Medical students and residents learn to view the uterus and the women who have them negatively. To quote from a widely used gynecological textbook:

> No drastic results are found following the removal of the uterus. . . . Indeed, it should be not construed as callous if many gynecologists feel that, in the woman who has completed her family, the uterus is a rather worthless organ. (Novak et al. 1970:26)

This attitude has been described as quite common: "This is indeed the attitude of most gynecologists. While it may seem harsh and ill-phrased, it is a logical viewpoint and one with which I personally agree" (Paulshock 1976:26). Scully (1980) points out, and the data in this article supports, that these attitudes provide the basis on which residents learn and use a regular "sales pitch" for hysterectomies.

Summary

As I pointed out, no patients in the Faculty Clinic received hysterectomies, while 7 out of 13 women in the Community Clinic did receive hysterectomies. It is logical to deduce, as Caress (1975, 1977) and Larned (1977) suggest, that if doctors believe that hysterectomies are in women's best interest, the number of hysterectomies will continue to increase.

It is likely that staff physicians and residents bring different sets of practical concerns into the examining room that affect how language is used and how treatment decisions are reached. It is also reasonable that patients referred from the private sector to professors of medicine in the Faculty Clinic are less likely to be treated with hysterectomies than are patients referred from the public sector to residents in the Community Clinic. The Faculty and Community Clinics provide very different settings in which to deliver and receive medical care.

Faculty and Community Clinics were organized in different ways, to serve a different population of patients and were staffed in a different manner. The Faculty Clinic was staffed by gynecological oncologists who were professors of medicine. There were no residents rotating in and out of the clinic; thus, there was a kind of continuity of care not normally found in teaching settings. The physical layout honored the humanness of patients. There was a separation of public and private space. The waiting room was separated from the backstage medical area. Examining rooms were separated from consulting offices.

The Community Clinic, on the other hand, was staffed in a rotating fashion. Everybody rotated—residents, support personnel, and supervising staff; thus heightening the lack of continuity of care. Assignment to the Community Clinic, the narrow definition of the medical problem under their care, and the constant rotation also increased the fragmentation of the care delivered. In addition, the physical layout of the clinic did not honor the humanness of patients. There was no separation of public and private space. There was no waiting room. Patients sat in the hall outside of the examining room overhearing medical talk that frightened them. There were also no consulting offices. All talk with patients occurred either in the halls (in the presence of other patients) or in the examining rooms. I suspect that it is a very different experience to sit across the desk from a doctor, fully clothed, discussing your medical problem from having a similar discussion with a resident while you are sitting undressed on the examining table.

The data discussed in this chapter support the view that although the doctor–patient relationship is an asymmetrical one, the asymmetry increases when patients are perceived as poor and powerless and medical practitioners are residents rather than staff physicians. It seems that the need for surgery experience and the lack of an outside advocate plus internal norms of medical adequacy contribute to the differential outcomes in the Faculty Clinic and Community Clinic. It follows, quite naturally, that these structural and organizational features of the delivery of health care are manifested during medical interviews in the exchange of information between participants, negotiated through the use of linguistic strategies, and have consequences for the treatment decision reached.

The linguistic and ethnographic data discussed here further suggest that the medical interview is organized in predictable ways. A detailed examination of how language is used and treatment decisions are negotiated provides information not available in an analysis of the medical and social facts underlying medical decision making. It displays the processes through which treatment decisions are jointly accomplished. First, medical practitioners and patients, exchanging the information necessary to reach treatment decisions, use language strategically, thus doing communicational work. In addition to specifying how treatment decisions are negotiated in the activities of participants, this kind of an analysis suggests that the communicational work of the participants is oriented toward the specific end of a treatment decision, thus linking interaction (or communication) to outcomes (or treatment decisions). Finally, this kind of analysis places the decision-making process in a specific organizational context.

By placing linguistic phenomena in their social context and analyzing how that context organizes linguistic structures, three levels of analysis (structural, organizational, and interactional) that are normally treated separately are linked. The detailed analysis of the communicational process through which treatment decisions are negotiated displays how the negotiation of hysterectomies is produced and constrained by structural, organizational, and interactional contexts and accomplished through the communication between participants.

There are theoretical, methodological, and practical ramifications inherent in the documentation of the communicational work through which treatment decisions are reached. Theoretically and methodologically, a systematic analysis of the communicational strategies used to accomplish treatment decisions provides insights not normally available when the subtleties of the practitioner–patient relationship are not examined. These insights can have practical consequences for medical education, resident training, and the creation of informed consumers.

In an era in which both medical practitioners and patients are displaying increasing dissatisfaction with the way things are—the high costs of medical care, the increasing performance of unnecessary medical procedures, the difficulties with patient compliance, the problems with informed consent, and the use and possible abuse of medical malpractice procedures—awareness of the processes used to communicate hold the potential for improving communication and improving the delivery of health care.

References Cited

Bernstein, Basil, 1971. *Class, Codes and Control*. London: Routledge & Kegan Paul.

Caress, Barbara, 1975. *Sterilization*. Health/PAC Bulletin #62, January/February, pp. 1–13.

———, 1977. *Womb-boom*. Health/PAC Bulletin, July/August.

Chafe, Wallace L., 1976. Givenness, contrastiveness, definiteness, subjects, topics and point of view. IN *Subject and Topic*, Charles H. Li, Ed., pp. 25–56. New York: Academic Press.

Cicourel, Aaron V., 1974. Interviewing and memory. IN *Pragmatic Aspects of Human Communication*, Colin Cherry, Ed., pp. 51–82. Dordrecht: Reidel.

————, 1975. Discourse and text: Cognitive and linguistic processes in studies of social structure. To appear in *Versus*. (Portions presented at 1975 American Sociological Association Meetings.)

Cost and Quality of Health Care: Unnecessary Surgery Report by the Committee on Oversight and Investigations of the Committee on Interstate and Foreign Commerce, House of Representatives, Ninth Congress Second Session, January, 1976. YN.IN 8/4 H 34/35.

Ehrenreich, Barbara, and John Ehrenreich, 1970. *The American Health Empire.* Health-PAC Book. New York: Vintage.

Ervin-Tripp, Susan, and Claudia Mitchell-Kernan, 1977. *Child Discourse.* New York: Academic Press.

Fisher, Sue Carole, 1979a. The Negotiation of Treatment Decisions in Doctor/Patient Communications and Their Impact on Identity of Women Patients. Doctoral dissertation, University of California, San Diego, California.

————, 1979b. Mirror, mirror on the wall; Women's identities and women's role. Paper presented at annual meetings of the Mid-South Sociological Association, Memphis, Tennessee, November 1979.

Freidson, Eliot, 1970. *Profession of Medicine.* New York: Dodd, Mead.

Halliday, Michael A., and Ruqaiya Hasan, 1976. *Cohesion in English.* London: Longmans.

Hymes, Dell, 1962. The ethnography of speaking. In *Anthropology and Human Behavior.* Washington, D.C.: Anthropological Society of Washington.

————, 1972. Models of the interaction of language and social life. In *Directions in Sociolinguistics: The Ethnography of Communication,* John J. Gumperz and Dell Hymes, Eds., pp. 38–71. New York: Holt, Rinehart and Winston.

————, 1974. *Foundations of Sociolinguistics.* Philadelphia: University of Pennsylvania Press.

Important Cost and Quality Issues of Health Care Hearings before the Subcommittee on Oversight and Investigations of the Committee on Interstate and Foreign Commerce, House of Representatives, 95 Congress/First Session, April 25 and 29, May 2 and 9, 1977. V/4. IN 8/4:95–32.

Keenan, Elinor Ochs, and Bambi B. Schieffelin, 1976. Topics as a discourse notion: A study of topic in the conversations of children and adults. In *Subject and Topic,* Charles N. Li, Ed., pp. 335–384. New York: Academic Press.

Kuno, Susumu, 1976. Subject, theme, and the speaker's empathy—a reexamination of relativization in phenomena. In *Subject and Topic,* Charles N. Li, Ed., pp. 417–444. New York: Academic Press.

Labov, William, 1972. *Sociolinguistic Patterns.* Philadelphia: University of Pennsylvania Press.

Labov, William, and David Fanshel, 1977. *Therapeutic Discourse: Psychotherapy as Conversation.* New York: Academic Press.

Larned, D., 1977. The epidemic in unnecessary hysterectomy. In *Seizing Our Bodies: The Politics of Women's Health,* Claudia Dreifus, Ed. New York: Vintage Books.

Mechanic, David, 1968. *Medical Sociology.* New York: The Free Press.

National Center for Health Statistics, 1976. Surgical operation in short-stay hospitals, US, 1973. In *Vital and Health Statistics,* Series 13, No. 21. Washington, D.C.: Author.

Navarro, Vincente, 1973. *Health and Medical Care in the U.S.: A Critical Analysis.* Farmingdale, N.Y.: Baywood Publishing Co.

Novak, E. R. et al., 1970. *Novak's Textbook of Gynecology.* Baltimore: Williams and Wilkens.

Paulshock, B. Z., 1976. What every woman should know about hysterectomy. *Today's Health* 54(2) (February):23–26.

Philips, Susan, 1972. Participant structures and communicative competence: Warm Springs children in community and classroom. In *Functions of Language in the Classroom*, Courtney Cazden, Vera John, and Dell Hymes, Eds., pp. 370–394. New York: Teachers College Press.

Scully, Diana, 1980. *Men Who Control Women's Health: The Miseducation of Obstetricians-Gynecologists.* Boston: Houghton Mifflin.

Scully, Diana, and P. Bart, 1973. A funny thing happened on the way to the orifice: Women in gynecological textbooks. *American Journal of Sociology* 78(4): 1045–1050.

Shatz, Marilyn, 1975. Towards a Developmental Theory of Communicative Competence. Doctoral dissertation, University of Pennsylvania.

Shatz, Marilyn, and Rochel Gelman, 1973. The Development of Communication Skills; Modifications in the Speech of Young Children as a Function of Listener. *Monographs of the Society for Research in Child Development* 38.

Shuy, Roger W., 1983. Three types of interference to an effective exchange of information in the medical interview. In *The Social Organization of Doctor–Patient Communication*, Sue Fisher and Alexandra Dundas Todd, Eds., pp. 189–202. Washington, D.C.: The Center for Applied Linguistics.

Stevens, Rosemary, 1966. *Medical Practice in Modern England: The Impact of Specialization and State Medicine.* New Haven: Yale University Press.

Virginia Department of Health, 1977. Uterine cancer and the Pap test. *Virginia Health Bulletin* 29, Series 2, Number 3. Richmond, Va.: Author.

Waitzkin, Howard B., and Barbara Waterman, 1974. *The Exploitation of Illness in Capitalist Society.* Indianapolis: Bobbs-Merrill.

Content Questions

1. What did Fisher observe about the likelihood of women receiving a hysterectomy when referred to the Faculty Clinic as opposed to the Community Clinic?

2. In terms of the balance of talk, how do medical interviews differ from regular conversations?

3. Explain the difference between "presentational" and "persuasional" strategies.

4. What role does a patient's demonstration of competence have in the treatment suggested by the doctor?

5. In the cases noted by Fisher, what relationship existed between the patients' use of questioning strategies and the likelihood of their being given a hysterectomy?

6. In Pat's case her question included some information that the doctor could use to justify his recommendation. What was that information and what decision did it contribute to?

Questions for Analysis and Discussion

1. In light of Fisher's research, what should patients consulting with a doctor keep in mind about how they participate in the consultation? What should doctors consider about the way they consult with their patients?

2. Comment on the importance of discourse analysis in understanding the dynamics of communication between individuals.

3. How do you think research into the discourse between doctors and patients could improve medical care?

4. What kinds of larger features of context must be considered when analyzing the way certain utterances will be interpreted?

5. Given the size of the sample that was considered in this research, how cautious do we need to be about generalizations that we make about all other medical settings and clinics?

Understanding Basic Medical Terminology

Janet Amundson Romich

Morphological analysis might seem like something that people do just to satisfy linguistics course requirements. But among other things, it can be useful to people interacting with or involved in medical-related fields when they need to learn many new vocabulary words. Janet A. Romich, a doctor of veterinary medicine whose article first appeared in *Veterinary Technician*, illustrates how someone outside the field of linguistics could use linguistic tools to approach this task. The morphological approach to learning medical terminology, while outlined briefly in this article, can be extensive. There are some books that take medical students through many pages of morphemes, morphological rules, terms, and exercises. But the brief outline below will serve to illustrate the kind of relevance morphology can have for people, whether they are studying to become neurosurgeons or veterinarians, or whether they are outside observers who want to better understand the discourse of medical professionals.

If you work in a veterinary setting, you use medical terminology every day. In addition to using medical terminology on the job, you, as a consumer, are exposed to medical terms and procedures on television, in magazines, and on any public information system. Becoming familiar with how medical terms are organized will enable you to understand words you may encounter at work and will allow you to figure out new words as you are exposed to them.

Studying medical terminology is like learning a new language. At first, the words look different and complicated. By understanding a few important guidelines, however, medical terminology can become interesting and seem like solving a logical puzzle. There are several basic rules to remember in analyzing medical terms; these rules are presented in the following discussion.[1]

When a medical word is first encountered, it should be analyzed structurally and divided into basic components. These components consist of a prefix (an affix occurring at the beginning of a word), a root (the foundation of a word), and a suffix (an affix occurring at the end of a word). For

---

[1]Chabner DE: *Medical Terminology: A Short Course*. Philadelphia, WB Saunders Co, 1991, pp 2–98.

example, the word *hyperglycemia* would be divided into the following parts:

hyper • glyc • emia.

The prefix is *hyper-*, the root is *glyc,* and the suffix is *-emia.* After dividing the word into basic components, the definition can be gleaned by analyzing the suffix, followed by the prefix, and then by the root(s). If two roots are present, the word that occurs first in the word is analyzed first.

In the example of hyperglycemia, *-emia* is the suffix, meaning blood condition; *hyper-* is the prefix, meaning excessive; and *glyc* is the root, meaning sugar. By putting these components together, it becomes apparent that hyperglycemia is a blood condition of excessive sugar. Hyperglycemia is seen in conjunction with several disease processes, including diabetes mellitus.

In some words, a combining vowel may be used between the root and the suffix to make the spoken form of the word flow more easily. The combining vowel is often *o,* but *i* and *a* are also used. If the suffix begins with a vowel, the combining vowel is usually not used. For example, in the word *cystitis,* the suffix is *-itis* (meaning inflammation) and the root is *cyst* (meaning bladder). Cystitis means inflammation of the bladder. A combining vowel is not used in this example because the suffix *-itis* begins with a vowel. In the word *hematology,* the suffix is *-logy* (meaning study of) and the root is *hemat* (meaning blood). Hematology is the study of blood. Because *-logy* does not begin with a vowel, the combining vowel, *o,* appears between the root and the suffix.

In approximately 90% of definitions of medical words, the part of the word that appears first comes last in the definition. In the word *cardiology,* for example, the definition can be gleaned by first analyzing the suffix and then the root. Therefore, cardiology is the study of the heart: *-logy* (meaning study of) and *cardi-* (meaning heart). The letter *o* is the combining vowel.

When defining words describing body systems, the words are usually built in the order in which the organs function. For example, gastroenteritis is divided into the suffix *-itis* meaning inflammation, the two roots *gastr* meaning stomach and *enter* meaning intestine, and the combining vowel *o.* Gastroenteritis is the inflammation of the stomach and intestines. In the digestive system, the stomach comes first structurally and is followed by the intestines; the term *gastroenteritis* is arranged in the same manner.

Some basic rules can be kept in mind to aid in determining the definition of a medical term. Most shorter suffixes mean *pertaining to.* Handouts and textbooks can provide information on basic anatomy and physiology concepts.

In medical writing, the correct spelling of a word is crucial; the slightest spelling error can completely alter the meaning of a word. Consider the

Table 1 Suffix List

SUFFIX	DEFINITION	EXAMPLE
-al or -eal	pertaining to	tracheal (pertaining to the trachea)
-ar	pertaining to	hilar (pertaining to a hilus)
-ary	pertaining to	maxillary (pertaining to the maxilla)
-centesis	surgical puncture to remove fluid	cystocentesis (puncture to remove urine)
-cyte	cell	monocyte (a cell with one nucleus)
-ectomy	removal, excision, resection	appendectomy (removal of the appendix)
-emia	blood condition	anemia (lack of blood)
-gram	record	electroencephalogram (a record of brain waves)
-graphy	process of recording	electroencephalography (the recording of brain waves)
-ia	condition, disease	glycosuria (the condition of glucose in the urine)
-ic	pertaining to	icteric (pertaining to jaundice)
-ism	condition, state	aneurysm (state of dilatation of the wall of an artery, a vein, or the heart)
-itis	inflammation	endocarditis (inflammation of the endo cardium)
-logist	specialist in the study of	cardiologist (one who studies the heart)
-logy	study of	cardiology (the study of the heart)
-lysis	separation, breakdown, destruction	autolysis (breakdown of tissue after death)
-megaly	enlargement	hepatomegaly (enlargement of the liver)
-oma	tumor, mass	hematoma (mass of blood)
-osis	abnormal condition	arthrosis (disease of the joints)
-pathy	disease	hepatopathy (disease of the liver)
-plasty	surgical repair	rhinoplasty (surgical repair of the nose)
-rrhea	flow, discharge	amenorrhea (lack of menstruation)
-rrhage	bursting forth of blood	hemorrhage (bleeding)
-scope	instrument to visually examine	laryngoscope (instrument to visualize the larynx)
-scopy	process of visually examining	endoscopy (visual examination of body cavities with an endoscope)
-sis	state of	hemostasis (state of arrested bleeding)
-stomy	opening	urethrostomy (creation of an opening in the urethra)
-therapy	treatment	chemotherapy (therapy with chemicals)
-tomy	process of cutting	urethrotomy (incision into the urethra)
-um	structure	epithelium (structure of tissue that covers the body)
-uria	condition of urine	hematuria (bloody urine)

Table 2 Prefix List

PREFIX	DEFINITION	EXAMPLE
a-, an-	no, not, without	atypical (not typical)
ab-	away from	abstain (to stay away from)
ad-	toward, near	adjacent (situated next to)
anti-	against	antimicrobial (active against microorganisms)
bi-	two, both	bipedal (pertaining to or using both feet)
brady-	slow	bradycardia (slow heartbeat)
con-	with, together	concurrent (occurring at the same time)
dys-	bad, painful, difficult	dysfunctional (difficulty in functioning)
ec-	out	ectocytic (outside the cell)
endo-	within, in	endoskeleton (skeleton within the body)
epi-	above, upon	epidural (above the dura mater)
ex-	out	exhale (to breathe out)
hyper-	excessive, above	hyperglycemia (excessive blood sugar)
hypo-	below, deficient	hypoglycemia (deficient blood sugar)
in-	in, into	intubation (insertion of a tube into the body)
infra-	below, beneath	infrapatellar (below the patella)
inter-	between, among	interfemerol (between the thighs)
intra-	within	intraarterial (within an artery)
mal-	bad, abnormal	malocclusion (abnormal occlusion of the maxilla and the mandible)
lumbo-	pertaining to the loins	lumbosacral (pertaining to the loins and sacrum)
meta-	beyond, change	metamorphosis (a striking change)
neo-	new, different	neoplasm (a new, abnormal growth)
para-	near, beside	paraomphilac (beside the umbilicus)
peri-	around, about	periosteum (connective tissue that covers all bones)
poly-	many	polymorphic (occurring in many forms)
post-	after, later	postsurgical (after surgery)
pre-	before, earlier	presynaptic (occurring before a synapse is crossed)
pro-	before, anterior	proleptic (occurring before the usual time)
re-	back, again	reassess (to evaluate again)
sacro-	related to the sacrum	sacrodynia (pain in the sacral region)
sclero-	hardening	sclerostenosis (hardening combined with contraction)
sub-	below, under, beneath	subpulmonary (below the lungs)
tachy-	fast	tachycardia (rapid heartbeat)
tri-	three	triamine (compound containing three amino groups)
uni-	one	unilobar (consisting of one lobe)

Table 3 Root List

ROOT	DEFINITION	EXAMPLE
abdomin	abdomen (part of the body between the thorax and pelvis)	abdominal (pertaining to the abdomen)
arthr	joint	arthritis (inflammation of the joints)
cardi	heart ·	cardiovascular (pertaining to the heart and blood vessels)
cervic	neck	cervical (pertaining to the neck)
chem	drug or chemical	chemistry (science of elements and atomic matter)
crani	skull	cranium (upper part of the head)
cyst	urinary bladder	cystalgia (pain in the bladder)
cyt	cell	cytology (the study of cells)
enter	intestine	enteritis (inflammation of the intestine)
epithel	skin, tissue lining surfaces	epithelium (skin)
erythr	red	erythrocyte (red blood cell)
gastr	stomach	gastritis (inflammation of the stomach)
glyc	sugar	glycogenesis (production of sugar)
hem, hemat	blood	hematocrit (tube used to determine the volume of packed red blood cells)
hepat	liver	hepatic (pertaining to the liver)
lapar	abdomen	laparotomy (incision into the abdomen)
later	side	lateral (pertaining to a side)
leuk	white	leukocyte (white blood cell)
nephr	kidney	nephron (functional unit of the kidney)
neur	nerve	neuron (conducting cell of the nervous system)
ophthal	eye	ophthalmology (excision of the eyeball)
oste	bone	osteoplaque (a layer of bone)
ot	ear	otitis (inflammation of the ear)
path	disease	pathogenesis (development of disease)
ren	kidney	reniculus (one of the lobules that forms the kidney)
septic	pertaining to infection	septicemia (infection of organisms in the blood)
thorac	thorax or chest	thoracic (pertaining to the thorax)
vertebr	vertebra or backbone	vertebrate (having a vertebral column)

words *ileum* and *ilium*. Both words are pronounced the same but have different meanings. *Ileum* is part of the small intestine, and *ilium* is part of the pelvic bone.[2]

By keeping these rules in mind, understanding medical terminology can be much easier. The meaning of an unfamiliar word can often be determined simply by dividing it into the suffix, prefix, and root; of course, the meaning can be confirmed by a dictionary. Dividing words to determine meaning and subsequently looking them up in a dictionary is an excellent way for technicians to expand their medical vocabulary. The tables list basic suffixes, prefixes, and roots. Although these lists are not all-inclusive, they are a good starting point for people interested in learning or expanding their medical vocabulary.

Content Questions

1. Romich suggests that an analysis of a medical term begins with a morphological analysis that breaks down the word into its basic parts. After doing that, which part of the word should then be examined first in order to get at the meaning?

2. Describe what occurs with a "combining vowel" when a root is combined with a suffix. Why is there no combining vowel in the word *cystitis?*

3. In forming the word *gastroenteritis,* what is significant about the ordering that puts the root *gastr* before *enter?*

4. Using the first table provided in the article, identify the suffixes that mean "pertaining to."

Questions for Analysis and Discussion

1. Using the tables provided in the article, break down the following terms into their morphemes and label each morpheme according to whether it is a root, prefix, or suffix. Then try to determine the meaning of these terms based on the combined meanings of the morphemes:

leukemia

hepatitis

intrathoracic

2. Why might a morphological approach to learning medical terminology be easier than just memorizing the meaning of every term?

[2]Chabner DE: *The Language of Medicine,* ed 4. Philadelphia, WB Saunders Co, 1991, pp 3–7.

3. Which kind of suffixes would you say are listed in this article, derivational or inflectional? Explain.

4. What does the presence of a form such as *-logist* in the list of suffixes indicate about whether that list has always broken forms down to their morphemic level? Explain.

5. How does this article show that morphological analysis is not just an area of interest to linguists?

Facilitating Grammatical Development: The Contribution of Pragmatics

Laurence B. Leonard and Marc E. Fey

Laurence B. Leonard of Purdue University and Marc E. Fey of the University of Kansas both work in speech pathology and audiology. This field benefits from research in linguistics, just as linguistics can learn much from the work done by speech pathologists and audiologists. Many people have narrow notions about what speech pathology involves. Speech pathologists do not work only with children, and they do not work only with speech articulation and pronunciation. Though pronunciation is of course important, there are larger communicative concerns as well. In the article below, which first appeared in *Pragmatics of Language: Clinical Practice Issues,* Leonard and Fey consider the interrelated nature of pragmatic and grammatical knowledge and how such information could be important to clinicians working with younger children who have a language impairment.

In Fey and Leonard (1983), we reviewed the growing literature on the pragmatic abilities of children with specific language impairment. We concluded that, as in other areas, these children do not represent a homogeneous group with respect to their pragmatic skills. Rather, we proposed that there are at least three different groups of children with specific language impairment as determined by their profiles of social-conversational participation.

The first pattern is represented by children who are neither as assertive nor as responsive to their social partners as expected, based on the formal linguistic means at their disposal. These children have general pragmatic deficits that extend well beyond any delays they are experiencing in the acquisition of language forms. Fey (1986) referred to these children as inactive conversationalists. The second group of children are considerably more cooperative in conversational settings. Indeed, many of these children are highly responsive to the requestive and nonrequestive acts of their conversational partners. Importantly, however, they are either unwilling or unable to make frequent substantive contributions to the conversation. They have the linguistic resources to initiate and extend topics and to perform assertive speech acts, such as requests for information and action, but they do so infrequently. Fey (1986) referred to these children as passive conversationalists. The third group of children are less pragmatically impaired than children in the first groups. These children, referred to by Fey (1986) as active conversationalists, are limited by deficits in language form, but they use their limited linguistic resources to participate actively in conversations. They typically produce a wide range of both assertive and responsive conversational acts, and they appear to attend to the informational requirements of their partners.

Fey (1986) added a fourth category of children, verbal noncommunicators, to our original formulation. These children willingly and frequently produce assertive conversational acts. In so doing, however, they seem relatively unconcerned with making semantic ties between their own utterances and those of their partners. Their narratives may also be characterized by incoherence. Their reasonably well-formed sentences simply do not make sense in the context.

Prior to the introduction of pragmatics into speech-language pathology, this type of categorization of children with language impairment would have been difficult to conceive. But the impact of pragmatics on language assessment and intervention extends well beyond simply making it possible to categorize children based on their pragmatic performance. Pragmatics gives speech-language pathologists the theoretical rationale for developing intervention objectives that are not based on language form. Furthermore, it obligates them to search for intervention approaches that are effective in achieving these nonformal goals.

For example, if a child does not perform a variety of illocutionary acts and is not participating actively both as speaker and as listener, it probably is not appropriate to focus the intervention program on the child's grammar (Fey, 1986). This is precisely the case for inactive conversationalists. A new Auxiliary or Article is not likely to have any significant effect on the communicative effectiveness of a child who is unwilling or unable to use existing formal abilities. Instead, intervention may focus on spontaneous talking, the use of topic initiations and extensions, the use of more assertive acts, and greater responsivity (Fey, 1986; Hubbell, 1977, 1981).

A similar case can be made for verbal noncommunicators. Omitted Auxiliaries, Articles, and inflectional morphemes seem rather insignificant obstacles to effective communication for a child who seems to have a basic deficit in the sense-making capacity (Lund & Duchan, 1988). At least initially, intervention must focus instead on helping the child to attend more carefully and respond more consistently to the informational requirements of the conversational partner.

By directing attention toward language as a tool for social action, pragmatics has freed speech-language pathologists from the necessity to focus on grammatical or even lexical form in intervention programs. But there are some children, especially active conversationalists, for whom the primary obstacle to effective communication is their delay in grammatical development. How can pragmatics, with its emphasis on language in context, inform speech-language pathologists in such cases? It is crucial to recognize, in this regard, that the emphasis on communication mandated by a pragmatic perspective in no way minimizes the importance of grammar (Kamhi & Nelson, 1988). In fact, a primary objective of functionalist theorists (e.g., Bates & MacWhinney, 1987) is to demonstrate how grammatical structure derives from semantic and pragmatic sources.

> Indeed, one of the basic principles of functional linguistics is that clause-internal morphosyntax can only be understood with reference to the semantic and pragmatic functions of its constituent units, and consequently the major task is to describe the complex interaction of form and function in language. (Foley & Van Valin, 1984, p. 14)

Clearly, then, the application of pragmatic principles to language intervention does not require the abandonment of grammar as a potential treatment objective. To the contrary, grammar must share center stage with semantic and pragmatic functions.

In this chapter, some of the ways in which pragmatics and grammar interact will be illustrated. The emphasis will be on how clinicians can capitalize on knowledge of pragmatics to facilitate the grammatical development of children with language impairment.

Some Links Between Grammar and Pragmatics

Any attempt to integrate pragmatics and grammar must recognize the reciprocal nature of their relationship. On the one hand, pragmatics is needed to define the conditions under which syntactic and semantic phenomena apply. For example, *do* is not simply optional in affirmative declarative sentences. It is used for contrast or emphasis. Auxiliaries are not free to appear in either sentence-initial or sentence-medial position. They appear in sentence-initial position when a question or indirect request is intended. Pragmatics is also necessary to explain apparent violations of grammatical rules. For example, in English a Sentence cannot consist entirely of a Prepositional Phrase. Yet, utterances such as *To the farm* are perfectly appropriate in the context of a prior utterance such as *Where is Maggie going?*

On the other hand, certain pragmatic abilities seem to depend on grammar. Because this is not the direction of influence usually considered in discussions of the relationship between pragmatics and grammar, a number of details will be provided here.

Speech Acts

Studies of children's pragmatic abilities often include an examination of the speech acts, or communicative functions served by the children's utterances. Three such speech acts are indirect requests (e.g., *Can you give me the pencil?*), permission requests (e.g., *May I go?*), and rules (e.g., *You should/hafta spin the dial*). It is doubtful that a child could be given credit for expressing the first two of these unless he or she included the Modal Auxiliary verb. Quite possibly, Auxiliary inversion would be required as well. In the case of rules, it is difficult to see how a child could receive credit for this speech act without producing the Modal or Semi-Auxiliary.

Conversational Replies

One of the bulwarks of conversation is ellipsis. Without it, much of a conversationalist's speech would simply be a repetition of material already contained in prior utterances. However, ellipsis, too, requires control of aspects of grammar. Consider the utterance in (1):

(1) ADULT: Who eats worms?
    CHILD: I don't!

In the child's response, *don't* replaces an entire Verb Phrase, *eats worms*. A response to the same question such as *Brenda!* would also require knowledge of the category Verb Phrase, for it is precisely this category that is deleted.

The pragmatic device called the follow-on (McShane, 1980) also appears to depend on knowledge of grammatical categories. The following utterance pair provides an example:

(2) ADULT: The truck is pulling a car
    CHILD: A broken car

The child's elaboration of the point made by the adult requires extraction of a Noun Phrase.

Conversational Repair and Regulation

When the child receives feedback from a listener that his or her original message requires modification, any repair that the child can muster will be dependent in part on his or her grammatical abilities. For example, the repair below seems to require knowledge of the category Noun Phrase:

(3) CHILD: It's crying
    ADULT: What?
    CHILD: The baby bird's crying

The child's attempts to obtain clarification from others also seems dependent on this type of knowledge:

(4) ADULT: Gonna take that tidbit
CHILD: Take what?
ADULT: That little piece

Code Switching

Adults are not the only ones to simplify their speech when talking to young children. Other children show evidence of this behavior as well. But to engage in this type of modification, children must have implicit knowledge of which categories can be reduced. For example, in (5), the child seems to recognize that a Modal Auxiliary is dispensable and that a full Prepositional Phrase can be replaced by a deictic term:

(5) We should put the toys on the shelf.
See? We put the toys here.

Cohesion

Perhaps the best example of an interaction between grammar and pragmatics can be found in the rules for using pronouns. From the standpoint of pragmatics, one can say that a pronoun is used whenever the referent is obvious from the physical context, or when the referent has already been made explicit in the prior discourse. However, if we limit ourselves to these considerations, we would be unable to explain why, for example, *him* can refer to *Dante* in (6) but not in (7):

(6) Dante thinks that Kevin might hurt him
(7) Dante might hurt him

To explain the difference in these two utterances, we must recognize that him cannot refer to another Noun Phrase that is within the same embedded clause. In (6), *him* can refer to Dante because Dante is outside the embedded clause, *Kevin might hurt him*. In (7), *him* can only refer to some male other than Dante. It is difficult to see how these constraints on pronoun interpretation could be explained by pragmatic principles alone.

Implications for Intervention

There are at least three ways in which information about pragmatics can play an important part in grammatical intervention. The first involves the selection of goals. In particular, a pragmatic skill found to be deficient in a child with language impairment may, on close inspection, require some grammatical knowledge and/or ability that the child has not yet attained. Effective intervention might require a focus on the child's acquisition of the prerequisite grammatical forms.

The second contribution made by pragmatics concerns the activities within which intervention takes place. Activities represent the physical and social contexts in which clinical procedures are implemented (Fey, 1986). The pragmatic focus on language as a means for social expression motivates clinicians to carry out intervention in more naturalistic and functional contexts than previously believed necessary. Pragmatic principles provide clinicians with some methods for enhancing the naturalness of even relatively structured intervention activities.

The third area in which pragmatics has influenced approaches to grammatical intervention concerns the specific procedures that are employed within the activities. In particular, knowledge of pragmatics provides clinicians with information about how to alter the specific conversational context to highlight the targeted grammatical form or, in some cases, to exemplify its communicative function. These three contributions will be discussed in turn.

Using Pragmatic Functions to Dictate Grammatical Goals

The literature on children who are language impaired reveals a number of specific pragmatic areas that can be deficient in these children (see Chapter 6). In some cases, these deficits clearly are not attributable to limitations in grammar. For example, some limitations might be due primarily to a poor understanding of listener needs or to a low degree of conversational assertiveness (Fey, 1986). As a case in point, Conti-Ramsden and Friel-Patti (1983) found that children with language impairment initiated fewer conversational turns when speaking with their mothers than did a group of younger normally developing children at a comparable stage of language development. This reluctance of many children with specific language impairment to initiate conversational bids cannot be easily attributed to deficient grammatical abilities.

In some cases, however, the pragmatic difficulties of children with language learning problems seem to be dependent on particular grammatical attainments. Accordingly, a reasonable strategy would be to select for treatment those areas of grammar that seem linked to documented pragmatic difficulties. A few examples are provided here.

Craig and Evans (1989) compared the turn exchanges of children with language impairment and younger normally developing children at a similar stage of language development. They found that when the normally developing children began an utterance in the middle of an adult's utterance, it occurred in a "transition-relevant position." That is, although the utterance overlapped with the adult's utterance, it followed the adult's completion of (or elliptical reference to) a simple proposition expressed in structures such as Subject + Verb, or Subject + Verb + Object. The overlaps of the children with language impairments were not so strategically placed. If children with language impairment who show inappropriate turn exchanges were found to have problems with grammatical structures of this type, such structures would be an especially appropriate goal for intervention.

MacLachlan and Chapman (1988) found that communication breakdowns frequently occurred in the narratives of children with language impairment, even when they showed relatively few such breakdowns in conversation. The largest proportion of breakdowns took the form of stalls (filled pauses and repetitions). Because the narratives involved utterances of greater length and complexity than in conversation, MacLachlan and Chapman suggested that the increases in communication breakdowns they observed might have reflected an interaction between the longer narrative utterances and the children's limited linguistic skills. If these children were more facile with grammatical elaborations, such as relative clauses and various forms of sentence coordination and subordination, such breakdowns might have been less frequent. It might be noted in this regard that Tyack (1981) presented evidence that increased use of complex sentences was related to improvements in story recall in a 10-year-old child who was learning disabled.

In a well-known study by Gallagher and Darnton (1978), the conversational repairs of children with language impairment were investigated. Relative to a group of younger normally developing children with similar mean utterance length, the children with language impairment showed less use of a repair involving a constituent substitution:

(8) CHILD: He ride bike
     ADULT: What?
     CHILD: He ride it

As noted earlier, these substitutions seem to require greater knowledge of syntactic categories such as Noun Phrase. If evidence of such knowledge were not otherwise available from the child, these categories would constitute an appropriate intervention goal.

Liles (1985) conducted an investigation of use of cohesion in narratives by children with language impairment. Relative to a group of normally developing children, the children with language impairment used fewer personal pronouns as cohesive devices and showed a greater number of incomplete and erroneous cohesive ties. Although several different factors might contribute to problems of this type, before intervention were to proceed with children experiencing such difficulties, it would be important to ensure that they knew which grammatical structures permitted pronouns to refer to preceding Noun Phrases (see [6] and [7]).

In summary, although not all pragmatic limitations will have a grammatical basis, an examination of the interactions between pragmatics and grammar can alert clinicians to some of the grammatical underpinnings that might serve as important goals in language intervention. What is important for the present discussion is that without attention to the child's pragmatic abilities, some grammatical deficiencies critical to the child's communication success may go undetected.

Consideration of the Intervention Activity

Perhaps the greatest disappointment stemming from early efforts to teach grammar to children was the finding that, in many cases, the abilities children displayed in the treatment context were not used outside the clinical setting (Hughes, 1985; Leonard, 1981). The literature on pragmatics made it clear that in at least some cases, this failure was due to the fact that these early efforts focused almost entirely on language form. Children were given direct intervention on what to say but were provided with very little evidence of when to use their new acquisitions or how their new forms could be socially useful (Rees, 1978; Spradlin & Siegel, 1982). Under these circumstances, children may be inclined to learn rules that enable them to play "the therapy game" yet fail to recognize the broader communicative relevance of the target forms (Johnston, 1988).

The solution to this problem that is offered by pragmatics lies in the basic principle that language form cannot be meaningfully dissociated from its social function. This principle has two broad implications for creating intervention activities. First, the principle suggests that activities should provide the clinician with many opportunities to model grammatical targets under semantically and pragmatically appropriate conditions. Under such conditions, the child is likely not only to hear the new grammatical form but to identify its meaning and pragmatic function. Second, the principle suggests that activities should provide numerous opportunities for the child to produce communicative acts in which the target form is useful, if not obligated. If the child uses the target form under these circumstances, the child's act can be consequated naturally by the adult's appropriate conversational and/or nonverbal response.

The activities that result from the application of these basic principles will look different in several respects from the drills commonly used in the 1960s and 1970s. In these drills, children are required to produce lists of sentences containing the target forms in response to unrelated pictures or events acted out by the clinician. The child's utterances serve no communicative function, such as informing, requesting, or clarifying, and are in no way related to the accomplishment of some higher objective, such as telling a story, making sandwiches, or baking cookies.

In pragmatically motivated activities, the child's production of the target form constitutes only a part of a broader goal. It is a means to an end rather than an end in itself. This can be the case whether the activity is loosely or tightly structured.

In loosely structured, highly naturalistic activities, the motivation for producing an utterance that obligates the use of a target form arises from within the child. For example, the incidental teaching approach of Hart and Risley (1975, 1980; see also Warren & Kaiser, 1986) takes place during the child's play periods. Intervention episodes arise only when the child initiates a communicative bid, usually a request or command.

The clinician can increase the number and quality of teaching episodes in natural contexts by altering the play environment in ways that make communication necessary. Suppose, for example, that a particular child enjoyed the art center in the classroom. If all relevant materials were stored where the child could get them without assistance, there would be no need for the child to communicate to complete the art project. The clinician could create a need to communicate, however, by placing necessary materials out of reach. Similarly, the clinician could "sabotage" the art activity by providing, say, crayons of only one color, coloring books that were already completed, or scissors that didn't work properly (see Constable, 1983; Fey, 1986; Lucas, 1980, for additional examples). Note that by modifying the physical setting in this way, the clinician has not done anything that directly facilitates grammatical development. Such changes in grammar must rest with the specific intervention procedures adopted within these activities (see below). However, it seems likely that these procedures can be more effective if the activities in which they take place increase the child's motivation to communicate, and if the child's communicative efforts have a potent effect on the listener's behavior.

In many instances, more tightly structured activities may be necessary. This is especially true in cases of low frequency grammatical forms such as passives. However, such activities are also helpful when the clinician feels the child needs to hear relatively common forms even more frequently and/or have a large number of opportunities to use the target form. For example, during a restaurant activity, the child might be asked to be the server and convey to the cook how many of each item on the menu the customer (alias clinician) orders. The structure of this activity would make it easier for the clinician to model, and the child to practice, a large number of noun plurals in an appropriate communicative context. Fey (1986) gives numerous examples of how structured activities can be made natural.

Child-Initiated and Clinician-Initiated Procedures

The potential influence of pragmatics goes beyond the selection of activities. The specific intervention procedures employed within these activities can also be significantly shaped by pragmatic considerations. In this section, the case is made that two quite different classes of intervention procedures can accommodate pragmatic notions, those in which the child initiates the occasion for grammatical instruction and those in which the clinician is the initiator.

In child-initiated procedures the clinician follows the child's lead and responds to the child's communicative attempts in a way that is presumed to facilitate language learning. Such procedures can be a useful means of presenting new grammatical information to the child. For example, if the clinician repeats the child's prior utterance and, in so doing, adds grammatical details, the child might be quite likely to register the changes (Nelson, 1989). Because the child's interest in the topic and knowledge of the basic vocabulary are assured (by virtue of the child's having just said essentially the same thing a moment before), the child's attention can focus more directly on these grammatical additions. This state of affairs seems to correspond to Johnston's (1985) proposal that intervention "fit the child's social purposes, interpretive resources and emergent meanings" while advancing his or her knowledge one step beyond its current level (p. 128).

Several specific procedures can be considered to be child-initiated. One of these is expansion, first employed as an intervention approach by Cazden (1965) and later adopted in a range of studies (e.g., Farrar, 1990; Scherer & Olswang, 1984). In this procedure, the child and clinician engage in an activity that promotes conversation and the clinician responds to the child's utterance with a grammatically expanded version of the utterance:

> (9) CHILD: Baby go sleep
> ADULT: The baby's going to sleep
> CHILD: Now want water
> ADULT: Oh, now she wants some water

Because expansions are intended to capture the child's original meaning, the grammatical details that are added in the clinician's subsequent utterance will vary by necessity, as seen in (9). Thus, expansion might be most accurately characterized as providing more general grammatical stimulation. A clinician who wishes to emphasize certain grammatical forms and not others must be highly selective in the utterances he or she expands.

Alternatively, the clinician might employ a related procedure, such as recasting. This procedure was first used in an intervention study by Nelson, Carskaddon, and Bonvillian (1973), and subsequently by Nelson (1977). In this case, the clinician uses the child's prior utterance as the basis for a modified sentence that contains the grammatical form that the clinician wishes to emphasize. For example, if the clinician's goal were to facilitate the child's use of questions, the following types of recasts might be appropriate:

> (10) CHILD: Car's gonna crash
> ADULT: Is the car gonna crash?
> CHILD: Yeah, and driver's hurt
> ADULT: Is the driver hurt? Oh no

For some children, it may not be sufficient to present new grammatical information in this way. These children might detect the new grammatical form in the clinician's speech, but fail to see how it adds to the original message. For these children, it may be necessary to highlight the precise function of the grammatical form.

Procedures in which the clinician initiates the interchange can be called on for this purpose. By manipulating the specific conversational context, the clinician can create instances in which the role of the grammatical form is demonstrated on an intensive basis. This format permits the clinician to conform to another of Johnston's (1985) tenets—that focused input be provided, to "narrow the child's search for order" (p. 130).

A number of examples of how both child- and clinician-initiated procedures can be used to facilitate the development of a range of grammatical structures are presented in the next section. Although the two types of procedures differ in the nature of their contributions, both can be pressed into service of Johnston's (1985) final principle, that intervention provide the child with "functional language tools" (p. 131).

New Syntactic Categories   Syntactic categories include Preposition, Auxiliary, and Noun Phrase, among others. These categories often pose problems for children with language impairment. Consider how a clinician might facilitate a child's acquisition of Prepositions, using expansion. The grammatical requirements for this category (see Valian, 1986) should first be considered. One of these is that a Preposition takes a Noun Phrase as an object but, unlike Verbs, is not inflected for Tense (e.g., one can say *He placed the dish in the refrigerator* but not **He place the dish inned the refrigerator*). Another requirement is that a Preposition must sometimes precede full Noun Phrases, not just single Nouns. The first of these requirements calls for the clinician to ensure that he or she expands utterances that vary in Tense, so that the child is in a position to note that Tense is marked on the Verb, not the Preposition:

> (11) CHILD: Put cup table
> ADULT: Put the cup on the table
> CHILD: Drop floor
> ADULT: Yup, it dropped on the floor.

The second requirement suggests the need to expand utterances in which a full Noun Phrase follows the Preposition, as well as those in which only a Noun follows:

> (12) CHILD: Hat Bob
> ADULT: The hat's on Bob
> CHILD: Now cowboy
> ADULT: Now the hat's on this big cowboy

The syntactic category Noun Phrase is also difficult for some children with language impairment. Before a child is credited with this category, considerably more is required than an ability to use Nouns (see Valian, 1986). First, Determiner + Noun combinations must be seen (e.g., *the car, a frog*). There must also be evidence that these combinations can serve as a single unit in the child's speech. This might be seen in the substitution of a single term such as *it* for, say, *the ball*. In addition, these combinations must appear in several different sentence positions with the same Determiner, namely, pre-Verb (e.g., *The frog fell*), post-Verb (e.g., *She hit the ball*), and post-Preposition (e.g., *Put it in the box*).

How might information on pragmatics facilitate teaching new categories such as Noun Phrase? Consider a clinician-initiated procedure that makes use of two interacting pragmatic notions, ellipsis and the given-new distinction. Ellipsis permits the child to begin the task of using Determiner + Noun in two-word utterances without violating conversational conventions. Further, the clinician's questions that permit ellipsis can vary in the type of information given and the type of (new) information that is requested such that the Determiner + Noun responses of the child represent constituents that are pre-Verb, post-Verb, and post-Preposition, as seen in (13), (14), and (15), respectively:

(13) ADULT: What's making that noise?
     CHILD: A bear
(14) ADULT: What's Dinah pushing?
     CHILD: A car
(15) ADULT: What's Mom putting the bird in?
     CHILD: Cage
     ADULT: Yeah, a cage. Mom's putting him in a cage

Thus, the linguistic context provided by the clinician makes it appropriate for the child to respond with a Noun Phrase only. Under these conditions, the child may be more likely to utilize his or her developing knowledge of Determiner + Noun. Note, however, that if the child fails to use a well-formed Noun Phrase, as in (15) above, the clinician has an opportunity to expand the child's utterance.

Once the child's use of Determiner + Noun in two-word utterances becomes established, the clinician can make use of the given-new distinction to assist the child in using Determiner + Noun in longer utterances. For example, by using sequence pictures in which only the action and object change, the child's ability to use post-verb Determiner + Noun might be enhanced. By using pictures in which only the agent changes, the use of pre-Verb Determiner + Noun might be facilitated.

The remaining criterion for crediting a child with the category Noun Phrase is that *it* (or *him, her,* etc.) must replace Determiner + Noun on occasion. This, too, can be promoted through the given-new distinction. For example, by keeping the object acted upon constant while varying the agent and action, subsequent reference to the object can be made with a pronoun:

(16) ADULT: Tell me a story about these pictures
CHILD: A hat
ADULT: Now what (indicating next picture)
CHILD: Monkey take it
ADULT: Yes, but now what? (next picture)
CHILD: Put hat in tree
ADULT: Yeah, he put it in a tree

Again, if the child fails to use the target form as planned, an expansion or recast can be used to create a learning opportunity.

Another syntactic category that is often problematic for children with language impairment is Auxiliary (e.g., Fletcher & Garman, 1988). In current theories of grammar, Auxiliary is separate from the Verb Phrase, which enables one to explain how Auxiliary verbs can be so easily separated from main verbs (e.g., *John will surely pass the test this time,* but not *John will pass surely the test this time*). Another illustration of the separate status of Auxiliary can be seen in ellipsis, in which the Auxiliary verb can stand alone:

(17) I don't know if she's going to the party, but I am.

It seems that this property of Auxiliary can be utilized in the initial teaching of this category. For example, a question-and-answer activity can be devised such that for all affirmative answers the child must use the form *yes, I* + Auxiliary. Initially, Auxiliary verbs that require no agreement marking for person or number can be used, such as the Modal *can:*

(18) ADULT: Can you ride a bike?
CHILD: Yes, I can

Subsequently, Auxiliary verbs requiring person and number agreement can be used:

(19) ADULT: Is the girl riding a bike?
CHILD: Yes, she is

Eventually, the child could be required to change the form of the Auxiliary verb to agree with the Subject:

(20) ADULT: Are you sitting on the table?
CHILD: Yes, I am

Expansions and recasts of the child's responses in these circumstances might be highly useful to the child:

(21) ADULT: Are the girls going to fall?
CHILD: Yes, they is
ADULT: They are. They are going to fall

At this point, there seem to be two possible directions to proceed in helping the child acquire Auxiliary. One is to devise activities in which the child asks questions using sentence-initial Auxiliary verbs (e.g., *Can you see my toes? Are you watching cartoons?*). An advantage of this option is that the Auxiliary verb is uncontractible and more salient in this context. However, because the sentence-initial position is not the typical location of Auxiliary verbs, and because the child's only other practice with Auxiliary verbs was in elliptical utterances, there is no assurance that the child will understand the proper placement of Auxiliary in the phrase structure tree (viz., Noun Phrase + Auxiliary + Verb Phrase).

For this reason, it might be advantageous to proceed directly to the use of Auxiliary in full declarative sentences. By making use of the principle of contrast, as in Fey's (1986) "false assertion" technique, this step might be somewhat easier to accomplish. For example, the clinician and child might monitor each other's descriptions of pictures, providing corrections when needed. Some of the clinician's descriptions can be in error, for example, by stating that some action is not being performed when it actually is. Because corrections in these cases could be elliptical (e.g., *Oh yes she is*), each description could contain two or more actions appropriate to the picture. Consider a picture in which some children are sleeping and some are not:

(22) ADULT: Let's see who's sleeping in this picture. This baby is not sleeping, she's eating; this boy is not sleeping, and this girl is not sleeping, she's reading a book
CHILD: Uh uh, the boy *is* sleeping
ADULT: Oh, now I see. The girl is not sleeping, but the boy *is* sleeping

Note how these manipulations make it possible to place pragmatically appropriate stress on the target form. This, in turn, might make the form more salient to the child.

New Grammatical Functions   If children have good command of the syntactic categories of the language, they possess one necessary ingredient for sentence construction. However, they must also learn the grammatical functions of these categories. Some of these functions are obligatory in all (English) sentences (except, as we know, when certain pragmatic conditions come into play). A prime example is Subject. Others are obligated when certain types of verbs are used. For example, *hit* requires Object, but *sleep* does not. In addition, there are functions, such as Adjunct, that are not obligated at all grammatically, but do serve to elaborate the meaning of the sentence. For example, in the sentence *Hugh ate his lunch on the terrace,* the Adjunct *on the terrace* is not required to make the sentence well-formed.

Although young normally developing children often omit Subjects from their early sentences (e.g., P. Bloom, 1989; Gerken, 1990), it appears that children with language impairment may do so even more frequently (Leonard, 1972). Although there are several factors at work in the use of this grammatical function, children's inclusion of Subjects might be promoted initially through use of the given-new distinction. Again, a clinician-initiated procedure with sequence pictures might be employed:

> (23) ADULT: Tell me a story about these pictures. It's about our old friends Archie, Betty, and Veronica. I'll start, and you finish. Here, Veronica is kissing Archie. And here?
> CHILD: Betty kissing him
> ADULT: Yes, it's Betty. She's kissing Archie

It can be seen that the final adult turn in (23) contains a recast in which the Subject is pronominalized. This might help the child recognize that Subjects are obligatory in English even when the referent is already established in the discourse.

Adjunct is a grammatical function that can be useful because it provides the child with a means of elaborating sentences at little cost in the form of syntactic complexity. To teach Adjuncts, the principle of contrast might be used:

> (24) ADULT: Well, Betty's washing her hair in the sink. But what about Archie?
> CHILD: Washing hair in swimming pool

Syntactic Features   Children with language impairment often have great difficulty with features such as Person, Number, Tense, Definiteness, and Case. For example, language-impaired children seem to omit the Past Tense inflection *-ed* more frequently than younger normally developing children at comparable levels of mean length of utterance (MLU) (Johnston & Schery, 1976). To assist a child in acquiring this inflection, a clinician might use a child-initiated procedure in which he or she selectively expands those utterances of the child that seem to refer to past events:

> (25) CHILD: Daddy watch tv. But mommy, no
> ADULT: Daddy watched tv. But mommy didn't?
> CHILD: No. Work
> ADULT: Oh, she worked

Case constitutes another difficult feature. For example, children with language impairment appear to substitute Accusative Case for Nominative Case more often than younger MLU-matched controls (Loeb & Leonard, 1991). Utterances such as *Me do it* and *Them not here* are quite frequent in the speech of these children.

Connell (1986) presented an interesting (clinician-initiated) method of facilitating children's use of Nominative Case. Noting that the use of forms such as *him* and *her* in pre-Verb position might reflect the children's expression of the topic of the sentence, Connell attempted to separate the topic function from the Subject function. Each child was taught to respond in a specific manner in carefully selected sentence pairs. For example, a picture depicting different persons performing diverse actions was presented, and the clinician and child proceeded as follows:

(26) ADULT: Which one is walking?
     CHILD: Him, he is walking
     ADULT: What is the man doing?
     CHILD: He is walking

As can be seen from (26), in the response to the first question there was a greater need for the topic to be highlighted. Yet, the following pronoun *(he)* contrasted with the topic pronoun *(him)* in Case and agreed in Person and Number with the Auxiliary Verb. Hence, it served as a clear indication that the notion of topic is not identical to Subject.

Another feature that might prove troublesome to children with language impairment is Definiteness, as reflected in Articles. Because children with language impairment frequently omit Articles, clinicians often focus principally on teaching the inclusion of these forms. However, inclusion of an Article does not necessarily mean that the child knows the distinction between *the* and *a*.

By highlighting the use of the Definite Article as a cohesive tie, this distinction might become clearer. For example, suppose the activity involves shopping. The clinician is the storekeeper and the child is the shopper. On the table, the clinician has arranged several objects. The child must buy several of them.

(27) ADULT: Welcome to our store. We have books, crayons, pens, and balls. What do you want?
     CHILD: Book
     ADULT: A book. You want a book, ok. But wait, we also have other nice things. Do you still want the book? Or do you want a pen?
     CHILD: A pen
     ADULT: Good, you'll like it. Here it is. Now, we also have a ball. Or do you want the book?
     CHILD: The book

As can be seen from (27), the clinician introduces each object with the Indefinite Article, but proceeds to the Definite Article when re-introducing the object.

Eventually, the child must be able to make the distinction between *the* and *a* without the support of the clinician's cues. For example, in a later procedural step, the child might be asked to describe his or her shopping experience using multi-utterance turns. In the first utterance of the turn, the child might name the objects purchased. Then, the child would be asked to describe each, focusing on some salient attribute such as size or color:

(28) ADULT: So, what did you buy at the new store?
      CHILD: I bought three pens and a book.
      The pens blue and the book red

The crucial aspect of this task is that the child learn that the initial reference to an object should be made using an Indefinite Article, and that subsequent reference to it should employ the Definite Article. To foster Indefinite Article use, the objects should probably not be visible to the clinician. By ensuring that several different objects are depicted at the same time, the clinician can increase the likelihood that the child will use a Noun and not a Pronoun in his or her second utterance. The use of plural objects (e.g., three pens) as well as single objects (one book) might lead the child to produce, for example, *one book* instead of *a book*. Such use is not a problem, provided that the child uses *the* only in the second utterance. Subsequently, the clinician can employ only single objects (e.g., one ball, one doll) to reduce the salience of number.

Alternate Word Orders   Although word order errors in production are not frequently reported for children with language impairment who are acquiring English, comprehension studies suggest that these children may not understand the variation in word order that is permitted in the language (van der Lely & Harris, 1990). One such variation is Dative alternation. It is assumed that children eventually learn that certain verbs (e.g., *give*) permit two different subcategorization frames, one making use of a Prepositional Phrase, as in (29), the other involving a double-Object construction, as in (30):

(29) Tina gave the microphone to Mick
(30) Tina gave Mick the microphone

It appears that Dative alternation can be made clearer to children with language impairment through use of procedures that capitalize on the given-new distinction. A task devised by McKee and Emiliani (in press) might be adapted for this purpose. For example, assume that while a confederate is blindfolded, the child and clinician manipulate toys or puppets in a prescribed manner. Upon questioning by the confederate, the child must then describe what transpired. As can be seen from (31) and (32), the nature of the confederate's question can highlight different elements in the activity, prompting either of the word orders:

> (31) ADULT: Well, I still see Olive Oyl and Popeye. But why is he hugging her?
>   CHILD: Because she gave him some spinach
> (32) ADULT: Well, there's Olive Oyl. But why doesn't she have her spinach?
>   CHILD: Because she gave it to Popeye

Another troublesome construction that implicates word order is the passive. Because attempts at this construction are not especially frequent, a procedure such as expansion may not be plausible. However, another child-initiated procedure, recasting, might prove quite effective in this case. Here, the clinician restates the child's utterance in such a manner that the original Object serves as Subject:

> (33) CHILD: The guy hit the ball
>   ADULT: Yeah, the ball was really hit by that guy
> (34) CHILD: Mommy bought these presents
>   ADULT: These presents were all bought by Mommy?

Clinician-initiated procedures can be designed to illustrate the important point that passives are employed in English when the Object receives focus. The following example demonstrates this use along with some relevant adult responses to the child's attempts:

> (35) ADULT: Here is a picture with a boy and a girl. First, tell me about the boy
>   CHILD: The dog bited him
>   ADULT: Yeah, he was bitten by that dog. What happened to the girl?
>   CHILD: She was bit by a raccoon
>   ADULT: Yeah, she was bitten by the raccoon. The boy was bitten by a dog, and the girl was bitten by a raccoon. They both were bitten by an animal. Ouch!

Conjunction and Relativization As clinicians employed in school settings can attest, many children who reach school age continue to exhibit problems with spoken language (see reviews in Aram & Hall, 1989; Weiner, 1985). Problems center not only on understanding humor, metaphors, and other aspects of figurative language, but also on aspects of grammar such as the use of complex sentences.

Here, too, pragmatics can be used to full advantage. Consider first simple conjunction. When two independent clauses are joined by *and,* three types of relationships can be expressed: additive (e.g., *Here's the corn and there's the endive*), temporal (e.g., *I got up and brushed my teeth*), and causal (e.g., *He saw the reflection of his face in the water and screamed*) (Bloom, Lahey, Hood, Lifter, & Fiess, 1980). The clinician might make use of any or all of these relationships to produce an expansion of the child's utterance that includes *and*. Consider, for example, the following procedure, adapted from Schwartz, Chapman, Terrell, Prelock, and Rowan (1985):

(36) CHILD: Baby lie down
ADULT: Oh, and now what?
CHILD: She go night-night
ADULT: The baby lies down and goes night-night

Relativization is a complex sentence construction that seems to be acquired after conjunction and complementation (Bloom et al., 1980). Relative clauses are used to modify Noun Phrases. This construction might be taught through use of the classic referential communication task (e.g., Glucksberg, Krauss, & Higgins, 1975). Assume that a child and clinician are seated at opposite sides of a table and that a screen blocks each participant's view of the other. Each person is given a set of drawings depicting, for example, a dog running, a dog sleeping, a cat running, and a cat sleeping. The child's task is to select a picture and instruct the clinician to select the identical one in his or her possession, using a particular sentence frame:

(37) CHILD: Pick up the cat
ADULT: Which one? Remember our rule.
CHILD: Pick up the one that's running
ADULT: Good . . . Or do you mean the dog that's running?
CHILD: The cat!

The value of this task is that the most communicatively relevant aspect of the child's instruction (the specification of which dog or cat is to be selected) is contained in the relative clause, thus highlighting the function of this construction.

Summary

In this chapter, ways in which grammar and pragmatics interact, and how this interaction has clinical relevance, have been discussed. Although some children may have pragmatic limitations that are unrelated to grammar, children with grammatical difficulties—even active conversationalists—appear to be at risk for certain problems in pragmatics. This is because a number of pragmatic abilities seem to rely on knowledge of some grammatical category, function, feature, or construction. Clinicians can take advantage of this dependency by using it as a basis for choosing grammatical targets during intervention: Of those grammatical problems exhibited by the child, choose for intervention one that seems to be hindering the development of some pragmatic skill.

Even when a child's grammatical limitations are a concern in their own right, the effectiveness of intervention might be bolstered through application of pragmatic principles. We have attempted to show that the activities and procedures selected can go a long way toward teaching the child the relevant social contexts in which to use particular grammatical forms, and the specific communicative functions these forms serve.

The intervention examples that were provided are only suggestive; future research must determine their ultimate worth. However, we are more confident in the larger message, that pragmatics and grammar should be considered together when plotting the course of intervention for a child with language impairment.

References

Aram, D., & Hall, N. (1989). Longitudinal follow-up of children with preschool communication disorders: Treatment implications. *School Psychology Review, 18*, 487–501.

Bates, E., & MacWhinney, B. (1987). Competition, variation, and language learning. In B. MacWhinney (Ed.), *Mechanisms of language acquisition* (pp. 157–193). Hillsdale, NJ: Lawrence Erlbaum.

Bloom, L., Lahey, M., Hood, L., Lifter, K., & Fiess, K. (1980). Complex sentences: Acquisition of syntactic connectives and the semantic relations they encode. *Journal of Child Language, 7*, 235–262.

Bloom, P. (1989). Why do children omit subjects? *Papers and Reports on Child Language Development, 28*, 57–63.

Cazden, C. (1973). Environmental assistance to the child's acquisition of syntax. Unpublished doctoral dissertation. Harvard University, Cambridge, MA.

Connell, P. (1986). Teaching subjecthood to language-disordered children. *Journal of Speech and Hearing Research, 29*, 481–492.

Constable, C. (1983). Creating communicative context. In H. Winitz (Ed.), *Treating language disorders: For clinicians by clinicians* (pp. 97–120). Baltimore, MD: University Park Press.

Conti-Ramsden, G., & Friel-Patti, S. (1983). Mothers' discourse adjustments to language-impaired and non-language-impaired children. *Journal of Speech and Hearing Disorders, 48*, 360–367.

Craig, H., & Evans, J. (1989). Turn exchange characteristics of SLI children's simultaneous and nonsimultaneous speech. *Journal of Speech and Hearing Disorders, 54*, 334–347.

Farrar, M. (1990). Discourse and the acquisition of grammatical morphemes. *Journal of Child Language, 17,* 607–624.

Fey, M. (1986). *Language intervention with young children.* San Diego, CA: College-Hill Press.

Fey, M., & Leonard, L. (1983). Pragmatic skills of children with specific language impairment. In T. Gallagher & C. Prutting (Eds.), *Pragmatic assessment and intervention issues in language* (pp. 65–82). San Diego, CA: College-Hill Press.

Fletcher, P., & Garman, M. (1988). Normal language development and language impairment: Syntax and beyond. *Clinical Linguistics and Phonetics, 2,* 97–113.

Foley, W., & Van Valin, R. (1984). *Functional syntax and universal grammar.* Cambridge, UK: Cambridge University Press.

Gallagher, T., & Darnton, B. (1978). Conversational aspects of the speech of language-disordered children: Revision behaviors. *Journal of Speech and Hearing Research, 21,* 118–135.

Gerken, L. (1990). Performance constraints in early language: The case of subjectless sentences. *Papers and Reports on Child Language Development, 29,* 54–61.

Glucksberg, S., Krauss, R., & Higgins, E. (1975). The development of referential communication skills. In F. Horowitz (Ed.), *Review of child development research* (Vol. 4, pp. 305–346). Chicago: University of Chicago Press.

Hart, B., & Risley, T. (1975). Incidental teaching of language in the preschool. *Journal of Applied Behavioral Analysis, 8,* 411–420.

Hart, B., & Risley, T. (1980). In vivo language intervention: Unanticipated general effects. *Journal of Applied Behavioral Analysis, 13,* 407–432.

Hubbell, R. (1977). On facilitating spontaneous talking in young children. *Journal of Speech and Hearing Disorders, 42,* 216–232.

Hubbell, R. (1981). *Children's language disorders: An integrated approach.* Englewood Cliffs, NJ: Prentice-Hall.

Hughes, D. (1985). *Language treatment and generalization: A clinician's handbook.* San Diego, CA: College-Hill Press.

Johnston, J. (1985). Fit, focus and functionality: An essay on early language intervention. *Child Language Teaching and Therapy, 1,* 125–134.

Johnston, J. (1988). Generalization: The nature of change. *Language, Speech, and Hearing Services in Schools, 19,* 314–329.

Johnston, J., & Schery, T. (1976). The use of grammatical morphemes by children with communication disorders. In D. Morehead & A. Morehead (Eds.), *Normal and deficient child language* (pp. 239–258). Baltimore, MD: University Park Press.

Kamhi, A., & Nelson, L. (1988). Early syntactic development: Simple clause types and grammatical morphology. *Topics in Language Disorders, 8,* 26–43.

Leonard, L. (1972). What is deviant language? *Journal of Speech and Hearing Disorders, 37,* 427–446.

Leonard, L. (1981). Facilitating linguistic skills in children with specific language impairment. *Applied Psycholinguistics, 2,* 89–118.

Liles, B. (1985). Cohesion in the narratives of normal and language-disordered children. *Journal of Speech and Hearing Research, 28,* 123–133.

Loeb, D., & Leonard, L. (1991). Subject case marking and verb morphology in normally developing and specifically language-impaired children. *Journal of Speech and Hearing Research, 34,* 340–346.

Lucas, E. (1980). *Semantic and pragmatic language disorders: Assessment and remediation*. Rockville, MD: Aspen Systems.

Lund, N., & Duchan, J. (1988). *Assessing children's language in naturalistic contexts* (2nd ed.). Englewood Cliffs, NJ: Prentice-Hall.

MacLachlan, B., & Chapman, R. (1988). Communication breakdowns in normal and language learning-disabled children's conversation and narration. *Journal of Speech and Hearing Disorders, 53*, 2–7.

McKee, C., & Emiliani, M. (in press). Some Italian two-year-olds' morphosyntactic competence and why it matters. *Natural Language and Linguistic Theory.*

McShane, J. (1980). *Learning to talk*. Cambridge, UK: Cambridge University Press.

Nelson, K. E. (1977). Facilitating children's syntax acquisition. *Developmental Psychology, 13*, 101–107.

Nelson, K. E. (1989). Strategies for first language teaching. In M. Rice & R. Schiefelbusch (Eds.), *The teachability of language* (pp. 263–310). Baltimore, MD: Paul H. Brookes.

Nelson, K. E., Carskaddon, G., & Bonvillian, J. (1973). Syntax acquisition: Impact of experimental variation in adult verbal interaction with the child. *Child Development, 44*, 497–504.

Rees, N. (1978). Pragmatics of language: Applications to normal and disordered language development. In R. Schiefelbusch (Ed.), *Bases of language intervention* (pp. 191–268). Baltimore, MD: University Park Press.

Scherer, N., & Olswang, L. (1984). Role of mothers' expansions in stimulating children's language production. *Journal of Speech and Hearing Research, 27*, 387–396.

Schwartz, R., Chapman, R., Terrell, B., Prelock, P., & Rowan, L. (1985). Facilitating word combination in language-impaired children through discourse structure. *Journal of Speech and Hearing Disorders, 50*, 31–39.

Spradlin, J., & Siegel, G. (1982). Language training in natural and clinical environments. *Journal of Speech and Hearing Disorders, 47*, 2–6.

Tyack, D. (1981). Teaching complex sentences. *Language, Speech, and Hearing Services in Schools, 12*, 49–53.

Valian, V. (1986). Syntactic categories in the speech of young children. *Developmental Psychology, 22*, 562–579.

van der Lely, H., & Harris, M. (1990). Comprehension of reversible sentences in specifically language-impaired children. *Journal of Speech and Hearing Disorders, 55*, 101–117.

Warren, S., & Kaiser, A. (1986). Incidental language teaching: A critical review. *Journal of Speech and Hearing Disorders, 51*, 291–299.

Weiner, P. (1985). The value of follow-up studies. *Topics in Language Disorders, 5*, 78–92.

Content Questions

1. What three labels do Leonard and Fey indicate have previously been used by Fey to describe the pragmatic competence of language-impaired children?

2. One additional category is added which, as the article explains, would not have been easy to conceive without bringing pragmatics into speech pathology. What is this category, and what does it involve?

3. Based on examples 3 and 4 given in the section on conversational repair and regulation, what would you say conversational repair is? In example 5, which deictic word replaces the prepositional phrase?

4. In what three major ways does a knowledge of pragmatics assist in the intervention work of clinicians?

5. What do Leonard and Fey indicate was a serious problem with intervention activities that focused mostly on form?

6. Describe the clinical procedures of expansion and recasting.

7. Which verb type do the authors suggest might be developed through a question-and-answer activity?

8. Explain how the stress on the auxiliary verb in example 22 is pragmatically determined.

9. Which type of grammatical distinction is being developed through the storekeeper exercise described in 27?

10. What two word orders are specifically mentioned as sometimes problematic to language-impaired children?

11. What specific task is mentioned as a possible strategy for working on relativization?

Questions for Analysis and Discussion

1. Comment on the connection between grammatical form and pragmatics. Why should the two be considered together?

2. Explain how a knowledge of grammar, even if unconscious knowledge, relates to how we form replies involving ellipsis.

3. Explain what the authors mean when they say that "without attention to the child's pragmatic abilities, some grammatical deficiencies critical to the child's communication success may go undetected."

4. How has the linguistic study of pragmatics contributed to some useful insights for those working in speech pathology?

5. How do you think a speech pathologist can benefit from having a linguistic background?

The Acquisition of Language*

Breyne Arlene Moskowitz

An understanding of how a person's native language is normally acquired is important to specialists treating individuals with abnormal language development. In this classic article, which originally appeared in the *Scientific American*, Professor Breyne Arlene Moskowitz discusses how children acquire their language, noting environmental factors that contribute to this development and its stages. While the article is not directly aimed at speech pathologists, it addresses a number of issues that would be of importance to specialists who work with language development.

An adult who finds herself in a group of people speaking an unfamiliar foreign language may feel quite uncomfortable. The strange language sounds like gibberish: mysterious strings of sound, rising and falling in unpredictable patterns. Each person speaking the language knows when to speak, how to construct the strings and how to interpret other people's strings, but the individual who does not know anything about the language cannot pick out separate words or sounds, let alone discern meanings. She may feel overwhelmed, ignorant and even childlike. It is possible that she is returning to a vague memory from her very early childhood, because the experience of an adult listening to a foreign language comes close to duplicating the experience of an infant listening to the "foreign" language spoken by everyone around her. Like the adult, the child is confronted with the task of learning a language about which she knows nothing.

The task of acquiring language is one for which the adult has lost most of her aptitude but one the child will perform with remarkable skill. Within a short span of time and with almost no direct instruction the child will analyze the language completely. In fact, although many subtle refinements are added between the ages of five and 10, most children have completed the greater part of the basic language-acquisition process by the age of five. By that time a child will have dissected the language into its minimal separable units of sound and meaning; she will have discovered the rules for recombining sounds into words, the meanings of individual words and the rules for recombining words into meaningful sentences, and she will have internalized the intricate patterns of taking turns in dialogue. All in all she will have established herself linguistically as a full-fledged member of a social community, informed about the most subtle details of her native language as it is spoken in a wide variety of situations.

The speed with which children accomplish the complex process of language acquisition is particularly impressive. Ten linguists working full time for 10 years to analyze the structure of the English language could not program a computer with the ability for language acquired by an average child in the first 10 or even five years of life. In spite of the scale of the task and even in spite of adverse conditions—emotional instability, physical disability and so on—children learn to speak. How do they go about it? By what process does a child learn language?

What Is Language?

In order to understand how language is learned it is necessary to understand what language is. The issue is confused by two factors. First, language is learned in early childhood, and adults have few memories of the intense effort that went into the learning process, just as they do not remember the process of learning to walk. Second, adults do have conscious memories of being taught the few grammatical rules that are prescribed as "correct" usage, or the norms of "standard" language. It is difficult for adults to dissociate their memories of school lessons from those of true language learning, but the rules learned in school are only the conventions of an educated society. They are arbitrary finishing touches of embroidery on a thick fabric of language that each child weaves for herself before arriving in the English teacher's classroom. The fabric is grammar: the set of rules that describe how to structure language.

The grammar of language includes rules of phonology, which describe how to put sounds together to form words; rules of syntax, which describe how to put words together to form sentences; rules of semantics, which describe how to interpret the meaning of words and sentences; and rules of pragmatics, which describe how to participate in a conversation, how to sequence sentences and how to anticipate the information needed by an interlocutor. The internal grammar each adult has constructed is identical with that of every other adult in all but a few superficial details. Therefore each adult can create or understand an infinite number of sentences she has never heard before. She knows what is acceptable as a word or a sentence and what is not acceptable, and her judgments on these issues concur with those of other adults. For example, speakers of English generally agree that the sentence "Ideas green sleep colorless furiously" is ungrammatical and that the sentence "Colorless green ideas sleep furiously" is grammatical but makes no sense semantically. There is similar agreement on the grammatical relations represented by word order. For example, it is clear that the sentences "John hit Mary" and "Mary hit John" have different meanings although they consist of the same words, and that the sentence "Flying planes can be dangerous" has two possible meanings. At the level of individual words all adult speakers can agree that "brick" is an English word, that "blick" is not an English word but could be one (that is, there is an accidental gap in the adult lexicon, or internal vocabulary) and that "bnick" is not an English word and could not be one.

How children go about learning the grammar that makes communication possible has always fascinated adults, particularly parents, psychologists and investigators of language. Until recently diary keeping was the primary method of study in this area. For example, in 1877 Charles Darwin published an account of his son's development that includes notes on language learning. Unfortunately most of the diarists used inconsistent or incomplete notations to record what they heard (or what they thought they heard), and most of the diaries were only partial listings of emerging types of sentences with inadequate information on developing word meanings. Although the very best of them, such as W. F. Leopold's classic *Speech Development of a Bilingual Child*, continue to be a rich resource for contemporary investigators, advances in audio and video recording equipment have made modern diaries generally much more valuable. In the 1960's, however, new discoveries inspired linguists and psychologists to approach the study of language acquisition in a new, systematic way, oriented less toward long-term diary keeping and more toward a search for the patterns in a child's speech at any given time.

An event that revolutionized linguistics was the publication in 1957 of Noam Chomsky's *Syntactic Structures*. Chomsky's investigation of the structure of grammars revealed that language systems were far deeper and more complex than had been suspected. And of course if linguistics was more complicated, then language learning had to be more complicated. In the 21 years since the publication of *Syntactic Structures* the disciplines of linguistics and child language have come of age. The study of the acquisition of language has benefited not only from the increasingly sophisticated understanding of linguistics but also from the improved understanding of cognitive development as it is related to language. The improvements in recording technology have made experimentation in this area more reliable and more detailed, so that investigators framing new and deeper questions are able to accurately capture both rare occurrences and developing structures.

The picture that is emerging from the more sophisticated investigations reveals the child as an active language learner, continually analyzing what she hears and proceeding in a methodical, predictable way to put together the jigsaw puzzle of language. Different children learn language in similar ways. It is not known how many processes are involved in language learning, but the few that have been observed appear repeatedly, from child to child and from language to language. All the examples I shall discuss here concern children who are learning English, but identical processes have been observed in children learning French, Russian, Finnish, Chinese, Zulu and many other languages.

Children learn the systems of grammar—phonology, syntax, semantics, lexicon and pragmatics—by breaking each system down into its smallest combinable parts and then developing rules for combining the parts. In the first two years of life a child spends much time working on one part of the task, disassembling the language to find the separate sounds that can be put together to form words and the separate words that can be put together to form sentences. After the age of two the basic process continues to be refined, and many more sounds and words are produced. The other part of language acquisition—developing rules for combining the basic elements of language—is carried out in a very methodical way: the most general rules are hypothesized first, and as time passes they are successively narrowed down by the addition of more precise rules applying to a more restricted set of sentences. The procedure is the same in any area of language learning, whether the child is acquiring syntax or phonology or semantics. For example, at the earliest stage of acquiring negatives a child does not have at her command the same range of negative structures that an adult does. She has constructed only a single very general rule: Attach

(1)	(2)	(3)	(4)	(5)	(6)
boy		boys	boysəz	boys	boys
cat		cats	catsəz	cats	cats
			catəz		
man	men	mans	mansəz	mans	men
			menəz		
house		house	housəz	houses	houses
foot		foots	footsəz	feets	feet
feet		feets	feetsəz		

Sorting out of competing pronunciations that results in the correct plural forms of nouns takes place in the six stages shown in this illustration. Children usually learn the singular forms of nouns first (1), although in some cases an irregular plural form such as "feet" may be learned as a singular or as a free variant of a singular. Other irregular plurals may appear for a brief period (2), but soon they are replaced by plurals made according to the most general rule possible: To make a noun plural add the sound "s" or "z" to it (3). Words such as "house" or "rose," which already end in an "s"- or "z"-like sound, are usually left in their singular forms at this stage. When words of this type do not have irregular plural forms, adults make them plural by adding an "əz" sound. (The vowel "ə" is pronounced like the unstressed word "a.") Some children demonstrate their mastery of this usage by tacking "əz" endings indiscriminately onto nouns (4). That stage is brief and use of the ending is quickly narrowed down (5). At this point only irregular plurals remain to be learned, and since no new rule-making is needed, children may go on to harder problems and leave final stage (6) for later.

"no" to the beginning of any sentence constructed by the other rules of grammar. At this stage all negative sentences will be formed according to that rule.

Throughout the acquisition process a child continually revises and refines the rules of her internal grammar, learning increasingly detailed subrules until she achieves a set of rules that enables her to create the full array of complex, adult sentences. The process of refinement continues at least until the age of 10 and probably considerably longer for most children. By the time a child is six or seven, however, the changes in her grammar may be so subtle and sophisticated that they go unnoticed. In general children approach language learning economically, devoting their energy to broad issues before dealing with specific ones. They cope with clear-cut questions first and sort out the details later, and they may adopt any one of a variety of methods for circumventing details of a language system they have not yet dealt with.

Prerequisites for Language

Although some children verbalize much more than others and some increase the length of their utterances much faster than others, all children overgeneralize a single rule before learning to apply it more narrowly and before constructing other less widely applicable rules, and all children speak in one-word sentences before they speak in two-word sentences. The similarities in language learning for different children and different languages are so great that many linguists have believed at one time or another that the human brain is preprogrammed for language learning. Some linguists continue to believe language is innate and only the surface details of the particular language spoken in a child's environment need to be learned. The speed with which children learn language gives this view much appeal. As more parallels between language and other areas of cognition are revealed, however, there is greater reason to believe any language specialization that exists in the child is only one aspect of more general cognitive abilities of the brain.

Whatever the built-in properties the brain brings to the task of language learning may be, it is now known that a child who hears no language learns no language, and that a child learns only the language spoken in her environment. Most infants coo and babble during the first six months of life, but congenitally deaf children have been observed to cease babbling after six months, whereas normal infants continue to babble. A child does not learn language, however, simply by hearing it spoken. A boy with normal hearing but with deaf parents who communicated by the American Sign Language was exposed to television every day so that he would learn English. Because the child was asthmatic and was confined to his home he interacted only with people at home, where his family and all their visitors communicated in sign language. By the age of three he was fluent in sign language but neither understood nor spoke English. It appears that in order to learn a language a child must also be able to interact with real people in that language. A television set does not suffice as the sole medium for language learning because, even though it can ask questions, it cannot respond to a child's answers. A child, then, can develop language only if there is language in her environment and if she can employ that language to communicate with other people in her immediate environment.

Caretaker Speech

In constructing a grammar children have only a limited amount of information available to them, namely the language they hear spoken around them. (Until about the age of three a child models her language on that of her parents; afterward the language of her peer group tends to become more important.) There is no question, however, that the language environments children inhabit are restructured, usually unintentionally, by the adults who take care of them. Recent studies show that there are several ways caretakers systematically modify the child's environment, making the task of language acquisition simpler.

Caretaker speech is a distinct speech register that differs from others in its simplified vocabulary, the systematic phonological simplification of some words, higher pitch, exaggerated intonation, short, simple sentences and a high proportion of questions (among mothers) or imperatives (among fathers). Speech with the first two characteristics is formally designated Baby Talk. Baby Talk is a subsystem of caretaker speech that has been studied over a wide range of languages and cultures. Its characteristics appear to be universal: in languages as diverse as English, Arabic, Comanche and Gilyak (a Paleo-Siberian language) there are simplified vocabulary items for terms relating to food, toys, animals and body functions. Some words are phonologically simplified, frequently by the duplication of syllables, as in "wawa" for "water" and "choo-choo" for "train," or by the reduction of consonant clusters, as in "tummy" for "stomach" and "scambled eggs" for "scrambled eggs." (Many types of phonological simplification seem to mimic the phonological structure of an infant's own early vocabulary.)

Perhaps the most pervasive characteristic of caretaker speech is its syntactic simplification. While a child is still babbling, adults may address long, complex sentences to her, but as soon as she begins to utter meaningful, identifiable words they almost invariably speak to her in very simple sentences. Over the next few years of the child's language development the speech addressed to her by her caretakers may well be describable by a grammar only six months in advance of her own.

The functions of the various language modifications in caretaker speech are not equally apparent. It is possible that higher pitch and exaggerated intonation serve to alert a child to pay attention to what she is hearing. As for Baby Talk, there is no reason to believe the use of phonologically simplified words in any way affects a child's learning of pronunciation. Baby Talk may have only a psychological function, marking speech as being affectionate. On the other hand, syntactic simplification has a clear function. Consider the speech adults address to other adults: it is full of false starts and long, rambling, highly complex sentences. It is not surprising that elaborate theories of innate language ability arose during the years when linguists examined the speech adults addressed to adults and assumed that the speech addressed to children was similar. Indeed, it is hard to imagine how a child could derive the rules of language from such input. The wide study of caretaker speech conducted over the past eight years has shown that children do not face this problem. Rather it appears they construct their initial grammars on the basis of the short, simple, grammatical sentences that are addressed to them in the first year or two they speak.

Correcting Language

Caretakers simplify children's language-analysis task in other ways. For example, adults talk with other adults about complex ideas, but they talk with children about the here and now, minimizing discussion of feelings, displaced events and so on. Adults accept children's syntactic and phono-

(1)	(2)	(3)	(4)	(5)	(6)
walk		walked	walkedəd	walked	walked
play		played	playedəd	played	played
need		need	needəd	needed	needed
come	came	comed	camedəd	comed	came
			comedəd		
go	went	goed	goed	goed	went
			wentəd		

Development of past-tense forms of verbs also takes place in six stages. After the present-tense forms are learned (1) irregular past-tense forms may appear briefly (2). The first and most general rule that is postulated is: To put a verb into the past tense add a "t" or "d" sound (3). In adult speech verbs such as "want" or "need," which already end in a "t" or "d" sound, are put into the past tense by adding "əd" sound. Many children go through brief stage in which they add "əd" endings to any existing verb forms (4). Once the use of "əd" ending has been narrowed down (5), only irregular past-tense forms remain to be learned (6).

logical "errors," which are a normal part of the acquisition process. It is important to understand that when children make such errors, they are not producing flawed or incomplete replicas of adult sentences; they are producing sentences that are correct and grammatical with respect to their own current internalized grammar. Indeed, children's errors are essential data for students of child language because it is the consistent departures from the adult model that indicate the nature of a child's current hypotheses about the grammar of language. There are a number of memorized, unanalyzed sentences in any child's output of language. If a child says, "Nobody likes me," there is no way of knowing whether she has memorized the sentence intact or has figured out the rules for constructing the sentence. On the other hand, a sentence such as "Nobody don't like me" is clearly not a memorized form but one that reflects an intermediate stage of a developing grammar.

Since each child's utterances at a particular stage are from her own point of view grammatically correct, it is not surprising that children are fairly impervious to the correction of their language by adults, indeed to any attempts to teach them language. Consider the boy who lamented to his mother, "Nobody don't like me." His mother seized the opportunity to correct him, replying, "Nobody likes me." The child repeated his original version and the mother her modified one a total of eight times until in desperation the mother said, "Now listen carefully! Nobody likes me." Finally her son got the idea and dutifully replied, "Oh! Nobody don't likes me." As the example demonstrates, children do not always understand exactly what it is the adult is correcting. The information the adult is trying to impart may be at odds with the information in the child's head, namely the rules the child is postulating for producing language. The surface correction of a sentence does not give the child a clue about how to revise the rule that produced the sentence.

It seems to be virtually impossible to speed up the language-learning process. Experiments conducted by Russian investigators show that it is extremely difficult to teach children a detail of language more than a few days before they would learn it themselves. Adults sometimes do, of course, attempt to teach children rules of language, expecting them to learn by imitation, but Courtney B. Cazden of Harvard University found that children benefit less from frequent adult correction of their errors than from true conversational interaction. Indeed, correcting errors can interrupt that interaction, which is, after all, the function of language. (One way children may try to secure such interaction is by asking "Why?" Children go through a stage of asking a question repeatedly. It serves to keep the conversation going, which may be the child's real aim. For example, a two-and-a-half-year-old named Stanford asked "Why?" and was given the nonsense answer: "Because the moon is made of green cheese." Although the response was not at all germane to the conversation, Stanford was happy with it and again asked "Why?" Many silly answers later the adult had tired of the conversation but Stanford had not. He was clearly not seeking information. What he needed was to practice the form of social conversation before dealing with its function. Asking "Why?" served that purpose well.)

In point of fact adults rarely correct children's ungrammatical sentences. For example, one mother, on hearing "Tommy fall my truck down," turned to Tommy with "Did you fall Stevie's truck down?" Since imitation seems to have little role in the language-acquisition process, however, it is probably just as well that most adults are either too charmed by children's errors or too busy to correct them.

Practice does appear to have an important function in the child's language-learning process. Many children have been observed purposefully practicing language when they are alone, for example in a crib or a playpen. Ruth H. Weir of Stanford University hid a tape recorder in her son's bedroom and recorded his talk after he was put to bed. She found that he played with words and phrases, stringing together sequences of similar sounds and of variations on a phrase or on the use of a word: "What color . . . what color blanket . . . what color mop . . . what color glass . . . what color TV . . . red ant . . . fire . . . like lipstick . . . blanket . . . now the blue blanket . . . what color TV . . . what color horse . . . then what color table . . . then what color fire . . . here yellow spoon." Children who do not have much opportunity to be alone may use dialogue in a similar fashion. When Weir tried to record the bedtime monologues of her second child, whose room adjoined that of the first, she obtained through-the-wall conversations instead.

The One-Word Stage

The first stage of child language is one in which the maximum sentence length is one word; it is followed by a stage in which the maximum sentence length is two words. Early in the one-word stage there are only a few words in a child's vocabulary, but as months go by her lexicon expands with increasing rapidity. The early words are primarily concrete nouns and verbs; more abstract words such as adjectives are acquired later. By the time the child is uttering two-word sentences with some regularity, her lexicon may include hundreds of words.

When a child can say only one word at a time and knows only five words in all, choosing which one to say may not be a complex task. But how does she decide which word to say when she knows 100 words or more? Patricia M. Greenfield of the University of California at Los Angeles and Joshua H. Smith of Stanford have suggested that an important criterion is informativeness, that is, the child selects a word reflecting what is new in a particular situation. Greenfield and Smith also found that a newly acquired word is first used for naming and only later for asking for something.

Superficially the one-word stage seems easy to understand: a child says one word at a time, and so each word is a complete sentence with its own sentence intonation. Ten years ago a child in the one-word stage was thought to be learning word meanings but not syntax. Recently, however, students of child language have seen less of a distinction between the one-word stage as a period of word learning and the subsequent period, beginning with the two-word stage, as one of syntax acquisition. It now seems clear that the infant is engaged in an enormous amount of syntactic analysis in the one-word stage, and indeed that her syntactic abilities are reflected in her utterances and in her accurate perception of multiword sentences addressed to her.

Ronald Scollon of the University of Hawaii and Lois Bloom of Columbia University have pointed out independently that important patterns in word choice in the one-word stage can be found by examining larger segments of children's speech. Scollon observed that a 19-month-old named Brenda was able to use a vertical construction (a series of one-word sentences) to express what an adult might say with a horizontal construction (a multiword sentence). Brenda's pronunciation, which is represented phonetically below, was imperfect and Scollon did not understand her words at the time. Later, when he transcribed the tape of their conversation, he heard the sound of a passing car immediately preceding the conversation and was able to identify Brenda's words as follows:

BRENDA: "Car [pronounced 'ka']. Car. Car. Car."
SCOLLON: "What?"
BRENDA: "Go. Go."
SCOLLON: [Undecipherable.]
BRENDA: "Bus [pronounced 'baish']. Bus. Bus. Bus. Bus. Bus. Bus.
    Bus. Bus."
SCOLLON: "What? Oh, bicycle? Is that what you said?"
BRENDA: "Not ['na']."
SCOLLON: "No?"
BRENDA: "Not."
SCOLLON: "No. I got it wrong."

Brenda was not yet able to combine two words syntactically to express "Hearing that car reminds me that we went on the bus yesterday. No, not on a bicycle." She could express that concept, however, by combining words sequentially. Thus the one-word stage is not just a time for learning the meaning of words. In that period a child is developing hypotheses about putting words together in sentences, and she is already putting sentences together in meaningful groups. The next step will be to put two words together to form a single sentence.

The Two-Word Stage

The two-word stage is a time for experimenting with many binary semantic-syntactic relations such as possessor-possessed ("Mommy sock"), actor-action ("Cat sleeping") and action-object ("Drink soup"). When two-word sentences first began to appear in Brenda's speech, they were primarily of the following forms: subject noun and verb (as in "Monster go"), verb and object (as in "Read it") and verb or noun and location (as in "Bring home" and "Tree down"). She also continued to use vertical constructions in the two-word stage, providing herself with a means of expressing ideas that were still too advanced for her syntax. Therefore once again a description of Brenda's isolated sentences does not show her full abilities at this point in her linguistic development. Consider a later conversation Scollon had with Brenda:

> BRENDA: "Tape corder. Use it. Use it."
> SCOLLON: "Use it for what?"
> BRENDA: "Talk. Corder talk. Brenda talk."

Brenda's use of vertical constructions to express concepts she is still unable to encode syntactically is just one example of a strategy employed by children in all areas of cognitive development. As Jean Piaget of the University of Geneva and Dan I. Slobin of the University of California at Berkeley put it, new forms are used for old functions and new functions are expressed by old forms. Long before Brenda acquired the complex syntactic form "Use the tape recorder to record me talking" she was able to use her old forms—two-word sentences and vertical construction—to express the new function. Later, when that function was old, she would develop new forms to express it. The controlled dovetailing of form and function can be observed in all areas of language acquisition. For example, before children acquire the past tense they may employ adverbs of time such as "yesterday" with present-tense verbs to express past time, saying "I do it yesterday" before "I dood it."

Bloom has provided a rare view of an intermediate stage between the one-word and the two-word stages in which the two-word construction—a new form—served only an old function. For several weeks Bloom's daughter Alison uttered two-word sentences all of which included the word "wida." Bloom tried hard to find the meaning of "wida" before realizing that it had no meaning. It was, she concluded, simply a placeholder. This case is the clearest ever reported of a new form preceding new functions. The two-word stage is an important time for practicing functions that will later have expanded forms and practicing forms that will later expand their functions.

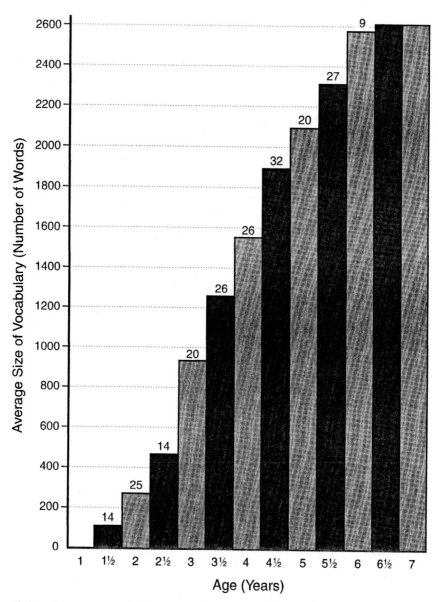

Children's average vocabulary size increases rapidly between the ages of one and a half and six and a half. The number of children tested in each sample age group is listed above the columns. Data are based on work done by Madorah E. Smith of University of Hawaii.

Telegraphic Speech

There is no three-word stage in child language. For a few years after the end of the two-word stage children do produce rather short sentences, but the almost inviolable length constraints that characterized the first two stages have disappeared. The absence of a three-word stage has not been satisfactorily explained as yet; the answer may have to do with the fact that many basic semantic relations are binary and few are ternary. In any case a great deal is known about the sequential development in the language of the period following the two-word stage. Roger Brown of Harvard has named that language telegraphic speech. (It should be noted that there is no specific age at which a child enters any of these stages of language acquisition and further that there is no particular correlation between intelligence and speed of acquisition.)

Early telegraphic speech is characterized by short, simple sentences made up primarily of content words: words that are rich in semantic content, usually nouns and verbs. The speech is called telegraphic because the sentences lack function "words": tense endings on verbs and plural endings on nouns, prepositions, conjunctions, articles and so on. As the telegraphic-speech stage progresses, function words are gradually added to sentences. This process has possibly been studied more thoroughly than any other in language acquisition, and a fairly predictable order in the addition of function words has been observed. The same principles that govern the order of acquisition of function words in English have been shown to operate in many other languages, including some, such as Finnish and Russian, that express the same grammatical relations with particularly rich systems of noun and verb suffixes.

In English many grammatical relations are represented by a fixed word order. For example, in the sentence "The dog followed Jamie to school" it is clear it is the dog that did the following. Normal word order in English requires that the subject come before the verb, and so people who speak English recognize "the dog" as the subject of the sentence. In other languages a noun may be marked as a subject not by its position with respect to the other words in the sentence but by a noun suffix, so that in adult sentences word order may be quite flexible. Until children begin to acquire suffixes and other function words, however, they employ fixed word order to express grammatical relations no matter how flexible adult word order may be. In English the strong propensity to follow word order rigidly shows up in children's interpretations of passive sentences such as "Jamie was followed by the dog." At an early age children may interpret some passive sentences correctly, but by age three they begin to ignore the function words such as "was" and "by" in passive sentences and adopt the fixed word-order interpretation. In other words, since "Jamie" appears before the verb, Jamie is assumed to be the actor, or the noun doing the following.

Function Words

In spite of its grammatical dependence on word order, the English language makes use of enough function words to illustrate the basic principles that determine the order in which such words are acquired. The progressive tense ending "-ing," as in "He going," is acquired first, long before the present-tense third-person singular ending "-s," as in "He goes." The "-s" itself is acquired long before the past-tense endings, as in "He goed." Once again the child proves to be a sensible linguist, learning first the tense that exhibits the least variation in form. The "-ing" ending is pronounced only one way, regardless of the pronunciation of the verb to which it is attached. The verb endings "-s" and "-ed," however, vary in their pronunciation: compare "cuts (s)," "cuddles (z)," "crushes (əz)," "walked (t)," "played (d)" and "halted (əd)." (The vowel "ə," called "shwa," is pronounced like the unstressed word "a.") Furthermore, present progressive ("-ing") forms are used with greater frequency than any other tense in the speech children hear. Finally, no verb has an irregular "-ing" form, but some verbs do have irregular third-person present-tense singular forms and many have irregular past-tense forms. (The same pattern of learning earliest those forms that exhibit the least variation shows up much more dramatically in languages such as Finnish and Russian, where the paradigms of inflection are much richer.)

The past tense is acquired after the progressive and present tenses, because the relative time it represents is conceptually more difficult. The future tense ("will" and a verb) is formed regularly in English and is as predictable as the progressive tense, but it is a much more abstract concept than the past tense. Therefore it is acquired much later. In the same way the prepositions "in" and "on" appear earlier than any others, at about the same time as "-ing," but prepositions such as "behind" and "in front of," whose correct usage depends on the speaker's frame of reference, are acquired much later.

It is particularly interesting to note that there are three English morphemes that are pronounced identically but are acquired at different times. They are the plural "-s," the possessive "-s" and the third-person singular tense ending "-s," and they are acquired in the order of listing. Roman Jakobson of Harvard has suggested that the explanation of this phenomenon has to do with the complexity of the different relations the morphemes signal: the singular-plural distinction is at the word level, the possessive relates two nouns at the phrase level and the tense ending relates a noun and a verb at the clause level.

The forms of the verb "to be"—"is," "are" and so on—are among the last of the function words to be acquired, particularly in their present-tense forms. Past- and future-tense forms of "to be" carry tense information, of course, but present-tense forms are essentially meaningless, and omitting them is a very sensible strategy for a child who must maximize the information content of a sentence and place priorities on linguistic structures still to be tackled.

(1)	(2)	(3)
Laura (2:2): Her want some more. Her want some more candy.	Laura (2:2): Where my tiger? Where my tiger book?	Laura (2:2): Let's dooz this. Let's do this. Let's do this puzzle.

(4)	(5)	(6)
Andrew (2:0): Put that on. Andrew put that on.	Andrew (2:1): All wet. This shoe all wet.	Benjy (2:3): Broke it. Broke it. Broke it I did.

(7)	(8)
Jamie (6:0): Jamie: Why are you doing that? Mother: What? Jamie: Why are you writing what I say down? Mother: What? Jamie: Why are you writing down what I say?	Jamie (6:3): Jamie: Who do you think is the impor-tantest kid in the world except me? Mother: What did you say, Jamie? Jamie: Who do you think is the specialest kid in the world not counting me?

(9)	(10)
Jamie (6:6): Jamie: Who are you versing? Adult: What? Jamie: I wanted to know who he was playing against.	Jamie (6:10): Jamie: I figured something you might like out. Mother: What did you say? Jamie: I figured out something you might like.

Children correct their speech in ways that reflect the improvements they are currently making on their internal grammar. For example, Laura (1–3) is increasing the length of her sentences, encoding more information by embellishing a noun phrase. Andrew (4, 5) and Benjy (6) appear to be adding subjects to familiar verb-phrase sentences. Jamie (7–10) seems to be working on much more subtle refinements such as the placement of verb particles, for example the "down" of "writing down." (Each child's age at time of correction is given in years and months.) Corrections shown here were recorded by Judy S. Reilly of University of California at Los Angeles.

Plurals

When there are competing pronunciations available, as in the case of the plural and past tenses, the process of sorting them out also follows a predictable pattern. Consider the acquisition of the English plural, in which six distinct stages can be observed. In English, as in many other (but not all) languages, nouns have both singular and plural forms. Children usually use the singular forms first, both in situations where the singular form would be appropriate and in situations where the plural form would be appropriate. In instances where the plural form is irregular in the adult model, however, a child may not recognize it as such and may use it in place of the singular or as a free variant of the singular. Thus in the first stage of acquisition, before either the concept of a plural or the linguistic devices for expressing a plural are acquired, a child may say "two cat" or point to "one feet."

When plurals begin to appear regularly, the child forms them according to the most general rule of English plural formation. At this point it is the child's overgeneralization of the rule, resulting in words such as "mans," "foots" or "feets," that shows she has hypothesized the rule: Add the sound /s/ or /z/ to the end of a word to make it plural. (The slashes indicate pronounced sounds, which are not to be confused with the letters used in spelling.)

For many children the overgeneralized forms of the irregular nouns are actually the earliest /s/ and /z/ plurals to appear, preceding "boys," "cats" and other regular forms by hours or days. The period of overgeneralization is considered to be the third stage in the acquisition of plurals because for many children there is an intermediate second stage in which irregular plurals such as "men" actually do appear. Concerned parents may regard the change from the second-stage "men" to the third-stage "mans" as a regression, but in reality it demonstrates progress from an individual memorized item to the application of a general rule.

In the third stage the small number of words that already end in a sound resembling /s/ or /z/, such as "house," "rose" and "bush," are used without any plural ending. Adults normally make such words plural by adding the suffix /əz/. Children usually relegate this detail to the remainder pile, to be dealt with at a later time. When they return to the problem, there is often a short fourth stage of perhaps a day, in which the child delightedly demonstrates her solution by tacking /əz/ endings indiscriminately onto nouns no matter what sound they end in and no matter how many other plural markings they may already have. A child may wake up one morning and throw herself into this stage with all the zeal of a kitten playing with its first ball of string.

Within a few days the novelty wears off and the child enters a less flamboyant fifth stage, in which only irregular plurals still deviate from the model forms. The rapid progression through the fourth stage does not mean that she suddenly focused her attention on the problem of /əz/ plurals. It is more likely that she had the problem at the back of her mind throughout the third stage. She was probably silently formulating hypotheses about the occurrence of /əz/ and testing them against the plurals she was hearing. Finding the right rule required discovering the phonological specification of the class of nouns that take /əz/ plurals.

Arriving at the sixth and final stage in the acquisition of plurals does not require the formulation of any new rules. All that is needed is the simple memorizing of irregular forms. Being rational, the child relegates such minor details to the lowest-priority remainder pile and turns her attention to more interesting linguistic questions. Hence a five-year-old may still not have entered the last stage. In fact, a child in the penultimate stage may not be at all receptive to being taught irregular plurals. For example, a child named Erica pointed to a picture of some "mouses," and her mother corrected her by saying "mice." Erica and her mother each repeated their own version two more times, and then Erica resolved the standoff by turning to a picture of "ducks." She avoided the picture of the mice for several days. Two years later, of course, Erica was perfectly able to say "mice."

Negative Sentences

One of the pioneering language-acquisition studies of the 1960's was undertaken at Harvard by a research group headed by Brown. The group studied the development in the language of three children over a period of several years. Two members of the group, Ursula Bellugi and Edward S. Klima, looked specifically at the changes in the children's negative sentences over the course of the project. They found that negative structures, like other subsystems of the syntactic component of grammar, are acquired in an orderly, rule-governed way.

When the project began, the forms of negative sentences the children employed were quite simple. It appeared that they had incorporated the following rule into their grammar: To make a sentence negative attach "no" or "not" to the beginning of it. On rare occasions, possibly when a child had forgotten to anticipate the negative, "no" could be attached to the end of a sentence, but negative words could not appear inside a sentence.

In the next stage the children continued to follow this rule, but they had also hypothesized and incorporated into their grammars more complex rules that allowed them to generate sentences in which the negatives "no," "not," "can't" and "don't" appeared after the subject and before the verb. These rules constituted quite an advance over attaching a negative word externally to a sentence. Furthermore, some of the primitive imperative sentences constructed at this stage began with "don't" rather than "no." On the other hand, "can't" never appeared at the beginning of a sentence, and neither "can" nor "do" appeared as an auxiliary, as they do in adult speech: "I can do it." These facts suggest that at this point "can't" and "don't" were unanalyzed negative forms rather than contractions of "cannot" and "do not," but that although "can't" and "don't" each seemed to be interchangeable with "no," they were no longer interchangeable with each other.

STAGE 1	STAGE 2	STAGE 3
No . . . wipe finger.	I can't catch you.	We can't make another broom.
No a boy bed.	I can't see you.	I don't want cover on it.
No singing song.	We can't talk.	I gave him some so he won't cry.
No the sun shining.	You can't dance.	No, I don't have a book.
No money.	I don't want it.	I am not a doctor.
No sit there.	I don't like him.	It's not cold.
No play that.	I don't know his name.	Don't put the two wings on.
No fall!	No pinch me.	I didn't did it.
Not . . . fit.	Book say no.	You didn't caught me.
Not a teddy bear.	Touch the snow no.	I not hurt him.
More . . . no.	This a radiator no.	Ask me if I not made mistake.
Wear mitten no.	No square . . . is clown.	Because I don't want somebody
	Don't bite me yet.	to wake me up.
	Don't leave me.	I didn't see something.
	Don't wake me up . . .	I isn't . . . I not sad.
	again.	This not ice cream.
	He not little, he big.	This no good.
	That no fish school.	I not crying.
	That no Mommy.	That not turning.
	There no squirrels.	He not taking the walls down.
	He no bite you.	
	I no want envelope.	
	I no taste them.	

Three stages in the acquisition of negative sentences were studied by Ursula Bellugi of the Salk Institute for Biological Studies and Edward S. Klima of the University of California at San Diego. They observed that in the first stage almost all negative sentences appear to be formulated according to the rule: Attach "no" or "not" to the beginning of a sentence to make it negative. In the second stage additional rules are postulated that allow the formation of sentences in which "no," "not," "can't" and "don't" appear after the subject and before the verb. In the third stage several issues remain to be worked out, in particular the agreement of pronouns in negative sentences (medium gray), the inclusion of the forms of the verb "to be" (dark gray) and the correct use of the auxiliary "do" (light gray). In adult speech the auxiliary "do" often carries tense and other functional markings such as the negative; children in third stage may replace it by "not" or use it redundantly to mark tense that is already marked on the main verb.

In the third stage of acquiring negatives many more details of the negative system had appeared in the children's speech. The main feature of the system that still remained to be worked out was the use of pronouns in negative sentences. At this stage the children said "I didn't see something" and "I don't want somebody to wake me up." The pronouns "somebody" and "something" were later replaced with "nobody" and "nothing" and ultimately with the properly concorded forms "anybody" and "anything."

Many features of telegraphic speech were still evident in the third stage. The form "is" of the verb "to be" was frequently omitted, as in "This no good." In adult speech the auxiliary "do" often functions as a dummy verb to carry tense and other markings; for example, in "I didn't see it," "do" carries the tense and the negative. In the children's speech at this stage "do" appeared occasionally, but the children had not yet figured out its entire function. Therefore in some sentences the auxiliary "do" was omitted and the negative "not" appeared alone, as in "I not hurt him." In other sentences, such as "I didn't did it," the negative auxiliary form of "do" appears to be correct but is actually an unanalyzed, memorized item: at this stage the tense is regularly marked on the main verb, which in this example happens also to be "do."

Many children acquire negatives in the same way that the children in the Harvard study did, but subsequent investigations have shown that there is more than one way to learn a language. Carol B. Lord of U.C.L.A. identified a quite different strategy employed by a two-year-old named Jennifer. From 24 to 28 months Jennifer used "no" only as a single-word utterance. In order to produce a negative sentence she simply spoke an ordinary sentence with a higher pitch. For example, "I want put it on" spoken with a high pitch meant "I don't want to put it on." Lord noticed that many of the negative sentences adults addressed to Jennifer were spoken with an elevated pitch. Children tend to pay more attention to the beginning and ending of sentences, and in adult speech negative words usually appear in the middle of sentences. With good reason, then, Jennifer seemed to have hypothesized that one makes a sentence negative by uttering it with a higher pitch. Other children have been found to follow the same strategy. There are clearly variations in the hypotheses children make in the process of constructing grammar.

Semantics

Up to this point I have mainly discussed the acquisition of syntactic rules, in part because in the years following the publication of Chomsky's *Syntactic Structures* child-language research in this area flourished. Syntactic rules, which govern the ordering of words in a sentence, are not all a child needs to know about language, however, and after the first flush of excitement over Chomsky's work investigators began to ask questions about other areas of language acquisition. Consider the development of the rules of semantics, which govern the way words are interpreted. Eve V. Clark of Stanford reexamined old diary studies and noticed that the development in the meaning of words during the first several months of the one-word stage seemed to follow a basic pattern.

The first time children in the studies used a word, Clark noted, it seemed to be as a proper noun, as the name of a specific object. Almost immediately, however, the children generalized the word based on some feature of the original object and used it to refer to many other objects. For example, a child named Hildegard first used "tick-tock" as the name for her father's watch, but she quickly broadened the meaning of the word, first to include all clocks, then all watches, then a gas meter, then a firehose wound on a spool and then a bathroom scale with a round dial. Her generalizations appear to be based on her observation of common features of shape: roundness, dials and so on. In general the children in the diary studies overextended meanings based on similarities of movement, texture, size and, most frequently, shape.

As the children progressed, the meanings of words were narrowed down until eventually they more or less coincided with the meanings accepted by adult speakers of the language. The narrowing-down process has not been studied intensively, but it seems likely that the process has no fixed end point. Rather it appears that the meanings of words continue to expand and contract through adulthood, long after other types of language acquisition have ceased.

One of the problems encountered in trying to understand the acquisition of semantics is that it is often difficult to determine the precise meaning a child has constructed for a word. Some interesting observations have been made, however, concerning the development of the meanings of the pairs of words that function as opposites in adult language. Margaret Donaldson and George Balfour of the University of Edinburgh asked children from three to five years old which one of two cardboard trees had "more" apples on it. They asked other children of the same age which tree had "less" apples. (Each child was interviewed individually.) Almost all the children in both groups responded by pointing to the tree with more apples on it. Moreover, the children who had been asked to point to the tree with "less" apples showed no hesitation in choosing the tree with more apples. They did not act as though they did not know the meaning of "less"; rather they acted as if they did know the meaning and "less" meant "more."

Subsequent studies have revealed similar systematic error making in the acquisition of other pairs of opposites such as "same" and "different," "big" and "little," "wide" and "narrow" and "tall" and "short." In every case the pattern of learning is the same: one word of the pair is learned first and its meaning is overextended to apply to the other word in the pair. The first word learned is always the unmarked word of the pair, that is, the word adults use when they do not want to indicate either one of the opposites. (For example, in the case of "wide" and "narrow," "wide" is the unmarked word: asking "How wide is the road?" does not suggest that the road is wide, but asking "How narrow is the road?" does suggest that the road is narrow.)

CHILD'S LEXICAL ITEM	FIRST REFERENTS	OTHER REFERENTS IN ORDER OF OCCURRENCE	GENERAL AREA OF SEMANTIC EXTENSION
mooi	moon	cake round marks on windows writing on windows and in books round shapes in books tooling on leather book covers round postmarks letter "O"	shape
bow-wow	dog	fur piece with glass eyes father's cufflinks pearl buttons on dress bath thermometer	shape
kotibaiz	bars of cot	large toy abacus toast rack with parallel bars picture of building with columns	shape
bébé	reflection of child (self) in mirror	photograph of self all photographs all pictures all books with pictures all books	shape
vov-vov	dog	kittens hens all animals at a zoo picture of pigs dancing	shape
ass	goat with rough hide on wheels	things that move: animals, sister, wagon . . . all moving things all things with a rough surface	movement texture
tutu	train	engine moving train journey	movement
fly	fly	specks of dirt dust all small insects child's own toes crumbs of bread a toad	size
quack	duck on water	all birds and insects all coins (after seeing an eagle on the face of a coin)	size

koko	cockerel's crowing	tunes played on a violin	sound
		tunes played on a piano	
		tunes played on an accordion	
		tunes played on a phonograph	
		all music	
		merry-go-round	
dany	sound of a bell	clock	sound
		telephone	
		doorbells	

Children overgeneralize word meanings, using words they acquire early in place of words they have not yet acquired. Eve V. Clark of Stanford University has observed that when a word first appears in a child's lexicon, it refers to a specific object but the child quickly extends semantic domain of word, using it to refer to many other things. Eventually meaning of the word is narrowed down until it coincides with adult usage. Clark found that children most frequently base the semantic extension of a word on shape of its first referent.

Clark observed a more intricate pattern of error production in the acquisition of the words "before" and "after." Consider the four different types of sentence represented by (1) "He jumped the gate before he patted the dog," (2) "Before he patted the dog he jumped the gate," (3) "He patted the dog after he jumped the gate" and (4) "After he jumped the gate he patted the dog." Clark found that the way the children she observed interpreted sentences such as these could be divided into four stages.

In the first stage the children disregarded the words "before" and "after" in all four of these sentence types and assumed that the event of the first clause took place before the event of the second clause. With this order-of-mention strategy the first and fourth sentence types were interpreted correctly but the second and third sentence types were not. In the second stage sentences using "before" were interpreted correctly but an order-of-mention strategy was still adopted for sentences that used "after." Hence sentences of the fourth type were interpreted correctly but sentences of the third type were not. In the next stage both the third and the fourth sentence types were interpreted incorrectly, suggesting that the children had adopted the strategy that "after" actually meant "before." Finally, in the fourth stage both "before" and "after" were interpreted appropriately.

It appears, then, that in learning the meaning of a pair of words such as "more" and "less" or "before" and "after" children acquire first the part of the meaning that is common to both words and only later the part of the meaning that distinguishes the two. Linguists have not yet developed satisfactory ways of separating the components of meaning that make up a single word, but it seems clear that when such components can be identified, it will be established that, for example, "more" and "less" have a large number of components in common and differ only in a single component specifying the pole of the dimension. Beyond the studies of opposites there has been little investigation of the period of semantic acquisition that follows the early period of rampant overgeneralization. How children past the early stage learn the meanings of other kinds of words is still not well understood.

Phonology

Just as children overgeneralize word meanings and sentence structures, so do they overgeneralize sounds, using sounds they have learned in place of sounds they have not yet acquired. Just as a child may use the word "not" correctly in one sentence but instead of another negative word in a second sentence, so may she correctly contrast /p/ and /b/ at the beginnings of words but employ /p/ at the ends of words, regardless of whether the adult models end with /p/ or /b/. Children also acquire the details of the phonological system in very regular ways. The ways in which they acquire individual sounds, however, are highly idiosyncratic, and so for many years the patterns eluded diarists, who tended to look only at the order in which sounds were acquired. Jakobson made a major advance in this area by suggesting that it was not individual sounds children acquire in an orderly way but the distinctive features of sound, that is, the minimal differences, or contrasts, between sounds. In other words, when a child begins to contrast /p/ and /b/, she also begins to contrast all the other pairs of sounds that, like /p/ and /b/, differ only in the absence or presence of vocal-cord vibration. In English these pairs include /t/ and /d/, and /k/ and the hard /g/. It is the acquisition of this contrast and not of the six individual sounds that is predictable. Jakobson's extensive examination of the diary data for a wide variety of languages supported his theory. Almost all current work in phonological theory rests on the theory of distinctive features that grew out of his work.

My own recent work suggests that phonological units even more basic than the distinctive features play an important part in the early acquisition process. At an early stage, when there are relatively few words in a child's repertory, unanalyzed syllables appear to be the basic unit of the sound system. By designating these syllables as unanalyzed I mean that the child is not able to separate them into their component consonants and vowels. Only later in the acquisition process does such division into smaller units become possible. The gradual discovery of successively smaller units that can form the basis of the phonological system is an important part of the process.

At an even earlier stage, before a child has uttered any words, she is accomplishing a great deal of linguistic learning, working with a unit of phonological organization even more primitive than the syllable. That unit can be defined in terms of pitch contours. By the late babbling period children already control the intonation, or pitch modulation, contours of the language they are learning. At that stage the child sounds as if she is uttering reasonably long sentences, and adult listeners may have the impression they are not quite catching the child's words. There are no words to catch, only random strings of babbled sounds with recognizable, correctly produced question or statement intonation contours. The sounds may accidentally be similar to some of those found in adult English. These sentence-length utterances are called sentence units, and in the phonological system of the child at this stage they are comparable to the consonant-and-vowel segments, syllables and distinctive features that appear in the phonological systems of later stages. The syllables and segments that appear when the period of word learning begins are in no way related to the vast repertory of babbling sounds. Only the intonation contours are carried over from the babbling stage into the later period.

No matter what language environment a child grows up in, the intonation contours characteristic of adult speech in that environment are the linguistic information learned earliest. Some recent studies suggest that it is possible to identify the language environment of a child from her babbling intonation during the second year of life. Other studies suggest that children can be distinguished at an even earlier age on the basis of whether or not their language environment is a tone language, that is, a language in which words spoken with different pitches are identifiable as different words, even though they may have the same sequence of consonants and vowels. To put it another way, "ma" spoken with a high pitch and "ma" spoken with a low pitch can be as different to someone speaking a tone language as "ma" and "pa" are to someone speaking English. (Many African and Asian languages are tone languages.) Tones are learned very early, and entire tone systems are mastered long before other areas of phonology. The extremely early acquisition of pitch patterns may help to explain the difficulty adults have in learning the intonation of a second language.

Phonetics

There is one significant way in which the acquisition of phonology differs from the acquisition of other language systems. As a child is acquiring the phonological system she must also learn the phonetic realization of the system: the actual details of physiological and acoustic phonetics, which call for the coordination of a complex set of muscle movements. Some children complete the process of learning how to pronounce things earlier than others, but differences of this kind are usually not related to the learning of the phonological system. Brown had what has become a classic conversation with a child who referred to a "fis." Brown repeated "fis," and the child indignantly corrected him, saying "fis." After several such exchanges Brown tried "fish," and the child, finally satisfied, replied, "Yes, fis." It is clear that although the child was still not able to pronounce the distinction between the sounds "s" and "sh," he knew such a systematic phonological distinction existed. Such phonetic muddying of the phonological waters complicates the study of this area of acquisition. Since the child's knowledge of the phonological system may not show up in her speech, it is not easy to determine what a child knows about the system without engaging in complex experimentation and creative hypothesizing.

Children whose phonological system produces only simple words such as "mama" and "papa" actually have a greater phonetic repertory than their utterances suggest. Evidence of that repertory is found in the late babbling stage, when children are working with sentence units and are making a large array of sounds. They do not lose their phonetic ability overnight, but they must constrain it systematically. Going on to the next-higher stage of language learning, the phonological system, is more important to the child than the details of facile pronunciation. Much later, after the phonological system has been acquired, the details of pronunciation receive more attention.

In the period following the babbling period the persisting phonetic facility gets less and less exercise. The vast majority of a child's utterances fail to reflect her real ability to pronounce things accurately; they do, however, reflect her growing ability to pronounce things systematically. (For a child who grows up learning only one language the movements of the muscles of the vocal tract ultimately become so overpracticed that it is difficult to learn new pronunciations during adulthood. On the other hand, people who learn at least two languages in early childhood appear to retain a greater flexibility of the vocal musculature and are more likely to learn to speak an additional language in their adult years without the "accent" of their native language.)

In learning to pronounce, then, a child must acquire a sound system that includes the divergent systems of phonology and phonetics. The acquisition of phonology differs from that of phonetics in requiring the creation of a representation of language in the mind of the child. This representation is necessary because of the abstract nature of the units of phonological structure. From only the acoustic signal of adult language the child must derive successively more abstract phonological units: first intonations, then syllables, then distinctive features and finally consonant-and-vowel segments. There are, for example, few clear segment boundaries in the acoustic signal the child receives, and so the consonant-and-vowel units could hardly be derived if the child had no internal representation of language.

At the same time that a child is building a phonological representation of language she is learning to manipulate all the phonetic variations of language, learning to produce each one precisely and automatically. The dual process of phonetics and phonology acquisition is one of the most difficult in all of language learning. Indeed, although a great deal of syntactic and semantic acquisition has yet to take place, it is usually at the completion of the process of learning to pronounce that adults consider a child to be a full-fledged language speaker and stop using any form of caretaker speech.

Abnormal Language Development

There seems to be little question that the human brain is best suited to language learning before puberty. Foreign languages are certainly learned most easily at that time. Furthermore, it has been observed that people who learn more than one language in childhood have an easier time learning additional languages in later years. It seems to be extremely important for a child to exercise the language-learning faculty. Children who are not exposed to any learnable language during the crucial years, for example children who are deaf before they can speak, generally grow up with the handicap of having little or no language. The handicap is unnecessary: deaf children of deaf parents who communicate by means of the American Sign Language do not grow up without language. They live in an environment where they can make full use of their language-learning abilities, and they are reasonably fluent in sign language by age three, right on the developmental schedule. Deaf children who grow up communicating by means of sign language have a much easier time learning English as a second language than deaf children in oral-speech programs learning English as a first language.

The study of child language acquisition has made important contributions to the study of abnormal speech development. Some investigators of child language have looked at children whose language development is abnormal in the hope of finding the conditions that are necessary and sufficient for normal development; others have looked at the development of language in normal children in the hope of helping children whose language development is abnormal. It now appears that many of the severe language abnormalities found in children can in some way be traced to interruptions of the normal acquisition process. The improved understanding of the normal process is being exploited to create treatment programs for children with such problems. In the past therapeutic methods for children with language problems have emphasized the memorizing of language routines, but methods now being developed would allow a child to work with her own language-learning abilities. For example, the American Sign Language has been taught successfully to several autistic children. Many of these nonverbal and antisocial children have learned in this way to communicate with therapists, in some cases becoming more socially responsive. (Why sign language should be so successful with some autistic children is unclear; it may have to do with the fact that a sign lasts longer than an auditory signal.)

There are still many questions to be answered in the various areas I have discussed, but in general a great deal of progress has been made in understanding child language over the past 20 years. The study of the acquisition of language has come of age. It is now a genuinely interdisciplinary field where psychologists, neurosurgeons and linguists work together to penetrate the mechanisms of perception and cognition as well as the mechanisms of language.

Content Questions

1. In general what kinds of things must children learn when they acquire their own language?

2. What is caretaker speech? Describe some of the features that characterize this speech. How does caretaker speech relate to a young child's ability to acquire a first language?

3. What explanation does Moskowitz give for the fact that a small child might continue to use a particular incorrect form even after being corrected a number of times?

4. Explain what a "vertical construction" is in the one-word and two-word stage.

5. What is telegraphic speech? What are some of its characteristics?

6. According to Roman Jakobson, why are the plural -s, possessive -s, and third-person singular verb suffix -s not acquired together by children learning English?

7. Explain why a child's shifting of usage from a form like "men" to "mans" could indicate a further development in his or her language abilities rather than a regression.

8. Describe the three stages of development that children go through when acquiring negative sentences.

9. How does the markedness of a term (whether it is marked or unmarked) relate to the order of language acquisition?

10. What does it mean to speak of the acquisition of distinctive features rather than sounds? Provide a couple of examples of distinctive features that can be acquired.

Questions for Analysis and Discussion

1. In what ways would it be true to say that small children are the ultimate linguists?

2. Explain what overgeneralization is and what it shows about the formulation of rules by small children.

3. Why might children's phonetic output not be an accurate representation of their phonological knowledge about the language? What implication could this have for speech therapists?

4. What contribution could the study of normal acquisition of language make toward the development of appropriate strategies for helping those with impaired language abilities?

Additional Activities and Paper Topics

1. Listen to the speech of a small child, outlining those sounds with which he or she seems to have trouble. Note the phonetic substitutions, if any, made by the child and briefly report on which features, if any, that those substitutions share with the target (intended or "proper") sounds. (**Phonetics & Phonology**)

2. Create a list of ten to fifteen common medical terms you have heard such as *paralysis* or *diagnosis*. Then look up these terms in a dictionary that provides information about the morphology and etymology of particular words. Report on what you discover about the morphology and etymologies of your words. (**Morphology & Historical Linguistics**)

3. Listen to and record the speech of a medical doctor conversing about his or her profession. If you record someone in a live setting (not the television or radio), you should have his or her permission. Make note of any jargon, interesting euphemisms, and so on. Report any interesting findings. (**Language Varieties**)

4. Record the discourse of a radio talk show in which individuals call in for medical advice. Observe discourse patterns such as turn taking, devices for closing off the conversation, methods by which the host of the show establishes rapport or indicates authority, and so on. Then prepare a report describing any significant patterns you noticed. (**Semantics & Pragmatics**)

5. Videotape or make an audio recording of the speech of several small children (six months to three years old) from differing age groups. Remember to get permission from their parent or guardian before doing so. Contrast the developmental level among the children in terms of phonology, morphology, syntax, and semantics. It would probably be a good idea to review Moskowitz's article before beginning your investigation. Report on your findings. (**Phonology, Morphology, Syntax, Semantics, & Language Acquisition**)

Linguistics, Business, and the Workplace

The contributions that linguistics can make to business and the workplace are numerous. The articles in this chapter are representative of a number of ways in which linguistic study can be applied toward creating effective advertising and marketing, developing products and services, and helping to provide a safer and more effective workplace.

In "Pidgin English Advertising," Suzanne Romaine notes the increasing amount of advertising being directed at pidgin speakers in New Guinea. She demonstrates that an ignorance or superficial understanding of pidgin or its speakers' culture can result in advertising that does not work. Bob Cohen's article, "There's More to a Name," explains how his company, Lexicon Naming (a consulting agency for companies seeking advice on product naming), has worked with a linguist to study people's reactions to particular sounds. This research provides significant insights into the relationship between specific sounds and the impressions they make or the connotations they raise in people's minds. Of course, this information is not only theoretically interesting but also has vital implications for companies seeking to name products that will attract buyers.

The contribution of linguistics to business is not only in the area of research and consulting with companies that already have a product to sell. Linguists also have important contributions to make in the development of products and services that can themselves be marketed. We can, for example, consider the unusual service that Marc Okrand provided. Most people might not imagine that there could possibly be a market or demand for an invented alien language. But when producers at Paramount Pictures needed Klingon dialogue for one of its *Star Trek* movies, Okrand made up dialogue and vocabulary, as well as a phonology, morphology, and syntax to go along with it. He has since published a Klingon dictionary, which explains some of the basics of his invented language and which has become popular among seriously devoted *Star Trek* fans. This reader includes a chapter about nouns from that dictionary.

A knowledge of linguistics is also important for business products that are designed to inform us about language, to assist us in the retrieval of information, or to mimic in some degree the capability of a human speaker. In the article "A Place for Phonetics in High Technology," Melvin J. Luthy discusses the importance of phonetic and phonological information in his work with a "rhymer" software project and with the creation of a program that would read people's electronic mail to them. And in their article "Dimensions of Usage and Dictionary Labeling," William Card, Raven I. McDavid, Jr., and Virginia McDavid explain the type of information about language that is necessary for dictionary makers to consider in preparing usage labels for the various entries.

The final reading in this chapter, "Fatal Words: Communication Clashes and Aircraft Crashes," examines some of the air accidents that have occurred as a result of faulty communication and misunderstanding. In this article, Steven Cushing explores the valuable role that discourse study and its applications could serve in helping to introduce greater safety measures in the airline industry.

These applications are by no means a complete representation of the possibilities for applying linguistics to business and the workplace, as evidenced by further applications found elsewhere in this reader. One might, for example, consider the research by Deborah Tannen into gender differences in language and how such differences can affect a woman's situation in the workplace. In the chapter on "Linguistics and Issues of Gender, Race, and Culture," I have included an article representative of her research. Beyond this reader there are, of course, many other articles by a variety of authors who have looked at the various features of discourse that occur in a number of work settings.

Other business applications by linguists have included the examination of cross-cultural differences and their relationship to the effectiveness of product naming or advertising. Some linguists have also helped develop books and software for educational or recreational purposes. And others are involved in developing computer capabilities in machine translation and artificial intelligence (see Victor Raskin's article in the chapter on "Linguistics and Translation"). While some of these latter applications are still in developmental stages, they will have increasingly more important business and commercial uses.

Pidgin English Advertising

Suzanne Romaine

As businesses look to increase their markets, they begin to target new groups. In many situations, advertisers will be preparing sales campaigns for linguistic groups with which they have not previously had much, if any, experience. Such is the case with Tok Pisin ("talk pidgin"), a pidgin spoken in New Guinea. In the article below, Suzanne Romaine, a linguist at Oxford University and a scholar in pidgin and creole languages, explains some of the cultural and linguistic factors that should be considered when preparing advertisements for use in Papua New Guinea.

There have recently been attempts to use pidgin English as a medium of advertising in Papua New Guinea, and these have given rise to a number of linguistic and cross-cultural dilemmas. Tok Pisin ("talk pidgin") is an English-based pidgin spoken in Papua New Guinea. Like all pidgin languages, it arose as a lingua franca among speakers of many different languages. It shares with other pidgin languages the characteristic that its lexicon is drawn mainly from one language, in this case English (hence it is referred to as an English-based rather than, say, a French-based pidgin). Its grammar is drawn from another source, in this case, the numerous indigenous languages of Melanesia. This means that even when items derived from English are used to express grammatical categories in pidgin, the syntactic patterning and meanings of them often follow structures found in the indigenous languages. One such instance can be found in the distinction between inclusive and exclusive first person plural pronouns, which is made in Tok Pisin and most, if not all, of the indigenous languages of Melanesia but not in English. Thus, where English has only *we*, Tok Pisin has *yumi* (from English *you* + *me*), which is inclusive in its reference, and *mipela* (from English *me* + *fellow*), which is exclusive. One must always distinguish in pidgin between "we" which includes the speaker and addressee(s) and "we" which includes the speaker and others, but not the addressee(s). Although the lexical material used to make this distinction is clearly drawn from English, the meanings encoded by it can be understood only by reference to grammatical categories present in Melanesian languages. The use of the suffix *-pela* (from English *fellow*) is another case in point. While *fellow* does not have any grammatical function in English, it has been taken over into pidgin as an affix or classifier marking the word class of attributive adjectives. Thus, we have *gutpela man* ("a good man"), *naispela haus* ("a nice house"), *wanpela meri* ("a/one woman"), and so on.

183

In the pronoun system it appears as a formative in the first and second person plural, *mipela* ("we" exclusive) and *yupela* ("you" plural).[1]

Tok Pisin is the descendant of a number of varieties of a Pacific Jargon English which was spoken over much of the Pacific during the nineteenth century and used as a lingua franca between English-speaking Europeans and Pacific Islanders. This jargon was learned by Papua New Guineans on plantations in Queensland, Samoa, Fiji, and in Papua New Guinea itself. The typical pattern of acquisition was for Melanesian workers to pick up the pidgin or jargon on the plantation and then bring it back to villages, where it was passed on to younger boys. Tok Pisin crystallized in a distinctive form in the New Guinea islands and spread from there to the mainland.

Although Tok Pisin was born in and kept going by colonialization, it quickly became more than just a means of communication between the indigenous population and their European colonizers. Since its origin in about 1880, Tok Pisin has become the most important lingua franca for Papua New Guineans, who, according to one estimate, have around 750 indigenous languages. Although it was originally learned as a second language, it is now being acquired by children as their first language. When this happens in the life cycle of a pidgin language, we can speak of creolization. In sociolinguistic terms, then, Tok Pisin can be described as an expanded pidgin which is currently undergoing creolization. It now has a sizable number of native speakers (about 20,000), and roughly 44 percent of the population claim to speak it. Indeed, the question of whether Tok Pisin should become the national language of Papua New Guinea has recently been the subject of much discussion. At the moment it has official status, along with two other languages: English, and another pidgin, Hiri Motu, which is based on Motu, one of the indigenous languages of what was, until independence in 1975, the Territory of Papua. Hiri Motu is, however, regionally restricted, and only about 9 percent of the population speak it. The name Tok Pisin was officially adopted for English-based pidgin in 1981. It had been previously referred to as Neomelanesian, Melanesian pidgin, *Tok boi* (from English *talk* + *boy*), or just pidgin.[2] It is now, since independence, the preferred language in the House of Assembly, though English is the official medium of education.

One of the things which happens when a pidgin expands and stabilizes, and possibly then creolizes, is that new linguistic resources have to be created or borrowed to fulfil the new functions to which the language is put. For instance, there is an increase in vocabulary so that new concepts

---

[1] See S. Romaine, *Pidgin and Creole Languages* (London, 1988).

[2] This word order pattern in *tok boi* also illustrates the use of English items in compound constructions based on those found in indigenous languages. Compare *kot ren* (from English *coat* + *rain*—"raincoat"), *haus man* (from English *house* + *man*—"men's house"), and so on. The word *boi* was used by Europeans to refer to an indigenous man of any age, particularly in indentured service. It has recently been "reborrowed" in its English sense to refer to young men in order to replace Tok Pisin *mangki* (from English *monkey*).

can be expressed: *nesional baset* ("national budget"), *minista bilong edukesan/edukesan minista* ("education minister"). More complicated syntactic structures such as relative clauses emerge, which allow the creation of more sophisticated discourse and stylistic alternatives. Tok Pisin is used now in political debates in the House of Assembly, in media broadcasts, and in journalism.

Tok Pisin has drawn heavily on English in all its new functions. So much English has been borrowed into the language, particularly by urban educated speakers, that many linguists have recognized two separate varieties of the language, urban and rural (or bush) pidgin. Consider this example in which a student being interviewed on a radio broadcast in 1972 said:

> Mi salim eplikeson bilong mi na skul bod [me send application belong me and school board] i konsiderim na bihain ekseptim mi na mi go [consider and behind accept me and me go] long skul long fama [to school of farmer].[3]

"I sent my application to the school board and then they considered and accepted me and I'm going to agricultural school."

Here *eplikeson, skul bod, konsiderim,* and *ekseptim* are all recent loans from English. In some cases there are established pidgin equivalents which could have been used. For example, instead of *ekseptim,* one could say *ol givim orait long dispela* or *long mi* ("they gave the okay for this/to me"). Nowadays students would probably not use the term *skul long fama* but say *agricultural college.* In many cases we can see that borrowing a word in English fills a lexical gap or expresses a concept which is foreign and which could be expressed in pidgin only by means of a lengthy circumlocution. For example, *baset* ("budget") could be paraphrased as *ol man i lukautim mani bilong gavman i raitim daun ol samting bilong mani bilong gavman* ("the people who look after the government's money write down things having to do with the government's money"). The circumlocution is self-explanatory, whereas the borrowing is not. People often do not understand the meanings of very frequently used English borrowings. When the country became independent in 1975, the term *independens* was used, but many people then did not understand what it meant, and still do not. I worked with bush informants in 1986 and 1987 who said they were happy their country was independent because it meant that Australia would help them, when in fact it means just the opposite. In practical terms, increased borrowing from English in urban areas has the effect of making town pidgin unintelligible to rural dwellers. But in other cases, though there are equivalent pidgin words, English is borrowed simply because English has

---

[3] This example is taken from L. R. Healey, "When is a word not a pidgin word?," *Tok Pisin i go we?* (Where is Tok Pisin going?), ed. K. McElhanon, Special Issue of *Kivung* (Linguistic Society of Papua New Guinea, 1975), pp. 36–42.

more prestige. For example, pidgin uses the term *askim* (from English *ask*) as both a verb and a noun, but increasingly in urban pidgin a more recently borrowed term, *kwesten* (from English *question*), appears too. Thus, one could say either *Mi gat askim* or *mi gat kwesten* ("I have a question") or *mi laik askim kwesten* ("I want to ask a question"). Another example is *infomesen* (from English *information*) and *toksave* (from Tok Pisin *tok* + *save*, that is, talk know), which means "information, knowledge, advice." Tok Pisin *toksave* can be used as either a noun or a verb, whereas the English *infomesen* can be used only as a noun.[4] There has also been an increase in the use of English plurals ending in *-s*—*ol gels* (from English *girls*), for example, as opposed to *ol meri* ("the girls/women").

Until the last few decades Tok Pisin was only a spoken language. Now it is written too and more and more literature is published in it. One main vehicle for Tok Pisin as a written language is the weekly newspaper *Wantok*, founded in 1970. (The word *wantok* means "one language" and is used to refer to a person who is part of the same social or kin group, or village.) Written almost entirely in pidgin, *Wantok* has a circulation of over 10,000 and more than 50,000 readers in Papua New Guinea, and its staff now consists entirely of nationals. Most of the material that appears in it is a translation of news releases from the Department of Information and Extension Services in Port Moresby. It is in *Wantok* that we find the most extensive use of pidgin in advertising.

Advertising creates special problems for newspapers aimed at a Papua New Guinean public. Most of the products are Australian and geared to western lifestyles, which were originally accessible only to expatriates. Now, increasingly a new market is found in the indigenous urban elite. While products like cars, trucks, and refrigerators are still luxuries for the average Papua New Guinean and therefore advertised largely in English, even in *Wantok*, it is no longer uncommon for Highlanders at the end of the coffee season to come into town and pay cash for a vehicle. Consequently, ads for cars and trucks—for instance, Toyota—are starting to appear occasionally in pidgin. While the names of such products mean something to Australians, they carry no meaning, and correspondingly have no use, for most Papua New Guineans. Products like Vegemite, Omo, and Pine-O-Cleen are just foreign words. For advertising to be successful, the product has to be not only advertised, but also explained in such a way as to create a need for it. One very simple ad which is effective, at least from the advertiser's point of view, is that used by the Wopa biscuit company. The Wopa ad shows a muscular man holding the product and saying, "Mi kaikai" (I eat). The implication is that the product is good for you because it makes you strong and big. Bread and flour-based products are not part of traditional diets, so they have to be explained and made appealing,

---

[4] The word *save* is from Spanish/Portuguese (*sabir/saber*—"to know") and is widespread in pidgin and creole languages throughout the world and not just in those of Spanish/Portuguese base. This is one of the few cases where English has borrowed a term from pidgin: that is, *savvy*. Though it can be used only as a noun or adjective in English, in Tok Pisin it can be used as a noun or verb.

whether they are nutritious or not. These products increasingly find their way into every village trade store.

The ad for Sunflower tinned fish, in which the product is clearly illustrated, is effective primarily because of its use of idiomatic Tok Pisin. The slogan says: *Em i bun bilong mi stret* ("it bone belong me straight"), a colloquial expression which means that it is just the thing to serve as the foundation of a good diet. In the literal sense *bun* means "bone" or "skeleton"; one who is *bun nating* (from English *bone + nothing*) would be very skinny.

The ad for Paradise Pineapple Crunch biscuits, however, is probably much less effective because it relies too heavily on English borrowing. The ad boasts of *tropikal fleva insait long bisket* ("tropical flavor inside a biscuit"). The words *tropikal* and *fleva* are new English borrowings and won't be understood by those who do not know English. The Anchor milk company uses a heavily anglicized description of the product, next to which is a photograph of a jug of milk, a cup of coffee, and a can bearing a label in English, "full cream vitamin enriched instant milk powder." To a reader who knows no English, it could as well be an ad for coffee. Most Papua New Guineans have no experience of real milk, let alone powdered milk.

The kinds of clever and catchy advertising slogans typical in Western societies like *drinka pinta milka day, go to work on an egg,* and *if your clothes aren't becoming to you, you should be coming to us* are impossible to translate literally into another language because they rely on linguistic devices like vowel reduction ("*drink a pint of milk a day*"), alliteration, rhyme ("*Beanz meanz Heinz*"), and so on. Although presumably these strategies are available to some degree in most languages, the extent to which they are used and the purposes for which they are used will vary.

There are also other kinds of difficulties in literal translations of slogans, even where special devices like rhyme or punning are not brought into play in the original. For example, the Omo soap company wanted to advertise their product in *Wantok* and say simply that this is the best powdered soap you can buy. But in pidgin two product names for soap powder have become generic now in the same way as the brandname Hoover is used in Britain to refer to any vacuum cleaner or the name Jello is used in the United States for any fruit-flavored gelatin. (One can even use the name Hoover as a verb, at least in Britain, where it is more usual to "hoover" a carpet than to "vacuum" it.) Pidgin speakers use both *rinso,* another brandname, and *omo* to refer to all soap powders, which would lead to an advertisement that said something like: Omo is the best rinso you can buy, or Rinso is the best omo you can buy.[5] It would be like saying in English: I've just bought an Electrolux hoover.

The difference here is that English already has generic terms like soap powder, detergent, vacuum cleaner, carpet sweeper, and so on, whereas

---

[5] See the comments of the first editor and founder of *Wantok,* in F. Mihalic, "Interpretation Problems from the Point of View of a Newspaper Editor," in *New Guinea Area Languages and Language Study,* ed. S. A. Wurm, vol. 3 of *Language, Culture, Society and the Modern World* (Canberra, 1977), pp. 1117–26.

pidgin did not until it pressed a particular brandname into service. In the case of pidgin omo and rinso, the particular brand provides the first name for such a substance and thus is synonymous with it. The status and desirability of brandnames used as generics are debatable. The American Heritage Dictionary includes an entry for example for Kleenex ("a trademark for a soft cleansing tissue") and one for Jello ("a trademark for a gelatin dessert"). But of course the whole point of brandnames is to establish uniqueness. One can assume from the advertising campaign mounted by the Coca Cola Company—"coke is the real thing" or simply "coke is it"—that it is not unequivocably pleased with the use of Coke as a generic term for a cola drink. Nevertheless, it can also be advantageous for a company's product to become a "household" word. If Kleenex is synonymous with tissues, then the consumer may be predisposed to seek this brandname when buying tissues.

A related problem arises from the lack of specialized terms in pidgin to refer to foodstuffs which have already undergone a certain degree of processing and are therefore "table-ready" or "oven-ready." (Traditionally, of course, Papua New Guineans do not sit down at tables to eat.) The distinction between English "pork" and "pig" and "beef" and "cow" is of course well known. Interestingly, English has borrowed from French the terms which refer to the edible version of the animal on the table, while it has used its own native terms to refer to the animal on the hoof, so to speak. There is a current ad for chicken which mixes English and pidgin and refers to its product in a confusing way as *Niugini table birds kakaruk* ("New Guinea table birds chicken"). This is also the company's name. The term *table bird* is a collocation specific to English referring to the product in a-ready-to-cook-and-serve state (and possibly even grown for that special purpose). Neither the term nor its concept is known to pidgin speakers. Presumably the idea is to establish an equation between ready-to-cook (as opposed to live) chickens and this particular company through invoking the pidgin term *kakaruk*, "chicken."

At the moment there is very little exploitation of linguistic devices like rhyme, alliteration, and punning to achieve catchy slogans in Tok Pisin. I found only one example in an advertisement for eggs, and it plays on the English word *eggs* rather than the Tok Pisin term *kiau* (from Tolai, one of the indigenous languages of Papua New Guinea). It describes eggs as "eggcellent," "eggciting," and "ineggspensive," and then says in pidgin that they are good value for money. A pidgin speaker who does not know English will not of course know what these blends mean. There is plenty of scope for creative advertising slogans drawing on native pidgin terms and devices. For instance, one Australian rice producer has named its product *Trukai* (Tok Pisin *tru* + *kaikai*—"true food").

Tok Pisin also has a number of named special registers which could provide a productive source for advertisers. *Tok piksa* ("talk picture") is a term for a way of speaking which relies on analogy and similes. *Tok pilai* ("talk play") refers to the jocular use of extended metaphors. *Tok bilas* ("talk decoration") is used to say things which are potentially offensive but can later be denied. *Tok bokis* ("talk box") is a deliberate attempt to disguise meaning by the substitution of familiar words with hidden meanings. There are many others. Advertisers would, however, have to be careful here because some brand names already figure in certain registers. For instance, a common tok piksa term for beer is *spesel Milo* ("special Milo"), and Milo is already a brand name for a chocolate drink. Biscuit advertisers would benefit from knowing that Tok Pisin *switbisket* (from English *sweet biscuit*) and *draibisket* (from English *dry biscuit*) have metaphorical meanings. The former can refer to a sexually attractive woman, and the latter to a woman past her prime.

Some of the advertising techniques used by Western advertisers would simply not work in Papua New Guinea because they would be offensive and/or culturally inappropriate—for example, the innuendo and overt display of sexuality in the sale of perfumes, cars, and other luxury items. *Wantok* newspaper refused an ad from the Gillette company because it showed a European couple in the bathroom nude from the waist up, the woman admiring the face of the smoothly shaven man. Shaving does not interest women in Papua New Guinea, and sexuality would not sell razor blades. On the contrary, it would discourage them.[6]

Conversely, however, many bodily functions do not have the same taboo surrounding them in Papua New Guinea as they do in Western culture, and euphemisms for these things are only just beginning to emerge in Tok Pisin under the influence of western practices. Euphemism is widely used in advertising, even for nontaboo subjects. Take, for instance, the use of "fun-size" for small candy bars. I was amazed when a young schoolgirl I was interviewing used a new euphemistic term, *troimwe excretia* ("to throw away excretia"), for the normal pidgin *pekpek* ("to defecate"), which is used in all contexts. Similarly, *pispis* is the normal term for "urinate," though there is a new Tok Pisin euphemism now: *kapsaitim wara* (from English *capsize + water*). The kind of subtlety and allusion used by Western advertisers to sell toilet tissue (for example, fluffy puppies playing with toilet rolls in gleaming bright bathrooms) and sanitary products (not even advertised until recently in Western media) will be lost on most Papua New Guineans from rural areas who have no experience of modern sanitation facilities. Ads for sanitary napkins, which have just recently begun to appear in *Wantok*, do not explicitly describe or depict the product. Although the language itself is not heavily anglicized and would be intelligible, the advertisers do not explain what the product is or does. Thanks to western taboo, the reader is simply told that Johnson and Johnson have *ol gutpela samting* ("good things"), and shown a picture of a girl daydreaming. The dividing line between euphemism and mystification is very fine in

---

[6] See Mihalic, "Interpretation Problems," for his discussion of the newspaper's policy.

this case. It may well be, however, that this phrase does carry unintended sexual overtone and would therefore offend, because the Tok Pisin term *samting* ("something") is used in *tok bokis* to refer to genitals.

Other familiar Western-style household products are increasingly aimed at Papua New Guineans: for example, Pine-O-Cleen, Mortein, and similar detergents and cleaning agents, and insect sprays. Here it is essential that the product be displayed as well as explained. In these ads an appeal is typically made to the notion of protecting your family against disease. We see here the introduction of Western metaphors into local culture.[7] When such products are advertised in Western media, women are usually portrayed as the protectors of the household, warding off dirt, germs, and other hazards with the right product. Ads for insurance also use the protection metaphor. Then there are also many ads which are used to explain institutions that are culturally alien: banks, taxes, telephones. The effectiveness of the ads depends on how successfully they can render into pidgin the concepts involved. For example, in an ad for PTC (Post and Telecommunication Corporation) the Western metaphor "time is money" (*yu save olsem taim em i mani*—"you know that time is money") is invoked to get people to use the telephone to conduct transactions which would ordinarily be done face-to-face in casual encounters and not by appointment. The concepts "social call" and "business call" are thus introduced.

These are a few of the difficulties presented by advertising in pidgin English. Some of these derive from the problems of the linguistic medium itself, which is in the process of expanding, while others have more to do specifically with the pragmatics of cross-cultural communication. In order to resolve some of the difficulties I have noted here, cooperation between linguists, manufacturing industries, and advertising agencies is essential.

Content Questions

1. What is Tok Pisin? How did it originate and where is it now spoken?

2. Contrast the use of the first-person plural pronoun (we) in Tok Pisin and English with regard to what it does or does not distinguish in its reference.

3. What happens to a pidgin language when it acquires native speakers?

4. What developments occur within a pidgin when it becomes a creole?

5. In Tok Pisin the expression *skul long fama* can be translated as "agricultural college." But what does that pidgin expression literally mean?

6. What has prompted the recent increase in advertisements using Tok Pisin?

---

[7]See G. Lakoff and M. Johnson, *Metaphors We Live By* (Chicago, 1980), for their discussion of some of these metaphors.

7. Why would the advertisement for Paradise Pineapple Crunch biscuits probably not be effective?

8. What does the situation with Omo soap show about one possible difficulty in translating advertisements into Tok Pisin?

9. Does Tok Pisin lend itself to any kinds of wordplay? Explain.

Questions for Analysis and Discussion

1. Romaine indicates that Tok Pisin has both an urban and rural variety. Do you think that fact is surprising? Why or why not?

2. As the article points out, English has different terms to distinguish between a particular type of animal when it appears in the field as opposed to its prepared state as food on the table. As far as translation is concerned, what does this article indicate about how safely one can assume that such distinguishing terms will be available in other languages?

3. Explain the relationship between taboos and the use of euphemisms. To what extent are some taboos culturally specific? How could a knowledge of euphemisms and taboos in a particular culture be useful to advertisers?

4. What kinds of problems could the difference in metaphors between cultures pose to an advertiser?

5. Romaine's conclusion indicates that more effective advertising could result from "cooperation between linguists, manufacturing industries, and advertising agencies." Why would this be the case?

There's More to a Name

Bob Cohen

Linguists have been aware of sound symbolism for many years. It has been noted, for example, that [gl-] is frequently associated by many with light or shininess as in *gloss, gleam, glow,* and so on. But while this area of linguistics has represented an interesting curiosity within the field, it has not been given much serious attention. In this article, however, Bob Cohen explains the results of linguistic research into the sound symbolism of consonants and how such research could be applied to more effective marketing. The research was performed by his company Lexicon Naming, a business devoted to creating successful product names. You might note within this article how natural categories of sounds you have studied in phonetics seem to correspond to actual categories that emerge when people are tested about their perceptions. This article originally appeared in the *Stanford Business School Magazine.*

If you're naming a new product, take note: traditional meaning is only one part of the communication equation.

Here's a simple puzzle. Which one of the two nonsense words *taketa* and *naluma* do you think goes with each of these pictures?

If you're like virtually everyone else, you'll pair *taketa* with the angular illustration and *naluma* with the curved one. That's because all the consonants in *taketa* are what linguists call obstruents, and all the consonants in *naluma* are sonorants. Obstruents are perceived as harder and more masculine; sonorants as softer and more feminine. Consider the two brand names Clorox, a hard-working laundry product, and Chanel, a perfume, and you'll get the idea.

Welcome to the world of sound symbolism—a concept whose implications linguists have debated for years.

At Lexicon Naming, we are trying to understand more about how sound symbolism can affect the way brand names are perceived. If a product can be perceived as faster, bigger, or even more reliable depending on the sound that starts its name, we have an entirely new set of tools to add to our creative process.

Under the direction of Stanford linguistics professor Will Leben, Lexicon's brand language group has initiated a research program to determine

---

Pick a brand name

Subjects in the pilot study were asked questions like the ones that follow. Ask yourself these questions and see if your answers match the test results.

a. Which headache tablet sounds faster?

     Pavil   Bavil

b. Which computer sounds more compact?

     Gortan   Kortan

c. Which car sounds faster?

     Sarrant   Tarrant

d. Which computer sounds more compact?

     Syndron   Zyndron

e. Which car sounds faster?

     Faldon   Valdon

f. Which computer sounds faster?

     Taza   Paza

g. Which car sounds more dependable?

     Bazia   Vazia

h. Which computer sounds more dependable?

     Gamza   Damza

Answer Key

h. Damza

g. Bazia

f. Taza

e. Valdon

d. Zyndron

c. Sarrant

b. Kortan

a. Pavil

---

if certain consonant sounds do a better job of communicating specific attributes than others.

Last year we completed a pilot study with 144 students from Stanford and UC–Berkeley. The students answered an extensive series of questions about possible names for three hypothetical new products—a performance sedan, a laptop computer, and a headache tablet. Written descriptions of each product were included to make the questionnaire seem like a true name test.

Because existing research had already demonstrated that certain vowel sounds are associated with certain physical attributes, we decided to test specific consonant sound groups for similar attributes. We chose two: size and speed. To push beyond simple physical attributes, we included a representative abstract attribute—dependability—an important marketing characteristic but a complete unknown in the world of sound symbolism.

We created fictitious brand name pairs in which the two choices differed only in their initial consonant—the most powerful position in a name. In order not to influence perception by inherent meaning, the names were created to carry little or no semantic value. (See table for sample questions.)

The results of our pilot study, significant at the 95 percent confidence level and independent of both product category and respondent gender, were quite dramatic and validate the powerful impact sound symbolism can have on the communication of both physical and abstract attributes by a brand name. Here are some partial conclusions about initial consonants:

- Voiceless stops (*p, t, k*) carry a greater connotation of speed than do voiced stops (*b, d, g*). E.g., *Pavil* sounds faster than *Bavil*.
- Voiceless stops (*p, k*) connote smallness better than voiced stops (*b, g*). E.g., *Kortan* seems smaller than *Gortan*.
- Fricatives (*v, f, z, s*) connote speed better than stops (*b, p, d, t*). E.g., *Sarrant* seems faster that *Tarrant*.
- *z* connotes smallness better than *s*. E.g., *Zyndron* seems more compact than *Syndron*.
- Voiced fricatives (*v* and *z*) connote speed better than voiceless fricatives (*f* and *s*). E.g., *Valdon* seems faster than *Faldon*.
- Dentals (*d* and *t*) connote speed better than labials (*b* and *p*). E.g., *Taza* seems faster than *Paza*.
- Stops (*b, p, d*) connote dependability better than fricatives (*v, f, z, s*). E.g., *Bazia* seems more dependable than *Vazia*.
- *d* seems relatively dependable, while *g* seems relatively undependable. E.g., *Damza* seems more dependable than *Gamza*.

At Lexicon, we are quite confident that these conclusions can be applied to names with real semantic value. Think about the name Lexicon created for Apple Computer—PowerBook. According to our research results, the initial *p* in "Power" supports compactness and speed, while the initial *b* in "Book" supports the perception of dependability. These are both important underlying messages for the product.

As an important next step, we are in the process of completing studies in Japan and three European countries to identify where meaningful cross-language generalizations are possible. These studies include an expanded list of abstract attributes. In an economy where global brands are becoming the norm rather than the exception, a greater understanding of sound symbolism is putting us that much closer to our ultimate goal—deciphering and implementing what we call "the universal language of branding."

Content Questions

1. What is sound symbolism?

2. How is this notion applied to the invention of product names?

3. In the study that was conducted, which position of the word do the generalizations about consonants relate to?

4. According to the reported research results in the article, why is a nickname such as *Bubba* unlikely to be given to a small individual (except perhaps as a joke)?

5. Explain how the name *PowerBook* relates to the generalizations made about particular consonant sounds and their associations.

6. Describe what a "next step" will be for Cohen's company.

Questions for Analysis and Discussion

1. What possible reason could you provide for why fricatives are associated with greater speed than stops?

2. The research results cluster around natural classes such as voiceless stops or fricatives. Should that be surprising? Why or why not?

3. The research tested differences between consonants by using minimal pairs such as *Pavil* versus *Bavil*. Why would the research have used minimal pairs?

4. Why was it important for the experiment to use fictitious brand names?

5. How reliable would a creation of product names that take only sound symbolism into account be? What other factors should be considered in name selection?

Nouns (A Chapter Excerpt from *The Klingon Dictionary*)

Marc Okrand

When movie producers for *Star Trek III* needed someone to prepare alien-sounding dialogue for the Klingons, they hired Marc Okrand, a linguist who has done scholarly work in Native American languages. Okrand, however, didn't limit himself to creating lines of dialogue; he also developed a language, complete with phonological, morphological, and syntactic rules in addition to vocabulary. His hard work paid off not only by providing him with subsequent film work, but also by making him into a sort of celebrity among *Star Trek* fans across the country, who are studying Klingon as an artificial language they can use among themselves. The following excerpt is taken from *The Klingon Dictionary* that Okrand produced. The excerpt discusses the morphology of nouns in Klingon. Within Okrand's book, this excerpt follows a chapter on the phonology of Klingon. For the purposes of your work with this chapter, however, do not worry about pronouncing Klingon correctly. But if you are serious about learning Klingon, you might wish to refer to the dictionary Okrand produced.

3. Nouns

There are various types of nouns in Klingon.

3.1. Simple Nouns

Simple nouns, like simple nouns in English, are simple words; for example, **DoS** *target* or **QIH** *destruction.*

3.2. Complex Nouns

Complex nouns, on the other hand, are made up of more than one part.

3.2.1. Compound Nouns

Compound nouns consist of two or three nouns in a row, much like English *earthworm* (*earth* plus *worm*) or *password* (*pass* plus *word*). For example, **jolpa'** *transport room* consists of **jol** *transport beam* plus **pa'** *room.*

3.2.2. Verb plus -wI'

A second type of complex noun consists of a verb followed by a suffix meaning *one who does* or *thing which does.* The English suffix *-er* (as in *builder* "one who builds" or *toaster* "thing which toasts") is a rough equivalent. In Klingon, the suffix is **-wI'**. It occurs, for example, in **baHwI'** *gunner,* which consists of the verb **baH** *fire (a torpedo)* plus **-wI'** *one who does.* Thus, **baHwI'** is literally "one who fires [a torpedo]." Similarly, **So'wI'** *cloaking device* comes from the verb **So'** *cloak* plus **-wI'** *thing which does.* **So'wI'** is a "thing which cloaks."

A noun formed by adding **-wI'** to a verb is a regular noun, so it may be used along with another noun to form a compound noun. For example, **tIjwI'ghom** *boarding party* comes from **tIjwI'** *boarder* plus **ghom** *group;* and **tIjwI'** comes from **tIj** *board* plus **-wI'**.

3.2.3. Other Complex Nouns

There are a good many nouns in Klingon which are two or, less frequently, three syllables long, but which are not complex nouns of the types described above. These nouns probably at one time were formed by combining simple nouns, but one or all of the nouns forming the complex noun are no longer in use, so it is not possible (without extensive etymological research) to know what the individual pieces mean.

For example, **'ejDo'** means *starship.* The syllable **'ej** also occurs in **'ejyo'** *Starfleet.* There are, however, no known Klingon words **'ej, Do',** or **yo'** that have anything to do with Starfleet, starships, the Federation, or space vehicles of any kind. It is quite likely that **Do'** is an Old Klingon word for *space vessel* (the modern Klingon word is **Duj**) that is used nowhere except in the noun **'ejDo'**. Of course, without further study, that remains pure conjecture.

3.3. Suffixes

All nouns, whether simple or complex, may be followed by one or more suffixes. If there are two or more suffixes, the suffixes must occur in a specific order. Suffixes may be classified on the basis of their relative order after the noun. There are five types of suffixes (which, for convenience, will be numbered 1 through 5). Suffixes of Type 1 come right after the noun; suffixes of Type 2 come after those of Type 1; suffixes of Type 5 come last. This may be illustrated as follows:

NOUN-1-2-3-4-5

Of course, if no suffix of Type 1 is used but a suffix of Type 2 is used, the Type 2 suffix comes right after the noun. If a suffix of Type 5 is the only suffix used, it comes right after the noun. Only when two or more suffixes are used does their order become apparent.

There are at least two suffixes in each suffix type. Only one suffix of each type may be used at a time. That is, a noun cannot be followed by, for example, two or three Type 4 suffixes.

The members of each suffix type are as follows.

3.3.1. Type 1: Augmentative/Diminutive

-**'a'** *augmentative*   This suffix indicates that what the noun refers to is bigger, more important, or more powerful than it would be without the suffix.

SuS *wind, breeze*	**SuS'a'** *strong wind*
Qagh *mistake*	**Qagh'a'** *major blunder*
woQ *power*	**woQ'a'** *ultimate power*

-**Hom** *diminutive*   This is the opposite of the augmentative suffix. It indicates that what the noun refers to is smaller, less important, or less powerful than it would be without the suffix.

SuS *wind, breeze*	**SuSHom** *wisp of air*
roj *peace*	**rojHom** *truce, temporary peace*

3.3.2. Type 2: Number

As in English, a singular noun in Klingon has no specific suffix indicating that it is singular: **nuH** *weapon* refers to a single weapon of any type. Unlike English, however, the lack of a specific suffix for plural does not always indicate that the noun is singular. In Klingon, a noun without a plural suffix may still refer to more than one entity. The plurality is indicated by a pronoun, whether a verb prefix or a full word, or by context. For example, **yaS** *officer* may refer to a single officer or to a group of officers, depending on other words in the sentence or the context of the discussion.

Compare:

yaS yImojpu' *I became an officer.*
yaS DImojpu' *We became officers.*

yaS jIH *I am an officer.*
yaS maH *We are officers.*

In the first pair of sentences, the only difference is the verb prefix (here only partially described): **vI-** *I*, **DI-** *we*. In the second pair, the pronouns are different: **jIH** *I*, **maH** *we*.

Under certain circumstances, the only way to know whether the noun refers to one or more than one entity is by context. Thus, **yaS mojpu'** can be translated either *he/she became an officer* or *they became officers*. Those taking part in any discussion in which this sentence is used would presumably already know whom is being talked about, so they would also know whether *he* or *she* or *they* is the correct meaning.

Fortunately for students of Klingon, it is never incorrect to add a plural suffix to a noun referring to more than one entity, even in those cases where it is unnecessary to do so. Accordingly, both **yaS maH** and **yaSpu' maH** are correct, both meaning *we are officers* (-**pu'** is a plural suffix). On the other hand, a plural suffix cannot be added to a noun referring to only one thing, even if pronouns are present in the sentence. In Klingon, **yaSpu' jIH** *I am officers* is as incorrect as its English translation.

There are three different plural suffixes in Klingon.

-**pu'** *plural for beings capable of using language*   This suffix can be used to indicate plurality for Klingons, Terrans, Romulans, Vulcans, and so on, but not for lower animals of any kind, plants, inanimate objects, electromagnetic or other beams or waves, etc.

yaS *officer*	**yaSpu'** *officers*
Duy *emissary*	**Duypu'** *emissaries*

-**Du'** *plural for body parts*   This suffix is used when referring to body parts of those beings capable of using language as well as of any other animal.

qam *foot*	**qamDu'** *feet*
tlhon *nostril*	**tlhonDu'** *nostrils*

-**mey** *plural, general usage*   This suffix is used to mark the plural of any noun.

mID *colony*	**mIDmey** *colonies*
yuQ *planet*	**yuQmey** *planets*

It can also be used with nouns referring to beings capable of using language (those nouns which take -**pu'**). When it is so used, it adds a notion of "scattered all about" to the meaning. Compare:

puq *child*
puqpu' *children*
puqmey *children all over the place*

The suffix -**mey** cannot be used with body parts. It should be noted, however, that Klingon poets often violate this grammatical rule in order to evoke particular moods in their poetry. Thus, forms such as **tlhonmey** *nostrils scattered all about* do occur. Until the subtle nuances of such constructions are firmly grasped, however, it is suggested that students of Klingon stick to the rules.

Finally, some nouns in Klingon are inherently or always plural in meaning, and therefore never take plural suffixes.

> **ray'** *targets*
> **cha** *torpedoes*
> **chuyDaH** *thrusters*

The singular counterparts of such words are utterly distinct:

> **DoS** *target*
> **peng** *torpedo*
> **vIj** *thruster*

The singular forms may take the **-mey** suffix, but the meaning always carries the "scattered all about" connotation:

> **DoSmey** *targets scattered all about*
> **pengmey** *torpedoes all over the place*

Inherently plural nouns are treated grammatically as singular nouns in that singular pronouns are used to refer to them. For example, in the sentence **cha yIghuS** *Stand by torpedoes!* or *Get the torpedoes ready to be fired!* the verb prefix yI-, an imperative prefix used for singular objects, must be used even though the object (**cha** *torpedoes*) has a plural meaning.

3.3.3. Type 3: Qualification

Suffixes of this type indicate the speaker's attitude toward the noun, or how sure the speaker is that the noun is being used appropriately.

-qoq *so-called*   This suffix indicates that the noun is being used in a false or ironic fashion. Saying **rojqoq** *so-called peace,* rather than simply **roj** *peace,* indicates that the speaker does not really believe that peace is legitimate or likely to endure.

-Hey *apparent*   This suffix indicates that the speaker is pretty sure the object referred to by the noun is accurately described by the noun, but has some doubts. For example, if the scanner on a Klingon ship senses an object, and the officer reporting the presence of this object assumes, but is not yet sure, that the object is a vessel, he will probably refer to the object as **DujHey** *an apparent vessel,* rather than simply **Duj** *vessel.*

-na' *definite*   This is the counterpart of **-Hey**. It indicates that there is no doubt in the speaker's mind as to the accuracy of his or her choice of words. Once the Klingon officer referred to above is sure that the object the scanner has found is a vessel, he might report the presence of **Dujna'** *a definite vessel, undoubtedly a vessel.*

3.3.4. Type 4: Possession/Specification

Type 4 is the largest class of noun suffixes. It consists of all the possessive suffixes, plus suffixes which can be translated as English *this* and *that.*
   The possessive suffixes are:

-wIj *my*	**-maj** *our*
-lIj *your*	**-raj** *your (plural)*
-Daj *his, her, its*	**-chaj** *their*

   Thus, **juH** *home* occurs in **juHwIj** *my home,* **juHlIj** *your home,* **juHchaj** *their home,* etc.
   When the noun being possessed refers to a being capable of using language, a special set of suffixes is used for first- and second-person possessors:

-wI' *my*	**-ma'** *our*
-lI' *your*	**-ra'** *your (plural)*

   These suffixes occur in, for example, **joHwI'** *my lord* and **puqlI'** *your child.* It is grammatically correct to use the regular possessive suffixes with nouns referring to beings capable of speech (as in **puqlIj** *your child*), but such constructions are considered derogatory; **joHwIj** for *my lord* borders on the taboo. Students of Klingon should bear this in mind.
   To indicate that one noun is the possessor of another noun (e.g., *enemy's weapon*), no suffix is used. Instead, the two nouns are said in the order possessor–possessed: **jagh nuH** *enemy's weapon* (literally, *enemy weapon*). This construction is also used for phrases translated by *of the* in English, such as *weapon of the enemy.* (See also section 3.4.)
   There are two suffixes indicating how close to the speaker the object referred to by the noun is.

-vam *this*   Like its English translation, this suffix indicates that the noun refers to an object which is nearby or which is the topic of the conversation.

   nuHvam *this weapon (near me as I speak)*
   yuQvam *this planet (that we've been talking about)*

When used with a plural noun (one with a plural suffix or an inherently plural noun), **-vam** is translated *these:*

nuHmeyvam *these weapons*

-vetlh *that*   This suffix indicates that the noun refers to an object which is not nearby or which is being brought up again as the topic of conversation.

nuHvetlh *that weapon (over there)*
yuQvetlh *that planet (as opposed to the one we were just talking about)*

When used with a plural noun, -vetlh is translated *those:*

nuHmeyvetlh *those weapons*

There is no Klingon equivalent for English *a, an, the.* In translating from Klingon to English, one must use context as a guide to when to use *a* or *an* and when *the*. In this book, *a* or *an* and *the* are used in translations to make the English sound more natural.

3.3.5 Type 5: Syntactic Markers

These suffixes indicate something about the function of the noun in the sentence. As in English, subjects and objects are normally indicated by the position of the noun or nouns in the sentence. The following two English sentences have the same words, but the sentences have different meanings due to the order of the words:

Dogs chase cats.
Cats chase dogs.

Subjects and objects in Klingon are likewise indicated by word order.

In other instances, English indicates the function of nouns in a sentence by adding words, particularly prepositions. In the following English sentence, the word *around* before *canaries* indicates that the canaries are neither chasing nor being chased:

Dogs chase cats around canaries.

Similarly, in Klingon, nouns which indicate something other than subject or object usually must have some special indication of exactly what their function is. Unlike English, this is accomplished by using suffixes.

-Daq *locative*   This suffix indicates that something is happening (or has happened or will happen) in the vicinity of the noun to which it is attached. It is normally translated by an English preposition: *to, in, at, on.* The exact translation is determined by the meaning of the whole sentence.

For example, **pa'Daq** is **pa'** *room* plus the suffix **-Daq**. It may occur in sentences such as the following:

> **pa'Daq jIHtaH** *I'm in the room.*
> **pa'Daq yIjaH** *Go to the room!*

In the first sentence, **jIH** *I* is used in the sense of *I am*, so *in* is the most reasonable translation of **-Daq**. In the second sentence, the verb is **jaH** *go*, so *to* makes the most sense as a translation of **-Daq**. An English preposition need not be part of the translation. Klingon **Dung** means *area above,* and **DungDaq** is *overhead,* literally something like "at the area above." For further discussion on prepositional concepts, see section 3.4.

It is worth noting at this point that the concepts expressed by the English adverbs *here, there,* and *everywhere* are expressed by nouns in Klingon: **naDev** *hereabouts,* **pa'** *thereabouts,* **Dat** *everywhere.* These words may perhaps be translated more literally as "area around here," "area over there," and "all places," respectively. Unlike other nouns, these three words are never followed by the locative suffix. (Note that **pa'** *thereabouts* and **pa'** *room* are identical in sound; **pa'Daq,** however, can mean only *in/to the room.*)

There are a few verbs whose meanings include locative notions, such as **ghoS** *approach, proceed.* The locative suffix need not be used on nouns which are the objects of such verbs.

> **Duj ghoStaH** *It is approaching the ship.* (**Duj** *ship, vessel,* **ghoStaH** *it is approaching it*)
> **yuQ wIghoStaH** *We are proceeding toward the planet.* (**yuQ** *planet,* **wIghoStaH** *we are proceeding toward it*)

If the locative suffix is used with such verbs, the resulting sentence is somewhat redundant, but not out-and-out wrong.

> **DujDaq ghoStaH** *It is approaching toward the ship.*

-vo' *from*   This suffix is similar to **-Daq** but is used only when action is in a direction away from the noun suffixed with **-vo'.**

> **pa'vo' yIjaH** *Leave the room!*

A more literal translation of this sentence might be "Go from the room."

-mo' *due to, because of*   This suffix occurs in sentences such as:

> **SuSmo' joqtaH** *It is fluttering in the breeze.*

The noun **SuSmo'** means *due to the breeze,* so the whole sentence is literally "due to the breeze, it [a flag] is fluttering."

-vaD *for, intended for*   This suffix indicates that the noun to which it is attached is in some way the beneficiary of the action, the person or thing for whom or for which the activity occurs.

> **Qu'vaD lI' De'vam** *This information is useful for the mission.*

The noun **Qu'vaD** means *for the mission,* and in this sentence -vaD indicates that the information is intended to be used somehow for the mission under discussion.

-'e' *topic*   This suffix emphasizes that the noun to which it is attached is the topic of the sentence. In English, this is frequently accomplished by stressing the noun (saying it emphatically) or by special syntactic constructions.

> **lujpu' jIH'e'** *I, and only I, have failed.*
> *It is I who has failed.*
> **De"e' vItlhapnISpu'** *I needed to get the INFORMATION. It was the information (and not something else) that I needed.*

Without the 'e', these same sentences would have no noun singled out for emphasis:

> **lujpu' jIH** *I have failed.*
> **De' vItlhapnISpu'** *I needed to get the information.*

3.3.6. Relative Ordering of the Suffixes

As briefly illustrated in the discussion of -vam *this* and -vetlh *that* (section 3.3.4), when a noun is followed by more than one suffix, the suffixes must occur in the proper order, according to the classification just described. It is rare for a noun to be followed by five suffixes, but it does happen from time to time. Some examples of nouns with two or more suffixes follow. (Suffix types are indicated by numbers.)

QaghHommeyHeylIjmo'		*due to your apparent minor errors*
Qagh	(noun)	*error*
-Hom	(1)	*diminutive*
-mey	(2)	*plural*
-Hey	(3)	*apparent*
-lIj	(4)	*your*
-mo'	(5)	*due to*

pa'wIjDaq		*in my quarters*
pa'	(noun)	*room*
-wIj	(4)	*my*
-Daq	(5)	*locative*

Duypu'qoqchaj		*their so-called emissaries*
Duy	(noun)	*emissary*
-pu'	(2)	*plural*
-qoq	(3)	*so-called*
-chaj	(4)	*their*

qamDu'wIjDaq		*at my feet*
qam	(noun)	*foot*
-Du'	(2)	*plural*
-wIj	(4)	*my*
-Daq	(5)	*locative*

rojHom'e'		*the truce* (as topic)
roj	(noun)	*peace*
-Hom	(1)	*diminutive*
-'e'	(5)	*topic*

All examples of suffixes given so far show only simple nouns. Suffixes are attached to complex nouns (section 3.2) in exactly the same fashion.

DIvI'may'DujmeyDaq		*at/to the Federation battle cruisers*
DIvI'may'Duj	(noun)	*Federation battle cruiser*
-mey	(2)	*plural*
-Daq	(5)	*locative*

baHwI'pu'vam		*these gunners*
baHwI'	(noun)	*gunner*
-pu'	(2)	*plural*
-vam	(4)	*this*

3.4. The Noun–Noun Construction

Some combinations of two (or more) nouns in a row are so common as to have become everyday words. These are the compound nouns (as discussed in section 3.2.1). In addition, it is possible to combine nouns in the manner of a compound noun to produce a new construct even if it is not a legitimate compound noun ("legitimate" in the sense that it would be found in a dictionary).

The translation of two nouns combined in this way, say N1–N2 (that is, noun #1 followed by noun #2), would be *N2 of the N1.* For example,

nuH *weapon* and **pegh** *secret* combine to form **nuH pegh** *secret of the weapon.* An alternate translation would be *N1's N2,* in this case, *the weapon's secret.* As discussed in section 3.3.4, this is the Klingon possessive construction for a noun possessed by another noun.

When the noun–noun construction is used, only the second noun can take syntactic suffixes (Type 5). Both nouns, however, may take suffixes of the other four types. For example:

nuHvam pegh		*secret of this weapon*
nuH	(noun)	*weapon*
-vam	(4)	*this*
pegh	(noun)	*secret*

jaghpu' yuQmeyDaq		*at/to the enemies' planets*
jagh	(noun)	*enemy*
-pu'	(2)	*plural*
yuQ	(noun)	*planet*
-mey	(2)	*plural*
-Daq	(5)	*locative*

puqwI' qamDu'		*my child's feet*
puq	(noun)	*child*
-wI'	(4)	*my*
qam	(noun)	*foot*
-Du	(2)	*plural*

English prepositional phrases are also rendered in Klingon by this noun–noun construction. Prepositional concepts such as *above* and *below* are actually nouns in Klingon, best translated as "area above," "area below," etc. The locative suffix (section 3.3.5) follows the second noun. For example:

nagh DungDaq		*above the rock*
nagh	(noun)	*rock*
Dung	(noun)	*area above*
-Daq	(5)	*locative*

More literally, this is "at the area above the rock" or "at the rock's above-area."

Content Questions

1. Klingon has an equivalent suffix to the English agentive *-er* suffix (as with the word *writer*). Provide the Klingon suffix form and an example of a word containing that suffix.

2. How many suffix types may be used at the end of a Klingon word? List the main types.

3. What role do the augmentative and diminutive suffixes serve in Klingon?

4. Which suffix type seems to indicate something about the speaker's attitude?

5. What is the locative suffix and when is it used? Which verbs would make the use of the locative suffix redundant?

Questions for Analysis and Discussion

1. Okrand's discussion of complex nouns using the morphemes '*ej, Do*', and *yo*' (as in '*ejDo*' and '*ejyo*') indicates that these morphemes no longer appear independently, so their individual meaning is unavailable "without extensive etymological research." Does this morphological phenomenon in Klingon (a single word with an etymological history as a compound noun) have any parallel in English? Explain. (You might look at the history of a word such as *lord*.)

2. The Klingon language rules seem to have exceptions or unnecessary complexities from the standpoint of creating a language that would be easy for outsiders to learn. What reason might Okrand have had for building such features into the language rather than inventing a clearly ordered language that is more characteristic of other artificial languages?

3. The article indicates that Klingon poets do not always follow one of the grammatical rules for the plural in Klingon. How does this practice by Klingon poets compare with the linguistic behavior of poets on earth? Are you familiar with the work of any poets who violate grammatical rules in their poetry? Explain.

4. Elsewhere in *The Klingon Dictionary*, we can see that the Klingon word for *hand* is *ghop*. Provide the linguistic form that should be created to say "her small hands." Remember the obligatory ordering of suffixes.

5. The Klingon word for *father* is *vav*. Why would the possessive form *vavlIj* (your father) be insulting?

6. Klingon has a particular order for suffix forms as they are added to a word. Does English follow any particular order in the suffixes that it adds? Explain.

7. *The Klingon Dictionary* identifies *Human* as the Klingon word for *human*. Assuming for a moment that Klingon is a natural language and that its use of *Human* is not a coincidence, how would you account for the fact that the Klingons use such a word in their language?

8. Marc Okrand, the creator of Klingon, is a linguist. How might people with no linguistic training have been limited in their ability to create a language that differs widely from their own?

9. The Klingon language has been studied at universities such as MIT. What value could there be in studying an artificial language such as Klingon?

A Place for Phonetics in High Technology

Melvin J. Luthy

Virtually every introductory linguistics textbook introduces its students to phonetics and phonology, including some exposure to phonetic transcription and concepts associated with phonemes and allophones. To some students it may not be apparent how such information could be of any use in the "real" world. But in the article below, Melvin J. Luthy of Brigham Young University shows how such information can be important beyond the classroom. Luthy illustrates how he applied a knowledge of phonetic transcription and the sound system of English to the development of software for a couple of different high-technology business ventures.

Articulatory phonetics is one of the oldest and probably best known of the linguistic subdisciplines. Even nonlinguists in many countries know of Henry Higgins' phonetic magic in making Eliza Doolittle, George Bernard Shaw's fictitious cockney flower girl, speak like a duchess. Students of the English language know of Jacob Grimm's contributions to our understanding of the systematic phonetic differences between Germanic and other Indo-European languages. More recently, many linguistic students remember Professor Harold Whitehall discussing how he had worked with Scotland Yard to identify the London origins of suspected criminals, by studying their pronunciations. Indeed, the British have long had a fondness for phonetics and have contributed much, including the establishment of the International Phonetic Association, from which we have the International Phonetic Alphabet (IPA). Although Americans and others have introduced their own variations, the IPA remains a standard, and many linguists lobby for its exclusive adoption worldwide to minimize confusion. Time will tell whether American linguists will be willing to give up some of their phonetic habits that they find convenient for transcribing English. Regardless of the outcome of this initiative, the discipline of phonetics will continue to affect many lives.

In addition to the investigative and acting applications already mentioned, other uses for phonetics include work in speech therapy, vocal music training, foreign accent reduction, and linguistic field work. Each of these endeavors requires a thorough knowledge of articulation and phonetic transcription. Those who use phonetics professionally to help others effect a difference in speech follow the Henry Higgins tradition of careful

209

analysis, prescription and practice. Others, such as dialectologists, use their phonetic expertise to study systematic differences in pronunciation, which allow them to identify dialect differences and their subtle changes. Anthropological linguists use phonetic transcription as the first step in recording the languages of preliterate peoples so they can analyze the languages in more detail. Without a fundamental understanding of articulation and how to record it, we would be unable to progress in these important areas of study.

Sometimes we find applications for phonetics where we least expect them. Such was the case when a young man named Robert Stevens appeared at my office for advice. He was a computer programmer for WordPerfect Corporation and wanted to make a rhyming dictionary that would be a word processing add-on feature. He knew how to write the computer program, but was not sure how to construct the data base on which the program would work. His first impulse was to consult the dictionary makers to see if he could retrieve the pronunciation information for each word from their computer tapes. Some were willing to share the information, but at a cost that was prohibitive. I assured him that the form in which the pronunciations were represented in dictionaries was not what he wanted, and that he would be better advised by constructing his own customized broad phonetic data base with syllables marked according to phonetic criteria rather than spelling conventions. He asked if I could help him do such a thing. I agreed to help, and a kind of partnership was born.

His original idea was to produce a dictionary of words that rhymed on specific syllables, but it soon became clear that with the power of the computer in our hands we could and should do more than produce a way for finding rhymes. It could be a tool for finding words that shared any set of sounds in any particular sequence or pattern. Surely, we reasoned, linguists, teachers, advertisement writers, song writers, game players—anyone with a need to come up with words with specific sounds would welcome such a tool. After we had developed a prototype of the program, we presented it to the owners of WordPerfect Corporation to see if they were interested in paying us to complete the project and include it in their line of software. We found them to be receptive to innovations, and they quickly agreed to finance the development. In retrospect I realize they had little to lose. It was a product that would cost very little to develop and could help give them the image of a company committed to meeting a wide variety of word processing needs.

The development process was really quite simple. Robert had helped develop the WordPerfect thesaurus and spell checker, so he was thoroughly acquainted with the code that had been used. He wrote a program that placed all the spell checker words in a scrolling list on the left side of my computer monitor screen. My job was to provide a phonetic representation for each word that I chose to be in the dictionary. His job was to write the program that would retrieve words that shared specific phonetic properties that the user would define. Since the program was intended to recognize entire rhyming syllables, as well as sequences of individual sounds, syllables needed to be identified, each phoneme had to be represented, and each syllable nucleus had to be represented as a single unit (speakers identify syllables by the presence of a nucleus that carries significant acoustic energy). Our initial goal was to produce a dictionary of 50,000 words. We ended up with over 93,000.

The transcription system we used was a modified version of the international phonetic alphabet, as below:

SYMBOL	SOUND	SYMBOL	SOUND	SYMBOL	SOUND
p	pan	č	cheer	o	boat
b	ban	ǰ	jeer	ɔ	caught
t	tan	m	man	a	cot
d	dan	n	man	ɚ	curt
k	can	ŋ	sing	ai	tie
g	gain	l	let	aiɚ	tire
f	fine	r	red	au	cow
v	vine	w	wash	auɚ	our
θ	thigh	j	yes	aɚ	car
ð	thy	i	beet	ɔɚ	wore
s	sip	ɪ	bit	ɔi	toy
z	zip	e	bait	ʊɚ	sure
š	ship	E	bet	ɪɚ	fear
ž	azure	æ	bat	Eɚ	bear
h	home	ə	butt	æɚ	clarity
		u	boot		
		ʊ	foot		

In the transcription, syllables were marked with hyphens, which seems simple enough, but often the words spelled the same way needed to appear with different syllable boundaries, depending on where the stress was placed. For example, the word *suspect* may be either a noun, an adjective, or a verb. If it is a noun or an adjective, the primary stress will fall on the first syllable, producing the pronunciation [sə́s-pEkt], but if it is a verb, the primary stress will fall on the second syllable, producing the pronunciation [sə-spEkt]. Even though in some words the syllable boundary does not change with a change of stress, the vowels change, as in the word spelled *subject,* which is either [sə́b-ǰɪkt] (noun) or [səb-ǰEkt] (verb). Even when the primary stress does not change with the shift of grammatical category, and the syllable boundary does not change, a different vowel often communicates the difference. Such is the case with a word like *syndicate*. If *syndicate* is a noun, the pronunciation is [sɪn-dɪ-kət], but if it is a verb, the pronunciation is [sɪn-də-ket]. Even though the meaning of a word may not change it may have slightly different pronunciations that determine where the syllable boundaries fall. For example, one may pronounce *stumbling* either [stəm-blɪŋ] or [stəm-bə-lɪŋ]. All such differences needed to be considered in building a data base so that variant pronunciations would be available to the user. Finally, the data base took on the following look:

WORD	PRONUNCIATIONS
stumbling	stəm-bə-lɪŋ, stəm-blɪŋ
syndicate	sɪn-də-ket, sɪn-dɪ-kət
subject	səb-jɛkt, səb-jɪkt
standby	stæn-bai, stænd-bai
strictly	strɪkt-li, strɪk-li
stance	stæns, stænts
etc.	

In addition to coping with different pronunciations of words spelled the same, there was a need to accommodate divergent pronunciations from different dialect areas. For example, in some parts of the United States, the distinction between the vowels [ɔ] and [a] does not exist. Thus, the words *caught* and *cot* are pronounced the same, and words like *taught* and *ought* rhyme with *hot* rather than a more Eastern pronunciation of *caught*. Such dialect differences also needed to be included within reason; however, British English pronunciations that differ from American English were not included in this first version.

As I developed the data base, Robert was busy preparing the computer interface that gave the user the option of finding words that had similar rhymes in particular syllables, or finding words that had the same phonetic sequences that users could define by entering the phonetic symbols from the chart on the computer monitor. This feature, which we called the "phonetic finder," proved to be a very useful option for teachers and researchers. For example, a teacher in our English Language Center was concerned that Spanish-speaking students learning English had difficulty pronouncing two syllables at the end of words ending in the sound [i] plus the sound [ɪŋ]. Thus, they tended to pronounce a word like *studying* as *studding*. She needed words that ended in these sounds, so she could incorporate them into conversation exercises, but she could only think of a few. By using the phonetic finder she found 126 words in a matter of seconds, words such as *accompanying, agreeing, copying, babying, emptying, freeing, envying, foreseeing, lobbying, skiing,* and *worrying.*

Another teacher wanted to help students understand when the initial *th* sound was voiced as in *then* or voiceless as in *thin*. Using the phonetic finder to retrieve words that began with these sounds, she found the following interesting data:

Sample words beginning with a voiced *th* sound [ð]:

the, then, there, that, these, this, thus, they, thou

Sample words beginning with a voiceless *th* sound [θ]:

thank, thaw, theater, theme, theft, theory, thumb, thrill, throwaway, thespian, thunder, thistle, thorough, through

A cursory glance at the data reveals that the initial [ð] sound occurs with only a small group of pronouns, adverbs and function words, but the [θ] sound occurs with a large number of other words. What otherwise would have taken many hours of analysis was accomplished in a matter of seconds.

As other students and teachers became aware of the data retrieval capabilities of the phonetic word finder, several of them began using it to retrieve words for their own studies. One professor who does research in second language vocabulary acquisition was interested in studying how various sound combinations in words affected the ease with which non-native speakers could learn English vocabulary. She found that certain sounds definitely made a difference, depending on what the learner's native language was. Another was interested in studying phonetic patterns for teaching phonics to younger learners. That project is still underway. Another was studying how our alphabetical symbols correspond to the sounds of words. When asked how the vowel in *blue* is represented in English spelling at the ends of words, she found 20 different spellings, including the following: *bamboo, through, coup, debut, shoe, view, hugh, milieu, mantoux, muumuu, queue, ragout, rendezvous,* and *two.* It is little wonder that English spelling and pronunciation are problematic. Another student writing humorous poetry wanted to find two-syllable words that contained repetitive p̲ sounds. He found 221 words, including *bagpipe, flip-flop, pamper, papa, papoose, perplex, pinprick, playpen,* and *purple.* Anyone who has tried to "think up" such data has learned that it is very difficult, indeed. Our minds are very inefficient in retrieving data in this manner.

It became clear that the data base we had constructed had other applications, as well. Attempting to look into the future and take advantage of new developments such as e-mail and speech synthesis, we agreed with WordPerfect Corporation to refine the data base so it could be used for speech synthesis. The idea was to produce a program that would allow an e-mail user to call his e-mail by telephone from any location, and have the program read the user's e-mail messages with a synthesized voice. Another company called Firstbyte had developed an "engine" that could read printed English, and produce synthetic speech according to general pronunciation rules based on spelling; however, one of the major problems was that not all written English fits into general pronunciation rules, so the program mispronounced many of the English words. We felt that if we could produce an "exceptions dictionary" of correct pronunciations for the program to query before following its own logic, most of the mispronunciations could be eliminated. So, it was back to the phonetic drawing board.

We took our data base and recoded it to match the Firstbyte transcription system. For example *č* was replaced by *tSH,* ɪ by *IH,* a by *AA,* etc. It was not a simple one-for-one matching, because in this task it became necessary to make distinctions that native English speakers are seldom aware of. For example, native speakers are unaware that they add a puff of air (aspiration) when they pronounce either *p, t,* or *k,* as the first sound of a word as in *pan, tan,* and *can.* This aspiration is lacking when an *s* precedes the sound as in *span, Stan,* or *scan.* These variations are natural, so we pay little or no attention to them; we are accustomed to thinking that every occurrence of *p, t,* or *k* sounds the same, but it doesn't. Each variation is called an *allophone,* and all of the allophones considered as a class make up what is called a *phoneme.* Such phonetic differences occur with almost all sounds, depending on what other sounds surround them or what position they occupy in a word.

In synthesizing speech it was important to discriminate between allophones, rather than simply transcribe the broad phonemic symbols. In addition to the difference in aspiration that affects the initial *t* consonant, a *t* occurring in words such as *button, sentence,* or *mutton* needed still another symbol that would be synthesized as a sound like a glottal stop, a closing of the vocal bands, that generally substitutes for a *t* in such words in American English. A *t* in words like *butter* or *fatter* required still another symbol that would sound more like a flap of the tip of the tongue on the alveolar ridge. In short, the data base needed to be refined to show narrow allophonic variations and differences in syllable stress, so the synthesized speech would sound as natural as possible. After adjusting the existing transcription system, we added many words (names and expressions) that might appear in e-mail, but were not in our original data base. When Novell, the large computer networking corporation, merged with WordPerfect Corporation in 1994, the possibility of having our voice-synthesized e-mail on a business network came closer to reality.

We are pleased that this program is now a feature of Novell Groupwise called "Telephone Access Server (TAS)." The "Rhymer and Phonetic Finder" is available from WriteExpress Corporation.

In a time of unprecedented technological opportunities, we can expect more phonetic innovations to aid communication and other language-related activities. The Rhymer and the Phonetic Finder are just the beginning of what can be done. Phonetics will continue to have a place in technology as work continues in speech recognition and voice synthesis. All such innovations will augment our current capabilities to check spelling and grammar and consult a thesaurus as we compose. But already the information age has benefitted from the rich tradition of phonetics.

Content Questions

1. In his introduction, what uses of phonetics does Luthy identify?

2. What product did Luthy and Stevens initially prepare for WordPerfect Corporation?

3. What kinds of variables among speakers did Luthy take into account as he prepared his phonetic transcriptions?

4. What are some of the useful applications of the "phonetic finder"?

5. Why was it so important in the e-mail project to transcribe phonetically, taking into account allophones and not just phonemes?

Questions for Analysis and Discussion

1. Why would it be necessary to transcribe words according to their sound rather than their spelling in order for a computer to be able to recognize rhymes? Provide one example in which two words spelled very differently would still rhyme.

2. Luthy provides a couple of examples showing how syllable stress changes between the noun and verb meanings in words such as *suspect* and *subject*. Provide a couple of other examples of words that behave the same way.

3. Other than the allophones of the phonemes /p/ and /t/, which the author mentioned, provide another example of a phoneme that would have different allophonic forms. Provide both the phoneme and at least two allophonic forms along with words that would contain these allophones.

4. What other applications can you imagine might benefit from an informed use of phonetic transcription?

5. Prior to the course, what did you think a phonologist's activities were limited to? What might you now tell someone about the possible applications of phonology?

Dimensions of Usage and Dictionary Labeling

William Card, Raven I. McDavid, Jr., and Virginia McDavid

Knowing the vocabulary of a language involves much more than knowing a set of definitions. Native speakers with a sensitivity to the language also become familiar with a variety of usage considerations connected with each word. The following article by William Card, a scholar in the structure of English, and the McDavids, well known for their work in dialect studies, explains and outlines nine dimensions of usage that are relevant to dictionary labeling. This article was written a number of years ago and was more recently published in the *Journal of English Linguistics*. The issues it outlines are nonetheless relevant today, whether they are considered in relation to mainline dictionaries or for more specialized usage dictionaries.

The practice of labeling words or senses in English dictionaries is far from a new one. Among seventeenth-century dictionaries Edward Phillips in the various editions of the *New World of Words* used symbols like a dagger or a check to indicate words whose use he thought should be restricted in some way. Those which he marked included hybrid words, hard words—unassimilated Latin terms—and terms of art—what we would call technical terms.

In his revision of Phillips and in his own dictionary John Kersey also used symbols. He marked an almost entirely new set of words, but again included hard words as well as obsolete words and technical terms. Kersey also condemned low words—what we might call popular terms, including cant, argot, and sometimes dialect terms.

Nathaniel Bailey in his dictionaries marked words also; his groups again fall into hard words, obsolete terms, and low words—cant and dialect. The same categories are found among the words Benjamin Martin marked in his dictionary of 1749. N. E. Osselton in *Branded Words in English Dictionaries Before Johnson* (1958) concludes that before Johnson the corpus of "branded words" was about two thousand.

In his *Plan of an English Dictionary* of 1747, Samuel Johnson announced his intention of marking several classes of words by symbols, including poetic words, obsolete words, "words used in burlesque and familiar compositions," and "barbarous or impure words and expressions" so that these might be "carefully eradicated wherever they are found."

In the *Dictionary* itself Johnson includes frequent subjective, prescriptive labels: "a barbarous contraction," "a colloquial abuse of the word," "this sense is somewhat low," "an unauthorized word," "a word out of use and unworthy of revival," "a word introduced unnecessarily from the French by a Scottish author," "a word that has crept into conversation and low writing but ought not to be admitted into the language," and "a low barbarous cant word." He calls *abhominable* "low and ludicrious." *Bamboozle* is "cant." *To banter* is "barbarous." *To color* 'to blush' is "low," and so, too, is *to cuddle.*

One of the ways in which Noah Webster tried to change traditional English spellings was by the use of restrictive labels. Among his restrictions that failed are *epitome* "better written Epit'omy," and *fashion* "more correctly Fash'on."

The *Oxford English Dictionary* also uses labels, much more extensively than earlier dictionaries. Among them are "dialectal," "popularly," "in ecclesiastical usage," and "in commercial usage." The 1972 and later *Supplements* continue the practice, as do most modern American dictionaries.

Labels, of course, are not the only way in which a dictionary indicates restrictions upon usage. Sometimes restrictions appear in the synonymies, sometimes through cross-references. The *American Heritage Dictionary* (1969) has some five hundred usage notes of varying lengths, of which about two hundred and thirty present in percentage form the results of voting by a usage panel. A thorough analysis of these usage notes and of the treatment of usage in general in dictionaries appears in Creswell 1975. The *Random House College Dictionary* (1972) has some two hundred and fifty usage notes but often gives usage information in synonymies.

A dictionary may also exercise a restrictive function by the omission of a word or sense. Terms considered vulgar have commonly been left out. *Webster's New World Dictionary* (1970) omitted these and ones thought to be racially or ethnically offensive, like *wop* and *bohunk.* The *American Heritage Dictionary* omits a definition of *infer* in the sense "imply" but has a nine-line usage note distinguishing the two.

Usage varies not only for words and meanings, for grammatical forms and constructions, and for pronunciations, but for other aspects of communication as well—for such prosodic features as intonation, stress, and juncture, for the various vocal modulations known as para-language (over-loudness and over-softness, over-high and over-low pitch, drawl, nasality, etc.), and for the gestures and spatial relationships between speakers. But some of these aspects of human communication have been studied only in the last few decades. Agreement is slowly emerging on how these phenomena should be described, and there is only fragmentary evidence of what past usage may have been.

The most significant development in the study of usage in the past few decades has been the increasing awareness that usage varies in many dimensions, and not simply between "good" and "bad" or along a single scale of excellence (see bibliography). The status of any linguistic form— word or meaning, grammatical structure, or pronunciation—involves a number of dimensions. The label employed in a dictionary normally indicates the place the particular item has in the dimension with which the person interested in this item is most frequently concerned. Thus *ain't* is generally labeled "nonstandard" or "substandard." However, it may be used jocosely, for effect, as in *Ain't it the truth* or *You ain't kidding*. Furthermore, in some communities, especially in the South, it is used freely in the informal conversation of cultivated speakers with those whom they consider their social equals—but never by them in a formal situation or in ordinary writing.

The number of dimensions in which usage varies is not agreed upon. But it is safe to say that the number is larger than that which might have satisfied observers a generation ago. Nine such dimensions and the associated labels will be considered here: 1) history, 2) maturity, 3) association, 4) relationship to reader or hearer, 5) medium, 6) attitude, 7) territory, 8) social position, and 9) responsibility. This classification and the labels associated with it have been developed by the authors over many years and draws upon their work as consultants on usage levels and dialect distribution for the editors of *Random House Dictionary of the English Language,* unabridged edition (1966). No one has mastered for all the language the full range of these dimensions. It is the part of sophistication to recognize an increasing number of nuances on a larger number of scales, just as the skilled musician comes to recognize the potentialities of a larger number of instruments in the orchestra.

1. *History.* The historical dimension is related to the development of the language. Some forms and senses are not used at all today or not widely used by educated people. The traditional labels for such words are **obsolete** and **archaic**. To these might be added **old-fashioned**.

A form may be labeled obsolete if there is no evidence of its use after a certain date. For *Webster's Third New International Dictionary* the cut-off date is 1755, that of the appearance of Johnson's *Dictionary*. In *Webster's New International Dictionary, Second Edition* (1934) "all literary or colloquial words and all meanings that have not appeared in print since 1660" are considered obsolete. For the *Random House Dictionary* the criterion is that the form be out of use for at least a century. Such senses as *hint* 'occasion' and *act* 'motivate' would thus be labeled obsolete.

A form is archaic if there is little evidence for its use more recently than an arbitrary date or if the instances of its use are normally in a context which shows that the speaker or writer is trying to create an effect of a bygone age. For *Webster's Third* archaic means "standard after 1755 but surviving in the present only sporadically or in special context." For the *Random House Dictionary* archaic means "current of an earlier time but rare in present-day usage." Among forms which would be labeled archaic are *forsooth, acre* 'plot,' and *know* 'to have sexual relations with.'

A term might be labeled old-fashioned if it is commonly used—too widely used to be attributed to a given region—but by those who are older, less educated, and less sophisticated members of the community. Examples are *nigh, yon, betwixt,* the pronunciation /dif/ for *deaf,* and a multiple negative like *There ain't nobody never makes no pound cake no more.* Further examples of old-fashioned forms are *abide* 'to put up with,' *powerful* 'very,' *almighty* 'very,' and *sight* 'a lot,' as in *He's seen a sight of trouble.*

In some dictionaries forms like these are labeled "dial." for dialectal. But such a label is misleading. If the word is restricted geographically, it should be possible to state these restrictions. If it is not so restricted but is fairly widely used among the older and less-sophisticated users of the language, a label like old-fashioned is more accurate.

Two cautions are necessary about historical labels. It is possible that a word or meaning may be in wide and reputable use at a later date than that for which lexicographers have evidence. A well-known case is that of *disinterested* in the sense of 'apathetic' or 'uninterested'—the oldest meaning attested for it in English. Because the readers for the *OED* found no citation later than 1797 for this sense, the editors of Volume III labeled it "? Obs." However, when the 1930 *Supplement* appeared, the editors had found several examples of this sense as late as 1928 and consequently deleted the label. Though the distinction between *disinterested* 'unbiased' and *uninterested* 'apathetic' may be a useful one and dear to the hearts of purists, it is a fact that the older sense of *disinterested* has never died out in English and that the word is susceptible of misinterpretation unless there is a full context.

The second caution is that obsolescence of a word or meaning should not be confused with obsolescence of the cultural setting within which it was used. Chattel slavery is extinct within the United States, but terms such as *quarters* 'slave residences' or *driver* 'male slave charged with organizing labor on a plantation' must still be used to describe plantation life before emancipation. Similarly many terms from medieval warfare would not be labeled obsolete though the technology of warfare has changed.

It is also true that forms which are dated may be used occasionally for rhetorical effect. A notable example is President Kennedy's "Ask not what your country can do for you." Present-day practice would normally require "Do not ask . . . ," but the older form—echoing the practice of the King James Bible—impressed the audience as being more reverential and in keeping with the dignity of the occasion.

2. *Maturity.* The scale of maturity, involving the life of the individual, is analogous to that of history, involving the life of the speech community. Here there is a further analogue to the public expectations of behavior and dress. Such forms as *doggie, dollie, pee-pee,* and *yummy* may

fit the speech of small children but are out of place among teenagers, let alone adults. Such forms may be labeled **juvenile,** meaning used by children or in talking to children about topics of interest to them.

It is this scale of maturity that makes baby talk by elderly aunts and grandparents distasteful to parents, or attempts by middle-aged professors to repeat the latest slang a cause of amusement among their students. Conversely, a high-school freshman who talks too seriously about the latest diplomatic crisis or too technically about the most recent discoveries in nuclear physics is often pitied by strangers as missing the alleged joys of childhood. Here practice varies both geographically and socially. English middle-class and upper-class children are expected to speak and dress more formally than Americans of the same age.

3. *Association.* Another dimension, or group of dimensions, is that of association. It may involve the **technical** language of a vocation or avocation and so have such field labels as "astronomy" or "biology." It may be **argot.** It may involve a passing vogue and be **slang.** All associational varieties of language, however, are looked upon as outside the main stream and are usually subject to fairly rapid change.

Between technical vocabulary and argot there is really very little difference except perhaps in one's attitude towards the activity. An English professor might accept the specialized terminology of T. S. Eliot's criticism, like *objective correlative,* as essential to his critical approach; waver at *existentialism* as a philosophical term; sneer at *upwardly mobile* as used by sociologists; and be completely mystified by the noun *send* 'to send a prospective victim home for more money' as employed by high-grade confidence men. In essence, however, each term is used as part of a way of life which a speaker has deliberately entered. In each of these subcultures, the use of specialized terminology sets off the initiate from the outsider.

Technical terminology has grown very rapidly in the past century as new specialized occupations have developed or older occupations have become more specialized and technical. Sometimes this new knowledge and new specialization have led to an entirely new vocabulary; x-ray therapy and antibiotics have created special vocabularies for medicine and pharmacy. *Roentgen,* as a unit of radiation, and *Aureomycin,* the registered trademark for a type of antibiotic, are relatively new.

Most of the new words in *6,000 Words: A Supplement to Webster's Third New International Dictionary* (1976) are from science and technology. We have *quasars* and *pulsars,* the *genetic code,* FORTRAN and COBOL, and ABMs and MIRVs.

In addition to such new terms, older ones have acquired special meanings: *transformation* in grammar, *fission* and *fusion* in nuclear physics (*fusion* also has a special meaning in politics). Any of these terms may spread into common use by way of metaphor; which ones will be so generally used that their technical origin will be forgotten (like *leeway* from sailing ships and *aftermath* from farming) will be left to history. In any event, the label of the field, whether "linguistics," "biophysics," or "astronomy," to give three random examples, indicates a technical term or meaning.

Though the line between technical terminology and argot is a thin one, it nevertheless can be drawn. The technical terminology of endocrinology, for example, can be picked up from reading textbooks and professional journals. The day-to-day argot of doctors and nurses, like that of forgers and counterfeiters, is picked up only by association. It has been said by some observers, notably David Maurer, that a narcotics addict may not have mastered the argot, but that it is impossible to master the argot without becoming addicted. Contrary to myth, argot is rarely used for concealment (pickpockets, who often work in crowds, are exceptional), but more as a badge of identification, to indicate—using a term from show business—that one is *with it*. A word or meaning, of course, may migrate from one argot into another, or from argot into slang, or even into standard usage. Many narcotics terms have been picked up by jazz musicians (some of whom are addicts), and thence by teenage or college fans. Terms originating in the bordellos of New Orleans may be used offhand by girls who have no inkling of their obscene significance.

Slang, the other kind of associational language, is a matter of vogue as well as interest. It is often transitory. What was *square* may become *straight*. Some years back a general adjective of approval was *hot*; more recently it was *cool*, still more recently *tough, boss, mean*, and *evil*. Among the terms labeled slang in *6,000 Words* are *key* 'kilogram, especially of marijuana or heroin,' *Mary Jane* 'marijuana,' *mule* 'an individual who smuggles or delivers illicit drugs,' *rainbow* 'a drug in a tablet or capsule of several colors,' *red devil* 'secobarbital or its sodium derivative in a red capsule,' and *scag* 'heroin'—all reflecting concern with drugs.

So transient is most slang that some observers have questioned whether this is an appropriate usage label in a dictionary: by the time slang is caught in the lexicographer's net, the term or sense is usually either dated or adopted into standard use. But there are exceptions: *booze* and *bones* 'dice' have lasted for centuries without losing their status as slang.

A further category is that of old-fashioned slang. To this would belong *geek* 'person,' *jack* 'money,' *sashay, sheik* 'a romantically attractive man,' and *skidoo.*

4. *Relationship to reader or hearer.* The relationship to the reader or hearer is one of the more troublesome scales to label, perhaps because it is such a natural kind of variation. At one end of the scale comes the conversation of two close friends who can suggest a thousand details in the intonation of a syllable; at the other, the highly compressed and richly meaningful statement of a great artist. Between these are several shades of formality, depending on the subject matter, the number of people participating, and the degree to which the participants know each other. Martin

Joos in *The Five Clocks* (1962) terms these relationships intimate, casual, consultative, formal, and frozen.

In general, the more formal varieties are found in written exposition, the more informal in everyday speech, but there are casual essays and there are formal court pleadings or parliamentary debates. At an earlier period, when the norm of written discourse was more formal than it is now, the label "colloquial" was applied to the more casual speech forms, such as the contractions *it's, don't,* and *wouldn't.* This label did not mean that forms so labeled were inferior to those unlabeled; it merely described situations in which they were considered appropriate. However, "colloquial" was misunderstood in two ways: on the one hand, any label was considered derogatory by some; on the other, it was often confused with "local," even by literary scholars, and the label was thought to mean what are called "regionalisms." More appropriate, less easily misunderstood, and more common in recent dictionaries is the label **informal.** While admitting that formal and informal usage blend into each other, one may still sort out the distinction, and such forms as *breakthrough, buy* 'accept,' *cagy* 'shrewd,' and *comfy* would be considered by most as needing some label like informal. Slang is more likely in informal than in formal discourse. The deliberate use of an epithet like *doubledome* or *cheapskate* or the homely pronunciation *passel* achieves an effect by the incongruity. The accidental use is grotesque and jarring.

Also part of the relation of user to hearer or reader is the use of **jocular** terms, such as *carcass* 'body,' *splendiferous,* and *boo-boo.*

5. Medium. It has already been noted that speech and writing differ partially on the scale of formality. It is also true that certain usages are found in one medium rather than another. The awesome polysyllables of organic chemistry are rarely pronounced, even in papers read by professional chemists. And such words as *lave, bard, pacific* 'peaceful,' and *malefic* are most common in writing. Conversely, such a word as *larroes,* as in the Southern description of a mysterious package as *larroes to catch meddlers,* is almost never written. As we acquire education, we learn that some very common words are taboo in writing—including *ain't*—which is rare in the writing of even the minimally literate.

6. Attitude. A few linguistic forms are associated with definite attitudes on the part of the speaker or hearer or both. If a word is used with intent to disparage a person or thing or institution, it is **derogatory.** If it is received with resentment by the hearer or reader, it is **offensive.** *Dago* 'Italian' is both. If a term especially connotes bluntness of attitude, it is **crude, vulgar,** or **restricted.** If it suggests unwonted delicacy, it is a **euphemism.** All these labels (as, indeed, all usage labels but these more than most) indicate that reaction to the word may prevent the speaker's or writer's meaning from being accepted on its own merits.

Derogatory terms are especially common where cultural or ethnic tensions are found. The term *kike* probably originated in the speech of Jews of German derivation, as disparagement of less-acculturated Jews from Eastern Europe. Adopted by *goyim,* it is an index of anti-Semitism and is almost never used except with intent to hurt.

Offensive terms involve the reaction of the reader or hearer; a term may be used with no derogatory intent but stir up deep resentment. The pronunciation of *Negro* as /nɪgər/ is a normal phonetic development, but the associations of the word make it impossible to use without creating misunderstanding. The stigma has recently spread to the pronunciation /nɪgrə/, which educated Southerners have traditionally accepted as a polite form.

Crude or restricted or vulgar forms are especially associated with sexual and excretory functions. Here we find not only such traditionally taboo items as the classic "four-letter words," but related metaphorical terms as well. The label indicates that the terms should be avoided unless the situation is very uninhibited or the user wants to achieve the effect of shock.

If the effect of a crude term is a gasp, that of a euphemism is often a nervous giggle. Because of the Victorian taboo on the cruder sexual and excretory terms, there is a wide range of supposedly more delicate terms. *Toilet* originally was a euphemism, but it has more delicate synonyms such as *lavatory, powder room, little boys'* (or *girls'*) *room.* Euphemism also extends to occupations and institutions, as *undertakers* (originally itself a euphemism) become *morticians* or *funeral directors* and now *funeral consultants* and *bereavement counsellors.* Book salesmen become *educational advisers* and adolescent criminals are handled as *juvenile delinquents.*

It is sometimes as necessary to keep up with current euphemy as with current slang. When a euphemism is clearly identified, it takes on the coloring of the taboo term for which it is substituted, and some new term must be created. *Privy* was once an elegantly polite term; it now provokes giggles. And social workers are hard put to discover a term which will adequately describe some inhabitants of our slums without offending them. *Culturally deprived* seems elegant enough, but it soon had to be replaced by *culturally disadvantaged* and even *culturally discouraged.* And the course of study for high school students who will not continue beyond the age of compulsory attendance is sadly labeled in many cities the *basic curriculum.*

7. Territory. The language spoken over a wide area, like English, is bound to develop **territorial** variations in the use of words, meanings, grammatical forms, and pronunciations. Some of these may be very local: *caps* as a synonym for the Northern *corn husks* or the Southern *corn shucks* is confined to the Eastern Shore of Chesapeake Bay; *cripple* 'scrapple' is limited to the Savannah Valley; *chay!* as a call to summon cows from the pasture is unknown outside the Williamsburg settlement in eastern South Carolina. Other terms may be used throughout a very wide area: in English-speaking North America all trains have *conductors;* the synonym *guard* is a Briticism.

The labels for local and regional usage are as specific as the available evidence permits. Since the size of the vocabulary is perforce limited in any general-purpose dictionary, highly localized words will be few. For American usage, the labels are, wherever practical, those based upon the archives of the various autonomous regional atlases which make up the Linguistic Atlas of the United States and Canada and the publications derived from these. Among these atlases are those of New England, the Middle and South Atlantic States, the Gulf States, the North–Central States, and the Upper Midwest. Thus the term "Northern," as for *whippletree,* designates a term known principally in the area of New England settlement; "Midland," as for *bawl,* the noise made by a calf, indicates the usage of Pennsylvania and settlements west and south deriving from Pennsylvania; "Southern," as for *lightwood* 'rosin-rich pine,' refers to the area of the South in which the plantation system was dominant.

National labels are likewise as specific as the evidence warrants. *Poteen* to designate illicitly-distilled whiskey, usually derived from potatoes, is "Irish"; *station* 'ranch' is "Australian"; *veldt* is "South African."

Sometimes a territorial label must be used with one indicating association. Canadians use *homer* in baseball as Americans do to mean a home run; however, in hockey they apply it, as it is not applied in the United States, to a referee suspected of favoring the home team. *Dinkum,* as an adjective of approbation, is Australian; more specifically, it is Australian slang. The birds designated by the term *robin* in Britain, North America, and Australia suggest territorial differences in the meanings of words.

A related class of words may be labeled **eye dialect.** Among them are *vittles* 'victuals,' *likker* 'liquor,' *kinda, sorta, fer* 'for,' and *'n'* 'and.' Skilled writers of dialect like Mark Twain and Joel Chandler Harris make little use of such devices. The intention of such misspellings is that if the user of these words could mispronounce them, he would.

8. *Social position.* Within a speech community, one finds social differences as well as regional ones. Where the class structure is more rigidly defined, family descent is an important marker; where the overt class distinctions are few, formal education or social position or wealth—or a combination of the three—may give prestige. In any event, the most subtle—and consequently the most important—distinctions in a given community are best learned by living there.

Within North American English the most generally recognized social differences are to be found in grammar. As the preterit of *see, saw* is everywhere recognized as standard; *seen* as preterit is widespread but **nonstandard;** *see* and *seed* as preterits are regionally restricted and also nonstandard. And some people have all four forms—the standard one and the three nonstandard ones.

For to with a following infinitive of purpose, as in *He went there for to tell the neighbors,* is everywhere nonstandard. With certain restrictions *ain't* is usually nonstandard as a substitute for *am not, is not, are not,* and almost always nonstandard as a substitute for *have not, has not* and *do not, does not,* and *did not.* The alternative *hain't* is less widely distributed and is always nonstandard.

Pronunciations are more often regionally than socially distributed. Nevertheless, certain pronunciations are widely recognized as nonstandard, like the final /i/ instead of /ə/ or /o/ in *China* and *borrow,* or the initial /ai/ in *Italian* with a following open juncture, or stressing *theater* on the second syllable rather than on the first. With other pronunciations, such as the intrusive /r/ in *wash* and *Washington,* the social significance is less clear, though the intrusive /r/ seems to be more characteristic of rural than of urban speech.

Another class of words may be labeled **popular.** The term has been used for half a century, for example in George Philip Krapp's *The English Language in America* (1925). These words and senses are too widely used by persons of some or considerable education to be considered nonstandard, yet the use of them is not so universal that they do not need some sort of restrictive label. Among them are *spread* and *eats* meaning a meal; *outfit* for clothes; *gent* for gentleman; *complected;* and *enthuse.*

9. Responsibility. The scale of responsibility is possibly one of the most important dimensions of usage but one of the most difficult to measure. The general principle is the classical one of decorum—of conformity to the expectations that a particular situation creates. It is easy in general to describe speaking or writing as too careless or sloppy for the situation in which it is used; it is perhaps more difficult to label it too precise or finicky. And yet there is plenty of evidence that the use of excessively formal devices in a conversational situation may be as disastrous as the unwitting use of slang in a sermon. The label "literary" for such words as *bard* or *beauteous* designates a usage with an effect of elegance and one most often found in writing. Usually, however, a failure in decorum is not traceable to any single word or phrase but to the whole design of the utterance.

Two final cautions are necessary. First, usage is seldom a matter of a single dimension; many people are bidialectal in several dimensions. Because there are cultural backwaters, certain regional forms of speech, like those of the Maine coast, the Eastern Shore of Chesapeake Bay, and Eastern North Carolina, are likely to be conservative and preserve archaic forms. Some grammatical usages, such as the unmarked third person singular present of the verb (*he walk, she eat, it make*) are fairly common in all uneducated speech in the South. In such northern cities as Chicago and Detroit, they are associated with Negro speech. And in some parts of the

South such features of Midwest speech as the strongly-articulated /r/ in *born, beard,* and *barn* may be associated with uneducated poor whites.

A second caution is that since language practices keep changing, no set of usage labels will be valid for all time. What was favored yesterday, as *them boys* was preferred by Noah Webster, may be denigrated today as nonstandard. The most elaborate statements we write cannot do more than set out principles by which a reader or listener may evaluate what he hears and sees. Specific judgments are always subject to modification as practice and opinion change; users of the language need to rely on evidence and observation.

References

Dictionaries

The American College Dictionary. 1947. New York: Random House.
The American Heritage Dictionary of the English Language. 1969. New York: American Heritage Publishing Co., and Houghton-Mifflin.
Dictionary of American Slang, 2nd ed. 1975. New York: Crowell.
Funk and Wagnalls Standard College Dictionary: Text Edition. 1963. New York: Harcourt, Brace and World.
The Oxford English Dictionary. 1888–1928. Oxford: Oxford University Press.
The Random House College Dictionary. 1972. New York: Random House.
The Random House Dictionary of the English Language: Unabridged Edition. 1966. New York: Random House.
A Supplement to the Oxford English Dictionary, vols. I and II. 1972, 1976. Oxford: Oxford University Press.
Webster's New Collegiate Dictionary, 8th ed. 1973. Springfield, MA: Merriam.
Webster's New International Dictionary of the English Language: Second Edition: Unabridged. 1959. Springfield, MA: Merriam.
Webster's New World Dictionary of the American Language: Second College Edition. 1972. New York: World.
Webster's Third New International Dictionary of the English Language: Unabridged. 1961. Springfield, MA: Merriam.
6,000 Words: A Supplement to Webster's Third New International Dictionary. Springfield, MA: Merriam.

Usage Guides and Studies

Baker, Sheridan. 1966. *The Complete Stylist.* New York: Crowell.
Bernstein, Theodore M. 1958. *Watch Your Language.* Manhasset, NY: Channel Press.
———— 1965. *The Careful Writer.* New York: Atheneum.
———— 1971. *Miss Thistlebottom's Hobgoblins.* New York: Farrar, Straus, and Giroux.
———— 1977. *Dos, Don'ts and Maybes of English Usage.* New York: Times Books.

Bryant, Margaret M. 1962. *Current American Usage.* New York: Funk and Wagnalls.

Copperud, Roy H. 1960. *Words on Paper.* New York: Hawthorn Books.

———— 1964. *A Dictionary of Usage and Style.* New York: Hawthorn Books.

———— 1970. *American Usage: The Consensus.* New York: Van Nostrand.

Creswell, Thomas. 1975. *Usage in Dictionaries and Dictionaries of Usage. Publication of the American Dialect Society,* 63–64.

Crisp, Raymond M. 1971. *Changes in Attitudes Toward English Usage.* Diss., University of Illinois.

Ebbitt, Wilma R., and David R. Ebbitt. 1977. *Index to English.* 6th ed. Glenview: Scott, Foresman.

Evans, Bergen, and Cornelia Evans. 1957. *A Dictionary of Contemporary American Usage.* New York: Random House.

Flesch, Rudolph. 1964. *The ABD of Style.* New York: Harper and Row.

Follett, Wilson. 1966. *Modern American Usage: A Guide.* Edited by Jacques Barzun, with Carlos Baker, Frederick W. Dupee, Dudley Fitts, James D. Hart, Phyllis McGinely, and Lionel Trilling. New York: Hill and Wang.

Fowler, Henry W. 1957. *A Dictionary of Modern English Usage.* London: Oxford University Press.

———— 1965. *A Dictionary of Modern English Usage.* 2nd ed., rev. by Sir Ernest Gowers. London: Oxford University Press.

Fries, Charles Carpenter. 1940. *American English Grammar.* New York: Appleton-Century-Crofts.

Hall, J. Lesslie. 1917. *English Usage: Studies in the History and Uses of English Words and Phrases.* Chicago: Scott, Foresman.

Krapp, George P. 1927. *A Comprehensive Guide to Good English.* Chicago: Rand McNally.

Leonard, Sterling A. 1932. *Current English Usage.* English Monograph No. 1, National Council of Teachers of English. Chicago: NCTE.

Mager, N. H., and S. K. Mager. 1974. *Encyclopedia Dictionary of English Usage.* Englewood Cliffs, NJ: Prentice-Hall.

Marckwardt, Albert H., and Fred Walcott. 1938. *Facts About Current English Usage.* English Monograph No. 7, National Council of Teachers of English. New York: Appleton-Century-Crofts.

Morris, William, and Mary Morris. 1975. *Harper Dictionary of Contemporary Usage.* New York: Harper and Row.

Nicholson, Margaret. 1957. *A Dictionary of American English Usage* (based on H. W. Fowler, *A Dictionary of Modern English Usage*). New York: Oxford University Press.

Perrin, Porter G. 1972. *Writer's Guide and Index to English.* 5th ed., revised by Wilma R. Ebbitt. Glenview: Scott, Foresman.

White, Richard G. 1899. *Words and Their Uses.* Boston: Ginn.

Works Consulted

Allen, Harold B. 1940. *Samuel Johnson and the Authoritarian Tradition in Linguistic Criticism.* Diss., University of Michigan.

————, ed. 1964. *Readings in Applied English Linguistics.* 2nd ed. New York: Appleton-Century-Crofts.

———, Enola Borgh, and Verna Newsome, eds. 1975. *Focusing on Language: A Reader.* New York: Crowell.

Baker, Sheridan. 1972. The Sociology of Dictionaries and the Sociology of Words. In Weinbrot 1972:138–51.

Bishop, Morris. 1969. Good Usage, Bad Usage. In *The American Heritage Dictionary of the English Language,* xxi–xxiv.

Cassidy, Frederic G. 1963. Restrictive Labels. *Funk and Wagnalls Standard College Dictionary,* xiii–xxiv.

——— *Toward More Objective Labelling in Dictionaries.* (bibliographical information unavailable.)

Dobbins, Austin C. 1956. The Language of the Cultivated. *College English* 18:46–47.

Friske, Ernest F. 1969. Student's Guide for *The American Heritage Dictionary of the English Language.* Boston: Houghton-Mifflin.

Follett, Wilson. 1962. Sabotage in Springfield. *The Atlantic,* January, 73–77.

Fries, Charles Carpenter. 1953. Usage Levels and Dialect Distribution. In *The American College Dictionary,* xxvii–xxviii.

Gove, Phillip B. 1961. Linguistic Advances and Lexicography. *Word Study* 36:3–8.

——— 1966. Usage in the Dictionary. *College English* 37:285–292.

——— 1972. The English Dictionaries of the Future. In Weinbrot 1972:151–168.

———, ed. 1967. *The Role of the Dictionary.* New York: Bobbs-Merrill.

Hall, Robert A., Jr. 1962. Telling the Truth. *Quarterly Journal of Speech,* December, 434–435.

Hartung, Charles V. 1956. Doctrines of English Usage. *English Journal* 45: 517–525.

Hill, Archibald A. 1970. Laymen, Lexicographers, and Linguists. *Language* 46: 245–258.

Householder, Fred W., and Sol Saporta, eds. 1962. *Problems in Lexicography.* Bloomington: Indiana University Press.

Joos, Martin. 1962. *The Five Clocks.* Bloomington: Indiana University Press.

Kenyon, John S. 1948. Cultural Levels and Functional Varieties of English. *College English* 10:31–36.

Kilburn, Patrick. 1970. The Gentleman's Guide to Linguistic Etiquette. *Union College Symposium* 9:2–6.

——— 1968. Labeling the Language. *Word Study* 44:1–7.

Krapp, George Philip. 1925. *The English Language in America.* 2 vols. New York: Century, for the Modern Language Association.

Laughlin, Rosemary M. 1972. Prescriptivism, Psychology, and THAT Dictionary. In *Studies in Linguistics in Honor of Raven I. McDavid, Jr.,* edited by Lawrence M. Davis (University, AL: University of Alabama Press), 377–396.

Leonard, Sterling Andrus. 1929. *The Doctrine of Correctness in English Usage 1700–1800. University of Wisconsin Studies in Language and Literature,* 25. Madison: University of Wisconsin Press.

Lynes, Russell. 1970. Usage, Precise and Otherwise. *Harper's Magazine,* April, 32–36.

Marckwardt, Albert H. 1963. Dictionaries and the English Language. *English Journal* 52:336–345.

———— 1973a. Lexicographical Method and the Usage Survey. In *Lexicography and Dialect Geography,* edited by Harald Scholler and John Reidy (Wiesbaden: Steiner), 134–146.

———— 1973b. Questions of Usage in Dictionaries. In McDavid and Duckert 1973:172–178.

McDavid, Raven I., Jr. 1966. A Review of the Reviews of *Webster's Third New International Dictionary of the English Language: Unabridged.* Unpublished report prepared for Encyclopedia Britannica Co.

———— 1967. Dialect Labels in the Merriam Third. *Publication of the American Dialect Society* 47:1–22.

———— 1969. Dictionary Makers and Their Problems. In *Language and Teaching: Essays in Honor of Wilbur W. Hatfield,* edited by Virginia Glenn McDavid (Chicago: Chicago State College), 70–79.

———— 1971a. False Scents and Cold Trails: The Prepublication Criticism of the Merriam *Third. Journal of English Linguistics* 5:101–121.

———— 1971b. Usage, Dialects, and Functional Varieties. In *The Random House Dictionary of the English Language,* xxi–xxii.

———— 1973. The English Language in the United States. In *Current Trends in Linguistics* (Vol. 10: *Linguistics in North America*), edited by Thomas A. Sebeok (The Hague: Mouton), 1–39.

———— and Audrey Duckert, eds. 1973. *Lexicography in English. Annals of the New York Academy of Sciences,* 211. New York: New York Academy of Sciences.

McDavid, Virginia G. 1973. Variations in Dictionary Labeling Practices. In McDavid and Duckert 1973:187–207.

McKnight, George H. 1956. *Modern English in the Making.* New York: Appleton-Century-Crofts.

McMillan, James B. 1964. Dictionaries and Usage. *Word Study* 39:1–4.

Mencken, H. L. 1963. *The American Language.* Abridged edition, edited by Raven I. McDavid, Jr. with the assistance of David W. Maurer. New York: Knopf.

Meyers, Walter E. 1972. A Study of Usage Items Based on an Examination of the Brown Corpus. *College Composition and Communication* 23:155–169.

Monson, Samuel C. 1973. Restrictive Labels—Descriptive or Prescriptive? In McDavid and Duckert 1973:208–212.

Morris, William. 1969. The Making of a Dictionary. *College Composition and Communication* 20:198–203.

A New Guide to Dictionary Use. 1967. Springfield, MA: Merriam. Pamphlet.

Osselton, N. E. 1958. *Branded Words in English Dictionaries Before Johnson.* Groningen: (no publisher).

Read, Allen Walker. 1963a. Desk Dictionaries. *Consumer Reports* 28:547–550.

———— 1963b. That Dictionary or the Dictionary? *Consumer Reports* 28:488–492.

————1965. Is American English Deteriorating? *Word Study* 41:1–3.

———— 1973. Approaches to Lexicography and Semantics. In *Current Trends in Linguistics* (Vol. 10: *Linguistics in North America*), edited by Thomas A. Sebeok (The Hague: Mouton), 145–205.

Roberts, Paul. 1952. Pronominal *This:* A Quantitative Analysis. *American Speech* 27:170–178.

Sledd, James. 1972. Dollars and Dictionaries: The Limits of Commercial Lexicography. In Weinbrot 1972:119–137.

———, and Wilma R. Ebbitt, eds. 1962. *Dictionaries and THAT Dictionary.* Chicago: Scott, Foresman.

———, and Gwin J. Kolb. 1955. *Doctor Johnson's Dictionary: Essays in the Biography of a Book.* Chicago: University of Chicago Press.

Stafford, Jean. 1973. Plight of the American Language. *Saturday Review World,* December 4, 14–18.

Vonnegut, Kurt, Jr. 1967. The Latest Word. In Gove 1967:58–60. Reprinted from the *New York Times Book Review,* 30 October 1966:1, 56.

Weinbrot, Howard D., ed. 1972. *New Aspects of Lexicography: Literary Criticism, Intellectual History, and Social Change.* Carbondale: Southern Illinois University Press.

Wells, Ronald A. 1973. *Dictionaries and the Authoritarian Tradition: A Study in English Usage and Lexicography.* The Hague: Mouton.

Wolk, Anthony. 1972. Linguistic and Social Bias in *The American Heritage Dictionary. College English* 33:930–935.

Woolf, Henry B. 1972. Dear Mr. Webster: The Letters Dictionary Users Write. *College Composition and Communication* 23:283–288.

Zgusta, Ladislav. 1971. *Manual of Lexicography.* Prague: Czechoslovak Academy of Sciences.

Content Questions

1. In what ways do dictionaries indicate usage restrictions?

2. Besides through words and meanings, how else does usage differ among individuals?

3. What are the nine usage dimensions identified by the authors?

4. Explain what determines when the labels *obsolete, archaic,* and *old-fashioned* are used.

5. Explain why a word such as *doggie* would be labeled according to the dimension of *maturity.*

6. What does "medium" refer to in this article? How does the medium we are using affect some of our word choices?

7. With which dimension would a euphemism be associated? Why do euphemisms sometimes need to be replaced?

8. What kinds of issues are included in the social position dimension?

9. Linguists frequently speak of the fact that there is no standard pronunciation, but the authors of this article indicate a few pronunciations that are viewed by many as nonstandard. What examples are given to illustrate a nonstandard pronunciation?

Questions for Analysis and Discussion

1. What kinds of linguistic knowledge do dictionary makers need besides the meaning of particular words? Why might a linguist be useful to such a project?

2. Comment on the nine dimensions listed by the authors. Which of these dimensions might not have occurred to you if you were compiling a dictionary?

3. How could the labeling of words according to these dimensions help a non-native speaker who is studying the vocabulary of our language?

4. Which orientation do you believe the authors of this article have—prescriptive or descriptive? Explain.

5. Why do you think a dictionary would still need to record obsolete meanings despite the fact that those meanings are no longer in use?

6. Provide some examples of argot or technical terminology with which you are familiar through an occupation or hobby. Define the terms and comment on which group or groups of people might be familiar with the terms.

Fatal Words: Communication Clashes and Aircraft Crashes

Steven Cushing

The study of discourse as a means of understanding what kind of miscommunication has led to a particular disaster is becoming more common. Such a study can lead to important solutions that can help avoid similar tragedies in the future. Cushing has conducted extensive research into the discourse that has led up to aircraft accidents and has published a book about his findings. In the article below, he identifies some of the kinds of linguistic misunderstandings that have contributed to such disasters. He also briefly explains some of his current work to develop technology that would help prevent future miscommunication between pilots and control tower personnel.

The kind of misstatements and misunderstandings that we all make and experience in ordinary conversation could have fatal consequences in the communication between a pilot and an air-traffic controller. On March 27, 1977, the pilot of a KLM 747 radioed "We are now at take-off," as his plane began rolling down the runway in Tenerife, the Canary Islands (*Figure 1*). The air-traffic controller mistakenly took this statement to mean that the plane was at the take-off point, waiting for further instructions, and so did not warn the pilot that another plane, a Pan Am 747 that was not visible in the thick fog, was already on the runway. The resulting crash killed 583 people in what is still the most destructive accident in aviation history.

The KLM pilot's otherwise perplexing use of the very nonstandard phrase *at take-off*, rather than the more standard phrase *taking off*, can be explained as a subtle form of what linguists refer to as code-switching. Careful studies of bilingual and multilingual speakers have shown that, for reasons that are not well understood, they habitually switch back and forth from one of their languages to another in the course of a conversation. In the KLM pilot's case, the present progressive tense of a verb, which is expressed in English by the verb's -*ing* form, is expressed in Dutch by the equivalent of *at* plus the infinitive of the verb. For whatever reason, perhaps fatigue or stress, the Dutch pilot inadvertently switched into Dutch grammatical construction while keeping the English words. The Spanish-speaking controller had no clue that this was going on and so interpreted the *at* most naturally as a locative word indicating a place, the take-off point.

Figure 1

Los Rodeos Airport, Tenerife, The Canary Islands, March 27, 1977.

1705:44.6 <u>KLM 4805:</u> The KLM <u>*four eight zero five*</u> is now ready for takeoff and we are waiting for our ATC clearance (1705:50.77).

1705:53.41 <u>Tower:</u> KLM *eight seven zero five* you are cleared to the Papa Beacon, climb to and maintain flight level nine zero, right turn after takeoff, proceed with heading four zero until intercepting the three two five radial from Las Palma VOR (1706:08.09).

1706:09.61 <u>KLM 4805:</u> Ah—Roger sir, we are cleared to the Papa Beacon, flight level nine zero until intercepting the three two five. <u>We are now at takeoff</u> (1706:17.79).

1706:18.19 <u>Tower:</u> O.K. . . . <u>Stand by for takeoff,</u> I will call you (1706:21.79).

Note: A squeal starts at 1706:19.39 and ends at 1706:22.06.

PAA: And we're still taxiing down the runway. The Clipper one seven three six (1706:23.6).

1706:21.92 <u>PAA 1736:</u> Clipper one seven three six (1706:23.39).

1706:25.47 <u>Tower:</u> Ah—Papa Alpha one seven three six report the runway clear (1706:28.89).

1706:29.59 <u>PAA 1736:</u> O.K., will report when we're clear (1706:30.69).

1706:61 [sic].<u>69 Tower:</u> Thank you.

1706:50: <u>COLLISION:</u> KLM on takeoff run collides with PAA on ground.

A different form of code-switching contributed to the accident that occurred at John Wayne Orange County Airport in Santa Ana, California, on February 17, 1981 (*Figure 2*). Air Cal 336 was cleared to land at the same time as Air Cal 931 was cleared to taxi into position for take-off, but the controller decided that more time was needed between the two scheduled events and so told 336 to go around. For some reason, the 336 captain resisted this instruction by having his copilot radio for permission to continue landing, but he used the word *hold*, inadvertently switching from technical aviation jargon to ordinary English vernacular. (In aviation parlance, *hold* always means stop what you are now doing; in this case, that would mean the pilot would continue circling rather than attempt to land.) But in ordinary English *hold* can also mean to continue what you are now doing; in this case, to land. The controller's seemingly self-contradictory instruction to 931 to *go ahead and hold* at almost exactly the same time further exacerbated the situation, especially in view of the near-indistinguishability of the two aircrafts' identifying call signs and the consequent uncertainty as to just who was being addressed with that instruction. The resulting confusion led to thirty-four injuries, four of them serious, and the complete destruction of the aircraft when Air Cal 336 landed with its gear retracted, the pilot having finally decided to follow instructions to go around, with it too late actually to do so.

Figure 2

John Wayne Orange County Airport, Santa Ana, California, February 17, 1981.

0133:11 <u>Tower:</u> <u>Air California three thirty six</u> you're cleared to land.

0133:33 <u>Tower:</u> <u>Air California nine thirty one</u> let's do it. Taxi into position and hold, be ready.

0133:37 <u>AC931:</u> Nine thirty one's ready.

0133:52 <u>Tower:</u> Air Cal nine thirty one traffic clearing at the end, clear for takeoff sir, Boeing seven thirty seven a mile and a half final.

0133:57 <u>AC931:</u> In sight we're rolling.

0134:13 <u>Tower:</u> Okay Air Cal three thirty six <u>go around three thirty six. Go around.</u>

(0134:15 <u>AC336:</u> Captain: Can we <u>hold.</u> Ask if if we can—<u>hold.</u>)

0134:18 <u>Tower:</u> Air Cal <u>nine thirty one</u> if you can just <u>go ahead and hold—</u>.

0134:21 <u>AC336:</u> Can we <u>land</u> tower?

0134:22 <u>Tower:</u> Behind you Air Cal nine thirty one just <u>abort.</u>

0134:25 <u>Tower:</u> Air Cal three thirty six, please go around air traffic is going to abort on the departure.

(0134:27 <u>AC336:</u> Captain: Gear up.)

0134:36 <u>IMPACT:</u> Aircraft lands with gear retracted.

Uncertainty of reference, rather than of addressee, contributed substantially to an accident in the Florida Everglades on December 29, 1972 (*Figure* 3). The Eastern Airlines plane's pilot and crew had been preoccupied with a nose-gear problem, which they had told several controllers about during their trip. When the Miami International Airport approach controller noticed on radar that their elevation was declining, he radioed, "How are things comin' along up there?" and they responded, "OK." The crew was referring to the nose-gear problem, which, as it happens, they had just managed to fix, entirely unaware that there was any problem with elevation. However, the controller interpreted the *OK* as referring to the elevation problem, because that is what he had had in mind when he radioed the question. There were 101 deaths from the resulting crash.

In my book *Fatal Words: Communication Clashes and Aircraft Crashes* (University of Chicago Press, 1993), I discuss over 200 incidents, some of which, like these three, resulted in disastrous accidents—all of which easily could have been prevented if the communication circumstances in each case had been only slightly different. Some of these incidents were caused by mundane factors: distractions, fatigue, impatience, obstinacy, uncooperativeness, frivolousness, or crew conflict, and could have been prevented or ameliorated through better conditions, training, or discipline. But the more serious—and more interesting—communication problems are those that arise from inherent characteristics of language itself, from reference confusion, or from the inferences that are drawn in the course of linguistic communication.

Figure 3

Miami International Airport, Miami, Florida, December 29, 1972.

2334:05 <u>EAL 401:</u> Ah, tower this is Eastern, ah four zero one, it looks like we're gonna have to circle, <u>we don't have a light on our nose gear yet.</u>

2334:14 <u>Tower:</u> Eastern four oh one heavy, roger, pull up, climb straight ahead to two thousand, go back to approach control, one twenty eight six.

2334:21 <u>EAL 401:</u> Okay, going up to two thousand, one twenty eight six.

2335:09 <u>EAL 401:</u> All right, ah, <u>approach control.</u> Eastern four zero one, we're right over the airport here and climbing to two thousand feet, in fact, we've just reached two thousand feet and <u>we've got to get a green light on our nose gear.</u>

2336:27 <u>MIA App Con:</u> Eastern four oh one, turn left heading three zero zero.

2338:46 <u>EAL 401:</u> Eastern four oh one'll go ah, out west just a little further if we can here and, ah, see if we can get this light to come on here.

2341 <u>Second Officer within cockpit:</u> I can't see it, it's pitch dark and I throw the little light, I get, ah, nothing.

2341:40 <u>MIA App Con:</u> Eastern, ah, four oh one how are <u>things</u> comin' along out there?

2341:44 <u>EAL 401:</u> <u>Okay,</u> we'd like to turn around and come, come back in.

2341:47 <u>MIA App Con:</u> Eastern four oh one turn left heading one eight zero.

2342:12 <u>IMPACT:</u> Aircraft crashes into the Everglades.

Language is replete with ambiguity. The presence in a word or phrase of more than one possible meaning or interpretation, such as *at* in the Tenerife case or *hold* in the John Wayne case; and with *homophony,* different words that sound exactly or almost alike, such as *to* and *two,* which actually led to a fatal accident at a southeast Asian airport, or *left* and *west;* peculiarities of punctuation or intonation, such as *back on—the power* vs. *back—on the power;* and the complexity of speech acts, which correspond only in the most indirect ways to sentence or statement types— all these can wreak havoc in even the simplest of situations. For example, when a pilot misconstrued the phrase *traffic . . . level at 6000* to be an instruction for himself meaning [descend to and remain] *level at 6000* [because of traffic], rather than an assertion about his traffic meaning [the traffic is] *level at 6000,* as the controller intended.

Pronouns, such as *him* or *it,* or indefinite nouns such as *things* in the Everglades case, can have multiple references that are not easily distinguished in a conversation, and the use of a word like *anticipate* or of unfamiliar terminology can create expectations that have no factual basis. Extensive repetition of essentially the same instruction, such as *cleared to _____ feet* or *expedite,* can lull a pilot into inattention. Similarly, overlapping number ranges that are shared by several aviation parameters (for example, *240* can be a flight level, a heading, or an air speed) inevitably breed confusions, requiring almost constant mutual or self-correction.

Problems with radios, such as being tuned to the wrong frequency, can prevent an instruction from being heard even when the message itself is clear. A perfectly well-formed and meaningful message can still cause problems when, for some reason, it is not sent; is sent, but is not heard; is sent and heard, but still not understood; or is sent, heard, and understood, but not remembered by the listener.

One source of the problem is that the aviation protocol was not designed systematically, but is a hodgepodge that grew *ad hoc* as new inventions and innovations were introduced. However "re-engineering" the system, that is, redesigning it from scratch, would require closing the world down for several years as pilots and controllers try to forget what they have learned and get retrained in whatever new procedures and terminologies might be developed.

A more realistic approach would involve intensive efforts to teach pilots and controllers about the subtle nuances of language and communication and about how their own and other people's safety depend on their willingness to use language more mindfully. For example, the Aviation Safety Reporting System of NASA-Ames Research Center in Mountain View, California, the center that funded the study reported in *Fatal Words,* issues alerts on threats to aviation safety that it finds to be particularly prevalent. Some of them involve issues of language and communication. And the Centre de Linguistique Appliquée of the Université de Franche-Comté in Besançon, France, develops linguistically sophisticated training materials for pilots and controllers and sponsors a triennial International Aviation English Forum, at which I presented some of the results reported in *Fatal Words* in 1991.

However, much more needs to be done in this area, especially in the United States, where English is taken for granted as a language that everyone is expected to speak in a standard way. In Europe, by contrast, where there are multiple languages, people have to take linguistic issues more seriously.

Another path that needs to be pursued is the development of appropriate communication tools. There are no sure fixes for emergency situations, which require split-second decisions by human beings, but technology can be used to reduce the number of emergency situations that arise. A close-to-ideal solution to at least some of these sorts of problems would be the development of an intelligent voice interface for aviation communication. Such a device would monitor communications and filter out potential linguistic confusions, checking with the speaker for clarification before conveying messages, and monitoring the aircraft's state, providing needed callouts automatically. Such a system would be valuable on-line as a safety device in real-time, but would be useful also as a training device, an aid to developing an awareness in both pilots and controllers of the kinds of linguistic constructions they ought to avoid, while conditioning them, to some extent, to do so.

Developing such a system would require extensive further research to solve many still open questions of scientific linguistics, such as the problem of speech recognition (how to extract a meaningful signal from an acoustic wave). This problem has become tractable technologically for individual words but still resists solution for more extended utterances.

There are also many unsolved problems of what linguists call *pragmatics,* or the ways in which *context* can affect the meaning of an utterance. For example, the sentence *I have some free time* means one thing during a discussion about one's work schedule, but means something quite different when driving up to a parking meter. With very little effort, people routinely distinguish such meanings in real conversations but exactly how they do that and how a device could duplicate this process remains to be discovered. The only certainty is that a workable intelligent voice interface is not likely to be developed for this or the next generation of aviation.

In the meantime, and in parallel with that research, it may be more fruitful to develop limited systems, in which a visual interface for processing a more restricted English-like language is used. A prototype version of such a system, the Aviation Interface Research (AIR) System, has been developed under my supervision by some of my graduate students at Boston University and is described in *Fatal Words.*

AIR uses a system of nested menus to send messages back and forth between two Macintosh computers, which simulate pilot and controller interfaces. When a message is entered from one of the user interfaces, a program called a *parser* checks that it is correctly formed with respect to the restricted English-like language that is used by the system. If it is acceptable, it is transmitted to the other interface, where it appears at the top of the screen; if necessary, an error message is returned to the sender instead. Menu screens are invoked by selecting icons, and messages are constructed by selecting buttons that contain actual words or phrases that are echoed at the bottom of the sending screen. As the system is currently set up, the selections are made by mouse. But they could just as well be made by touch-screen.

As it now stands, AIR serves mainly to illustrate the concept and demonstrate the feasibility of an error-resistant visual message-sending-and-receiving system for two-way air-ground pilot-controller communication. Work has begun on a second version that is envisioned as having further features that will improve on the current system in several ways. For example, it will be possible to provide bilingual screens, in English and in the user's own language, to enable the crew or controller to check the correctness of messages they want to send or to test their understanding of messages they receive. It will also be possible to have the system choose randomly from a set of synonymous alternative formulations of an instruction in order to preempt the semi-hypnotic boredom that is induced by repeatedly receiving instructions in exactly the same form.

Content Questions

1. What specific linguistic misunderstanding occurred between the KLM pilot and the control tower? How was this related to code switching?

2. How did an ambiguity of reference contribute to disaster in the accident in the Everglades?

3. Explain what the ambiguities were in the examples involving homophony, intonation, and speech acts.

4. Why is it dangerous for particular messages to come to pilots in the same form time after time?

5. What kind of system does the author describe as a future possibility to help avoid communication disasters among airline personnel?

Questions for Analysis and Discussion

1. With regard to pragmatics, why would an effective and reliable linguistic interface be difficult to develop? What kinds of linguistic issues must be considered?

2. The advantage of having a language such as English used internationally is obvious. But why does the use of a single language among pilots and personnel in control towers still require special attention to possible misunderstandings?

3. Speakers regularly switch speaking styles. What made the switch from jargon to more ordinary speech a problem in the case of Air Cal 931?

Additional Activities and Paper Topics

1. Select ten product names of prominently advertised products. Using the table presented in Cohen's article, report on the degree to which you think the sounds within the product names might enhance or promote the image that the producers of the product probably want to connote. (**Phonetics and Phonology**)

2. Contact a native speaker of a foreign language or a speaker who is knowledgeable about a foreign language and ask that speaker to spell out ten names used by native speakers of that language. Then ask for the pronunciation of those names. Record those pronunciations with phonetic transcription, so that you can later recall how those names should be pronounced. For the purpose of this assignment, it would be better to work with an Indo-European language, since you likely have not learned some of the necessary symbols for transcribing sounds commonly found in other language families. Report on your list and how you might have pronounced some of the names if you had briefly encountered them and forgotten to record them phonetically. Also comment on any sounds for which you may not have known the transcription symbol. Finally, report on how learning transcription could benefit someone who works in a multinational business setting. (**Phonetics and Phonology**)

3. Assume that you have to create a new language for a movie or computer software game and that that language must have a morphology and syntax that differs from Modern English. As an initial demonstration of the kind of language you will create, provide ten new words and describe three morphological rules and three syntactic rules of this language that are distinctive of this new language (rules that differ from Modern English). Do not use rules found within a foreign language with which you may already be familiar. (**Morphology and Syntax**)

4. Research some of the customs and expectations of another culture. Then identify and discuss some English-based advertisements that would not be effective in that culture. Explain why those advertisements would not be effective. (**Semantics or Language Varieties**)

5. Consult a usage dictionary (a dictionary that provides information about the usage concerns with selected terms, rather than providing definitions for all the terms in a language). Discuss several entries in that dictionary and provide examples from contemporary usage in the media showing how traditional prescriptive declarations about how language should be used are violated even by educated public personalities. (**Language Varieties**)

Linguistics and
Issues of Gender, Race,
and Culture

The readings in this chapter are important for what they show us about the value of linguistic study in contributing to a greater understanding among different groups, whether those groups are distinguished by their gender, race, or culture. Measuring the effect of such research is more difficult than in earlier mentioned applications, such as a verdict in a court case. But the importance of this linguistic study can be just as significant and can result in a greater degree of sensitivity and respect between one group and another, and perhaps in some cases can even enhance cooperation and accommodation between groups.

The first three articles in this chapter deal with issues of gender. In the first article, "The Power of Talk: Who Gets Heard and Why," Deborah Tannen examines the discourse features that often distinguish women's speech from men's speech. She identifies ways in which some characteristics of women's speech "may put women at a disadvantage" in cross-gender situations, particularly in the workplace. In "Penguins Don't Care, But Women Do: A Social Identity Analysis of a Whorfian Problem," Fatemeh Khosroshahi looks at the issue of pronoun usage. She reports on empirical research she conducted to examine whether the choice of the pronouns *he, he or she,* or *they* to indicate the generic singular shapes our perception about the subject's gender. Edith H. Raidt discusses the influence that women speakers in the Cape colony in South Africa had on the development of Dutch into Afrikaans, beginning in the 17th century. Her article, "The Role of Women in Linguistic Change," reports her research of specific patterns that characterized women's speech at that time and shows how these women influenced the development of the language. She also considers the social networks that influenced these women's speech patterns.

Many people are familiar with the claim that the Eskimo language has many more terms for snow than other languages and what this shows about the importance of snow in their culture. Laura Martin's article, " 'Eskimo Words for Snow': A Case Study in the Genesis and Decay of an Anthropological Example," challenges the validity of this popular example and serves as a cautionary reminder not only about the carelessness that is occasionally found in academic work, but also the tendency among many who are too quick to believe unfounded claims about a group of people with whom they have little knowledge or contact. In his article, "American Sign Language: 'It's Not Mouth Stuff—It's Brain Stuff,' " Richard Wolkomir discusses the history and use of American Sign Language. His discussion also explores what sign language can teach us about the acquisition and nature of language.

The final reading in this chapter is a classic article by Paul Thieme titled "The Indo-European Language." This article illustrates the kind of knowledge we can gain about an ancient people by studying their language. What makes Indo-European a particularly interesting example is that, in contrast with languages such as Greek and Latin, it is a language that linguists first had to reconstruct, because no actual writings of Indo-European have been discovered.

This chapter can only represent a fraction of the possible contributions of linguistics to cross-cultural understanding. Other linguistic research dealing with cross-cultural issues in language has examined the differences that exist between particular social or regional varieties of a language and the standard variety of that language. This research has, for example, considered social varieties such as Black English or Chicano English and regional varieties such as Appalachian English. Examples of how a knowledge of differences in social or regional varieties might be applied can be seen in several of the following chapters. Additional illustrations of linguistic involvement in cross-cultural research are found in the work of linguists who have recorded, and in some cases helped to preserve endangered languages before those languages have disappeared altogether. The urgency of this type of work is underscored when it is realized that there are many languages that have been reduced to so few speakers, with few of them being younger, that the languages face a real threat of extinction.

A central feature of this chapter is that its readings help us to understand other individuals or groups. This is true of much of the research in linguistics. And while a significant portion of this reader illustrates utilitarian applications, this chapter demonstrates how linguistic research contributes to genuine cross-cultural understanding for its own sake.

The Power of Talk:
Who Gets Heard and Why*

Deborah Tannen

Deborah Tannen, a linguist at Georgetown University, is well known for her work in gender and language. Tannen's research suggests that in some ways the communication between men and women can be considered cross-cultural communication. Just as misunderstandings can occur between speakers of two different languages or dialects, such misunderstandings can also occur between men and women. Tannen has recently examined the role that linguistic differences between men and women can have in putting women "at a disadvantage in the workplace." In the article below, which appeared in the *Harvard Business Review,* she provides an overview of many important issues involved in the communication between men and women in the workplace. She also indicates how an understanding of such differences could lead to some positive changes.

The head of a large division of a multinational corporation was running a meeting devoted to performance assessment. Each senior manager stood up, reviewed the individuals in his group, and evaluated them for promotion. Although there were women in every group, not one of them made the cut. One after another, each manager declared, in effect, that every woman in his group didn't have the self-confidence needed to be promoted. The division head began to doubt his ears. How could it be that all the talented women in the division suffered from a lack of self-confidence?

In all likelihood, they didn't. Consider the many women who have left large corporations to start their own businesses, obviously exhibiting enough confidence to succeed on their own. Judgments about confidence can be inferred only from the way people present themselves, and much of that presentation is in the form of talk.

The CEO of a major corporation told me that he often has to make decisions in five minutes about matters on which others may have worked five months. He said he uses this rule: If the person making the proposal seems confident, the CEO approves it. If not, he says no. This might seem like a reasonable approach. But my field of research, sociolinguistics, suggests otherwise. The CEO obviously thinks he knows what a confident person sounds like. But his judgment, which may be dead right for some people, may be dead wrong for others.

Communication isn't as simple as saying what you mean. How you say what you mean is crucial, and differs from one person to the next, because using language is learned social behavior: How we talk and listen are deeply influenced by cultural experience. Although we might think that our ways of saying what we mean are natural, we can run into trouble if we interpret and evaluate others as if they necessarily felt the same way we'd feel if we spoke the way they did.

Since 1974, I have been researching the influence of linguistic style on conversations and human relationships. In the past four years, I have extended that research to the workplace, where I have observed how ways of speaking learned in childhood affect judgments of competence and confidence, as well as who gets heard, who gets credit, and what gets done.

The division head who was dumbfounded to hear that all the talented women in his organization lacked confidence was probably right to be skeptical. The senior managers were judging the women in their groups by their own linguistic norms, but women—like people who have grown up in a different culture—have often learned different styles of speaking than men, which can make them seem less competent and self-assured than they are.

What Is Linguistic Style?

Everything that is said must be said in a certain way—in a certain tone of voice, at a certain rate of speed, and with a certain degree of loudness. Whereas often we consciously consider what to say before speaking, we rarely think about how to say it, unless the situation is obviously loaded— for example, a job interview or a tricky performance review. Linguistic style refers to a person's characteristic speaking pattern. It includes such features as directness or indirectness, pacing and pausing, word choice, and the use of such elements as jokes, figures of speech, stories, questions, and apologies. In other words, linguistic style is a set of culturally learned signals by which we not only communicate what we mean but also interpret others' meaning and evaluate one another as people.

Consider turn taking, one element of linguistic style. Conversation is an enterprise in which people take turns: One person speaks, then the other responds. However, this apparently simple exchange requires a subtle negotiation of signals so that you know when the other person is finished and it's your turn to begin. Cultural factors such as country or region of origin and ethnic background influence how long a pause seems natural. When Bob, who is from Detroit, has a conversation with his colleague Joe, from New York City, it's hard for him to get a word in edgewise because he expects a slightly longer pause between turns than Joe does. A pause of that length never comes because, before it has a chance to, Joe senses an uncomfortable silence, which he fills with more talk of his own. Both men fail to realize that differences in conversational style are getting in their way. Bob thinks that Joe is pushy and uninterested in what he has to say, and Joe thinks that Bob doesn't have much to contribute. Similarly, when Sally relocated from Texas to Washington, D.C., she kept searching for the right time to break in during staff meetings—and never found it. Although in Texas she was considered outgoing and confident, in Washington she was perceived as shy and retiring. Her boss even suggested she take an assertiveness training course. Thus slight differences in conversational style— in these cases, a few seconds of pause—can have a surprising impact on who gets heard and on the judgments, including psychological ones, that are made about people and their abilities.

Every utterance functions on two levels. We're all familiar with the first one: Language communicates ideas. The second level is mostly invisible to us, but it plays a powerful role in communication. As a form of social behavior, language also negotiates relationships. Through ways of speaking, we signal—and create—the relative status of speakers and their level of rapport. If you say, "Sit down!" you are signaling that you have higher status than the person you are addressing, that you are so close to each other that you can drop all pleasantries, or that you are angry. If you say, "I would be honored if you would sit down," you are signaling great respect—or great sarcasm, depending on your tone of voice, the situation, and what you both know about how close you really are. If you say, "You must be so tired—why don't you sit down," you are communicating either closeness and concern or condescension. Each of these ways of saying "the same thing"—telling someone to sit down—can have a vastly different meaning.

In every community known to linguists, the patterns that constitute linguistic style are relatively different for men and women. What's "natural" for most men speaking a given language is, in some cases, different from what's "natural" for most women. That is because we learn ways of speaking as children growing up, especially from peers, and children tend to play with other children of the same sex. The research of sociologists, anthropologists, and psychologists observing American children at play has shown that, although both girls and boys find ways of creating rapport and negotiating status, girls tend to learn conversational rituals that focus on the rapport dimension of relationships whereas boys tend to learn rituals that focus on the status dimension.

Girls tend to play with a single best friend or in small groups, and they spend a lot of time talking. They use language to negotiate how close they are; for example, the girl you tell your secrets to becomes your best friend. Girls learn to downplay ways in which one is better than the others and to emphasize ways in which they are all the same. From childhood, most girls learn that sounding too sure of themselves will make them unpopular with their peers—although nobody really takes such modesty literally. A group of girls will ostracize a girl who calls attention to her own superiority and criticize her by saying, "She thinks she's something"; and a girl who tells others what to do is called "bossy." Thus girls learn to talk in ways that balance their own needs with those of others—to save face for one another in the broadest sense of the term.

Boys tend to play very differently. They usually play in larger groups in which more boys can be included, but not everyone is treated as an equal. Boys with high status in their group are expected to emphasize rather than downplay their status, and usually one or several boys will be seen as the leader or leaders. Boys generally don't accuse one another of being bossy, because the leader is expected to tell lower-status boys what to do. Boys learn to use language to negotiate their status in the group by displaying their abilities and knowledge, and by challenging others and resisting challenges. Giving orders is one way of getting and keeping the high-status role. Another is taking center stage by telling stories or jokes.

This is not to say that all boys and girls grow up this way or feel comfortable in these groups or are equally successful at negotiating within these norms. But, for the most part, these childhood play groups are where boys and girls learn their conversational styles. In this sense, they grow up in different worlds. The result is that women and men tend to have different habitual ways of saying what they mean, and conversations between them can be like cross-cultural communication: You can't assume that the other person means what you would mean if you said the same thing in the same way.

My research in companies across the United States shows that the lessons learned in childhood carry over into the workplace. Consider the following example: A focus group was organized at a major multinational company to evaluate a recently implemented flextime policy. The participants sat in a circle and discussed the new system. The group concluded that it was excellent, but they also agreed on ways to improve it. The meeting went well and was deemed a success by all, according to my own observations and everyone's comments to me. But the next day, I was in for a surprise.

I had left the meeting with the impression that Phil had been responsible for most of the suggestions adopted by the group. But as I typed up my notes, I noticed that Cheryl had made almost all those suggestions. I had thought that the key ideas came from Phil because he had picked up Cheryl's points and supported them, speaking at greater length in doing so than she had in raising them.

It would be easy to regard Phil as having stolen Cheryl's ideas—and her thunder. But that would be inaccurate. Phil never claimed Cheryl's ideas as his own. Cheryl herself told me later that she left the meeting confident that she had contributed significantly, and that she appreciated Phil's support. She volunteered, with a laugh, "It was not one of those times when a woman says something and it's ignored, then a man says it and it's picked up." In other words, Cheryl and Phil worked well as a team, the group fulfilled its charge, and the company got what it needed. So what was the problem?

I went back and asked all the participants who they thought had been the most influential group member, the one most responsible for the ideas that had been adopted. The pattern of answers was revealing. The two other women in the group named Cheryl. Two of the three men named Phil. Of the men, only Phil named Cheryl. In other words, in this instance, the women evaluated the contribution of another woman more accurately than the men did.

Meetings like this take place daily in companies around the country. Unless managers are unusually good at listening closely to how people say what they mean, the talents of someone like Cheryl may well be undervalued and underutilized.

One Up, One Down

Individual speakers vary in how sensitive they are to the social dynamics of language—in other words, to the subtle nuances of what others say to them. Men tend to be sensitive to the power dynamics of interaction, speaking in ways that position themselves as one up and resisting being put in a one-down position by others. Women tend to react more strongly to the rapport dynamic, speaking in ways that save face for others and buffering statements that could be seen as putting others in a one-down position. These linguistic patterns are pervasive; you can hear them in hundreds of exchanges in the workplace every day. And, as in the case of Cheryl and Phil, they affect who gets heard and who gets credit.

Getting Credit

Even so small a linguistic strategy as the choice of pronoun can affect who gets credit. In my research in the workplace, I heard men say "I" in situations where I heard women say "we." For example, one publishing company executive said, "I'm hiring a new manager. I'm going to put him in charge of my marketing division," as if he owned the corporation. In stark contrast, I recorded women saying "we" when referring to work they alone had done. One woman explained that it would sound too self-promoting to claim credit in an obvious way by saying, "I did this." Yet she expected—sometimes vainly—that others would know it was her work and would give her the credit she did not claim for herself.

Managers might leap to the conclusion that women who do not take credit for what they've done should be taught to do so. But that solution is problematic because we associate ways of speaking with moral qualities: The way we speak is who we are and who we want to be.

Veronica, a senior researcher in a high-tech company, had an observant boss. He noticed that many of the ideas coming out of the group were hers but that often someone else trumpeted them around the office and got credit for them. He advised her to "own" her ideas and make sure she got the credit. But Veronica found she simply didn't enjoy her work if she had to approach it as what seemed to her an unattractive and unappealing "grabbing game." It was her dislike of such behavior that had led her to avoid it in the first place.

Whatever the motivation, women are less likely than men to have learned to blow their own horn. And they are more likely than men to believe that if they do so, they won't be liked.

Many have argued that the growing trend of assigning work to teams may be especially congenial to women, but it may also create complications for performance evaluation. When ideas are generated and work is accomplished in the privacy of the team, the outcome of the team's effort may become associated with the person most vocal about reporting results. There are many women and men—but probably relatively more women—who are reluctant to put themselves forward in this way and who consequently risk not getting credit for their contributions.

Confidence and Boasting

The CEO who based his decisions on the confidence level of speakers was articulating a value that is widely shared in U.S. businesses: One way to judge confidence is by an individual's behavior, especially verbal behavior. Here again, many women are at a disadvantage.

Studies show that women are more likely to downplay their certainty and men are more likely to minimize their doubts. Psychologist Laurie Heatherington and her colleagues devised an ingenious experiment, which they reported in the journal *Sex Roles* (Volume 29, 1993). They asked hundreds of incoming college students to predict what grades they would get in their first year. Some subjects were asked to make their predictions privately by writing them down and placing them in an envelope; others were asked to make their predictions publicly, in the presence of a researcher. The results showed that more women than men predicted lower grades for themselves if they made their predictions publicly. If they made their predictions privately, the predictions were the same as those of the men—and the same as their actual grades. This study provides evidence that what comes across as lack of confidence—predicting lower grades for oneself—may reflect not one's actual level of confidence but the desire not to seem boastful.

These habits with regard to appearing humble or confident result from the socialization of boys and girls by their peers in childhood play. As adults, both women and men find these behaviors reinforced by the positive responses they get from friends and relatives who share the same norms. But the norms of behavior in the U.S. business world are based on the style of interaction that is more common among men—at least, among American men.

Asking Questions

Although asking the right questions is one of the hallmarks of a good manager, how and when questions are asked can send unintended signals about competence and power. In a group, if only one person asks questions, he or she risks being seen as the only ignorant one. Furthermore, we judge others not only by how they speak but also by how they are spoken to. The person who asks questions may end up being lectured to and looking like a novice under a schoolmaster's tutelage. The way boys are socialized makes them more likely to be aware of the underlying power dynamic by which a question asker can be seen in a one-down position.

One practicing physician learned the hard way that any exchange of information can become the basis for judgments—or misjudgments—about competence. During her training, she received a negative evaluation that she thought was unfair, so she asked her supervising physician for an explanation. He said that she knew less than her peers. Amazed at his answer, she asked how he had reached that conclusion. He said, "You ask more questions."

Along with cultural influences and individual personality, gender seems to play a role in whether and when people ask questions. For example, of all the observations I've made in lectures and books, the one that sparks the most enthusiastic flash of recognition is that men are less likely than women to stop and ask for directions when they are lost. I explain that men often resist asking for directions because they are aware that it puts them in a one-down position and because they value the independence that comes with finding their way by themselves. Asking for directions while driving is only one instance—along with many others that researchers have examined—in which men seem less likely than women to ask questions. I believe this is because they are more attuned than women to the potential face-losing aspect of asking questions. And men who believe that asking questions might reflect negatively on them may, in turn, be likely to form a negative opinion of others who ask questions in situations where they would not.

Conversational Rituals

Conversation is fundamentally ritual in the sense that we speak in ways our culture has conventionalized and expect certain types of responses. Take greetings, for example. I have heard visitors to the United States complain that Americans are hypocritical because they ask how you are but aren't interested in the answer. To Americans, How are you? is obviously a ritualized way to start a conversation rather than a literal request for information. In other parts of the world, including the Philippines, people ask each other, "Where are you going?" when they meet. The question seems intrusive to Americans, who do not realize that it, too, is a ritual query to which the only expected reply is a vague "Over there."

It's easy and entertaining to observe different rituals in foreign countries. But we don't expect differences, and are far less likely to recognize the ritualized nature of our conversations, when we are with our compatriots at work. Our differing rituals can be even more problematic when we think we're all speaking the same language.

Apologies

Consider the simple phrase *I'm sorry.*

> CATHERINE: How did that big presentation go?
> BOB: Oh, not very well. I got a lot of flak from the VP for finance, and I didn't have the numbers at my fingertips.
> CATHERINE: Oh, I'm sorry. I know how hard you worked on that.

In this case, *I'm sorry* probably means "I'm sorry that happened," not "I apologize," unless it was Catherine's responsibility to supply Bob with the numbers for the presentation. Women tend to say *I'm sorry* more frequently than men, and often they intend it in this way—as a ritualized means of expressing concern. It's one of many learned elements of conversational style that girls often use to establish rapport. Ritual apologies— like other conversational rituals—work well when both parties share the same assumptions about their use. But people who utter frequent ritual apologies may end up appearing weaker, less confident, and literally more blameworthy than people who don't.

Apologies tend to be regarded differently by men, who are more likely to focus on the status implications of exchanges. Many men avoid apologies because they see them as putting the speaker in a one-down position. I observed with some amazement an encounter among several lawyers engaged in a negotiation over a speakerphone. At one point, the lawyer in whose office I was sitting accidentally elbowed the telephone and cut off the call. When his secretary got the parties back on again, I expected him to say what I would have said: "Sorry about that. I knocked the phone with my elbow." Instead, he said, "Hey, what happened? One minute you were there; the next minute you were gone!" This lawyer seemed to have an automatic impulse not to admit fault if he didn't have to. For me, it was one of those pivotal moments when you realize that the world you live in is not the one everyone lives in and that the way you assume is the way to talk is really only one of many.

Those who caution managers not to undermine their authority by apologizing are approaching interaction from the perspective of the power dynamic. In many cases, this strategy is effective. On the other hand, when I asked people what frustrated them in their jobs, one frequently voiced complaint was working with or for someone who refuses to apologize or admit fault. In other words, accepting responsibility for errors and admitting mistakes may be an equally effective or superior strategy in some settings.

Feedback

Styles of giving feedback contain a ritual element that often is the cause for misunderstanding. Consider the following exchange: A manager had to tell her marketing director to rewrite a report. She began this potentially awkward task by citing the report's strengths and then moved to the main point: the weaknesses that needed to be remedied. The marketing director seemed to understand and accept his supervisor's comments, but his revision contained only minor changes and failed to address the major weaknesses. When the manager told him of her dissatisfaction, he accused her of misleading him: "You told me it was fine."

The impasse resulted from different linguistic styles. To the manager, it was natural to buffer the criticism by beginning with praise. Telling her subordinate that his report is inadequate and has to be rewritten puts him in a one-down position. Praising him for the parts that are good is a ritualized way of saving face for him. But the marketing director did not share his supervisor's assumption about how feedback should be given. Instead, he assumed that what she mentioned first was the main point and that what she brought up later was an afterthought.

Those who expect feedback to come in the way the manager presented it would appreciate her tact and would regard a more blunt approach as unnecessarily callous. But those who share the marketing director's assumptions would regard the blunt approach as honest and no-nonsense, and the manager's as obfuscating. Because each one's assumptions seemed self-evident, each blamed the other: The manager thought the marketing director was not listening, and he thought she had not communicated clearly or had changed her mind. This is significant because it illustrates that incidents labeled vaguely as "poor communication" may be the result of differing linguistic styles.

Compliments

Exchanging compliments is a common ritual, especially among women. A mismatch in expectations about this ritual left Susan, a manager in the human resources field, in a one-down position. She and her colleague Bill had both given presentations at a national conference. On the airplane home, Susan told Bill, "That was a great talk!" "Thank you," he said. Then she asked, "What did you think of mine?" He responded with a lengthy and detailed critique, as she listened uncomfortably. An unpleasant feeling of having been put down came over her. Somehow she had been positioned as the novice in need of his expert advice. Even worse, she had only herself to blame, since she had, after all, asked Bill what he thought of her talk.

But had Susan asked for the response she received? When she asked Bill what he thought about her talk, she expected to hear not a critique but a compliment. In fact, her question had been an attempt to repair a ritual gone awry. Susan's initial compliment to Bill was the kind of automatic recognition she felt was more or less required after a colleague gives a presentation, and she expected Bill to respond with a matching compliment. She was just talking automatically, but he either sincerely misunderstood the ritual or simply took the opportunity to bask in the one-up position of critic. Whatever his motivation, it was Susan's attempt to spark an exchange of compliments that gave him the opening.

Although this exchange could have occurred between two men, it does not seem coincidental that it happened between a man and a woman. Linguist Janet Holmes discovered that women pay more compliments than men (*Anthropological Linguistics,* Volume 28, 1986). And, as I have observed, fewer men are likely to ask, "What did you think of my talk?" precisely because the question might invite an unwanted critique.

In the social structure of the peer groups in which they grow up, boys are indeed looking for opportunities to put others down and take the one-up position for themselves. In contrast, one of the rituals girls learn is taking the one-down position but assuming that the other person will recognize the ritual nature of the self-denigration and pull them back up.

The exchange between Susan and Bill also suggests how women's and men's characteristic styles may put women at a disadvantage in the workplace. If one person is trying to minimize status differences, maintain an appearance that everyone is equal, and save face for the other, while another person is trying to maintain the one-up position and avoid being positioned as one down, the person seeking the one-up position is likely to get it. At the same time, the person who has not been expending any effort to avoid the one-down position is likely to end up in it. Because women are more likely to take (or accept) the role of advice seeker, men are more inclined to interpret a ritual question from a woman as a request for advice.

Ritual Opposition

Apologizing, mitigating criticism with praise, and exchanging compliments are rituals common among women that men often take literally. A ritual common among men that women often take literally is ritual opposition.

A woman in communications told me she watched with distaste and distress as her office mate argued heatedly with another colleague about whose division should suffer budget cuts. She was even more surprised, however, that a short time later they were as friendly as ever. "How can you pretend that fight never happened?" she asked. "Who's pretending it never happened?" he responded, as puzzled by her question as she had been by his behavior. "It happened," he said, "and it's over." What she took as literal fighting to him was a routine part of daily negotiation: a ritual fight.

Many Americans expect the discussion of ideas to be a ritual fight—that is, an exploration through verbal opposition. They present their own ideas in the most certain and absolute form they can, and wait to see if they are challenged. Being forced to defend an idea provides an opportunity to test it. In the same spirit, they may play devil's advocate in challenging their colleagues' ideas—trying to poke holes and find weaknesses—as a way of helping them explore and test their ideas.

This style can work well if everyone shares it, but those unaccustomed to it are likely to miss its ritual nature. They may give up an idea that is challenged, taking the objections as an indication that the idea was a poor one. Worse, they may take the opposition as a personal attack and may find it impossible to do their best in a contentious environment. People unaccustomed to this style may hedge when stating their ideas in order to fend off potential attacks. Ironically, this posture makes their arguments appear weak and is more likely to invite attack from pugnacious colleagues than to fend it off.

Ritual opposition can even play a role in who gets hired. Some consulting firms that recruit graduates from the top business schools use a confrontational interviewing technique. They challenge the candidate to "crack a case" in real time. A partner at one firm told me, "Women tend to do less well in this kind of interaction, and it certainly affects who gets hired. But, in fact, many women who don't 'test well' turn out to be good consultants. They're often smarter than some of the men who looked like analytic powerhouses under pressure."

The level of verbal opposition varies from one company's culture to the next, but I saw instances of it in all the organizations I studied. Anyone who is uncomfortable with this linguistic style—and that includes some men as well as many women—risks appearing insecure about his or her ideas.

Negotiating Authority

In organizations, formal authority comes from the position one holds. But actual authority has to be negotiated day to day. The effectiveness of individual managers depends in part on their skill in negotiating authority and on whether others reinforce or undercut their efforts. The way linguistic style reflects status plays a subtle role in placing individuals within a hierarchy.

Managing Up and Down

In all the companies I researched, I heard from women who knew they were doing a superior job and knew that their coworkers (and sometimes their immediate bosses) knew it as well, but believed that the higher-ups did not. They frequently told me that something outside themselves was holding them back and found it frustrating because they thought that all that should be necessary for success was to do a great job, that superior performance should be recognized and rewarded. In contrast, men often told me that if women weren't promoted, it was because they simply weren't up to snuff. Looking around, however, I saw evidence that men more often than women behaved in ways likely to get them recognized by those with the power to determine their advancement.

In all the companies I visited, I observed what happened at lunchtime. I saw young men who regularly ate lunch with their boss, and senior men who ate with the big boss. I noticed far fewer women who sought out the highest-level person they could eat with. But one is more likely to get recognition for work done if one talks about it to those higher up, and it is easier to do so if the lines of communication are already open. Furthermore, given the opportunity for a conversation with superiors, men and women are likely to have different ways of talking about their accomplishments because of the different ways in which they were socialized as children. Boys are rewarded by their peers if they talk up their achievements, whereas girls are rewarded if they play theirs down. Linguistic styles common among men may tend to give them some advantages when it comes to managing up.

All speakers are aware of the status of the person they are talking to and adjust accordingly. Everyone speaks differently when talking to a boss than when talking to a subordinate. But, surprisingly, the ways in which they adjust their talk may be different and thus may project different images of themselves.

Communications researchers Karen Tracy and Eric Eisenberg studied how relative status affects the way people give criticism. They devised a business letter that contained some errors and asked 13 male and 11 female college students to role-play delivering criticism under two scenarios. In the first, the speaker was a boss talking to a subordinate; in the second, the speaker was a subordinate talking to his or her boss. The researchers measured how hard the speakers tried to avoid hurting the feelings of the person they were criticizing.

One might expect people to be more careful about how they deliver criticism when they are in a subordinate position. Tracy and Eisenberg found that hypothesis to be true for the men in their study but not for the women. As they reported in *Research on Language and Social Interaction* (Volume 24, 1990/1991), the women showed more concern about the other person's feelings when they were playing the role of superior. In other words, the women were more careful to save face for the other person when they were managing down than when they were managing up. This pattern recalls the way girls are socialized: Those who are in some way superior are expected to downplay rather than flaunt their superiority.

In my own recordings of workplace communication, I observed women talking in similar ways. For example, when a manager had to correct a mistake made by her secretary, she did so by acknowledging that there were mitigating circumstances. She said, laughing, "You know, it's hard to do things around here, isn't it, with all these people coming in!" The manager was saving face for her subordinate, just like the female students role-playing in the Tracy and Eisenberg study.

Is this an effective way to communicate? One must ask, effective for what? The manager in question established a positive environment in her group, and the work was done effectively. On the other hand, numerous women in many different fields told me that their bosses say they don't project the proper authority.

Indirectness

Another linguistic signal that varies with power and status is indirectness—the tendency to say what we mean without spelling it out in so many words. Despite the widespread belief in the United States that it's always best to say exactly what we mean, indirectness is a fundamental and pervasive element in human communication. It also is one of the elements that vary most from one culture to another, and it can cause enormous misunderstanding when speakers have different habits and expectations about how it is used. It's often said that American women are more indirect than American men, but in fact everyone tends to be indirect in some situations and in different ways. Allowing for cultural, ethnic, regional, and individual differences, women are especially likely to be indirect when it comes to telling others what to do, which is not surprising, considering girls' readiness to brand other girls as bossy. On the other hand, men are especially likely to be indirect when it comes to admitting fault or weakness, which also is not surprising, considering boys' readiness to push around boys who assume the one-down position.

At first glance, it would seem that only the powerful can get away with bald commands such as, "Have that report on my desk by noon." But power in an organization also can lead to requests so indirect that they don't sound like requests at all. A boss who says, "Do we have the sales data by product line for each region?" would be surprised and frustrated if a subordinate responded, "We probably do" rather than "I'll get it for you."

Examples such as these notwithstanding, many researchers have claimed that those in subordinate positions are more likely to speak indirectly, and that is surely accurate in some situations. For example, linguist Charlotte Linde, in a study published in *Language in Society* (Volume 17, 1988), examined the black-box conversations that took place between pilots and copilots before airplane crashes. In one particularly tragic instance, an Air Florida plane crashed into the Potomac River immediately after attempting take-off from National Airport in Washington, D.C., killing all but 5 of the 74 people on board. The pilot, it turned out, had little experience flying in icy weather. The copilot had a bit more, and it became heartbreakingly clear on analysis that he had tried to warn the pilot but had done so indirectly. Alerted by Linde's observation, I examined the transcript of the conversations and found evidence of her hypothesis. The copilot repeatedly called attention to the bad weather and to ice buildup on other planes:

> COPILOT: Look how the ice is just hanging on his, ah, back, back there, see that? See all those icicles on the back there and everything?
> PILOT: Yeah.
> [The copilot also expressed concern about the long waiting time since deicing.]
> COPILOT: Boy, this is a, this is a losing battle here on trying to de-ice those things; it [gives] you a false feeling of security, that's all that does.
> [Just before they took off, the copilot expressed another concern—about abnormal instrument readings—but again he didn't press the matter when it wasn't picked up by the pilot.]
> COPILOT: That don't seem right, does it? [3-second pause] Ah, that's not right. Well—
> PILOT: Yes it is, there's 80.
> COPILOT: Naw, I don't think that's right. [7-second pause] Ah, maybe it is.

Shortly thereafter, the plane took off, with tragic results. In other instances as well as this one, Linde observed that copilots, who are second in command, are more likely to express themselves indirectly or otherwise mitigate, or soften, their communication when they are suggesting courses of action to the pilot. In an effort to avert similar disasters, some airlines now offer training for copilots to express themselves in more assertive ways.

This solution seems self-evidently appropriate to most Americans. But when I assigned Linde's article in a graduate seminar I taught, a Japanese student pointed out that it would be just as effective to train pilots to pick up on hints. This approach reflects assumptions about communication that typify Japanese culture, which places great value on the ability of people to understand one another without putting everything into words. Either directness or indirectness can be a successful means of communication as long as the linguistic style is understood by the participants.

In the world of work, however, there is more at stake than whether the communication is understood. People in powerful positions are likely to reward styles similar to their own, because we all tend to take as self-evident the logic of our own styles. Accordingly, there is evidence that in the U.S.

workplace, where instructions from a superior are expected to be voiced in a relatively direct manner, those who tend to be indirect when telling subordinates what to do may be perceived as lacking in confidence.

Consider the case of the manager at a national magazine who was responsible for giving assignments to reporters. She tended to phrase her assignments as questions. For example, she asked, "How would you like to do the X project with Y?" or said, "I was thinking of putting you on the X project. Is that okay?" This worked extremely well with her staff; they liked working for her, and the work got done in an efficient and orderly manner. But when she had her midyear evaluation with her own boss, he criticized her for not assuming the proper demeanor with her staff.

In any work environment, the higher-ranking person has the power to enforce his or her view of appropriate demeanor, created in part by linguistic style. In most U.S. contexts, that view is likely to assume that the person in authority has the right to be relatively direct rather than to mitigate orders. There also are cases, however, in which the higher-ranking person assumes a more indirect style. The owner of a retail operation told her subordinate, a store manager, to do something. He said he would do it, but a week later he still hadn't. They were able to trace the difficulty to the following conversation: She had said, "The bookkeeper needs help with the billing. How would you feel about helping her out?" He had said, "Fine." This conversation had seemed to be clear and flawless at the time, but it turned out that they had interpreted this simple exchange in very different ways. She thought he meant, "Fine, I'll help the bookkeeper out." He thought he meant, "Fine, I'll think about how I would feel about helping the bookkeeper out." He did think about it and came to the conclusion that he had more important things to do and couldn't spare the time.

To the owner, "How would you feel about helping the bookkeeper out?" was an obviously appropriate way to give the order "Help the bookkeeper out with the billing." Those who expect orders to be given as bald imperatives may find such locutions annoying or even misleading. But those for whom this style is natural do not think they are being indirect. They believe they are being clear in a polite or respectful way.

What is atypical in this example is that the person with the more indirect style was the boss, so the store manager was motivated to adapt to her style. She still gives orders the same way, but the store manager now understands how she means what she says. It's more common in U.S. business contexts for the highest-ranking people to take a more direct style, with the result that many women in authority risk being judged by their superiors as lacking the appropriate demeanor—and, consequently, lacking confidence.

What to Do?

I am often asked, What is the best way to give criticism? or What is the best way to give orders?—in other words, What is the best way to communicate? The answer is that there is no one best way. The results of a given way of speaking will vary depending on the situation, the culture of the company, the relative rank of speakers, their linguistic styles, and how those styles interact with one another. Because of all those influences, any way of speaking could be perfect for communicating with one person in one situation and disastrous with someone else in another. The critical skill for managers is to become aware of the workings and power of linguistic style, to make sure that people with something valuable to contribute get heard.

It may seem, for example, that running a meeting in an unstructured way gives equal opportunity to all. But awareness of the differences in conversational style makes it easy to see the potential for unequal access. Those who are comfortable speaking up in groups, who need little or no silence before raising their hands, or who speak out easily without waiting to be recognized are far more likely to get heard at meetings. Those who refrain from talking until it's clear that the previous speaker is finished, who wait to be recognized, and who are inclined to link their comments to those of others will do fine at a meeting where everyone else is following the same rules but will have a hard time getting heard in a meeting with people whose styles are more like the first pattern. Given the socialization typical of boys and girls, men are more likely to have learned the first style and women the second, making meetings more congenial for men than for women. It's common to observe women who participate actively in one-on-one discussions or in all-female groups but who are seldom heard in meetings with a large proportion of men. On the other hand, there are women who share the style more common among men, and they run a different risk—of being seen as too aggressive.

A manager aware of those dynamics might devise any number of ways of ensuring that everyone's ideas are heard and credited. Although no single solution will fit all contexts, managers who understand the dynamics of linguistic style can develop more adaptive and flexible approaches to running or participating in meetings, mentoring or advancing the careers of others, evaluating performance, and so on. Talk is the lifeblood of managerial work, and understanding that different people have different ways of saying what they mean will make it possible to take advantage of the talents of people with a broad range of linguistic styles. As the workplace becomes more culturally diverse and business becomes more global, managers will need to become even better at reading interactions and more flexible in adjusting their own styles to the people with whom they interact.

Content Questions

1. What effect can a difference of expectations between speakers about the appropriate length of pauses in a conversation have on the way they view

each other? What factors can contribute to this difference in expectations between speakers?

2. Explain what Tannen means when she says that "every utterance functions on two levels."

3. On what basis does Tannen make the claim that communication between men and women is cross-cultural? How do their childhood experiences contribute to those differences?

4. How can conversational style affect "who gets credit" in the workplace?

5. What does the experiment that involved students predicting their own grades seem to show about the differences between male and female discourse norms?

6. How could a male employer's perception of an employee who asks many questions be different from the perception held by a female employer? How is this related to different expectations in conversational style?

7. What is a "conversational ritual"? What are some of the types of conversational rituals identified in the article?

8. In the example of the plane crash, what role did the indirect speech of the copilot play in the subsequent disaster? Explain.

Questions for Analysis and Discussion

1. Prepare a list of some of the conversational differences between men and women that are identified in this article.

2. Tannen is careful to point out that the generalizations she makes about women and men do not characterize all women and men. Do you think your own behavior corresponds to the observations that Tannen makes in her article?

3. How can different expectations about what constitutes a conversational ritual lead to a breakdown in communication? Comment on the differences that seem to exist between men and women with their use of apologies and compliments.

4. How might people interpret and react to "ritual opposition" in a particular setting if they do not recognize it for what it is?

5. Is Tannen's point that we should develop one type of speech style or another? Explain.

6. Based on what you have read, to what extent do you believe that Tannen places responsibility on one gender or another for the linguistic styles that might disadvantage women?

7. How might a business benefit from management and employees who are more aware of differences in conversational styles? To what extent do you believe that individuals could improve their own interpersonal communication by being aware of such differences?

Penguins Don't Care, but Women Do: A Social Identity Analysis of a Whorfian Problem[*]

Fatemeh Khosroshahi

Social movements often see language as a powerful tool that must be modified in some cases in order to initiate more appropriate thoughts or attitudes in people's minds. Such goals for language change are based on the type of assumption embodied in the Sapir–Whorf hypothesis (also known as the "Whorfian hypothesis"). This hypothesis suggests that the language we speak influences our perception. In the article below, which first appeared in the journal *Language in Society,* Fatemeh Khosroshahi develops and discusses an experiment she conducted to see the extent to which the generic usage of pronoun forms such as *he, he or she,* or *they* for the third-person singular affects our perception. Her experiment resulted in some interesting findings. The article contains a section of statistics and formulas. You do not need to understand all the specifics about how to interpret those figures, but pay particular attention to the conclusions that are drawn based on those numbers and formulas.

Abstract

The Sapir–Whorf hypothesis is often implicitly assumed to be true independent of its empirical status. Feminist attempts to eliminate the generic *he* must assume that language somehow affects thought, since there is no intrinsic harm in the word itself. Research to date has, in fact, shown that generic *he* tends to suggest a male referent in the mind of the reader. This study asks whether people's interpretation of a generic sentence varies depending on whether or not they have followed feminist proposals and re-

*Roger Brown's work in social psychology has influenced me deeply. His substantive contributions to this research and his unfailing generosity have seemed limitless. The following individuals have also been invaluable at various stages of this work: Paul Andreassen, Frank Bernieri, Irene Goodale, Monica Harris, Leora Heckelman, Ellen Langer, James MacKay, Eigil Pedersen, Robert Rosenthal (who went far beyond the call of duty in helping me), Gregg Solomon, and Elena Yuan. Dell Hymes and another, anonymous reader of an earlier draft of this article provided engaged and engaging comments. Thanks are also due to the subjects who freely gave of their time to this study and to those friends at Harvard who volunteered as pilot subjects. This research was supported by a scholarship from Fonds pour la Formation de Chercheurs et l'Aide à la Recherche of Quebec. Their generosity went far beyond expectations and I wish to express my deepest gratitude to them for it.

formed their own language. Fifty-five college students read sex-indefinite paragraphs involving either the generic *he, he or she,* or *they,* and made drawings to represent the mental images evoked by what they read. The sex of the figure drawn was the dependent variable. Students' term papers were used to determine whether their own language was "reformed" or "traditional." *He* was found to be least likely to evoke female referents, *he or she* most likely, and *they* in between. However, regardless of the pronoun, men drew more male and fewer female pictures than women. Moreover, whereas men did not differ in their imagery, whether their language was reformed or traditional, women did. Traditional-language women had more male images than female. Reformed-language women showed the opposite. Results are discussed in terms of the theory of social identity (Tajfel 1981), and it is concluded that the weak, correlational form of Whorf's thesis applies to women, the group that initiated the reform in the first place.

A father and his son are out driving. They have an automobile accident. The father is killed, and the son is rushed to the hospital and prepared for operation. The doctor comes in, sees the patient, and exclaims, "I can't operate on this patient, it's my son!"

Give, if you will, a little bit of thought to this problem. Can you find a simple solution for it? Many, perhaps most people cannot. The best answer is, of course, that the doctor was the mother of the patient. Yet this seemingly obvious solution does not occur to many of us.

Feminists have argued for the existence of an archetypal assumption that, by default, all creatures are male unless they are explicitly specified as female (e.g., Silveira 1980). Our language, the argument goes, reflects this "male-as-norm syndrome" (Miller & Swift 1976).[1] Thus, in generic contexts the word *man* is supposed to include women. Or, as our grammar teachers have taught us, we are to use the masculine pronoun *he* in sex-indefinite sentences, for example, "Everyone views his grammar rules as written in stone." This linguistic asymmetry can be viewed as an instance of *markedness,* a general phenomenon in languages (see Baron 1986; Lakoff 1973; Silveira 1980). Unmarked forms are simple and, presumably, neutral, whereas marked forms represent "the deviation from some basic simple form" (Baddeley 1976:320). In English, female terms are marked. They "are formed by the addition of suffixes, as in *actor–actress* . . . and it is the male term that neutralizes to cover both sexes, as in . . . *mankind*" (H. Clark & E. Clark 1977:543).

---

[1] In the context of our vignette, perfectly realistic statistics justify such an assumption. Most doctors *are* male. But only *most* doctors are male. Why then does the possibility of a female doctor not even occur to so many of us?

The unmarkedness of masculine words in English has been interpreted as making women invisible and is thus thought to embody and transmit a sexist view of social relations (Baron 1986; Cameron 1985; Henley 1977; Kramarae 1981; McConnell-Ginet 1984; Miller & Swift 1976; Silveira 1980). An analogy has been drawn between generic terms such as *he* and *man* and brand names such as *Kleenex* (Moulton, Robinson, & Elias 1978; Silveira 1980). The manufacturers of Kleenex are probably proud because people all over the world use the name of their product not only to refer to that particular brand but also to paper tissues in general. Similarly, men, or at least English-speaking men, must be proud because, the argument goes, generic terms such as *he* and *man* are not gender-neutral, just as *Kleenex* is not brand-neutral. Feminists have argued that if *he* and *man* were truly generic, sentences like these would be legitimate: "Man, being a mammal, breast-feeds his young" (Martyna 1980a:489). "Un homme sur deux est une femme" ('one man out of two is a woman'—a slogan of the French Mouvement de la Libération de la Femme)!

The claim that masculine generic words help to perpetuate an andro-centric world view assumes more or less explicitly the validity of the Sapir–Whorf hypothesis, according to which the structure of the language we speak affects the way we think (e.g., Whorf 1956). That different languages make us think and feel differently is a compelling experience for many of us. However, the empirical tests of the hypothesis of linguistic relativity have yielded more equivocal results (for reviews see Brown 1976, 1986; see also Carroll & Casagrande 1958; Kay & Kempton 1984). But independently of its empirical status, Whorf's view is quite widely held.[2] In fact, many social movements have attempted reforms of language and have thus taken Whorf's thesis for granted (Brown 1986).

Furthermore, a large body of empirical work has shown that in ethnic revival movements and situations of intergroup conflict, language can become a powerful symbol of group identity and cultural pride and thus can acquire social significance far beyond its function as a medium of communication (e.g., Giles 1977; Lambert 1967; Ryan & Giles 1982; Taylor, Bassili, & Aboud 1973). This line of research has been deeply influenced by Tajfel's (e.g., 1981) theory of social identity, according to which people are interested in enhancing the value of their ethnic group because a favorable group identity elevates their self-esteem (see also Giles, Bourhis, & Taylor 1977).

Much of this work has focused on ethnolinguistic groups, such as French Canadians, and has tended to scant the supreme and most primitive social distinction of all times and all cultures, that is, gender. However, a framework based on the theory of social identity permits us to see the

---

[2]I am indebted to Dell Hymes for pointing out that rejections or adoptions of Whorf's view, and of Chomsky's for that matter, tend to be based on subjective preferences rather than on decisive evidence.

canonical structure shared by various resurgences of ethnic pride as well as the women's movement (Brown 1986; Kramarae 1981; Ryan & Giles 1982; Smith 1985; Williams & Giles 1978). There are at least three linguistic strategies that ethnic groups as well as women adopt in search of a positive social identity. These strategies can be thought of as expressing something like this:

> "We are an O.K. people.
>
> 1. In fact, our language is good.
> 2. So don't address us like that.
> 3. And don't talk about us like that."

1. "Our Language Is Good": The Positive Reevaluation of "Minority" Languages

Again and again language has been a battleground of political conflicts, and there have been recurrent attempts by ethnic groups (e.g., in Quebec and Belgium) to reevaluate their languages positively. From the perspective of the theory of social identity, such attempts are instances of social action (or "voice") aimed at ameliorating the negative identity of the group and, thus, increasing the pride of its members (see Brown 1986).

In an influential article, Lakoff (1973) speculated that women are expected to speak like "ladies" and that they do in fact speak in ways different from men. Lakoff's article has been criticized not only because some of her predictions have failed the empirical tests (e.g., Edelsky 1979; Holmes 1986), but also because she implied that she didn't *like* "women's language." She is therefore accused of "identification with the aggressor" (Dubois & Crouch 1978), a phenomenon reminiscent of Lambert's (e.g., 1967) French Canadian subjects who showed disdain for their own language. Today, there is more and more voice about women's traits, including women's speech style (e.g., Henley 1977), and more recent research in this area emphasizes the *stereotyping* of female speakers (Edelsky 1979; Kramarae 1982; Smith 1985).

2. "Don't Address Us Like That": Ideologically Motivated Attempts to Reform Terms of Address

In their influential study, Brown and Gilman found a close association between terms of address and "two dimensions fundamental to the analysis of all social life—the dimensions of power and solidarity" (1960:253). Given the social meaning of terms of address, it is not surprising that egalitarian political revolutions attempt to make these symbols of social structure compatible with their ideals. Two things usually happen, however. First, some people soon become "more equal" than others, and second, the language finds a new way of expressing this fact.

Nevertheless, attempts to reform terms of address are frequent, and the women's movement has been no exception (Henley 1977). The title of a report by Wolfson and Manes (1980)—"Don't 'dear' me!"–nicely captures their main finding and is reminiscent of the man who was arrested in 1913 for accosting a woman with the greeting "Hello, chicken" (in Baron 1986:162). The woman who says "don't 'dear' me" shows that she tacitly knows the rule that Roger Brown has made explicit: "If form X is used to inferiors it is used between intimates, and if form Y is used to superiors it is used between strangers" (1965:92). If there is no intimacy between her and the person who "deared" her, then that person must have assumed that she is of lower status. Such an assumption is often challenged when a group attempts to raise its negative identity.

3. "Don't Talk About Us Like That": Eliminating Pejorative Forms of Reference

In social movements, the way members of a subordinate group are referred to can also become subject to reform. Thus, feminists have attempted to eliminate reference forms that are thought to deprecate and trivialize women, ignore them, or subordinate their identity to men (Baron 1986; Cameron 1985; Graham 1975; Henley 1977; Kramarae 1981; Lakoff 1973; Martyna 1980a; McConnell-Ginet 1984; Miller & Swift 1976).

The generic pronoun *he*, the prime target of reform, was apparently prescribed by grammarians in the 18th century, which probably has something to do with the sex of these grammarians (Bodine 1975). Prior to such prescriptions, singular *they* seems to have been the accepted generic pronoun, and it still is very much a part of American English (Baron 1986; MacKay 1983; Miller & Swift 1976). In *written* language, however, *he or she* seems to be the most commonly used alternative, but it is cumbersome and since *he* always comes first, gender asymmetry is preserved in any case.

Feminist attempts to change masculine generic words have been strongly resisted (e.g., Kilpatrick 1976). From the perspective of the theory of social identity, such resistance is not surprising. As Giles, Bourhis, and Taylor put it, when threatened, "dominant groups do not lie idle" (1977:307). Nevertheless, a view of the generic *he* and *man* which goes against Whorf does seem plausible. One can reasonably argue that people might interpret these terms as truly unmarked for sex (Dubois & Crouch 1978) and that there might exist a cognitive isolation between the sex-specific and the generic meanings of the terms. Fortunately, this is an empirical question and it has been investigated. The following informal experiment, suggested by Shepelak, can be thought of as the "script," in Schank and Abelson's (1977) sense, of these studies:

> I would like to conduct a small experiment with you, the reader. Take a
> sheet of paper and draw your conception of what the Neanderthal man

looked like. Finished? . . . Why did you picture a male to represent the Neanderthal man, especially since the noun "man" was being used generically (or was it?) . . . When one says Neanderthal man, one imagines a male, not a female. (Shepelak, in Kilpatrick 1976:90–91)

In this experiment, the procedure was one of asking the subject to draw, and the dependent variable was the sex of the picture drawn. Other studies, using a variety of comprehension tasks, have consistently found that both *man* and *he* tend to be interpreted as referring only to males, despite generic contexts (e.g., Crawford & English 1984; MacKay 1980; MacKay & Fulkerson 1979; Martyna 1980b; Moulton et al. 1978; Schneider & Hacker 1973). Although we are far from Whorf's (1956) speculation that the structure of language affects one's "ideology of nature," this finding is one case where language has cognitive consequences.

Rationale for the Present Experiment

Given the result that *he* can be interpreted as excluding women even in generic contexts, a natural question is whether people who have reformed their own language and no longer use the masculine generic would differ in their interpretation of generic sentences from those who still use the traditional form. In other words, are those who are more egalitarian in their language also more egalitarian in their thought? Is a reform in language production associated with one in comprehension? Does saying *he or she* mean thinking *he or she?*

Language production can be thought to be typically more deliberate than comprehension, which seems to be a relatively spontaneous process involving tacit knowledge and automatic operations (see Frederiksen & Dominic 1981). Producing language, especially *written* language, can be regarded as typically much more "mindful" (Langer 1983) than understanding language. Language production is therefore more likely to reflect one's deliberately chosen, conscious ideological values (e.g., feminism) than the habitual, automatic thought processes involved in comprehension. Thus, unless the ideology has become second nature, it is more likely to be reflected in the public task of writing than in the private process of comprehension.

The present study examined the comprehension of generic pronouns by college students and its relationship to their own language usage. Students who consistently used the generic *he* in a term paper were considered to be "traditional" in their language production. Those who, at least some of the time, replaced the generic *he* with, say, *he or she* were regarded as having "reformed" their usage. The comprehension task that was presented to these two groups of men and women involved sex-neutral paragraphs containing the generic *he*, *he or she*, or singular *they*.

Because the very purpose of the study was to compare the spontaneous (comprehension) with the deliberate (production), it was important that subjects be naive with respect to the study and do the comprehension task with minimal effect of those egalitarian values which have not become part of their tacit knowledge. They were therefore told that the experiment was on "mental imagery and language" and were asked to read each paragraph and sketch on paper their mental imagery relevant to it. The question was, when people are asked to draw their mental imagery about a sentence referring to a generic person, what will be the sex of the person they draw? Obviously, images cannot be equated with comprehension and they may even not occur unless they are asked for (see Lang 1984). However, it is probably reasonable to assume that images are in some way related to comprehension and consistent with it.

Method

Subjects

Fifty-five students (28 women, 27 men) in Harvard University introductory psychology courses participated voluntarily in the study. The subjects were either native speakers of English or said that English was their better language.

Materials

Six paragraphs were generated, each of which could include any one of the three forms of the possessive third person generic pronoun (i.e., *his, his or her,* and singular *their*). To give the reader a feel for the material used, here is one of the paragraphs:

> It is usually believed that crying reflects sadness and smiling reflects happiness. However, things are not always this simple, and ambiguous cases do exist. For example, an unhappy person could still have a smile on his/her or her/their face.

An attempt was made to have the paragraphs be as sex-neutral as possible. Thus, the pronouns used are more or less accepted forms of reference to a generic person, and present tense and indefinite antecedents preceded by the article *a* were used (MacKay & Fulkerson 1979). A pilot study had suggested that nouns referring to predominantly male groups (e.g., *plumber*) tend to be interpreted invariably as referring exclusively to males. Therefore, the present study used only sex-neutral nouns (i.e., *person*, in the paragraph presented here, and *child, resident, human, adult,* and *teenager,* in the remaining five paragraphs). Furthermore, an attempt was made to render the semantic context within which these nouns occurred neutral with respect to sex role stereotypes.

Procedure

The students were tested individually by a female experimenter (me) and each session lasted about 40 minutes. The students first read instructions that led them to believe that what was being studied was their mental imagery during reading, its role in the "comprehension of abstract sentences," and its relationship to their "ability to hold digits in memory." These precautions proved worthwhile: no one guessed the purpose of the study. After having read the instructions, the students were presented with written paragraphs one by one. They read each paragraph and sketched their mental imagery in response to it.

The pilot study had shown that subjects' drawings are often very sketchy (e.g., stick figures), and determining the sex of the figures drawn can be impossible. Therefore, once all the drawings were completed, each student was asked: "Tell me *whether or not* you can give this person [or child, etc.] an age and a name." The age question was a distractor but the name question was intended to reveal the sex of the person that the students had in mind. However the words "whether or not" were emphasized in each case in order to prevent *forcing* sex-specific interpretations.

Throughout the entire session, I was blind with respect to the language-production group to which each student belonged, and with respect to the pronoun used in each paragraph. At the end of the session, students were thoroughly debriefed and asked demographic questions as well as questions about their exposure to the issue of sexism in language.

Design

The experiment involved four variables. The two variables *between* subjects were their sex and their language usage as reflected in their term paper (reformed vs. traditional). Thus, there were four groups of students. The two variables *within* subjects, on the other hand, were the pronoun presented (*he, he or she, they*) and the sex of the image drawn (female, male, or generic).

Each student was presented with all six paragraphs, two per pronoun. But paragraph and pronoun were not confounded: each paragraph was used with all three pronouns across students. Thus, all possible paragraph–pronoun combinations were used and different students received different paragraph–pronoun combinations. The order of presentation of paragraphs and pronouns was independently counterbalanced via a Greco-Latin rectangle (Rosenthal & Rosnow 1984; Winer 1962), and students were randomly assigned to sequence conditions.

Coding Procedure

Students' sketches of human figures were categorized as male or female when gender was reflected in the sketches or explicitly mentioned or when the figures were given sex-specific proper names. Figures that students refused to name or to provide further sex-relevant information about were classified as generic. The generic category also included the cases where students produced both male and female figures in response to a paragraph.

As mentioned, students' papers were used to determine whether or not they had reformed their own language. The fact that all papers were written to fulfill the same requirement of the same class taught by the same instructor increases the comparability of the language-production data across students. In fact, it is reasonable to suppose that the use of generic pronouns in written language varies depending on the purpose, task demands, and the audience.

Different cases (e.g., nominative, possessive, etc.) of generic *he* were considered traditional, and different cases of *he or she, s/he, (s)he,* as well as the generic *she,* were considered reformed. However, when generic *she* referred to a stereotypically female group (e.g., nurse), it was viewed as traditional usage. Obviously, many people who are sympathetic to the ideal of gender equality and are aware of bias in language do not use generic pronouns, considered here to be reformed, because they find these forms inadequate for one reason or another. However, it is only when a writer does use such forms that we can tell for sure that deliberate reform of language has occurred.

The use of singular *they*—not a rarity—was not classified as either reformed or traditional. The very high frequency of singular *they* in students' spoken language suggests that instances of singular *they* in papers are likely to be slips of spoken language into the written mode rather than motivated attempts to use nonsexist language.

The unexpected finding from the students' papers was that although all students had had some exposure to the issue of sexism in language, only seven of them (four women and three men) consistently used the reformed pronouns and never the traditional ones. Therefore, students who had included *one or more* instances of reformed pronouns in their papers were considered to have done so in a motivated, deliberate fashion and were thus viewed as having attempted to reform their language. Of the 55 students, 25 (13 women, 12 men) were categorized as having reformed their own language on the basis of this minimal criterion.

Results

The data were subjected to a repeated-measures analysis of variance. The main effect of image was large (eta = .82) and statistically reliable,

Table I. Mean Numbers of
Female, Male, and Generic Images
Produced, Pooled over Sex,
Language, and Pronoun

	IMAGE	
Female	Male	Generic
0.525	1.224	0.251

Note: Maximum score = 2.

$F(2,102) = 102.05$, $p < .001$ (see Table 1). The number of male images was much higher than the number of female images, $F(1,102) = 99.08$, $p < .001$, $r = .81$. Furthermore, the number of male images was highest, generic images lowest, and female images in between, $F(1,102) = 191.99$, $p < .001$, $r = .89$. However, although these findings generally hold for both of the language groups and all three pronouns, when the sex of the students and its interaction with their language use are considered, they have to be qualified.

The Sex × Image interaction was significant and quite strong, $F(2,102) = 46.31$, $p < .001$, eta $= .69$. Not surprisingly, relative to women, men drew more male images, $F(1,102) = 50.89$, $p < .001$, $r = .71$, and fewer female figures, $F(1,102) = 41.32$, $p < .001$, $r = .67$; men and women did not differ, however, with respect to generic images, $F(1,102) < 1$. Men also produced significantly more male images than female images, $F(1,102) = 190.94$, $p < .001$. This difference is simply enormous ($r = .94$). Women, on the other hand, did not show a difference in the number of male and female figures they produced, $F(1,102) < 1$. This latter result, however, is modified by the language group to which a woman belongs (see later discussion).

The interaction of language and image did not reach the conventional level of significance, $F(2,102) = 2.40$, $p = .096$, eta $= .21$. Contrary to what one might expect, the two language groups did not differ significantly in the number of female, $F(1,102) = 1.37$, $p > .20$, $r = .16$, male, $F(1,102) = 3.09$, $p > .08$, $r = .24$, or generic figures produced, $F(1,102) < 1$. But these results must be qualified when the sex of the students is taken into account.

The three-way Sex × Language × Image interaction, though not very large (eta $= .24$), was marginally significant, $F(2,102) = 2.98$, $p = .056$. A series of contrasts revealed that the conclusion of no difference between the two language groups holds for men but not for women (see Table 2). That is, whereas reformed- and traditional-language men did not differ significantly in the number of female, male, and generic images that they generated (all three Fs < 1), reformed women produced significantly more female figures, $F(1,102) = 4.91$, $p < .05$, $r = .40$, and fewer male images,

$F(1,102) = 4.70, p < .05, r = .39$, than traditional women; there was virtually no difference, however, for generic figures, $F(1,102) < 1$.

Given the finding that reform of language is associated with differences of imagery among women but not among men, a reasonable question is whether men and women who had reformed their pronoun usage in their papers had done so to the same extent. On the average, 57 percent of the generic pronouns used by reformed-language men in their papers included *she*, whereas 50 percent of the generic pronouns used by reformed-language women could be considered reformed. Thus, although men's language reform was more general than women's, it mattered less than theirs.

As mentioned, men produced fewer female and more male figures than women but almost as many generic images. Furthermore, men drew many more male characters than female ones. These results are true of both language groups (see Table 2). However, the result already given that there is no significant difference between the number of male and female images that women produced has to be reformulated. Reformed-language women produced significantly more female than male figures, $F(1,102) = 4.03, p < .05, r = .50$, whereas traditional-language women generated significantly more male images than female ones, $F(1,102) = 5.62, p < .025, r = .54$ (see Table 2).

The Pronoun $\times$ Image interaction was statistically reliable, $F(4,204) = 2.56, p = .04$, but not very large (eta $= .22$) (see Table 3). *He or she* and *they* did not differ significantly in the number of female, $F(1,204) = 1.62, p > .20, r = .18$, male, $F(1,204) = 2.17, p > .10, r = .20$, and generic images, $F(1,204) < 1$, they elicited in the minds of the students. Similarly, *he* and *they* did not differ in the number of female, $F(1,204) = 1.23, p > .20, r = .15$, male, $F(1,204) < 1$, and generic figures, $F(1,204) < 1$, they evoked.

Table 2. Mean Numbers of Female, Male, and Generic Images Produced, Pooled over Pronoun

		IMAGE		
SEX	**LANGUAGE**	**FEMALE**	**MALE**	**GENERIC**
Women	Reformed ($n = 13$)	1.000	0.718	0.282
	Traditional ($n = 15$)	0.689	1.022	0.289
Men	Reformed ($n = 12$)	0.167	1.556	0.278
	Traditional ($n = 15$)	0.244	1.600	0.156

Note: Maximum score = 2.

Table 3. Mean Numbers of Female, Male, and Generic
Images Produced, Pooled over Sex and Language

PRONOUN	IMAGE		
	FEMALE	MALE	GENERIC
He	0.374	1.331	0.295
He or she	0.683	1.075	0.243
They	0.518	1.266	0.216

Note: Maximum score = 2.

However, imagery associated with *he or she* did differ from that associated with *he* (see Table 3). In fact, after reading paragraphs involving *he or she,* students produced more female characters, $F(1,204) = 5.67, p < .025,$ $r = .32,$ and fewer male figures, $F(1,204) = 3.89, p < .05, r = .27,$ than after reading the *he* paragraphs. The difference was small and unreliable, however, for generic images, $F(1,204) < 1.$ Also, *he* evoked the lowest number of female images, *he or she* the highest number, and *they* in between, $F(1,204) = 5.67, p < .025, r = .32.$ The reverse linear contrast predicting the number of *male* images to be highest in response to *he,* lowest for *he or she,* and in between in the case of *they* was also significant, $F(1,204) = 3.89, p < .05, r = .27.$

Overall, the differences among the three pronouns were not as many and as large as what one might expect on the basis of the empirical literature cited earlier, and in fact, male figures were produced significantly more than female figures, regardless of whether the pronoun was *he,* $F(1,306) = 56.64, p < .001, r = .73,$ *he or she,* $F(1,306) = 9.50, p < .005, r = .40,$ or *they,* $F(1,306) = 34.60, p < .001, r = .64$ (see Table 3). As reported earlier, only women who had reformed their language showed the opposite pattern, that is, they produced more female than male images; and they did so for all three pronouns.

All high-level interactions involving the pronoun variable were both nonsignificant and rather small.

Discussion

What have we learned? First, the use of generic *he* in written language is much more widespread than might appear from language used in academic journals. When Harvard University undergraduates used a generic pronoun, it was usually *he.*

Second, feminists are right in suggesting that the generic *he* can be psychologically nongeneric. In fact, after reading paragraphs involving the generic *he,* students drew sketches of male figures 67 percent of the time.

The data suggest that from the perspective of a feminist, *he or she* is best, *he* is worst, and *they* in between. Thus overall, *he or she* evoked the highest number of female images (34%), *he* the lowest number (19%), and *they* an intermediate number (26%). This pattern was also obtained in a study by Moulton et al. (1978). However, the effect of the pronoun was not very strong. The largest difference was between the number of female referents that *he or she* elicited in the minds of the students and those that *he* evoked. The size of this effect was .32. But this rather small effect is reliable. It was statistically significant in this study and, more important, it replicates the findings of many previous studies. As Bertilson, Springer, and Fierke put it, this pronoun effect is "*robust* and *not attenuated* by a variety of stimulus and response conditions" (1982:924). The effect is not enormous, but it is there.

Those who believe that generic *he* is not sexist *have* had plausible arguments for their position. Nevertheless, they are wrong. In fact, despite the *prima facie* plausibility, given what we know about the structure of memory, the finding that generic *he* is biased is not surprising. Students of memory have repeatedly demonstrated that the presentation of a word leads to the memorial activation of its associates (e.g., Meyer & Schvaneveldt 1971). Considering the frequent association of *he* with male referents, *he* must activate such referents even in generic contexts (Silveira 1980).

In a series of ingenious experiments, Swinney (1979) demonstrated that *both* meanings of an ambiguous word are evoked, even when the word is presented in a context where only one of its two readings is relevant. The context plays its role in making the meaning clear only after that initial activation. This finding is consistent with information-processing theories that postulate a bottom-up, fast, and automatic spread of activation to the associates of a stimulus, and a top-down, slower control process of selection of relevant entries and inhibition of irrelevant ones (e.g., Posner & Snyder 1975).

The presumed pride of the manufacturers of Kleenex therefore does not seem baseless. Words that have a generic meaning or a specific one, depending on the context, do seem to have the potential to bias people even when their unmarked, generic sense is intended. Like *Kleenex*, *he* refers to a category and to one of its members (Moulton et al. 1978; Silveira 1980). Given the well-documented, robust phenomenon of associative activation, the finding that generic *he* unwittingly misleads people into thinking of males, instead of both females and males, should not be newsworthy.

However, our results suggest that even *he or she* is often interpreted mostly in terms of male figures. One of the groups (reformed-language women) showed the opposite pattern, but then for that group even the *he*-paragraphs were interpreted mostly in terms of female referents. It thus appears that while relative to *he*, *he or she* evokes more female referents in the mind of the reader, *who* that reader is is also very important.

Reformed-language women thought more of women even when presented with generic *he,* presumably because they have developed top-down, controlled processes to inhibit the automatically evoked masculine associates of *he.*

A third finding is a pattern of sex differences corresponding to what one might expect. Regardless of their own usage and of the pronoun involved, when women read a generic sentence they were more likely than men to draw female figures and less likely than they to draw male figures. This is a straightforward sex difference that is *not* the same as finding that women drew more female than male figures and that men drew more male than female ones. *This* was also found but not for all groups, and this brings us to the fourth and last set of results, a set having to do with group differences.

To summarize several results involving group differences in one statement, we can say: *all groups were androcentric except the women who had reformed their language* (see Table 4); androcentric in the sense that when they read a paragraph that was ambiguous with respect to gender, they were more likely to interpret it as referring to a male than to a female character. Even if the paragraph used *he or she* or *they,* feminine referents did not become more salient than masculine ones.

Table 4. Mean Numbers[a] of Female and Male Images Produced by Four Groups of Subjects

[a] Actually, entries are roughly *proportional* to the mean numbers of male and female figures drawn (see Table 2). Generic figures are ignored.

Research on natural categories has shown that "not all members of a concept are equal.... Concepts possess an internal structure that favors typical members over less typical ones" (Smith & Medin 1981:35). Our conception of people should be no exception; some people are probably thought of as "more person" than others (Silveira 1980). For three of our four groups, the typical person seems to be male by default.

If someone says "I saw a bird . . . ," we assume, tacitly, that the bird was, say, a robin or a sparrow, and we tend to ignore the possibility that it might have been a penguin or a chicken; such atypical birds would have been explicitly named, just as doctors would have to be explicitly characterized as female or else assume the default, male gender (see Silveira 1980). As Brown pointed out, however,

> there are differences between natural categories for ethnic [or gender] groups and natural categories for the nonhuman world. The main difference is that in the latter domain there is no one to take offense if you use a highly prototypical example to stand for the category.... It is just that *birds don't care but people do.* (emphasis added, 1986:595)

Given the repeatedly documented fact that women are significantly under-represented in a variety of literatures (e.g., Bertilson et al. 1982; Graham 1975), the finding that the masculine tends to be read as representative is not very surprising. We just don't read about women as much. In fact, some writers have questioned the very existence of common-gender terms (see Baron 1986; Cameron 1985). In a literature dominated by male characters, initially sex-indefinite words must quickly develop masculine connotations.

Thus, some people, some doctors, some birds, and some paper tissues seem to be more "activated" than others; hence the androcentrism of three of our four groups, for whom women seem to be marginal members of the person category, just like penguins and chickens are on the fringes of the category bird (see Silveira 1980). Our "Hello chicken" man in 1913 might have had a point!

However, although both men and traditional-language women were androcentric, men's androcentrism was much more extreme (see Table 4). In fact, the difference between the number of male and female images that men drew was simply huge. A post-hoc test contrasting men's androcentrism to that of traditional women (number of male minus number of female images) indicated a large and significant difference between them, $F(1,40) = 38.62$, $p < .001$, $r = .70$.[3] Moreover, not everyone was androcentric; women who *had* changed, at least to some extent, their pronoun

---

[3] Given the rather large size of the effect and the number of degrees of freedom involved, the difference would be significant even if a conservative approach such as the Bonferroni procedure or the Scheffé test were adopted (see Rosenthal & Rosnow 1984).

usage according to feminist proposals did not interpret most generic sentences as referring to males. What did they do? Did *they* interpret such sentences in an egalitarian fashion, that is, as referring to males and females equally? No; they tended to interpret them as referring mostly to female characters. Thus, like men, the images that these women associated to a text which was ambiguous with respect to gender was biased towards their own sex.

This finding allows us to summarize the results in an alternative fashion: *all groups were biased towards their own sex except the women who had not reformed their usage* (see Table 4). When the students read about a person of unspecified sex, they tended to think of a person of their own sex. A bias towards one's own sex is analogous to ethnocentrism, the tendency to favor one's own ethnic group. This tendency, which has been extensively documented by Tajfel (1981) and his colleagues, seems to be a very general one (Brown 1986).

Note however that ethnocentrism—or more accurately "gendercentrism"—was much stronger among men than among (reformed-language) women (see Table 4). A post-hoc test contrasting the gendercentrism of these two groups (number of own-sex images minus number of opposite-sex images) indicated a large and significant difference between them, $F(1,38) = 35.42$, $p < .001$, $r = .69$.[4] Moreover, not everyone was "gendercentric." Women who had not changed their use of pronouns and still consistently used the generic *he* interpreted paragraphs which were ambiguous with respect to gender more in terms of the *opposite* sex than in terms of their own sex. Their behavior is reminiscent of the black American children, in the classic study by K. Clark and M. Clark (1947), who expressed preference for a white doll over a black doll. The androcentric imagery of these women also reminds one of the Québécois who denigrated the speech style of their own group. And it is analogous as well to the behavior of those Welsh people who, ashamed of their ethnic identity, attenuated their Welsh accent when interacting with an English outgroup speaker (see Bourhis 1982; Bourhis & Giles 1977; Lambert 1967). This reverse ethnocentrism indicates the acceptance of an inferior social identity, and *that* is what social movements attempt to eliminate (Tajfel 1981).

In fact, some of the later doll-preference studies (e.g., Hraba & Grant 1970) have failed to replicate the early findings of K. Clark and M. Clark, suggesting that the "Black is Beautiful" campaign did indeed promote black pride (see Brown 1986). The ethnocentric (or gendercentric) imagery of the *reformed*-language women is analogous to the behavior of the black children in these later studies who preferred *black* dolls. Their responses are also reminiscent of the Québécois in some of the more recent studies who rated the language of their own group more favorably, just as the *proud* Welsh emphasized their accent when responding to an English inter-

---

[4] See note 3.

locutor (see Bourhis 1982; Bourhis & Giles 1977; Lambert 1967). The androcentric behavior of the men, on the other hand, resembles that of the white children or the Anglophones in Quebec who were invariably ethnocentric whether tested in the 1940s and 1950s (traditional language) or in the 1970s and 1980s (reformed language).[5]

What can we say about the relation of language and thought? Because the language variable (reformed vs. traditional) was not experimentally manipulated in this study, causal inferences cannot be drawn about its relation to thought (comprehension as reflected in pictures sketched). The pattern of association between the two sets of data does suggest some interesting relationships, however.

Traditional-language men and women still consistently use the generic *he* in their writing and they also interpret generic sentences primarily in terms of male referents; both their language and their thought are androcentric. Reformed-language women, on the other hand, have changed their pronoun usage according to feminist ideology, *and* their comprehension of generic sentences is not androcentric. Their language includes women and so does their thought. Thus, like the traditional-language men and women, their language and thought are consistent. However, the men who have reformed their language and use pronouns in the new way do not show a compatible pattern of thought. Their language includes women; their thought does not, or at least not yet. Thus, if we consider the *weak* form of the Sapir–Whorf hypothesis, which states that differences in language are *correlated* with differences in thought (Brown 1958), we can restate our conclusion in this form: *all groups conformed to Whorf's thesis except the men who had reformed their language* (see Table 4).

The question of whether language and thought are congruent is analogous to a problem that has preoccupied social psychologists for decades: the relation between action and cognition.[6] Do people act (e.g., use language) according to what they think (e.g., image)? The empirical work on this question has provided mixed results, and if you expect overt action to be predicated upon cognition, you will be surprised by the small size of the correlations that have been found in some of the studies. In fact, as McGuire (1985:251) put it, "the low correlations . . . have been the scandal of the field for a half century." However, if you expect to find discrepancy between what people do and what they think, you will be impressed that reliable correlations between action and cognition have been empirically established *at all*. Much of the research in this area has focused on the

---

[5] It should be pointed out, however, that some of the recent studies *have* replicated Lambert's early findings in Quebec (e.g., Maurice 1985). Similarly, negative identity among black children in the United States seems to have reappeared (e.g., Jenkins 1985). Even Michael Jackson has lightened his skin color. Once again, different seems to be bad. Attitude change is evidently not a linear process.

[6] I am indebted to Dell Hymes for pointing out the relevance of this literature to the findings, and for providing very constructive comments in this regard.

correspondence between what people think about members of an outgroup and the way they act towards them. Numerous studies have found congruence between prejudicial thinking and discriminatory behavior in intergroup relations; many others, however, have found discrepancies (see Stephan 1985, for a review).

The results of the present study are consistent with both sets of findings. The women who have changed their activity and use reformed pronouns show a compatible pattern of thought. This is analogous to the correspondence which has been found between, say, attending an NAACP meeting and impartiality towards blacks (see Stephan 1985).[7] On the other hand, the men who have reformed their language behavior show no congruent thinking, a discrepancy reminiscent of the U.S. Army men who collaborated (behaviorally) with their brainwashing captors during the Korean War without changing their inner beliefs (see McGuire 1985).

It seems that whether new behavior is associated with new thought depends in part on the depth of the underlying change of attitude. The men who have adopted the new linguistic behavior seem to have undergone a relatively superficial change of attitude, a change induced by situational demands, interpersonal pressures, or other extraneous influences, rather than by inner convictions. A number of those who have studied the processes of social influence have contrasted this overt compliance with deeper, more private attitude change. Thus, Moscovici (1985), for instance, made a distinction between "compliance" and "conversion," and Kelman (1974) between "compliance" and "internalization." Compliance involves the public acquiescence to a position without private commitment to it. The person adheres to an emerging norm of behavior in order to gain a specific reward or to avoid disapproval. Internalization, on the other hand, goes beyond conformity to social pressures. The person accepts influence because of an authentic modification of old values and a personal integration of new ones (Kelman 1974). The women who have altered their pronoun usage seem to have changed attitude at this level, that is, not just in what they regard as interactionally appropriate, but in their actual conception of who the generic person is. They are concerned not just with the social effect of their behavior, but seem to have incorporated a redefinition of persons. Their action and cognition are congruent because they have undergone a deeper attitude change than men.

As mentioned, however, many studies have found a discrepancy between action and thought. After all, what people do under the constraints of a social situation need not correspond to what they think privately. Our behavior can change depending on whether or not others might know about it (Stephan 1985). Behavior that is based on compliance tends to manifest itself only under conditions of surveillance, whereas behavior adopted through internalization can manifest itself even when it is not observable (Kelman 1974).

---

[7]NAACP = National Association for the Advancement of Colored People.

In the present study, the imagery method probably did tap the private thoughts of the students, and our results suggest that for women, the deliberate adoption of a new linguistic practice for ideological reasons is associated with an authentic change of heart which is thus expressed even under relatively private circumstances. For men, on the other hand, reform of language seems to be a relatively superficial change, operative only at the level of a deliberate and public task such as writing a term paper, with no repercussions, so far at least, on private, tacit knowledge. Once these men become oblivious to some of the rules for appropriate behavior, their responses change. What seems to have motivated them to change their use of generic pronouns, then, is a concern about the impression they make on others. To avoid the costs of appearing prejudiced, they have modified their verbal, public responses, but such facework seems to have left their genuine, private beliefs intact, at least for the time being.

The research on action and cognition is not only concerned with the consistency between the two but also with the underlying causal patterns (see McGuire 1985). Just as Whorf (1956) had speculated that language *affects* thought, some investigators have maintained that change in action *produces* cognitive change, as in Pascal's word of advice: "Pray, and faith will follow" (cited in Moscovici 1985:393). There is actually quite a bit of empirical support for this idea (see McGuire 1985; Stephan 1985), and it is an idea with social implications of great importance. In fact, the notion that a change in what people do can lead to a change in what they think has been part of the rationale for significant programs of social change, such as racial desegregation in the United States (see Stephan 1985).

However, as mentioned earlier, the design of this study does not permit the inference that the reform of women's language necessarily preceded the change in their thinking. We cannot say much, then, either about the strong form of Whorf's hypothesis or about the effect of action on thought. Still, the results of this study are consistent with Kelman's (1980) contention that cognitive change always occurs in the context of action, because in these data, when there *was* change of thought, there was also change of action. If these results could be replicated with a better selected reformed-language group and with comprehension tasks other than the imagery method used here, it would suggest that people who *initiate* linguistic reform are likely to experience correlated reform of thought. Changing language does not necessarily produce alteration at the cognitive level, but it doesn't seem to hinder it either. Perhaps, as Kelman put it, "the conditions for attitude change are most likely to be present in an action situation" (1980:138). Reforming language according to feminist ideals was proposed for the most part *by women* and it does seem to work *for women,* the group that, according to the social identity theory of group relations (Tajfel 1981), needed it.

Gender categories are very probably obligatory, the result of a most natural line of fracture. The big question is the extent to which they have turned into social constructs with a life of their own, byproducts of cultural and linguistic dichotomizations, producing differences that need not exist.

References

Baddeley, A. D. (1976). *The psychology of memory.* New York: Basic.

Baron, D. (1986). *Grammar and gender.* New Haven, Conn.: Yale University Press.

Bertilson, H. S., Springer, D. K., & Fierke, K. M. (1982). Underrepresentation of female referents as pronouns, examples, and pictures in introductory college textbooks. *Psychological Reports* 51:923–31.

Bodine, A. (1975). Androcentrism in prescriptive grammar: Singular "they," sex-indefinite "he," and "he or she." *Language in Society* 4:129–46.

Bourhis, R. Y. (1982). Language policies and language attitudes: Le monde de la francophonie. In E. B. Ryan & H. Giles (eds.), *Attitudes towards language variation.* London: Edward Arnold. 34–62.

Bourhis, R. Y., & Giles, H. (1977). The language of intergroup distinctiveness. In H. Giles (ed.), *Language, ethnicity, and intergroup relations.* London: Academic. 117–35.

Brown, R. (1958). *Words and things.* Glencoe, Ill.: Free Press.

——— (1965). *Social psychology.* New York: Free Press.

——— (1976). Reference: In memorial tribute to Eric Lenneberg. *Cognition* 4:125–53.

——— (1986). *Social psychology. The second edition.* New York: Free Press.

Brown, R., & Gilman, A. (1960). The pronouns of power and solidarity. In T. A. Sebeok (ed.), *Style in language.* Cambridge, Mass.: Technology Press. 253–76.

Cameron, D. (1985). What has gender got to do with sex? *Language and Communication* 5:19–27.

Carroll, J. B., & Casagrande, J. B. (1958). The function of language classifications in behavior. In E. E. Maccoby, T. M. Newcomb, & E. L. Hartley (eds.), *Readings in social psychology* (3rd ed.). New York: Holt, Rinehart & Winston. 18–31.

Clark, H. H., & Clark, E. V. (1977). *Psychology and language.* New York: Harcourt Brace Jovanovich.

Clark, K. B., & Clark, M. P. (1947). Racial identification and preference in Negro children. In T. M. Newcomb & E. L. Hartley (eds.), *Readings in social psychology.* New York: Holt. 169–78.

Crawford, M., & English, L. (1984). Generic versus specific inclusion of women in language: Effects on recall. *Journal of Psycholinguistic Research* 13:373–81.

Dubois, B. L., & Crouch, I. M. (1978). Introduction. *International Journal of the Sociology of Language* 17:5–15.

Edelsky, C. (1979). Question intonation and sex roles. *Language in Society* 8:15–32.

Frederiksen, C. H., & Dominic, J. F. (eds.) (1981). *Writing: The nature, development, and teaching of written communication* (Vol. 2). Hillsdale, N.J.: Erlbaum.

Giles, H. (ed.) (1977). *Language, ethnicity, and intergroup relations.* London: Academic.

Giles, H., Bourhis, R. Y., & Taylor, D. M. (1977). Towards a theory of language in ethnic group relations. In H. Giles (ed.), *Language, ethnicity, and intergroup relations.* London: Academic. 307–48.

Graham, A. (1975). The making of a nonsexist dictionary. In B. Thorne & N. Henley (eds.), *Language and sex: Difference and dominance.* Rowley, Mass.: Newbury House. 57–63.

Henley, N. M. (1977). *Body politics: Power, sex, and nonverbal communication.* Englewood Cliffs, N.J.: Prentice-Hall.

Holmes, J. (1986). Functions of *you know* in women's and men's speech. *Language in Society* 15:1–22.

Hraba, J., & Grant, G. (1970). Black is beautiful: A reexamination of racial preference and identification. *Journal of Personality and Social Psychology* 16:398–402.

Jenkins, A. (1985). *Hearts and minds: The relationship between racial attitudes and self-esteem in young children.* Unpublished honors thesis, Harvard University, Cambridge, Mass.

Kay, P., & Kempton, W. (1984). What is the Sapir–Whorf hypothesis? *American Anthropologist* 86:65–79.

Kelman, H. C. (1974). Social influence and linkages between the individual and the social system. In J. T. Tedeschi (ed.), *Perspectives on social power.* Chicago: Aldine. 125–71.

———— (1980). The role of action in attitude change. In H. E. Howe, Jr. & M. M. Page (eds.), *Nebraska symposium on motivation: Beliefs, attitudes, and values, 1979.* Lincoln: University of Nebraska Press. 117–94.

Kilpatrick, J. J. (1976). And some are more equal than others. *American Sociologist* 11:85–93.

Kramarae, C. (1981). *Women and men speaking.* Rowley, Mass.: Newbury House.

———— (1982). Gender: How she speaks. In E. B. Ryan & H. Giles (eds.), *Attitudes towards language variation.* London: Edward Arnold. 84–98.

Lakoff, R. (1973). Language and woman's place. *Language in Society* 2:45–80.

Lambert, W. E. (1967). A social psychology of bilingualism. *Journal of Social Issues* 23:91–109.

Lang, P. J. (1984). Cognition in emotion: Concept and action. In C. E. Izard, J. Kagan, & R. B. Zajonc (eds.), *Emotions, cognition, and behavior.* Cambridge: Cambridge University Press. 192–226.

Langer, E. (1983). *The psychology of control.* Beverly Hills: Sage.

MacKay, D. G. (1980). Psychology, prescriptive grammar, and the pronoun problem. *American Psychologist* 35:444–49.

———— (1983). A reply to Pateman on singular *they. Language in Society* 12:75–76.

MacKay, D. G., & Fulkerson, D. C. (1979). On the comprehension and production of pronouns. *Journal of Verbal Learning and Verbal Behavior* 18:661–73.

Martyna, W. (1980a). Beyond the "he/man" approach: The case for nonsexist language. *Signs: Journal of Women in Culture and Society* 5:482–93.

———— (1980b). The psychology of the generic masculine. In S. McConnell-Ginet, R. Borker, & N. Furman (eds.), *Women and language in literature and society.* New York: Praeger. 69–78.

Maurice, S. (1985). Evaluative reactions to spoken languages: Attitudes of French Canadians. *McGill Student Journal of Psychology* 1:84–97.

McConnell-Ginet, S. (1984). The origins of sexist language in discourse. *Annals of the New York Academy of Sciences* 433:123–35.

McGuire, W. J. (1985). Attitudes and attitude change. In G. Lindzey & E. Aronson (eds.), *Handbook of social psychology* (3rd ed., Vol. 2). New York: Random House. 233–346.

Meyer, D. E., & Schvaneveldt, R. W. (1971). Facilitation in recognizing pairs of words: Evidence of a dependence between retrieval operations. *Journal of Experimental Psychology* 90:227–34.

Miller, C., & Swift, K. (1976). *Words and women*. New York: Anchor.

Moscovici, S. (1985). Social influence and conformity. In G. Lindzey & E. Aronson (eds.), *Handbook of social psychology* (3rd ed., Vol. 2). New York: Random House. 347–412.

Moulton, J., Robinson, G. M., & Elias, C. (1978). Psychology in action: Sex bias in language use: "Neutral" pronouns that aren't. *American Psychologist* 33: 1032–36.

Posner, M. I., & Snyder, C. R. R. (1975). Attention and cognitive control. In R. L. Solso (ed.), *Information processing and cognition: The Loyola symposium*. Hillsdale, N.J.: Erlbaum. 55–85.

Rosenthal, R., & Rosnow, R. L. (1984). *Essentials of behavioral research*. New York: McGraw-Hill.

Ryan, E. B., & Giles, H. (eds.) (1982). *Attitudes towards language variation*. London: Edward Arnold.

Schank, R. C., & Abelson, R. P. (1977). *Scripts, plans, goals, and understanding: An inquiry into human knowledge structures*. Hillsdale, N.J.: Erlbaum.

Schneider, J. W., & Hacker, S. L. (1973). Sex role imagery and use of the generic "man" in introductory texts: A case in the sociology of sociology. *American Sociologist* 8:12–18.

Silveira, J. (1980). Generic masculine words and thinking. *Women's Studies International Quarterly* 3:165–78.

Smith, E. E., & Medin, D. L. (1981). *Categories and concepts*. Cambridge, Mass.: Harvard University Press.

Smith, P. M. (1985). *Language, the sexes, and society*. Oxford: Basil Blackwell.

Stephan, W. G. (1985). Intergroup relations. In G. Lindzey & E. Aronson (eds.), *Handbook of social psychology* (3rd ed., Vol. 2). New York: Random House. 599–658.

Swinney, D. A. (1979). Lexical access during sentence comprehension: (Re)consideration of context effects. *Journal of Verbal Learning and Verbal Behavior* 18:645–59.

Tajfel, H. (1981). *Human groups and social categories*. Cambridge: Cambridge University Press.

Taylor, D. M., Bassili, J. N., & Aboud, F. E. (1973). Dimensions of ethnic identity: An example from Quebec. *Journal of Social Psychology* 89:185–92.

Whorf, B. L. (1956). *Language, thought, and reality. Selected writings of Benjamin Lee Whorf* (ed. by J. B. Carroll). Cambridge, Mass.: MIT Press.

Williams, J., & Giles, H. (1978). The changing status of women in society: An intergroup perspective. In H. Tajfel (ed.), *Differentiation between social groups*. London: Academic. 431–46.

Winer, B. J. (1962). *Statistical principles in experimental design*. New York: McGraw-Hill.

Wolfson, N., & Manes, J. (1980). "Don't 'dear' me!" In S. McConnell-Ginet, R. Borker, & N. Furman (eds.), *Women and language in literature and society.* New York: Praeger. 79–92.

Content Questions

1. What does it mean to say that in English the masculine terms are unmarked whereas the feminine terms are marked?

2. What is the Sapir–Whorf hypothesis and how does it relate to attempts by particular groups to initiate reforms in the language?

3. What are three "linguistic strategies" adopted by ethnic groups and women trying to improve their own identity? Briefly identify what each of these involves.

4. As far as terms of address are concerned, explain the relationship between terms that show power and those that show solidarity. How does this relate to a woman who does not want to be called "dear" by a stranger?

5. What does it mean to speak of the generic use of *he?*

6. What was the main experiment, as described in this article, set up to discover?

7. Comment on the results of the experiment as far as which of the generic forms (*he, he or she,* or *they*) was found to be the best from the standpoint of feminist goals.

8. How were the experimental results of the "reformed-language women" different from the results of others in the experiment?

9. What does the author mean when she states that "all groups were biased towards their own sex except the women who had not reformed their usage"?

10. How does the author explain the fact that the men who used reformed language seemed to perceive things in the same way as the men who used traditional language?

Questions for Analysis and Discussion

1. Comment on the procedures of the experiment described in this article. What kinds of precautions were taken to ensure more reliable results?

2. A comparison is made between the generic use of *he* and the product name of *Kleenex.* In what way is the use of these two terms similar?

3. What is the point of the part of the title that says that "penguins don't care, but women do"? Relate your answer to the author's discussion of natural categories.

4. What does this research suggest about how accurate it would be to use a male speaker's use of traditional versus reformed language as a basis for judging his perceptions?

5. Comment on the degree to which you believe language shapes our perception (and behavior) or merely reflects our own views.

The Role of Women in Linguistic Change

Edith H. Raidt

Any thorough examination of the history of a particular language must go beyond the more immediately accessible texts produced by leaders and literary figures because a language is shaped by its speakers whether or not they happen to be featured in later history books. It is also a mistake to consider only written as opposed to oral patterns and tendencies within a language if orally based information is available. Professor Edith H. Raidt of the University of the Witwatersrand, Johannesburg, South Africa, examines the significant effect that women's speech had on the development of Afrikaans. Afrikaans is a language that developed in South Africa from Dutch. In order to more completely understand the nature of its development, Raidt examined not only women's speech but also their particular social network. As you read her article, do not concern yourself with understanding every Dutch or Afrikaans form. Just follow the discussion as it reveals some of the important ways that women influenced the development of Afrikaans.

Introduction

Sparked off by Robin Lakoff's famous article on "Language and woman's place" (1973), the controversy around linguistic sex differentiation has resulted in a veritable flood of sociolinguistic studies during the last two decades. Although there is a fair amount of agreement that the differences are not sex-exclusive but rather "on average," explanations for this rather interesting linguistic phenomenon differ greatly. According to Trudgill (1983), however, linguistic differences between men and women is the "single most consistent finding to emerge from sociolinguistic studies over the past 20 years" (Trudgill 1983:162), a statement that is borne out by studies of Labov (1966), Milroy (1980), Gerritsen (1980), Schatz (1985) and others. Furthermore, it has been found that in 20th century Western societies, women use the most advanced forms in their own casual speech (Labov 1978:303). Labov argues that women show a special sensitivity to linguistic change and that the sexual differentiation of speech may play a major role in the mechanism of linguistic evolution (Labov 1978:301).

The genesis of Afrikaans bears this out. In the transition from 17th century Dutch to Afrikaans—i.e. in the period from 1652 till approximately 1775—women seem to have played a major role. Strangely enough, despite an explicit and well-known 18th century remark on the sexual differentiation of speech in Cape Dutch, the role of women in the linguistic change that led to the evolution of Afrikaans had never been investigated prior to my pilot study in 1984 (Raidt 1984). On analysing archival texts, either written by or recorded as being spoken by women during the 18th century, I found that the women of the rather primitive, colonial society at the Cape of Good Hope, exerted both a conservative and a progressive influence on the evolution of a new language. On the one hand, their speech was more natural than that of the men because they were less acquainted with Dutch, the official language of the small colony which was governed by the Dutch East India Company. This partly explains why numerous lexical and phonological forms of 17th century Dutch dialects were preserved in their speech. On the other hand, women picked up and unwittingly promoted simplified forms of foreigner speech, resulting from linguistic interference in the speech of immigrants, Asian slaves and local Khoikhoi speakers. In many instances typical Afrikaans forms appear 70–100 years earlier in the texts of women than in those of men. Naturally, one is tempted to ask, did the women "invent" these new forms, in other words, were they the cause of linguistic changes, or were they the catalysts through whom change was facilitated? The data indicate that the latter was the case.

Mentzel's Comment on Sex Differentiation in Cape Dutch

A casual comment by the German traveller Otto Friedrich Mentzel who worked at the Cape of Good Hope between 1733 and 1741 may shed some light on early linguistic differentiation between men and women in the Cape Colony. In his monumental *Vollständige geographische und topographische Beschreibung des . . . afrikanischen Vorgebirges der Guten Hoffnung*, published 45 years after his return to Germany, he comments in a derogatory fashion on the speech habits in the Cape colony:

> Die Sprache der Landleute ist so wenig reine Holländische Mundart als die teutschen Bauern reines Teutsch sprechen. Die Mannspersonen nehmen das Maul dabei sehr voll, und das Frauenvolk hat Redensarten angenommen, die zuweilen recht lächerlich sind. Zum exempel. Man frägt etwan, ob sie keine Bibel haben, so erfolgt die Antwort: Onz heeft geen Bijbel . . . Wann man sie aber alsdann frägt: Wie viel Unzen gehen auf ein Pfund? so werden sie schamroth.
>
> (Mentzel 1787: II, ch. 7)
>
> *(The language of the country people is just as far from being pure Dutch, as that of the German peasants is from pure German. The men have a*

bombastic way of speaking and the women folk use expressions that are
sometimes really ridiculous. For instance, if one were to ask them whether
they have a Bible, the reply is: Onz heeft geen Bijbel [Us has no Bible.] If
one were then to ask them: "How many 'onze' [ounces] in a pound?" they
would blush with shame.)

Clearly, Mentzel is referring here to the use of the personal pronoun *ons* instead of *wij* (objective instead of subjective form) and the reduced verbal
form without conjugational endings; both are typical of Afrikaans. Earlier
instances of the same phenomena have been recorded in the language of
slaves and Khoikhoi. Does this mean that only the women, and not the
men, used forms that were characteristic of foreigner and pidgin speech,
usually associated with slaves and blacks? The subjective *ons* remained a
stigmatised form until the late 19th century. Although it is difficult to assess how accurate Mentzel's account really is, his comment certainly raises
the question as to whether there was something like a "women's language"
in the early colony at the Cape of Good Hope. Furthermore, his reference
to the "ridiculous" expressions used by women indicates that he noticed
something of a linguistic change in progress which seemed to be particularly evident in the speech of women.

Text Collection and Social Networks

In order to investigate both the characteristics of women's speech and the
possible role women played in linguistic change in the 18th century I examined a corpus of 57 archival texts, i.e. all the available texts either written
by women or recording women's language that have so far been found in
Cape archives. The corpus covers the period 1710–1805; it consists of 20
official and 15 personal letters, 16 affidavits and 6 verbatim reports of witnesses in courts proceedings. The letters are usually short (60–200 words),
whereas the affidavits and witness reports vary in length between 30 and
1000 words. All but four of these women were born and bred Cape colo-
nialists.

Apart from these heterogeneous texts there are 2 diaries written by
women of the upper class, namely a delightful journal of Helena and Johanna Swellengrebel, written as a report of their sea voyage to Holland in
1751 (Schutte 1978:34–39); and the fragments of a diary written in 1797
by Johanna Duminy, wife of French naval officer Francois Duminy
(Franken 1938). While the two young daughters of the retired governor
Hendrik Swellengrebel write a remarkably good Dutch, it does show many
signs of Cape Dutch influences. The girls were already third generation of
Cape colonists, born and bred at the Cape of Good Hope. The same applies to Johanna Duminy, the daughter of a German immigrant, but she
clearly was already Afrikaans speaking although she tried to write in

Dutch. These two texts differ from the others by their length, contents and the respective authors' degree of proficiency in writing, especially in Dutch.

After an initial pilot study in which I concentrated almost exclusively on the linguistic form and variation in each text with little attention given to biographical detail (Raidt 1984), I realized that it was of the utmost importance to reconstruct—as far as possible—the social networks of each of these women. Considering the fragmented records of the early colonial period it is always extremely time-consuming and often well-nigh impossible to research these social networks comprehensively; however, once they are laid bare, significant patterns of variation and of gradual linguistic change emerge (cf. Raidt 1986). Unfortunately, no writings of female slaves, Khoikhoi and black women could be found. The recorded affidavits of such women are so fragmentary that it is impossible to reconstruct any social network. This is a serious gap in the available data.

In the reconstruction of social networks, marriage and family patterns play a vital role. It emerged that 15 of these women had been married twice and 3 of them three times to local and immigrant men of totally different cultural and linguistic backgrounds. Of the 34 women who had been married only once, 18 had husbands of Cape extraction, the other 16 were married to European immigrants. Another important factor was the number of children each woman bore. It was not unusual for a woman to have ten or more children (Lichtenstein 1811:I.173); and often the husband brought a number of children from a previous marriage into the fold, which meant that women were exposed to children's language over long periods of time.

The marriage and family patterns reveal that women were right in the centre of language contact, linguistic variation and imperfect learning; and since the conflict of linguistic norms was directly or indirectly linked to conflictive social norms, women found themselves again in the centre of an emerging colonial society.

Apart from the family patterns, the role of women in the household had an influence on their linguistic behaviour. As reported by many European travellers, the women in the Cape colony were in charge of the numerous domestic servants which meant the Asian slaves in the Cape district, and the Khoikhoi in the interior of the country. Thus housewives in a colonial household at the Cape were in a daily situation of personal interaction with servants of varying linguistic backgrounds and varying degrees of faulty Cape Dutch. In individual cases we have proof that women were proficient in a Khoi-language. All these factors explain why women were continuously exposed to linguistic variation, imperfect learning and linguistic change.

In the attached table (see the Appendix) an attempt is made at placing the texts of women within the respective social networks in regard to marriage and family patterns and geographic distribution, viz-a-vis the linguistic variation in each text.

Language Behaviour and Self-Image

A further factor which influenced the linguistic behaviour of women was the numerical relationship between men and women. Until the end of the 18th century there was a serious shortage of women. At the beginning of the century there was 1 woman for every 2 men; this improved slightly in the second and third quarters when there were 2 women for every 3 men (Nienaber 1953:172). Women certainly were in great demand; this may be one of the reasons why one finds no trace of uncertainty in the style and contents of the texts, on the contrary, the style of the women writers is self-assured, forceful, and often even aggressively direct. So-called characteristics of women's speech in modern societies, such as negative and rhetorical questions, repetition, diminutives and emphatic articles (cf. Trudgill 1983: 165) are altogether absent in these texts. In contrast to the men who strove hard to write correct, official Dutch, women were far less concerned about standard forms; they conveyed their message in a more spontaneous manner which seems to reveal their speech patterns in spite of the disguise of written Dutch. Being aware of their importance in society they had a strong self-esteem; they were less dependent on the status of their husbands than their modern counterparts. Although women were sensitive about their social standing, this did not show in a more refined speech according to European Dutch norms, in contrast to the men for whom the language always was a prestige factor on which they depended for possible promotion in the services of the Dutch East India Company.

The use of swear words and other expletives shows a quantitative difference between men and women. Such words appear more in the recorded speech of men than in that of women; there are relatively few examples of expletives in the writings of women. Furthermore, a gradual decrease in the frequency of expletives is noticeable. In the early 18th century, when the rough military language of ex-soldiers and sailors was still prevalent, women used expletives more frequently, although in relation to their husbands the expressions were less coarse. With the development of a more homogeneous society there was a noticeable decrease in the use of expletives in women's language.

The specific contribution of women towards speech patterns in the Cape colony was certainly not in the area of greater linguistic politeness, high-status pronunciation and standard grammatical forms. Exactly the opposite was the case. They preserved in their speech old dialect forms inherited from Dutch and at the same time they unconsciously promoted "new" forms derived from foreigner speech and imperfect learning, thereby accelerating the process of linguistic change.

Agents of Linguistic Change

Were the women the agents of linguistic change? It is certainly striking that in the texts of women we find the earliest recorded forms in the language of whites, of the Afrikaans personal pronouns *ons, julle* and *hulle* (which are derived from Dutch dialectal forms) for 18th century-standard Dutch *wij, jijlui* and *hunlieden;* likewise the earliest instances of the possessive pronoun *mij* for Dutch *mijn*—also of Dutch dialect origin—and the relative pronoun *wat* for Dutch *die* appear in women's writings. A number of innovations, especially among the pronouns, were based on or had developed out of old Dutch dialectal variants. In regard to reduced verbal forms without inflectional endings women again seem to have taken the lead. However, if one takes into account that some of these typically Afrikaans forms had been recorded much earlier in the pidginised or at least faulty speech of Khoikhoi and Asian slaves (Ten Rhyne 1671, Kolbe 1719; cf. Franken 1953:188–207, Scholtz 1963:27), then it seems unlikely that women were the originators. On analysing the data it becomes evident that women picked up and promoted these new forms despite the fact that pronouns like *ons, julle* and *hulle* in subjective function were highly stigmatised forms which were carefully avoided by whites until the mid-19th century.

The main changes that led to the genesis of Afrikaans happened in the noun and verb systems as a result of morphological reduction, simplification and regularisation (Raidt 1983:108–161). It is exactly here that the written and spoken language of women provides some of the earliest records of linguistic change in progress.

Pronouns

In regard to personal, possessive and relative pronouns women's language proves to be most revealing. The fact that women consistently wrote the pers. pronoun sing. *ik* according to Dutch spelling tradition and *wij* for the plural instead of *ek* and *ons* as spoken by them shows that they, too, were norm-conscious as far as the stigmatised forms were concerned. However, in their recorded spoken language they provide us with the earliest records of the Afrikaans forms in the mouths of burghers. All the more valuable are isolated cases of these substandard forms.

The earliest recorded examples of the personal pronouns *ons, julle* and *hulle* (for Dutch *wij, jijlui* and *zijlieden*) appear in affidavits of two women in 1770, one living in Paarl, a village in the west, the other living at the eastern border of the Cape Colony, an indication therefore that these pronouns were in use everywhere.

The 37-year-old widow Hanna Wagenaar (of the Camdebo in the Eastern part of the colony) is expecting a baby; to the investigations of her brothers-in-law who try to find out who the father of the child is, she gives the sharp reply:

"Het *hulle* dan overal geloop waar *ons* geloop het, hoe weet *hulle* dat of het *hulle* de neus daar beij gehad?"

(Scholtz 1972:24)

(Did they walk everywhere where we walked, how should they know it, or did they poke their nose into it?)

In this one sentence which contains other typical Afrikaans forms, we not only get *ons*, but also 3 times *hulle*. Further examples of *hulle* appear in 1772 in an affidavit of another young woman, Catharina Pienaar of Swellendam. If at this point we add the information given by Mentzel concerning the use of the subjective *ons* instead of *wij* as a characteristic of women's speech in the 1730's, then the women are ahead of the male colonists by some 70 years in revealing the actual forms used in the spoken language of all, women and men, white and black. Like the pronoun *ons* in subjective function, the personal pronoun *hulle* belonged to the stigmatised and carefully avoided forms in the writings of the burghers. The attested cases of *hulle* in the writings of women are more than 30 years older than those in writings by men.

One of the earliest examples of the Afrikaans personal pronoun *julle* (Dutch *jijlui*) as subjective form for the second person plural appears in 1770, in an affidavit of Elsje Hofman, daughter of an emancipated slave woman and wife of Jean du Buis of Huguenot descent. It is interesting to note that another witness in this courtcase, a Khoi "bastard," used the same form. In 1772 Catharina Pienaar of Swellendam uses *julle* 3 times in the nominative in her own, handwritten affidavit. Even Johanna Duminy uses the personal pronoun *julle* twice in a recorded conversation (Franken 1938:91, 95). These data together with similar forms like *julluij*, *jullij* indicate that *julle* must have been in frequent use since about the middle of the 18th century (cf. Scholtz 1963:84); again, the language of the women merely betrays colloquial forms much sooner.

Another case in question is the personal pronoun *U* in the polite form of address. One of the earliest examples of *U* in subjective function appears in a letter of Catharina van As in 1727. Still with polite forms of address, the indirect form of address deserves to be mentioned. In a letter of Elsebe Meijer, the daughter of a Cape colonist, addressed to her in-laws, she uses the then polite form of indirect address:

"Nu is mijn versoek seer vriendelyk aan *vader en moeder* of ik dat gelt dat wij van *vader* hebbe . . ."

(MOOC 3/9, Ao.1742)

This is but the second case of this form of address found up till now in Cape Dutch texts.

In 1774, one of the earliest examples of *hom* (Dutch *hem*), the pers. pronoun third person sing. in objective function, appears in the letter of a young girl Alida Janzen from Paarl.

In 1805, the stigmatised and carefully avoided form *ek* (Dutch *ik*) suddenly breaks through in full force 23 times in a letter written by the widow and business woman Francina van Dyk living at the northern border of the colony.

The very first example of the possessive pronoun *mij* instead of Dutch *mijn* appears in a short letter of Elisabeth du Perez of Huguenot descent, written in 1710.

Even the Afrikaans relative pronoun *wat* instead of Dutch *die* appears for the first time in a letter written in 1766 by an angry woman, Alida de Swart, addressed to her estranged husband (cf. Scholtz 1972:40). Considering that *wat* belonged to the stigmatised and carefully avoided forms till the mid-19th century, this early case gains extra significance.

Innovations in Verbal Forms

The evolution of the Afrikaans verbal form system was marked by the abolition of difference in number and person, i.e. the loss of conjugational endings and the suffix *-en* of infinitives, furthermore the use of verbal forms *is* and *het* for all persons, singular and plural, instead of the respective forms of *zijn* and *hebben*. The earliest simplified verbal forms are recorded in the speech of Khoikhoi and slaves already before 1700, but it is mainly in texts written by women or in recorded women's speech, that such forms appear for the first time as being part of the speech of the white settlers as well, especially of those who were born and bred Cape colonists.

The simplified verbal forms *hij hebt* (for *heeft*), *sal* (for *zullen*), *zouw* (for *zouden*), *is* (for *zijn*), *sien* (for *ziet*), which appear in letters of Jannetie Clerk (1711, of Huguenot descent and married to a Frenchman), Catharina van As (1727, second generation Cape colonist, married to a Dutchman and two German immigrants), Maria van Hoeven (1734, born in Zeeland and married to a German immigrant), belong to the earliest recorded forms of reduced verb without the suffixes for person and number in the language of whites. Similarly, the simplified infinitive forms, e.g. *mag geniet* (for *genieten*), *is* (for *zijn*), *niet te weet* (for *weten*), *moete betaal* (for *betalen*) appear in women's letters considerably earlier than in those of Cape-born men. Earlier cases of such faulty, truncated infinitives were recorded in foreigner speech, especially that of French immigrants (Pheiffer 1980:95–101).

Simplified and regularised past participles occur early in women's language, e.g. *geloop*, *afgewast* and *wedervaart* (for *gelopen*, *afgewassen*, *wedervaren*). Women also show a clear preference for the use of the perfect tense instead of the preterite and pluperfect, thus leading in the evolution of the Afrikaans tense system which only retains the original Dutch perfect tense. Although it is evident that the women were still fully acquainted with the ablaut of strong verbs in the preterite and pluperfect form of the verbs, they give a clear preference to the use of the perfect tense.

In all these cases where women use the most advanced forms much earlier than the men—at least on paper—they were not the originators of these new variants. Being more uninhibited in their speech and written language, they merely picked up and unconsciously promoted existing new forms from the foreigner speech of Khoikhoi, slaves and European immigrants. In this way they contributed towards an acceleration of linguistic change in the course of the 18th century.

Contribution of Dutch Dialect Variants

As mentioned earlier on, women not only played a role in the use and promotion of new forms, they were also the most powerful agents in the retention of old Dutch dialect forms. The development of the Afrikaans pronominal system, which is largely based on Dutch dialectal forms, bears this out. This preserving role of women can be attributed to two factors: on the one hand their nonchalant attitude towards the official Dutch language, on the other their continuous presence in the early Cape society. In contrast to the constantly changing male population with an influx of thousands of immigrant men especially in the 18th century, the women— with very few exceptions in the early period—were born and bred at the Cape. It is indeed striking to see such a persistent continuation of Dutch dialect forms in the language of women. Considering their role in the family and local society, one may safely conclude that their speech patterns profoundly influenced that of their immediate environment. This may explain the surprisingly high survival of typically Dutch (Hollands) dialectal sound patterns, lexical and syntactic variants until the late 19th century. It was only with the rise and gradual impact of standardisation that many of these dialect forms disappeared from spoken and written Afrikaans. In the mid-nineteenth century they were still very much alive in spoken Afrikaans throughout the country.

Phonological Variants

The most conspicuous phenomenon is the neutralisation of full vowels in unstressed syllables. This has always been a typical characteristic of the Dutch dialect of Holland (cf. Scholtz 1972:82). The text complexes of women show a remarkable increase in schwa-forms. More than 60 cases of vowel neutralisation were found, where the neutral [ə] replaces full vowels such as [i], [y], [a], [o:] and [ε], e.g. *in* (en), vr*i*ndin, wedewee, d*e* Pree, rewiene (ruine), h*i*m, br*i*nge, omtr*i*nt, etc.

The exact opposite is also the case, namely the replacement of [ə] by a full vowel, e.g. *ommers, hom* (for immers, hem/him), *ravier* (rivier, revier). The old Dutch variants *ken* and *sel* for *kan* and *sal* which are so prevalent in the 19th century, are present in the 18th century texts, but they are not as frequent as one would expect. Other dialectical variants of Dutch origin include *er/ar* (smerte/smart, dartig/dertig), *eu/o* (meugen/mogen), *ee/eu* (veel/veul), frequent loss of unstressed medial vowel (syncope) such as *korpraal, trug* (korporaal, terug), and the reversal of the order of /r/ and vowel (metathesis), e.g. *seckertaris* (for sekretaris), *pertoris* (for Pretorius), *persense* (for presentie).

In the field of consonants, the earliest recorded example of the transition of *v* to *w* appears in a letter of Jannetie Clerk (1711) where she writes the place name *Waveren* as *Waweren*. A more conspicuous phenomen is the unvoicing of *v* to a voiceless *f*. Early cases are recorded in letters by women with voiceless *f* in the anlaut and inlaut position, e.g. *fader, frouw, friende; feragten, fersneijde, ofer, leefen, schrijfen*. Even the well-educated daughters of governor Swellengrebel repeatedly use the unvoiced fricative *f* in words like *beneffens, fulden* (for vulden), which goes to show that the unvoicing of fricatives was socially acceptable by the mid-18th century.

Syncope and vocalisation of intervocalic *d* is extremely frequent; it reflects the colloquial language of the time.

Simplification of consonant clusters reflects well-known dialectal tendencies of 17th and 18th century Dutch. Apocope of auslaut *t* after unvoiced plosives, fricatives and nasals had established itself in Cape Dutch as early as the beginning of the 18th century.

The use of the cluster *sk* in anlaut position which has developed into a phonological rule in Afrikaans, is derived from the Dutch dialectal *sk*-pronunciation (Weijnen 1966, Daan 1983:59, Goossens 1972:35, Van Bree 1987:161). Although sporadic incidents have been recorded as early as 1711 (Scholtz 1972:85, Ponelis 1989:117), they are scarce in the writings of women, the spelling norm seems to have been particularly strong in this respect.

Syntactic Variation

Although the women were so close to colloquial speech it is remarkable how successfully they avoided the stigmatised negation pattern with the double *nie*. Instead, they make use of the pattern *niet . . . en* which must have been very much in use in both European and Cape Dutch speech (Raidt 1974). However, they frequently write emphatic forms such as *als dat, wanneer dat, alschoon dat, sodra dat;* furthermore the frequent use of the adverbial and conjunctive *zoo* seems to indicate the tendency towards repetition. In one letter it appeared 33 times at the start of a sentence.

Lexical and Idiomatic Patterns

Apart from a number of lexical items which occur earliest in women's writings, such as *kabaai, pokkel, vroetmoer, gebuurte,* the use of idiomatic expressions is rather conspicuous and seems to have been a characteristic of women's speech, e.g.

als men een hont slaen wilt dan kan men wel een stok krijgen (1733)
Beeter bijtijds dan alte laat (1795)
Hij versuip seijn gespes van seyn schoen (1802)

The strong continuation of dialectal forms of Dutch is less conspicuous in the syntactic and lexical patterns. It shows up mainly and most forcefully in the sound patterns. The fact that these dialectal sound patterns were strongly and widely in vogue in the mid-19th century, prior to the process of gradual standardisation, indicates how much vitality they had shown over 200 years in the spoken language at the Cape. Given the fact that so many men were foreigners, the women must have played a major role in the preservation and handing on of these inherited dialectal forms.

Conclusion

This investigation into the role of women in the process of linguistic change lends support to Labov's statement that "women use the most advanced forms in their own casual speech" and that this behaviour of women must therefore play an important part in the mechanism of linguistic change (Labov 1970, 1978:301–303).

However, this behaviour must be seen within its social context, especially in regard to the social role women play in a particular community. In the colonial community which I investigated, it was the men rather who corrected more sharply to the other extreme in their formal speech by trying to speak and write the official language. On closer investigation it becomes clear that the sexual differentiation of speech depends to a large extent on the patterns of social interaction in everyday life.

The fact that the women in the Cape Colony played a double role in linguistic change—a progressive and a conservative one—is directly linked to their place in society. Women's greater sensitivity to new forms may be a gender-related characteristic, but the promotion of these new forms is largely society-bound; here the social networks and the patterns of social interaction play the decisive role. In the case of emerging Afrikaans, women's language as reflected in their writings and recorded speech is not a sex-specific language, but a more reliable reflection of the actual colloquial speech of all inhabitants, male and female, master and servant, white and black. In this colloquial speech they may have given the lead in linguistic change simply by being more spontaneous, and less restricted by the norms of the official language. Although they were not the initiators of the new forms they promoted them, and in doing so they unconsciously sanctioned the new patterns of speech and accelerated the process of linguistic change.

References

Brouwer, Débé and Dorian de Haan, eds. 1987. *Women's language, socialization and self-image.* Dordrecht: Foris.

Daan, Jo. 1983. "*sk* en *sch.*" *Nederlands Dialectonderzoek* ed. by J. Stroop, 59–60. Amsterdam.

Franken, J. L. M. 1938. *Duminy-Dagboeke.* Cape Town: Van Riebeeck-Society, 19.

———. 1953. *Taalhistoriese bydraes.* Cape Town: Balkema.

Geerts, G. and A. Hagen. 1980. *Sociolinguistische studies 1: Bijdragen uit het Nederlandse taalgebied.* Groningen: Wolters-Noordhoff.

Gerritsen, Marinel. 1980. "Een kwantitatief onderzoek naar sexeverschillen in het Amsterdams." Geerts & Hagen 1980. 154–179.

Labov, William. 1966. *The social stratification of English in New York City.* Washington, D.C.: Center for Applied Linguistics.

———. 1978. *Language and woman's place.* New York: Harper and Row.

Lichtenstein, Hinrich. 1811. *Reisen im südlichen Afrika in den Jaren 1803, 1804, 1805 und 1806.* 2 Vols. Berlin 1811, 1812.

Mentzel, Otto Friedrich. 1787. *Vollständige geographische und topographische Beschreibung des ... afrikanischen Vorgebirges der Guten Hoffnung.* Vol. 2. Glogau.

Milroy, Lesley. 1980. *Language and social networks.* Oxford: Basil Blackwell.

Nienaber, G. S. 1953. *Oor Afrikaans.* Vol. 2. Cape Town: Tafelberg.

Odendal, F. F. 1974. *Taalkunde –'n Lewe.* Cape Town: Tafelberg.

Pheiffer, R. H. 1980. *Die gebroke Nederlands van Franssprekendes aan die Kaap in die eerste helfte van die agtiende eeu.* Pretoria/Cape Town: Academica.

Ponelis, F. A. 1989. *Historiese klankleer van Afrikaans.* Unpublished Manuscript. University of Stellenbosch.

Raidt, Edith H. 1974. "Nederlandse en Kaapse spreektaal in die 17de en 18de eeu." Odendal 1974.90–104.

———. 1983. *Einführung in Geschichte und Struktur des Afrikaans.* Darmstadt: Wissenschaftliche Buchgesellschaft.

———. 1984. "Vrouetaal en taalverandering." *Tydskrif vir Geesteswetenskappe* 24(4).256–286.

———. 1986. "Taalvariasie in agtiende-eeuse vrouwetaal." *S. A. Journal of linguistics* 4(4). 101–145.

Schatz, Henriëtte F. 1985. "Tussen standaardtaal en stadsdialect: De norm van vrouwen." *Taal en Tongval* 37(1–2).23–34.

Scholtz, J. du P. 1963. *Taalhistoriese opstelle.* Pretoria: Van Schaik.

———. 1972. *Afrikaans-Hollands in die agtiende eeu.* Cape Town: Nasou.

Schutte, G. J. 1978. "Een damesverslag van een scheepsreis in 1751." *Mededelingen van de Nederlandse Vereniging voor Zeegeschiedenis* 36.

Trudgill, P. 1974. *Sociolinguistics: An Introduction.* Harmondsworth: Penguin.

———. 1983. *On dialect: Social and geographical perspectives.* Oxford: Basil Blackwell.

Van Bree, C. 1987. *Historische Grammatica van het Nederlands.* Dordrecht: Foris.

Weijnen, A. 1966. *Nederlandse dialectkunde.* Assen: Van Gorcum.

Appendix

	SOCIAL NETWORKS	WOMEN/TEXTS	LINGUISTIC VARIATION
DRAKENSTEIN	x P. J. van Marseveen (D) 3 children	1710 *Elisabeth du Preez* (F): Letter to Orphan Chamber	SYNT: *nit en heb . . . en heb; nit . . . nit en* hebben verdient; daer ue ons *oover* hebt *over* geschreven; poss.p. *mij (mijn)*
DRAKENSTEIN	x C. van Niekerk (D) 6 children / xx S. Walters (G) 3 children	1710 *Maria van der Westhuyzen* (C): Letter to Orphan Chamber	PHON: kient, kienderen, vriendien; voornomde(2), kannen(2), antwort; seckertaris, resenderende, onvaesoendelijk; houwen(2) / SYNT: *niet en*
DRAKENSTEIN	x André Gaucher (F) 3 children / xx Pieter Becker (G) 6 children	1711 *Jannettie Clerk* (F-D): Business Letter	PHON: pertoris, Wauveren, Jannetie, hebt (heeft), te gekregen (krijgen)
CAPE TOWN/ STELLENBOSCH	x A. B. Gildenhuyzen (G) 9 children	1712 *Margaretha Hoefnagels* (D): Letter to Orphan Chamber	PHON: gekoft; most; souwen, ouwe, woonigh; selver; / SYNT: *niet en*(3), *als dat, en doe/dan*(3) / MORPH: ekeurt, brieftien. LEX: *gicht* (jicht)
CAPE TOWN	x G. van Aart (D) 2 children	1718 *Levijntie Theunis (van Aart)* (D): Affidavit	PHON: levijntie(9), bartie(4), wast (was), klop, belanght (belandt), hert, rewiene / SYNT: *als dat, en . . . niet*(4). LEX: *kabaai, kooi*
STELLENBOSCH	x J. Botma (C) 3 children	1720 *Christina de Bruijn* (D): Letter to Orphan Chamber	PHON: hertelijk, beleijt (belegd) / SYNT: *als dat, niet . . . en*
CAPE TOWN	x J. H. Vlok (G) 5 children	1723 *Maria Schroers* (G): Letter to heirs	PHON: hert, sel, ken (kan), tetel, Aprel, oekkasee *Muee/Mutee* / SYNT: *als dat*(3)
PAARL/ STELLENBOSCH	x J. Carstens (D) 5 children / xxx J. Sprengel (G) / J. L. Mollevanger (G)	1727 *Catharina van As* (C): Business Letter / Libel case	PHON: vrint; aeverens(2), onkkostigh / MORPH: sal (zullen)(2), souw (zouden), *U* as subj / SYNT: *als dat*(3)
TYGERBERG	x J. P. v. d. Heever (G) 9 children	1733 *Maria van Hoeven* (D): 4 love letters	PHON: hert(6), ken(7), ofer(8), leefen(2), schrijfen(3), liefer, hoefen(2), gefergt, gefen; feragten, fersnijde, ok(2), ommers; meugen(3), sulckt / MORPH: is (zijn), ik heeft, mag geniet (inf.), siem (ziet), mij (mijn), *die* (rel. wat) / LEX: "als men een hont slaen wilt dan ken men wel een stok krijgen"

Place	Husband(s)	Date	Woman / Document	Linguistic notes
WAVEREN	x H. van Dyk (C) 9 children	1737	Maria du Preez (C-F):	PHON: wedewee, De Pree
CAPE TOWN	x C. H. Feyr (G) 4 children	1737·	Maria Koster (C): Letter to Council of Policy	PHON: hedens, selfs (zelf) — LEX: kompareren
RONDEBOSCH	xx G. C. Opperman (G) 2 children	1741	Susanna Elisabeth Duymeling (C): 2 letters to boyfriend	PHON: couris (Kobus)(2), moeje (moet je)(3), hije, houwen; vuul (veul), ken/kan, as (als)
CAPE TOWN	x F. van den Berg (C)			
DRAKENSTEIN	x J. H. Melius (G) 4 children	1741	Hester Roux (C-F): Affidavit	PHON: in (en); op ge zaalt (opgezadelt) — MORPH: ge tijkende (getekende); koppie; blau ooge; heef (heeft)
CAPE TOWN	x H. Gildenhuyzen (C) 2 children; xx S. Hasewinkel (C) 3 children; 1 illeg. child	1742	Elsebe Meijer (C): Letter to parents-in-law	PHON: vrindelijk, capetal, Elsebe; barmhertigheijt; sijfele. MORPH: kinders(3) — SYNT: Always indirect form of polite address — LEX: roode loop (buikloop); instalt, sifile intres, prettendeerde
PAARL	x F. Hübner (G) 1 child	1745	Catharina Hoffman (C): Affidavit	PHON: eskuus, reviet, maqueren, Dir (Dirk) — LEX: maqueren, consenteren — SYNT: alsoo (2)
OVERT GOURITS	xx F. Scheepers (C) 2 children	1745	Magdalena Roussouw (C-F): Affidavit	PHON: Jan Louwis — MORPH: Niet te weet
DRAKENSTEIN	xxx W. Landman (D) 3 children			
WAVEREN	x J. L. du Plessis (C-F) 11 children	1752	Elisabeth Loret (C): Affidavit	PHON: en (in); mits (met) — MORPH: verklarings, obligasies — SYNT: Nooijt geen
PIKETBERG	x D. Bockelenberg (G) 9 children	1754	Marta Pienaar (Erasmus) (C): Letter to children	PHON: en (in), dartig, saal (zadel); febriaris, kouwe bokke velt — MORPH: wy ben (bennen/zijn); uwe heeft; de man syn naam is
-?	x L. Erasmus (C) 15 children	1754	Martha Souilliers (C-F): Libel case	MORPH: Jy (UE), jou
CAPE TOWN	x Renault Berthault de St Jean (F) 5 children	1759	Widow Gildenhuijs: Letter	PHON: Weeduwe, De Sardini baij (Saldanhabaaii), vanditie; wegens — MORPH: ik hebt(3), zijn (is) — SYNT: en . . . niet. LEX: malkanderen
-?		1760	Johanna Terrier(C-F): Letter	PHON: vrendelijk, vrenschap, Abram Cruijwenkel, botter, fat, motje — MORPH: ik komt
SWELLENDAM	x J. Cordier (C-F) 1 child; xx P. Pienaar (C) 7 children	1761	Hendrina v.d. Westhuijsen (C): Letter to boyfriend	PHON: vrind(3), ken (kan)(4), hert(2), smerte(3), scryven(2) — MORPH: ik is, wij ben, je heeft
SWARTLAND	x M. A. Basson (C) 2 children			

Location		Date, Name, Document	Linguistic features
CAPE TOWN	x A. de Neys (D) 6 children	1761 *Maria Magdalena Meyer* (C): Business Letter	PHON: *vrindin; laetje* (dat je), *kost* (kon), *teegens* MORPH: *ik het*(3); indirect form of address SYNT: *als dat*
DRAKENSTEIN	x H. J. Potgieter (C) 6 children	1762 *Elsie Botha* (C), *Cornelia Potgieter* (C), *Sara van de Caab* (Slave woman) Divorce case	PHON: *teegens* MORPH: *kooijen* (sleep with) SYNT: *voor mij geven*. LEX: *nonje* (address)
CAPE TOWN	x J. M. Koppen (C)	1766 *Anna Elisabeth Kluijsman* (C): Letter to boyfriend	PHON: *megiel* (Michael), *mondelings* SYNT: *niet en* (neg.)
DRAKENSTEIN	x A. du Toit (C-F) 2 children xx H. G. Heyns (C) (2)	1766 *Alida Maria de Swart* (C): Letter to husband	PHON: *ken*(kan), *in*(en) (2), *vendiesie, geruewemeert, scaemte* MORPH: *betael, suvig* (inf.); *wat* (rel.) LEX: *bedelbrok, bij dese tijt*
CAPE TOWN	x J. Mostert (C) 10 children xx J. C. Bresler (Danish) 2 children	1768 *Neeltje van Os* (*Brasler*) (C): Letter to husband	PHON: *leugens, friende, fader, frouw, befelen, verscheije, pokkies* MORPH: *U* (subj.), *com* (komt)(2) SYNT: *wanneer dat, als dat*
PAARL	x J. du Buis (C-F) 7 children	1770 *Elsje Hofman* (C): Evidence in court case	MORPH: *julle* (jijlui) (2), *moet* (moeten)
CAMDEBO	x J. C. Wagner (G) 11 children 1 illeg. child	1770 (1772) *Johanna Maria Lubbe* (*wid. Wagenaar*) (C): Evidence	MORPH: *ons* (wij), *hulle* (zij) (3); *geloop* (gelopen), *ons het* (wij hebben), *hulle weet hulle het* (hebben)
ROGGELAND	x J. M. van den Berg (C) 7 children	1771 *Jacoba van Wyk* (*Wid. Johannes Meintjes v. d. Bergh*) (C): Letter to Governor	PHON: *goewerwner*(3), *fiif, en* (in), *apriel, wienne* (wennen), *sieg* (zich), *ciendere* (kinderen), *buerie* (buren), *nit* (niet) (2) MORPH: *ont ferm* (ontfermt)
CAPE TOWN SWELLENDAM	x J. F. van Staden (C) 13 children xx G. Stolts (C) (10)	1772 *Isabella de Jager* (C): Affidavit	PHON: *dingsdag*(2), *hersenpannen*(3), *troep*(2), *bitje, neffens* MORPH: *afgevast* (afgewassen), *geschieden* (geschied); *wat* (rel.) (2) LEX: *voor mijn part, voor mijn deel, "Goe moer!", soebadden* SYNT: *zoo* (conj.) (33)
SWELLENDAM	x J. du Buis (C)	1772 *Catherina Pienaar* (C): Affidavit	PHON: *breejezavier*(2), *gereje*(4), *reije*(2), *beseije, gelaaje*(2), *stilgehouwe, hartsepan, overkant, Swellemdam*(2) MORPH: *ik/wij het*(6), *wij ben, ik doet/zlaat; julle*(2), *hulle*(2); perf. for pret. (20:34), perf. for pluperf.(2)
STELLENBOSCH	x G. van Nimwegen (D) 8 children	1773 *Maria Beyers* (C): Libel case	LEX: *uithaalders*

SWELLENDAM
x B. Pieters (G) 7 children

1773 *Anna Christina Pieters* (C): Affidavit

PHON: revier, vendaan, in, begost, tegens(3), afferika, vernoemde (voornoemde)
MORPH: zij gorg (gingen), weij sal/komt
LEX: spits krijge

STELLENBOSCH
x A. Mouton (C) 7 children
xx J. A. Botma (C) 3 children

1774 *Jacoba Keiser (Wid. Johannes Botma)*: Letter to magistrate

PHON: in/en; weedewee, pouwel (Paull), revieren, Menheer

PAARL
x F. Jordaan (C) 9 children

1774 *Alida Elisabeth Janzen* (C): Letter to aunt

PHON: dingstag, sellefs, parel, hom, Stevanis, drumpel, om behotlijke
LEX: weder vart (wedervaren), ik bet(2), perf. for pret.(14)
LEX: muij(2), kabaai (gown)
SYNT: na . . . toe; indir address

DRAKENSTEIN
x G. Joubert (C-F) 5 children
xx H. Hoppe (G) 2 children

1775 *Margarita de Villiers* (C): Affidavit

PHON: bekinne, revier, Jacobes(2), gewonelik
MORPH: plaasie

STELLENBOSCH
CLAPMUTS
x G. van der Byl (C)
xx D. J. Bleumer (G)

1777 *Elisabeth Grové* (C): Letter to husband

PHON: maa (maar). LEX: assurantie(2),
LEX: assuranttie(2), geapsenteert, meriteerd, consientie, acespteeren

RUYGTEVLEI
PAARL
x I. de Villiers (C) 3 children
xx J. W. Dojema (D) 2 children

1777 *Susanna de Villiers (Dojema)* (C): Affidavit

MORPH: jeij heb, jeij heeft(2)
MORPH: is (zijn)

GROENEKLOOF
x P. Jensen (G) 1 child

1778 *Sophia Oluagen* (C): Letter

PHON: vrindelijk, vrindinne, houwen, waarschouwen.
SYNT: als dat
MORPH: rondebossie, wil (wilt)
LEX: hoe eer hoe liever

SWELLENDAM
x H. de Bruyn (C) 7 children
xx J. van der Merwe (C) 3 children

1780 *Anna Loots* (C): Letter

PHON: kommen (komen)|(2)
MORPH: verklarings

LANGEKLOOF
x B. Boijens (C) 9 children

1783 *Elisabeth Strijdom* (C): Affidavit

PHON: compenis, condiese, goewerneur, revier
MORPH: verkog(2), genuamp (genaamd); ben (is/zijn), heef (heb)

LANGEKLOOF
STELLENBOSCH
x J. Oelofse (C) 5 children
xx J. A. Vosloo (C) 2 children

1783 *Johanna Rooje* (C): Affidavit

PHON: Raevier(2), behulpelik, konnen
SYNT: repetitive en

VERKEERDE-VALLEI
x W. J. van Rensburg (C) 4 children
xx J. Pienaar (C) 8 children

1786 *Anna Sophia Burger* (C): Letter to magistrate

PHON: revier(2), verdinke

SWELLENDAM
x P. C. du Preez (C) 7 children
xx G. N. Siebold (G) 1 child

1789 *Aletta Elis, Besuidenhout* (C): Affidavit

MORPH: siektens, ik woont, my (poss.pr.)(4)
PHON: vlep de pre(2); persense, welle (willen), ende (in de), huigen (heugen), leijijen
MORPH: hoor (behoort), heef(6)
SYNT: niet . . . niemant niet; meijn man seijn vee, voor kleijnhans seijn teijt

Location			Year	Name (status): Document	Linguistic features
GRAAFF-REINET	x	R. A. Jansen (C) 2 children	1790	*Elsie Elis, Vlotman* (C): Affidavit	PHON: pritorius(3), bin, uitgesneije LEX: *pokkel, mallebaar* SYNT: *vne dat, niet en, geen een*
SWELLENDAM		-?	1790	*Helena Becker* (C): Affidavit	PHON: in (en). LEX: *vroetmoer*
SWELLENDAM	x	J. Fourie (C) 10 children	1793	*Elsie van Eden* (C): Affidavit	PHON: mot (met)\(5), kleer MORPH: *eet, drink, slaap* (inf.), *laat was* (wassen)
OLIFANTS RIVER	x	J. Vosloo (C) 4 children	1794	*Catharina H. van de Bank* (C): Affidavit	PHON: det(2), en (in), ken (kan), revier, Crestoffel; *sulley*
UYLEKRAAL	x	N. Jonas (C) 6 children	1795	*Sacharia Deventer* (C): Petition of four women to magistrate	PHON: *De Winter* (Deventer), ken (kan)(3), herten, sel(2); destreksie, risselveren, schryfen; corpraal, mankeer, matewis SYNT: *als dat*(2). LEX: *ter oore nemen*
HEKSRIVER	x	L. Erasmus (C) 13 children	1795	*Margarita de Bruyn* (C): Letter to magistrate	PHON: in(9)/en(11); him(3), mit(3); binne (bennen), bringe, omtrint, Swellimdam; ombekwaam; revier, ken(5), sels, trug; korprraal, broeie. MORPH: stukkies(2), beenties(2), troppie, kinders(2) wij heb(2) SYNT: *als dat, sodra dat, alschoon dat; onmogelyk geen* (neg.). LEX: *broeie, gebuurte*
SWELLENDAM	x	I. M. Ferreira (C) (2) 7 children	1795	*Margarita M. S. Schutte* (C): Letter	PHON: *wel* (wil) LEX: *beeter bijtids dan alte laat*
STELLENBOSCH	x	J. P. Janse v. Rensburg (C) 3 children	1795	*Hester van der Merwe* (C): Letter	PHON: bennende, kent, wel, dins, welgen MORPH: oogies, is (zijn), ben (is); sulij gat SYNT: *kent seyn ser mont* LEX: *braaf* (bra), *seer*(2)
PAARL	x	J. Roos (D) 1 child	1802	*Christina Vlotman (Roos)* (C): Letter to magistrate	PHON: verdom, maak, versuip, verlos, bestraf, meshandel; bewus, seeder, gewees, nag, vlug; ken(5), begen, mender, meshandel; gestringe, bin(3), dinke, in(2); dussend MORPH: mry(6); 23 inf. without *-en* SYNT: *menheer*(10) as address LEX: *versuip seijn gespes van seyn schoen; hoe eer hoe liever; voorgang* (example)
PIKENIERSKLOOF	x	J. Kotze (C) 13 children	1805	*Francina van Dyk (Wid. Johannes Kotzee)* (C): Letter of petition	PHON: ek(23), vrendleyk(2), vrendene, pekneers kloof(3), vergadereng, kooreng; savens, rukemduse (rekognitie); es, ken, welt (wild), en (in)

Note on Family Relationships

[1712] Margaretha Hoefnagels was the (first) mother-in-law of [1742] Elsabe Meijer.

[1737] Maria Koster and [1752] Elisabeth Loret were in-laws.

[1745] Catharina Hoffman was the older sister of [1770] Elsje Hof(f)man.

[1754] Marta Pienaar (Erasmus) was the mother-in-law of [1795] Margarita de Bruyn.

[1760] Johanna Terrier's second husband Pieter Pienaar was the uncle of [1786] Anna Sophia Burger's second husband Johannes Pienaar.

[1770] Elsje Hofman was married to Jean du Buis, the uncle of [1772] Catherina Pienaar's husband Jacob du Buis.

[1780] Anna Loots' first husband Hendrik de Bruyn was the uncle of [1795] Margarita de Bruyn's husband Lourens.

[1783] Johanna Rooje and [1794] Catharina Hendrina van den Bank were married to the cousins Johannes Arnoldus Vosloo and Johannes Vosloo.

[1790] Elsie Vlotman and [1802] Christina Vlotman were sisters.

[1795] Hester van der Merwe and Jacob van der Merwe, second husband of [1780] Anna Loots, were first cousins. Hester was also related to [1786] Anna Sophia Burger, her husband Johannes Petrus van Rensburg was the grandson of Willem van Rensburg, first husband of Anna Sophia Burger.

This list is by no means complete, but it gives an indication of the many and often closely knit family ties of the small colonial community in which these women functioned.

Content Questions

1. Which language's development did Raidt study in order to understand how it had arisen from Dutch? Which time period did she study?

2. What special factors affected the situation of women in the Cape colony to make them particularly significant agents of language change?

3. Contrast the degree to which the men and women in the Cape colony adhered to standard forms of Dutch. What accounted for this difference?

4. Raidt notes that in writing, the women were careful to avoid the stigmatized pronoun forms. How then was Raidt able to get an idea about the pronoun forms that were being used in their speech during the period? What kinds of texts were especially helpful?

5. Even before the women began dropping verb suffixes that indicated person and number, which group appears to have begun the process of suffix dropping on the verbs?

6. What role did women play in preserving old dialectal forms of Dutch?

7. List some of the phonological changes that occurred in the language.

Questions for Analysis and Discussion

1. Why was it important for Raidt to study the "social networks" of the women in the Cape colony?

2. To what extent do you believe that the kinds of circumstances which favored the Cape colony women's linguistic influence on language change are also present with American English–speaking women, today?

3. Comment on the extent to which speakers of a less prestigious language variety can influence a more prestigious variety of the language.

4. The article mentions that verbs lost distinctions of number and person. Has such a loss of verb complexity made the Afrikaans language inadequate? As you answer this question, consider the English present tense verb system. How many different forms exist (do not look at the exceptional verb *be* with its forms)?

5. Why would it be wrong to assume that the linguistic influence of women on the language somehow harmed it?

6. Raidt lists different phonological changes within the Dutch language of the Cape colony such as vowel neutralization, metathesis, and simplification of consonant clusters. Can you provide any examples of these processes occurring in English? Explain.

7. What value is there in studying the history of a particular language?

"Eskimo Words for Snow":
A Case Study in the Genesis and Decay of an Anthropological Example

Laura Martin

One of the most widely cited examples to show the relationship between culture and language is the claim that Eskimos have many more words for snow than other languages do. In the following article, however, Professor Laura Martin of Cleveland State University explains that this widely reported claim about the Eskimo language is an example of sloppy scholarship that has unfortunately taken on a life of its own. Martin's article first appeared in the journal *American Anthropologist*.

A common example purportedly documenting the inextricable linkage of language, culture, and thought refers to "Eskimo words for snow." According to this example, undifferentiated "Eskimo"[1] languages are credited with some variable number of unique words for snow and are compared to English, which has but one. As most commonly expressed, the example refers to the power that cultural interests or setting have on the structure of language (e.g., Pyles 1964:16). A somewhat more sophisticated version applies the putative Eskimo categorization of snow to theories of grammatical influence on perception (e.g., Smith and Williams 1977:143). Other examples of vocabulary elaboration are sometimes used for similar explanatory purposes, but none is as widely cited as this one. Such popularity is at once ironic and unfortunate because the evolution of the example, a curious sequence of distortions and inaccuracies, offers both a case study in the creation of an oral tradition and an object lesson on the hazards of superficial scholarship.

The earliest reference to Eskimos and snow was apparently made by Franz Boas (1911:25–26). Among many examples of cross-linguistic variation in the patterns of form/meaning association, Boas presents a brief citation of four lexically unrelated words for snow in Eskimo: *aput* 'snow on

---

[1] Various debates exist over the proper terminology and classification for languages of the Arctic. What is usually referred to as the Eskimo language family encompasses several important dialect divisions, most prominently those of Yupik and Inuit-Inupiaq; for details regarding both linguistic classification and description, consult Woodbury (1984) and the extensive body of references cited therein. "Eskimo" is used here in reference to the snow example in recognition of the fact that those who perpetuate it, like those who originated it, fail to make any linguistically significant distinctions among speakers.

the ground,' *qana* 'falling snow,' *piqsirpoq* 'drifting snow,' and *qimuqsuq* 'a snow drift.' In this casual example, Boas makes little distinction among "roots," "words," and "independent terms." He intends to illustrate the noncomparability of language structures, not to examine their cultural or cognitive implications.

The example became inextricably identified with Benjamin Whorf through the popularity of "Science and Linguistics," his 1940 article (see Carroll 1956:207–219) exploring the same ideas that interested Boas, lexical elaboration not chief among them. Although for Boas the example illustrated a similarity between English and "Eskimo," Whorf reorients it to contrast them (1956:216). It is a minor diversion in a discussion of pervasive semantic categories such as time and space, and he develops it no further, here or elsewhere in his writings.

Of particular significance is Whorf's failure to cite specific data, numbers, or sources. His English glosses suggest as many as five words, but not the same set given by Boas. Although Whorf's source is uncertain, if he did rely on Boas, his apparently casual revisions of numbers and glosses are but the first mistreatments to which the original data have been subjected.

Anthropological fascination with the example is traceable to two influential textbooks, written in the late 1950s by members of the large group of language scientists familiar with "Science and Linguistics," and adopted in a variety of disciplines well into the 1970s. One or both of these were probably read by most anthropologists trained between 1960 and 1970, and by countless other students as well during that heyday of anthropology's popularity.

In the first, *The Silent Language*, Edward Hall mentions the example only three times (1959:107–108, 110), but his treatment of it suggests that he considered it already familiar to many potential readers. Hall credits Boas, but misrepresents both the intent and extent of the original citation. Even the data are misplaced. Hall inexplicably describes the Eskimo data as "nouns" and, although his argument implies quite a large inventory, specific numbers are not provided. Hall introduces still another context for the example, using it in the analysis of cultural categories.

At approximately the same time, Roger Brown's *Words and Things* (1958) appeared, intended as a textbook in the "psychology of language." Here the example is associated with Whorf and thoroughly recast. Brown claims precisely "three Eskimo words for snow," an assertion apparently based solely on a drawing in Whorf's paper. Psychological and cognitive issues provide still another context in Brown's discussion of a theory about the effects of lexical categorization on perception (cf. Brown and Lenneberg 1954).

Brown's discussion illustrates a creeping carelessness about the actual linguistic facts of the example; this carelessness is no less shocking because it has become so commonplace. Consider Brown's application of Zipf's Law to buttress arguments about the relationship between lexicon and perception. Since Zipf's Law concerns word length, Brown's hypothesis must assume something about the length of his "three" "Eskimo" "snow" words; his argument stands or falls on the assumption that they must be both short and frequent. Eskimo words, however, are the products of an extremely synthetic morphology in which all word building is accomplished by multiple suffixation. Their length is well beyond the limits of Zipf's calculations. Furthermore, precisely identical whole "words" are unlikely to recur because the particular combination of suffixes used with a "snow" root, or any other, varies by speaker and situation as well as by syntactic role (Sadock 1980).

A minimal knowledge of Eskimo grammar would have confirmed the relevance of these facts to the central hypotheses, and would, moreover, have established the even more relevant fact that there is nothing at all peculiar about the behavior or distribution of "snow words" in these languages. The structure of Eskimo grammar means that the number of "words" for snow is literally incalculable, a conclusion that is inescapable for any other root as well.

Any sensible case for perceptual variation based on lexical inventory should, therefore, require reference to distinct "roots" rather than to "words," but this subtlety has escaped most authors.[2] Brown, for example, repeatedly refers to linguistic units such as "verbal expression," "phrase," and "word" in a way that underscores the inadequacy of his understanding of Eskimo grammar. His assumption that English and "Eskimo" are directly comparable, together with his acceptance of pseudo-facts about lexical elaboration in an unfamiliar language, cause him to construct a complex psychocultural argument based on cross-linguistic "evidence" related to the example with not a single item of Eskimo data in support (1958:255). This complete absence of data (and of accurate references) sets a dangerous precedent because it not only prevents direct evaluation of Brown's claims but suggests that such evaluation is unnecessary.

As scholarship in linguistic anthropology, this treatment is wholly inadequate. It is particularly unfortunate, then, that this particular treatment was perpetuated and disseminated to a new generation of students in Carol Eastman's 1975 survey of linguistic approaches in anthropology, *Aspects of Language and Culture*. Eastman summarizes the Sapir–Whorf hypothesis, which she calls "the worldview problem," entirely by reference to the snow example, quoting Brown's "modifications" of Whorf's ideas (1975:76).

---

[2] There seems no reason to posit more than two distinct *roots* that can be properly said to refer to snow itself (and not, for example, to drifts, ice, storms, or moisture) in any Eskimo language. In West Greenlandic, these roots are *qanik* 'snow in the air; snowflake' and *aput* 'snow (on the ground)' (Schultz-Lorentzen 1927; cf. Boas's data). Other varieties have cognate forms. Thus, Eskimo has about as much differentiation as English does for 'snow' at the monolexemic level: snow and flake. That these roots and others may be modified to reflect semantic distinctions not present in English is a result of gross features of Eskimo morphology and syntax and not of lexicon. Any consequences that those grammatical differences may have for perception or cognition remain undocumented.

Even more striking than the distortion of Whorf's writing and thinking, which is implicit in the association of him with it, is the powerful influence the snow example exerts even on an experienced linguistic anthropologist. With Brown's reference to "three words" only six lines away, Eastman still asserts that "Eskimo languages have many words for snow."

Thus is the complexity of the interrelations of linguistic structure, cultural behavior, and human cognition reduced to "Eskimo words for snow." These and other textbooks have disseminated misinterpretations of the example throughout the educated American population since the late 1950s. Boas's small example—ironically, one intended as a caution against superficial linguistic comparisons—has transcended its source and become part of academic oral tradition. Like folk beliefs about English vowels (Walker 1970), tenaciously held folk theories about Arctic snow lexicon are not easily contradicted. Unlike the vowel example, however, this folklore has not been promulgated by secondary-school teachers but by anthropologists and linguists who should know better and by professors in other fields who first learned it from them.

Textbook references to the example have reached such proliferation that no complete inventory seems possible, but examination of a representative set reveals several common features: lack or inaccuracy of citations; application of the example to diverse (and contradictory) theoretical purposes; wholesale reanalysis of the example and its history. Thus, according to a text on acoustics and speech physiology (Borden and Harris 1980:4f.), the Whorfian hypothesis "was based on comparative linguistic data which show that languages differ in the number of terms for such things as color or snow." Even a recent introductory anthropology text cites the example as typical of those upon which Whorf founded his conclusions about the effects of linguistic categorization on thought (Cole 1982:69). From time to time, linguists and anthropologists have attempted to restore a sensible interpretation and proper context to the example (e.g., Hymes 1967:213; Lyons 1981:306), but these efforts have probably only succeeded in increasing its visibility. References in serious texts are testimony to the example's widespread acceptance, but they are only the most easily traceable of its manifestations. Casual classroom use is startlingly frequent and much more often accompanied by apocryphal numbers, which usually range from about a dozen to more than one hundred.

Even if academic use were suddenly to cease, years of carelessness have taken their toll. Although awareness of the example is largely an artifact of higher education, the process of its transmission as a folk myth no longer depends on that context. The gradual filtering of the example into the educated lay population has established its vitality beyond university walls. Consider a diverse random sample of recent references: "many words" in the *Journal of American Photography* 3:1.19 (March 1984); "fifty" in Lanford Wilson's 1978 play *The Fifth of July*; "nine" in a trivia encyclopedia called *The Straight Dope: A Compendium of Human Knowledge* (Chicago Review Press, 1984), which includes a droll explanation for the variety: "[Eskimos] have a limited environment to talk about, so they have to make up a lot of words to fill up their conversations"; a *New York Times* editorial (February 9, 1984), citing Whorf in reference to a "tribe" distinguishing "one hundred types of snow"; *Time*'s July 1, 1985, comparison of the Beirut glossary of descriptive terms for shelling to the Eskimos' "many" words for snow; and the inevitable local television references to "two hundred words" during winter snow forecasts (e.g., WEWS–Cleveland, 1984).

How may we account for such remarkable persistence and ubiquity? No doubt exoticism plays some role. Arctic peoples, among the most easily recognized ethnographic populations, remain a poorly understood group about whom other easy generalizations are routine: they eat only raw meat, they give their wives as gifts to strangers, they rub noses instead of kissing, they send their elderly out on ice floes to die. We are prepared to believe almost anything about such an unfamiliar and peculiar group. (See Hughes [1958] for another example of scholarly misinterpretation of Eskimo culture.)

The context of such generalizations is not altogether negative. There is in them an element of respect for the creative adaptability of people who live in the almost unimaginably harsh Arctic environment. The tendency to inflate the numbers associated with the snow example is a reflection of admiration, not simply of linguistic creativity but of human variability and survival as well. Taken in this way, a self-evident observation—what is in our environment is likely to be reflected in our language—has become imbued with exaggerated meaning. Through repetition in print or in lecture, the snow example has become cloaked in scholarly importance. Its patina of sophistication reflects on the lecturer who appears to be in possession of specialized knowledge and impresses any listener to whom close attention to the details of language or culture may be a novel enterprise. Its "meaning" remains vague but seems generally simple: human beings are very different from each other. (Or, depending on the version of the example that is used and the theoretical matrix in which it is grounded, human beings are much the same.)

Students constantly seek such simplicities and are abetted in their quest by their teachers. Many facts about Eskimo languages are fascinating and even astonishing. However, providing the detail, the careful reasoning, and the technical sophistication required to draw conclusions about language or culture or psychology from those facts is a demanding task. Too often the search for shorthand and simple-minded ways to talk about the complexities of language and culture results in excessive reliance on inadequately detailed illustrations. In the case of the snow example, sheer repetition reinforces it, embedding it ever more firmly in folk wisdom where it is nearly immune to challenge. Whenever issues in language, culture, and thought are raised, a substantial proportion of listeners are unwilling to abandon the notion that "It's all just like Eskimos and snow."

Such a trivialization of the complexity inherent in linguistic structures, linguistic behaviors, and the relationships among them distorts the requirements of research into these relationships by implying that counting words is a suitable method of pursuing such investigations. It may not be excessive to speculate that, through this process, the example has come to substantiate for some the bias that these investigations are either impossible, irrelevant, or unscientific.

In this twisted form, the snow example returns to the academic context and is adduced as "proof" that Whorf's ideas were superficial or lacked insight (cf. Lehman 1976:267). At a time when Whorfian hypotheses are receiving renewed attention among serious scholars whose approaches to them are of exemplary rigor (e.g., Bloom 1981), it is especially unfortunate that the frivolousness of the snow example should continue to be so prominent and to obscure the true dimensions of such research problems. Relying increasingly on the dubious value of surveys and summaries instead of on original sources, even graduate students may never understand that Whorf's work—like that of other linguistic anthropologists—is not only not primarily concerned with snow words, but not even primarily concerned with vocabulary. Such misunderstandings are especially hurtful when they underpin much of the training given to today's students about the role of linguistic investigations in anthropology.

Certainly, we have little control over the processes of folklorization that can remove scholarly statements from their rightful context and cause misinterpretation. However, greater alertness to the dangers inherent in careless disregard for the essential requirements of responsible scholarship might have prevented the sorry evolution of the snow example within our own discipline. Now that we have its history before us, perhaps it is not too late to introduce yet another—and, we may hope, final—context for it: the cautionary tale that serves to remind us of the intellectual protection to be found in the careful use of sources, the clear presentation of evidence, and, above all, the constant evaluation of our assumptions.

Acknowledgments

An earlier version of this paper was presented at the 1982 annual meeting of the American Anthropological Association. Since then, many students and colleagues have contributed new data, examples, and editorial comments; although indebted to them all, I owe particular thanks to Jill Brody, Nora C. England, and Victor Golla. Any flaws are, of course, my own responsibility.

References Cited

Bloom, Alfred H., 1981. The Linguistic Shaping of Thought: A Study in the Impact of Language on Thinking in China and the West. Hillsdale, NJ: Laurence Erlbaum Associates.

Boss, Franz, 1911. Introduction to The Handbook of North American Indians. Smithsonian Institution Bulletin 40, Part 1. (*Reissued by* the University of Nebraska Press, 1966.)

Borden, Gloria J., and Katherine S. Harris, 1980. Speech Science Primer: Physiology, Acoustics, and Perception of Speech. Baltimore: Williams & Wilkins.

Brown, Roger W., 1958. Words and Things. New York: Free Press.

Brown, Roger W., and Eric H. Lenneberg, 1954. A Study in Language and Cognition. Journal of Abnormal and Social Psychology 48:454–462.

Carroll, John B., ed., 1956. Language, Thought and Reality: Selected Writings of Benjamin Lee Whorf. Cambridge, MA: MIT Press.

Cole, Johnetta B., 1982. Anthropology for the Eighties: Introductory Readings. New York: Free Press.

Eastman, Carol M., 1975. Aspects of Language and Culture. San Francisco: Chandler.

Hall, Edward T., 1959. The Silent Language. Garden City, NY: Doubleday/Anchor Books.

Hughes, Charles Campbell, 1958. Anomie, the Ammassalik, and the Standardization of Error. Southwestern Journal of Anthropology 14:352–377.

Hymes, Dell, 1967. Objectives and Concepts of Linguistic Anthropology. *In* The Teaching of Anthropology. David G. Mandelbaum, Gabriel W. Lasker, and Ethel M. Albert, eds. Pp. 207–234. Berkeley: University of California Press.

Lehman, Winifred P., 1976. Descriptive Linguistics. 2nd edition. New York: Random House.

Lyons, John, 1981. Language and Linguistics: An Introduction. New York: Cambridge University Press.

Pyles, Thomas, 1964. The Origins and Development of the English Language. New York: Harcourt, Brace & World.

Sadock, Jerrold M., 1980. Noun Incorporation in Greenlandic Eskimo. Language 56:300–319.

Schultz-Lorentzen, C. W., 1927. Dictionary of the West Greenlandic Eskimo Language. Meddeleser om Grønland, 69. Copenhagen: Reitzels.

Smith, Dennis R., and L. Keith Williams, 1977. Interpersonal Communication: Roles, Rules, Strategies and Games. 2nd edition. Dubuque, IA: Wm. C. Brown.

Walker, Willard, 1970. The Retention of Folk Linguistic Concepts and the *Tíyčtr* Caste in Contemporary Nacireman Culture. American Anthropologist 72:102–105. (*Reprinted in* Nacirema: Readings on American Culture, James P. Spradley and Michael A. Rynkiewich, eds., pp. 71–75, Boston: Little, Brown, 1975.)

Whorf, Benjamin Lee, 1940. Science and Linguistics. Technology Review (MIT) 42:229–231, 247–248. (*Reprinted in* Language in Action, S. I. Hayakawa, ed., pp. 302–321, 1941; Readings in Social Psychology, T. Newcomb and E. Hartley, eds., pp. 207–218, 1947; Collected Papers on Metalinguistics, Foreign Service Institute, 1952; and Language, Thought and Reality, John B. Carroll, ed., pp. 207–219, 1956.)

Woodbury, Anthony C., 1984. Eskimo and Aleut Languages. *In* Handbook of North American Indians, Vol. 5: Arctic. David Damas, ed. Pp. 49–63. Washington, DC: Smithsonian Institution.

Content Questions

1. Briefly summarize what the Eskimo snow example involves and the type of theory about language and culture or thought for which the Eskimo snow example is widely used.

2. How many roots does Martin in fact indicate that Eskimo has (see footnote 2 in her article)? How does this number of roots in Eskimo compare with the number in English?

3. Why is it important to distinguish between words and roots when making a count about the number of words for snow in Eskimo? What makes it possible to argue that Eskimo has potentially an unlimited number of words for snow? To what extent could that same claim be made about Eskimo words for other concepts?

4. Summarize the development of the exaggerated claims about Eskimo terms for snow as outlined in Martin's article.

5. What factors related to culture and human nature have probably contributed to the rapid spread and popularity of the Eskimo snow example?

Questions for Analysis and Discussion

1. Aside from the whole issue of just how many words Eskimo has for snow, those who refer to the Eskimo language also perpetuate a sort of fiction about the identity of Eskimo. Why is it problematic even to speak of the "Eskimo language" (see footnote 1)?

2. In one respect, this article is not really even about the Eskimo terms for snow. What issue is the article really addressing?

3. In light of what this article points out, how important do you believe that academic conventions such as proper citations, bibliographies, and the like, are?

4. How familiar with Eskimo do you think those people are who teach or present the typical snow claims?

5. How does the Eskimo snow example relate to the Whorfian hypothesis (also known as the "Sapir–Whorf hypothesis")?

American Sign Language:
"It's Not Mouth Stuff—It's Brain Stuff"

Richard Wolkomir

There are many misconceptions about American Sign Language. One common misconception about American Sign Language, or ASL, is that the language is merely a visual representation of English. ASL is in fact a completely different language from English, even possessing its own syntax. And while the most important reason for anyone to study ASL is its communicative value, some linguists have also found it to be an important object of study as they look for answers about how all of us acquire and use language. In the article below, Richard Wolkomir, a writer for *Smithsonian*, traces some of the history and current use of American Sign Language and how the study of ASL can help linguists with unresolved questions about the nature and acquisition of language.

Research on how deaf people communicate gives them a stronger hand in our culture, and casts new light on the origin of language.

In a darkened laboratory at the Salk Institute in San Diego, a deaf woman is signing. Tiny lights attached to her sleeves and fingers trace the motions of her hands, while two special video cameras whir.

Computers will process her hands' videotaped arabesques and pirouettes into mathematically precise three-dimensional images. Neurologists and linguists will study these stunning patterns for insight into how the human brain produces language.

Sign has become a scientific hot button. Only in the past 20 years have linguists realized that signed languages are unique—a speech of the hand. They offer a new way to probe how the brain generates and understands language, and throw new light on an old scientific controversy: whether language, complete with grammar, is innate in our species, or whether it is a learned behavior. The current interest in sign language has roots in the pioneering work of one renegade teacher at Gallaudet University in Washington, D.C., the world's only liberal arts university for deaf people.

When Bill Stokoe went to Gallaudet to teach English, the school enrolled him in a course in signing. But Stokoe noticed something odd: among themselves, students signed differently from his classroom teacher.

311

"Hand Talk": A Genuine Language

Stokoe had been taught a sort of gestural code, each movement of the hands representing a word in English. At the time, American Sign Language (ASL) was thought to be no more than a form of pidgin English. But Stokoe believed the "hand talk" his students used looked richer. He wondered: Might deaf people actually have a genuine language? And could that language be unlike any other on Earth? It was 1955, when even deaf people dismissed their signing as "slang." Stokoe's idea was academic heresy.

It is 37 years later. Stokoe—now devoting his time to writing and editing books and journals and to producing video materials on ASL and the deaf culture—is having lunch at a café near the Gallaudet campus and explaining how he started a revolution. For decades educators fought his idea that signed languages are natural languages like English, French and Japanese. They assumed language must be based on speech, the modulation of sound. But sign language is based on the movement of hands, the modulation of space. "What I said," Stokoe explains, "is that language is not mouth stuff—it's brain stuff."

It has been a long road, from the mouth to the brain. Linguists have had to redefine language. Deaf people's self-esteem has been at stake, and so has the ticklish issue of their education.

"My own contribution was to turn around the thinking of academics," says Stokoe. "When I came to Gallaudet, the teachers were trained with two books, and the jokers who wrote them gave only a paragraph to sign language, calling it a vague system of gestures that looked like the ideas they were supposed to represent."

Deaf education in the '50s irked him. "I didn't like to see how the hearing teachers treated their deaf pupils—their expectations were low," he says. "I was amazed at how many of my students were brilliant." Meanwhile, he was reading the work of anthropological linguists like George Trager and Henry Lee Smith Jr. "They said you couldn't study language without studying the culture, and when I had been at Gallaudet a short time, I realized that deaf people had a culture of their own."

When Stokoe analyzed his students' signing, he found it was like spoken languages, which combine bits of sound—each meaningless by itself—into meaningful words. Signers, following similar rules, combine individually meaningless hand and body movements into words. They choose from a palette of hand shapes, such as a fist or a pointing index finger. They also choose where to make a sign; for example, on the face or on the chest. They choose how to orient the hand and arm. And each sign has a movement—it might begin at the cheek and finish at the chin. A shaped hand executing a particular motion creates a word. A common underlying structure of both spoken and signed language is thus at the level of the smallest units that are linked to form words.

Stokoe explained his findings on the structure of ASL in a book published in 1960. "The faculty then had a special meeting and I got up and said my piece," he says. "Nobody threw eggs or old vegetables, but I was bombarded by hostility." Later, the university's president told Stokoe his research was "causing too much trouble" because his insistence that ASL was indeed a *language* threatened the English-based system for teaching the deaf. But Stokoe persisted. Five years later he came out with the first dictionary of American Sign Language based on linguistic principles. And he's been slowly winning converts ever since.

"Wherever We've Found Deaf People, There's Sign"

Just as no one can pinpoint the origins of spoken language in prehistory, the roots of sign language remain hidden from view. What linguists do know is that sign languages have sprung up independently in many different places. Signing probably began with simple gestures, but then evolved into a true language with structured grammar. "In every place we've ever found deaf people, there's sign," says anthropological linguist Bob Johnson. But it's not the same language. "I went to a Mayan village where, out of 400 people, 13 were deaf, and they had their own Mayan Sign—I'd guess it's been maintained for thousands of years." Today at least 50 native sign languages are "spoken" worldwide, all mutually incomprehensible, from British and Israeli Sign to Chinese Sign.

Not until the 1700s, in France, did people who could hear pay serious attention to deaf people and their language. Religion had something to do with it. "They believed that without speech you couldn't go to heaven," says Johnson.

For the Abbé de l'Epée, a French priest born into a wealthy family in 1712, the issue was his own soul: he feared he would lose it unless he overcame the stigma of his privileged youth by devoting himself to the poor. In his history of the deaf, *When The Mind Hears,* Northeastern University psychologist Harlan Lane notes that, in his 50s, de l'Epée met two deaf girls on one of his forays into the Paris slums and decided to dedicate himself to their education.

The priest's problem was abstraction: he could show the girls a piece of bread and the printed French word for "bread." But how could he show them "God" or "goodness"? He decided to learn their sign language as a teaching medium. However, he attempted to impose French grammar onto the signs.

"Methodical signing," as de l'Epée called his invention, was an ugly hybrid. But he did teach his pupils to read French, opening the door to education, and today he is a hero to deaf people. As his pupils and disciples proliferated, satellite schools sprouted throughout Europe. De l'Epée died happily destitute in 1789 surrounded by his students in his Paris school, which became the National Institution for Deaf-Mutes under the new republic.

Other teachers kept de l'Epée's school alive. And one graduate, Laurent Clerc, brought the French method of teaching in sign to the United States. It was the early 1800s; in Hartford, Connecticut, the Rev. Thomas Hopkins Gallaudet was watching children at play. He noticed that one girl, Alice Cogswell, did not join in. She was deaf. Her father, a surgeon, persuaded Gallaudet to find a European teacher and create the first permanent school for the deaf in the United States. Gallaudet then traveled to England, where the "oral" method was supreme, the idea being to teach deaf children to speak. The method was almost cruel, since children born deaf—they heard no voices, including their own—could have no concept of speech. It rarely worked. Besides, the teachers said their method was "secret." And so Gallaudet visited the Institution for Deaf-Mutes in Paris and persuaded Laurent Clerc to come home with him.

During their 52-day voyage across the Atlantic, Gallaudet helped Clerc improve his English, and Clerc taught him French Sign Language. On April 15, 1817, in Hartford, they established a school that became the American School for the Deaf. Teaching in French Sign Language and a version of de l'Epée's methodical sign, Clerc trained many students who became teachers, too, and helped spread the language across the country. Clerc's French Sign was to mingle with various "home" signs that had sprung up in other places. On Martha's Vineyard, Massachusetts, for example, a large portion of the population was genetically deaf, and virtually all the islanders used an indigenous sign language, the hearing switching back and forth between speech and sign with bilingual ease. Eventually, pure French Sign would blend with such local argots and evolve into today's American Sign Language.

After Clerc died, in 1869, much of the work done since the time of de l'Epée to teach the deaf in their own language crumbled under the weight of Victorian intolerance. Anti-Signers argued that ASL let the deaf "talk" only to the deaf; they must learn to speak and to lip-read. Pro-Signers pointed out that, through sign, the deaf learned to read and write English. The Pros also noted that lipreading is a skill that few master. (Studies estimate that 93 percent of deaf schoolchildren who were either born deaf or lost their hearing in early childhood can lip-read only one in ten everyday sentences in English.) And Pros argue correctly that the arduous hours required to teach a deaf child to mimic speech should be spent on real education.

"Oralists" like Horace Mann lobbied to stop schools from teaching in ASL, then *the* method of instruction in all schools for the deaf. None was more fervent than Alexander Graham Bell, inventor of the telephone and husband of a woman who denied her own deafness. The president of the National Association of the Deaf called Bell the "most to be feared enemy of the American deaf." In 1880, at an international meeting of educators of the deaf in Milan, where deaf teachers were absent, the use of sign language in schools was proscribed.

After that, as deaf people see it, came the Dark Ages. Retired Gallaudet sociolinguist Barbara Kannapell, who is cofounder of Deafpride, a Washington, D.C. advocacy group, is the deaf daughter of deaf parents from Kentucky. Starting at age 4, she attended an "oral" school, where signing was outlawed. "Whenever the teacher turned her back to work on the blackboard, we'd sign," signs Kannapell. "If the teacher caught us using sign language, she'd use a ruler on our hands."

Kannapell has tried to see oralism from the viewpoint of hearing parents of deaf children. "They'll do anything to make their child like themselves," she signs. "But, from a deaf adult's perspective, I want *them* to learn sign, to communicate with their child."

In the 1970s, a new federal law mandated "mainstreaming." "That law was good for parents, because they could keep children home instead of sending them off to special boarding schools, but many public schools didn't know what to do with deaf kids," signs Kannapell. "Many of these children think they're the only deaf kids in the world."

Gallaudet's admissions director, James Tucker, an exuberant 32-year-old, is a product of the '70s mainstreaming. "I'd sit in the back, doing work the teacher gave me and minding my own business," he signs. "Did I like it? Hell no! I was lonely—for years I thought I was an introvert." Deaf children have a right to learn ASL and to live in an ASL-speaking community, he asserts. "We learn sign for obvious reasons–our eyes aren't broken," he signs. Tucker adds: "Deaf culture is a group of people sharing similar values, outlook and frustrations, and the main thing, of course, is sharing the same language."

Today, most teachers of deaf pupils are "hearies" who speak as they sign. "Simultaneous Communication," as it is called, is really signed English and not ASL. "It looks grotesque to the eye," signs Tucker, adding that it makes signs too "marked," a linguistic term meaning equally stressed. Hand movements can be exaggerated or poorly executed. As Tucker puts it: "We have zealous educators trying to impose weird hand shapes." Moreover, since the languages have entirely different sentence structures, the effect can be bewildering. It's like having Japanese spoken to English-speaking students with an interpreter shouting occasional English words at them.

The Silent World of Sign

New scientific findings support the efforts of linguists such as Bob Johnson, who are calling for an education system for deaf students based on ASL, starting in infancy. Research by Helen Neville, at the Salk Institute, shows that children *must* learn a language—any language—during their first five years or so, before the brain's neural connections are locked in place, or risk permanent linguistic impairment. "What suffers is the ability to learn grammar," she says. As children mature, their brain organization becomes increasingly rigid. By puberty, it is largely complete. This spells trouble because most deaf youngsters learn language late; their parents are hearing and do not know ASL, and the children have little or no contact with deaf people when young.

Bob Johnson notes that more than 90 percent of all deaf children have hearing parents. Unlike deaf children of deaf parents, who get ASL instruction early, they learn a language late and lag educationally. "The average deaf 12th-grader reads at the 4th-grade level," says Johnson. He believes deaf children should start learning ASL in the crib, with schools teaching in ASL. English, he argues, should be a second language, for reading and writing: "All evidence says they'll learn English better." It's been an uphill battle. Of the several hundred school programs for the deaf in this country, only six are moving toward ASL-based instruction. And the vast majority of deaf students are still in mainstream schools where there are few teachers who are fluent in ASL.

Meanwhile, researchers are finding that ASL is a living language, still evolving. Sociolinguist James Woodward from Memphis, who has a black belt in karate, had planned to study Chinese dialects but switched to sign when he came to Gallaudet in 1969. "I spent every night for two years at the Rathskeller, a student hangout, learning by observing," he says. "I began to see great variation in the way people signed."

Woodward later concentrated on regional, social and ethnic dialects of ASL. Visiting deaf homes and social clubs in the South, he found that Southerners use older forms of ASL signs than Northerners do. Southern blacks use even more of the older signs. "From them, we can learn the history of the language," he says.

Over time, signs tend to change. For instance, "home" originally was the sign for "eat" (touching the mouth) combined with the sign for "sleep" (the palm pillowing the cheek). Now it has evolved into two taps on the cheek. Also, signs formerly made at the center of the face migrate toward its perimeter. One reason is that it is easier to see both signs and changes in facial expressions in this way, since deaf people focus on a signer's face—which provides crucial linguistic information—taking in the hands with peripheral vision.

Signers use certain facial expressions as grammatical markers. These linguistic expressions range from pursed lips to the expression that results from enunciating the sound "th." Linguist Scott Liddell, at Gallaudet, has noted that certain hand movements translate as "Bill drove to John's." If the signer tilts his head forward and raises his eyebrows while signing, he makes the sentence a question: "Did Bill drive to John's?" If he also makes the "th" expression as he signs, he modifies the verb with an adverb: "Did Bill drive to John's inattentively?"

Sociolinguists have investigated why this unique language was for so long virtually a secret. Partly, Woodward thinks, it was because deaf people wanted it that way. He says that when deaf people sign to the hearing, they switch to English-like signing. "It allows hearing people to be identified as outsiders and to be treated carefully before allowing any interaction that could have a negative effect on the deaf community," he says. By keeping ASL to themselves, deaf people—whom Woodward regards as an ethnic group—maintain "social identity and group solidarity."

A Key Language Ingredient: Grammar

The "secret" nature of ASL is changing rapidly as it is being examined under the scientific microscope. At the Salk Institute, a futuristic complex of concrete labs poised on a San Diego cliff above the Pacific, pioneer ASL investigator Ursula Bellugi directs the Laboratory for Cognitive Neuroscience, where researchers use ASL to probe the brain's capacity for language. It was here that Bellugi and associates found that ASL has a key language ingredient: a grammar to regulate its flow. For example, in a conversation a signer might make the sign for "Joe" at an arbitrary spot in space. Now that spot stands for "Joe." By pointing to it, the signer creates the pronoun "he" or "him," meaning "Joe." A sign moving toward the spot means something done *to* "him." A sign moving away from the spot means an action *by* Joe, something "he" did.

In the 1970s, Bellugi's team concentrated on several key questions that have been of central concern ever since MIT professor Noam Chomsky's groundbreaking work of the 1950s. Is language capability innate, as Chomsky and his followers believe? Or is it acquired from our environment? The question gets to the basics of humanity since our language capacity is part of our unique endowment as a species. And language lets us accumulate lore and pass it on to succeeding generations. Bellugi's team reasoned that if ASL is a true language, unconnected to speech, then our penchant for language must be built in at birth, whether we express it with our tongue or hands. As Bellugi puts it: "I had to keep asking myself, 'What does it mean to be a language?'"

A key issue was "iconicity." Linguistics has long held that one of the properties of all natural languages is that their words are arbitrary. In English, to illustrate, there is no relation between the sound of the word "cat" and a cat itself, and onomatopoeic words like "slurp" are few and far between. Similarly, if ASL follows the same principles, its words should not be pictures or mime. But ASL does have many words with transparent meanings. In ASL, "tree" is an arm upright from the elbow, representing a trunk, with the fingers spread to show the crown. In Danish Sign, the signer's two hands outline a tree in the air. Sign languages are rife with pantomimes. But Bellugi wondered: Do deaf people *perceive* such signs as iconic as they communicate in ASL?

One day a deaf mother visited the lab with her deaf daughter, not yet 2. At that age, hearing children fumble pronouns, which is why parents say, "Mommy is getting Tammy juice." The deaf child, equally confused by pronouns, signed "you" when she meant "I." But the sign for such pronouns is purely iconic: the signer points an index finger at his or her own torso to signify "I" or at the listener to signify "you." The mother corrected the child by turning her hand so that she pointed at herself. Nothing could be clearer. Yet, as the child chattered on, she continued to point to her mother when she meant "I."

Bellugi's work revealed that deaf toddlers have no trouble pointing. But a pointing finger in ASL is linguistic, not gestural. Deaf toddlers in the "don't-understand-pronouns" stage do not see a pointing finger. They see a confusing, abstract word. ASL's roots may be mimetic, but—embedded in the flow of language—the signs lose their iconicity.

By the 1980s, most linguists had accepted sign languages as natural languages on an equal footing with English, Italian, Hindi and others of the world. Signed languages like ASL were as powerful, subtle and intricately structured as spoken ones.

The parallels become especially striking in wordplay and poetry. Signers creatively combine hand shapes and movements to create puns and other humorous alterations of words. A typical pun in sign goes like this: a fist near the forehead and a flip of the index finger upward means that one understands. But if the little finger is flipped, it's a joke meaning one understands a little. Clayton Valli at Gallaudet has made an extensive study of poetry in ASL. He finds that maintenance or repetition of hand shape provides rhyming, while meter occurs in the timing and type of movement. Research with the American Theater of the Deaf reveals a variety of individual techniques and styles. Some performers create designs in space with a freer movement of the arms than in ordinary signing. With others, rhythm and tempo are more important than spatial considerations. Hands may be alternated so that there is a balance and symmetry in the structure. Or signs may be made to flow into one another, creating a lyricism in the passage. The possibilities for this new art form in sign seem bounded only by the imagination within the community itself.

The special nature of sign language provides unprecedented opportunities to observe how the brain is organized to generate and understand language. Spoken languages are produced by largely unobservable movements of the vocal apparatus and received through the brain's auditory system. Signed languages, by contrast, are delivered through highly visible movements of the arms, hands and face, and are received through the brain's visual system. Engagement of these different brain systems in language use makes it possible to test different ideas about the biological basis of language.

The prevailing view of neurologists is that the brain's left hemisphere is the seat of language, while the right controls our perception of visual space. But since signed languages are expressed spatially, it was unclear where they might be centered.

To find out, Bellugi and her colleagues studied lifelong deaf signers who had suffered brain damage as adults. When the damage had occurred in their left hemisphere, the signers could shrug, point, shake their heads and make other gestures, but they lost the ability to sign. As happens with hearing people who suffer left-hemisphere damage, some of them lost words while others lost the ability to organize grammatical sentences, depending on precisely where the damage had occurred.

Conversely, signers with right-hemisphere damage signed as well as ever, but spatial arrangements confused them. One of Bellugi's right-hemisphere subjects could no longer perceive things to her left. Asked to describe a room, she reported all the furnishings as being on the right, leaving the room's left side a void. Yet she signed perfectly, including signs formed on the left side. She had lost her sense of *topographic* space, a right-hemisphere function, but her control of *linguistic* space, centered in the left hemisphere, was intact. All of these findings support the conclusion that language, whether visual or spoken, is under the control of the left hemisphere.

One of the Salk group's current efforts is to see if learning language in a particular modality changes the brain's ability to perform other kinds of tasks. Researchers showed children a moving light tracing a pattern in space, and then asked them to draw what they saw. "Deaf kids were way ahead of hearing kids," says Bellugi. Other tests, she adds, back up the finding that learning sign language improves the mind's ability to grasp patterns in space.

Thinking and Dreaming in Signs

Salk linguist Karen Emmorey says the lab also has found that deaf people are better at generating and manipulating mental images. "We found a striking difference in ability to generate mental images and to tell if one object is the same as another but rotated in space, or is a mirror image of the first," she says, noting that signers seem to be better at discriminating between faces, too. As she puts it: "The question is, does the language you know affect your other cognitive abilities?"

Freda Norman, formerly an actress with the National Theater of the Deaf and now a Salk research associate, puts it like this: "English is very linear, but ASL lets you see everything at the same time."

"The deaf *think* in signs," says Bellugi. "They *dream* in signs. And little children sign to themselves."

At McGill University in Montreal, psychologist Laura Ann Petitto recently found that deaf babies of deaf parents babble in sign. Hearing infants create nonsense sounds like "babababa," first attempts at language. So do deaf babies, but with their hands. Petitto watched deaf infants moving their hands and fingers in systematic ways that hearing children not exposed to sign never do. The movements, she says, were their way of exploring the linguistic units that will be the building blocks of language—their language.

Deaf children today face a brighter future than the generation of deaf children before them. Instruction in ASL, particularly in residential schools, should accelerate. New technologies, such as the TDD (Telecommunications Device for the Deaf) for communicating over telephones, relay services and video programs for language instruction, and the recent Americans with Disabilities Act all point the way to a more supportive environment. Deaf people are moving into professional jobs, such as law and accounting, and more recently into computer-related work. But it is not surprising that outside of their work, they prefer one another's company. Life can be especially rewarding for those within the ASL community. Here they form their own literary clubs, bowling leagues and gourmet groups.

As the Salk laboratory's Freda Norman signs: "I love to read books, but ASL is my first language." She adds, smiling: "Sometimes I forget that the hearing are different."

Content Questions

1. What "old scientific controversy" do some linguists hope to be able to resolve through the study of sign languages?

2. What is meant by the "oral method"? How effective is it for members of the deaf community?

3. Who was Gallaudet University named after and what was that person's significant contribution to sign language in the United States?

4. Trace the origins of American Sign Language. How was it modified by different influences?

5. What is meant by "simultaneous communication"? What special challenge does this present to deaf speakers?

6. Why is it so important for a deaf child to be exposed to sign language early?

7. Languages naturally develop dialectal differences and also change through time. Is there any evidence that American Sign Language has done so? Explain.

8. What is significant about the fact that, as far as their interpretation is concerned, the signs in American Sign Language are only arbitrarily connected with their meaning?

9. How can sign language create poetry?

Questions for Analysis and Discussion

1. Why do you think it is more accurate to speak of American Sign Language as a natural language than as some kind of pidgin? What do you think has caused some to resist giving fuller recognition to this language?

2. The article mentions that there are many different native sign languages throughout the world, all of which are incomprehensible to each other. Is that because they are based on spoken languages that are mutually incomprehensible? In other words, would American Sign Language be incomprehensible to users of a sign language in China because English is so different from Chinese? Explain.

3. Explain why Bellugi's research into brain hemisphere damage and Petitto's research into deaf children's babbling seem to indicate that there is validity in studying sign language to better understand psycholinguistic issues involving other natural languages.

The Indo-European Language*

Paul Thieme

Most people are aware of how archaeology can provide information about the past, but fewer people realize the extent to which linguistic study can contribute to such knowledge. In the article below, which originally appeared in *Scientific American*, Paul Thieme shows how a reconstruction of the Indo-European language can yield important insights into the history of that group of people whose language was the ancestral tongue for modern languages stretching from India to Europe (and through subsequent colonization to the Americas, Australia, New Zealand, and Africa). Indo-European has been given much attention by linguists in the last two hundred years. More recently, some linguists have been turning their attention to a classification of other language families such as those that can be found in the Americas, Africa, or Asia. But the essay below is a good illustration of what can be learned through the study of any language family's proto-language.

The descendants of this forgotten tongue include English, Sanskrit and Greek. By comparing its "daughter languages" with one another, linguists have learned how it sounded and even where it originated.

Every educated person knows that French and Spanish are "related" languages. The obvious similarity of these tongues is explained by their common descent from Latin; indeed, we could say that French and Spanish are two dialects of "modern Latin," forms of the ancestral language that have grown mutually unintelligible through long separation. Latin has simply developed somewhat differently in these two fragments of the old Western Roman Empire. Today these dialects are called Romance languages.

The other great family of European languages is of course the Germanic. It includes English, Dutch, German and the Scandinavian tongues, all descended from an ancient language—unfortunately unrecorded—called Teutonic.

Romance languages and Teutonic, plus Greek—these were once the center of our linguistic universe. During the past 200 years, however, linguistics has been undergoing a kind of prolonged Copernican revolution. Now the familiar European tongues have been relegated to minor places in a vaster system of languages which unites Europe and Asia. Known collectively as the Indo-European languages, this superfamily is far and away the most extensive linguistic constellation in the world. It is also the most thor-

oughly explored: while other language families have remained largely unknown, the Indo-European family has monopolized the attention of linguists since the 18th century. The modern discipline of linguistics is itself a
product of Indo-European studies. As a result of these intensive labors we
have come to know a great deal about both the genealogy and the interre-
lationships of this rich linguistic community.

If we look at the family as a whole, several questions spring to mind.
Where did these languages come from? Every family traces its descent from
a common ancestor: what was our ancestral language? What did it sound
like? What manner of men spoke it? How did they come to migrate over
the face of the earth, spreading their tongue across the Eurasian land mass?

Linguistics can now provide definite—if incomplete—answers to
some of these questions. We have reconstructed in substantial part the
grammar and sound-system of the Indo-European language, as we call this
ultimate forebear of the modern Indo-European family. Although much of
the original vocabulary has perished, enough of it survives in later languages so that we can contrive a short dictionary. From the language, in
turn, we can puzzle out some characteristics of Indo-European culture. We
can even locate the Indo-European homeland.

We can never hope to reconstruct the Indo-European language in complete detail. The task would be immeasurably easier if the Indo-Europeans
had only left written records. But the Indo-Europeans, unlike their Egyptian and Mesopotamian contemporaries, were illiterate. Their language
was not simply forgotten, to be relearned by archaeologists of another day.
It vanished without a trace, except for the many hints that we can glean
and piece together from its surviving daughter languages.

The Discovery of the Language

The first clue to the existence of an Indo-European family was uncovered
with the opening of trade with India. In 1585, a little less than a century after Vasco da Gama first rounded the Cape of Good Hope, an Italian mer-
chant named Filippo Sassetti made a startling discovery in India. He found
that Hindu scholars were able to speak and write an ancient language, at
least as venerable as Latin and Greek. Sassetti wrote a letter home about
this language, which he called *Sanscruta* (Sanskrit). It bore certain resemblances, he said, to his native Italian. For example, the word for "God"
(*deva*) resembled the Italian *Dio;* the word for "snake" (*sarpa*), the Italian
serpe; the numbers "seven," "eight" and "nine" (*sapta, ashta* and *nava*),
the Italian *sette, otto* and *nove.*

What did these resemblances prove? Sassetti may have imagined that
Sanskrit was closely related to the "original language" spoken by Adam
and Eve; perhaps that is why he chose "God" and "snake" as examples.
Later it was thought that Sanskrit might be the ancestor of the European

languages, including Greek and Latin. Finally it became clear that Sanskrit was simply a sister of the European tongues. The relationship received its first scientific statement in the "Indo-European hypothesis" of Sir William Jones, a jurist and orientalist in the employ of the East India Company. Addressing the Bengal Asiatic Society in 1786, Sir William pointed out that Sanskrit, in relation to Greek and Latin, "bears a stronger affinity, both in the roots of verbs and in the forms of grammar, than could possibly have been produced by accident: so strong, indeed, that no philologer could examine them all three without believing them to have sprung from some common source, which, perhaps, no longer exists; there is similar reason, though not quite so forcible, for supposing that both the Gothick and the Celtick, though blended with a very different idiom, had the same origin with the Sanskrit."

Sir William's now-famous opinion founded modern linguistics. A crucial word in the sentence quoted is "roots." Jones and his successors could not have done their work without a command of Sanskrit, then the oldest-known Indo-European language. But they also could not have done it without a knowledge of traditional Sanskrit grammar. Jones, like every linguist since, was inspired by the great Sanskrit grammarian Panini, who sometime before 500 B.C. devised a remarkably accurate and systematic technique of word analysis. Instead of grouping related forms in conjugations and declensions—as European and U.S. school-grammar does to this day—Panini's grammar analyzed the forms into their functional units: the roots, suffixes and endings.

Comparative grammar, in the strict sense, was founded by a young German named Franz Bopp. In 1816 Bopp published a book on the inflection of verbs in a group of Indo-European languages: Sanskrit, Persian, Greek, Latin and the Teutonic tongues. Essentially Bopp's book was no more than the application to a broader group of languages of Panini's technique for the analysis of Sanskrit verbs. But Bopp's motive was a historical one. By gathering cognate forms from a number of Indo-European languages he hoped to be able to infer some of the characteristics of the lost language—the "common source" mentioned by Jones—which was the parent of them all.

In the course of time Bopp's method has been systematically developed and refined. The "affinities" which Jones saw between certain words in related languages have come to be called "correspondences," defined by precise formulas. The "Indo-European hypothesis" has been proved beyond doubt. And many more groups of languages have been found to belong to the Indo-European family: Slavonic, Baltic, the old Italic dialects, Albanian, Armenian, Hittite and Tocharian. The "family tree" of these languages has been worked out in some detail. It should be borne in mind, however, that when it is applied to languages a family-tree diagram is no more than a convenient graphic device. Languages do not branch off from one another at a distinct point in time; they separate gradually, by the slow accumulation of innovations. Moreover, we cannot be sure of every detail in their relationship. The affinities of the Celtic and Italic languages, or of the Baltic and Slavonic, may or may not point to a period when each of these pairs formed a common language, already distinguished from the Indo-European. Some Indo-European languages cannot be placed on the family tree because their lineage is not known. Among these are Tocharian and Hittite. These extinct languages (both rediscovered in the 20th century) were spoken in Asia but descend from the western branch of the family.

Reconstruction

Let us see how a linguist can glean information about the original Indo-European language by comparing its daughter tongues with one another. Take the following series of "corresponding" words: *pra* (Sanskrit), *pro* (Old Slavonic), *pro* (Greek), *pro* (Latin), *fra* (Gothic), all meaning "forward"; *pitā* (Sanskrit), *patēr* (Greek), *pater* (Latin), *fadar* (Gothic), all meaning "father." Clearly these words sprang from two words in the original Indo-European language. Now what can we say about the initial sounds the words must have had in the parent tongue? It must have been "p," as it is in the majority of the languages cited. Only in Gothic does it appear as "f," and the odds are overwhelmingly in favor of its having changed from "p" to "f" in this language, rather than from "f" to "p" in all the others. Thus we know one fact about the original Indo-European language: it had an initial "p" sound. This sound remains "p" in most of the daughter languages. Only in Gothic (and other Teutonic tongues) did it become "f."

Now let us take a harder example: *dasa* (Sanskrit), *deshimt* (Lithuanian), *deseti* (Old Slavonic), *deka* (Greek), *dekem* (Latin), *tehun* (Gothic), all meaning "ten"; *satam* (Sanskrit), *shimtas* (Lithuanian), *suto* (Old Slavonic), *he-katon* (Greek), *kentum* (Latin), *hunda-* (Gothic), all meaning "hundred." (The spelling of some of these forms has been altered for purposes of exposition. The hyphen after the Gothic *hunda-* and certain other words in this article indicates that they are not complete words.)

Certainly the "s," "sh," "k" and "h" sounds in these words are related to one another. Which is the original? We decide that "k" changed into the other sounds rather than *vice versa*. Phoneticians tell us that "hard" sounds like "k" often mutate into "soft" sounds like "sh." For example, the Latin word *carus* ("dear") turned into the French word *cher;* but the reverse change has not occurred.

Reconstruction would be much easier sailing but for two all-too-common events in the history of language: "convergence" and "divergence." In Sanskrit the three old Indo-European vowels "e," "o" and "a" have converged to become "a" (as in "ah"). In the Germanic languages the Indo-European vowel "e" has diverged to become "e" (as in "bet") next to certain sounds and "i" (as in "it") next to others.

Like most procedures in modern science, linguistic reconstructions require a certain technical skill. This is emphatically not a game for amateurs. Every step is most intricate. Some people may even wonder whether there is any point to the labors of historical linguists—especially in view of the fact that the reconstructions can never be checked by immediate observation. There is no absolute certainty in the reconstruction of a lost language. The procedure is admittedly probabilistic. It can only be tested by the coherence of its results.

But the results in the reconstruction of ancestral Indo-European are heartening. By regular procedures such as those I have illustrated, we have reconstructed a sound system for Indo-European that has the simplicity and symmetry of sound systems in observable languages. We have discovered the same symmetry in our reconstructions of roots, suffixes, endings and whole words. Perhaps even more important, the Indo-European words we have reconstructed give a convincing picture of ancient Indo-European customs and geography!

The Indo-European Culture

Consider the words for "mother," "husband," "wife," "son," "daughter," "brother," "sister," "grandson," "son-in-law," "daughter-in-law," all of which we can reconstruct in Indo-European. As a group they prove that the speakers lived in families founded on marriage—which is no more than we might expect! But we obtain more specific terms too: "father-in-law," "mother-in-law," "brother-in-law," "sister-in-law." Exact correspondences in the speech usage of the oldest daughter languages which have been preserved lead to the conclusion that these expressions were used exclusively with reference to the "in-laws" of the bride, and not to those of the groom. There are no other words that would designate a husband's "father-in-law," and so on. The inference is unavoidable that the family system of the old Indo-Europeans was of a patriarchal character; that is, that the wife married into her husband's family, while the husband did not acquire an official relationship to his wife's family as he does where a matriarchal family system exists. Our positive witnesses (the accumulation of designations for the relations a woman acquires by marriage) and our negative witnesses (the complete absence of designations for the relations a man might be said to acquire by marriage) are trustworthy circumstantial evidence of this.

The Indo-Europeans had a decimal number system that reveals traces of older counting systems. The numbers up to "four" are inflected like adjectives. They form a group by themselves, which points to an archaic method of counting by applying the thumb to the remaining four fingers in succession. Another group, evidently later arrivals in the history of Indo-European, goes up to "ten" (the Indo-European *dekmt-*). "Ten" is related to "hundred": *kmtom*, a word which came from the still earlier *dkmtom*, or "aggregate of tens." In addition to these four-finger and ten-finger counting systems there was a method of counting by twelves, presumably stemming from the application of the thumb to the twelve joints of the other four fingers. It is well known that the Teutonic languages originally distinguished a "small hundred" (100) from a "big hundred" (120). The latter is a "hundred" that results from a combination of counting by tens (the decimal system) and counting by twelves (the duodecimal system). Traces of duodecimal counting can also be found in other Indo-European languages.

Reconstruction yields an almost complete Indo-European inventory of body parts, among them some that presuppose the skilled butchering of animals. The Indo-European word for "lungs" originally meant "swimmer." We can imagine a prehistoric butcher watching the lungs float to the surface as he put the entrails of an animal into water. There is no reference in the word to the biological function of the lungs, which was presumably unknown. The heart, on the other hand, appears to have been named after the beat of the living organ.

So far as tools and weapons are concerned, we are not quite so lavishly served. We obtain single expressions for such things as "arrow," "ax," "ship," "boat," but no semantic system. This poverty is due partly to an original lack of certain concepts, and partly to the change of usage in the daughter languages. It is evident that new terms were coined as new implements were invented. We do find words for "gold" and perhaps for "silver," as well as for "ore." Unfortunately we cannot decide whether "ore" was used only with reference to copper or to both copper and bronze. It is significant that we cannot reconstruct a word for "iron," which was a later discovery. In any case we need not picture the people who spoke Indo-European as being very primitive. They possessed at least one contrivance that requires efficient tools: the wagon or cart. Two Indo-European words for "wheel" and words for "axle," "hub" and "yoke" are cumulative evidence of this.

The Indo-European Homeland

Especially interesting are the names of animals and plants, for these contain the clue to the ancient Indo-European homeland. It is evident that our reconstructed language was spoken in a territory that cannot have been large. A language as unified as the one we obtain by our reconstruction suggests a compact speech community. In prehistoric times, when communication over long distances was limited, such a community could have existed only within comparatively small boundaries.

These boundaries need not have been quite so narrow if the people who spoke Indo-European had been nomads. Nomads may cover a large territory and yet maintain the unity of their language, since their roamings repeatedly bring them in contact with others who speak their tongue. The Indo-Europeans, however, were small-scale farmers and husbandmen rather than nomads. They raised pigs, which kept them from traveling, and they had words for "barley," "stored grains," "sowing," "plowing," "grinding," "settlement" and "pasture" (*agros*), on which domesticated animals were "driven" (*ag*).

We cannot reconstruct old Indo-European words for "palm," "olive," "cypress," "vine," "laurel." On the strength of this negative evidence we can safely eliminate Asia and the Mediterranean countries as possible starting points of the Indo-European migrations. We can, however, reconstruct the following tree names: "birch," "beech," "aspen," "oak," "yew," "willow," "spruce," "alder," "ash." The evidence is not equally conclusive for each tree name; my arrangement follows the decreasing certainty. Yet in each case at least a possibility can be established, as it cannot in the case of tree names such as "cypress," "palm" and "olive."

Of the tree names the most important for our purposes is "beech." Since the beech does not grow east of a line that runs roughly from Königsberg (now Kaliningrad) on the Baltic Sea to Odessa on the northwestern shore of the Black Sea, we must conclude that the Indo-Europeans lived in Europe rather than in Asia. Scandinavia can be ruled out because we know that the beech was imported there rather late. A likely district would be the northern part of Middle Europe, say the territory between the Vistula and Elbe rivers. It is here that even now the densest accumulation of Indo-European languages is found—languages belonging to the eastern group (Baltic and Slavonic) side by side with one of the western group (German).

That the Indo-Europeans came from this region is indicated by the animal names we can reconstruct, all of them characteristic of the region. We do not find words for "tiger," "elephant," "camel," "lion" or "leopard." We can, however, compile a bestiary that includes "wolf," "bear," "lynx," "eagle," "falcon," "owl," "crane," "thrush," "goose," "duck," "turtle," "salmon," "otter," "beaver," "fly," "hornet," "wasp," "bee" (inferred from words for "honey"), "louse" and "flea." We also find words for domesticated animals: "dog," "cattle," "sheep," "pig," "goat" and perhaps "horse." Some of these words are particularly significant. The turtle, like the beech, did not occur north of Germany in prehistoric times.

The Importance of the Salmon

It is the Indo-European word for "salmon" that most strongly supports the argument. Of all the regions where trees and animals familiar to the Indo-Europeans live, and the regions from which the Indo-Europeans could possibly have started the migrations that spread their tongue from Ireland to

India, it is only along the rivers that flow into the Baltic and North seas that this particular fish could have been known. Coming from the South Atlantic, the salmon ascends these rivers in huge shoals to spawn in their upper reaches. The fish are easy to catch, and lovely to watch as they leap over obstacles in streams. Without the fat-rich food provided by the domesticated pig and the salmon, a people living in this rather cold region could hardly have grown so strong and numerous that their migration became both a necessity and a success.

The Indo-European word for "salmon" (*laks-*) survives in the original sense where the fish still occurs: Russia, the Baltic countries, Scandinavia and Germany (it is the familiar "lox" of Jewish delicatessens). In the Celtic tongues another word has replaced it; the Celts, migrating to the West, encountered the Rhine salmon, which they honored with a new name because it is even more delectable than the Baltic variety. The Italic languages, Greek and the southern Slavonic tongues, spoken where there are no salmon, soon lost the word. In some other languages it is preserved, but with altered meaning: in Ossetic, an Iranian language spoken in the Caucasus, the word means a large kind of trout, and the Tocharian-speaking people of eastern Turkestan used it for fish in general.

Several Sanskrit words echo the importance of the salmon in Indo-European history. One, *laksha,* means "a great amount" or "100,000," in which sense it has entered Hindustani and British English with the expression "a lakh of rupees." The assumption that the Sanskrit *laksha* descends from the Indo-European *laks-* of course requires an additional hypothesis: that a word meaning "salmon" or "salmon-shoal" continued to be used in the sense of "a great amount" long after the Indo-European immigrants to India had forgotten the fish itself. There are many analogies for a development of this kind. All over the world the names of things that are notable for their quantity or density tend to designate large numbers. Thus in Iranian "beehive" is used for 10,000; in Egyptian "tadpole" (which appears in great numbers after the flood of the Nile) is used for 100,000; in Chinese "ant," for 10,000; in Semitic languages "cattle," for 100; in Sanskrit and Egyptian "lotus" (which covers lakes and swamps), for "large number." Several words in Sanskrit for "sea" also refer to large numbers. In this connection we may recall the words in *Hamlet:* ". . . to take arms against a sea of troubles, and by opposing end them."

A second Sanskrit word that I believe is a descendant of the Indo-European *laks-* is *lākshā,* which the dictionary defines as "the dark-red resinous incrustation produced on certain trees by the puncture of an insect (*Coccus lacca*) and used as a scarlet dye." This is the word from which come the English "lac" and "lacquer." *Lākshā,* in my opinion, was originally an adjective derived from the Indo-European *laks-;* meaning "of or like a salmon." A characteristic feature of the salmon is the red color of its flesh. "Salmonlike" could easily develop into "red," and this adjective could be used to designate "the red (substance)," *i.e.,* "lac."

There is even a third possible offshoot: the Sanskrit *laksha* meaning "gambling stake" or "prize." This may be derived from a word that meant "salmon-catch." The apparent boldness of this conjecture may be vindicated on two counts. First, we have another Indo-European gambling word that originally was an animal name. Exact correspondences of Greek, Latin and Sanskrit show that the Indo-Europeans knew a kind of gambling with dice, in which the most unlucky throw was called the "dog." Second, in Sanskrit the gambling stake can be designated by another word, a plural noun (*vijas*) whose primary meaning was "the leapers." The possibility that this is another old word for "salmon," which was later used in the same restricted sense as *laksha*, is rather obvious.

By a lucky accident, then, Sanskrit, spoken by people who cannot have preserved any knowledge of the salmon itself, retains traces of Indo-European words for "salmon." Taken together, these words present a singularly clear picture of the salmon's outstanding traits. It is the fish that appears in big shoals (the Sanskrit *laksha,* meaning "100,000"); that overcomes obstacles by leaping (the Sanskrit *vijas,* meaning "leapers," and later "stake"); that has red flesh (*lākshā,* meaning "lac"); that is caught as a prized food (*vijas* and *laksha,* meaning "stake" or "prize").

The Age of the Language

If we establish the home of our reconstructed language as lying between the Vistula and the Elbe, we may venture to speculate as to the time when it was spoken. According to archaeological evidence, the domesticated horse and goat did not appear there much before 3000 B.C. The other domesticated animals for which we have linguistic evidence are archaeologically demonstrable in an earlier period. Indo-European, I conjecture, was spoken on the Baltic coast of Germany late in the fourth millennium B.C. Since our oldest documents of Indo-European daughter languages (in Asia Minor and India) date from the second millennium B.C., the end of the fourth millennium would be a likely time anyhow. A thousand or 1,500 years are a time sufficiently long for the development of the changes that distinguish our oldest Sanskrit speech form from what we reconstruct as Indo-European.

Here is an old Lithuanian proverb which a Protestant minister translated into Latin in 1625 to show the similarity of Lithuanian to Latin. The proverb means "God gave the teeth; God will also give bread." In Lithuanian it reads: *Dievas dawe dantis; Dievas duos ir duonos.* The Latin version is *Deus dedit dentes; Deus dabit et panem.* Translated into an old form of Sanskrit, it would be *Devas adadāt datas; Devas dāt* (or *dadāt*) *api dhānās.* How would this same sentence sound in the reconstructed Indo-European language? A defensible guess would be: *Deivos ededōt dntns; Deivos dedōt* (or *dōt*) *dhōnās.*

Content Questions

1. What was the Indo-European language? Name some of the modern languages that have "descended" from it.

2. What contribution did Sir William Jones make to modern linguistics and our knowledge of the Indo-European language?

3. Who was Panini and why was his work also important to our knowledge of the Indo-European language?

4. What is linguistic reconstruction? How has it been important to the study of the Indo-European language?

5. The article provides two examples of how data from known languages can be used to reconstruct Indo-European. Identify the two separate strategies that are illustrated in the two examples given.

6. What do the kinship terms of Indo-European tell us about Indo-European society? What can we learn from their animal and plant names?

7. When was Indo-European probably spoken?

Questions for Analysis and Discussion

1. The tree metaphor and the family metaphor are frequently used to show the relationships among Indo-European languages. In what ways can these two metaphors be misleading?

2. Thieme mentions some Sanskrit terms that may have descended from the Indo-European word for *salmon*. How convincing do you find his explanations?

3. Compare and contrast the type of knowledge about a culture that can be gained through linguistic reconstruction as opposed to finding old ruins or artifacts such as pottery.

Additional Activities and Paper Topics

1. Acquaint yourself with some of the phonological features of a particular regional or social dialect. Assume now that you are a director of a theatrical production and responsible for helping the actors and actresses to produce authentic pronunciations in the speech of characters who would be speakers of that dialect. Transcribe some of the distinctive pronunciations of that dialect so that you have readily available information for yourself as you coach the actors and actresses on their pronunciation. Then report on the features that you have noted and provide a copy of the transcriptions you have made. (**Phonology**)

2. Familiarize yourself with some of the signs used in American Sign Language. Then report on those signs that at least appear to have once been iconically based (whether or not they are now regarded as such among ASL speakers). (**Language Varieties**)

3. Along the lines of Deborah Tannen's work, observe a mixed-gender conversation, business setting, or recreational activity. Record some of the cross-gender dynamics. Do you see any interesting patterns (do not force yourself to see things that might not be there)? You might watch for things such as which gender does more of the talking, who seems to do more of the interrupting, to what extent are self-effacing remarks used and who uses more of them, and so on. Report on your observations and explain to what extent gender may or may not have been a factor in the particular interactions you were observing. Remember that in some situations, other explanations might be more relevant. (**Language Varieties**)

4. Prepare an annotated bibliography of twenty articles or books that discuss linguistic research related to gender. Report on the kinds of specific topics that have been explored by linguists working in this area. (**Language Varieties**)

5. Consult a dictionary of Indo-European roots and identify five words with interesting etymologies. Discuss what makes those personally interesting to you. (**Historical Linguistics**)

Linguistics, Education, and Social Policy

The relationship between linguistic research and education is becoming increasingly more significant. Much of this increased significance is related to recent developments in the study of sociolinguistics and discourse analysis. These developments have come at an important time, when our country's school systems are struggling with how best to accommodate the many differing cultures and backgrounds of our students. Shirley Brice Heath has examined the different discourse styles that exist within the classroom. In her article "Teacher Talk: Language in the Classroom," she shows how some students, because of their background, differ in the degree to which their discourse style matches the style of their teacher. These differences can have a significant effect on the interactions between teachers and their students. Heath illustrates some of the issues that teachers should consider about the language background of their students and how a greater awareness of such issues might enhance classroom communication.

Linguistics has also studied the effects of differing dialects on the way subject matter should be taught. While some people have incorrectly assumed that Black English Vernacular (BEV) is a more primitive language that limits the cognitive abilities of its speakers, linguistic research challenges those assumptions. In "Recognizing Black English in the Classroom," William Labov discusses some of the complex features of BEV and how a knowledge of these features could be applied when teaching children who speak that dialect how to read.

As a teacher, it is easy to take certain kinds of skills and knowledge for granted with students. When teaching reading, for example, a logical starting point for teachers would seem to be the teaching of sound-symbol correspondences and the "sounding out" of alphabetic sequences. Such an approach, however, takes some prereading skills for granted, which in fact some beginning readers have never developed. In the article "Phonemic Awareness Training: Application of Principles of Direct Instruction," Janet E. Spector examines a critical component in reading readiness, known as phonemic awareness. She considers ways in which this skill can be developed in students.

In his article "Beyond Black English: Implications of the Ann Arbor Decision for Other Non-Mainstream Varieties," Walt Wolfram reminds us that Black English is not the only nonstandard dialect in American English that can put its speakers at a disadvantage in the classroom. In his article he looks specifically at Appalachian English. After identifying some of the features that characterize Appalachian English, he considers it in relation to the classroom, noting how some students could be improperly evaluated in other skills, based on an ignorance among some educators about Appalachian English.

Linguistics can contribute to teaching in many ways. In fact, several chapters in this book deal with teaching in some specialized senses, whether in the teaching of literature, composition, or language. I have separated articles into those other chapters, but it is worth noting here that education-related applications are not limited to the types of applications shown in this chapter.

Another important area in which linguistics has much to contribute is in the field of social policy. While social policies often involve educational issues, these policies may also involve other issues that extend well beyond the educational setting. In "Applied Linguistics and Language Policy and Planning," Robert B. Kaplan examines some of the important and complex issues that should be considered when governmental policy or social policy makers must make decisions that prioritize some languages over others. Kaplan's article introduces us to a whole field of application that could benefit immensely from well-trained applied linguists.

In an earlier chapter we looked at the valuable role that a linguist as expert witness could play in court cases. In "Testimony before the State Legislature on California Proposition 63," we can see another example of a linguist providing expert testimony. This situation involves Geoffrey Nunberg, who testified before a state legislature as it considered upcoming legislation that would designate English as the official language. As part of his testimony, Nunberg considers some of the relevant history of our language and what it might show about the relative advisability of legislating language use.

Teacher Talk: Language in the Classroom

Shirley Brice Heath

Shirley Brice Heath of Stanford University is an anthropologist and linguist whose work in ethnography and education has been influential. The article below originally appeared in connection with the National Institute of Education, U.S. Department of Health, Education, and Welfare. In this article Heath illustrates how linguistic differences, even among English-speaking children, can relate to their conduct and the type of treatment they receive from their teachers. Heath notes the varied backgrounds of the young children entering school and how these background differences relate to important discourse differences. She explains that teachers should not take for granted that particular discourse patterns will be equally clear to all of their students. Her research shows the importance of discourse analysis in illuminating certain dynamics of the classroom and enhancing the effectiveness of teachers.

*Who knows where our story for today takes place?
I do—Switzerland.
*Good. Now, Jeremy, can you point Switzerland out on the map?

*I don't think you really want to be talking when our guests come, do you?

*I see two boys who are going to be stepping outside in a minute.

Anyone who has been through the formal educational system in the United States will recognize the speakers in the starred passages as teachers and the setting as a classroom. Teacher talk is immediately recognizable. What is unique about the talk of teachers in classrooms? Why does it have specific features that set it apart from the talk of doctors to patients, waitresses to customers, public service personnel to clients, or the general remarks of adults to children?

Studies of classroom language have focused on the communication patterns—both verbal and nonverbal—of teachers and students.[1] Teachers

---

[1] The study of teacher talk is only one aspect of recent research into the social events of the classroom that examines the social, linguistic, and cognitive events of instructional settings. Students have to reflect their learning within the communication system the teacher establishes. Major research efforts in classroom language began in the late 1960s with the Flanders Instrument Analysis Categories System (1970). Researchers coded units of communication in which the teacher's

learn these patterns through their own home and school experiences and from reinforcement in their teacher training. Students are expected to learn these patterns before they enter school and to have them continually reinforced at home and in other institutional settings. The patterns are conventionalized; many relate to the use of space and time, and respect for others.

It's clean-up time now!

What are we supposed to be doing?

Why don't you try the method on page 76?

What on earth are you doing?

Is that where the crayons belong?

For those with classroom experience, each of these expressions brings to mind a particular range of situations in which these directives or requests for action would be used. To be familiar with any of these routines one must have learned (1) the lexical and grammatical features of these structures, (2) the situations in which they occur, and (3) the rules for interpreting and responding to them. Many homes and communities, however, do not share these conventions, and students from these environments have difficulty interpreting the meanings, situations, and rules of classroom language. Teachers are often unaware of the need to make these conventions explicit, because they seem only 'natural' to them.

Descriptions of these mainstream customs and their manifestation in classroom language may therefore seem self-evident to many teachers or mainstream parents. However, the rules that govern these social interactions are neither self-evident nor simple. Description and analysis reveal their complexities and the extent to which their correct interpretation and appropriate response depend on prior experience or explicit translations of their meanings.

To provide a framework for the discussion of classroom language, we need first to characterize it in terms of some of its special features as a 'register' or style appropriate to the particular situation of teaching or caregiv-

language stimulated a student response. Analyses of frequencies of coded behavior revealed that teachers did two-thirds of the talking in the classroom. Critical points in the facilitation of decision making were identified in an effort to influence teachers to make their instructional strategies less directive. Recent work has been more qualitative and has emphasized preservation and analysis of the actual classroom language data in order to describe the skills teachers and students use for appropriate interpretation of verbal or nonverbal events. The most comprehensive summary of this type of research on classroom language appears in Mehan et al. (1976). Other studies are reported in Stubbs and Delamont (1976), Cicourel et al. (1974), Gumperz and Herasimchuk (1975), and Cazden, John and Hymes (1972). In the bibliography that follows, several citations include research on various types of teacher talk.

ing. A register is a conventionalized way of speaking used in particular situations. Numerous registers (baby talk, for example) are part of the linguistic repertoire of members of every speech community, and though they vary in detail from individual to individual, they are recognized and transmitted from generation to generation. A second feature of classroom language is the connected units that make up the 'discourse' or flow of speech in interaction between teacher and students. Teacher or student comments cannot be analyzed in isolation; they must be examined within the context of their occurrence with other stretches of speech. In addition to having particular characteristics of register and discourse, classroom language can be described in terms of the special provinces of control to which many of the 'directives,' or requests for action, refer: i.e., time and space usage, and respect for others.

What else can be gained—in addition to helping teachers make their directives more explicit—by the study of classroom language? Are there particular insights to teaching language arts skills in English as well as other languages that can be obtained from analysis of teacher talk? Examination by teachers and students of the features of teacher talk as register, discourse, and specialized language of control can help supplement traditional methods of teaching language arts. Teachers of foreign languages and English as a second language can also benefit from examining their own uses of the special register and discourse features of their classrooms and discussing these with students. Bilingual teachers, who in addition to adopting various registers in their classrooms also switch languages for specific types of interactions, can also gain a better understanding of these strategies. In the following discussion, suggestions are provided for variations of teacher talk and ways of involving students in the analysis of classroom language.

The Nature of the Talk of Teachers as 'Caregivers'

Language can vary according to user and use. 'Baby talk,' 'foreigner talk,' and 'doctor talk' are registers we can differentiate easily. Linguists view teacher talk as a style of speaking having special features shared with other types of talk used by caregivers. The talk used by parents to children or infants reflects emotional attachment and the goal of instruction (Brown 1977). 'Baby talk' across numerous speech communities—indeed, perhaps all—is a simplified register used to clarify, show expressiveness, and emphasize identification of infant as addressee (Ferguson 1977).

Within their role of controlling standards of citizenship and order, teachers become intimate caregivers to students.[2] Prior to schooling,

---

[2] The findings presented here that are not specifically credited to published studies are based on research conducted at Winthrop College between 1970 and 1975 by myself and by graduate

children learn from parents, kin, siblings, playmates; they learn few, if any, rules and norms of behavior from strangers. They are warned in particular against strangers who act like caregivers and become solicitous, give directions, or tell them what their intentions should be. In schools, as in other institutional settings (e.g., hospitals), interactions between strangers assuming the role of intimates have to become acceptable. Teachers, nurses, school officials, and counselors are strangers providing guidance in intimate areas of values and behaviors.

The special register or use of language that develops in these situations enables both parties to give notice of their recognition of the circumstances (Greene 1973). Both parties admit that caregivers have to teach things that only they and those internal to the structure of the institution agree should be taught. To project an easy, 'friendly' relationship between caregiver and care-recipient, teachers adopt certain verbal formulae: e.g., "Don't you think it's time you settled down to work?" This formula appears to be a question. However, students who know how to interpret teacher talk will hear this as a detailed directive: "Time has been marked for a specific task; you should do your task in this period of time; if you do not, you are wasting time, and you and your work will suffer as a consequence." Characteristics of the caregiver register are distributed differently across age groups, institutional settings, and between sexes. However, all intra-register varieties exhibit similar prosodic, lexical, and grammatical features. The characteristics of the caregiver's language co-occur regularly enough and are so interrelated that they constitute a register.

Prosodic elements are the most notable characteristics of the speech addressed by teachers to very young schoolchildren. Teachers in day-care centers, kindergartens, and early primary grades use overall high pitch and

---

students. Data were collected in rural and urban traditional and open classrooms, day-care centers, elementary, junior and senior high schools. The graduate student research was reported in unpublished papers on the following topics: reading instructional settings in an elementary school (Helen Guinness 1974); principals and teachers in interaction (Vance Bettis 1974); third and fourth grade math and reading instruction in an open school (Judy Adams and Patricia Threatt 1971–1972); mainstream kindergarten (Ann Barron and Mary Watson 1970); monitoring motivations, intentions, and responsibility in reading instruction (Betsy Forrest 1974); modified discourse patterns in open science classes, secondary level (Patricia Norris 1972); opening discussion in a fifth grade social studies class (Margaret Saleeby 1973); monitoring politeness formulae and rules for eating in an elementary school (Barbara Abell 1970). Field notes made by teachers in similar educational settings supplemented these papers. The data were obtained across grade levels and in varied subject areas and ability groupings by three different methods: (1) observation and participation by team teachers or teacher, and class observer writing down sequences of interactions; (2) audio taping of encounters relating to discipline between teachers and students, or administrators and students; (3) videotaping of lessons on similar topics (organizing an answer, responding to a fire drill). The bulk of the data was gathered by the first method; weaknesses in this form of data collection were in part compensated for by repeated observations of the same classrooms by different students, simultaneous observations by several students and myself, and comparisons of observations of the same teacher or subject area made during different semesters. Ethnographic fieldwork conducted in two communities in which many of the students lived supplemented classroom observations. These school and community data will be presented in expanded form in Heath, *Ethnography and Education: Community to Classroom* (in preparation).

exaggerated intonation contours in addition to slow, carefully enunciated speech. There is often much nonverbal reinforcement through facial gestures and body movements. Why are these used? There is evidence that the high pitch may be imitative of what young children themselves produce. In addition, high pitch not only attracts the young child's attention, but it also identifies the talk as directed specifically toward the child and excluding all others. A teacher talking to a parent bringing a young child to school for the first time will shift pitch and contour pattern to engage the child's attention when ending the conversation with the parent. Furthermore, teachers in the early primary grades use high pitch more frequently during the first weeks of the school year, and individually with new pupils coming in later in the year.

Teachers working with children they believe to be deficient in language skills (Head Start programs as opposed to upper-class church kindergartens) use prosodic features extensively. Perhaps they feel unconsciously that prosodic changes clearly mark boundaries between utterances. Enunciating short, distinct sentences in which stress is given to particular words attracts attention and alerts learners to what they are expected to provide in answers to questions: "Tomorrow will be a *color* day. Our special *color* will be *red*." The child is given a cue that answers to questions asked the next day will be about 'color' and should contain the words 'color' and 'red.' Teacher handbooks caution new teachers to speak slowly and distinctly so that they may serve as models for students' speech. Providing students with language for imitation is not the goal of this modelling; instead, teachers' questions point out the slots and fillers students must use to provide correct answers. All these characteristics elicit the child's attention and cooperation in verbal interaction and mark the teacher's speech as learner directed; moreover, many teachers assume that these cues clarify the linguistic structure of the speech and thus help in comprehension and acquisition of language control.

Grammatical modifications in the language of teachers are often more obvious to the casual observer than are prosodic changes. In the early grades, teacher talk is marked by shorter sentences, fewer subordinate clauses, and more frequent repetitions than normal adult-to-adult speech or the language used in higher grades. Teachers in remedial programs for high school students or in vocational educational programs for adults often remark that the speech normally directed to early learners is not appropriate for older students, yet they often slip into it when teaching what they consider simple subject matter. They use full forms instead of contractions, insist on complete sentences, and use 'will' instead of 'going to' to indicate intention. Students interpret these features as signs that teachers are 'talking down' to them.

Vocabulary modifications tend to be determined in part not only by teacher manuals but also by rules of discipline established by the school. In the primary grades, respect for the school, school officials, teachers, and students is a desired goal, and campaigns are often launched to orient young children to display such respect. Discipline rules are personified. If the school has a campaign to keep a new building clean, admonishments to children about marking on walls or not putting trash in containers will often invoke the symbolism of a mascot or the authority of the principal:

> Do you think Giggly Glowworm would be very happy about your desk, David?

> What would Mr. Morris say if he could see the floor around the wastepaper basket?

In the higher grades, teachers may substitute 'the boss' or 'the big man' for 'Mr. Morris,' or they may refer students to other authority sources. Handbooks, wallboard messages, and monitoring systems run by peers make real the abstractions of cleanliness, orderliness, respect, and responsibility.

The Nature of Classroom Discourse

Linguists also analyze classroom language as segments of discourse—sequences of units of language arranged to produce interaction for particular functions. Sometimes these functions are straightforward; other times they must be inferred; and on other occasions they may be purposefully concealed from specific parties in the interaction.

Analysis of discourse focuses on the function of units of language larger than the sentence. In general, discourse analysis starts from the premise that most statements carry an informative intent, commands a directive intent, and interrogatives an elicitation intent. However, this is not always the case. Directives may come in the form of questions *or* statements: "Can you open the window?" "I won't be patient with two gabby girls much longer." Ervin-Tripp (1976) points out the varied forms directives can take in American English. However, all these become functional not as single sentences nor pieces of language, but as connected units dependent upon prior and subsequent units.

Interpretation is highly dependent upon the setting, social relations between speakers, and the speakers' expectations in regard to the situation. For example, the forms of the questions and responses given in the materials below are determined by all of these factors:

And what is your name?	Your name, please?
Belinda Gayle.	Allen Smith.
Why, that's a nice name.	Yes, here it is; right this way, please.

It is not difficult to guess which discourse would occur in a classroom and which would be heard in a restaurant. The internal forms and the intent of each unit vary. It would seem inappropriate for the headwaiter to use a complete sentence in the first unit; it would be rude for the teacher to ask the question as the headwaiter did. The third unit is an evaluation in teacher talk, a directive in headwaiter talk.

Unlike general conversation, in which a series of replies and responses determines the direction (Goffman 1976), classroom language has overriding rules that reflect the teacher's authority to decide who speaks, on what topics, and for how long. Many teachers have a high regard for the conversational mode, yet the goals of instruction and learning prevent them from allowing uncontrolled classroom conversation. Thus they provide rules for discussion, class meetings, or lessons that prescribe for students the limits of their powers of decision making about such talk. Prescriptions for classroom social interaction are given in terms of adhering to norms of order, good citizenship, good manners, respect for others, and the need to adhere to constraints of time and space on talk in the classroom.

Modifications in teacher talk are predominantly in the area of discourse. Questions asked in certain forms, frequent use of 'tag questions' ("—O.K.?" "—right?" "—hmm?" "—isn't it?"), failure to wait for answers, and a predominance of third person pronouns are only a few of the features of discourse found in teacher talk. These modifications are often thought to give classroom interaction a conversational tone, but the use of certain of these and the timing between discourse segments often rule out true conversation. Students who succeed in classroom discourse must stay on the subject and not monopolize the discussion, and they must also recognize special cues indicating when their turn has ended or if their remarks were inappropriate.

For example, in a junior high class discussion of environmental problems, the student who makes the following contribution may get no response from the teacher or other classmates: "I saw this neat program on TV last night that showed all these problems of pollution on another planet in the space age." The absence of a response from other participants signals negative reaction. Youngsters in reading-circle time in the elementary grades must learn that their contributions have to be directly related to the story or have a high interest quotient; othewise, their conversational participation will elicit no response from the teacher. Students must learn that verbal strictures ("Jerry, now is not the time to talk about that"), nonverbal signals (a cocked head and raised eyebrow), or the absence of a signal are measures teachers employ to control the direction of discourse.

Examination of teacher talk has shown that in the classroom, much discourse has a tripartite structure, with the teacher offering in the third unit some adjective of positive evaluation.

TEACHER: What products did the colonists provide the mother country?

STUDENT: Tobacco, cotton, and lots of other stuff they could grow over here.

TEACHER: Good. Now, why were these products important?

What is the relative impact of this formula? Is "good" truly praise, or is it primarily a signal to the student that participation in this segment of discourse is closed? Or is it merely a filler, a space-holder until the teacher can formulate the next question? Is this third unit necessary if it does not serve the purpose of positive reinforcement for the student? Could something else be used in this slot that would encourage the student to offer new information, to think more carefully, or to ask a question? Moreover, if positive reinforcement is used continuously in this type of exchange, what does the teacher say when there is a real need to praise?

Those who study classroom language view its detailed description as necessary for answering these and other questions and for making teachers and students of language aware of what does and does not happen when people communicate with each other. The purpose is to examine these interactions, not to evaluate past practices. In addition, knowing the structure of discourse and the characteristics of register variation used in the classroom helps in the teaching of language skills and testing of general knowledge. Detailed descriptions of how register and discourse work can also help teachers adjust their use of language to pedagogical goals.

What kinds of interrogatives and pronouns are used in general classroom discussions led by teachers? A subsample of data drawn from junior high English classes observed by Kluwin (1977) showed that most questions were introduced by *wh*-words, and the most frequent type was the *what* question. *Why, how,* and *when* questions occurred much less frequently. The present tense was used most often, suggesting that teachers ask questions about immediate concerns and do not call on students to formulate hypotheses. Most questions sought answers that were labels—names of items, actions, or agents. In another study, teachers who subscribed to the 'inquiry' or 'discovery' approach favored *what* or *who* questions in general classroom discussion periods (Heath, in preparation). In small-group work or written tests, however, these teachers asked questions that stressed *why, how, in comparison with,* and *in what context.*

TEACHER: [Stopping by to work briefly with a group of five fourth grade students assigned the project of preparing a bulletin board showing how language varies] What main ideas will you stress?

STUDENT A: Different kinds of writing and talking.

TEACHER: How will you do that?

STUDENT D: We're gonna use cartoons, pictures, and pieces out of magazines 'n stuff.

TEACHER: How will you compare types of writing? Will you talk about business letters and literature, or different types of literature?

STUDENT B: We'll do all that.

TEACHER: Can you show who writes these different ways and when?

STUDENT A: Maybe we better do a skit, too!

In the habit of leading general classroom discussion, teachers maintained an unconscious preference for questions calling for brief answers—questions that would not allow one student to 'monopolize the floor.'

TEACHER: [In fourth grade language arts class, after students had read a series of poems] What do we have here?

[No response]

TEACHER: What have you been reading?

STUDENT K: Stories.

TEACHER: Is that what they are, class?

STUDENTS A, D, L: No.

TEACHER: What are they?

STUDENT A: Poems.

TEACHER: Who writes poems?

[No response]

TEACHER: L—, can you write a poem? What makes a poem 'special'?

STUDENT L: I don't know.

A comparison of selected portions of tapes and transcripts of their questions in total class instruction and in small-group work helped these teachers recognize that their goal in using the 'discovery' approach (i.e., to generate creative and expanded answers) was being achieved only in small-group settings.

The study of teacher language can also focus on particular uses of verbal and nonverbal communication. Are there special ways of showing appreciation, scolding, reviewing, repeating? If so, what are the principles governing the occurrence of these, how do they vary from one type of classroom to another (e.g., open or traditional), or from one grade level to another, or perhaps from one topic area to another? Some teachers use restatement: "Bill has told us the dog doesn't find the bird, remember?" Others ask a question, and after a student responds, they add "Good," "O.K.," or "All right" (as mentioned previously, brief praise is the third unit of the question-response-evaluation pattern). Other instructors provide positive reinforcement by paying attention to the process used in obtaining the answer:

TEACHER: Who doesn't get the prize in this story?

STUDENT: Well, I can't tell, because we're not sure whether or not Leann gets the award, and the letter at the beginning of the story—you know, where Don is writing after the contest all about it to his cousin—tells me Don didn't get the prize either. He tells Ted what happened, and if he'd gotten that prize, he would've for sure told that first.

TEACHER: Good! You recognized the value of that letter way back at the beginning of the story as a clue to the actual ending. That's one way writers hold our attention; they introduce clues, and we read the story, in part, to figure out how the clue fits in. But we have to remember the clue as we go along. Have any of you ever played the game "Clue"?

In this exchange, the teacher points out the process the student used to reach his conclusion. She also relates this process to the author's intentions in designing the story. In addition, other students who may have played "Clue" are reminded that they use their abilities to collect, store, and relate facts to reach a final conclusion in situations other than reading lessons.

At the junior and senior high levels, subject areas played a strong role in determining how teachers reviewed, repeated, praised, or scolded, and the extent to which they used direct or indirect physical contact for praise or punishment (Heath, in preparation). Classes in social studies and English contained more discussion of the reasoning process, more latitude for varying interpretations, and more restatements of questions than did those in math or science. In the latter subjects, students were directed to a text or an object when they offered an incorrect answer; they were not frequently given the opportunity to think about their replies or restate them. Instead, they were told to "look at the problem again," "work it through another way," or "check the solution on page 14." Teachers' sentences in math/science classes were shorter, offered students fewer opportunities for interruptions with questions, and focused more attention on specific procedures, prescribed actions, or characteristics of objects than did classes in the humanities. When these analyses were discussed with them, teachers in various classes defined their roles very differently with respect to language. Math and science teachers believed students should be as brief, concise, and precise as possible. Teachers in the humanities courses talked in terms of self-expression, creativity, and style development through multiple approaches to answers.

Discussions based on data collected from their own classrooms helped teachers recognize that some of their classroom language was habitual, nonadaptive, and stereotyped. Science and math teachers admitted that although ideally they wanted students to be able to expand their ideas orally and explain concepts in acceptable expository prose, they had relegated opportunities for acquiring these skills to classes in the humanities. After technical reports and discussions of science/math concepts from local laboratories and businesses were introduced as classroom materials, discussion styles began to reflect teacher and student recognition of the use of different types of language—formulaic and expository, abbreviated and expanded—in the science/math fields as well as in other subject areas.

Perhaps the most important benefit of analyzing discourse in the classroom is the recognition of those nonadaptive features that may have negative value. There are students, such as newcomers or particularly reticent individuals, for whom caregiver register and predictable discourse patterns of question-response-evaluation provide positive stimuli or reinforcement. However, to use aspects of the caregiver register to 'talk down' to an entire group stereotyped as slow or underachieving is nonadaptive. Similarly, to use discourse patterns in science and math classes that allow for little verbal expansion—written or oral—is to operate from the assumption that math and science students lack verbal abilities.

Such talk of flexibility and variation in classroom language and the opening up of formerly restricted opportunities for verbal expression may make instructors fearful of being unable to maintain class discipline. A look at some of the ways teachers preserve control may provide ideas for altering these routines while still preserving a sense of discipline. Or, if individuals do not wish to relinquish these routines, discussion of their *implicit* meanings may help teachers present them in a more concrete way to students whose preschool socialization has not prepared them for this type of communication.

The Nature of the Talk of Teachers as Arbiters of 'Good Citizenship' and 'Order'

I hope we shall be friends.

When I am talking to you, I want you to hear.

I am paid to teach you. One of the things I have to teach you is good manners. You are old enough to know better than to. . . .

A Hoosier schoolmaster in the 1860s spoke these words, yet they sound very much like present-day teacher talk. This kind of talk has been a consistent characteristic of American education—indeed probably of all education in formal institutions. The very fact that one individual—the teacher—has to control or facilitate control of a number of individuals leads to the need for special verbal and nonverbal strategies of organization. These strategies are variously called 'good manners' or 'discipline'; they are in reality procedures for predicting certain limits of behavior in the classroom. Students are expected to follow these procedures on cue from ritualistic verbal formulae that incorporate values about how people in a situation of one-to-many should treat each other. Ideally, the specific behaviors to which these formulae refer are known to all, and students as well as teachers recognize them as necessary for managing a classroom in an atmosphere conducive to learning.

Furthermore, the image of the ideal teacher is of a person who wants what is best for the student. This implicit assertion of intimate concern allows the teacher-as-stranger to assign responsibilities and to judge and prescribe intentions and moral choices—areas of behavior generally set down directly by intimates only, or indirectly by abstract codes in our society. As a single figure of control, the teacher must rely on the predictability of responses from students accepting an assertion that he or she will act in their best interests.

Let's be sure we know this.

The grading period is almost over.

I had hoped to have time for some films.

We'll have to get our work done.

The familiar phrase, "You are old enough to know better than to . . ." reflects a basic underlying premise that many of the routines—and the values underlying them—should not have to be taught. In their middle class/ mainstream home socialization or institutional professional education, teachers learn unconsciously or implicitly the following values associated with verbal and nonverbal strategies of organization in the classroom:

- Displays of respect for generalized 'others,' usually in the order of 'school' (either as the specific institution or as formal education in general), school officials, teachers, and students. Ideally, if students place respect for 'school' at the top of the list, then respect for all others will follow automatically;
- The right of the teacher to determine rules and standards of talk in school: who may talk, why, when, how, and where;
- Behavior in accordance with a belief in the value of present tasks—especially those related to competition and evaluation—for future goals;
- Management of time in blocks designated for specific purposes;
- Recognition of specific spaces for designated functions.

Learned in mainstream settings, these values and the behaviors expected to accompany them are associated with certain verbal formulae:

Is that how we treat classmates?

It's time to clean up now.

Is this where the scissors belong?

Remember someone else will be using this book next year.

What's that on the floor?

Is that the way to talk to a teacher?

These routines reflect the tension between individual and group rights in school. Toward students who violate the norms behind these routines, teachers address these cues with the expectation that they will be appropriately interpreted as directives. Understanding the requests for action these routines carry, students are supposed to reorient their behavior. Because routines that maintain discipline are so embedded in the past experiences of teachers, they rarely think of the need to make explicit the rules for interpreting the language of control in the classroom.

Appropriate interpretations of directives are particularly difficult to make explicit. Ervin-Tripp (1977) has identified several types of directives in terms of the social relationships that exist between the person giving the directive and the individual or group to whom the directive is given. The following examples are taken directly from the classroom:

- Statements of personal need or desire:
  I need someone to help prepare the new bulletin board.
- Imperatives:
  Give me your attention.
- Embedded imperatives:
  Can we get ready on time?
- Permission directives:
  May I talk to Mr. James without interruption, Billy?
- Question directives:
  Have you finished your work?
- Hints:
  This room is certainly messy.

These directives are by no means clear. For example, embedded imperatives do not make the *task* obvious, but subtly refer to the *attitude* of the addressee, who is expected to recognize in these commands the call to displays of willingness and ability. Embedded imperatives are declaratives as well as questions:

Are you going to check out those slides?

You can clear out the supply cabinet, Mary, and you might want to check the orders, Joe.

Could you straighten out the bookshelves, Tom?

A positive response is expected from the hearer; the assertion of recognition of a compliant attitude is implied in the use of such modals as 'can,' 'could,' 'will,' 'would,' and 'going to.' Interpreting the *intention* behind directives is often critical to determining the appropriate response. The same statement or question may be interpreted as sarcasm, a request for sympathy, a warning, or a directive. Perhaps the most common examples of this are found in expressions using 'may,' 'might,' 'do you think you could,' or containing the word 'favor': "Ron, do you think you could do all of us a favor—and be quiet?"

In these cases, the intention is to remind the student that he is infringing on the rights of others by putting his own desires ahead of those of the class. To suggest, however, that he would be doing something special, i.e., a 'favor' for the class by being quiet, is to imply the student is ignorant of classroom rules. Other students recognize this implication; the sequence below is a typical example of the remarks that follow a directive such as that noted above:

BOB: [In response to teacher's comment to Ron] Yeah—sit down 'n shut up!
TEACHER: Bob, was that necessary?

In this interchange, students and teacher are united in chastising Ron; the teacher's comment to Bob is directed more toward Ron than Bob.

The use of tag questions is another common way of neutralizing assertions about intentions, motivations, and responsibility (see p. 341). In the classroom, teachers use tag questions less to request confirmation or agreement than they do to weaken their assertions about moral and ethical attitudes of students: "You knew better, didn't you?" Tag questions are actually declarative in intent; "You don't want that grade to drop this term, do you?" does not call for a response so much as it asserts from the teacher "You should not intend that that grade drop." In 'polite society,' we are not supposed to make assertions about the wants or desires of others. However, in instructional or counseling settings, such assertions seem necessary. Those who use these forms do not expect verbal responses— only eye contact or other signals of attention and respect. In fact, students who supply verbal support to these tag questions are considered disrespectful. Students are also considered disruptive for offering verbal responses to directives phrased as questions:

Are you about ready to hand that in now?

How about settling down to work?

Why don't you check the encyclopedia?

Would you like to come in now?

Students who come from home environments or cultures where questions-as-directives, hints, or tag questions are not used, have to learn—if they are to become acceptable members of the school's speech community—not to respond verbally. They also have to learn the values and behaviors implied in these directives. Teachers who use these devices can help by recognizing when and how often they use them and by making an effort to spell out the values and behaviors behind these routines.

Routines relating to time and space usage are an integral part of the language of teachers. The assignment of segments of time for specific purposes begins early in the formal educational system. Individuals are trained to expect certain events to occur at certain times of the day, and for specific events to follow one another. Head Start and day-care programs reflect this regimentation in the use of time by the posting of schedules of activities on classroom doors and in the classroom. Parents are asked to talk about the 'wise use' of time and the need to cooperate in such periods as 'clean-up time,' so that the class may move to the next time block.

This kind of training is familiar to individuals from mainstream settings. Here, children have been oriented traditionally to eating at specific hours, sleeping during certain hours, and playing at particular times. The value mainstream society attaches to the proper use of blocks of time is indicated by the fact that the most frequent request for specific information about how 'baby' is doing is a question about whether or not the feeding schedule and sleeping routine have been established. This regimentation teaches children from mainstream cultures to recognize boundaries of time between daily activities. Particular questions, directives, and statements are used to formalize these expected uses of time:

Now is not the time for that.

Your time is almost up.

It's about time for _____.

It's mealtime (naptime, gametime, reading time, etc.).

The speech used in children's games—'times,' 'time in,' or 'time out'—reflects the notion that time is seen as blocks to be manipulated, delayed, suspended, or put into action. A value is placed on 'using' time well by using it for the purpose for which it has been designated. Misuse of one's time is not something that is understood by young children as requiring apology. Older children and adults, however, are expected to understand the need to say "I'm sorry I'm late" or "Thank you for spending your time to do this for me."

Children from mainstream middle class homes are trained to perform in blocks of time; schools and other institutions providing human services stress this as well. Conformity to rules occurs, therefore, insofar as children come from cultures that share the rules related to the use of time as well as the verbal formulae of the classroom. Underlying the acceptance of the need to use time well is a fundamental notion of responsibility to use one's time to the best advantage in order to obtain future benefits and to avoid wasting others' time. Teachers often question unconsciously whether or not an individual who is not conforming to the required use of a time period does so knowingly and intends to involve others in the shift of the use to which that unit of time will be put. Open classroom strategies have weakened these notions, and students are operating increasingly according to schedules they establish for themselves. However, for many the use of time remains a moral issue, a test of character and self-discipline:

Time is money.

Time on your hands.

A stitch in time saves nine.

Space is another unit used for specific functions in school. The organization and use of space in the classroom are critical to notions of discipline. Value-laden terms, such as 'neat' or 'orderly,' are applied to bulletin boards, areas around trash cans, lines of desks, and the work of students. Implicit in the 'correct' or 'normal' use of space in the classroom are the notions of linearity and space-function ties. Many mainstream children grow up in rooms containing units rectangular or square in shape, in which things are kept lined up (either horizontally or vertically) if they are to be considered 'tidy,' and not 'messy.' Arranging objects and work areas in linear fashion reflects general norms of neatness in mainstream institutions. Similarly, specific objects or activities 'belong' in special places. Mainstream parents say the following to their children when they are very young:

Put your books away.

Your coat doesn't belong there.

You want the lines of the spread to be straight.

Line your blocks up, and they will fit in the box.

Many of these expressions are heard in classrooms, as teachers reflect norms of neatness and order. Things are put 'up,' 'away,' 'where they belong,' because "that's how we make the room look nice." Non-mainstream/middle class kindergarten and first grade children instructed to 'put things up' often take this as a literal directive and hold objects up in the air, not realizing that the teacher means that the object goes back in a linear position on 'its' shelf. Explicit directions clarifying these verbal formulae of space usage are necessary for students from home environments in which neither these formulae nor the norms they reflect are part of socialization.

Learning Teacher Talk: Why Study It?

What, then, does it mean to be a speaker of teacher talk? To be a speaker of any language, one must know the rules of sentence formation and how to use the language in different settings and for special purposes among members of the same culture. In the classroom and elsewhere, teachers use utterances to communicate; they as well as their listeners must know the grammar and uses of these utterances in order for communication to take place. Many of the sentences (or parts of sentences) used in the classroom have particular characteristics: they are fixed in form and do not show the variety of internal structures of messages in other contexts. They are idiomatic, sometimes even idiosyncratic: "Do I have to use my special voice?" "Do you want to take our special seat today, Mark?" They do not carry literal meanings. Many have come to be automatic parts of sequences of sentences. Communication depends on shared knowledge between teacher and students not only about the structure of these utterances, but also about the norms and behaviors to which they refer. If the principles of behavior to which the routines refer exist only in the teacher's mind, it will be necessary to make explicit to students the intent and behaviors meant by these formulaic routines.

Consider the situation of the student as a newcomer in the following classroom episodes that occur within the same day:

[Teacher and students working at a table with boxes and objects of different shapes]

Hold the red box *up*.

Put the blue circle *in* the red box.

Hold the sheet of brown paper *over* the red box.

In this reading readiness setting, the students are learning to deal with a paradigm: they learn to display, to be exact, and—most important—to pay attention to the examiner's actions. They learn to learn by following directions; they probably learn little about the meaning of prepositions—the explicit focus of the lesson.

Contrast the use of prepositions in the following routine expressions as the teacher attempts to maintain classroom control throughout the day:

We've got to get *over* this habit of everyone stopping at the water fountain on the way to lunch.

Let's put the scissors *up* now.

Are we all *in* line?

Hold your work at your desk until reading circle is *over.*

As part of reading readiness, the child has had specific drills in the understanding of prepositions in particular contexts. Yet these same prepositions occur without explanation in the verbal formulae of control. The child may learn words and the rules of their operation in readiness settings; however, this knowledge alone is not enough to enable comprehension of norms and behaviors implied in certain rituals of routine.

Analysis of the way people teach others in an instructional setting is relevant to the larger question of how children acquire their mother tongue, as well as to the ways in which they learn skills and view the information gained in these settings. Questions sort out for children what it is that adults see as relevant in a myriad of objects to be labelled, described, and manipulated. For example, in many middle class institutional settings, small children told to look at a cloth picture book will see a single item on a page (usually with no context) and be asked "What is this?" "Where is the ball?" "Show me the ball." Rarely will they be asked "What do we do with a ball?" Children from mainstream homes learn early to handle *what* questions and to recognize that names of things, agents, and events are of major importance to show what one has 'learned.' If the language addressed to children to request information is markedly different from the ordinary conversation of adults or from questions directed to adults, it seems plausible that this difference might help or hinder the child in language development or cognitive categorizing.

The study of the talk of instructional personnel to children should also include considerations of how language varies according to topic, function, and age and sex of listener. If the variation is not random, or if it changes according to regular patterns over the span of the school years, it is not only part of teachers' linguistic repertoires, but it is also part of the stimuli from which students draw in order to determine their own range of registers and their estimations of the respective topics, listeners, and settings for each.

All of these purposes for examining teacher talk seem reasonable. We learn about the structure of the language and its particular uses, and we begin to realize what teachers actually do with language in the classroom as opposed to the use of language in other contexts. Alternatives to unconscious use of teacher talk can come only when teachers are made aware of the structural and functional features of their own language. The goal of change is not only for teachers to shift from a role of direct influence to an indirect one, but to provide them with imaginative alternatives to many of the strategies and routines of classroom that have become fossilized and make teaching and learning boring for everyone concerned. Moreover, the limited and often simplified register of teacher talk has implications for learning strategies, and the observation of register and discourse in context can offer insights to students and teachers interested in the study of the ethnography of communication.

Alternatives and Recommendations

In spite of a strong impetus toward a return to traditional teaching strategies and a curriculum of the 'basics,' many aspects of alternative approaches to classroom organization may be retained by some schools or individual teachers. Numerous schools moving from traditional to modified or open systems of operation have altered their uses of time and space as well as their standards for noise level and turn taking. Teachers who have adopted both the philosophy and the methods of the open classroom have altered their talk. They do not talk as much as they did before; they have increased their use of the future tense and of second and first person (singular) pronouns:

You will need to schedule your project presentations before June 13.

I don't understand what you're trying to do.

I think Mary is scheduled to use that space for her presentation.

You check the sign-up sheet to see who has supply room duty.

You'll have a tight schedule if you try another project before the end of the term.

You'll have to decide about the safety patrol meeting before two o'clock.

The use of politeness formulae has decreased; when asked why they no longer said "please," "thank you," etc. as frequently as they had before adopting the open classroom philosophy, teachers answered, "We don't feel we're asking students to work for *us*. They set their own schedules, lay out their tasks, and determine their project presentations to be given before classmates. None of the process is oriented toward pleasing us or doing what we want. We feel free to express opinions, say what we think, and admit we are not the central factor in their learning."

Approaches to written discourse can be altered as well. At the junior and senior high levels, the format of tests has been modified. The usual procedure is to ask questions of students and request that they provide answers in designated forms (lists, short essays, true or false designations, multiple choices). New tests have been devised that consist solely of answers; the students have to provide the questions. This procedure has helped students focus on information organization and transfer. For example, if the answer given on a test is simply a name, e.g., 'Napoleon Bonaparte,' students have to recognize that there are many questions that could have generated that answer. In providing the possible questions, students may reflect much more knowledge than when required simply to come up with 'Napoleon Bonaparte.' Some teachers have provided short paragraph essays as answers for which students have to provide the best-fitting question. Analysis of these answers has allowed students to utilize their compositional and organizational processes; the questions have to include clauses or phrases that are appropriate stimuli for each portion of the essay.

Students in higher-level advanced classes and in remedial classes have expressed satisfaction with this approach to information exchange. The majority of middle range students, however, have been very unhappy about this method. Presumably, many average level students have managed in part to maintain their grades by means of their ability to predict the kinds of answers called for by specific types of questions. In other words, they are adept at taking tests and participating in class. Their school experiences have not prepared them for providing questions to answers. On the other hand, both advanced and remedial classes are more inclined to believe most teacher-made questions are unfair or inadequate ways of judging 'what someone really knows' and see this alternative method as a decided improvement. Teachers involved in this answer-question process find that students often see information possibilities never considered previously. Many teachers also judge the procedure far less boring than their usual methods of testing.

Adaptations of this reversal have occurred also in middle level classrooms where language arts, social studies, and math are taught by the same teacher. 'Stores' and 'businesses' are set up around the room, and groups of students are sent to these 'to do business.' Numerical problems (4 @ 29, 6% of $400, 2 lbs. @ .19) are placed on the board. Students go to the grocery, variety store, or bank to negotiate transactions that fit the problems on the board. Some students are observers; others are buyers, sellers, bankers, etc. Observers have to record the transactions on appropriate forms or in proper formats (receipts for groceries, including prices, totals, tax, and department abbreviations; bank loan notes; charge forms for store purchases). Other observers have to write out the transaction as a 'word problem' or a story, or use a tape recorder to describe the transaction as if they were an 'on-the-scene' TV reporter.

As a result of these activities, language skills have improved; abilities to interpret word problems in math have increased; and language, math, and social studies have become integrated in situations using various language skills. Particular attention is paid by students to the language used by the banker, the TV reporter, or the clerk. Who is courteous? Who is rude? How do observers judge politeness between individuals taking part in the transactions?

Some elementary grade teachers who have participated in programs to analyze their own talk have decided to use the same technique with their students in order to make them aware of the various uses of language and to enable students from non-mainstream home environments to learn in school settings the meanings and rationale of teacher talk. Students have been asked to record (in writing or on tape recorders) the language between Batman and Robin. Their conversation abounds with politeness formulae, and Batman excels in the stiff talk of caregivers: short sentences, moral pronouncements, use of the first person plural, full comparisons ("Robin is smarter than the Joker is") and 'will' for 'going to.' In class, these data are used for discussions about language variation: 'polite' talk and ways of talking that don't sound 'right,' 'natural,' or 'like we talk.' Students often make comparisons: "Batman sounds just like Mr. Allen when he talks to one of the sixth graders." Older students have been asked to record the language of Captain Kangaroo and note politeness formulae, direct and indirect orders, real and 'false' questions. Teachers with cooperative (and unself-conscious) principals have recorded portions of their remarks to teachers, parents, and students. Students analyzing these tapes have discovered that even their teachers and parents are sometimes 'talked down to' and have to use certain formulae in particular settings with specific individuals.

The introduction of innovative techniques in language arts, social studies, and even math no longer has to depend on inservice teacher training or summer school courses at nearby universities. The creative use of language—examined, recorded, and analyzed—transfers into new classroom practices. Student assessments of what makes a good teacher reflect the effect of these changes: "Good teachers don't talk down to us." "Good *good* teachers explain what they mean by 'good,' 'neat,' 'right,' 'straight'; they don't think we are mind-readers."

It is generally recognized—especially by those who have been in classrooms, where they are sometimes outnumbered 35 to 1—that change is

not so easy, especially in those areas where predictability is most comforting. However, specific strategies modifying teacher talk help open the way
to what are ultimate teaching goals across curricula: assuming an open attitude about learning about language, becoming aware of variations in structure and function, and understanding and accepting the reasons for these
variations. The following recommendations for observing and analyzing
language variation are not meant to be exhaustive, but simply first steps in
this process. Most important, they are introduced here to expand classroom instruction, not to suggest that teachers introduce variation for its
own sake.

> (1) Discuss the language of routines with students. This tactic applies
>   across grade levels. A social studies unit on the Civil War can bene-
>   fit from a discussion of the language of military routine; a first
>   grade class can benefit from discussing Captain Kangaroo's talk to
>   Mr. Greenjeans.
> (2) Be conscious of the behaviors of routine that differ for the school
>   as a whole and within your class. Think about the different strate-
>   gies used to deal with misbehavior in the lunchroom: the principal
>   makes a general announcement, but he or she also asks you to talk
>   with your class. What is different about the language (and the as-
>   sumptions of responsibility and respect) in the two settings?
> (3) Ask the students what can be accomplished when it is someone's
>   turn to talk. Strategies of reversing questions and answers between
>   teacher and students help. Another useful device is to give several
>   individuals an impromptu turn at talking with each other in front
>   of the class for a short period each day, or to give an opportunity
>   to 'take the whole floor' to one individual who has been 'disturb-
>   ing' the class by talking.
> (4) Whenever you catch yourself offering ambiguous instructions
>   ("Straighten up," "Don't leave a mess"), change these to explicit
>   directions.
> (5) Recognize when you are asserting a motivation or intention on the
>   part of a student ("You did that just to get out of spelling," "You
>   never intended to bring that homework in, did you?"). If you wish
>   to express an opinion about a student's behavior, do so directly ("I
>   believe . . . ," "I think . . ."). Accept the fact that the student may
>   have another explanation.

It is obvious that there is no end to the number of alternatives to 'standard teacher talk.' The more we attempt to understand how our messages
are structured, how they function, and how they are received, the greater
our chances of communicating with students from different environments
and cultures. The real test of meaning lies in our ability to be aware of
what we have intended in our messages and how we have been understood.

Selected Bibliography

Brown, Roger. 1977. Introduction. *Talking to children: language input and acquisition,* Catherine E. Snow and Charles E. Ferguson, eds. Cambridge: Cambridge University Press.

Cazden, Courtney B., Vera P. John and Dell Hymes, eds. 1972. *Functions of language in the classroom.* New York: Teachers College Press.

Chanan, Gabriel and Sara Delamont, eds. 1975. *Frontiers of classroom research.* London: National Foundation for Educational Research.

Cicourel, Aaron V. et al. 1974. *Language use and school performance.* New York: Academic Press.

Dunkin, Michael J. and Bruce J. Biddle. 1974. *The study of teaching.* New York: Holt, Rinehart & Winston.

Ervin-Tripp, Susan. 1976. Is Sybil there? The structure of American English directives. *Language in Society* 5 (April), 25–67.

———. 1977. Wait for me, roller skate! In *Child discourse,* Susan Ervin-Tripp and Claudia Mitchell-Kernan, eds. New York: Academic Press.

Ferguson, Charles E. Baby talk as a simplified register. 1977. In *Talking to children: language input and acquisition,* Catherine E. Snow and Charles E. Ferguson, eds. Cambridge: Cambridge University Press.

Flanders, N. A. 1970. *Analyzing teacher behavior.* Reading, Mass.: Addison-Wesley.

Galloway, Charles H., ed. 1977. *Nonverbal.* Theory into Practice 16 (3). Columbus: The Ohio State University Press.

Goffman, Erving. 1976. Replies and responses. *Language in society* 5 (December), 257–315.

Greene, Maxine. 1973. *Teacher as stranger: educational philosophy for the modern age.* Belmont, Mass.: Wadsworth.

Gumperz, John J. and Eleanor Herasimchuk. 1975. The conversational analysis of social meaning: a study of classroom interaction. In *Sociocultural dimensions of language use,* Mary Sanches and Ben O. Blount, eds. New York: Academic Press.

Heath, Shirley Brice. *Ethnography and education: community to classroom.* In preparation.

Hurt, H. Thomas et al. 1978. *Communication in the classroom.* Reading, Mass.: Addison-Wesley.

Hymes, Dell H. 1977. *Language in education: forward to fundamentals.* Working Papers in Education, No. 1. Philadelphia: University of Pennsylvania.

Kluwin, Thomas. 1977. *A discourse analysis of the language of the English classroom.* Ph.D. dissertation, Stanford University.

McDermott, R. P. 1976. *Kids make sense.* Ph.D. dissertation, Stanford University.

———. 1977. The ethnography of speaking and reading. In *Linguistic theory: what does it have to say about reading?* Newark, Del.: International Reading Association.

McNaughton, Patricia. 1973. *A selected bibliography on sociolinguistics: classroom verbal interaction and discourse analysis.* (*Supplement,* 1976.) Claremont, Calif. [mimeograph]

Mehan, Hugh et al. 1976. *The social organization of classroom lessons.* San Diego: University of California Center for Human Information Processing.

Payne, Charles and Carson Bennett. 1977. Middle class 'aura' in public schools. *The Teacher Educator* 13 (Summer), 16–26.

Philips, Susan. 1974. *The invisible culture: communication in classroom and community on the Warm Springs Indian Reservation.* Ph.D. dissertation, University of Pennsylvania.

——. 1976. Some sources of cultural variability in the regulation of talk. *Language in Society* 5 (April), 81–98.

Sinclair, J. McH. and R. M. Coulthard. 1975. *Towards an analysis of discourse: the English used by teachers and pupils.* London: Oxford University Press.

Stubbs, Michael and Sara Delamont, eds. 1976. *Explorations in classroom observation.* London: John Wiley.

Content Questions

1. List some of the characteristics of teacher talk as it is directed to young students.

2. What are the reasons given for the high-pitched speech directed at young children?

3. As far as teacher talk in the classroom is concerned, explain what the "tripartite structure" is and why the final response by the teacher, as it is frequently given, may be problematic.

4. Heath explains that some teachers were able to examine transcripts and tapes of their classroom questioning patterns. What became apparent to those teachers about how they constructed questions for the larger classroom situations versus the smaller group activities?

5. The article contains a list of directive types that have been observed in the classroom. Identify the six types of directives that are mentioned.

6. What is the common function of tag questions used by teachers? How are students expected to respond? Should a teacher, particularly of younger students, take it for granted that all students are familiar and understand this particular usage of tag questions? Explain.

7. What are some of the reasons given for studying teacher talk?

Questions for Analysis and Discussion

1. To what extent do you think that teachers using teacher talk are even consciously aware of the features that they are using?

2. Why is it necessary for interpretation to take into account such larger issues as the relationship of speakers to each other, the setting, and so on?

3. Why do you think that junior and senior high school math and science teachers might prefer shorter answers than English teachers might? How could the subject area contribute to this pattern?

4. Under what circumstances can "nonadaptive" or stereotypical speech patterns be offensive to students? Consider for example a situation in which a teacher refers to himself or herself in the third person such as "Your teacher likes it when you hand in your assignments on time." This works well with small children, but how would older students react?

5. Imagine a situation in which you need to ask a professor of yours the directions to another campus building. Which ones of the directive types would you consider using? Which ones would you probably avoid? How would the set of possibilities change if you were asking directions from a close friend?

6. What kinds of communication problems can result when students from a particular background do not have the same discourse behaviors as their teachers?

7. What could students learn about language use if a teacher has them study discourse used by others (or even themselves) in varying situations?

8. Comment on the value of discourse analysis in illuminating classroom aspects that might otherwise go unnoticed. Could an analysis of discourse help teachers to be more effective? Explain.

Recognizing Black English
in the Classroom

William Labov

In 1979 a U.S. district court judge in Detroit ruled that a school district in
Ann Arbor, Michigan, needed to be more accommodating in its treatment
of children who spoke Black English. Parents had complained that the
children were being prematurely labeled as deficient intellectually because
of inaccurate views by the teachers toward the children's dialect. Important to the judge's decision was evidence presented by linguists about the
linguistic structure and features of Black English. William Labov, who is
well known for his research in dialect studies, was one of the linguists
who served as an expert witness in the case. In the article below, Labov
discusses some structural characteristics of Black English and then indicates how such knowledge could be applied by teachers of reading to help
them be more effective in dealing with speakers of Black English Vernacular (BEV).

The Ann Arbor decision must be considered an important step in the effort
to achieve racial integration of American society. In recognizing Black English as a linguistic system, Judge Charles Joiner, Jr. acted to bring teachers
and Black children closer together, arguing that teachers should have a better knowledge of the resources children bring to school. He also brought
together linguists and educators: an immediate consequence of the Ann Arbor decision is that linguists must do a better job of making their research
findings available to those who need them. This presentation is intended as
an effort to organize our present knowledge of Black English in a form that
will be useful to designers of reading programs.[1]

Research on Black English was begun by Black scholars particularly
conscious of Black people's African heritage and the resemblance between

---

[1] The analysis of Black English presented here rests on the work of many other people besides
my own. The research in New York City was a joint effort, and I am greatly indebted to my colleagues Paul Cohen, Clarence Robins, and John Lewis at every stage of field work and analysis. The
work of Walt Wolfram and Ralph Fasold forms an essential part of our present knowledge of Black
English, though I have not provided all the references identifying their contributions. My debt to
John Baugh, John Rickford, and other scholars from the Black community appears throughout: the
most creative work of the last decade comes from participant-observers who have drawn upon their
entire social experience to solve linguistic problems. Finally, I must acknowledge my debt to Beryl
Bailey, William Stewart, and Joey Dillard, who never stopped insisting on the importance of parallels between Black English and the creoles of the Caribbean, until even the most backward members
of the linguistic community were at last convinced, including myself.

the language used in the Caribbean and the Black speech forms of the United States. Lorenzo Turner's research on the African elements in Gullah (1949) and Beryl Bailey's description of Jamaican Creole English (1966) provide an excellent foundation for the study of inner-city Black dialects. This type of research began in the mid 1960's, a time when violent protests throughout the country called attention to high levels of unemployment and a low degree of educational success in the cities. My own work in Harlem, funded by the Office of Education, was concerned with the issue of reading failure. The biracial team of researchers addressed two main questions:

1. How great were the differences between the linguistic systems used by Black and white youth in the inner-cities?
2. Do language differences contribute to the reading problems of Black children in inner-city schools?

If the Ann Arbor case had emerged at that time, the court would have found very little agreement among linguists. There were violent controversies between traditional dialectologists and students of Caribbean creoles, particularly on the historical origins of the dialects spoken in the United States. The dialectologists argued that Blacks spoke regional dialects no different from white speakers of the same southern region. Those familiar with the creoles of the Caribbean argued that Black English was a creole language with an underlying structure very different from other dialects and quite similar to the Caribbean English-based creoles. Dialectologists traced features of Black English to British dialect patterns: creolists maintained that those features were derived from a general American creole with Caribbean roots and ultimately from African grammar and semantics.

On the second question, the causes of reading failure, there was even less agreement. Most psychologists endorsed the verbal deprivation theory: that the language of Black children was impoverished as a result of deficiencies in their early environment (Deutsch, Katz, & Jensen, 1968). An alternative view developed, partly as a result of the alleged failure of enrichment programs, that lack of educational success was attributable to genetic defects in certain children (Jensen, 1969). Linguists and anthropologists as a whole disagreed with both of these views. They argued that Black children had very rich verbal resources which remained untapped because of ignorance on the part of children and teachers.

One might have expected the Ann Arbor Black English trial to become a battleground for these opposing points of view. One would think that the defense could find psychologists and linguists who would argue that there was no such thing as Black English, or that it was only a regional dialect, or that it was just the bad English of non-standard speakers. But this did not happen. There were no witnesses for the defense. The plaintiffs presented Joiner with a consistent testimony that appeared to represent the consensus of all scholars involved in the study of Black English and its educational implications. Although there was disagreement, the defense attorneys, who did a tremendous amount of research on the question, could not find anyone who would support a significantly different position.

How did such a remarkable consensus come about? Three distinct streams of events leading to this result can be identified. First, having weighed the evidence advanced by the other side, linguists and dialectologists achieved a certain consensus by the time of the trial. Second, the existence of Black English became recognized as a social fact, partly through the legitimation of the Black experience and of the term *Black,* and partly through the publication of such books as Dillard's *Black English* (1972). Third, a new generation of young Black linguists entered the field in the 1970's: John Baugh, Mary Hoover, John Rickford, Milford Jeremiah, Jerrie Scott, Geneva Smitherman, Arthur Spears, Anna Vaughn-Cooke, and many others. Their research has deepened our knowledge of Black English and its educational implications. For all these reasons, the testimony given at the trial carried far more weight than if the proceedings had taken place ten years earlier.

Judge Joiner's summary of the evidence (1979) was a model of clarity in its treatment of the general character of Black English, the relationship between Black English and other kinds of English, and the historical origins of this language variant. He saw clearly that Black English is a distinct linguistic system but that it is not a foreign language, that it has many features in common with southern dialects since most Blacks lived in the South for several centuries, and that it has distinct marks of an Afro-Caribbean ancestry, reflecting the earlier origins of the Black community. Joiner concluded that the law must therefore recognize a distinct linguistic form historically derived, in part, from Black people's heritage of slavery and segregation.

Joiner was not as clear on the details of these linguistic differences, on how Black English interferes with reading, or on what can be done to overcome any such interference. The opinion lists the twelve features of Black English that figured most prominently in the testimony. As it now stands, this list is not likely to be very useful to teachers who want to know if the children in their school use Black English, or to curriculum writers who want to take it into account in building reading programs. Yet the testimony did include many of the elements that we need for these purposes. The aim of this paper is to reorganize the descriptions of Black English presented at the trial into a form that will be more useful to teachers and educators.

With the trial over, Black English grammar is seldom discussed. A great deal of attention has been paid to the teachers' attitudes toward the use of Black English in their classrooms, and to children's attitudes toward the use of standard English. Judge Joiner himself concluded:

If a barrier exists because of the language used by the children in this case, it exists not because the teachers and students cannot understand each other, but because in the process of attempting to teach the children how to speak standard English the students are made somehow to feel inferior and are thereby turned off from the learning process. (1979, p. 6)

This was not the trial's original orientation. At first the judge had ruled out consideration of cultural and political factors, and insisted on an exact description of the *linguistic* barriers in question.[2] My own testimony was accordingly aimed at the grammatical description of the language used by Ann Arbor Black children, showing that it was the same as the Black English vernacular used in New York, Washington, Chicago and Los Angeles. I then presented evidence showing structural interference with the use of the alphabet and other steps in reading. The defense lawyers appeared to have read most of my written work, including unpublished galleys. They asked how I could reconcile my testimony with the earlier conclusion (Labov, Cohen, Robins, & Lewis, 1968; Labov & Robins, 1969) that structural differences between Black English and standard English could not in themselves account for massive reading failure. We had concluded that the principal problem was a cultural and political conflict in the classroom and that Black English had become a symbol of this conflict.

I responded to the defense's query with three main points. First, we know more about the structural differences between Black English and standard American English than we did ten years ago due largely to research conducted by Black linguists in the 1970's. Second, there is no reason to think that educational programs informed by popular attitudes alone can make major improvements in the teaching of reading. Teachers need to incorporate concrete information on the features of Black English into their daily lesson plans. Finally, the contradiction is only apparent since negative attitudes can be changed by providing people with scientific evidence of the language's validity.

Judge Joiner's opinion indicates that he may not have accepted this point of view. He did accept an educational program, initiated by the Ann Arbor Board of Education, designed to change general attitudes. No reading curriculum has yet been established using information on Black English.[3]

---

[2] Because the Judge's preliminary instructions to the plaintiffs seemed to convey a very narrow notion of linguistic description, the plaintiffs did not include in their presentation the problem of barriers caused by differences in the use of language: the area named by Hymes the "ethnography of communication." It is likely that cultural and linguistic conflicts contribute not only to educational failure, but also to behavioral differences in areas such as ways of showing attention, of turn-taking, and of showing respect and deference to adults.

[3] Only one educational program was presented by the plaintiffs to show how knowledge of Black language and culture could be used in reading programs: BRIDGE, written by Gary Simpkins, Grace Holt, and Charlotte Simkins, and published by Houghton Mifflin. Simpkins testified on the

The gap between general discussion and concrete practice has not gone unnoticed. At a symposium on the outcome of the trial held in February, 1980, Benjamin Alexander, President of Chicago State University, argued that Black English was obviously a myth, since no one had been able to describe it to his satisfaction. At the conference held by the NIE in June, 1980, a teacher at the King School agreed that her attitude towards Black English may have been improved by the new training program, but said that she had not yet had instruction on what to do when faced with a child who had not learned to read.

This paper will apply our present linguistic knowledge to the teaching of reading. It will present not merely a list of Black English features, but a coherent view of its linguistic system that is accessible to non-linguists. I will then indicate how this system may interfere with the business of learning to read standard English, and where in a reading method this information may be taken into account.

1. Terminology

Throughout the trial, the term "Black English" was used to refer to the vernacular system that was the home language of children living in the Green Road housing project, and to the system used by the majority of American Black people in their casual conversation (Joiner, 1979, p. 12). It is normally used in quotes by the judge, who notes at the outset two equivalent terms: "Black vernacular" and "Black dialect." *Black English* will undoubtedly remain the most commonly used term following Dillard's book (1972) of that title.

For more precise discussions, I prefer to apply the term *Black English* to the entire range of linguistic forms used by Black Americans. The term *Black English Vernacular* or BEV will be used to refer to the grammar used by children growing up in the Black community and by adults in the most intimate in-group settings.[4] *Standard Black English* refers to the speech forms used by educated Black speakers in formal and public situations. It contains phonological variation from standard forms, but the same standard English syntax. There are, of course, many intermediate forms, but no

---

cognitive difficulties of Black youth who had to translate the standard English semantic system into their own framework as well as decode the alphabet. BRIDGE avoids this problem by a smooth transition between tapes and reading texts in BEV, an intermediate form, and standard English. The content draws on Black culture and folklore throughout. BRIDGE is written for adolescent youth who are returning to the problem of learning to read, while the focus in the Ann Arbor Black English case was more on younger children in their first approach to reading. The same general problems, however, are addressed in both.

[4]Research in the 1960's was concentrated primarily among Black youth in the inner cities, and it is their use of BEV that is reported. Baugh's research in Pacoima, California (1979) demonstrated that adults who lived and worked in the Black community used exactly the same linguistic system in peer group and family contexts.

intermediate system has been identified clearly enough to deserve a separate name:

BLACK ENGLISH

Standard Black English   ←————————→   Black English Vernacular

[SBE]   [BEV]

This paper focuses on the Black English Vernacular, since it is the home language in the Ann Arbor case, and the linguistic system the great majority of Black children bring to their first reading experiences. This vernacular is not known perfectly to six- or seven-year-olds; there is considerable language learning that continues into late adolescence (Labov et al., 1968). Furthermore, there are many individuals in the Black community who are influenced by other dialects as they grow up. The most consistent vernacular is found among adolescents who are centrally located in their peer groups (Labov, 1972, Ch. 7) or among adults who live and work within the Black community (Baugh, 1979). It is not always possible for teachers to recognize these differences in social and linguistic status, with the result that classroom observations are often blurred (Garvey & McFarlane, 1968).

In this discussion, I will present some of the features that distinguish BEV from intermediate forms. Even though studies show that inner-city teachers can assume that the majority of their Black students participate in the BEV linguistic and cultural system, and that their approach to reading is profoundly influenced by it, it is important that teachers recognize intermediate forms. I will also suggest a number of strategies for applying our knowledge of BEV to the teaching of reading: these will apply equally well to children who use BEV in its most consistent form and those whose system is shifted some distance towards classroom English.

Educators are often presented with stereotypic descriptions of BEV far-removed from linguistic systems used in everyday life. Media coverage of the Ann Arbor Black English case described BEV with examples never used by anyone anywhere, such as, "He am so big an cause he so, he think everybody do what him say" (*U.S. News & World Report*, 3/31/80, p. 64).[5] More often, educators are exposed to stereotypes that preserve only those forms of BEV that most differ from classroom English, eliminating all variation as the result of "borrowing" or "code-switching." This is sometimes a hold-over from the earlier days of controversy, when creolists were interested only in isolating those forms that resembled the Caribbean creoles. Sometimes these stereotypes are proffered by people who have

---

[5] One exception to this was the series of newspaper stories generated by Geneva Smitherman in Detroit before the trial. These included accurate descriptions of the BEV tense and aspect system.

never studied tape recordings of the language as it is spoken. But in any case, BEV is a full-fledged linguistic system, with the range of inherent variation that all such systems have. BEV has some obligatory rules where other dialects have optional rules, some variable rules where the others have obligatory ones, and some rules that don't exist in any other dialects.

Many educators have borrowed Robert L. Williams' term "Ebonics" to refer to both the linguistic and cultural systems particular to Black Americans. The term is not widely used by linguists, but discussions of Ebonics programs refer to many of the linguistic features presented at the Black English trial. There is considerable convergence between proponents of Ebonics and those who prefer the concepts Black English and Black English vernacular.

Finally a word must be said about the question of *language* vs. *dialect.* "Is BEV a separate language?" The answer is that linguistics does not make a technical distinction between languages and dialects; the difference is more political than linguistic. It is therefore factually correct to say that Black people have a language of their own. But if it appears that BEV is closer to classroom English than, say, Hawaiian creole English or Jamaican English, then I would prefer to say that BEV differs much more from regional dialects of the North than from Hawaiian creole English or Jamaican English, and in its tense and aspect system, is quite distinct from the dialects spoken by white Southerners.

2. The Tense and Aspect System of BEV

Much of the Ann Arbor Black English trial testimony made reference to the *aspect* system of BEV, and newspaper accounts have usually featured one example of habitual *be,* as in *She be sick.* This is the most prominent and the most frequent of the BEV aspects: Geneva Smitherman's texts of conversations with the Green Road children recorded seventeen examples of habitual *be.* Tito B. alone used the aspect eight times over the course of a short interview. His statement, *When it be raining, I be taking it to school* is a good example of the habitual *be.*

Habitual *be* is especially important because it does not exist in any other American dialect.[6] It also exemplifies the positive side of BEV grammar. Its survival in the classroom demonstrates better than any other aspect how BEV makes useful distinctions that aren't made as easily in classroom English. Tito B.'s sentence (1) cannot be accurately translated as (2), but requires the expanded version (3) to convey the same meaning in classroom style:

---

[6]Rickford (1974) shows how the *doz be* forms of Gullah shift gradually to the invariant *be,* with the same "habitual meaning," responding to the overt stigmatization of the *doz.* He considers an alternative origin in the Anglo-Irish *does be,* but rejects this since Anglo-Irish dialects do not generally delete the first word.

(1) They be hitting on peoples.
(2) They are hitting people.
(3) They go around hitting people all the time.

Of all linguistic categories, the concept of *aspect* is the hardest to understand, and linguists disagree more about aspect than anything else. The meaning of *tense* is easier to comprehend for it situates an event at a point in time. Aspect communicates the *shape* of the event in time: Did it happen all at once (punctual), at many separate times (iterative or habitual), or was it spread out in time (durative)? Was it just beginning (inceptive) or was it finished and done with (perfective)? These are not clear and distinct ideas, but rather (as the term "aspect" implies) they represent ways of looking at things. Aspect is seldom found in pure form; it is often combined with questions of causation (is the event relevant to the present?) and reality (was it really so?). Finally, it is often combined with tense, so that we speak of a "tense-aspect system." Given all these complications, it isn't surprising that there is so little agreement on the meaning of general English aspects. There are almost as many theories to explain the contrast of (4) and (5) as there are linguists to argue about them.

(4) They hit people.
(5) They have hit people.

Since there is so little agreement about this topic in other languages, we should avoid dogmatism about the meanings of BEV aspects.

Before considering the meanings, we should look at the forms that these meanings hang on. Aspect can be expressed by independent adverbs like *already* or *really*, but the grammatical system we are interested in depends on short, one-syllable words placed before the verb. They usually don't carry stress, and as will be shown, in BEV the tendency for unstressed words to wear down or even disappear in speech is even greater than in other dialects. This tendency is triggered by the reduction of a short vowel in these monosyllables (*is, was, had, will*, etc.) to the obscure shwa. This reduction does not occur if the vowel is long. It is no accident that the BEV tense and aspect system is built on three words with long vowels: *be, do,* and *go*. In building on these three root words, BEV makes use of a single ending, the one inflection that does not tend to disappear in spontaneous speech. In other dialects, these auxiliary words preceding the verb are often reduced to single consonants like the future *'ll*, the present *'s* or *'re*, the past perfect or conditional *'d* or the present perfect *'ve*. In BEV, these single consonants / l, s, z, r, d, v, / are more often missing than present. But final /n/ does not disappear entirely: if it is not heard as a consonant, it is heard as a nasal quality of the preceding vowel. The basic BEV aspect system is made up of six words:

be	do	go
been	done	gon'

Notice that although the vowel quality changes when we add the *-n*, it does not disappear even in fast speech.

The three root words carry the same basic meanings as other dialects of English. *Be* refers to existence, *do* to action, and *go* to movement. But in the auxiliary, they have become specialized: *be*, as we have seen, indicates a special kind of habitual or repeated state; *do* has lost its content, and is used to emphasize other actions or carry the negative particle *n't*, as in other dialects; and *go* takes on a sense of movement towards confrontation, as in the standard English *go and*.

When we add the *n*, a new set of meanings emerge that move the action away from the immediate present. *Be + n* has developed a complex meaning in BEV unknown in any other dialect or language.[7]

(6) I *been* know your name.
(7) I *been* own that coat.

In psychological terms, the speaker in example (6) is saying that he or she first got to know the other person's name, and in example (7) that he or she got the coat a long time ago. Both speakers stress that their respective situations remain true right up to the present.

When *n* is added to *do*, the meaning is *perfective:* the event referred to is completely and recently done, or really and truly done:

(8) You don't have it 'cause you done used it in your younger age.
(9) I done forgot my hat! I done forgot my hat!

(Labov et al., 1968, p. 265)

The addition of *n* to *go* produces the future, as in many other dialects. In the following example, the contrast between *done* and *gone* is particularly clear.

(10) After you knock the guy down, he done got the works.
(11) You know he gon' try to sneak you.

(Labov et al., 1968, p. 265)

The richness of the BEV tense and aspect system is most clearly apparent when we look at combinations of these elements. To begin with, *be* is combined with *done* to yield *be done*, as in:

---

[7] The *been* with this meaning is always stressed and shows a low-pitch accent. Rickford (1975) reports a series of experiments showing dramatic differences in the interpretation of the sentence "She *been* married." 92 percent of his Black subjects answered "yes" to the question, "Is she still married?" and only 32 percent of the whites.

(12) I'll be done put—struck so many holes in him he'll wish he wouldna said it.

(Labov et al., 1968, p. 266)

This combination is normally translated as a future perfect, equivalent to *will have* (and is often preceded by *'ll*). But there are sentences where this translation cannot be made and where in fact there is no straightforward translation into other dialects:

(13) I'll be done killed that dude if he lays a hand on my child again.

(Baugh, 1979, p. 154)

What is the speaker's meaning? The statement was made with utmost seriousness by a man who had just witnessed his son being manhandled by a swimming pool aide. Normally, the English future perfect is the future form of the present perfect: it refers to the relevance of some future event for something else to follow. This is true of (12): the effect of sticking so many holes in the other person is that he will regret what he did. But in (13), we see a true perfect: the *be done* is attached to the result of the event. Instead of translating (13) into the nonsensical,

(14) I will have killed that dude if he lays a hand on my child again.

we would have to translate the perfective sense as something like "I will really and truly have to kill . . ." In trying to understand the cognitive differences between BEV and other dialects, considerable attention must be given to sentences like (13) which have no direct translation.

It also must be stressed that *done* is combined with *been* in a variety of ways to express events that have been completely accomplished in the past and are separated from the present.

A final use of the *n* suffix is the most familiar: it is in the progressive aspect that BEV shares with all other dialects of English. Here the *n* is usually combined with a short vowel, and variably with various forms of the verb *to be*, including the invariant *be* meaning "habitual." The meaning of *He's workin'* as opposed to *he works* is the same as in other dialects: it is a "durative," referring to extended activity that is actually carried out, usually simultaneously with some other event. With the habitual *be* in *he be workin'*, the progressive is freed from association with any particular time. BEV speakers rarely use the *-ing* and use *-in'* close to 100 percent of the time. The *-ing* appears primarily in writing and cannot be really considered a part of the vernacular language.

This symmetrical system of *do, be, go,* plus *n* is not all there is to the BEV tense and aspect system. The past tense *-ed* is firmly entrenched in the underlying grammar, though it is so often deleted after consonants that some speakers have trouble identifying it on the printed page (see sec. 3). In the auxiliary *had,* the final *d* appears again as a past tense marker. It is acquired early and is often used as the past perfect marker, meaning as in standard English, "occurred before the last event mentioned," and to denote other past tense meanings as well. In addition to *be*, there is an auxiliary *steady*, which is often combined with *be:*

(15) Them fools steady hustlin' everybody they see.
(16) Her mouth is steady runnin.'
(17) Ricky Bell be steady steppin' in them number nines.

(Baugh, 1980)

Though *be* refers to habitual action, *steady* refers to much more. Baugh defines its scope as covering actions that are "persistent, consistent and continuous." In other words, *steady* has a lawful character: whenever this event could take place, it did.

We should also note the alternative form of the future:

(18) I'm a do it.

This form is found only in BEV and apparently is a semantic equivalent of *gon'*. Fickett (1970) has argued that the *I'ma* form (which occurs only with the first person singular) is semantically distinct from *gon'* and it means "immediate future." The evidence is not all in on this: it is one of the many areas in the semantics of BEV that needs further work.

A near neighbor of these aspects is a special BEV use of *come* as in

(19) He come tellin' me I don't love my parents.

Spears (1980) demonstrates that this is a "camouflaged" modal. It often looks like the standard English *come*. But the BEV speaker can also say "He come comin' ..." or "He come goin' ..." The camouflaged modal *come* is a member of the BEV grammatical system that signals moral indignation: "He had the nerve to present himself doing this."

There are many similarities between these BEV forms and grammatical forms found in other dialects, and in creoles of the Caribbean and the Pacific.[8] Most of the BEV meanings, however, are unique combinations of semantic elements. There is every reason to think that BEV, like all other living languages, continues to develop its resources and enrich the cognitive system of its speakers.

To sum up, we can present the special features of the BEV tense and aspect system as:

---

[8]The perfective particle *done* is also used by white speakers throughout the Southern states. It remains to be shown whether the semantics of their use is the same as the semantics of the BEV *done*. The combination *be done* is not used by white speakers.

be	"habitual," applied to events that are generally so
been	"remote present perfect," conditions that were so a long time ago, and are still so
done	"perfective," events that are completely and/or really so
be done	"future perfective," events in the future that are completely, really so
been done	"past perfective," events in the past that are accomplished and really so
steady	"persistently, consistently, and continuously so"
gon'	"future and less really so"

The organization and symmetry of this system should now be evident. With the exceptions of the invariant *be* and *gon'*, these are seldom heard in the classroom and rarely in the Black English of radio and television. Even in intimate vernacular settings, many of them are rare: it is only when highly particular contexts arise that they are needed and used. If the tense and aspect system of BEV doesn't appear in the speech and writing of the classroom, how can it affect reading? The answer to this question will be easier if we look first at other features of BEV that have a more obvious connection with reading.

3. English Inflections in BEV

So far, we have looked at the special BEV system of conveying grammatical meaning by invariant words placed before the verb. Now we will look at the other end: how does BEV use the system of modifying meaning by putting inflections—usually single consonants—at the ends of words?

We have already noticed that many final consonants tend to disappear in BEV speech. This happens not only in the auxiliary, but at the ends of all words. The variable process of consonant deletion as it affects words and grammatical endings (the plural, the possessive, the past tense) has been studied in some detail. BEV is often described as a series of absences; to most people it looks like an over-simplified language "without grammar." It is said that BEV has no plural, no past tense, and no possessive, and that these categories are foreign to Black children. But a careful examination reveals that this view is highly exaggerated.[9]

We can first observe that some English inflections are present *more* often in BEV than in other dialects. One of these is the plural. While standard English has no plural inflection in words like *deer, sheep,* and *fish,* the

---

[9] The plural [s] suffix is often absent from "nouns of measure" when they are preceded by a number: *three cent, five year,* and so on. This is not peculiar to BEV: many other dialects show more systematic use of this feature, such as the north of England dialect of Leeds.

corresponding BEV plurals are regular *deers, sheeps,* and *fishes.*[10] Another example is the absolute possessive, as in:

(20) This is mines.

BEV has generalized the possessive inflection found in *John's, yours,* and *hers.*

The past tense category is also quite secure. BEV speakers use the strong verb forms *gave, told,* and *left,* in the same way as all other dialects. In fact, it is even more regular, since the historical present seems to be used less by BEV speakers than by others.

The problem with the past tense is related to regular verbs ending in *-ed,* where the signal of the past tense is confined to a single consonant, /t/ or /d/. This signal is sometimes present, sometimes absent. But we have ample evidence that it is firmly located in the underlying grammatical structure representing the linguistic knowledge of the speakers. First, it is always present more often than the /t/ or /d/ in consonant clusters that do not signal the past tense, like *fist* or *old.* Second, when *-ed* follows a /t/ or a /d/ as in *wanted,* and a vowel breaks up the cluster, the final *-ed* is always present. Third, the past tense *-ed* is dropped less often before a vowel, and more often in difficult consonantal combinations like *mixed batter.* Fourth, the *-ed* never occurs where it is not wanted: we never find the past tense used for the present, as in *He walked home these days.* For these and many other reasons, it is certain that present-day BEV has the grammatical suffix *-ed* and speakers have knowledge of it that they can draw on in reading standard English primers.

The rate of deletion may be so high, however, that BEV speakers may not recognize the *-ed* on the printed page as a carrier past tense of meaning. To determine the presence of this ability, we devised reading tests including such sentences as:

(21) Last month I read five books.
(22) When he passed by, he read the poster.

The task here is to transfer the past tense signal in the first half of the sentence to the unique homograph *read,* which demonstrates the form of the vowel, /riyd/ vs. /red/, whether the reader had the past tense in mind. For BEV speakers who had reached the fourth or fifth grade reading level, there was almost 100 percent success in transferring the past tense meaning from the adverb *last month;* but with the past tense *-ed* in *passed,* the results were not much better than chance (Labov, 1972, p. 30ff).

The case of the auxiliary and verb *to be* is parallel. The finite forms *is* and *are* are sometimes present in their full form, sometimes in contracted form, and sometimes entirely missing. There is now ample evidence indi-

---

[10] Jane Torrey (1972) found this in her research among second graders in Harlem.

cating that in present-day BEV, the dropping of the copula is simply an extension of the contraction process found in other dialects and in BEV (Labov, 1972, Ch. 3). Here, too, the full verb forms are available and are freely used by BEV speakers; in fact, young children use more full forms than adults. It is the contracted forms, or single consonants fused with the preceding word, that can cause problems. Young children find it very hard to connect chains like these:

$$\text{/ay aem/} \longleftrightarrow \text{/ay am/} \longleftrightarrow \text{/aym/} \longleftrightarrow \text{/ay/}$$

Several investigators have found that children in the second grade lack the ability to analyze *I'm* into *I am*, though all the facts surrounding them would suggest that connection.[11] Many BEV speakers of this age will respond:

(23) —You're not George Baker!
—Yes I'm am!

Finally we come to the class of English inflexions representing the maximum distance between BEV and classroom English. Although the third singular -*s* of *he works hard* is occasionally present in the speech and writing of BEV speakers, studies show that it is not present in the underlying linguistic knowledge that children bring to school. For each of the four points raised in the above discussion of -*ed*, the answers are the opposite for third singular -*s*. There is no general process of dropping final -*s* in other words. It does not appear more often after /s/ or /z/, when a vowel appears between the stem and the consonant. When third singular -*s* does appear, there is no effect on the surrounding consonants or vowels; there is not even a reverse effect. It often appears in the wrong context, from the point of view of classroom English, as in

(24) He can goes out.

(Labov et al., 1968, p. 166)

For these reasons and many others, we believe that the task of acquiring consistent use of third singular -*s* is harder for BEV speakers than is learning to use -*ed* consistently. Furthermore, the problem is harder for BEV speakers than for Spanish speakers. Though Spanish has no mark on the third singular, the notion of agreement between subject and verb is fundamental to Spanish grammar. In BEV, it is not simply third singular -*s* that is absent. The general machinery of number agreement between subject and verb is barely represented in the grammar. The irregular alterations

---

[11] William Stewart (1968) pointed this out in an early article and Torrey's work in Harlem found experimental confirmation.

have/has, do/does, and *was/were* are represented in BEV by invariant *have, do,* and *was.* It is only in the finite forms of the verb *to be* that we find some agreement between subject and verb.

We discussed the absolute form of the possessive as an example of a grammatical category that is fully represented, even over-represented, in BEV. The opposite is the case when the possessive *-s* relates two noun phrases. In the great majority of cases, the possessive *-s* is absent for BEV speakers, and demonstrates many of the traits of third singular *-s.* In some cases, the choice seems to be categorical: *whose book* is not heard and is very hard to reproduce in repetition tests.

Thus a portrait of BEV inflections can be drawn of three distinct situations: features entirely absent from the underlying grammar of BEV, features present in the grammar but variably deleted to a point hard to retrieve, and features that are generalized beyond the point of the standard language:

ABSENT	VARIABLE	GENERALIZED
subject-verb agreement: 3rd singular [s]	regular tense [ed]	regular plural [s]
possessive [s]: noun adjuncts	contracted copula [s] & [r]	possessive [s]: absolute form

4. Loss of Information at the Ends of Words

In most of the language families of the world, words gradually become worn away at their ends. There are many reasons for this. While a principle of least effort is certainly involved, it is also true that the distribution of information must also be taken into account. The first sound or letters of a word are the most useful in helping the listener determine the meaning of the word; the last few sounds or letters may be completely predictable. For example, if a one-syllable word begins *des-* there is only one way to finish it: with a *k.* Even if the /k/ was not pronounced, the word would have to be *desk.*

This tendency to lose information at the ends of words may be encouraged by the fact that the ends of words do not carry as much information as the beginnings, but it is not limited to cases where the information is not needed. In the course of linguistic history, sound changes in languages like Chinese and French have produced thousands of homonyms, words that have exactly the same sound, though they were once quite different. For languages that carry their grammatical information in the form of single consonants at the ends of words, this leads to a great deal of unhappiness in the grammatical system. English has lost most of its inflections through this wearing away process.

The Black English vernacular loses information at the ends of words in a more extreme fashion than other dialects.[12] But those who grow up speaking BEV, like speakers of other dialects, have many indirect ways to learn about the shapes of words. They do not necessarily pick the form of the word they hear most often as the base of their mental dictionary. If they are exposed to older speakers who have an underlying knowledge of the form of a particular word that includes all of the sounds in the standard dictionary entry, they will sometimes pronounce these full forms, particularly when the next word begins with a vowel. In some cases, where a stop consonant is sandwiched between two *s*'s, as in *wasps, tests,* or *desks,* the stop may never be pronounced. Still, the *t* in *tests* can be discovered if a *t* reappears in the word *testing.* When young children are first learning to read, they may not yet have put together all the bits of information they need to arrive at the final solution—the shape of the word in the grown-up dictionary. Just as some think that *I* has an extra sound /m/, they may also assume that *desk* has only three sounds, or that *old* has two or only one.

Because the tendency to delete final /r/, /l/, /t/, /d/, /v/, and other consonants is more extreme in BEV than in other dialects, the relation between the spelling forms and the spoken language can be much harder to figure out for children learning to read and write the standard language. The following list contains some of the words that can be heard the same way. Each word stands for a member of a class of words: all the words that rhyme with it.

(a) The deletion of final *t* or *d* can give:
   in simple words:

cold = coal	mist = miss	tent = ten
field = feel	paste = pace	pant = pan
world = whirl	must = muss	wand = wan

   in the regular past tense:

rolled = roll	missed = miss	fanned = fan
healed = heal	faced = face	penned = pen

   in the past tense of irregular verbs:

told = toll	lost = loss	went = when
held = hell	bent = Ben	meant = men

   with the general merger of /i/ & /e/ before /n/:
   penned = pinned = pen = pin
   send = sinned = sin

---

[12] The wearing away of inflections is a slow evolutionary process in most languages, but in the formation of pidgins and creoles it is much faster. The long history of BEV seems to be dominated by the reverse of this evolution, as inflections are replaced under the influence of the standard language. But the existence of this long-term decreolization does not end the normal process of wearing away in rapid and spontaneous speech. Grammatical particles like [ed] that have been replaced are still frequently deleted—even more drastically than in other dialects, since the earlier tradition without [ed] is not entirely eliminated from the scene.

(b) The deletion of *l* and *r* can give:
   with the Southern deletion of the glide after back vowels:
      told = toll = tore = toe
      sold = soul = sore = so
   with the more common Northern pronunciation:
      sore = Saul = saw
      cord = called = cawed
   and generally:

guard = God	tool = too
par = pa	jewel = Jew

   with the tensing of /e/ before /l/:
      held = hell = hail
      sailed = sail = sell
   with the monophthongization of /ay/:

wired = wide = why	wild = wowed = wow
fire = far = fa	piled = Powell = pow
mire = mar = ma	tiled = towel

The examples are not intended to suggest that all of these words are the same for all speakers of BEV. With the exception of a few cases (like *pen* and *pin*), identity is variable. But the frequency of deletion can be very high, and the experience of the learned does not yield enough information to keep these words apart.

The differences between the spoken and written form can cause problems at each step in the reading process. When the child reads a word correctly, the teacher may not recognize this success unless he or she can also recognize the equivalent sets of pronunciations outlined above. As early as 1965, these patterns were presented to the National College Teachers of English to illustrate some of the special problems confronting a speaker of BEV learning to read (Labov, 1967). It was then proposed that teachers who conduct oral reading practice begin to make clear distinctions between mistakes in reading and differences in pronunciation. Since that time, the principle has been widely accepted, but we do not know to what extent it has affected classroom practice.

It is now possible to put forward a more concrete program for reading curricula incorporating these special properties of BEV. A great deal of reading research is devoted to the fundamental problem of the acquisition of the alphabet. We are not only concerned here with the learning of the alphabetic principle, but also with its use as a general tool in decoding the printed page. In the Harlem study of 1965–1968, it was shown that many young people were effectively illiterate. Researchers found, for example, twelve-year-olds who scored at the first or second grade level on the Metropolitan Reading Test. Yet surprisingly enough, every one of them had mastered the alphabet. Early mastery of the alphabet was apparent in the patterns of reading mistakes on reading tests and standardized tests as well. When someone did not recognize a word, and had to guess, the guess almost always had the same first consonant as the printed form, and the same first vowel. But the rest of the guess showed no relation to the letters on the page. A typical example shows (25a) read as (25b):

(25) a. I sold my soul to the devil.
     b. I saw my sour to the deaf.

The sentence has not been read and understood. But in attempting to decode its meaning, the reader hasn't neglected the alphabet. The alphabet has been used for as long as it could be trusted: for the first several letters. The weak connection between the last letters on the page and the form of the word as it is perceived and grasped by the reader has led to this loss of confidence. The same pattern appears clearly when we analyze reading errors. For seventeen pre-adolescent youth in the Harlem study, ages ten through thirteen, we considered all those misread words whose pronunciation had some relation to the letters on the printed page. The number of letters read correctly in each position were:

		LETTERS READ CORRECTLY						
	N	1ST	2ND	3RD	4TH	5TH	6TH	7TH
3-letter words	11	8	4	6				
4-letter words	77	65	55	45	31			
5-letter words	46	45	30	34	25	24		
6-letter words	26	26	19	20	19	15	10	
7-letter words	11	11	10	9	10	10	8	3

The problem is not the mastery of the alphabet itself, but one of acquiring the confidence to use it consistently. The weak correlation between the spelling forms on the printed page and the forms of the words as they are spoken has apparently led many Black youth to limit their use of the alphabet to the first few letters—or more accurately, to lose all confidence in the value of the alphabet for the last few letters.

Preliminary results of reading research by J. Baron point in the same direction. Eleven Black and eleven white children were matched for their ability to read regular words (34 correct out of 51). On exception words, Black children scored better, averaging 30.3 correct out of 51, than white children, who averaged 27.6. But on nonsense words, which require alphabetic skills, the results were reversed: 30.9 correct out of 51 for Blacks, as against 32.5 correct for whites. Other tests confirm the small but significant tendency of Black readers to use the alphabet less than whites. If we were to distinguish the use of the alphabet at the ends of words from its use at the beginnings of words, this difference might well be magnified.

Though there are many unanswered questions on how the structure of BEV interacts with the business of learning to read, there are a number of clear findings that can be applied to reading curricula. But before considering strategies for putting this knowledge to use, we should complete our look at the whole picture. It isn't hard to see how the sound patterns of BEV affect reading. But what about the more abstract semantics of section 1? Forms like *be done* and *been done* do not appear very often in the classroom—neither in writing nor in speech. Is there any way in which the BEV aspect system enters into the process of learning to read standard English? The next section will show that this underlying semantic system may not be as far away from the classroom as it first appears.

5. Ambiguities of Tense and Aspect

The child who comes to school speaking BEV meets classroom English in two main forms: the teacher's speech and the printed words on the page. We've looked at some evidence about the result of interaction with the second: the full forms of words are hard to decipher, even when there is reason to think that adult speakers of BEV have the same full forms. It is also hard for children who speak BEV to make use of the final consonants that represent inflections, even when there is reason to believe that their own underlying grammars include this information.

There is no hard evidence on children's ability to interpret the speech of the teacher. But there are many indications that some of the speech signals of classroom English will be missed, and no reason to believe that children who speak BEV will automatically understand and absorb the standard system of tense and aspect.

We have seen that BEV-speaking children do use contractions like *We'll* and *They're* and *They'd*. But contractions are less common in BEV than in white dialects since they alternate with zero forms as well as with full forms. Among young children, full forms are more common than among older children and, as we have noted, contractions are often misinterpreted as in *Yes I'm am*. The *'ve* in *I've* or *they've* is particularly rare, and there is strong reason to doubt that the underlying grammar has a *have* auxiliary in the present perfect.

It is not generally realized that the full forms of auxiliaries are widely used in BEV. Typical BEV forms are shown below as (a) rather than as (b), which represents forms more common in white dialects:

(26) a. I had come over.
     b. I'd come over.
(27) a. We will have succeeded . . .
     b. We'll have succeeded . . .
(28) a. We have said it . . .
     b. We've said it . . .

The past perfect of (26a) is very common among young Black children, and the uncontracted form is normal in the most vernacular speech. The *will have* of (27a) is formal; but the informal shift is to the simple future or to the complex *be done.* (28a) is again formal. The informal alternate, however, is not (28b) but rather the past tense *We said it.* In a word, there are many contradictions that are common currency for white children but not for Black children.

This disparity results in multiple ambiguity in the contact situation. The BEV-speaking child's problem shows up in this input-output diagram:

Teacher's Production	Heard As	Interpreted As
They will be there ——► They'll be there They would be there ——► They'd be there	They be there	future habitual *be* conditional
They have been there ——► They've been there They had been there ——► They'd been there	They been there	present perfect remote present perfect past perfect

Here are two situations where the grammatical information of classroom English may be neutralized, and open to a three-way interpretation by the listener. The multiple ambiguities shown here are only some of the problems resulting from structural mismatch in the learning situation. It might be argued that context will usually make the teacher's intention less ambiguous. But this can be said for any part of language. We do not know how many misunderstandings are needed to produce cognitive confusion of a more permanent sort. Nonetheless, it is reasonable for the teacher to be aware of potential confusions and try to avoid them.

When the forms on the left are found on the printed page, the students' problems are much more evident. The contracted forms are hard for BEV readers to interpret and relate to their full forms or zero forms. The readers we are most concerned with interpret words one at a time—with some of the bizarre results exemplified by (25b) above. Any steps promoting the shift to reading meaningful sentences will be a major step forward in reading. Any mismatch on the printed page between the readers' grammatical knowledge and the letters to be read can only delay that process.

For all dialects, there are homonyms in speech that must be rendered unambiguous if they are going to be correctly connected to the printed page. To be helpful, teachers must know what words sound the same and what connections have to be made. Two other sets of homonyms in BEV illustrate the principle.

It was noted at the outset that BEV grammar does not rely on words with short, reducible vowels so much as on words with long vowels that never disappear. Two long nasal vowels do a great deal of work for BEV:

(a) long nasal *e:*
    They haven't = They ain't = They 'e'
    They aren't = They ain't = They 'e'
    They didn't = They ain't = They 'e'

Most people realize that *ain't* can correspond to standard *haven't, hasn't, amn't, isn't* and *aren't.* But few people realize that BEV can also use *ain't* where other dialects use *didn't.*

(b) long nasal *o:*
    They are going to = They gon' = They 'o'
    They do not = They don' = They 'o'
    They will not = They won' = They 'o'

Here we have two future forms and one present tense form, all expressed by the same vowel. Such drastic reductions can create problems in working out the relationship between the colloquial forms and the full forms of classroom English.

6. Five Strategies for Teaching Reading to Speakers of BEV

This last section will outline five strategies for bringing our knowledge of BEV grammar into the day-to-day teaching of reading. It is not intended as a series of suggestions of how to teach reading: that is the business of teachers and educators who know the full range of problems and practices involved. These principles are put forward as a means of making linguistic knowledge available to those who design reading curricula. My aim here is to put into practice the letter and spirit of the Ann Arbor Black English decision, so that knowledge of the Black English Vernacular can be taken into account in the teaching of reading.

Strategy 1: Recognize reading errors: Teachers should be ready to distinguish between mistakes in reading and features of pronunciation typical of BEV. This strategy rests on the fundamental principle put before the National College Teachers of English in 1965, that the teaching of reading should distinguish true reading errors from differences in the ways that words are pronounced. The underlying concept is generally recognized: that reading is a way of deriving meaning from the printed page. But discussions of the trial have focused far more attention on the way children speak or are allowed to speak in the classroom. Arguments about "Black English in the classroom" have little to do with the Ann Arbor decision, and distract from the main task at hand: helping children learn to read.

Oral reading is not used to the same extent in every classroom. When children do read aloud, however, corrections by the teacher have considerable impact: they affect both readers and listeners at the same time. Certainly teachers should know enough about the constants and variables of BEV pronunciation to be able to decide whether the reader has misunderstood the message on the printed page. Thus, in

(29) When I passed by, I read the posters.

we can use the pronunciation of *read* to draw such a conclusion, but not the pronunciation of *passed,* since the final /st/ cluster is variable. In

(30) He lost his tests and hers too.

we cannot tell from the presence or absence of the /t/ in *lost* or *tests* whether those words have been read correctly, since the first is variable and the second always absent in BEV pronunciation; but we can judge from the /s/ in *hers,* because *her* and *hers* are never confused in BEV.

It is generally agreed that success in reading is the critical first step in the acquisition of basic skills, and all programs must be weighed against this priority. If educators should decide that training in standard English pronunciation is an essential step in reading, that should be undertaken as a separate program. But the bulk of current research indicates that success in reading is not dependent on pronunciation. Practice in imitating the teacher's pronunciation will not necessarily add to children's underlying knowledge of the language, since it has been shown that such superposed dialects do not develop systematic knowledge. Strategies 4 and 5 below may be more effective in this respect.

Strategy 2: Pay attention to the ends of words: Evidence has been brought forward showing that the loss of information at the ends of words is a critical factor in the use of the alphabet by BEV speakers. Yet reading programs pay far more attention to the use of the alphabet for decoding letters at the beginnings of words. I have reviewed a number of phonics texts in current use, and found that the majority devote only a small fraction of their lesson plans to final consonants, and that only one gave roughly equal time to beginnings and ends of words.

This idea does not apply only to reading programs that rely heavily on phonics. No matter how the curriculum is designed, some means should be found to focus the BEV reader's attention on the *d* in *child* and the *ed* in *walked* at an early age. Some reading teachers avoid paying too much attention to the ends of words because of the danger of reading reversals: getting *saw* instead of *was.* It seems to me that this is usually a minor problem compared to the major difficulties documented in section 4 above, and it should not be allowed to dictate the fundamental strategies used in teaching of reading.

I have tried to show that the potential knowledge is often present. If the task of the educator is to build on that knowledge, the means must be found to make it available to the reading process. One such means is presented as Strategy 3.

Strategy 3: Introduce words in the most favorable contexts: The most common way to introduce a new word is in citation form: that is, in isolation, or at the end of a short presentative sentence:

(31) This is a *desk.*

This method has the advantage of focusing attention of the word, with full final stress, and minimizing confusion with other information. Yet for BEV speakers this is not the best way to introduce a word into the reading process. It has been shown that BEV differs from other dialects in that consonant cluster simplification is relatively high before pause, and lowest before a following vowel. For a speaker of BEV, the full form of the word will be recognized more fully in the context.

(32) There is a *desk* in this room.

This principle applies most obviously to spoken interaction, as when an adult is introducing a word for the first time, or reading a new lesson, or even correcting a mis-reading. But we have reason to think that it also affects individual and silent reading in the course of the complex feedback between decoding, recognition, and encoding.

This is one case where differences between dialects are most relevant to teaching strategies. For some white dialects, like that found in Philadelphia, consonant clusters are preserved most often in final position. In these cases citation form of instruction works very well. But for other dialects (New York City, BEV, Puerto Rican English) final position behaves like a following consonant. Here, a following vowel helps bring out the form of the word more clearly.

Adopting this strategy would not favor Black children at the expense of the others. For every speaker of English, final consonants are pronounced far more often before a following vowel than before the next word that begins with a consonant, and the advantage of final position is, at best, not very large.

Strategy 4: Use the full forms of words: This principle follows from all that has been said about the role of contracted forms in BEV. Contractions are not alien to BEV and are frequently used in speech. But for many young speakers of BEV, they are not easily analyzed as distinct from the word they are attached to, or related to the verb phrase. It would therefore be best to avoid the use of such contractions in reading texts and in the first steps of learning to read. Some textbook writers would interpret this alteration as a step backward, since they feel that

(33) This is Rex. He is my dog.

is stiff and traditional. They would tend to replace it with the more relaxed and colloquial

(34) This is Rex. He's my dog.

Although this second form is less stilted, it does not automatically help speakers of BEV. For them, the first form is likely to be more clear and natural. A more extreme kind of problem is created by

(35) This is Rex. He's my brother's dog.

which introduces the possessive 's sandwiched between two noun phrases, and is especially hard for BEV speakers to recognize and use. It might be easier for them to apprehend

(36) The name of this dog is Rex. He is my brother's.

which does not involve any letters that are hard to recognize.

The choice of sentence forms is not based on difficulty in understanding the basic message. BEV speakers will not necessarily misunderstand *He's my brother's dog.* But it will not be easy for them to interpret the two 's signals. If they ignore them, it will be one more step towards the loss of confidence in the alphabet we have already witnessed.

It might be argued that sooner or later all children must learn to read sentences like (34) and (35). This is certainly so. But the strategies suggested here are designed to facilitate the first steps in reading and to avoid any conflict of BEV and classroom English. The next strategy looks toward further reading steps and toward bridging the distances between linguistic systems.

Strategy 5: Relate full forms to contracted forms: Here we enter an area that goes beyond the first steps in the teaching of reading. The central principle involved is to make use of the child's own knowledge of language by developing the relation between the various forms that he or she uses in everyday speech, especially those that are closest to classroom English. Thus the relation between full, contracted, and deleted forms of the copula:

(37) a. He is on my side of the room.
    b. He's on my side of the room.
    c. He on my side of the room.

is implicit in the child's production of language but not necessarily available to him for further advances in reading. One of the most extreme examples of such expansion and contraction is found in the English periphrastic future, where the child's competence may include such forms as:

(38) a. I am going to do it.
    b. I'm going to do it.
    c. I'm goin' to do it.
    d. I'm gonna do it.
    e. I'm gon' do it.
    f. I'm 'on' do it.
    g. I'm 'o' do it.
    h. I'm a do it.

The child may recognize the relationship between any two of these. But faced with the contrast between (38a) and (38g) or (38h), most people will not see much relationship at all.

There are many ways in which this relationship can be developed within the reading program or in the more general teaching of English. At each step, specific linguistic information is needed, and this information has to be made available to those curriculum designers who are prepared to use it. Even if linguists were better at communicating their own knowledge of grammar to other scholars and to the general public, their suggestions alone are likely to be wide of the mark. This communication is submitted to educators as part of one effort to put our linguistic knowledge to use in the critical problem of improving the teaching of reading to American children.

References

Bailey, Beryl. *Jamaican creole syntax*. London: Cambridge University Press, 1965.

Baugh, John. Linguistic style-shifting in Black English. Ph.D dissertation. University of Pennsylvania, 1979.

———. Steady: Progressive aspect in Black English. Mimeographed, 1980.

Deutsch, Martin, Katz, Irwin & Jensen, Arthur. *Social class, race and psychological development*. New York: Holt, Rinehart & Winston, 1968.

Dillard, J. L. *Black English*. New York: Random House, 1972.

Fickett, Joan. *Aspects of morphemics, syntax and semology of an inner-city dialect*. West Rush, N.Y.: Meadowbrook Publications, 1970.

Garvey, Catherine & McFarlane, Paul T. A preliminary study of standard English speech patterns in the Baltimore city public schools. *Report No. 16.* Johns Hopkins University, 1968.

Jensen, Arthur. How much can we boost IQ and scholastic achievement? *Harvard Educational Review,* 1969, 39.

Joiner, Charles W. Memorandum opinion and order in Civil Action 7–71861, *Martin Luther King Junior Elementary School Children, et al. vs. Ann Arbor School District Board,* July 12, 1979.

Labov, William. Some sources of reading problems for speakers of non-standard Negro English. In A. Frazier (Ed.), *New directions in elementary English.* Champaign, Ill.: *National College Teachers of English, 1967.*

———. *Language in the inner city.* Philadelphia: University of Pennsylvania Press, 1972.

Labov, William & Robins, Clarence. A note on the relation of peer-group status to reading failure in urban ghettos. *Teachers College Record,* 1969, 70(5).

Labov, William, Cohen, P., Robins, C. & Lewis, J. A study of the non-standard English of Negro and Puerto Rican Speakers in New York City. *Cooperative Research Report 3288.* 2 vols. Philadelphia: U.S. Regional Survey, 1968.

Rickford, John. The insights of the mesolect. In D. DeCamp & I. Hancock (Eds.), *Pidgins and creoles: Current trends and prospects.* Washington, D.C.: Georgetown University Press, 1974.

———. Carrying a new wave into syntax: The case of Black English *been.* In R. Fasold & R. Shuy (Eds.), *Analyzing variation in language.* Washington, D.C.: Georgetown University Press, 1975.

Spears, Arthur. Come: a modal-like form in Black English. Paper read at the Winter meeting of the Linguistic Society of America, Los Angeles, 1980.

Stewart, William. Continuity and change in American Negro dialects. *The Florida FL Reporter,* 1968, 6, 14–16, 18, 304.

Torrey, Jane. *The language of Black children in the early grades.* New London: Connecticut College, 1972. [ERIC ED 067 690]

Turner, Lorenzo. *Africanisms in the Gullah dialect.* Chicago: University of Chicago Press, 1949.

Content Questions

1. Why according to Labov was the outcome of the Ann Arbor trial different from what it might have been if it had occurred ten years earlier?

2. Distinguish between the terms *Black English, Standard Black English,* and *Black English Vernacular.*

3. Why does Labov say that the use of the habitual *be* shows the "positive side of BEV grammar"?

4. What kinds of meanings are formed through the addition of *n* to *be, do,* and *go?*

5. Describe the use of the BEV "camouflaged" modal *come.*

6. Contrast the relative similarity between BEV and Standard English in the use of the inflections -*ed* and -*s*.

7. How does the deletion of particular consonants in BEV contribute toward a greater difficulty for BEV speakers in learning to read in the standard variety of English?

8. Which part of a word presents the greatest problems for BEV speakers relying on the alphabet to guide their reading?

9. How does the use of contractions by speakers of the standard dialect sometimes lead to ambiguities for a BEV speaker?

10. Explain each of the five strategies that Labov identifies for teaching BEV speakers to read.

Questions for Analysis and Discussion

1. Select a feature of BEV and explain how it illustrates that BEV is rule governed.

2. How would a knowledge of some features of BEV phonology help a teacher to distinguish a genuine error in reading from a mere pronunciation variant?

3. Comment on the contribution of linguistic research to our knowledge of strategies that might benefit particular individuals in the classroom.

Phonemic Awareness Training: Application of Principles of Direct Instruction

Janet E. Spector

Phonemic awareness has been receiving increased attention because of its importance to reading. While many students learn to read without much difficulty, for some the synthesizing of sounds presents real problems. In this article, which originally appeared in the *Reading & Writing Quarterly: Overcoming Learning Difficulties,* Janet Spector, an education professor at the University of Maine at Orono, discusses phonemic awareness and its importance to the reading process. She also notes the differing phonemic abilities that some students bring to the classroom and which could put them at a disadvantage as they begin learning the sound-symbol correspondences that are so important in learning to read. Spector provides useful information about how phonemic awareness can be developed. Her article thus provides another illustration of how linguistic knowledge can be applied in the classroom.

Why is phonemic awareness so critical to the learning-to-read process? Why do some readers fail to develop phonemic awareness? What can be done to foster phonemic awareness? The research on these three related questions is integrated. It is argued that learning how to read in an alphabetic system requires children to understand the complex relationship between print and speech. This understanding is not easily achieved by children who have difficulty detecting and manipulating the sounds within spoken words. Pre-reading and beginning reading instruction should be designed to facilitate the acquisition of phonemic awareness. Recommended practices include (a) engaging preschool children in activities that direct their attention to the sounds in words, (b) teaching students to segment and to blend, (c) combining training in segmentation and blending with instruction in letter–sound relationships, (d) teaching segmentation and blending as complementary processes, (e) systematically sequencing examples when teaching segmentation and blending, (f) teaching for transfer to novel tasks and contexts, and (g) teaching teachers the rationale behind phonemic awareness training.

Researchers have long tried to identify the cause of reading failure among students who otherwise have average intellectual abilities. Investigators now agree that no single cause is likely. Because reading is a multidimensional process, there are many points at which development may stall. At the same time, the elusiveness of a single cause does not preclude the existence of patterns or subtypes of reading disability. On the contrary, there is evidence that the majority of readers with persistent deficits experience difficulty at the level of word recognition, even when they are selected for study on the basis of scores on reading comprehension tests (Curtis, 1980; Perfetti et al., 1984; Stanovich et al., 1984b). Furthermore, the contrast between good and poor readers is greatest on tasks, such as pseudoword recognition, that depend heavily on the ability to decode (Frederiksen, 1978; Hogaboam & Perfetti, 1978; Juel, 1988; Perfetti & Hogaboam, 1975; Spector & Calfee, 1984).

According to Stanovich (1988), these problems reflect deficits in phonological processing. That is, poor readers have difficulty using the sounds of the language in processing written and oral information. This difficulty manifests itself in a wide range of tasks, including identifying the sounds heard within words; naming objects, letters, and numbers; and retaining sounds and words in short-term memory. Central to phonological processing is the ability to detect and manipulate the sounds within words. Many terms have been used to describe this ability: *Phonemic awareness* (Golinkoff, 1978), *phonetic analysis* (Bruce, 1964), *phonological awareness* (Rozin & Gleitman, 1977), and *auditory analysis* (Rosner & Simon, 1971) are but a few. For the sake of convenience, the term *phonemic awareness* is used herein.

An essential aspect of phonemic awareness is facility in perceiving a word as a sequence of sounds (Lewkowicz, 1980). The word *fish,* for example, comprises three phonemes: /f/, /ɪ/, and /š/. Phonemic awareness has been measured by performance on a wide range of tasks, including rhyming (e.g., Calfee et al., 1972); isolating beginning, medial, and ending sounds (e.g., Williams, 1980); breaking down words into their component sounds (e.g., Fox & Routh, 1975; Goldstein, 1976; Helfgott, 1976); saying words with target sounds deleted (e.g., Bruce, 1964; Rosner & Simon, 1971); and producing invented spellings (e.g., Mann et al., 1987; Morris & Perney, 1984; Read, 1971). Why is phonemic awareness so critical to the learning-to-read process, and why do some readers fail to develop this ability? How do instructional practices influence phonemic awareness? In this article, I summarize the research on these questions and provide instructional recommendations for developing phonological abilities.

Research on Phonemic Awareness

Role of Phonemic Awareness in Beginning Reading

The relationship between phonemic awareness and reading acquisition has been one of the most studied questions in the past two decades of research on beginning reading (for reviews, see Adams, 1990; Ehri, 1991; Golinkoff, 1978; Jorm & Share, 1983; Juel, 1991; I. Y. Liberman & Shank-weiler, 1985; Sulzby & Teale, 1991; Wagner & Torgesen, 1987; Williams, 1984, 1986). The conclusion across both correlational and experimental studies is that students who enter reading instruction unable to perform phonemic awareness tasks experience less success in reading than do students who score high in phonemic awareness when instruction commences (Bradley & Bryant, 1983; Calfee et al., 1973; Juel, 1988; Juel et al., 1986; I. Y. Liberman et al., 1974; Perfetti et al., 1987; Share et al., 1984; Spector, 1992; Stanovich et al., 1984a; Tunmer et al., 1988; Tunmer & Nesdale, 1985; Vellutino & Scanlon, 1987).

From a theoretical perspective, the link between phonemic awareness and reading acquisition is consistent with models of reading acquisition that emphasize the critical role that an understanding of the alphabetic principle plays in the initial stages of learning to read (Adams, 1990; Ehri, 1991; Elkonin, 1973; Gough & Hillinger, 1980; Juel, 1991; I. Y. Liberman, 1973; Perfetti, 1985; Rozin & Gleitman, 1977). That is, children must understand how print maps onto speech. They must realize that spoken words can be broken down into individual sounds, letters within words stand for sounds, and individual sounds blended together yield words.

Problems in Acquiring Phonemic Awareness   Children do not necessarily acquire knowledge of the alphabetic principle by virtue of being exposed to print in their environment. Even the focused experiences afforded by activities such as identification of labels on cereal boxes, fingerpoint reading, and shared storybook reading can be insufficient for some children in prompting phonemic awareness (Ehri & Sweet, 1991; Mason, 1980; Masonheimer et al., 1984; Yalden et al., 1989; also see reviews by Ehri, 1991; Sulzby & Teale, 1991). Although by the time they enter kindergarten many children possess considerable knowledge of the purposes and conventions of print and about the names of letters, the majority are unable to perform tasks such as phoneme segmentation (breaking down words into a sequence of sounds) until Grade 1 (I. Y. Liberman et al., 1974). In fact, there is evidence that adults who are poor readers still have difficulty identifying the component sounds within spoken words, despite years of reading instruction (I. Y. Liberman et al., 1985; Pratt & Brady, 1988). Similarly, fluent readers in a logographic writing system such as Chinese typically cannot isolate individual sounds within an utterance, presumably because this ability develops only to meet the demands of an alphabetic writing system (Read et al., 1986).

Why is phonemic awareness so seemingly unnatural and difficult to acquire for some readers? To answer this question, we need to consider characteristics of speech perception.

Differences between Speech and Reading   Although to fluent readers it seems obvious that the first sound of *cat* is /k/, A. M. Liberman et al. (1967) provided evidence that the speech stream cannot be neatly divided into segments corresponding to sounds. That is, if we were to tape record someone saying "cat," we could not splice the tape into three consecutive parts, corresponding to the sounds /k/, /a/, and /t/. Spectrographic analysis of speech waves reveals that, when transmitted, the sounds within words overlap. Thus, sound waves corresponding to the medial vowel /a/ reach us as we are still perceiving the sound waves corresponding to /k/. And then the sound waves for /t/ arrive, almost simultaneously. The phoneme, then, is not a discrete acoustic unit. As A. Liberman et al. concluded, we hear in syllables, not in individual sounds. This fact, however, presents no obstacles to us when we attempt to produce or understand speech. Speech comprehension requires that we attend to the meaning of the utterance that we hear and pay little attention to its sound qualities. For example, when someone asks me what time it is, my thoughts should turn to my watch and not to the fact that one of the words that I just heard contains the sound /t/ in the initial position.

According to A. Liberman (1982), we have an inborn capacity to process speech at the level of the phoneme. This ability builds on implicit, rather than explicit, knowledge about the sound structure of words. On listening tasks, for example, even infants can detect differences between similar phonemes such as /b/ and /p/ (Miller & Eimas, 1975). Similarly, preschool children can easily recognize that words such as *bill* and *pill* are different (Eimas, 1975). What young children and other nonreaders cannot readily do, however, is to reflect on that knowledge—to explain why the two words are different. And until children enter into reading instruction, they are not likely to be asked to provide such an explanation. Explicit phonemic awareness is required only to learn to read and write in an alphabetic system such as English (I. Y. Liberman, 1973). It is not a skill that either facilitates or develops automatically from speaking or understanding speech.

Effects of Instruction on Phonemic Awareness

Although phonemic awareness does not always come naturally, with instruction children can acquire explicit knowledge of the structural and phonological features of spoken language. The first explicit language analysis task that children are able to master is to break down an utterance into phrases or propositions (e.g., "I'm going"; "to the store"). Next in order of acquisition is segmentation into words, followed by analysis into syllables. The task that is most difficult to accomplish is breaking down words into sounds or phonemes (I. Y. Liberman et al., 1974).

Interestingly, the case with which children can be taught to break down language into constituent parts mirrors the development over time of writing systems (Gleitman & Rozin, 1977; Rozin & Gleitman, 1977). The first writing systems invented were ideographic systems (e.g., Native American petroglyphs), in which symbols stand for whole ideas. Next to appear were logographies, like Chinese and Japanese Kanji. In a logography, a symbol stands for a concept or word. The visual features of each symbol lead directly to the meaning that it communicates; the aural pronunciation of a symbol is not predicted by its form. In Chinese, for example, speakers of different dialects can read the same printed material because the symbols map onto meaning in the same way, regardless of dialect. They cannot converse with each other, though, because the spoken word equivalents of the logographs vary by dialect (Carroll, 1972).

After logography, the next writing systems to evolve were syllabaries, such as Japanese Kana and Hebrew. Each symbol in a syllabary represents a syllable. In Kana, for example, approximately 100 symbols represent all possible syllables in Japanese. The most recently developed and most abstract scripts are alphabetic writing systems such as English, in which symbols stand for phonemes.

Discovering the Alphabetic Principle   Case studies of emergent readers suggest that it is possible to gain insight into the alphabetic principle through discovery (Bissex, 1980; Sulzby, 1985; Yaden et al., 1989). Some children search for patterns and regularities in printed language that then allow them to crack the code with little or no formal reading instruction (Durkin, 1966). Other children, however, do not detect these "samenesses" (Carnine, 1991) in print-to-speech mapping when left to their own devices. Children with reading, writing, and learning disabilities, in particular, appear to be less sensitive to the sounds within words and thus may be less likely to detect the regularities that would lead them to discover the alphabetic principle on their own. For these children, systematic instruction may be necessary to ensure the development of phonemic awareness. Without such training, the impact of beginning reading will likely be diminished.

Does Phonics Develop Phonemic Awareness?   Many teachers assume that phonics, or code-based, programs ensure the development of phonemic awareness. This assumption appears unwarranted (Byrne & Fielding-Barnsley, 1991; Juel, 1991). Although phonics programs typically are organized to highlight letter–sound regularities, they vary in the degree to which they provide direct instruction in sound blending and phoneme segmentation. In some programs (e.g., Bloomfield & Barnhart, 1961), phonics is taught through "word families" (e.g., *mat, fat, bat; hip, tip, lip*). Sounds of single letters are intentionally not introduced. Although many children achieve insight into the alphabetic principle in such a program (just as they do in whole-word programs), there is evidence that others will not develop phonemic awareness from this type of instruction (Johnson & Baumann, 1984).

Similarly, even programs that provide direct instruction in letter–sound relationships (e.g., teaching that *p* says "puh") are likely to fall short for many children in achieving the goal of phonemic awareness. Why? Phonemic awareness implies the ability to analyze and synthesize the sound structure of words. That is, children must realize that words are made up of individual sounds (phonemes) and that sounds, when combined, yield words. Furthermore, they must recognize that some words share phonemes. For example, the *s* in *sun* is the same sound that is heard at the end of *bus*. Mastery of letter–sound correspondences, on the other hand, is nothing more than paired-associate learning or rote memory of facts. As anyone who has ever heard a beginning reader trying to blend knows, the sequence *puh-ah-tuh* yields a three-syllable word that is a far cry from *pat*. To blend, children must be able to abstract the phonemic "p-ness" from the syllable "puh," despite the fact that stop consonants, like *p*, cannot be pronounced in isolation without adding an unnecessary schwa sound. Similarly, a child must be able to reflect on the internal structure of words to be at all successful in spelling unknown words. Thus, a child might be able to tell you that "s" says *s*, but be unable to recognize that the medial sound in "ask" is *s*. Clearly, the successful reader or writer acquires both phonemic awareness and letter–sound knowledge; one is not a substitute or a prerequisite for the other (Byrne & Fielding-Barnsley, 1989, 1991).

Having acknowledged both the importance of phonemic awareness and the difficulties associated with acquisition, two related questions remain: What should we teach, and how should we teach it? In the remainder of this article, I offer some recommendations regarding phonemic awareness training. These recommendations are supported by research on phonemic awareness as well as by principles of direct instruction.

Recommendations for Instruction

At the Preschool Level, Engage Children in Activities That Direct Their Attention to the Sounds in Words   As mentioned earlier, young children appear to adopt an initial orientation to print that mirrors their orientation to spoken language: attention to meaning, rather than sound. Research on emergent literacy suggests that children's first approach to print is logographic (see reviews by Ehri, 1991; Juel, 1991). That is, to identify words, children use environmental context and other visual cues that relate to the meaning, rather than the sound structure of the word. For example, a child might be able to recognize the word *McDonald's,* but only if the golden arches are present. Alternatively, a child might recognize the word "dog" by noting the resemblance of the word to the physical features of a dog (e.g., the lowercase "g" looks like a tail). To move beyond this phase of development, children need to turn their attention, at least auditorily, to the similarities among words that share common sounds.

According to Bryant et al. (1989), memorization of nursery rhymes may enhance sensitivity to word sounds. Carefully selected read-alouds can similarly be used to encourage manipulation of the sounds of the English language. Griffith and Olson (1992) provided a list of trade books that play with language in ways that call attention to the sounds of words. They cite the alphabet book *Animalia* (Base, 1986), for example, for its use of alliteration (e.g., "Lazy lions lounging in the local library"). Books that highlight a less frequently considered pattern, assonance (the repetition of vowel sounds within words, e.g., "A leaf, a tree, a green bean green" from *Who Said Red,* Serfozo, 1988) are also included on the list. Additional activities that facilitate the development of phonemic awareness include rhyming and alliteration games, along with more structured lessons that provide the vocabulary needed to discuss the sound structure of words, such as "first sound" and "last sound" (Lundberg et al., 1988).

Teach Students to Segment and to Blend   Phonemic awareness is clearly not a unitary ability. Different tasks tap distinct aspects of phonemic awareness. Lewkowicz (1980) described 10 categories of tasks that have been used in research on phonemic awareness. On the basis of logical analysis, she identified two tasks that appear to be most directly related to beginning reading: phoneme segmentation (analysis) and phoneme blending (synthesis). A segmentation skill that is introduced in many phonemic awareness programs is identification of the sequence of sounds heard within a word (see the description below of Elkonin's, 1973, approach). Phoneme blending has long been taught in reading programs that emphasize decoding (e.g., Carnine et al., 1990; Engelmann & Bruner, 1974). Typically, students are asked to pronounce individual sounds and then to say them rapidly (and in order) to make a word.

Research confirms that the most successful phonemic awareness training programs provide instruction on segmentation and blending (Blachman, 1987; Wallach & Wallach, 1977; Williams, 1979, 1980). Skills that appear to be less important to teach are those that are more complex, such as phoneme deletion, a task that requires students to say a word with a target sound deleted (e.g., say *stand* without the /t/). The results of longitudinal studies suggest that complex phonemic awareness is best viewed as the result, rather than the cause, of reading and spelling instruction (Perfetti et al., 1987). Instruction, then, is best aimed at two basic skills: phoneme segmentation (analysis) and phoneme blending (synthesis).

There is some evidence that segmentation and blending can be taught as auditory skills apart from their relationship to reading and writing. One of the first training programs aimed at phoneme segmentation was developed by the Russian psychologist Elkonin (1973). Elkonin used tokens placed in a series of squares to represent sounds in words. He constructed cards that provided a picture of the word to be segmented and a series of squares corresponding to the number of sounds in the word. His teaching procedure requires the teacher to pronounce the word slowly. As the first sound in a spoken word is pronounced, the teacher places a token in the first square, places a token in the second square when the second sound is pronounced, and so on, through each sound in the word. After the teacher models the procedure, students apply it themselves to segment a variety of word types. Elkonin purposely made no attempt to link letters with sounds or to substitute letters for the blank tokens, reasoning that letters distract the child from attending carefully to the sounds within the word. Although Elkonin provided only anecdotal evidence to support the effectiveness of his procedure, in the years since he published his work, others have incorporated his approach as the first step in teaching phoneme segmentation (Ball & Blachman, 1991; Blachman, 1987; Clay, 1979, 1985; Williams, 1979, 1980).

Combine Training in Segmentation and Blending with Instruction in Letter–Sound Relationships   Although there is evidence that segmentation and blending can be taught successfully as auditory skills (e.g., Elkonin, 1973; Lundberg, 1987; Lundberg et al., 1988), the phonemic awareness programs that have had the most positive effect on reading achievement have been those that incorporate segmentation and blending training with letter–sound instruction (e.g., Ball & Blachman, 1991; Blachman, 1987; Bradley & Bryant, 1983; Byrne & Fielding-Barnsley, 1989, 1991; Clay, 1979, 1985; Treiman & Baron, 1983; Wallach & Wallach, 1977; Williams, 1979, 1980). That is, purely auditory approaches to developing phonemic awareness may succeed in focusing students' attention on the sound qualities of words and may thus improve phonemic awareness, but improvement in reading and spelling skills will not necessarily follow unless students also have letter–sound knowledge.

An optimal program, then, combines instruction in letter–sound correspondences with training in segmentation and blending. Thus, once a small set of letter–sound correspondences is mastered, letters can be substituted for Elkonin's blank tokens. For example, if the word were *sun,* the student would say "sun" slowly, placing an *s* in the first square as the first sound was uttered, a *u* in the second square as the second sound was pronounced, and an *n* in the third square as the third sound was spoken.

Teach Segmentation and Blending as Complementary Processes   The literature is ambiguous about which skill to teach first, segmentation or blending. Adams (1990) proposed that putting together sounds is easier than taking apart a word, an observation that suggests the desirability of working on blending before working on segmentation. At the same time, though, she acknowledged that children who are not familiar with the way sounds are pronounced in isolation will have difficulty blending. Perhaps the best solution is for the child to move back and forth between segmentation and blending. For example, after students have segmented a word using a modified version of Elkonin's procedure, they could be asked to "read back" the word that has just been segmented, pronouncing the word as a whole, while moving their fingers smoothly under each letter to emphasize the blending of sounds (for additional formats that reinforce blending, see Carnine et al., 1990; Kameenui & Simmons, 1990). Similarly, words that the student can read can be used for segmentation practice.

Systematically Sequence Examples When Teaching Segmentation and Blending

1. *Begin segmentation exercises with biphonemic words.* Studies on segmentation and blending indicate that the number of sounds within the word affects case of segmentation and blending (e.g., Lewkowicz & Low, 1979). Words that contain two sounds (e.g., *at* and *me*) are easier to segment or blend than words that contain three sounds (e.g., *fish* and *men*), and triphonemic words are segmented more readily than words with four sounds. An appropriate sequence for segmentation and blending training is to introduce words with two sounds first. When these words are mastered, words with three sounds can then be practiced.

2. *With students who can segment biphonemic words but cannot analyze more complex syllables, first practice breaking complex syllables into onsets and rimes.* If students have difficulty breaking down a word into three or more phonemes (e.g., *hit* and *stop*), an intermediate step that is more easily accomplished is to segment the word into onset and rime (Treiman, 1985a). The onset is the portion of the syllable prior to the vowel (*h* and *st* in the case of *hit* and *stop*), while the rime includes the vowel and the consonants that follow it (*it* and *op*). Even prereaders appear sensitive to onset and rime (see review by Adams, 1990).

3. *Have students practice words that begin with continuants before they practice words that begin with stop consonants.* Research on beginning reading also confirms that some words are more difficult than others to analyze and synthesize. For example, stop consonants that precede vowels are notoriously troublesome to blend or segment because they are impossible to say without adding a schwa sound. That is, initial *b* is likely to be pronounced "buh," just as *k* will be pronounced "kuh." Thus, the first examples that students practice should begin with vowels or continuant consonants that are easily pronounced in isolation (e.g., *f, s, m,* and *l*).

4. *Introduce words with simple consonants before words that contain consonant blends.* Consonant blends pose additional challenges to the student who is a novice at segmentation and blending. Apparently, it is our knowledge of English orthography that enables us to "hear" so clearly two distinct sounds within many blends. While we, as print experts, believe that we hear the sounds *s* and *p* as the first two sounds in *spoon*, recent research indicates that a more accurate representation of the second sound is *b* rather than *p* (Ehri &

Wilce, 1980, 1987; Treiman, 1985b). Similarly, in speech, the pronunciation of the consonant blend at the beginning of *truck* sounds like *ch* and the blend at the beginning of *dragon* sounds like *jr* (Read, 1971). In addition, some final consonant blends are not easily detected as two distinct sounds. Nasals (e.g., *ng* and *nd*), for example, are more difficult to segment than other blends (e.g., *-st* and *-ft*). When first teaching segmentation and blending, then, teachers should start with words that contain only simple consonants. Words such as *fun* and *name,* for example, should be mastered before students attempt words such as *sing, clap,* or *twist.*

Teach for Transfer to Novel Tasks and Contexts

1. *Provide opportunities for students to transfer newly acquired knowledge to words with different sound structures.* Once students have practiced segmentation or blending on a particular set of words, they should be provided with a new set of words to segment or blend. Also, just because students can segment triphonemic words that include single consonants (e.g., *sit* and *lap*), it should not be assumed that they will automatically be able to segment words with consonant blends (e.g., *sly* and *ask*). To ensure transfer, have students practice words with different sound structures.

2. *Vary the context within which segmentation and blending are practiced.* The range of segmentation and blending tasks should be expanded beyond the cards and tokens that may be used in initial teaching. Blachman (1987), for example, incorporated a modification of one of Slingerland's (1971) techniques in her phonemic awareness program to ensure that students generalized segmentation and blending beyond the Elkonin-inspired cards that were used to introduce segmentation. Students used small pocket-charts called *sound boards* to manipulate letter cards. First, the teacher slowly pronounced a word (e.g., "map"), emphasizing the sound of the medial vowel. The child then selected the letter card to represent the vowel and placed it in a pocket on the chart. Next, the teacher repeated the whole word and asked the child for the initial sound. Once the child supplied the initial sound, the teacher pronounced the initial two segments (e.g., "ma") and prompted the child to supply a card to represent the remaining sound in the word. After the child successfully produced cards to represent all sounds in a word, he or she pronounced all three segments together. The teacher then asked the child to modify the display to create a new word (e.g., "How could we change 'map' into 'mat'?"). The last step was then repeated to create additional words.

3. *Make explicit the link between phonemic awareness activities and reading and writing.* Once students have mastered segmentation us-

ing cards and tokens or sound boards, the teacher should demonstrate the application of the skill to more meaningful contexts. A recent study by Cunningham (1990) indicated the effectiveness of including a "metalevel" (i.e., metacognitive) component in phonemic awareness training programs. In Cunningham's approach, the teacher discussed with the children the application of phonemic awareness to reading tasks. For example, after learning about segmentation and blending, children were told that a good strategy to use when they came upon an unfamiliar word was "to 'cut the word up' into its smallest pieces, think about what that word sounds like, and then think if they know any words that resemble that combination of sounds" (Cunningham, 1990, p. 435). Similar instruction can be provided to demonstrate the connection between phonemic awareness and spelling (e.g., making explicit the applicability of phoneme segmentation to the task of spelling unknown words). Thus, after children have learned to pronounce the phonemes heard within spoken words, they can be told that when they are trying to spell a word they do not know, a good strategy is first to say each sound heard in the word and then to write the letter that "goes with" each sound. Reading Recovery, a currently popular program that includes segmentation and blending training, includes an exemplary series of activities that takes the student from contrived tasks (like Elkonin's procedure) to more naturalistic reading and writing situations (Clay, 1979, 1985). Clay and her followers in the United States claim what is perhaps the highest effectiveness rate of any remedial or compensatory program (Pinnell et al., 1988; Pinnell et al., 1990).

Teach Teachers the Rationale Underlying Phonemic Awareness Training

As I. Y. Liberman (1987) observed,

> Many teachers of beginning reading are being trained to teach reading in an alphabetic orthography without ever being taught how an alphabetic orthography represents the language, why it is important for beginning readers to understand how the internal structure of words relates to the orthography, or why it may be hard for children to understand this. Though its relevance has been confirmed over and over again, many prospective teachers are not being taught the critical role phonological awareness can play in the child's mastery of the alphabetic principle, or how to identify a child who is deficient in such awareness and what can be done about it. (p. 7)

Not surprisingly, the reading programs that have most successfully incorporated phonemic awareness training have been those that provide staff development to teach teachers the rationale behind the approach (e.g., Blachman, 1987; Clay, 1985). In the absence of such training, teachers are not flexible in applying instruction where needed and modifying instruction to meet individual needs.

Conclusions

The research to date provides clear evidence that phonemic awareness training works: Not only does it enhance the auditory skills of segmentation and blending in beginning readers, but also it results in increased reading achievement when it is combined with training in letter–sound correspondences. There is still substantial work to be done in identifying additional approaches to teaching phonemic awareness. Further research is needed, in particular, to identify the components of more versus less successful programs. In addition, the scope of experimental research needs to be expanded to include older students with long-standing histories of reading failure. The majority of phonemic awareness training studies have not targeted this group, but instead have focused on students in the early primary grades.

It is also important to recognize that phonemic awareness training is not a panacea. It is expected to benefit primarily those students who have difficulty acquiring basic decoding skills. It will not ameliorate deficits in vocabulary and reading comprehension, and it will not result in improved performance for those students who have difficulty with automatic recognition of visual symbols. As mentioned earlier, however, decoding problems account for the majority of cases of severe reading disability among students of otherwise average intellectual ability (see reviews by Stanovich, 1988; Vellutino & Denkla, 1991) and so the potential contribution of phonemic awareness training is great. At present, there is considerable optimism in the fields of literacy and special education that severe reading disability can be either prevented or improved.

References

Adams, M. J. (1990). *Beginning to read: Thinking and learning about print*. Cambridge, MA: MIT Press.

Ball, E. W., & Blachman, B. A. (1991). Does phoneme awareness training in kindergarten make a difference in early word recognition and developmental spelling? *Reading Research Quarterly, 26,* 49–66.

Base, G. (1986). *Animalia*. New York: Adams.

Bissex, G. L. (1980). *Gnys at wrk*. Cambridge, MA: Harvard University Press.

Blachman, B. A. (1987). An alternative classroom reading program for learning disabled and other low-achieving children. In W. Ellis (Ed.), *Intimacy with lan-*

guage: A forgotten basic in teacher education (pp. 49–55). Baltimore, MD: Orton Dyslexia Society.

Bloomfield, L., & Barnhart, C. L. (1961). *Let's read: A linguistic approach.* Detroit, MI: Wayne State University Press.

Bradley, L., & Bryant, P. (1983). Categorizing sounds and learning to read—a causal connection. *Nature, 301,* 419–421.

Bruce, D. J. (1964). An analysis of word sounds by young children. *British Journal of Educational Psychology, 34,* 158–170.

Bryant, P., Bradley, L., Maclean, M., & Crossland, J. (1989). Nursery rhymes, phonological skills and reading. *Journal of Child Language, 16,* 407–428.

Byrne, B., & Fielding-Barnsley, R. (1989). Phonemic awareness and letter knowledge in the child's acquisition of the alphabetic principle. *Journal of Educational Psychology, 81,* 313–321.

Byrne, B., & Fielding-Barnsley, R. (1991). Evaluation of a program to teach phonemic awareness to young children. *Journal of Educational Psychology, 83,* 451–455.

Calfee, R. C., Chapman, R. S., & Venezky, R. L. (1972). How a child needs to think to learn how to read. In L. Gregg (Ed.), *Cognition in learning and memory* (pp. 139–182). New York: Wiley.

Calfee, R. C., Lindamood, P., & Lindamood, C. (1973). Acoustic-phonetic skills and reading—kindergarten through twelfth grade. *Journal of Educational Psychology, 64,* 293–298.

Carnine, D. (1991). Curricular interventions for teaching higher order thinking to all students: Introduction to the special series. *Journal of Learning Disabilities, 24,* 261–269.

Carnine, D., Silbert, J., & Kameenui, E. J. (1990). *Direct instruction reading* (2nd ed.). Columbus, OH: Merrill.

Carroll, J. B. (1972). The case for ideographic writing. In J. Kavanaugh & I. Mattingly (Eds.), *Language by ear and by eye: The relationships between speech and reading* (pp. 103–109). Cambridge, MA: MIT Press.

Clay, M. M. (1979). *Reading: The patterning of complex behavior* (2nd ed.). Auckland, New Zealand: Heinemann.

Clay, M. M. (1985). *The early detection of reading difficulties* (3rd ed.). Auckland, New Zealand: Heinemann.

Cunningham, A. E. (1990). Explicit versus implicit instruction in phonemic awareness. *Journal of Experimental Child Psychology, 50,* 429–444.

Curtis, M. E. (1980). Development of components of reading skill. *Journal of Educational Psychology, 72,* 656–669.

Durkin, D. (1966). *Children who read early.* New York: Teachers College Press.

Ehri, L. C. (1991). Development of the ability to read words. In R. Barr, M. L. Kamil, P. Mosenthal, & P. D. Pearson (Eds.), *Handbook of research on reading* (Vol. 2, pp. 383–417). White Plains, NY: Longman.

Ehri, L. S., & Sweet, J. (1991). Fingerpoint-reading of memorized text: What enables beginners to process the print? *Reading Research Quarterly, 26,* 442–462.

Ehri, L. C., & Wilce, L. S. (1980). The influence of orthography on readers' conceptualizations of the phonetic structure of words. *Applied Psycholinguistics, 1,* 371–385.

Ehri, L. S., & Wilce, L. S. (1987). Does learning to spell help beginners learn to read words? *Reading Research Quarterly, 18*, 47–65.

Eimas, P. D. (1975). Distinctive feature codes in the short-term memory of children. *Journal of Experimental Child Psychology, 19*, 241–251.

Elkonin, D. B. (1973). U. S. S. R. In J. Downing (Ed.), *Comparative reading* (pp. 551–579). New York: Macmillan.

Engelmann, S., & Bruner, E. (1974). *DISTAR reading I.* Chicago: Science Research Associates.

Fox, B., & Routh, D. K. (1975). Analyzing spoken language into words, syllables, and phonemes: A developmental study. *Journal of Psycholinguistic Research, 4*, 331–342.

Frederiksen, J. R. (1978). Assessment of perceptual decoding and lexical skills and their relation to reading proficiency. In A. M. Lesgold, J. W. Pellegrini, S. E. Fokkems, & R. Glaser (Eds.), *Cognitive psychology and instruction* (pp. 153–169). New York: Plenum.

Gleitman, L., & Rozin, P. (1977). The structure and acquisition of reading: Relations between orthographies and the structure of language. In A. S. Reber & D. L. Scarborough (Eds.), *Toward a psychology of reading* (pp. 1–53). Hillsdale, NJ: Erlbaum.

Goldstein, D. M. (1976). Cognitive-linguistic functioning and learning to read in preschoolers. *Journal of Educational Psychology, 68*, 680–688.

Golinkoff, R. M. (1978). Critique: Phonemic awareness skills and reading achievement. In F. B. Murray & J. J. Pikulski (Eds.), *The acquisition of reading: Cognitive, linguistic, and perceptual prerequisites* (pp. 23–41). Baltimore, MD: University Park Press.

Gough, P., & Hillinger, M. L. (1980). Learning to read: An unnatural act. *Bulletin of the Orton Society, 30*, 179–196.

Griffith, P. L., & Olson, M. W. (1992). Phonemic awareness helps beginning readers break the code. *The Reading Teacher, 45*, 516–523.

Helfgott, J. A. (1976). Phonemic segmentation and blending skills of kindergarten children: Implications for beginning reading acquisition. *Contemporary Educational Psychology, 1*, 157–169.

Hogaboam, C. W., & Perfetti, C. A. (1978). Reading skill and the role of verbal experience in decoding. *Journal of Educational Psychology, 70*, 717–729.

Johnson, D. D., & Baumann, J. F. (1984). Word identification. In P. D. Pearson (Ed.), *Handbook of reading research* (Vol. 1, pp. 583–608). White Plains, NY: Longman.

Jorm, A. F., & Share, D. L. (1983). Phonological recoding and reading acquisition. *Applied Psycholinguistics, 4*, 103–147.

Juel, C. (1988). Learning to read and write: A longitudinal study of 54 children from first through fourth grades. *Journal of Educational Psychology, 80*, 437–447.

Juel, C. (1991). Beginning reading. In R. Barr, M. L. Kamil, P. Mosenthal, & P. D. Pearson (Eds.), *Handbook of research on reading* (Vol. 2, pp. 759–788). White Plains, NY: Longman.

Juel, C., Griffith, P. L., & Gough, P. B. (1986). Acquisition of literacy: A longitudinal study of children in first and second grade. *Journal of Educational Psychology, 78*, 243–255.

Kameenui, E. J., & Simmons, D. C. (1990). *Designing instructional strategies: The prevention of academic learning problems.* Columbus, OH: Merrill.

Lewkowicz, N. K. (1980). Phonemic awareness training: What to teach and how to teach it. *Journal of Educational Psychology, 72,* 686–700.

Lewkowicz, N. K., & Low, L. Y. (1979). Effects of visual aids and word structure on phonemic segmentation. *Contemporary Educational Psychology, 4,* 238–252.

Liberman, A. M. (1982). On finding that speech is special. *American Psychologist, 37,* 148–167.

Liberman, A. M., Cooper, F. S., Shankweiler, D., & Studdert-Kennedy, M. (1967). Perception of the speech code. *Psychological Review, 74,* 431–461.

Liberman, I. Y. (1973). Segmentation of the spoken word and reading acquisition. *Bulletin of the Orton Society, 23,* 65–77.

Liberman, I. Y. (1987). Language and literacy: The obligation of the schools of education. In W. Ellis (Ed.), *Intimacy with language: A forgotten basic in teacher education* (pp. 1–9). Baltimore, MD: Orton Dyslexia Society.

Liberman, I. Y., Rubin, H., Duques, S., & Carlisle, J. (1985). Linguistic abilities and spelling proficiency in kindergartners and adult poor spellers. In D. B. Gray & J. F. Kavanagh (Eds.), *Biobehavioral measures of dyslexia* (pp. 163–176). Parkton, MD: York Press.

Liberman, I. Y., & Shankweiler, D. (1985). Phonology and the problems of learning to read and write. *Remedial and Special Education, 6,* 8–17.

Liberman, I. Y., Shankweiler, D., Fischer, F. W., & Carter, B. (1974). Explicit syllable and phoneme segmentation in the young child. *Journal of Experimental Child Psychology, 18,* 201–212.

Lundberg, I. (1987). Phonological awareness facilitates reading and spelling acquisition. In W. Ellis (Ed.), *Intimacy with language: A forgotten basic in teacher education* (pp. 56–63). Baltimore, MD: Orton Dyslexia Society.

Lundberg, I., Frost, J., & Petersen, O. (1988). Effects of an extensive program for stimulating phonological awareness in preschool children. *Reading Research Quarterly, 23,* 263–284.

Mann, V. A., Tobin, P., & Wilson, R. (1987). Measuring phonological awareness through the invented spellings of kindergarten children. *Merrill-Palmer Quarterly, 33,* 365–391.

Mason, J. M. (1980). When do children begin to read: An exploration of four-year-old children's letter- and word-reading competencies. *Reading Research Quarterly, 15,* 203–227.

Masonheimer, P. E., Drum, P. A., & Ehri, L. C. (1984). Does environmental print identification lead children into word reading? *Journal of Reading Behavior, 26,* 257–271.

Miller, J. L., & Eimas, P. D. (1983). Studies on the categorization of speech by infants. *Cognition, 13,* 135–166.

Morris, D., & Perney, J. (1984). Developmental spelling as a predictor of first grade achievement. *Elementary School Journal, 84,* 441–457.

Perfetti, C. A. (1985). *Reading ability.* New York: Oxford University Press.

Perfetti, C. A., Beck, I., Bell, L. C., & Hughes, C. (1987). Phonemic knowledge and learning to read are reciprocal: A longitudinal study of first grade children. *Merrill-Palmer Quarterly, 33,* 283–319.

Perfetti, C. A., Finger, E., & Hogaboam, T. (1984). Sources of vocalization latency differences between skilled and less-skilled young readers. *Journal of Educational Psychology, 70,* 730–739.

Perfetti, C. A., & Hogaboam, T. (1975). Relationship between single-word decoding and reading comprehension skill. *Journal of Educational Psychology, 67,* 461–469.

Pinnell, G. S., DeFord, D. E., & Lyons, C. A. (1988). *Reading recovery: Early intervention for at-risk first graders.* Arlington, VA: Educational Research Service.

Pinnell, G. S., Fried, M. D., & Estice, R. M. (1990). Reading recovery: Learning how to make a difference. *The Reading Teacher, 43,* 282–295.

Pratt, A. C., & Brady, S. (1988). Relation of phonological awareness to reading disability in children and adults. *Journal of Educational Psychology, 80,* 319–323.

Read, C. (1971). Pre-school children's knowledge of English phonology. *Harvard Educational Review, 41,* 1–34.

Read, C., Yun-Fei, Z., Hong-Yin, N., & Bao-Qing, D. (1986). The ability to manipulate speech sounds depends on knowing alphabetic writing. *Cognition, 24,* 31–44.

Rosner, J., & Simon, D. (1971). The auditory analysis test: An initial report. *Journal of Learning Disabilities, 4,* 384–392.

Rozin, P., & Gleitman, L. (1977). The structure and acquisition of reading II: The reading process and the acquisition of the alphabetic principle. In A. Reber & D. Scarborough (Eds.), *Toward a psychology of reading* (pp. 55–141). Hillsdale, NJ: Erlbaum.

Serfozo, M. K. (1988). *Who said red?* New York: Macmillan.

Share, D. L., Jorm, A. F., Maclean, R., & Matthews, R. (1984). Sources of individual differences in reading achievement. *Journal of Educational Psychology, 76,* 1309–1324.

Slingerland, B. H. (1971). *A multisensory approach to language arts for specific learning disability children: A guide for primary teachers.* Cambridge, MA: Educators Publishing Service.

Spector, J. E. (1992). Predicting progress in beginning reading: Dynamic assessment of phonemic awareness. *Journal of Educational Psychology, 84,* 353–363.

Spector, J. E., & Calfee, R. C. (1984, May). *A comparison of decoding skills in learning-disabled and non-learning-disabled readers.* Paper presented at the annual meeting of the International Reading Association, Atlanta, GA.

Stanovich, K. E. (1988). Explaining the differences between the dyslexic and the garden-variety poor reader: The phonological-core variable-difference model. *Journal of Learning Disabilities, 21,* 590–612.

Stanovich, K. E., Cunningham, A. E., & Cramer, B. B. (1984a). Assessing phonological awareness in kindergarten children: Issues of task comparability. *Journal of Experimental Child Psychology, 29,* 175–190.

Stanovich, K. E., Cunningham, A., & Feeman, D. (1984b). Relation between early reading acquisition and word decoding with and without context: A longitudinal study of first grade children. *Journal of Educational Psychology, 76,* 668–677.

Sulzby, E. (1985). Children's emergent reading of favorite storybooks. *Reading Research Quarterly, 20,* 458–481.

Sulzby, E., & Teale, W. (1991). Emergent Literacy. In R. Barr, M. L. Kamil, P. Mosenthal, & P. D. Pearson (Eds.), *Handbook of research on reading* (Vol. 2, pp. 727–758). White Plains, NY: Longman.

Treiman, R. (1985a). Onsets and rimes as units of spoken syllables. *Journal of Experimental Child Psychology, 39,* 161–181.

Treiman, R. (1985b). Spelling of stop consonants after /s/ by children and adults. *Applied Psycholinguistics, 6,* 262–282.

Treiman, R., & Baron, J. (1983). Phonemic-analysis training helps children benefit from spelling-sound rules. *Memory & Cognition, 11,* 382–389.

Tunmer, W. E., Herriman, M. L., & Nesdale, A. R. (1988). Metalinguistic abilities and beginning reading. *Reading Research Quarterly, 23,* 134–158.

Tunmer, W. E., & Nesdale, A. R. (1985). Phonemic segmentation skill and beginning reading. *Journal of Educational Psychology, 77,* 417–427.

Vellutino, F. R., & Denkla, M. B. (1991). Cognitive and neuropsychological foundations of word identification in poor and normally developing readers. In R. Barr, M. L. Kamil, P. Mosenthal, & P. D. Pearson (Eds.), *Handbook of research on reading* (Vol. 2, pp. 571–608). White Plains, NY: Longman.

Vellutino, F. R., & Scanlon, D. M. (1987). Phonological coding, phonological awareness, and reading ability: Evidence from a longitudinal and experimental study. *Merrill-Palmer Quarterly, 33,* 321–363.

Wagner, R. K., & Torgesen, J. K. (1987). The nature of phonological processing and its causal role in the acquisition of reading skills. *Psychological Bulletin, 10,* 192–212.

Wallach, M., & Wallach, L. (1977). *Teaching all children to read.* Chicago: University of Chicago Press.

Williams, J. (1979). The ABD's of reading. A program for the learning disabled. In L. B. Resnick & P. A. Weaver (Eds.), *Theory and practice of early reading* (Vol. 3, pp. 179–195). Hillsdale, NJ: Erlbaum.

Williams, J. P. (1980). Teaching decoding with an emphasis on phoneme analysis and phoneme blending. *Journal of Educational Psychology, 72,* 1–15.

Williams, J. P. (1984). Phonemic analysis and how it relates to reading. *Journal of Learning Disabilities, 17,* 240–245.

Williams, J. P. (1986). The role of phonemic analysis in reading. In J. Torgesen & B. Wong (Eds.), *Psychological and educational perspectives on learning disabilities* (pp. 399–416). San Diego, CA: Academic Press.

Yaden, D. B., Smolkin, L. B., & Conlon, A. (1989). Preschoolers' questions about pictures, print convention, and story text during reading aloud at home. *Reading Research Quarterly, 24,* 188–214.

Content Questions

1. What is phonemic awareness?

2. What tasks does Spector explain have been used to measure phonemic awareness?

3. What kind of correlation exists between children's phonemic awareness as they begin reading instruction and their subsequent success in learning to read?

4. Why is phonics instruction sometimes insufficient in helping to develop phonemic awareness?

5. Why is merely teaching letter–sound correspondences, and suggesting that these sounds can be put together, sometimes insufficient in helping students to learn how to read words?

6. Spector provides some general recommendations for how to develop phonemic awareness. What are those recommendations?

7. Which two tasks seem to be particularly important to work with in beginning reading instruction?

8. Why is the suggestion given to work on words beginning with continuants rather than stops?

9. What kinds of reading problems would phonemic awareness training not address? What kinds of readers could it really help?

Questions for Analysis and Discussion

1. Why is phonemic awareness unimportant to Chinese speakers when they begin to study their writing system?

2. Think of literature you have seen that has been written for small children. What kinds of features are present that might assist small children in developing phonemic awareness? Provide specific examples from books you have seen.

3. How might teachers of reading benefit from the research that has been done on phonemic awareness?

Beyond Black English:
Implications of the Ann Arbor Decision
for Other Non-Mainstream Varieties

Walt Wolfram

A previous article considered some ways that teachers, in light of the Ann
Arbor case, could be more effective in addressing the needs of Black English speakers. But speakers of this dialect are not the only nonstandard
dialect speakers who could experience difficulty with a school system that
has little understanding or awareness of their local dialect. In the following article, Walt Wolfram, an English professor at North Carolina State,
who is nationally recognized for his work in dialectal studies, looks at
these types of issues in relation to Appalachian English.

Introduction

It is appropriate that "Black English" was the language variety in focus in
the landmark judicial decision involving educational equity and dialect diversity. As the non-mainstream variety used by a substantial proportion of
the largest minority population in the U.S., it deserves to be the dialect at
issue in a landmark legal decision. Despite laws which guarantee Blacks accessibility to the same schools as their White counterparts, it is apparent
that Blacks are not participating in the educational process in an equitable
way. There are no doubt many dimensions to this educational inequity, as
Judge Joiner pointed out in his opinion and order, and there is no simple
solution. Nonetheless, language differences deserve to be considered as a
possible barrier to educational equity.

The role of linguistic and sociolinguistic testimony in guiding Judge
Joiner's decision (Civil Action No. 7–71861, U.S. District Court, East
District, Detroit, Michigan) seems to be fairly obvious. The wealth of descriptive data brought to bear by expert linguistic testimony obviously influenced the following conclusion by the judge.

> The language of "black English" has been shown to be a distinct, defin-
> able version of English, different from standard English of the school and
> the general world of communications. It has definite language patterns,
> syntax, grammar, and history. (p. 23)

The systematic nature of the language patterns of Black English seem obvious to a linguist, but such a conclusion must be seen against a background of popular mythology which has considered this variety to be nothing more than an unworthy and haphazard distortion of the "standard" variety of English. Negative attitudes and unjustified stereotypes about Black English have persisted in the face of sociolinguistic knowledge concerning it, with all the implications that this negativism can mean for the educational process (Shuy and Fasold, 1973; Pietras, 1977). The discrepancy between the sociolinguistic facts about Black English and much of the popular opinion governing the education of Black English-speaking children thus led Judge Joiner to the following determination.

> The court cannot find that the defendant School Board has taken steps (1) to help teachers understand the problem; (2) to help provide them with knowledge about the children's use of a "black English" language system; and (3) to suggest ways and means of using that knowledge in teaching the students to read. (p. 32)

Thus, the precedent has been set, and a plan to address these concerns has been implemented by the Ann Arbor School Board. The implications of the decision, however, do not stop with Ann Arbor. The landmark decision would certainly seem to have applicability to other areas (and there are many of them) where similar circumstances exist. The lack of adequate progress in language-related tasks, particularly reading, is certainly evident in many areas of the U.S. where Black English speakers reside. The potential for application beyond Ann Arbor is, of course, part of the significance of the case.

While descriptive studies of Black English have certainly been prominent in sociolinguistics over the past two decades, we must be careful to point out that Black English is *not* the only non-mainstream variety of English. Current descriptions of dialects in the U.S. include a range of varieties which must be considered outside of standard English, some of which are ethnically correlated, but some of which are simply class or even regional varieties. What is the significance of this judicial decision for these varieties? Does it have a bearing on children who speak other non-mainstream varieties and do not appear to participate in the educational process in an equitable way?

The statute under which the action was pressed is as follows:

> No State shall deny equal educational opportunity to an individual on account of his or her race, color, sex or national origin, by—
>
> * * *
>
> (f) the failure by an educational agency to take appropriate action to overcome language barriers that impede equal participation by its students in its instructional programs. 20 U.S.C. 1073(f).

In the following sections, we shall examine the possible applicability of the Ann Arbor decision by setting forth parallel characteristics for other non-mainstream-speaking populations. Since it is not our intention to suggest a legal interpretation of the statute cited above, our argument does not revolve around the issue of which groups might qualify on the basis of "race, color, sex, or national origin." Our goal is simply to investigate some of the possible linguistic, sociolinguistic, and educational parallels for other groups of non-mainstream speakers. From this perspective, we can stay within the limits of our own expertise, and allow the judicial system to interpret the legal statute as it may or may not pertain to other groups.

The Linguistic Parallel

As a preliminary to establishing a particular dialect as a potential barrier to educational equity, it seems necessary to establish the variety as a distinct linguistic system. Thus, Black English is characterized in the decision as follows:

> . . . a language system, which is a part of the English language but different in significant respects from the standard English used in the school setting, the commercial world, the world of the arts and science, among the professions, and in government. . . . It [Black English] contains aspects of Southern dialect and is used largely by black people in their casual conversation and informal talk. (p. 14)

As evidence for the distinctness of Black English, a list of characteristic features is cited, including many of the structures found in summaries of this variety (e.g. Fasold and Wolfram, 1970; Burling, 1973). Certainly, other varieties of English must be admitted as distinct non-mainstream varieties along with Black English. Thus, studies of the rural working-class population in the Appalachian region lead to a similar conclusion about this, a variety conveniently labeled "Appalachian English."* Our own study has led to the following conclusion about this variety.

> . . . we use the term AE [Appalachian English] to refer to the variety of English most typically associated with the working class rural population found in one particular region of the Appalachian range. . . . there is evidence, both from our own informal comparisons of working class speakers from other rural areas and available descriptions of other sections of Appalachia, that many of the features we describe have relatively wide distribution within the central Appalachian range.

---

*For the sake of continuity, we shall consistently use "Appalachian English" as our reference dialect throughout the remainder of the paper. Other dialects certainly might have been used as a case in point.

... Quite obviously, there are many features we have described which are not peculiar to speakers within the Appalachian range. On the other hand, there also appear to be a small subset of features which may not be found in other areas. Even if this is not the case, we may justify our distinction of AE on the basis of the combination of features. (Wolfram and Christian, 1976:29)

As was done for Black English in the Ann Arbor case, a characteristic list might be set up for Appalachian English. Consider, for example, the following, abbreviated from a much more complete inventory of structures found in Wolfram and Christian (1976).

1. The use of a prefix *a-* on verb forms
   e.g. *I knew he was a-tellin' the truth.*
   He just kept a-beggin' and a-cryin'.
2. Subject-verb agreement patterns
   e.g. *Some people makes them this way.*
   You was quite busy.
3. Past tense irregular verbs
   e.g. *He hearn something.*
   He knowed he was right.
4. Completive *done*
   e.g. *I done forgot.*
   She's done sold it.
5. Intensifying adverbs
   e.g. *It liketa scared you plumb to death.*
   He stayed there a right smart little while.
6. Use of words with different meanings
   e.g. *I got blessed out.* ('scolded severely')
   I reckon to my age and the way I worked.
   ('acknowledge,' 'defer')
7. Absence of plural after noun of weights and measures
   e.g. *I got two pound of hull beans.*
   Twenty year ago things was different.
8. Use of object pronoun as "personal dative"
   e.g. *Well, I take me a pick and shovel.*
   She wanted her some liver pudding.
9. The use of "double subjects"
   e.g. *My mother, she went to the store.*
   And then my brother, he was fixin' to shoot it.
10. Use of *h* on *it* and *ain't*
    e.g. *Hain't a thing that'll hurt you.*
    When the winter set in hit set in.
11. Use of "intrusive" *t*
    e.g. *He done it oncet or twicet.*
    I started acrosst and found it was a big clifft.

12. Use of *they* or *it* for *there*
e.g. *They was five of them in the coop.*
It was five of them in the coop.

As with the Black English listed in the Ann Arbor decision, this inventory is only intended to be illustrative. Furthermore, some of these features are shared with other varieties of English. In fact, a number of the items (e.g. "double subjects" and *it* for *there*) are shared with Black English. Though the historical tradition which has resulted in Appalachian English (the language of isolated rural mountainous enclaves of early English settlers) is quite different from that hypothesized for Black English (a pidgin language of the slaves which became a creole and was further refined by contact with standard English), both varieties have established and maintained a distinct dialect of English.

We do not claim that a variety such as Appalachian English as we have defined it here is as different from standard English as Black English. Determining the extent of difference from a standard variety can be a rather complicated issue, since it depends on the kind of measure used to determine language differences. Quite clearly, some structures of Appalachian English are closer to standard English than comparable structures in Black English. By the same token, however, there are differences between Appalachian English and standard English that are not found in a comparison of Black English and standard English.

An important difference in the relationship between standard English and the non-mainstream variety might be maintained if a difference in intelligibility were established for Black English and standard English. But this type of evidence is not established in the Ann Arbor case. As a matter of fact, the opposite conclusion is reached.

> The teachers in King School had no difficulty in understanding the students or their parents in the school setting and the children could understand the teachers and other children in that setting. In other words, so far as understanding is concerned in the school setting, although there was initially a type of language difference, there was no barrier to understanding caused by the language.
> There seems to be no problem existing in this case relating to communication between the children and their teachers or between the children and other children in the school. (pps. 25 and 26)

On the basis of such a conclusion, the more stringent characteristic of dialect unintelligibility is eliminated as a requisite for the existence of a "language barrier." This is not to say that differences in language do not lead to some particular differences in comprehension. There is, in fact, some basis for maintaining that particular differences in comprehension patterns might arise from dialect differences. Notwithstanding these particular differences, substantive problems in general intelligibility are not a necessary condition for the language barrier. It seems sufficient to establish the integrity of a dialect which differs substantially from the standard variety as the linguistic norm in this case. Accordingly, we might include a range of varieties which meet these conditions of linguistic difference. For example, Appalachian English, as we have defined it above, matches the characteristics summarized in the decision for Black English (pps. 23–24):

(1) It is "a distinct, definable version of English, different from the standard English of the school and general world of communications."
(2) "It has definite language patterns, syntax, grammar, and history."
(3) "In some communities and among some people in this country, it is the customary mode of oral, informal communication."
(4) A significant number of Appalachians use or have used some version of Appalachian English in oral communications, and "many of them incorporate one or more aspects . . . in their more formal talk."
(5) It "is not a language used by the mainstream of society—black or white," nor is it "an acceptable method of communication in the educational world. . . . It is largely a system that is used in casual and informal communication among the poor and lesser educated."

In terms of its linguistic structure and its distribution within the community, a variety such as Appalachian English is quite parallel to a variety such as Black English.

The Sociolinguistic Parallel

Linguistic differences do not in themselves provide a basis for educational inequity. There exist many widely-recognized differences among the varieties of English which cause no apparent barrier to the educational process. For example, regional differences among mainstream, middle class groups seem to be readily tolerated. The middle class New Englander's absence of *r* in terms such as *car* (*cah*) or *court* (*cou't*), or the use of *tonic* to refer to an object labeled as *soda* or *pop* in other regions, is hardly considered a barrier to the educational process. In fact, various regional differences of this type are typically viewed with an attitude of bemused curiosity, even if they lead to initial confusion of a referent.

The sociolinguistic dimension of language differences in an educational setting arises when language differences are associated with socially "unacceptable groups." Ultimately, the value associated with a particular way of saying something is related to the social status of the people who are saying it that way. Thus, Black English is a stigmatized variety of English not because of its linguistic characteristics, but because it is predominantly used by working-class Blacks. Social and historical facts indicate that if the same variety were spoken by middle class White mainstream groups, it would be recognized as the standard variety.

From a sociolinguistic perspective, it is essential to observe (as stated previously) that Black English "is not a language used by the mainstream of society—black or white," and that it is "not an acceptable method of communication in the educational world, in the commercial community, in the community of the arts and science, or among professionals" (p. 23). It is socially stigmatized because it is most typically used "in many areas of the country where blacks predominate . . . particularly the poor and those with lesser education" (p. 17). The upshot, then, is that Black English is "commonly thought of as an inferior method of speech and those who use this system may be thought of as 'dumb' or 'inferior' " (p. 18). Conclusions about the low esteem in which Black English is held by the mainstream population are amply supported by research on language attitudes (cf. Williams, 1973; Shuy and Williams, 1973; Shuy et al., 1969). Ultimately, it is difficult to separate the issue of language esteem from underlying attitudes about race and status (e.g. Williams, 1973).

While we do not intend to diminish the significance of racism and classism, which have resulted in the stigmatization of Black English, we must admit that other groups and their concomitant language patterns have also become socially stigmatized. Consider, for example, what the distinguished English historian Arnold Toynbee concluded about the isolated rural communities of Southern Appalachia:

> The Appalachian has relapsed into illiteracy and into all the superstitions for which illiteracy opens the door. . . . The Appalachian mountain people are the American counterparts of the latter-day white barbarians of the Old World: . . . *ci-devant* heirs of the Western civilization who have relapsed into barbarism under the depressing effect of a challenge which has been inordinately severe . . . [Their] nearest social analogues are . . . certain "fossils" of extinct civilizations which have survived in fastness and have likewise relapsed into barbarism there. (Quoted in Mencken, 1962:116)

The noted literary authority on the English language, H. L. Mencken, was not as categorically condemning of Appalachian mountaineers and their dialect, but the low esteem of the people and the dialect still surfaces.

> It would be ridiculous to say that all the Appalachian mountaineers are on this low level, or to assume that their stock is wholly decayed. They produce, at somewhat longish intervals, individuals of marked ability— whether by chance adulteries or by some fortunate collocation and effervescence of Mendelian characters is not certain. But such individuals

usually escape from their native alps at the first chance, so that their genes do not improve the remaining population, which continues to go down-hill, with excessive inbreeding to help it along. The speech of these poor folk, who have been called "our contemporary ancestors," is ignorant but very far from unpleasant, as I can testify who have heard it used to preach the Word in the mountains of eastern Tennessee. (Mencken, 1962:117)

Mencken's professed intrigue with the language of Appalachia, unfortunately, does not compensate for the underlying negative attributes also contained in the description. In essence, mountain people are described as genetically inferior, incestuous, and ignorant, with the rare successful individual somehow managing to escape the heritage of the mountain culture. The analogy between type of assessment and the stereotyped caricature of Blacks and their language should be obvious. It is no wonder, then, that Dial (1970) summarizes current opinion of Appalachian English in the following manner.

The dialect spoken by Appalachian people has been given a variety of names, the majority of them somewhat less than complimentary. Educated people who look with disfavor on this particular form of speech are perfectly honest in their belief that something called the English Language, which they see as a completed work—unchanging and fixed for all time—has been taken and, through ignorance shamefully distorted by the mountain folk. (Dial, 1970:16)

Instead of being viewed as a distinct language variety, with "definite language patterns, syntax, grammar, and history" (p. 23), Appalachian English is commonly dismissed as an unworthy, unsystematic, and illegitimate distortion of English. Like Black English, it is a stigmatized variety of English, with all the negative sociolinguistic attitudes about its speakers that this status entails.

The Educational Parallel

While the establishment of linguistic and sociolinguistic parallels is an essential preliminary in examining the wider applicability of the Ann Arbor decision, the heart of the problem is ultimately an educational one. Judge Joiner stated this problem as follows:

The problem in this case revolves around the ability of the school system . . . to teach the reading of standard English to children who, it is alleged, speak "black English" as a matter of course at home and in their home community. . . . (p. 3)

According to Joiner, "a major goal of a school system is to teach reading, writing, speaking, and understanding standard English" (p. 3) and "a child who does not learn to read is impeded in equal participation in the educational program" (p. 18). Regardless of the non-mainstream variety, the correlation between speaking a non-mainstream variety and reading failure is not difficult to establish. Thus, a survey of existing research on this topic readily leads to the following conclusion:

> Research certainly shows that there is a correlation between speaking nonstandard varieties and reading failure; that is, the likelihood of reading problems developing is increased if a person is a member of a nonstandard English speaking population. (Wolfram, 1979:1)

Concluding that there is a correlation between reading failure and speaking a non-mainstream variety must, of course, be differentiated from saying that speaking a nonstandard dialect will necessarily *cause* reading failure. There are many variables that correlate with reading failure, many of which have no apparent relationship with language. The multi-dimensioned nature of reading failure is certainly admitted in Judge Joiner's order (p. 35), and it would be inappropriate to assume that the court concluded that speaking a nonstandard dialect was the sole, or even the prime, variable responsible for the reading failure of non-mainstream students. In the Ann Arbor decision, it was simply concluded that reading was made more difficult for Black English speaking children for the following reasons:

1. There is a lack of parental or other home support for developing reading skills in standard English, including the absence of persons in the home who read, enjoy it, and profit from it.
2. Students experience difficulty in hearing and making certain sounds used discriminatively in standard English, but not distinguished in the home language system.
3. The unconscious but evident attitude of teachers toward the home language causes a psychological barrier to learning by the student. (pp. 35–36)

Of the three, the first reason appears to have the least supportable research base. (It should, of course, be noted that the absence of research evidence does not necessarily mean that it is, in fact, the least significant, since there is no evidence to the contrary either.) Impressionistically, the situation as described for the Black community in this regard does not differ substantially from that found in other non-mainstream communities. At any rate, this argument does not appear to be crucial in this instance.

The second reason refers to our description of linguistic differences that exist between mainstream and non-mainstream varieties. Certainly, differences in the pronunciation and grammatical systems of a mainstream and non-mainstream variety "may be a cause of superficial difficulties in speaking standard English" (p. 36). While some of the differences are described as superficial in terms of their linguistic content, their cumulative effect may, in fact, be quite substantial. The substantive effect is most readily seen by examining how speakers of a non-mainstream variety might perform on an educational test which does not take the home dialect into account. It is somewhat surprising that the effect of a nonstandard dialect on testing was not discussed in more detail in the Ann Arbor decision, since it offers impressive evidence concerning the cumulative effect of a dialect difference on educational assessment (cf. Vaughn-Cooke). Language tests may be used for a wide range of purposes, including the assessment of language development for reading readiness, reading assessment, and diagnosis of learning disabilities. In this context, consider the effect of a test which uses only standard English as a norm for correctness, as is the case with most educational tests. For illustrative purposes, we can use a subtest of the Illinois Test of Psycholinguistic Abilities (ITPA), the "grammatic closure subtest" (Kirk et al., 1968). This subtest is designed to "assess the child's ability to make use of the redundancies of oral language in acquiring automatic habits for handling syntax and grammatical inflections" (*Examiner's Manual,* 1968:11). Such a battery is often used, among other things, as a basis for establishing reading readiness. In the grammatic closure subtest, the child is asked to produce a missing word as the tester points to a picture. For example, the examiner shows a plate with two pictures on it, one with one bed and the other with two beds. The examiner points to the first picture as he says, "Here is a *bed,*" then points to the second picture and says, "Here are two ____," with the child supplying the missing word. All of the responses must be in standard English in order to be considered correct.

With this background information in mind, consider how the "home dialect" might affect the responses and subsequent assessment based on this test. In this case, we shall look at the systematic divergence that might be expected from Black English and Appalachian English speakers who used their home dialect as the basis for giving an appropriate response. In terms of the rules of their home language, their response would be quite appropriate (i.e. "correct"), but in terms of the standard English norms assumed in the test, their responses would have to be considered "incorrect." In Table 1, the standard English responses considered correct according to the scoring manual are given, along with the systematic differences based on the language rules of Black English or Appalachian English.

Two conclusions can be drawn on the basis of Table 1. First, we see that the cumulative effect of the "home dialect" can be quite substantive. For both Black English and Appalachian English, 24 of the 33 items potentially reflect dialect differences on the basis of the home dialect rules. Second, the substantive effect is quite parallel for Black English and Ap-

Table 1 ITPA Grammatical Closure Subtest with Comparison of "Correct" Responses and Appalachian and Vernacular Black English Alternant Forms

STIMULUS WITH "CORRECT" ITEM ACCORDING TO ITPA TEST MANUAL	APPALACHIAN ENGLISH ALTERNANT	VERNACULAR BLACK ENGLISH ALTERNANT
(Items considered to be "correct" according to the procedures for scoring are italicized.)		
1. Here is a dog. Here are two *dogs/doggies*.		dog
2. This cat is under the chair. Where is the cat? She is *on/(any preposition—other than "under"—indicating location)*.		
3. Each child has a ball. This is hers, and this is *his*.	his'n	
4. This dog likes to bark. Here he is *barking*.		
5. Here is a dress. Here are two *dresses*.		dress
6. The boy is opening the gate. Here the gate has been *opened*.		open
7. There is milk in this glass. It is a glass *of/with/for/o'/lots of milk*.		
8. This bicycle belongs to John. Whose bicycle is it? It is *John's*.		John
9. This boy is writing something. This is what he *wrote/has written/did write*.	writed/writ, has wrote	writed/wrote
10. This is the man's home, and this is where he works. Here he is going to work, and here he is going *home/back home/to his home*.	at home	
11. Here it is night, and here it is morning. He goes to work first thing *in the morning*, and he goes home first thing *at night*.	of the night, a-paintin'	
12. This man is painting. He is a *painter/fence painter*.		
13. The boy is going to eat all the cookies. Now all the cookies have been *eaten*.	eat/ate/eated/et	ate
14. He wanted another cookie, but there weren't *any/any more*.	none/no more	none/no more
15. This horse is big. This horse is *bigger*.	more bigger	more bigger
16. And this horse is the very *biggest*.	most biggest	most biggest
17. Here is a man. Here are two *men/gentlemen*.	mans/mens	mans/mens
18. This man is planting a tree. Here the tree has been *planted*.		
19. This is soap, and these are *soap/bars of soap/more soap*.	soaps	soaps
20. This child has lots of blocks. This child has even *more*.		
21. And this child has the *most*.	mostest	mostest
22. Here is a foot. Here are two *feet*.	foots/feets	foots/feets
23. Here is a sheep. Here are lots of *sheep*.	sheeps	sheeps
24. This cookie is not very good. This cookie is good. This cookie is even *better*.	gooder	gooder
25. And this cookie is the very *best*.	bestest	
26. This man is hanging the picture. Here the picture has been *hung*.	hanged	hanged
27. The thief is stealing the jewels. These are the jewels that he *stole*.	stoled/stealed	stoled/stealed
28. Here is a woman. Here are two *women*.	womans/womens	womans/womens
29. The boy had two bananas. He gave one away and he kept one for *himself*.	hisself	hisself
30. Here is a leaf. Here are two *leaves*.	leafs	leafs
31. Here is a child. Here are three *children*.	childrens	childrens
32. Here is a mouse. Here are two *mice*.	mouses	mouses
33. These children all fell down. He hurt himself, and she hurt herself. They all hurt *themselves*.	theirselves/theirself	theirselves, theyselves, theirself/theyself

palachian English even though the two varieties differ in varying ways from the standard variety of English used as the test norm.

The potential educational effect of the dialect differences is more dramatically revealed when we examine how the raw scores on a test such as the grammatic closure are correlated with "psycholinguistic age norms." Consider the case of a ten-year-old Appalachian English or Black English speaker who applies the rules of his or her home dialect to this task. With a raw score of 8 to 10 correct, the ten-year-old child is diagnosed as having a psycholinguistic age norm of less than five years of age. And the sole basis of this discrepancy was the fact that the child used appropriate dialect forms which the test disallowed. Such a child might be misdiagnosed in terms of reading readiness, language development, and academic potential. Dialect differences, then, can have important implications for a child's educational experience.

With this kind of information in mind, it is easy to see how it might be concluded that the failure to recognize dialect differences can have a harmful effect on a child's educational experience, as was indicated in the decision:

> ... the evidence does clearly establish that unless those instructing in reading recognize (1) the existence of a home language used by children in their own community for much of their nonschool communications, and (2) that this home language may be the cause of the superficial difficulties in speaking standard English, great harm will be done. ... A language barrier develops when teachers, in helping the child switch from the home language ("black English") to standard English, refuse to admit the existence of a language that is the acceptable way of talking in his local community. (p. 36)

The situation we have described here seems to be a general one—one which seems to go beyond Black English in a given locale. The failure to recognize dialect differences in teaching reading can cause the kind of situation described above wherever non-mainstream students use stigmatized dialects of English, whether the dialect be Black English as found in Ann Arbor, Black English in another setting, Appalachian English as found in a rural county of West Virginia, or some other non-mainstream variety of English.

Conclusion

In the final judgment, it was determined that the Ann Arbor School Board had not taken the following steps:

> ... (1) to help the teachers understand the problem; (2) to help provide them with knowledge about the children's use of a "black English" lan-

guage system; and (3) to suggest ways and means of using that knowledge in teaching the students to read. (p. 32)

In essence, the judgment pointed to a gap between sociolinguistic research evidence and educational application. There existed a body of sociolinguistic knowledge with import for the equitable education of non-mainstream children, and the educational system had ignored it. And the failure to apply such a knowledge base had imposed an educational barrier for students who spoke this non-mainstream variety. Despite some sociolinguists who have accepted the challenge to apply their research in an educational setting, and some educators who have taken it upon themselves to use current knowledge of social dialects in the context of their classroom teaching, the gap still persists. In this regard, Ann Arbor is hardly atypical. Similar situations might be detailed for many contexts where Black English is spoken, and important parallels exist for other non-mainstream speaking groups that do not participate in the educational process in an equitable way.

The legal precedent has now been set, as the Ann Arbor School Board was ordered to submit to the court a plan that identified the exact steps to be taken (1) to help the teachers identify children speaking non-mainstream vernacular and (2) to use that knowledge in teaching students how to read standard English. If this kind of information is relevant for educators at Martin Luther King Jr. Elementary School in Ann Arbor, it seems just as relevant for other school settings, including those where Black English is the dominant non-mainstream variety and those where a different non-mainstream variety is in use. Educators in other regions need this kind of information just as much as those in Ann Arbor. The parallels seem too obvious to ignore.

Despite the preceding discussion, I am not calling for a new wave of litigation over the issue of equitable education and non-mainstream dialect speakers. Ultimately, this is an activity in which "losers" and "winners" can become obscured by the time-consuming, costly, embittering process. Hopefully, however, enough school systems will be convinced by the Ann Arbor decision that this is an issue of sufficient magnitude to take it upon themselves to provide the necessary information for teachers. In that way, the time, money, and energy would be invested in assuring that teachers elsewhere have the knowledge base necessary for dealing with dialect diversity in a way that is educationally equitable.

References

Burling, Robbins, *English in Black and White.* New York: Holt, Rinehart and Winston, 1973

Dial, Wylene P. "Folk Speech Is English Too." *Mountain Life and Work* February 1970, pp. 16–18

Fasold, Ralph W. and Walt Wolfram. "Some Linguistic Features of Negro Dialect."
    In Ralph W. Fasold and Roger W. Shuy, eds., *Teaching Standard English in the
    Inner City*. Washington, D.C.: Center for Applied Linguistics, 1970

Joiner, C. W. *Martin Luther King Junior Elementary School Children et al.* vs. *Ann
    Arbor School District Board*: Memorandum Opinion and Order. Detroit,
    Mich., 1979

Kirk, S., J. McCarthy, and W. Kirk. *Illinois Test of Psycholinguistic Abilities*. Ur-
    bana, Ill.: University of Illinois Press, 1968

Mencken, H. L. *The American Language: The Fourth Edition and the Two Supple-
    ments*. Abridged and edited by Raven I. McDavid. New York: Knopf, 1962

Pietras, Thomas P. "Teacher Expectancy Via Language Attitudes: Pygmalion from a
    Sociolinguistic Point of View." *The Journal of the Linguistic Association of the
    Southwest* 2: 105–110, 1977

Shuy, Roger W. and Ralph W. Fasold, eds., *Language Attitudes: Current Trends
    and Perspectives*. Washington, D.C.: Georgetown University Press, 1973

——— and Frederick Williams. "Stereotyped Attitudes of Selected English Dialect
    Communities." In Shuy and Fasold, eds., 1973

———, Joan C. Baratz, and Walt Wolfram. *Sociolinguistic Factors in Speech Iden-
    tification*. NIMH Final Report, Project No. MH 15048-01, 1969

Vaughn-Cooke and Fay Boyd. "Evaluating the Language of Black English Speakers:
    Implications of the Ann Arbor Decision." In Marcia Farr Whiteman, ed.,
    Reactions to Ann Arbor: Vernacular Black English and Education. Arlington,
    Va.: Center for Applied Linguistics, 1980.

Williams, Frederick. "Some Research Notes on Dialect Attitudes and Stereotypes."
    In Shuy and Fasold, 1973

Wolfram, W. *Speech Pathology and Dialect Differences*. (Dialects and Eductational
    Equity Series, 3.) Arlington, Va.: Center for Applied Linguistics, 1979

——— and Donna Christian. *Appalachian Speech*. Arlington, Va.: Center for Ap-
    plied Linguistics, 1976

———. *Dialogue on Dialects*. (Dialects and Educational Equity, 1.) Arlington, Va.:
    Center for Applied Linguistics, 1979

Content Questions

1. As an illustration of how the legal ruling on Black English might also affect other "non-mainstream" varieties, which dialect of English does Wolfram highlight?

2. Contrast the origins that Wolfram gives for Black English and Appalachian English.

3. Was intelligibility between one dialect and another the defining factor
for what counted as a "language barrier" in the Ann Arbor court decision?
Explain.

4. What shapes the perception people have of a particular dialect?

5. What relationship exists between speaking a nonstandard dialect and
having difficulty learning to read?

6. For how many of the thirty-three questions on the ITPA test that Wolfram mentions would the answers potentially be influenced by a child's dialect?

7. If a child uses a nonstandard form in response to a written question, does that indicate that the child has a problem with reading comprehension? Explain.

Questions for Analysis and Discussion

1. Have you ever used any of the features that are identified as characteristic of Appalachian English? If so, what have you used?

2. To what extent do you think prejudice against a particular dialect is shaped by actual inferiority in the linguistic structure or logic of that particular dialect?

3. What kinds of unfavorable consequences for a child could result from a reading assessment that does not distinguish between incorrect responses that result from the child's own dialect and answers that genuinely reflect reading deficiencies?

4. What implications does Wolfram's article have for a teacher with students who speak a nonstandard dialect?

5. Do you believe Wolfram's intent is for children not to receive instruction in standard English? Why or why not?

6. What role has linguistic research had in contributing to a greater understanding of the needs of children who speak nonstandard dialects in the classroom? How might this knowledge contribute to more appropriate teaching approaches?

Applied Linguistics and Language Policy and Planning

Robert B. Kaplan

Robert Kaplan, of the University of Southern California, is internationally respected for his work in language policy and planning. Policy makers in government are often uninformed about the consequences and implications of choices they make regarding the status of languages in communities over which they preside. In the following article, Kaplan discusses the situations in which language policy and planning occur and the issues that must be considered in relation to this important area of applied linguistics. He also suggests some strategies to follow when engaging in language planning.

Introduction

Imagine that a country has newly emerged from an old colonial empire. The individuals responsible for the nurturing of this new polity seek the means to unify a diverse population and to create a "history" that provides some sort of continuity and authenticity over time for the group of people who will now live together within the polity. But the new country is poor—it has limited natural resources, and it was constrained in its rate of modernization under the older regime. Thus, the new entity has an overwhelming need for education at all levels. The leaders believe that the modernization of the economy requires that the population be literate. It gradually becomes clear that the one device that can accomplish the objectives of unity, authenticity, and modernization is a national language. But the choice of a single language is complex, for a number of different languages are spoken by the citizens of the new country. Although one language is spoken by the largest number of people, the speakers of that language constitute only 40 percent of the total population, and, because they were a favored group under the colonial regime, they are not very popular. Many of the other languages widely spoken in the new country have no written form. The language of the particular colonial state itself might, of course, be chosen, but that language does not really contribute to the authenticity of the new polity. The leaders of the new polity are faced with a genuine language problem. This language problem requires some sort of solution.

Such a scenario is not uncommon, particularly since the 1960s when so many newly nonaligned countries achieved independence, and along with it the need to address a host of developmental problems. Looking back, it is clear that language policy and planning were issues widely recognized as deserving attention; it is equally clear that early efforts at such policy and planning were for the most part rather unsuccessful. In the decades intervening between the golden positivism of the language-planning experts and consultants of the 1960s and the more cautious policy/planning undertakings in the 1990s, it is possible to outline important principles of language-planning projects from around the world, and that represent an accumulation of trial and error knowledge on language policy and planning. Perhaps foremost among these slowly acquired principles is an organizational approach to language planning as an operational systems-design problem, one that begins with the basic questions: Who does what for whom? How is it done? And why is it done?

What Is Language Planning?

Generally speaking, a language problem occurs whenever there is linguistic discontinuity between segments of a population that are in contact. Such a discontinuity, of course, affects individuals as well as whole populations. A language policy recognizes the existence of such a discontinuity and proposes a principled solution to the discontinuity. A language plan is the vehicle for implementing a language policy; it tries to solve the problem by dealing with the individuals involved. In order to be effective, a language plan has to make it explicitly clear that adopting some other language behavior than that already practiced brings some palpable benefit to the individuals involved. If a language plan fails to recognize this relationship, it cannot succeed. Unfortunately, language plans tend to be couched in fairly altruistic terms; e.g., there is a tendency to try to motivate children to learn another language by telling them that doing so is somehow good for them. But an activity that promises a vague good in the distant future is not motivating. There is the additional problem of the level at which a plan originates and that at which it gets implemented. As in other areas, a plan may occur in a top-down fashion or in a bottom-up fashion; that is, a plan may be conceived by government as being good for the people and subsequently mandated downward to the individual, or a plan may be conceived at the level of an affected community, and subsequently government may be asked to help with it. It is difficult to generalize about the most successful approach, but if indeed the success of a policy depends upon its ability to deliver palpable benefits to individuals, it seems likely that bottom-up plans have a greater probability of success.

What Are Language Problems?

The above example illustrates one kind of situation in which language problems arise, but language problems may result from a vast variety of real-world events. For example, when one country invades another and occupies it, a language problem arises. When war, economic pressure, famine, or the weather create dislocations of populations, a language problem arises. When a particular in-group wishes to exclude a particular out-group in an existing polity, a language problem arises. The history of the world provides a vast range of examples. Using only contemporary history, one can point to countries like the Philippines, or Cameroon, or India after the Raj, as examples of the type of situation in which a national language had to be identified. The worldwide dispersal of Indo-Chinese refugees constitutes another kind of example—one in which the war-caused dislocation of large populations from Cambodia, Laos, and Vietnam has created language problems in Hong Kong, New Zealand, and the United States. A similar problem exists in the Southwest of the United States as the result of an influx of refugees from wars in Central America or from economic hardship in Mexico. The situation in Canada, where French-speaking Canadians reacted against domination by English speakers and have in fact reversed the language situation, so that, at least in Quebec, French speakers have dominance over English speakers, is an example of an in-group wishing to exercise some control over an out-group. When Japan invaded and occupied Taiwan, Malaysia, and Indonesia in the 1940s, a language problem was created there, and when the Nationalist government of China occupied Taiwan in the late 1940s, a different language problem was created. When the government of the People's Republic of China decided to choose Mandarin as the official language of China, a language problem was created, and when the same government changed its designation of first foreign language from Russian to English, a different language problem was created. When the newly emerged polity known as Israel elected Hebrew as its official language, a language problem was created. And the so-called English-only movement in the United States (cf. Judd) is creating a new language problem. There is a perception that language problems of the sort described here are all phenomena of the twentieth century. It has been claimed that the language problems of newly emerging nations are severe in part because these new nations are attempting to achieve in a decade what has evolved (implying accidental change) in nations with long histories over centuries. Neither claim is entirely true. Language problems have existed throughout recorded history, and the evolution of languages in nations with long histories was not as smooth as it appears in retrospect. In countries such as Spain and France, for example, where, respectively, Spanish and French are perceived to be long-established national languages, some groups are in revolt because, even now, they do not accept the domination of the national language. In Spain, the Basque people, and to some extent the Catalonian people, do not accept Spanish as their language and are demanding the recognition of their own languages in various sectors of the society, principally in schools. Only now are Catalonians being allowed to introduce their first language into the school systems of northeast Spain.

In France, where some Basque people also reside, there is a replication of the situation in Spain, though perhaps on an even greater scale. The Breton people are unhappy about the domination of their language by French. The speakers of Provençal and langue d'oc are unhappy about the imposition of northern metropolitan (standard) French in their southern regions. The Alsatian people are equally unhappy about the domination of their French/German dialect by French. In a country where over half the population were not speakers of standard French as late as the beginning of the twentieth century, the policy of the government has consistently been to develop the standard metropolitan variety of French at the expense of all other languages and French dialects. As late as the 1960s and 1970s, the language policy of the French government was one of brutal suppression of minority languages and dialects.

In Great Britain, there are ongoing efforts to maintain Welsh and Scots as living languages, though already in Great Britain Cornish and Manx have been lost, and Irish Gaelic is faltering despite heroic efforts by some concerned Irish scholars to reinvigorate it. In Soviet Azerbaizhan there is evidence that the Turkish minority is at present being victimized; again, this is not a new problem, but one based on an old migration. These are not twentieth-century problems; their roots lie far back in history.

What Are Language Questions?

The range of questions that can be addressed is vast. One set of questions deals with language preservation as the goal of language academies around the world (cf. language maintenance, which is primarily concerned with the preservation of minority languages/dialects). Much more is, of course, at issue. Perhaps by considering a few examples, one can determine the scope of language-policy activity. When the newly emerged state of Israel elected, for purposes of authenticity and unification, Hebrew as its official language, it was faced with a language which, though having a long written history, had become restricted in use largely to ritual functions. It was necessary to modernize Hebrew; to create within it whole new ranges of vocabulary, for example, to permit discussion of contemporary topics never dreamt of in classical Hebrew; to create mechanisms to permit the use of Hebrew in government, in auto mechanics, in the army, in banking, and so on. Some of the efforts were successful; some were not. In registers where a perfectly good non-Hebrew lexicon existed and was in common use among practitioners, the newly created Hebrew lexicon simply did not take hold (Hofman 1974a, 1974b). Similar problems were faced in Malaysia and Indonesia, as the language academies in those countries struggled to invent a greater lexicon in Bahasa Malaysia and Bahasa Indonesia to permit science and technology to be taught in those languages. In Japan, the problem was somewhat different; it was to permit the controlled entry of foreign lexicon into Japanese as the need for new lexicon in certain registers arose, and to control the way in which those new terms were written in the various orthographies of Japanese. In Japan, then, it was possible to make conscious decisions about areas that needed enhancement and to increase the influx in some registers and restrict it in others.

Language policy is not, however, only concerned with lexical development. In the Philippines, for example, where the population speaks some 250 languages, it was a political necessity to identify a national language. The 1976 constitution of the Philippines is a rather remarkable document; it recognizes a number of languages as having a certain status; e.g., Filipino and English are to be used for all official purposes (government documents, etc.), but a number of other Philippine languages (e.g., Ilocano, Cebuano, etc.) are recognized as having important status, and a number of smaller languages are recognized as simply existing. In addition, this constitution mandates as a national language a fiction—a language that does not exist. A language which, the drafters of the constitution believed, would come into existence over time—an amalgam of the languages of the Philippines—and which would be known as Filipino, was mandated as the national language.

This brief summary of language questions begins to suggest the range that may be subsumed under language policy and planning—the sorts of questions dealing with real-world problems that may be addressed. There are, of course, other kinds of issues that provide substance for planning and policy development.

Literacy, Numeracy, and Computer Literacy

In recent years there has been, both in developed and in developing countries, a great concern about literacy. In the minds of many people, literacy is equated with education, with intelligence, and with the notion of modernization and technical development. There are, of course, important questions to be asked in the context of literacy. Obviously, the first question is: "Literacy in what?" The answers to this question are not as obvious as they seem initially. In countries recently emerged out from colonial empires, there is a high probability that whatever literacy exists in the population is in the colonial language. When the colonial language is not chosen as the national language, some problems are created. In any circumstance, literacy implies that there is something to read; in languages recently elevated to prominence (or indeed, recently provided with an orthography), there is not likely to be anything to read. (That fact has created circumstances in which literacy painfully learned is rapidly lost because it has no significant function.)

There are other circumstances in which the written form of the language does not have a high intercorrelation with the spoken language. Written Chinese, for example, is not closely affiliated with many of the spoken varieties of China, and it has been observed that Cantonese-speaking children in Hong Kong attending English-medium schools are being asked to become trilingual: to control spoken Cantonese, written standard Chinese (which does not have a close affinity with spoken Cantonese), and English in both oral and written form. The nature of written Chinese simply complicates the problem; it has been observed that one must control seven or eight thousand characters to be considered really literate in Chinese and, as a consequence, staying literate in Chinese is like training for a boxing match.

But the issue of Chinese literacy raises an important additional question: "What does it mean to be literate?" Early definitions of literacy (e.g., those employed by UNESCO in the 1950s) tend to be fairly modest in their requirement, while the popular notion of literacy—usually the ability to read belletristic materials and to write letters, memos, and even books like this one—implies a very different standard. As the world has become more technologized, and as the quantity of available written material has increased at astonishing rates, the definition of literacy has changed. Furthermore, to what extent are literacy and numeracy intertwined? Is it a part of functional literacy to be able to read and manipulate numbers at some level? In the very recent past, developed societies have begun to discuss, in addition, something that has come to be called *computer literacy*. Is it reasonable to expect every high-school graduate to be able to manipulate numbers to a relatively high level of sophistication, to be able to decipher virtually any use of written text employing natural language, and also to be able to decipher and create text in computer languages? And is it further reasonable to expect the student to be able to do at least the first two kinds of activity in more than one natural language? These questions in turn raise important questions about the limits of human ability.

Given the preceding sample of various kinds of language-policy issues, it is necessary to introduce some sort of order into the activity. The sheer number and variety of issues is overwhelming. Without some sort of order—some system—the process would quickly become unmanageable. One way of introducing order is to categorize problems in some convenient way. One such categorization separates, at least formally, linguistic from political problems.

Corpus and Status Planning

Planning may occur either in a linguistic mode or in a political mode or both. Corpus planning is concerned with planning the language itself; that is, it deals with such issues as reaching standardization on questions of pronunciation, arriving at a means to represent the language orthographically (if it is not already so represented), arriving at an agreement on standardization of spelling, morphology, and grammar, and preparing and disseminating dictionaries and pedagogic grammars. Corpus planning begins with the current state of the language; to the extent that consensus already exists about the form of the language, that consensus constitutes the starting point for corpus planning. When, for example, it was determined that Bahasa Malaysia should be "modernized" (to allow that traditional language to deal with modernization-related subjects, e.g., science and technology), a principal function of corpus planning became the creation of new Bahasa Malaysia terminology to permit discussion of science and technology and, subsequently, the compilation and dissemination of dictionaries containing that new lexicon. The development of new terms in turn created morphological problems that needed attention (e.g., appropriate pluralization rules for the new terms).

Status planning is, on the other hand, frankly political; it has to do with "selling" new (or standardized) forms of a language to the language community. When Singapore decided to use Mandarin as the only standard and official variety of Chinese, it was necessary to persuade the Chinese-speaking community to accept that decision. That, in turn, required some understanding of the ways in which various dialects of Chinese were being used. Once understanding of the uses of different dialects of Chinese was understood, it became possible to devise a plan to encourage the Chinese-speaking community to switch to Mandarin. Such a plan requires the articulation of a set of reasons for changing and a set of rewards that would encourage the shift. (In some conditions, a set of sanctions may be imposed on those unwilling to make the shift.) Status planning receives by far the greatest amount of attention, and it is often a decision to create a status change that drives corpus planning. Like corpus planning, status planning requires research both to understand the existing situation and to rationalize a set of strategies that will enhance (or expedite) the desired change.

Both activities take a lot of time, require substantial investment, and necessitate constant back-checking to ascertain that the moves being made are in fact having the desired effect in the target population. Both activities are, in themselves, inadequate to ensure moderately rapid language change, in the sense that it takes more than a grammar text and a dictionary, and more than planned change to modify the behavior of a language community. Both corpus and status change must at some point result in planned enrichment; that is, lexicons must be available for all sorts of communication purposes; grammars must be available for all sorts of registers; and a genuine communicative need must exist. Once a language can be written, material must be written; a literature has to come into existence. The new language form must be used in the public media and in the educational system. Creating communicative need and disseminating the new form through every possible medium is still a function of status planning, but it is long-term status planning at a very sophisticated level.

In principle, both corpus and status planning are value-neutral; in fact, neither ever is. All of the decisions underlying the inception of status planning are political: to include or exclude some segment of the population from the power structure. To the extent that corpus planning is driven by status planning, it, too, is politicized. Even seemingly value-neutral decisions—e.g., the omission of some language from the inventory of languages to be taught in the official school system, when the omission is a genuine oversight or the result of budgetary (rather than political) considerations—take on value by virtue of being included in a language plan. Because language is so central to human behavior, any language policy, whether the outcome of formal planning or of accident, takes on value at least for those whose existence as a language community is threatened. It is simply a fact that political motivations are not always altruistic; thus a planner may be faced with difficult ethical questions at the (any) point of involvement.

In sum, corpus and status planning are two basic activities underlying all systematic language planning (and some accidental language policy). The former deals with changing the shape of a language, the latter deals with changing the attitudes of speakers toward a language. Corpus planning draws more heavily upon linguistic descriptions; status planning is more clearly political, and it tends to drive corpus planning. Up to this point, the problem of defining language planning has been the focus of discussion. Assuming that language planning can be understood in terms of the illustrations developed in the preceding pages, there is the question of who (or what) undertakes language planning.

Who Does Language Planning?

Governments, typically, determine a policy to solve a problem and then devise a plan to implement that policy. With respect to language problems, one way of proceeding is to articulate a language policy and then devise a set of strategies—a language plan—for the implementation of that policy. But the determination of a policy requires a great deal of information. For example, what languages are spoken by whom in that community? For what purposes are these various languages used; that is, in what language does one pray, get married, buy groceries, vote, get a haircut, buy clothes, get sent to jail, hire a taxi, etc.? What kind of language talent (resources) does the country need for modernization, for regional trade, for international trade, to undertake scientific and technological development, to expand the educational system, to produce newspapers and books that people can (and will) read, to develop a radio/television network? What kind of language talent is already in place—for what languages are there teachers immediately available; how well do teachers control the languages they profess to be able to teach; what literary talent exists, and in what language is literature created? These are by no means all of the questions that ought to be answered.

The reality, of course, is that these questions rarely get asked. The fact is that politicians, not very sophisticated in matters linguistic, make the decisions, and they tend to make those decisions largely with respect to their own individual language loyalties. (Much the same could be said for bilingual-education implementation in many school districts in the United States.) Such decisions may or may not be unpopular, but the extent to which they are unpopular, or merely unimplementable, creates a new set of language problems. And the new set of language problems creates a new set of linguistic questions that must be answered before a policy can be articulated to solve that new set of problems. These various sets of questions are the proper concern of applied linguists, indeed, the solution of such real-world language problems is exactly the kind of work that applied linguists are supposed to do, and language-policy/planning questions are in a sense the prototypical activity of applied linguistics. Of course, as the questions suggest, it is unlikely that any one person can possibly know enough to undertake such an activity. Teams of specialists are normally involved in language-planning activities, teams including (and probably headed by) applied linguists, but also taking advantage of the talents of anthropologists, economists, historians, professional planners, sociologists, and the like. There are, in addition, a number of structures already in place in some language communities which function to make language-policy decisions, some of them very old.

The Role of Language Academies

In the seventeenth and eighteenth centuries, a number of "language academies" sprang up across Europe. The original purpose of these academies was to preserve the purity of the languages over which they had authority and to prevent the perversion of those languages through the use of the languages spoken by uneducated peasants. The best known of the language academies is the Academie Française, but it is by no means the only such body. Language academies have been important shapers of policy throughout Europe, and more recently in the Middle East. In Portugal and Spain, these bodies have also influenced language policies in many Latin American countries and spawned language academies in a number of those countries. In addition, other nations have created their own language academies for various purposes in recent times; examples of these are the academies in Japan and Malaysia.

In the contemporary world, academies continue to strive to maintain the purity of languages, and they serve a pragmatic purpose by compiling dictionaries of the language and by acting as arbiters of correctness in grammar and usage. In Malaysia, the academy has been responsible for the creation of new indigenous lexicons in science and technology to assist in education and modernization. In Japan, the academy has been responsible for sorting out the limitations of the various orthographic systems that constitute written Japanese. Thus, they serve not only to keep languages "pure," but to promulgate rules regarding the "right" use of the language. In a sense, the academies have authenticated private champions of taste in countries where academies do not exist. For example, in the United States there is a long history of individuals who have assumed the role of arbiters of standards and have written (indeed, fulminated) about decaying standards and about the importance of preserving stylistic beauties of the past. After all, a language that has a Shakespeare in its relatively distant history has a great tradition to look back upon.

Other Functionaries in Language Planning

Governments are engaged in language policy and planning in a number of other ways that go beyond the activities of both official and quasi-official language academies. It would perhaps be most useful to distinguish between activities that are externally directed by governmental agencies and offices, and other activities that are internally directed by such policy-creating units. Each type of activity has far-reaching influences in shaping the use and disuse of languages and dialect varieties. In modern times, the externally oriented agencies (both official and quasi-official) are units engaged in a kind of linguistic imperialism through their mission of language dissemination. The internally oriented agencies are more typically engaged in the dissemination of educationally oriented decisions (as in Morocco and Singapore), support for other languages within communities (e.g., minority/majority-language policies in the People's Republic of China and the Soviet Union), and the standardization of scientific and technological terminology and usage to improve production and effectiveness in research and business.

Examples of structures whose principal function is to assist externally with language dissemination are the German Goethe Institute, the British Council, and the Alliance Française. Through branch offices in other countries, they provide language instruction at relatively low cost and offer a variety of other "cultural" services. The United States Information Agency (USIA; locally USIS) is a similar agency, though the language dissemination aspects of its mission do not receive nearly as high a priority. It does offer cultural services, but it does not to any significant degree engage in direct-language teaching, though it does support Binational Centers, which teach English, and provide teachers under the Fulbright-Hayes act, to local institutions that teach English. The government of Saudi Arabia, in the very recent past, without the creation of a special agency, has supported the spread of Islam and has funded Arabic-teaching operations in a number of countries.

Some governments have encouraged the flow of international students into their educational establishments, particularly their tertiary systems.

Students entering the tertiary educational structures of developed countries are expected, as a matter of course, to learn the instructional languages of those countries. Hundreds of thousands of 'foreign students' have, since the end of World War II, learned English in tertiary educational institutions in Australia, Britain, Canada, New Zealand, and the United States; but the English-speaking nations have not really exploited the foreign-policy implications of international student exchange. The Soviet Union and the Federal Republic of Germany have, on the other hand, made explicit use of international students and of the resultant language dissemination as a vehicle of foreign policy. A recent entrant into this sphere of activity is Japan, which seeks to increase its 'foreign-student' population to 100,000 individuals by the end of the century. The preceding discussion suggests that all planning is a conscious activity of agencies of government. That is not the case.

Accidental Language Policy

There are instances in which governments and other organizations (often businesses) create language policy entirely by accident; that is, the functions of certain nonlanguage-related branches of government create implicit policy. An interesting case in point is the U.S. Bureau of Indian Affairs, long a branch of the Department of the Interior. This body (like those bodies in Australia responsible for the lives of Australian aboriginal people or those in New Zealand responsible for the Maori people) inadvertently created policy by establishing schools in which Native American pupils were inhibited from speaking their indigenous languages and were required to learn English. Other examples include the Census Bureau (which until recently has collected information only in English), the Post office (which has delivered mail only in English), the local agencies responsible for elections (which have permitted voting only in English), the local welfare agencies (which have permitted access to benefits only in English), the Department of Commerce (which currently is deeply concerned about what it considers a language-based "technology hemorrhage"), and even the Department of Defense (which expects all personnel to be able to function in English). Some of these practices have been liberalized in the recent past, but implicit language restrictions continue to exist in many governmental policies, and the English-only political movement growing in the United States will only strengthen this bias.

The Role of Religion in Language Planning

The earlier discussion suggests that language policy is a function of government; in contemporary times, it often is, but it is certainly not uniquely the province of government. An important actor in language policy is institutionalized religion. The Roman Catholic Church was, for hundreds of years, responsible for the preservation of Latin as a liturgical language; it was a conscious decision by the Church, in quite recent times, to abandon Latin in favor of vernacular languages. Both the decision to maintain Latin and the decision to abandon it in favor of vernacular languages are language-policy decisions. The preservation of liturgical Greek in the Greek Orthodox Church is another similar example, and the spread of Classical Arabic in relation to the spread of Islam is perhaps the most apparent example. But various institutionalized religions have also played major roles in relation to other languages as well. For example, as sub-Saharan Africa was colonized by European powers, one of the major subsidiary activities of colonization was the spread of religion by missionaries. In a relatively short time after initial colonization, in many areas of Africa, the missionary groups became largely or exclusively responsible for education. There was a major difference in the language attitudes of Protestant missionary groups from those of Roman Catholic missionary groups. Many Protestant faiths take as an article of faith the notion that personal salvation can be achieved through direct access to the Gospels; the Roman Catholic Church does not share this belief. As a result, Protestant missionary groups were (and continue to be) responsible for the translation of the Gospels into vernacular languages—an activity that sometimes has required the development of an orthography.

In many instances, it was the Bible translators who were initially responsible for the creation of orthographies in vernacular languages, and it was through the availability of the Bible in vernacular languages that those languages were preserved, were made languages of education, and eventually became candidates for national or official status in emerging nations. The work of the Summer Institute of Linguistics (SIL) is an important example. The SIL, a function of the Wycliff Bible Translators, has done significant work in linguistics in the description of little known vernaculars. The Church of Jesus Christ of Latter-day Saints (LDS; Mormons) has had an equally important function through its Bible Translating Mission. The Roman Catholic Church has not engaged widely in such activities, but has, on the other hand, played a powerful role not only in the preservation of liturgical Latin but in the spread of colonial languages (e.g., French, Portuguese, and Spanish) because of the language loyalty of the clergy doing missionary work in various colonial areas. As institutionalized religious bodies have selected certain languages for use (and therefore preservation and/or dissemination), they have deselected other languages; an interesting example of deselection is the resistance of some missionary groups to the spread of Swahili on the grounds that Swahili is affiliated with Islam.

Private Efforts in Language Policy

It is, however, not only through such formal structures that language problems are attacked on a large scale. There are a number of nongovernmental entities, made up of individuals dedicated to the presumed beauties of some language, which are to greater or lesser degrees engaged in actively disseminating a particular language beyond its normal sphere of influence; an example of such a group is the English-Speaking Union. It has branches in most English-speaking countries and has the stated objective of promoting the use of English through scholarships to study in English-speaking countries, through book donation programs, and through a variety of other mechanisms. A new phenomenon in language activity has arisen through the emergence in the late twentieth century of multinational corporations. Such organizations maintain operations in many countries, and, precisely because they have linguistically diverse employee pools, these organizations have internal language policies that define what language is spoken within the corporation, what proficiency in what language and to what degree can make an individual eligible for senior-management status, and what languages are used for doing business in what context. Such organizations are also responsible for the international sale of hardware—e.g., airplanes, ships, etc.—that brings with it maintenance manuals usually written in the language of the country of origin (or in some cases in the official language of the corporation) and that creates a language problem related to the maintenance of that expensive hardware. In multilingual nations, advertisers have begun to be concerned with choosing an appropriate language for advertising particular products in minority areas; at the present time, advertising agencies in the southwestern part of the United States are spending significant sums of money to determine whether Hispanic populations can be addressed most effectively in standard English, standard Spanish, or a nonstandard variety of either.

Science and Technology in Language Policy

In the contemporary world, perhaps the single most important area of language activity is that of science and technology. It is a fact that academic disciplines, particularly in the hard sciences and engineering, have been responsible for language dissemination and for language policy. Disciplines sometimes have internal "language academies" that agree on the standardization of terminology for the things a particular discipline talks about. (This standardization also occurs in global functions, e.g., global maritime navigation and the global operation of commercial aircraft.) The key journals in each field take on important gatekeeping functions, since they determine in what language scholarly work may be published, and, even more important, they determine the conventions of presentation. The role of English in these contexts cannot be underestimated. At the end of World War II, a number of interesting accidents co-occurred to ensure the hegemony of English in the areas of science and technology: first, the United States was the only major industrialized nation to emerge from the war with its industrial and educational infrastructures completely intact and booming as a result of the war effort; second, the United States and Britain were on the winning side, and when the new international bodies (e.g., the UN,

UNESCO, etc.) came into being, the United States and Britain had a voice not only in the way these bodies would be structured and would function, but also about the languages in which they would function. There is a truism in science, which of necessity is cumulative in its activities (that is, all new science depends on all previous science), that those who contribute most new information are also, of necessity, those who most use the information resources, and those who most use and most contribute to information networks come to own them. Thus, it is not merely the case that, according to the Fédération Internationale de Documentation (FID), 85 percent of all the scientific and technical information available in the world today is either written or abstracted in English, but it is also the case that the information in the world's great information-storage and -retrieval networks is coded under an English-based sociology of knowledge, and the key terms used to access the system are English terms.

Language-in-Education Planning

So far, the discussion has involved to some extent organizations and agencies that are aimed outward; that is, they are to some extent concerned with the dissemination of languages beyond the areas in which those languages have cultural significance. In every polity, of course, there are also bodies concerned with the promulgation of the indigenous (official, national) language among the citizens of that polity. These responsibilities typically fall to the education sector. Not only does the education sector determine the way in which the national or official language will be taught; it also determines the amount of time that will be devoted to national-language instruction in the curriculum (which, after all, has finite limits because children can only be required to go to school so many hours per day, so many days per week, so many weeks per year). More important, the education sector also determines what other languages will be included in the curriculum, how they will be taught, and what fraction of the curricular day will be devoted to the learning of those other languages; a corollary of this function is the implicit right to determine what and who will *not* be taught. The area under discussion here is called *language-in-education planning,* and this entire area is discussed at length by Judd.

How Does One Do Language Planning?

Although it is true that the various bodies (governmental or not) involved in making language-policy decisions do not often turn to applied linguists for information on which to base those decisions, from time to time they have. Given that applied linguists have been involved, what precisely is it that they can do in such an environment? In order to deal with questions about language distribution and language use in communities, applied linguists have undertaken language-situation analyses through surveys. Language-use surveys attempt to establish who uses what language, for what purpose, under what circumstances in a given community. Basically, a language-use survey involves a number of steps that can be classified into three groups:

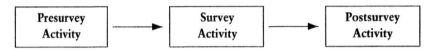

Presurvey

These activities fall basically into three categories: background research, instrument planning, and team training. For background research, obviously, it is necessary to have some sense of the language situation to the extent that information is available. That requires doing background reading about the area, its culture, the ethnic groups who live there, and so on; but it also involves talking with as many people as possible who are in a position to be helpful; that group would include academic linguists and anthropologists who are at the time working (or have in the past worked) in the area, but it would also include individuals in the media, government officials, and others who are likely to have an overview of the situation. The information gathered in this way must be systematized, recorded, and analyzed; it will be used in shaping the survey instrument.

Survey work involves collecting data from a large population and therefore requires instrument planning. In order to collect data, one must decide not only upon what information to collect, but also upon the sorts of collection devices to be employed. It is sometimes convenient to use a written instrument, but obviously the use of such a form depends on the distribution of literacy in the population; if large segments of the population are not literate, written collection will not do, although it may be used among some segments of the population (e.g., government officials, teachers, etc.). If a written survey is to be used with any segment of the population, it is necessary to determine how the instrument will be distributed and collected; e.g., will it be mailed to respondents, and if so are the mails dependable, are the respondents likely to return the form, etc.? Or will it be handed out to the respondents in some convenient setting, and if so what setting? How will the survey-team members be sure that respondents fill out the form and do their own work rather than simply copying from some perceived leader in the group? And how will the instrument be retrieved? More important, if a written survey is to be used, what language will it be in? What variety of that language? Are there enough people in the survey team who can read and write that language to make such collection effective? How will the team be certain that the questions collect the desired information (since semantic variability can make nonsense of a question)?

If a survey must be conducted orally, what segment of the population can be surveyed, under what social circumstances? What numbers of surveyors will be required to conduct the oral interviews? Are trained surveyors available or will it be necessary to recruit and train an essentially naive group? What safeguards can be built into the system to assure that surveyors are asking the right questions in the right order, are recording their findings accurately, etc.? Whether the survey is oral or written, can the instrument be structured in such a way as to facilitate data entry into some computer system? What system is available? Where is it physically located? How accessible is it? How secure is it? What will it cost to use it? What is the anticipated turnaround time for data analysis? Whatever sort of survey collection is chosen, it will be necessary to design a sample instrument and to try out that instrument on a sample population, making corrections and modifications on the basis of the trial data.

Team training depends upon a number of decisions deriving from the background check and the instrument design. In the first instance, before any work can be undertaken (even the background research), it is necessary to assemble the basic team. That is accomplished on the basis of the questions to be answered by the survey. Any team is likely to require members other than applied linguists. Once a basic team is assembled, and the team members understand the objectives of the survey task and the real-world constraints upon it, the background research can be undertaken, and once the background research has been accomplished, it is possible to begin to design the data-collection process, including the design and field testing of any data-collection instruments to be used. To the extent that the members of the basic team do not speak the local language(s), it will be necessary to augment the team with local specialists who can interview government officials, media people, and business leaders. These individuals need to be oriented to the project and trained in the method of conducting such interviews. Once instrument design is under way, it will be necessary to add translators sufficiently bilingual to be able to deal with the nuances of questions to be asked. The translators should be able to tell the team whether certain kinds of questions cannot be asked (that is, whether certain topics are taboo); how questions can be phrased in order to elicit reasonable answers; and how certain lexical items that may not have equivalences in the local language(s) can be dealt with. At the same time, it will be necessary to understand local experience with surveys in order to answer such questions as: How long (in time) can an oral interview be? What is the most likely site for an interview (e.g., in people's homes, in the marketplace, or in gathering places like bars or barbershops—and who is likely to gather in such places)? Can men and women be interviewed simultaneously? Where and under what circumstances can children be approached? If a written instrument is employed, how many questions can reasonably be asked? Can such techniques as semantic differential be employed?

Regardless of the type of survey to be used, it will be necessary to determine how large a segment of the population will be sampled. If field workers will be used, then, to distribute a written questionnaire or to administer an oral interview, such people will need to be recruited and trained. The overall timeline of the survey process will need to be calculated to permit for the time necessary to these recruitment and training activities. Care will need to be taken to assure that survey workers are paid a reasonable salary according to the standards of the local economy, and that they are employed for a sufficient period of time to permit both training and survey work. It is important that field workers be debriefed after the survey fieldwork to discover any problems they may have encountered and to get a sense of the cooperation of subjects. The instrument(s) will need to be field tested, and—once assumed to be ready—will need to be produced in sufficient quantity. If instruments are mailed, time must be allocated to permit delivery and return, and it is likely that at least one reminder will have to be sent to recalcitrant subjects. The completion of these and other steps will lead to the survey itself.

The Survey

The survey process consists essentially of the data-collection process. Data collection may go on simultaneously in several different ways; that is, if a written questionnaire is to be used among literate segments of the population, distribution of that questionnaire can go on at the same time that oral interviewing of other segments of the population is occurring. Oral interviewing may take different forms; e.g., one group of interviewers may be working with "the man in the street," collecting data in people's homes, or in the marketplace, or wherever, while another group of fieldworkers (perhaps the members of the basic team) may be conducting interviews of various government officials (in the ministries of education, tourism, communication, foreign affairs, and commerce, in the military, etc.), of the police and representatives of the judicial and social-welfare systems, of those people responsible for national census data, of postal officials, of religious leaders, of leaders in the business community (including advertisers), and of other segments of the community where there are stated or implied language concerns. As information is received, it can be entered for computer analysis. As information is entered, it will need to be checked for accuracy and completeness. It is possible that, in the actual process of data collection, some hole in the database may be discovered; should that be the case, it will be necessary to devise a strategy to collect the missing data. The actual survey process is the most mechanical portion of the activity, but it cannot be assumed that it will run smoothly simply because it is mechanical.

Feedback loops need to be built into the system that will permit correction of the process at any time. For example, data entry may demonstrate that some single fieldworker (or some group of fieldworkers) appears to be encountering extraordinary difficulty; the cause of the difficulty needs to be determined, and corrective measures taken. It is possible that an entire process (e.g., a written questionnaire, a section of the oral interview) may be found not to be functioning properly; such a discovery requires corrective action even if such action necessitates redoing the questionnaire or some portion of it.

The survey stage may be said to be completed when all of the anticipated data have been collected and entered for analysis and when all of the entries have been reviewed for accuracy and completeness. One set of data that is collected right at the end of the process, but which is crucial to the process, is that deriving from the debriefing of fieldworkers. Information from that debriefing, too, needs to be quantified and entered. The last stages of the survey process involve making determinations concerning the statistical procedures that will be employed in data analysis. Presumably, that determination has been made early in the process and assumptions about statistical analyses have governed the design of the collection instruments. What occurs at this stage is a final check to be certain that the data is in a format such that the desired statistical procedures can be undertaken. If it is found that data is not appropriately entered, again, corrective measures need to be taken.

The Postsurvey Process

The postsurvey process can also be divided into three stages: data analysis; determination of recommendations, report writing, and report dissemination; and policy formation and implementation. Data analysis is exactly what the name implies; that is, the various preplanned statistical procedures are applied, correlations are developed, and the raw data is converted into a form that will have meaning. The basic team members must understand the data and must be able to perceive what the data suggest. As the data set is developed, it is important to use the knowledge of local experts in trying to understand the implications of the information that has been gathered. To put it in a slightly different way, the information gathered needs to be understood in terms of the local situation.

Determination of recommendations, report writing, and dissemination are done by the team as a whole. Once the data have been carefully analyzed, the members of the team can begin formulating recommendations. The recommendations, while they must be applicable to the local situation, should bring to bear on the local situation parallel experience of which the members of the team are aware. Each recommendation must be tested with local people to determine whether it is feasible and at least potentially implementable in the local environment. There is no point in making a recommendation that will never be implemented; for example, if it is perceived that a local examination used to screen applicants to tertiary educational institutions is faulty, but it is known that the ministry of education is completely committed to the use of such an instrument for political and social reasons, it makes no sense to recommend the abolition of the instrument, but it may make some sense to suggest incremental modification.

As the various interpretations of the information collected and the various recommendations take shape, a formal report needs to be assembled. There arises the question of the language in which the report will be written; presumably, the initial contract will state the language in which the report is to be submitted, but it is useful to prepare the report bilingually. Preparing a two-language version of the report helps to assure that the report is accurate, and it provides a version the researchers can take away with them (assuming that the language in which the report is submitted is not the same as the native language of the team members).

The report and recommendations need to be confirmed informally with as many appropriate officers of government as possible while the report is being written. Indeed, by the time the formal report is submitted, it should contain no surprises; everyone concerned ought to be aware of precisely what the report has found the language situation to be, and of precisely what recommendations the report will offer.

The final report should be neatly printed and bound and, on a set date, simultaneously submitted to as many persons as possible. It is desirable to have some announcement of the availability of the report in the local media, and it is equally desirable to announce the existence of the report simultaneously in the professional journals. In making the submission, the basic team should indicate its willingness to answer questions about the report, but it should at the same time be fully prepared to disperse; in effect, once the report has been submitted, the work of the research team is finished. The purpose of a study and report is to provide information on the basis of which action can be taken; the work of the team is academic. Once the report is received, the conversion of the information and recommendations into action is a political process that is fully the responsibility of local authorities; the academic team should play no part in that process.

It is, however, appropriate for the report to include a section dealing with potential implementations, the policy-formation and -implementation recommendations. The members of the team will certainly have some thoughts on the staging of implementation, and it is important to build into the system feedback loops that will permit correction in the implementation process as the implications of various actions unfold over time.

It is sometimes the case that a report may be ignored by the government or governmental agency concerned. When that happens, it may be due to the fact that the report contains surprises—recommendations not anticipated by its recipients, or recommendations that are blocked by political or financial considerations. Proper review of recommendations in advance of the completion of the report will help to allay this problem. But it is also possible that, with the best of intentions on all sides, the government may be paralyzed by the magnitude of the task or by ignorance of how to proceed. When it is anticipated that such problems may be present in the environment, it is entirely appropriate that the report contain suggestions on the point at which implementation may begin, on the rate at which implementation may proceed, and on the sequencing of various stages in the process. Such discussion in the report probably should not seem to tell the government what to do, but rather should be couched as a number of alternatives available to the government as it moves to turn a team report into a viable plan, and the plan into a set of implementation stages.

A strategy that may be suggested as part of the report is the convening of an invitational conference, colloquium, or seminar at some point relatively early in the implementation process. Such a structure will permit some or all of the members of the team to return during implementation, and it will permit other language-planning experts to be invited to look at the report in a formal way, as well as look at the unfolding implementation process.

Why Language Policy and Planning Is Done

Aside from these rather basic questions, there are other sorts of issues that motivate language planning. Most of the illustrations discussed above deal with the question of identifying a national language within a polity for purposes of authentication, unification, and modernization. But language-policy issues may be motivated by political and economic considerations as well. For example, in 1987 Australia enacted a National Language Policy. To a large degree, that policy is economically motivated, stressing policies that promote languages of trading partners, and it is only partially directed to solving internal language problems (e.g., providing access to speakers of minority languages, to hard-of-hearing persons, and so on). It is significantly motivated by the recognition that Australia's primary trading neighbors are not the states of the European Economic Community, where French and German might be useful, but its neighboring states, where such languages as Chinese, Indonesian, Japanese, and Korean are spoken.

To some extent, the Australian policy takes account of certain internal economic and political issues. There is evidence that the highest arrest rates and conviction rates lie among certain linguistic minorities, and there is also evidence that the greatest draw upon social-welfare services originates in those same linguistic minorities. In order to reduce the societal costs imposed on the welfare system and to the criminal-justice system, certain linguistic minorities need to receive linguistic help; i.e., to have greater access to majority-language functions. There are other examples of polities in which linguistic problems have important economic effects; for example, in some cases, the production and delivery of goods is impeded by the fact that different segments of the process are "owned" by speakers of different languages or different varieties of a language. If, for example, produce is raised on farms whose owners speak one language; the produce is transported to market by a group speaking a different language or variety; and the retail distribution of the goods is in the hands of still a third linguistic minority, the entire process may be impeded.

In still other instances, a severe social problem can be created by differences between the language in which certain services can be delivered and the language of the population most in need of those services. This is most likely to occur in relation to medical services; it is often the case that medical practitioners are trained in a world language, but deliver medical services to populations who do not speak the language in which the medical practitioners were trained. Certainly that is the case in public-service medicine in places like Los Angeles, where medical practitioners are likely to be monolingual speakers of English, while their clients are likely to be speakers of Hmong, Korean, or Spanish. There is some evidence that a similar problem exists in much of sub-Saharan Africa in relation to AIDS. But the problem is certainly not unique to medical practice; it is equally an issue in relation to the law (cf. Maher for a discussion of both problems).

The reasons why language policy and planning are done also point to an important aspect of how, and to what extent applied linguists become involved in language-planning activities. It would be preferable to report that language planners are regularly trained and recruited for such tasks as have been outlined in this chapter; in fact, however, the activity of language policy and planning is much more haphazard. As this section suggests, language policy and planning are most often undertaken for larger political and economic reasons; that being the case, the persons in charge of these activities are most often not applied linguists, but politicians and business executives. And if an applied linguist is called as a consultant to help formulate a plan, the choice of specialist is as much a matter of accident and referral by an unknown third party as it is of seeking out a highly qualified applied linguist specializing in language policy and planning. Of course, such a scenario also means that applied linguists wishing to specialize in language-policy and -planning activities will not find it an easy source of employment unless they are already working for the influential political and economic groups that motivate the policy and planning activities in the first place.

Conclusion

The process of information gathering, surveying, and policy creating in language planning as described in this chapter is, as noted early in this chapter, the prototypical activity of applied linguistics. In the course of doing a language survey within a language-planning context, a whole range of applied-linguistic activities are employed. Questions about who uses what language for what purposes under what circumstances in a particular linguistic situation—the basic research interests of applied linguists—are addressed; the tools of the applied linguist are employed to answer these questions (e.g., through written- and oral-use surveys), and the report deriving from that undertaking presumably contains recommendations dealing with applied-linguistic issues: changes in the basic code, modifications of the code in special circumstances (e.g., law, medicine, social-services delivery), and educational questions regarding changes in the code: questions of first- and second-language acquisition, of literacy, of materials development, of curriculum design, of methodology. If indeed applied linguistics is the application of linguistic and other strategies to the solution of basic real-world language problems, it is all here.

Suggestions for Further Reading

Good overviews of the area are presented in Baldauf and Luke 1989; Cooper 1989; Fasold 1984; Kaplan et al. 1982; and Wardhaugh 1987. Important studies in the field include Beer and Jacobs 1985; Cobarrubias and Fishman 1983; Eastman 1983; Fishman 1972, 1974; Fishman, Ferguson, and Das Gupta 1968; Hagege (3 volumes) 1983; Haugen 1956; Kennedy 1983; Kloss 1977; Rubin and Jernudd 1971; Rubin et al. 1977; Weinreich 1953; and Weinstein 1983. There are a large number of country- or region-specific studies covering, for example, India, the Philippines, Canada, the Arab Middle East, East Asia, Australia, East Africa, Mexico, etc. Two illustrations of this broad genre are Ferguson and Heath 1981; McKay and Wong 1988.

There are also a number of important journals; e.g., *Language Problems and Language Planning, New Language Planning Newsletter, International Journal of the Sociology of Language,* and *Journal of Multilingual and Multicultural Development.* In addition, there are various edited collections of the work of key figures like Ferguson, Fishman, Haugen, and others.

References

Baldauf, R. and A. Luke (eds.). 1989. *Language planning and education in Australasia and the South Pacific.* Clevedon, Avon: Multilingual Matters.

Beer, W. and J. Jacobs (eds.). 1985. *Language policy and national unity.* Totowa, NJ: Crane Publishing.

Cobarrubias, J. and J. Fishman (eds.). 1983. *Progress in language planning.* New York: Mouton.

Cooper, R. 1989. *Language planning and social change.* Cambridge: Cambridge University Press.

Eastman, C. 1983. *Language planning: An introduction.* San Francisco: Chandler and Sharp.

Fasold, R. 1984. *The sociolinguistics of society.* New York: Basil Blackwell.

Ferguson, C. and S. Heath (eds.). 1981. *Language in the United States.* New York: Cambridge University Press.

Fishman, J. 1972. "The sociology of language." In P.P. Giglioli (ed.), *Language in social context.* Baltimore, MD: Penguin, 45–58.

Fishman, J. (ed.). 1974. *Advances in language planning.* The Hague: Mouton.

Fishman, J., C. Ferguson, and J. Das Gupta (eds.). 1968. *Language problems of developing nations.* New York: Wiley.

Hagege, C. 1983. *Language reform: History and future.* 3 Vols. Hamburg: Buske Verlag.

Haugen, E. 1956. *Bilingualism in the Americas: A bibliography and research guide.* Tuscaloosa, AL: University of Alabama.

Hofman, J. 1974a. The prediction of success in language planning: The case of chemists in Israel. *Linguistics: An Interdisciplinary Journal of the Language Sciences* 120.39–65.

Hofman, J. 1974b. Predicting the use of Hebrew terms among Israeli psychologists. *Linguistics: An Interdisciplinary Journal of the Language Sciences* 136.53–65.

Judd, E. 1992. Language-in-education policy and planning. In *Introduction to Applied Linguistics.* W. Grabe & R. Kaplan (eds.). Reading, MA: Addison-Wesley.

Kaplan, R.B. et al. (eds.). 1980–1990. *Annual review of applied linguistics,* Vols. 1–10. New York: Cambridge University Press.

Kennedy, G. 1983. *Language planning and education policy.* Winchester, MA: George Allen and Unwin.

Kloss, H. 1977. *The American bilingual tradition.* Rowley, MA: Newbury House.

Maher, J. & D. Rokosz. 1992. Language use and the professions. In *Introduction to Applied Linguistics.* W. Grabe & R. Kaplan (eds.). Reading, MA: Addison-Wesley.

McKay, S. and S. Wong (eds.). 1988. *Language diversity: Problem or resource?* New York: Newbury House.

Rubin, J. and B. Jernudd (eds.). 1971. *Can languages be planned?* Honolulu, HI: University of Hawaii Press.

Rubin, J. et al. (eds.). 1977. *Language planning processes.* The Hague: Mouton.

Wardhaugh, R. 1987. *Languages in competition.* New York: Basil Blackwell.

Weinreich, U. 1953. *Languages in contact.* New York: Linguistic Circle of New York.

Weinstein, B. 1983. *The civic tongue: Political consequences of language choices.* New York: Longman.

Content Questions

1. What does Kaplan say is necessary for a language plan to be effective? Is this more likely to occur with momentum from the top down or bottom up?

2. Provide a couple of examples of social or political events that have resulted in a "language problem."

3. What are some of the issues that must be considered in language policy and planning with regard to literacy?

4. What is the difference between corpus planning and status planning?

5. What kind of organization might try to control the "purity" of a language? Does the United States or England have this kind of organization?

6. Besides governments or government agencies, what other types of organizations are involved in language policy and planning?

7. What is the purpose of survey work in language policy and planning?

8. At the end of his article, Kaplan mentions some additional reasons behind language policy measures. Identify what these are.

Questions for Analysis and Discussion

1. Think about all of the issues that Kaplan mentions should be considered when preparing a survey to learn about a particular language situation. What does his discussion show about how carefully a survey should be set up in order to ensure accurate results? Explain.

2. How regularly are linguists included in language planning endeavors? What kinds of problems could linguists help an agency avoid that engages in language policy implementation?

3. What kinds of consequences might a country have to endure if it fails to carefully consider its decisions before implementing a new language policy?

Testimony before the State Legislature on California Proposition 63[*]

Geoffrey Nunberg

Proposition 63 was a measure designed to make English the official language of California. During the time that California was considering this measure, experts testified before the state legislature. One of those experts was Geoffrey Nunberg. The essay below is the actual testimony he gave to the state legislature in 1986. While some may ultimately disagree with his position not to make English the official language, his testimony illustrates the relevance of linguistic study and the insights it can bring to important contemporary issues. The issue has been decided in California, but it will continue to be debated for years to come in various states across the country.

I want to make a few remarks about Proposition 63 from my perspective as a linguist, and in particular as someone who has devoted a lot of time to studying and writing about the English language. I want to concentrate on making two points. First, measures like Proposition 63 fly in the face of everything we have learned about the processes of language shift and acculturation. And second, Proposition 63 demeans some of the basic traditions of the English-speaking world. I do not think it would be going too far to say that the U.S. English movement represents a greater threat to the English language than any group of immigrants could possibly pose.

I will start with the lessons of history. It is beyond doubt that people will learn a new language when they perceive the economic and social advantages of doing so. And if they do not want to change to a new language, legal measures are not going to do any good. Let me give you some examples. In Spain, Franco banned the use of Catalan, the language of the area around Barcelona, for more than 40 years. By the time of his death, there were more speakers of Catalan than ever before. The Polish language was submerged for two hundred years, but when the Polish state was established after World War I, lo and behold! there was a whole nation still speaking the language. Or you could look at what happened to English after the Norman Conquest, when French was made the language of justice, administration, and literature. For a period of about three hundred years,

---

*Verbatim testimony before the California State Legislature, September 29, 1986. See also Nunberg (1989).

in fact, we have almost no records in English at all—if that were all the evidence there were, you would think that the language had utterly disappeared. It is only when English re-emerges in the fourteenth century that we realize that people had been using it all along. Of course, sometimes you can impose a language in this way, if you go at it hard enough and long enough. For a number of centuries, it was actually illegal to use Gaelic in Ireland. (In fact, the use of Gaelic is restricted to this day in Northern Ireland.) And of course the English finally succeeded in establishing English as a common language in Ireland (Hudson-Edwards 1990). But the imposition of English scarcely resulted in an increased sense of British unity, or of loyalty to the Crown.

Now of course these situations are not like ours, in that people did not want to acquire the language that was being forced on them. But even in situations in which people do want to acquire the new language, we find that attempts to impose it officially invariably backfire. Not only do they wind up creating political turmoil and disunity, but they often actually slow down the spread of the national language. Take the example of the Soviet Union, where Russian is the native language of less than 60 per cent of the population. The use of Russian has been spreading ever since the Revolution, particularly among people who want to rise in the system or the party. But in the 1950s the Soviets began to get worried about the growth of non-Russian minorities, many of whom have much higher birthrates than the Russians do. They said to themselves, "We had better make sure that these people all speak Russian, in the interest of national unity." So they took a number of steps, such as restricting the use of languages other than Russian in higher education in certain republics. The result was that in areas like Soviet Georgia there were mass demonstrations protesting the policy. Now I think you can appreciate that the Soviet Union is not a place where people get together and demonstrate whenever somebody closes a neighborhood school. In fact, the Soviets have had to back off some from their schedule of "russification," as they call it. What they learned is that while people are willing to learn Russian, they do not like being forced to do so.

Or take the case of Sorbian, a Slavic language spoken in Eastern Germany. Hitler was so concerned that the Sorbians should become German-speaking that he actually instituted a policy of requiring Sorbian parents to hire German-speaking maids. When the communists came to power after the war, they discovered that the number of Sorbian speakers had increased. They took a diametrically opposite line on the language—they encouraged the use of Sorbian, and established Sorbian schools. The result was that the use of Sorbian fell off drastically. This might seem surprising, but here again you have to realize that the Sorbians really did want to learn German, but felt compelled to resist the imposition of German from outside.

Now let me turn to English itself. From the eighteenth century on, one thing that has made English almost unique among the major Western languages is that we have had a sharp separation between language and state. The French have an official academy and a society charged with encouraging the use of French abroad, but both the English and later the Americans have explicitly rejected this sort of approach. As the great lexicographer Samuel Johnson put it, any attempt to establish an official basis for the language must be destroyed by "the spirit of a free people." And his American counterpart, Noah Webster, who realized better than anyone else the importance of linguistic unity in forging a single nation, opposed any state interference in matters of language. Instead, these men argued that language use should be a matter of individual choice, precisely because they had faith that citizens would agree on language standards out of their own free will. This was the view adopted by the framers of our Constitution, who debated and rejected proposals to make English an official language (Marshall 1986).

This policy has been vindicated in the face of tests much more severe than anything we face today. We tend to lose sight of the fact that the use of foreign languages was much more common in the nineteenth century than it is now. Bilingual education was common, and the U.S. Commissioner of Education could write in 1870 that "the German language has actually become the second language of our Republic, and a knowledge of German is now considered essential to a finished education." In reaction, certain states tried to impose English by official means, particularly in the early years of this century, when xenophobic sentiment was at a high (often, these measures were coupled with attempts to restrict foreign immigration). In 1923, for example, the Nebraska legislature made it illegal to give instruction to primary-school students in any language other than English, and the law was upheld by the state supreme court, which held that such instruction would "inculcate in [students] the ideas and sentiments alien to the best interests of this country" (Weinstein 1990). Fortunately, the law was overturned by the U.S. Supreme Court on grounds of the Fourteenth Amendment.

Of course, this all seems silly now. The children and grandchildren of earlier immigrants are proficient in English, and the pockets of bilingualism that still exist—among the Pennsylvania Dutch, the Cajuns, or the Finns of Michigan's Upper Peninsula—are the pride of local tourist commissions. And I assure you that fifty years from now, Proposition 63 is going to appear just as absurd as the Nebraska law of 1923. The trouble with movements like the U.S. English group is that they lose sight of the enormous cultural and economic appeal of English, which have made it the most widely-used language in the world, without the help of official support.

Let me sum up my objections to this proposition. When you start to pass laws to protect English, you send off two signals. The first is to speakers of other languages; you tell them, in effect, that they must give up their native tongues. And they react as anyone would; they begin to see the measure as an attack on their group identity, and it becomes a point of pride with them to resist and to keep using their original language. But the second signal is even more pernicious. You say to English speakers: "Our language is not rich enough or strong enough to win speakers on its own; it needs to be bolstered by the full force of state authority" (Zeydel 1964: 345, as quoted in Heath 1981: 13). This is the mark of groups that have lost faith in the power of their language—people like the French and Italians, for example, who have enacted laws to restrict the use of English words in their newspapers. Whereas the wonderful thing about English, and particularly American English, is that we have not felt the need to protéct our language against foreign influences. Take such "all-American words" as *nix, bum, kibitzer, phooey, hoosegow, buckaroo, barbecue, stampede, tycoon, chow, pizza, canoe, skunk,* and *succotash.* What these words have in common is that they have all been taken into English from the languages of immigrants or native American groups. Now I do not know whether Proposition 63 would have the effect of actually preventing the official use of further loan words of this sort. But the important thing is not that, but rather that the "English language" that the proposition purports to protect is actually an amalgam of tongues, and that this enrichment has been possible precisely because English-speakers have had enough confidence in the strength and flexibility of their language to resist the temptation to try to protect it. For the sake of the English language, then, if for nothing else, I urge voters to reject the amendment.

References

Heath, S.B. 1981. English in our language heritage. In *Language in the USA,* ed. C. A. Ferguson and S. B. Heath, 6–20. Cambridge: Cambridge University Press.

Hudson-Edwards, A. 1990. Language policy and linguistic tolerance in Ireland. In *Perspectives on Official English,* ed. K.L. Adams and D.T. Brink, 63–81. Berlin: Mouton de Gruyter.

Marshall, D.F. 1986. The question of an official language: language rights and the English language amendment; Rebuttal. *International Journal of the Sociology of Language* 60: 7–75; 201–211.

Nunberg, G. 1989. Linguists and the official language movement. *Language* 65, 3:579–87.

Weinstein, J. 1990. Is language choice a constitutional right?: Outline of a constitutional analysis. In *Perspectives on Official English,* ed. K.L. Adams and D.T. Brink, 273–79. Berlin: Mouton de Gruyter.

Zeydel, E.H. 1964. The teaching of German in the United States from colonial times to the present. *German Quarterly* 37: 315–92.

Content Questions

1. How successful have most countries been in forcing a language to be adopted by their citizens?

2. What position did Samuel Johnson and Noah Webster take on individual linguistic choice?

3. What law was passed by the Nebraska legislature in 1923? What was the reaction of the U.S. Supreme Court?

4. Identify the two messages that Nunberg says would be sent if we set up laws to "protect" English.

5. How has the English language benefited from foreign language influences?

6. At the end of his testimony, what reason does Nunberg give for suggesting that Californians reject Proposition 63?

Questions for Analysis and Discussion

1. Do you find Nunberg's arguments convincing? Why or why not?

2. What role do you think Nunberg's knowledge of the history of the English language has played in the formulation of his opinion? What examples does he provide in his testimony to support his point?

3. Supporters of an officially designated language sometimes speak in terms of preserving the purity of a language. How would Nunberg react to this argument?

Additional Activities and Paper Topics

1. Consult some books written for small children and comment on the various types of language play in those books that might contribute to phonemic awareness. **(Phonology)**

2. Geoffrey Nunberg reports on some of the disadvantages of having an official language. What might some of the benefits of an official language be? What might some other disadvantages be?

3. Imagine yourself to be a linguistics expert who has been consulted by a university curriculum committee about whether to have a required language or linguistics course as part of teacher training. Prepare a report in which you explain how such a background could be useful for prospective teachers. You might also examine some later chapters of this book, which look at applications of linguistics to composition, literary analysis, and language instruction.

4. With your instructor's permission, tape-record or videotape a class period. Note any particularly interesting discourse interactions. Transcribe some of these and report on what you have observed. Include both your analysis and relevant transcriptions. Your transcriptions in this case will consist of written words (not phonetic or phonemic transcriptions). **(Semantics, Pragmatics, and Discourse Analysis)**

5. Consider the issue of "purifying" a language from foreign borrowings. If our country were to set up a language academy with a goal of removing, for example, all French borrowings from the English language, how extensive would its job be? Consult a sample of entries from the dictionary and report on what you find about the relative numbers of French-based vocabulary. You might also discuss the nature of some of the borrowings that you find. **(Historical Linguistics)**

Linguistics and Composition

The field of composition studies has experienced major changes in the last several decades. It is now widely recognized that the teaching of writing should involve much more than just helping students to correct their grammar, punctuation, and spelling. As composition studies have advanced, linguistic studies, while not always central to that discipline, have nonetheless provided some valuable insights. In this chapter I have included articles indicative of these insights, whether the insights deal with holistic concerns such as tone and rhetorical patterns or more mechanical writing problems such as punctuation.

The first article in this chapter, "Tone as a Function of Presupposition in Technical and Business Writing," by Kathryn Riley and Frank Parker, explains how problems in tone often result from unshared assumptions between a writer and his or her audience. These assumptions are often encoded within presuppositions. Riley and Parker identify some of the linguistic constructions in which presuppositions commonly occur and thus provide information that could help students in making decisions that affect the tone of their writing.

In "Transformational-Generative Syntax and the Teaching of Sentence Mechanics," Rei R. Noguchi shows an unexpected application of Chomsky's well-known linguistic model. Noguchi shows how native speakers' intuitive grammatical knowledge can be utilized to help them in editing fragments, comma splices, subject-verb agreement problems, and so on. Traditional approaches have often required a lot of grammatical explanation to help students avoid such features in their writing. But as Noguchi shows, students can do more with less training.

One situation that composition teachers might face when teaching students from varying cultural backgrounds involves differences in the way the students' own cultures typically organize and present material in their writing. William G. Eggington, in his article "Written Academic Discourse in Korean: Implications for Effective Communication," examines some rhetorical differences between Korean and English and the extent to which these differences can interfere with comprehension and recall among individuals who must read something written in a discourse style that differs from what they commonly use. Eggington's research raises interesting and significant issues about cross-cultural rhetorical differences and what training in one discourse style can mean for people who must communicate in writing with others who do not share that particular style.

Clarity is one of the most important goals in writing, and a large part of achieving clarity is the avoidance of ambiguity. While many individuals are used to thinking of word-meaning ambiguities, structural ambiguities, in which the intended structure of a phrase, clause, or sentence is ambiguous, can present some serious obstacles to the clarity of less experienced writers. In his article "Ambiguity in College Writing: (To a College Freshman)," Norman C. Stageberg identifies some of the major types of structural ambiguity and some strategies for revising or avoiding such structures. His discussion should help students in becoming more aware of how to avoid ambiguity in their own writing.

Often students' native language patterns interfere with their written compositions in a second language. In his article "A Linguistic Frame of Reference for Critiquing Chicano Compositions," Ricardo L. Garcia shows some of the kinds of linguistic interference that bilingual students with a Spanish-speaking background might experience. His article also serves as a cautionary reminder to teachers about how they might approach the critiquing of compositions that show such interference.

The potential contributions of linguistics to composition teaching of course are not limited to what has been shown above. One could look at linguistic research about the degree to which particular lexical and structural patterns are stigmatized and how this would affect the kinds of errors a teacher or intended audience focuses on. Other research has been done on coherence and cohesion. One might also look at the research work done with sentence-combining exercises, which seem to enhance the abilities of less experienced writers to create more syntactically sophisticated sentences. Such exercises of course do not guarantee that students will necessarily have anything significant to say with their more syntactically developed sentences. It is therefore also important for teachers to help their students learn how to develop topics and ideas and to organize these in appropriate ways.

Linguistic tools and research do not by any means represent a panacea for composition teachers. Many of the most important aspects of writing that must be taught by composition teachers may not be easily addressed by current linguistic research. But the field does provide valuable insights for alert and resourceful composition teachers who acquaint themselves with a variety of approaches. This chapter of readings should provide a brief glimpse of some of the kinds of research and strategies that linguistics has provided.

Tone as a Function of Presupposition in Technical and Business Writing

Kathryn Riley and Frank Parker

A skilled writer must consider the effect his or her writing will have on the intended audience. Such a consideration will include attention given to the effective and appropriate uses of tone. But explaining to students about how to distinguish appropriate from inappropriate tone can present a challenge. In the following article, Kathryn Riley, a professor of composition and linguistics at the University of Minnesota, Duluth, and Frank Parker, editor-in-chief of Parlay Press in Superior, Wisconsin, show how linguistic scholarship concerning presuppositions could help in more clearly identifying how to avoid inappropriate tone in writing. Their article, which originally appeared in the *Journal of Technical Writing and Communication,* thus provides some useful and specific applications of linguistic theory to a common problem in writing.

Abstract

Current treatments of tone rely on a hit-list approach in which writers are presented with lists of words to avoid and a few do and don't examples. Such treatments, however, do not constitute a theory of why certain linguistic elements create problems in tone. The linguistic concept of presupposition can be used to construct such a theory. Presuppositions are unstated propositions conveyed by the use of certain linguistic expressions called presupposition triggers. These presupposition triggers may convey the writer's beliefs about the truth of a proposition or the writer's value judgments about a proposition. Many problems in tone can be traced to one of two types of conflict between reader and writer: different beliefs about the truth of an implied proposition, and different attitudes toward a proposition whose truth is agreed upon.

The importance of tone in technical and business writing is indicated by its regular treatment by specialists in these fields. However, despite tone's acknowledged importance, it remains a somewhat poorly understood concept. As we illustrate in more detail below, standard discussions of tone usually consist of a general admonition to "avoid negative language," followed by a list of specific words and phrases to avoid or a few examples of *do and don't* sentences.

453

What this approach suggests is that writing specialists—editors, teachers, and skilled writers—have an intuitive understanding of tone; that is, they are able to identify problems in tone and to resolve them. Yet, on the other hand, there is no clearly articulated theory of the principles that govern tone; that is, of why problems in tone arise. We believe that an understanding of the linguistic principles that affect tone would strengthen research, practice, and pedagogy in technical and business writing.

An analogy from Riley may clarify the benefits of using linguistic principles to explain particular problems in writing [1]. Suppose an ESL student writes the sentence "I may taking physics next year." Any native speaker of English can, intuitively, suggest several ways to correct this sentence: for example, add *be* between *may* and *taking* (to yield "I may be taking physics next year") or change *taking* to *take* (to yield "I may take physics next year"). However, merely correcting this idiosyncratic error will not benefit the student in future writing tasks (unless, of course, the student uses exactly the same sentence again—an unlikely possibility). In order to avoid similar errors in the future, the student needs a set of *principles* for inflecting verb phrases in English, like the following: In an active sentence, the verb following a modal (e.g., *may*) is always uninflected; hence "I may be" or "I may take." The verb following the auxiliary *be* is always the present participle; hence "I may be taking." Given these general principles, the student has not only an explanation for the ungrammaticality of "I may taking physics next year," but also a way of solving similar problems in the future, regardless of the particular sentences in which they occur. In short, then, *correction* is idiosyncratic in that it applies to one particular problem in the past; on the other hand, *principles* are general in that they can be applied to a class of problems in the future.

We believe that the student of professional writing can benefit in a similar way if problems in tone are not just corrected but are also explained in terms of more general principles. For example, suppose a writer uses the following sentence in a job application letter: "When may I come in to see you?" As pointed out by Menning and Wilkinson, this sentence creates an overly presumptuous tone [2, p. 68]. The teacher may recommend revising this sentence to "May I have an interview at your convenience?" or "I would appreciate an interview at your convenience." While these revisions improve the tone, they do not point the writer toward any explicit, principled explanation of the original sentence's problem or of why the revisions alleviate this problem. In professional writing as in ESL, merely correcting isolated sentences leaves the student only with a way to solve past problems, not an understanding of how to recognize, analyze, and solve future ones—thereby perpetuating the *post hoc* task of correction for both student and teacher.

In addition to benefiting teachers and students, an understanding of some of the linguistic principles that govern tone is also of interest to theoreticians in professional communication. Anderson describes the goals of theory development as follows [3, p. 274]:

> Instead of trying to find out *what works best*—on the job or in the class-room—it tries to understand *how* things work. It asks such questions as, "What is a reasonable way of describing what happens when technical information is being communicated?" and "What is a reasonable way of explaining why one communication seems to work better than another?" When trying to select from alternative answers to such questions, the theoretical discipline applies criteria that ask, "Which most satisfactorily explains the phenomena under consideration, at least insofar as we presently understand these phenomena?"

Success in meeting these goals, however, has been limited, according to Anderson. He argues that theoreticians, as well as professionals and teachers, must

> look more actively at work being done outside our disciplines . . . one is tempted to believe that technical communication suffers from a kind of parochialism that prevents it from learning what is happening in other disciplines, such as those that are concerned with other kinds of communication or that look at communication in other ways [3, p. 277].

In short, then, specialists in professional communication have as their goal not only stating *what* works but also explaining *why* it works. One way to achieve this goal is to incorporate research from other disciplines. To this end, we propose that presupposition, a concept developed within logic and linguistics, can be used to refine the study of tone in two ways: first, to construct a partial definition of tone, and second, to identify several classes of linguistic elements that may create problems in tone. The remainder of our discussion works toward these purposes as follows. First, we briefly describe some typical treatments of tone by specialists in professional writing. Second, we offer an alternative treatment of tone, based on the concept of presupposition. Third, we use presupposition theory to identify several general classes of linguistic elements that may create problems in tone and demonstrate how this theory provides a more unified way of analyzing these problems.

Treatments of Tone by Writing Specialists

Two recent bibliographical essays have assessed research on areas related to tone in professional writing, and thus provide a starting point for assessing previous treatments of tone. According to Broadhead, many writing specialists have taken a "hit-list approach" to word choice in technical writing, listing "terms and phrases (whether technical or common) that should not be used" (or, alternatively, "terms and phrases that may be used while unlisted words are avoided") [4, p. 229]. Moran and Moran, in a survey of research on business correspondence, note that "the largest segment of articles on the business letter falls under the general category of 'tips.' Generally concerned with style, structure, and tone, these articles present a surprisingly consistent and redundant body of practical advice that amounts to a kind of folk wisdom based on tradition and blind faith rather than on research" [5, p. 315].

Both Broadhead and Moran and Moran reach similar conclusions about research on style and word choice. Broadhead observes that treatments of style have reflected "the absence of precise, generally adopted definitions" [4, p. 238] and "have only recently begun to draw significantly on theoretical and empirical studies in other fields" [4, p. 217]. Along similar lines, Moran and Moran state that "The majority of extant articles assume that certain principles of sound writing are givens and not deserving of serious research. This attitude has encouraged the research to remain at the level of description and practical advice" [5, p. 336]. More strongly, they state that researchers "have tended either to rely on a kind of folk wisdom handed down from generation to generation of writers or to depend on rather limited personal experience" [5, p. 313]. These criticisms echo those of Anderson, who says that writing specialists are "uncritically accepting a large number of beliefs about teaching technical communications, many of which are highly debatable . . . many of the articles on teaching merely repeat advice already given many times before" [3, p. 275]. In short, evaluations of research in professional writing have noted a uniformity of advice about matters related to tone, despite a widespread lack of evidence to support this advice.

This tendency to espouse commonly agreed-upon, but untested, advice is also apparent in textbook discussions of tone, where the "hit-list" approach is especially prevalent. Typically, these discussions of tone begin with a general admonition to "avoid negative language" and then offer a few examples of words or phrases to avoid. The following passage from Menning and Wilkinson illustrates this strategy:

> Keeping your messages positive also means deliberately excluding negative words. You can't be "sorry" about something without recalling the negative experience. You can't write "unfortunately" without relaying some gloomy aspect of a situation. Nor can you write in terms of "delay," "broken," "damages," "unable to," "cannot," "inconvenience," "difficulty," "disappointment," and other negatives without stressing some element of the situation which makes your reader react against you rather than with you [2, p. 66].

Similarly, Sherman and Johnson enumerate several other words to avoid:

> One cause of the negative suggestion is the use of words with a negative flavor. For example, "We have received your letter in which *you claim* that the last shipment was improperly packed," implies that the writer questions whether the statements of the reader are accurate.... Other characteristic negative terms are "you neglect," "you fail," "your complaint," and "your error" [6, p. 357].

A more recent work by Pauley and Riordan continues the "hit-list" tradition by advising writers to avoid sentences such as this: "I can't imagine why you chose to put the machine in that spot"; "Don't you think your treatment of the machine was careless?"; "We sent that check a couple of weeks ago. Why don't you review your records before writing?" [7, p. 441].

Treatments using the "hit-list" approach usually suffer from a number of shortcomings. One problem is that they do not define tone precisely, other than by example or as "language that may elicit a negative response from the reader." Second, the "hit-list" approach focuses on the effects of word choice on tone, when in fact syntactic structure may also play a role, as we demonstrate below. Third, this approach is more idiosyncratic than principled. As a result, one textbook's list of "words to avoid" may vary significantly from another's. This lack of a consistent, unified approach can create a potential problem for students, in that it provides them only with a vague sense of the need to "avoid negative language" and a few examples of what might constitute such language. What the student will *not* come away with is an understanding of more general principles that govern tone, principles that could be applied to texts other than those discussed in the student's particular textbook.

An Alternative Treatment of Tone

In this section we propose an alternative analysis of negative tone as a means of refining the rather vague notion of "language which elicits a negative response." Our analysis draws upon the concept of presupposition, a property of language that has long been of interest to logicians and linguists working in semantics and pragmatics (see Levinson [8, pp. 169–177] for a concise history of its treatment).

Defining Presupposition

In order to provide a sense of how presupposition is defined in language theory, we will begin by contrasting the ordinary usage of this term with its more specialized meaning. Following Levinson, we can say that the ordinary usage of the term *presupposition* describes "any kind of background assumption against which an action, theory, expression, or utterance makes sense or is rational" [8, p. 168]. In contrast, the technical sense of presupposition is more limited, being restricted to certain pragmatic inferences or assumptions that are "built into linguistic expressions and which can be isolated using specific linguistic tests (especially . . . constancy under negation . . .)." Thus, we can define a presupposition informally as an unstated proposition implied by a linguistic expression.

Informally, we may say that a *proposition* (a semantic construct) constitutes the meaningful content of a *sentence* (a syntactic construct). Propositions always take the form of declarative sentences, whereas sentences do not. Thus, for example, the sentence "Did John kiss Mary?" expresses the proposition 'John kissed Mary' but does not presuppose it; on the other hand, the sentence "When did John kiss Mary?" expresses the same proposition 'John kissed Mary' and does presuppose it.

The "constancy under negation" test mentioned by Levinson, although not without its problems [8, pp. 185–198], provides a fairly reliable and straight-forward way to isolate presuppositions. As an example of how this test works, consider sentence (1):

(1) John managed to solve the problem.

From this sentence we can infer a number of propositions, among them the following:

(2) Someone named *John* exists and is known to both speaker and listener.
(3) Some problem exists and is known to both speaker and listener.
(4) John tried to solve the problem.
(5) John solved the problem.

In order to determine which of these can be classified as presuppositions of (1), we will apply the "constancy under negation" test by negating the main clause in (1), thereby yielding (1'):

(1') John didn't manage to solve the problem.

From (1'), we can still infer propositions (2), (3), and (4). On the other hand, note that (5) is not a possible inference from (1'); i.e., it does not remain constant under negation. Therefore, we can classify (2–4), but not (5), as presuppositions of (1).

This property of constancy under negation can be stated more generally as follows:

(I) A proposition P is a presupposition of a sentence S if:
  • In all cases where S is true, P is true, and
  • In all cases where S is false, P is true.

The general definition in (I) applies regardless of whether we start with a positive sentence and render it negative, or start with a negative sentence and render it positive. For example, assume that the following negative sentence is true:

(6) John didn't manage to solve the problem.

In order to change the truth value of the sentence, we have merely to change it from negative to positive:

(6') John managed to solve the problem.

Note that presuppositions (2–4) remain constant for both (6) and (6'), even though we began with a negative sentence this time.

An additional example should serve to reinforce the definition given in (I), as well as to illustrate another form that presuppositions may take. Consider the following positive sentence and its negative counterpart:

(7) Mary forgave John for deleting the file.
(7') Mary didn't forgive John for deleting the file.

Both (7) and (7') carry the following presuppositions:

(8) Persons named *Mary* and *John* are known to both speaker and listener.
(9) John deleted a file.
(10) Mary believes that deleting the file was a negative action.

The presuppositions of (7 and 7') are in some respects similar in nature to those of (1 and 1'). As shown in (8), (7 and 7') presuppose the existence of an entity referred to in the discourse; thus (8) is similar in nature to (2 and 3). As shown in (9), (7 and 7') presuppose a specific behavior on the part of that entity; thus (9) is similar in nature to (4). However, (10) represents a type of presupposition conveyed by (7 and 7'), but not by (1 and 1'), namely an evaluation of the presupposed behavior.

To summarize, a sentence may convey two distinct types of presuppositions. As shown by (8 and 9), a sentence can convey presuppositions about the truth or falsity of a proposition (e.g., 'It is true that X exists'; 'It is true that X happened'). As shown by (10), a sentence can also convey presuppositions about an attitude toward a proposition (e.g., 'It is good that X happened'; 'It is bad that X happened'). Thus presuppositions can be either *existential* (e.g., 8 and 9) or *evaluative* (e.g., 10) in nature.

Extensions to Tone

So far we have examined the general nature of presuppositions, defining them as unstated propositions conveyed by particular linguistic expressions.

We have further classified presuppositions as either existential or evaluative. With respect to professional writing, we propose that these two types of presupposition can be used to account for a number of problems in tone. More specifically, many problems in tone can be traced to a conflict between two forces: the presuppositions conveyed by a writer and the assumptions held by a reader. One type of problem in tone may arise when the reader and writer hold different assumptions about the *truth* of a proposition. For example, the writer's language may presuppose the truth of a proposition that the reader believes to be false, or vice versa. This type of problem can be traced to disagreement about an *existential* presupposition. A second type of problem in tone may arise when the reader and writer maintain different *value judgments* about a proposition. For example, both reader and writer may agree that a proposition is true, but hold different attitudes toward it. This type of problem can be traced to disagreements about an *evaluative* presupposition.

We believe that this understanding of tone has several advantages. First, it identifies two discrete sources for problems in tone: disagreements about truth and disagreements about judgments. Second, the test for presuppositions outlined in (I) can be used to reveal the implicit propositions in a piece of writing, thus allowing the writer to isolate and examine these potential points of disagreement. Third, we can identify entire classes of words and structures that convey presuppositions, rather than relying merely on idiosyncratic lists of particular words. The cover term *presupposition triggers* has been used to discuss these classes in the literature on logic and linguistics. The next section discusses several major classes of presupposition triggers.

Presupposition Triggers

A number of linguistic elements have been found to trigger existential or evaluative presuppositions. Some of these elements are particular syntactic structures, while others are classes of particular words. The discussion below describes several types of presupposition triggers and provides examples of them. Where possible, we contrast each presupposition trigger with closely related linguistic elements that do not convey the same presupposition. In addition, we show how each type of presupposition trigger can be used to account for various effects in tone.

WH-Questions

English has the means for asking two different types of questions: the *yes/no*-question (e.g., "Did Jones inspect the building?") and the *wh*-question (e.g., "When did Jones inspect the building?"). One difference between the two is that a *yes/no*-question can be answered *yes* or *no*, whereas a *wh*-question cannot. Moreover, Levinson analyzes *wh*-words (e.g., *when*) as presupposing the proposition of which they are a part [8, p. 184]. Thus, for example, "When did Jones inspect the building?" presupposes that Jones inspected the building, but "Did Jones inspect the building?" does not. Consider also the following sentences, which contain other examples of *wh*-words:

(11) When did Jones inspect the building?
(12) Why did Jones inspect the building?
(13) Where did Jones inspect the building?
(14) How did Jones inspect the building?
(15) Who inspected the building?
(16) What did Jones inspect?

Each of these *wh*-questions presupposes the truth of the proposition which is being questioned. Sentences (11–14) all presuppose the truth of the proposition 'Jones inspected the building.' In these cases, the *wh*-words serve to question some aspect of this assumed action. Sentence (15) also triggers a presupposition, but of a slightly different nature. The presupposition here can be stated as 'Someone inspected the building'; the *wh*-word *who* in subject position questions the agent of this assumed action. In sentence (16), the presupposition is 'Jones inspected something'; the agent and action are assumed, and the *wh*-word questions the object of the agent's action.

The fact that *wh*-questions carry presuppositions can be used to explain certain problems in tone. Consider the following analysis [2, p. 68]:

> The application letter writer who so boldly and confidently asks
> *When* may I come in to see you?
> gives the impression that he thinks his reader has no alternative but to see him. With such presumptuousness he may irritate his reader.

The problem identified in this passage can be traced to an inappropriate presupposition on the writer's part. By using the *wh*-word *when*, the writer presupposes the truth of the proposition 'I may come in to see you.' In contrast, a *yes/no*-question such as "May I have an interview at your convenience?" carries no such presupposition and, thus, conveys a less presumptuous tone.

Structures containing *wh*-words may be contrasted not only with *yes/no*-questions but also with conditionals. Whereas *wh*-structures trigger presuppositions, conditionals actually suspend them.[1] This contrast can be

---

[1] Constructions that suspend presuppositions might be called *presupposition barriers,* although to our knowledge such a term is not currently used in the literature.

used to explain problems that arise from a tone that is too weak or unsuggestive, a problem discussed in the following passage [2, p. 67]:

> The sales correspondent who writes
>> *If you'd like* to take advantage of this timesaving piece of equipment, put your check and completed order blank in the enclosed envelope and drop it in the mail today
>
> would be better off if he did not remind the reader of his option to reject the proposal. Simply omitting the phrase *if you'd like* establishes a tone of greater confidence. The one word *if* is the most frequent destroyer of success consciousness.

In terms of its presuppositions, the conditional construction *If you'd like* can be analyzed as too weak in this context because it suspends the presupposition that the reader will order the equipment. Thus, in linguistic terms, the tone of "success consciousness" achieved by omitting this phrase results from a presupposition that the reader will carry out this action.

Because a conditional does not presuppose the truth of its complement, it may create an accusatory tone if the complement refers to an action that the reader was obliged to perform. For example, consider the following analysis from Murphy and Hildebrandt's discussion of "Courtesy" [9, p. 73]. Sentence (a) is offered as an example of a "tactless, blunt" approach, while sentence (b) is offered as a "tactful" revision:

(a) Obviously, if you'd read your policy carefully, you'd be able to answer these questions yourself.
(b) Sometimes policy wording is a little hard to understand. I'm glad to clear up these questions for you.

The concept of presupposition can be used to explain why sentence (b) is preferable to sentence (a) in this context. The use of the *if*-clause in (a) suspends the presupposition that the reader has read the policy carefully. The point to note, however, is that the too-weak tone in the first example and the too-strong tone in the second both have the same linguistic cause: The conditional construction suspends the truth of the proposition it expresses.

Lesikar raises a similar problem in his discussion of "Avoiding Anger" [10, p. 135]:

> Angry words destroy goodwill. They make the reader angry. And with both reader and writer angry, little likelihood exists that the two can get together on whatever the letter is about.
>
> To illustrate this effect, take the case of an insurance company correspondent who must inform a policyholder that the policyholder has made a mistake in interpreting the policy and is not covered on the case in ques-

tion. Feeling that any fool should be able to read the policy, the correspondent used these angry words:

> If you had read Section IV of your policy, you would know that you are not covered on accidents which occur on water.

In a sense, we might say that this statement tells it as it is. The information is true. But as it shows anger, it lacks tact.

Here again the problem in tone is created by the *if*-clause. Because this clause suspends the truth of the proposition it expresses, it raises questions about whether or not the reader actually read Section IV of the policy, thus creating a negative tone.

To summarize, *wh*-constructions trigger presuppositions about the truth of the propositions of which they are a part, while conditionals actually suspend such propositions. Because a *wh*-construction presupposes agreement between reader and writer, it may create an overly presumptuous tone if the writer is making unwarranted assumptions about the reader's beliefs. In contrast, a conditional does not convey any existential presuppositions; instead, it treats propositions as "open questions." This treatment may convey an uncertainty on the writer's part about actions being attributed to the reader.

Factive Predicates

The distinction between factive and nonfactive predicates, initially developed by Kiparsky and Kiparsky, can be used to identify a second class of presupposition triggers [11]. The most general way to characterize this distinction is to say that a factive predicate presupposes the truth of the proposition expressed by its complement, while a nonfactive predicate does not. Among the factive predicates discussed by Kiparsky and Kiparsky are the following [11, p. 347]:

> Smith [regrets, is aware, grasps, comprehends, takes into consideration, takes into account, bears in mind, makes clear, resents] that X is the case.

In contrast, the following predicates are analyzed as nonfactives:

> Smith [supposes, asserts, alleges, assumes, claims, charges, maintains, believes, concludes, conjectures, fancies, figures] that X is the case.

Under this analysis, a factive predicate presupposes the truth of the proposition expressed in the predicate's complement. For example, the writer of a sentence like

(17) Smith regrets that the order was misplaced.

presupposes the truth of the proposition 'The order was misplaced.' This can be verified by negating (17):

(17′) Smith doesn't regret that the order was misplaced.

Note that the same presupposition holds for (17 and 17′), as predicted by the test outlined earlier in (I).

Conversely, a nonfactive predicate does not presuppose the truth of the proposition expressed in the predicate's complement. As illustration, consider the following sentences:

(18) Smith assumes that the order was misplaced.
(18′) Smith doesn't assume that the order was misplaced.

Unlike (17 and 17′), neither of these sentences presupposes the truth of the proposition 'The order was misplaced.'

The distinction between factives and nonfactives can be used to account for some problems in tone that arise from conflicting assumptions by writer and reader about the truth of a proposition. For example, consider the following analysis [6, p. 357]:

> One cause of the negative suggestion is the use of words with a negative flavor. For example, "We have received your letter in which *you claim* that the last shipment was improperly packed," implies that the writer questions whether the statements of the reader are accurate. [emphasis in original]

Similar problems are discussed by other authors dealing with word choice. For example, Sigband and Bell write, "If we say . . . 'We received your letter in which you claim we did not ship,' we are certainly being tactless" [12, p. 586]. Likewise, Lesikar offers the following sentence as part of a letter whose "effect on the reader is destructive of goodwill": "We received your claim in which you *contend* that we were responsible for *damage* to three cases of Madame Dupree's lotion" [10, p. 131; emphasis in original]. And Murphy and Hildebrandt include "you claim that . . ." in their list of "irksome expressions to be avoided" [9, p. 74].

In the passages under discussion, the problematic phrases are "you claim" and its synonym "you contend." As Lesikar points out, "The words 'in which you contend' clearly imply some doubt of the legitimacy of the claim" [10, p. 132]. From a linguistic perspective, the problem in tone created by this phrase can be traced to its status as a nonfactive predicate. By phrasing the reader's assertion as the complement of a nonfactive, the writer suspends the presupposition that this assertion is true. Consequently, the use of *claim* or *contend* may result in an argumentative tone because the writer is attributing nonfactual status to a situation that the reader has presented as factual.

The factive/nonfactive distinction is also relevant when a writer is requesting an adjustment, rather than responding to such a request. Consider the following advice given by Sigband and Bell [12, p. 627]:

> When buyers are certain that their claim is correct from every point of view, and that the adjustment they are requesting is honest in every respect, then they should check their letter to be sure that the tone is positive (not accusing), the statements specific, and the details precise. . . .
>
> If the buyer's letter reflects a tone of uncertainty, the recipient will very probably seize upon that tone to delay an adjustment. In the following examples the revised phrases have a much more positive tone:

> Original: *We believe the damage took place* . . .
> Revised: *The damage took place* . . .

> Original: *We think you did not include* . . .
> Revised: *. . . was not included.*

In both of these examples, the original sentences contain nonfactive predicates (*believe, think*). These predicates create the "tone of uncertainty" described by Sigband and Bell, since they do not presuppose the truth of the propositions expressed in their complements. In contrast, the revised sentences simply assert the propositions that were formerly expressed in the complements of nonfactive verbs.

Another area in which the factive/nonfactive distinction can be observed is in the "review of the literature" section which often begins a research article. A number of inferences can be drawn about the writer's attitude toward another researcher's findings by examining whether the researcher uses factive or nonfactive predicates in discussing these findings. For example, compare the following, where the bracketed material represents alternative word choices:

> Smith [demonstrates, shows, proves, confirms, realizes, acknowledges, regrets, admits, notes, recognizes, points out] that X is the case.

> Smith [says, states, claims, argues, proposes, postulates, believes, thinks, assumes, maintains] that X is the case.

The predicates in the first set are factive, and consequently would be more appropriate where the writer agrees with Smith's argument. In contrast, the predicates in the second set are nonfactive, and consequently would be more appropriate where the writer is taking issue with Smith's argument.

Again, this contrast in tone can be traced to the distinction between factive and nonfactive predicates and to the corresponding differences in their presuppositions.

In summary, factive and nonfactive predicates may affect tone because they differ in their presuppositions. Factive predicates trigger existential presuppositions, thereby conveying the writer's certainty about the truth of a proposition. In contrast, nonfactive predicates suspend existential presuppositions, thereby conveying the writer's uncertainty about the truth of a proposition. In order to achieve the desired tone, the writer must be sensitive to the truth value presupposed by these different predicates.

Implicative Predicates

A third category of presupposition triggers, called implicative predicates, is discussed by Karttunen [13]. As suggested by their name, implicative predicates "commit the speaker to an implied proposition" [13, p. 340]. Thus, while a factive predicate presupposes the truth of a proposition explicitly stated in the complement, an implicative predicate does not. As illustration, compare (19 and 19′), containing the factive verb *realize,* and (20 and 20′), containing the implicative verb *manage:*

(19) John realized that he had solved the problem.
(19′) John didn't realize that he had solved the problem.
(20) John managed to solve the problem.
(20′) John didn't manage to solve the problem.

The proposition expressed in the complement, 'John solved the problem,' is a presupposition of (19 and 19′), since it remains true under negation. In contrast, it does not qualify as a presupposition of (20 and 20′) under this test. Unlike factive predicates, then, implicative predicates do not presuppose a proposition that is explicit in the complement.

The type of presupposition that is conveyed by implicative predicates is described by Karttunen as follows:

> The presuppositional content expresses the unstated beliefs of the speaker that underlie the proposition. Associated with each [implicative predicate], there are a number of suppositions that have to be fulfilled if the sentence is going to count as a felicitous utterance [13, p. 350].

These unstated beliefs do constitute presuppositions because they remain constant under negation. For example, from either (20) or (20′), the addressee can infer the speaker's belief that 'John tried to solve the problem.' Thus this can be classified as a presupposition triggered by the verb *manage.* Karttunen further elaborates on the presuppositions of *manage* as follows:

... the speaker must assume that whatever is meant by the complement sentence is in some way difficult for the subject to accomplish ... *manage* requires that the subject at least attempted the act described in the complement. ... It also seems that if the attempt is successful, this is credited to the skill or ingenuity of the subject; a failure ... is understood to show that those necessary qualities were not present to a sufficient degree [13, p. 351].[2]

Note that these presuppositions are cancelled if the implicative verb *manage* is removed, as in (21) and (21'):

(21) John solved the problem.
(21') John didn't solve the problem.

In the absence of *manage,* no presuppositions are triggered about the difficulty of the task or the subject's attempt to carry it out.

A number of other predicates behave like *manage* in the sense that they presuppose unstated conditions. As examples, consider the verbs *remember, bother,* and *happen.* Sentences (22 and 22') illustrate the relevant positive and negative uses of *remember:*

(22) John remembered to go to the meeting.
(22') John didn't remember to go to the meeting.

Such sentences, according to Karttunen, presuppose "that the subject was obligated to carry out the act described in the complement," and further presuppose "a basic willingness on the part of the subject to carry out his obligation" [13, p. 351]. Thus the presuppositions triggered by (22 and 22') are that 'John was committed and willing to go to the meeting.'[3]

Sentences (23 and 23') illustrate the relevant positive and negative uses of the implicative verb *bother:*

(23) John bothered to go to the meeting.
(23') John didn't bother to go to the meeting.

According to Karttunen, the use of *bother* presupposes that "some conscious effort is needed on the part of the subject, in order to carry out the

---

[2] This analysis explains the irony in a statement like "I managed to step on some chewing gum in the parking lot." Here, the implicative verb *manage* commits the speaker to the presupposition 'I tried to step on some chewing gum in the parking lot'—that is, the speaker attributes a sense of intention to an act that normally would not be intended.

[3] While Karttunen analyzes *remember* as presupposing 'willingness,' it may be valid to describe this as 'intention,' since certainly one may intend to perform an act that is not undertaken quite willingly, as in the following: "John remembered to send a check for $2500 to the Internal Revenue Service."

proposition expressed in the complement. It also suggests that the subject's willingness to make this effort is the crucial factor that determines the outcome" [13, p. 351].

Finally, sentences (24 and 24') illustrate the relevant positive and negative uses of the implicative verb *happen:*

(24) John happened to go to the meeting.
(24') John didn't happen to go to the meeting.

The presupposition of *happen* is analyzed by Karttunen as follows: "Whatever turns out to be the case is supposedly accidental; there is no other factor except chance that could have determined the outcome" [13, p. 351].

So far we have looked at some particular implicative predicates and have reviewed Karttunen's analysis of their individual presuppositions. It might be useful at this point to review their common properties:

> It is assumed that there is some necessary and sufficient condition, expressed by the main verb [i.e., the implicative predicate], which alone determines whether the event described in the complement took place. This crucial factor may consist of showing enough skill and ingenuity in one's attempt, as in *manage*, keeping one's commitment in mind, as in *remember*, or making an effort, as in *bother*, etc. [13, pp. 351–352].

Karttunen also mentions a sub-category of implicative predicates which he describes as "negative implicatives"; that is, implicative predicates that "seem to incorporate negation": *forget, fail, neglect, decline, avoid,* and *refrain* [13, p. 352]. Although these are discussed in less detail, it is a fairly simple matter to explicate the presuppositions for several of them. Consider first sentences (25 and 25'), which contain the relevant positive and negative uses of *forget:*

(25) John forgot to go to the meeting.
(25') John didn't forget to go to the meeting.

Like *remember,* which may be regarded as its positive counterpart, *forget* presupposes the subject's obligation to perform the act described in the complement, and also presupposes that the completion of this act "depends only on whether the subject kept his commitment in mind" [13, p. 353]. Thus, (25 and 25') share the same set of presuppositions as (22 and 22').

Sentences (26 and 26') contain the relevant positive and negative uses of *fail:*

(26) John failed to go to the meeting.
(26') John didn't fail to go to the meeting.

Both of these sentences convey presuppositions similar to those containing *manage,* that is, they imply that the subject attempted the act described in the complement and that the outcome of this attempt hinged on the subject's perseverance or ingenuity.

Sentences (27 and 27') contain positive and negative uses of *neglect:*

(27) John neglected to go to the meeting.
(27') John didn't neglect to go to the meeting.

The use of *neglect* presupposes that the subject was responsible for completing the act described in the complement, and that the completion of this act depended on the subject's willingness to carry out this responsibility.

The evaluative presuppositions triggered by implicative predicates may affect tone if the reader and writer disagree about these evaluations. For example, consider the verb *neglect* and the cognate noun *negligence,* which appear regularly on "hit lists" in discussions of tone [9, pp. 52, 74; 10, p. 135; 12, p. 586; 14, p. 60]. Menning and Wilkinson point out the "almost completely insensitive attitude" toward the reader conveyed by a letter containing the sentence "*You neglected* to specify which shade of sweater you desire" [2, p. 77]. The concept of implicative predicates allows us to analyze the source of this problem in tone. *Neglect* is an implicative verb, and further it presupposes that the agent (i.e., the reader) had a responsibility to complete the act described in the complement. The fact that the act was not completed is thus attributed to the subject's not carrying out this responsibility.

We may also analyze the verb *fail* and the noun *failure* using Karttunen's theory of implicative predicates. These words are mentioned frequently in discussions of tone [9, pp. 49, 52, 74; 10, p. 130; 14, pp. 59–60]. Some authors discuss strategies for eliminating the verb *fail.* For example, Blicq suggests revising sentence (a) to sentence (b) [14, p. 60]:

(a) You have failed to include motel receipts with your expense account.
(b) Please send motel receipts to support your expense account.

Similarly, Lesikar offers the following as "negative" and "positive" versions of the same message [10, p. 132]:

(a) You failed to give us the fabric specification of the chair you ordered.
(b) So that you may have the one chair you want, will you please check your choice of fabric on the enclosed card?

As analyzed following Karttunen's theory, the verb *fail* presupposes that the completion of the action described in the complement (e.g., "to include motel receipts"; "to give us the fabric specification") depends on the subject's perseverance or ingenuity. Consequently, *fail* presupposes that these qualities are lacking in the reader.

To summarize, implicative predicates presuppose attitudes toward a subject's willingness or ability to carry out an action. Consequently, they may affect tone when a writer uses them to discuss a reader's actions. Negative implicatives, especially, may introduce presuppositions about unmet obligations on the reader's part, thereby creating problems in tone.

Conclusion

Let us summarize the main points of our discussion. Within the field of professional writing, the problem of tone is usually treated on a case-by-case basis, using what has been termed a "hit-list" approach: "Say this; don't say that." This approach is useful insofar as it provides students, teachers, practitioners, and researchers with specific examples of problems in tone. At the same time, however, a more comprehensive theory of tone (or of any other phenomenon in professional writing) requires an articulation of the general principles that predict and explain particular examples.

We have proposed that the linguistic concept of presupposition (i.e., a proposition implied by a particular linguistic expression) helps to explain how and why a number of problems in tone arise. We have identified two types of presupposition that are relevant to these problems: *existential* presuppositions, which concern the truth of a proposition, and *evaluative* presuppositions, which concern the writer's attitude toward a proposition. These two types of presuppositions, in turn, account for two different sources of tone problems. One is where the writer and reader disagree about the *truth* of a proposition; the other is where they hold different *value judgments* about a proposition.

By way of illustration, we have discussed several constructions that affect presuppositions directly and tone indirectly.

- A *wh-question* presupposes the truth of the proposition it expresses (e.g., "When may I come in for an interview?" presupposes 'I may come in for an interview.'). In contrast, a *conditional* suspends the truth of the proposition it expresses (e.g., "If you want to place an order" allows either the proposition 'You want to place an order' or the proposition 'You do not want to place an order').

- A *factive predicate* presupposes the truth of the proposition expressed in the complement; a *non-factive predicate* suspends such a proposition (e.g., "You claim that the goods were damaged" suspends the truth of the proposition 'The goods were damaged').

- An *implicative predicate* presupposes a proposition expressing a particular attitude (e.g., "You failed to supply your credit card number" presupposes an unmet obligation on the part of the addressee).

We are not arguing that all problems in tone can be explained by presupposition theory in particular or by linguistic theory in general. Rather, we are merely proposing that some problems in tone can be explained by reference to the linguistic concept of presupposition. Nor are we suggesting that courses in professional writing be transformed into linguistic theory classes; such a move would clearly subordinate the ends of instruction to the means. Instead, we are simply arguing that a working knowledge of relevant areas of linguistic theory would facilitate the efforts of those involved in different areas of professional writing. In particular, we feel that our understanding of the relationship between presupposition and tone would enable researchers to gain deeper insights, practitioners to write more effectively, instructors to teach more efficiently, and students to learn less painfully.

Acknowledgments

The work of the first author was supported by a Faculty Research Award from the University of Tennessee.

References

1. K. Riley, Pragmatics and Technical Communication: Some Further Considerations, *The Technical Writing Teacher, 13,* pp. 160–170, 1986.
2. J. H. Menning and C. W. Wilkinson, *Communicating Through Letters and Reports,* 5th edition, Richard D. Irwin, Homewood, Illinois, 1972.
3. P. V. Anderson, The Need for Better Research in Technical Communication, *Journal of Technical Writing and Communication, 10,* pp. 271–282, 1980.
4. G. J. Broadhead, Style in Technical and Scientific Writing, in *Research on Technical Communication: A Bibliographic Sourcebook,* M. G. Moran and D. Journet (eds.), Greenwood Press, Westport, Connecticut, pp. 217–252, 1985.
5. M. H. Moran and M. G. Moran, Business Letters, Memoranda, and Resumes, in *Research on Technical Communication: A Bibliographic Sourcebook,* M. G. Moran and D. Journet (eds.), Greenwood Press, Westport, Connecticut, pp. 313–349, 1985.
6. T. A. Sherman and S. S. Johnson, *Modern Technical Writing,* 4th edition, Prentice-Hall, Englewood Cliffs, New Jersey, 1983.
7. S. E. Pauley and D. G. Riordan, *Technical Report Writing Today,* 3rd edition, Houghton Mifflin, Boston, 1987.
8. S. C. Levinson, *Pragmatics,* Cambridge University Press, Cambridge, 1983.
9. H. A. Murphy and H. W. Hildebrandt, *Effective Business Communications,* 4th edition, McGraw-Hill, New York, 1984.
10. R. V. Lesikar, *Business Communication: Theory and Application,* 4th edition, Richard D. Irwin, Homewood, Illinois, 1980.
11. P. Kiparsky and C. Kiparsky, Fact, in *Semantics: An Interdisciplinary Reader in Philosophy, Linguistics, and Psychology,* D. Steinberg and L. Jakobovitz (eds.), Cambridge University Press, Cambridge, pp. 345–369, 1971.

12. N. B. Sigband and A. H. Bell, *Communication for Management and Business,* 4th edition, Scott, Foresman, Glenview, Illinois, 1986.
13. L. Karttunen, Implicative Verbs, *Language, 47,* pp. 340–358, 1971.
14. R. S. Blicq, *Technically-Write!,* 3rd edition, Prentice-Hall, Englewood Cliffs, New Jersey, 1986.

Content Questions

1. Why would a principled approach to error correction be more valuable to someone interested in learning about effective writing than an approach that merely corrects errors in individual sentences?

2. What is meant by the "hit-list approach" when we consider tone?

3. What concept from linguistic research do Riley and Parker apply to a better understanding of tone in writing?

4. How are presuppositions different from propositions?

5. What is the "constancy under negation" test? How does it help identify presuppositions?

6. How do existential presuppositions differ from evaluative ones?

7. Explain what a presupposition trigger is. What examples of types of presupposition triggers do the authors provide?

8. According to the analysis provided in this article, why could the question "When may I come in to see you?" be problematic?

9. What kinds of problems can result from the use of conditionals?

10. Distinguish between factive and nonfactive predicates. How do factive predicates relate to presuppositions?

11. What are implicative predicates?

Questions for Analysis and Discussion

1. Do you believe that learning about presuppositions could help composition students in a way that traditional explanations about tone have not? Why or why not?

2. How do you respond to questions or statements containing presuppositions that you do not agree with?

3. Can you imagine ways in which a knowledge of presuppositions might be helpful in other contexts such as law and advertising? Explain.

4. How common do you think presuppositions are in our speech and writing? In what ways do you think the use of presuppositions assists us in our communication? In what ways could their use be inappropriate?

Transformational-Generative Syntax and the Teaching of Sentence Mechanics

Rei R. Noguchi

Since its appearance in 1957, Chomsky's transformational-generative grammar and subsequent revisions of that theoretical model have had an enormous influence on not only linguistics, but also related fields such as psychology, computer programming, and education. In the following essay, Rei R. Noguchi, a professor of English at California State University at Northridge, looks at how insights from Chomsky's model can help students in editing or avoiding some mechanical errors in their writing. This article, which originally appeared in the *Journal of Basic Writing*, has since been expanded into a book, *Grammar and the Teaching of Writing*, published by the National Council of Teachers of English.

Of the various skills needed in writing, the skill to detect and eliminate certain mechanical errors—run-ons, comma splices, unintentional sentence fragments, lack of subject-verb agreement—would seem one of the easiest to master. After all, such errors deal not with paragraphs or whole essays but with individual sentences. Further, as the often-used designation "sentence mechanics" suggests, such errors deal with "mechanics," something machinelike, automatic. Yet, teachers of writing all too often encounter native writers, both basic and nonbasic, who progress in the higher-level writing skills (e.g., invention and organization) but still write with run-ons, comma splices, fragments, and lack of subject-verb agreement. Indeed, the mechanical errors occur with such frequency that teachers begin to question not just their teaching methods but the linguistic competence of their students. Where exactly does the fault lie? More importantly, given that most students have had little or no formal training in traditional or modern grammar, what can be done to eliminate such persistent errors? This essay, written from the perspective of transformational-generative linguistics, suggests that these errors persist not because of the lack of language ability in students but because of the instructor's lack in exploiting that ability.

Basic writing instructors know that writing exhibiting run-on sentences, comma splices, unintentional sentence fragments, and errors in subject-verb agreement invites strongly negative linguistic and social criticism. Many in society, often in positions of power, view such mechanical errors as signs of illiteracy, if not mental incompetence. Given the constraints of the reader-writer relationship and the difference between writing and speech, instructors will have more success changing the habits of the offending writers rather than the habits of a censorious public. Yet, eliminating mechanical errors has proved a formidable task for both students and teachers of writing. Although the traditional handbooks offer "rules" to aid in the correction of these errors, the rules are in actual practice difficult to apply, especially if students have had little or no formal study of grammar. For example, traditional handbooks instruct students to make the verb of a sentence agree in number with its subject. But, this seemingly simple and straightforward rule is impossible to apply if students do not know what the term "subject" means or how to locate a subject in an actual sentence. Another seemingly accessible handbook rule states that a fragment is not a sentence and, hence, cannot be punctuated as one. For students to understand and apply this rule, however, they must first understand what is meant by "sentence"; but to understand what is meant by a sentence, they must understand what an independent clause is, and to understand the latter, they must understand what a subject and verb are.

For writing instructors, the path proves equally tortuous. To help students eliminate, for example, sentence fragments, instructors might try explaining the concept of fragment. But to do so inevitably leads to the concept of sentence, which, in turn, leads to the concepts of independent clause, subject, and verb. As most writing teachers can attest, the same tortuous route applies in explaining the concepts of run-on sentences and comma splices. The crux of the problem is obvious: much of conventional instruction to correct run-on sentences, comma splices, sentence fragments, and errors in subject-verb agreement makes reference not merely to opaque grammatical terms but, worse still, to opaque grammatical terms which interlink in their definitions with other equally opaque grammatical terms.

To help students correct sentence mechanics, writing instructors need a method which eliminates the dovetailing of grammatical concepts, one which enables students to identify the relevant grammatical categories *independently* of other grammatical categories. The standard, or classical, model of transformational-generative grammar can serve as a significant pedagogical aid here.[1] The model posits two levels of representation for sentences, an abstract deep structure of meaning relationships and a concrete surface structure of realized sentences. The surface structure is derived from the deep structure by a set of rules, or transformations. As I will demonstrate shortly, it is the transformational part which proves useful in the correcting of sentence mechanics. What makes the transformational part particularly useful is that transformational rules are sensitive to various syntactic categories.

---

[1] By the "standard" or "classical" model of transformational-generative grammar, I mean that model of language presented by Chomsky in *Aspects of the Theory of Syntax*. Those wishing a cogent history of the development and reception of transformational-generative linguistics in the United States can consult the two books by Newmeyer listed in the bibliography.

Take, for example, the rule of Tag-Formation, which relates the *a* and the *b* sentences in each pair of sentences below:

1a. John can swim.
 b. John can swim, can't he?
2a. The neighbors will be moving to Los Angeles.
 b. The neighbors will be moving to Los Angeles, won't they?
3a. The car with the mag wheels and the tinted windows has been washed.
 b. The car with the mag wheels and the tinted windows has been washed, hasn't it?
4a. Betty studied her chemistry last night.
 b. Betty studied her chemistry last night, didn't she?

If given only the *a* sentences above, native speakers of English can easily transform them into the corresponding *b* sentences—that is, into the tag-questions. Writing instructors can readily demonstrate this both to themselves and to their students by reading the *a* sentences in class and having their students orally produce the corresponding tag-questions.

But how is it possible that native speakers of English can perform such transformations so effortlessly? Specially, how do native speakers create the "tags" (e.g., the *can't he, won't they, hasn't it, didn't she*) at the ends of the original declarative sentences and thereby convert the declarative sentences into tag-questions? Native speakers certainly have not memorized the corresponding tag-question for each declarative sentence. Rather, they have internalized a rule, here the rule of Tag-Formation, which enables them to transform each declarative sentence into the corresponding tag-question. While linguists have formulated Tag-Formation in different ways,[2] most agree that the rule essentially copies certain constituents of a sentence to create the tag at the end. The grammatical elements which get copied are the first auxiliary verb (if none occurs, a form of *do* is added instead), the verb tense, the negative *not* in contracted form (if the sentence is positive), and the subject noun phrase in pronominal form. Although Tag-Formation is a complex rule involving several operations, all native speakers of English have an implicit knowledge of the rule; otherwise they would be unable in daily life to transform the *a* sentences in *1–4* into their corresponding tag-questions. This fact is highly important, for if native speakers already know the rule of Tag-Formation (although they may not be able to state it explicitly in the manner linguists do), instructors do not have to teach the rule. After all, instructors cannot teach students what they already know. A second and more important point follows: if native speakers

---

[2]For a classical version, see, for example, the formulation in Akmajian and Heny 1–11, 202–18. Further discussion and other treatments of Tag-Formation appear in Arbini; Huddleston; Cattel; and Culicover 131–43.

of English already know the rule of Tag-Formation, they must also know the syntactic categories involved in the rule; that is, native speakers of English, whatever their formal background in grammar, already have an underlying knowledge of such syntactic categories as sentence, auxiliary verb, tense, negative, and (subject) noun phrase. (How else could they correctly identify and copy these elements in the tag?) Stated in a somewhat different way, even though students may lack the ability to assign traditional labels to certain syntactic categories, they nevertheless unconsciously know what they are. It is precisely this unconscious knowledge of syntactic categories that writing instructors should exploit in the teaching and correcting of sentence mechanics.

Yet, just how can instructors exploit this underlying knowledge of syntactic categories? The correction of sentence fragments can serve as an illustration. To understand the notion of sentence fragment, students need to make use of the concept of sentence (i.e., a sentence fragment is only a "part" of a sentence). But herein lies a pedagogical problem. How can writing instructors introduce the concepts of sentence without also invoking such dovetailing concepts as independent clause, subject, and predicate? The solution is to bypass these latter concepts and to exploit directly the student's implicit underlying knowledge of the syntactic category "sentence." That students already have an intuitive knowledge of what constitutes a sentence is clearly evident in their ability to use the Tag-Formation rule to transform any declarative *sentence*—e.g., the *a* sentences in *1–4* above—into its corresponding tag-question. Put in a slightly different way, Tag-Formation operates on only declarative (and imperative) sentences, not fragments. If this is so, the rule will operate on sentences such as *1a, 2a, 3a,* and *4a* but not on sequences such as:

5. Although John will stay home.
6. Whatever was bothering the neighbors.
7. Who saw that she had been trying.
8. Waiting for the show to begin.

As suggested earlier, if students are asked to transform sentences like *1a, 2a, 3a,* and *4a* into their corresponding tag-questions, they can easily perform the transformation; however, with sequences like *5–8,* they will find the task impossible since Tag-Formation works only for declarative (and imperative) sentences, not fragments. Put in the most simplistic terms, if a sequence of words can be transformed into a proper tag-question, it is a sentence; if not, it's a fragment.[3] Worth emphasizing here is that students

---

[3] I use the term "simplistic" deliberately here, for some notable exceptions do occur. For example, from the fragment "A nice day," we can derive "A nice day, isn't it?" However, instructors can utilize such examples to reinforce the idea that all tag-questions derive from underlying declarative sentences and not parts of them. By undoing the effects of Tag-Formation and other transformational rules (e.g., deleting the -*n't* and putting the copied elements of the tag back into their original positions), instructors can demonstrate that "A nice day, isn't it?" actually derives from "It is a nice

do not need to know how to formulate the Tag-Formation rule to realize this fact; neither is it necessary for instructors to introduce transformational-generative linguistics as background. Yet, if instructors can get students to recognize the simple fact that tag-questions cannot be formed from fragments, then students will have an easily and always available means of testing for fragments—and without first having to undergo time-consuming and often confusing formal instruction in what constitutes a sentence, independent clause, subject, predicate, and so on.

The Tag-Formation rule can also help identify and correct run-on sentences and comma splices. This is so because, as suggested above, the Tag-Formation rule differentiates between two general types of word sequences: a sentence and a nonsentence. Technically speaking, neither a run-on nor a common splice is a bona fide sentence since each consists of two or more sentences incorrectly joined as one sentence. The value of the Tag-Formation rule is that it can be utilized to determine the "sentencehood" of the whole sequence (i.e., the run-on or comma splice) and its parts. For purposes of demonstration, instructors might ask their students to write the proper tag-questions for such sequences as the comma splice in *9* below, and the run-on in *10:*

9. Jerry decided to become an accountant, Susan became a doctor.
10. The guard made his nightly rounds all seemed in order.

With sequences like *9* and *10*, students either will be unable to produce a proper tag-question (in which case they will have strong evidence that the sequences are nonsentences), or they will produce the following sequences:

11. Jerry decided to become an accountant, Susan became a doctor, didn't she?
12. The guard made his nightly rounds all seemed in order, didn't it?

day" (the underlying declarative *sentence*) and not from "A nice day" (a *part* of the underlying declarative sentence). The derivation of "A nice day, isn't it?" proceeds thus: "It is a nice day" (underlying declarative sentence) to "It is a nice day, isn't it?" (derived sentence after the Tag-Formation rule has applied) to "A nice day, isn't it?" (derived sentence after another rule has deleted *it* and *is* in the main clause). This derivation, incidentally, reveals an exception to the simplified description of the Tag-Formation rule given in the text. Tag-Formation also copies forms of the main verb *be* in the tag if these *be* forms have no accompanying first auxiliary verb (e.g., "Bill is happy, isn't he?" vs. "Bill could be happy, couldn't he?"). Another notable exception involves sentences like "I believe (that) John will go to Las Vegas," where the appropriate tag-question seems to be "I believe (that) John will go to Las Vegas, won't he?" rather than the expected "I believe (that) John will go to Las Vegas, don't I?" Yet, the fact that we can still derive an acceptable tag-question by copying elements from *within* the original sentence suggests that, if not the whole sentence, at least the embedded clause (i.e., *John will go to Las Vegas*) is a sentence and not a fragment. Of interest here is that constructions like "I believe that. . . ." (with *that* being unstressed) can serve as another test of "sentencehood" since only sentences (and not fragments) can be immediately embedded after them. To demonstrate this, the instructor might ask that students try to embed fragments like *5–8* immediately after "I believe that. . . ." (Discerning readers may notice that the sequence "A nice day" cannot occur in this slot—hence, it is a fragment.) For a pragmatic explanation of why sentences containing cognition verbs (e.g., *believe, suppose, guess*) followed by an embedded clause behave differently in the formation of tag-questions, see Lakoff.

If asked to read sequences *11* and *12* aloud, however, most students will find them unnatural as individual sentences because one part sounds like a question and the remaining part does not. If requested to do so, most students can also separate the question part from the nonquestion part (it's generally easier to separate two unlikes than two likes). The separation point, of course, is the point where the run-on or comma splice actually occurs. Ignoring punctuation and capitalization, sequences *11* and *12* will thus divide into two parts:

13. Jerry decided to become an accountant // Susan became a doctor, didn't she?
14. The guard made his nightly rounds // all seemed in order, didn't it?

To demonstrate further that run-ons and comma splices incorrectly join sentences, instructors should ask students to form a tag-question from the remaining part (i.e., the first, or nonquestion, part) of *13* and *14*. Again, most students will be able to do so because this part, like the second part, is also a sentence.

The ability to use the Tag-Formation rule as a testing device can, of course, be highly valuable in the actual correction of run-ons and comma splices. Logically, the detection of run-ons and comma splices is necessarily prior to correction. The advantage of using the method outlined above is that if students are instructed not to join sentences with merely commas or no punctuation at all, they can use the Tag-Formation rule to identify just what parts of suspect sequences are individual sentences and then insert the correct form of punctuation. If the lack of a semicolon is the mechanical error, an added boon is that the method can be used to demonstrate (or verify) that a semicolon, in its primary function, should join sentences, not fragments.

Lastly, the use of underlying syntactic knowledge can help identify and correct errors in subject-verb agreement. With errors in subject-verb agreement, the primary source of error lies in locating the subject of the sentence—that is, the noun phrase (more specifically, the noun) constituent with which the verb agrees in number. To simplify matters here, I exclude from discussion collective noun phrases; noun phrases following the expletive, *there;* and compound noun phrases joined by *or;* all of which require special rules. I make these exclusions in order to focus on the more general type of error, namely, errors dealing with the simple misidentification of the subject. This kind of error usually occurs because some phrase (e.g., prepositional phrase, participial phrase) or some subordinate clause intervenes between the main clause subject and its verb. The following sentences (where the symbol * designates an ungrammatical sentence) exemplify this type of error:

15. *The use of electronic security devices have increased in the last decade.

16. *The company which operated several branch offices in New York, Chicago, and Los Angeles were going bankrupt.

In the two sentences above, the sources of the agreement errors are the intervening prepositional phrase (i.e., *of electronic security devices*) in *15* and the intervening relative clause (i.e., *which operated several branch offices in New York, Chicago, and Los Angeles*) in *16*.

Conventional instruction to eliminate agreement errors such as those in *15* and *16* is, however, fraught with difficulty. To help eliminate subject-verb agreement errors caused by intervening constructions, writing instructors might, for example, try explaining that prepositional phrases, or more accurately, objects of prepositions, can never serve as subjects of sentences; however, this leaves the onerous task of explaining just what constitutes a prepositional phrase or an object of a preposition, and, inescapably, what constitutes a preposition (not to mention what constitutes a subject). If instructors attempt to explain that relative clauses, or more specifically, noun phrases in relative clauses, also cannot serve as subjects of main clauses, an even greater store of proliferating categories lies on the horizon (e.g., main clause, dependent clause, relative pronoun, subject, verb, noun phrase).

To break the chain of interlinking categories, writing instructors can again make use of the implicit syntactic knowledge of their students. Since the Tag-Formation rule makes reference to the notion of subject (i.e., it's the subject which gets copied in pronominal form in the tag), the rule would seem to provide an effective means of identifying subjects of sentences. All one needs to do to locate the subject of a sentence is to form the derivative tag-question, locate the pronoun (or simply, the last word) in the tag, and determine which word in the sentence the pronoun refers to (i.e., "stands for"). However, a discomforting problem may arise here. In sentences like *15* and *16* above, the Tag-Formation rule will not always work in identifying subjects for all students. For example, given the grammatical declarative sentences *17a* and *18a* below, students will produce the corresponding grammatical tag-questions *17b* and *18b*:

17a. The use of electronic security devices has increased in the last decade.
  b. The use of electronic security devices has increased in the last decade, hasn't it?
18a. The company which operated several branch offices in New York, Chicago, and Los Angeles was going bankrupt.
  b. The company which operated several branch offices in New York, Chicago, and Los Angeles was going bankrupt, wasn't it?

However, if students begin unwittingly with the *un*grammatical sentences *15* and *16*, which I will repeat as *19a* and *20a* below, they are likely to produce unwittingly the ungrammatical tag-questions *19b* and *20b:*

19a.   *The use of electronic security devices have increased in the last decade.

   b.   *The use of electronic security devices have increased in the last decade, haven't they?

20a.   *The company which operated several branch offices in New York, Chicago, and Los Angeles were going bankrupt.

   b.   *The company which operated several branch offices in New York, Chicago, and Los Angeles were going bankrupt, weren't they?

In *19b*, the pronoun *they* in the tag substitutes not for the subject *use* but incorrectly for *devices* (the object of the preposition *of*); in *20b*, the pronoun *they* substitutes not for the subject *company* but apparently either for *offices* (the direct object of the relative clause) or for *New York, Chicago, and Los Angeles* (the compound objects of the preposition *in*).

The errors in forming the correct tag-question in *19* and *20* raise at least two important questions. First, do such errors mean that students do not really know how the Tag-Formation rule operates and, more specifically, do not know what the subjects of sentences are? The answer in both cases is no. Because of the greater length and complexity of declarative sentences *19a* and, particularly, *20a*, many writers—including sophisticated ones—will fall prey to errors in linguistic performance (not linguistic competence), more specifically, to limits of short-term memory. Producing the correct pronoun in the tag of a tag-question requires, among other things, holding the subject of the sentence in memory until the end of the sentence, a task which becomes more difficult as other constructions, particularly other noun phrases, increase the distance between the subject and the tag. (Instructors of writing can demonstrate to themselves and to their students that the underlying knowledge of subjects is still there with *19a* and *20a* by deleting the intervening constructions, changing the verbs *have increased* and *were going* to *increased* and *went*, respectively, and then having the students form the tag-questions.)

The second question is more pedagogical. If Tag-Formation does not always work in identifying subjects, particularly in long and complex sentences, is there some other means that writing instructors can use as a backup—or as an initial resource—to help students identify subjects? For example, let us say that a student has unwittingly produced the ungrammatical tag question in *19b* and insists that *devices* is the subject of the sentence since that is what the *they* in the tag refers to. An instructor who recognizes that *19a* and *19b* are ungrammatical versions of *17a* and *17b*, respectively, would insist just as strongly that the subject is *use*, not *devices*, since *use* is what *it* in the grammatical tag-question *17b* refers to. Because the instructor and student apply the Tag-Formation rule to different declarative sentences—the student to *19a* and the instructor to *17a*—they end with different results. Is there any way to resolve the issue?

Fortunately, in such situations, instructors and their students can use as a resource another question formation rule of transformational-generative linguistics, namely, the Yes-No Question rule. This transformational rule, known implicitly by all native speakers of English, transforms declarative sentences to questions of the following form:

21a. The gambler could have lost all of his money already.
  b. Could the gambler have lost all of his money already?
22a. The witness whom the police believe was threatened refuses to testify.
  b. Does the witness whom the police believe was threatened refuse to testify?
23a. Yesterday afternoon, Martha bought a new stereo.
  b. Yesterday afternoon, did Martha buy a new stereo?
24a. My friends from Canada, Joseph and Sandy, have been thinking about moving to Florida.
  b. Have my friends from Canada, Joseph and Sandy, been thinking about moving to Florida?
25a. Although having a bad cold, the child is planning to go to the party.
  b. Although having a bad cold, is the child planning to go to the party?

As evidenced from the illustrative sentences above, the Yes-No Question rule moves the first auxiliary verb (if there is one) and verb tense of the main clause to the immediate left of the subject noun phrase. If no auxiliary verb occurs in the main clause, as in *22a* and *23a,* another transformational rule known as Do-Support inserts a *do* form to take the place of the "missing" auxiliary verb. Again, neither the Yes-No Question rule nor the Do-Support rule need be taught formally in the classroom since all native speakers of English not only know these rules already but constantly use them in daily speech to produce grammatical yes-no questions.

What is significant about the Yes-No Question rule for the problem at hand is that it specifically makes reference to the subject noun phrase of a sentence. This means that students can use the Yes-No Question rule as another means to identify subjects. Specifically, after the application of the Yes-No Question rule (and, if necessary, the Do-Support rule) to a declarative sentence, the subject of a sentence will be that noun phrase which occurs to the *immediate right* of the auxiliary verb (or the inserted *do* form if no auxiliary verb occurs). Given that it is the auxiliary verb that always undergoes the movement (and not the subject), the location of the subject can be stated in a somewhat unorthodox yet simpler fashion: the (simple) subject of a sentence is the noun (i.e., "person, place, or thing") which stands to the nearest right of the word that has moved (or the nearest right of the *do* form if it has been inserted). Thus, in sentences *21–25,* the subject nouns (of the main clauses) are, respectively, *gambler, witness, Martha, friends, and child.*

While identifying subjects with the Yes-No Question rule does have the disadvantage of instructors having to explain what a noun phrase or a noun is, the rule has some clear benefits. For one, the use of the rule can resolve the problem encountered earlier in determining the actual subject of the sentences in *17* and *19* and other similar sentences. If students transform the declarative sentences in *17a* and *19a* not into tag-questions but into yes-no questions, the resulting questions would be, respectively:

26. Has the use of electronic devices increased in the last decade?
27. *Have the use of electronic devices increased in the last decade?

Disregarding for the moment the ungrammaticality of *27*, the application of the Yes-No Question rule here shows clearly that *use* and not *devices* is the actual subject of the sentence since *use* is the noun which stands to the nearest right of the moved auxiliary verb *have.* Transforming more complex sentences such as *18a* and *20a* results, respectively, in the following yes-no questions:

28. Was the company which operated several branch offices in New York, Chicago, and Los Angeles going bankrupt?
29. *Were the company which operated several branch offices in New York, Chicago, and Los Angeles going bankrupt?

Here (again ignoring ungrammaticality), the application of the Yes-No Question rule shows that *company* is the subject, not *offices* nor the compound noun phrase *New York, Chicago, and Los Angeles.*

The Yes-No Question rule, however, provides a still greater benefit with respect to resolving the subject-verb agreement problem. Because the Yes-No Question rule places the verb which carries number agreement and the subject back to back, students can perceive more clearly if indeed the verb and its subject agree in number. Put in another way, because the Yes-No Question rule can radically shorten the distance between the subject and the number-carrying verb, students are less prone to performance errors, such as lapses in short-term memory. Thus, if given sentences *27* and *29*, especially in contrast to sentences *26* and *28*, students will more clearly see not only the ungrammaticality of sentences *27* and *29* but also the reason why.[4] Again, none of this requires students to have prior schooling in grammar.

---

[4] As an added attraction, the Yes-No Question rule can be used to test for fragments, run-ons, and comma splices in the same way that the Tag-Formation rule can. This is so because the Yes-No Question rule, like the Tag-Formation rule, applies successfully only on bona fide sentences, not fragments, run-ons, or comma splices. Indeed, in many cases, the Yes-No Question rule may be an easier and more effective rule to use. I invite the reader to test these claims not only with the demon-

As with any method employed to attack persistent mechanical errors, the method of exploiting underlying syntactic knowledge has some drawbacks. It may not work in all cases in all dialects, and, obviously, it will not work for nonnative speakers of English, or at least, nonnative speakers with a weak command of the language. The method, however, does have some decided advantages. It works for most standard speakers of English; it requires no formal training in traditional or transformational-generative grammar (all an instructor needs are sample sentences and fragments for demonstration purposes); it can be employed from the elementary school level to the college level; it can be used both in a classroom setting and in individual tutoring sessions (it can be taught very easily to student tutors); it can be expanded to include other matters of sentence mechanics (e.g., explaining and applying punctuation rules which make reference to independent and dependent clauses). Lastly, and perhaps most important at least for basic writers, the method develops not only self-reliance but also self-confidence because it emphasizes what students already know rather than what they do not. The method is, in other words, intuitive rather than theoretical. Indeed, if anything, the method brings to the surface the immense, often untapped (and often unappreciated), store of linguistic knowledge that students bring to the classroom everyday.

Works Cited

Akmajian, Adrian, and Frank Heny. *An Introduction to the Principles of Transformational Syntax*. Cambridge, MA: MIT P, 1975.

Arbini, Ronald. "Tag-Questions and Tag-Imperatives." *Journal of Linguistics* 5 (1969): 205–14.

Cattel, Ray. "Negative Transportation and Tag Questions." *Language* 49 (1973): 612–39.

Chomsky, Noam. *Aspects of the Theory of Syntax*. Cambridge, MA: MIT P, 1965.

Culicover, Peter W. *Syntax*. New York: Academic, 1976.

Huddleston, Rodney. "Two Approaches to the Analysis of Tags." *Journal of Linguistics* 6 (1970): 215–22.

Lakoff, Robin. "A Syntactic Argument for Negative Transportation." *Papers from the Fifth Regional Meeting of the Chicago Linguistic Society*. Ed. Robert I. Binnick, Alice Davison, Georgia M. Green, and Jerry L. Morgan. Chicago: Dept. of Linguistics, U of Chicago, 1969. 140–47.

Newmeyer, Frederick J. *Grammatical Theory: Its Limits and Its Possibilities*. Chicago: U of Chicago P, 1983.

———. *Linguistic Theory in America: The First Quarter-Century of Transformational Generative Grammar*. New York: Academic, 1980.

stration data given for the Tag-Formation rule but also with other word sequences in English. When teaching students how to test for fragments with the Yes-No Question rule, instructors should make clear that no new words may be added to suspect sequences except, if necessary, some form of *do* (i.e., *do, does,* or *did*).

Content Questions

1. Why according to Noguchi are rules in traditional handbooks not successful in helping students to avoid mechanical errors?

2. What is a tag-question?

3. Describe how the Tag-Formation test helps determine whether an utterance is a fragment. Does this test require a conscious knowledge of grammatical rules or of transformational-generative grammar? Explain.

4. What other common mechanical errors can the Tag-Formation test be applied toward correcting?

5. What role can prepositional phrases, participial phrases, or subordinate clauses have in causing a subject-verb agreement problem?

6. What is the difference between linguistic performance and linguistic competence? How does linguistic performance relate to errors that a person might sometimes make?

7. In relation to the problems that sometimes occur with subject-verb agreement, what is proposed as a backup test for the Tag-Formation test?

8. What is the "Do-Support" rule?

9. Describe how a Yes-No Question is formed. How can this transformation help identify the subject of a sentence?

Questions for Analysis and Discussion

1. What do the Tag-Formation and Yes-No Question tests show about the difference between conscious and unconscious linguistic knowledge?

2. Why would the approach in this article probably not work well with nonnative speakers of English?

3. In what way does Noguchi's article show the application of theoretical linguistics to common writing problems?

Written Academic Discourse in Korean: Implications for Effective Communication

William G. Eggington

It would be easy to assume that good writers throughout the world organize and present material in a similar way, just encoded in a different language. But this is not the case. Indeed, to someone trained in a Western rhetorical style, the writing style of someone trained in Asia might appear chaotic and unfocused. The field of contrastive rhetoric looks at differences in organization and rhetorical styles across cultures. One scholar in this field is William Eggington of Brigham Young University, who has researched differences between Korean and English rhetorical styles. In the article below, he reports on some of his research, and he raises some issues that are important for composition teachers as they consider the cross-cultural background or future cross-cultural needs of their students.

This paper has two main purposes: the first, to conduct a general overview of Korean academic written discourse; and the second, to investigate an interesting feature of modern Korean discourse style.

Written Discourse Features

Although greatly influenced by China throughout their cultural heritage, the Korean people have been able to develop a distinctively Korean culture, philosophical approach, and artistic method—factors which, following Kaplan's (1972) assertion of the relationship between culture and discourse patterns, have contributed to equally distinctive rhetorical styles. In the following section, certain salient features of written Korean discourse will be briefly examined.

Korean discourse structure is described by Kaplan as being

> ...marked by what may be called an approach by indirection. In this kind of writing the development of the paragraph may be said to be "turning and turning in a widening gyre." The circles or gyres turn around the subject and show it from a variety of tangential views, but the subject is never looked at directly. Things are developed in terms of what they are not, rather than in terms of what they are (1972:46).

485

Example 1, which together with the ensuing samples has been translated from Korean, supports Kaplan's notion. From the initial sentence, the topic of the discourse unit, one is led away from, and then back to the subject, which is renewed in the first sentence of the second paragraph.

Example 1:

Foreigners who reside in Korea as well as those who study the Korean language in foreign countries are, despite their deep interest, ignorant of the basis on which the Korean alphabet, Hangul, was formulated. The Korean alphabet, composed of combinations of lines and curves, at first seems more difficult than Japanese kana for those who use the Roman alphabet, and as the combination of vowels and consonants multiplies, it appears more difficult to memorize all the combinations. This seemingly complicated combination of vowels and consonants can, on the contrary, be mastered with no more effort than is needed to learn the Roman alphabet or Japanese kana, for one must merely memorize two dozen vowels and consonants, the principal letters of the Korean alphabet.

The principal concern of foreign as well as Korean scholars has been on what foundation the Korean alphabet was formulated (Kang and Kim 1979:5).

Example 2 defines the topic in terms of what it is not rather than what it is.

Example 2:

The sounds of these five words are of the same kind as *k, t, p, s, ch,* however they are named hard sounds because the sounds are harder than *k, t, p, s, ch.* Some people think that these sounds are the same as *g, d, b, z, j,* because *st, sp, ps, sch* which are used with *g, d, b* as sounds today are combination words. And some people say, "The words which mark hard sounds are *sk, st, sp.*" They say, "*g, d, b* are not Korean. These were made to mark Chinese." So they wanted to take *g, d, b* out of Korean (Lee 1973:60).

Note also the use of the "some people say" formula, which appears very common in Korean discourse when one is taking a somewhat controversial stand, either to protect one's own position by enlisting anonymous support, or to appear not too direct when criticizing another's position. In a debate conducted in a national journal over the inclusion of Chinese characters in the public school curriculum, a professor of Liberal Arts and Sciences at Seoul National University used this formula, or one of its variations, seven times in a four-page article. Variations of the formula included "some claim that . . . ," "some scholars have . . . ," "there are men who . . . ," "a professor whom I know . . . ," "it is grievous to find some men holding the position that . . . ," and "it is also said that . . ." (Huh 1972). This may also be indicative of an oral influence on written discourse (Ong 1979).

An example of extended discourse comes from an article (Pae 1982) taken from the English edition (a direct translation of the Korean edition) of the *Korean Times,* one of the major newspapers in Korea. The author, Pae Yang-seo, is a Hanyang University professor. In the interests of space a paragraph-by-paragraph synopsis is given here.

Example 3:

Paragraph #1.

The Ministry of Home Affairs is planning to lengthen the period of training for public officials from 3 days to 6 days per year in order to solidify the spirituality of the public officials. The training is to be conducted at the Spiritual Cultural Institute which is rendered in English as the Institute for Korean Studies.

Paragraph #2.

A new meaning of "national" is attached to the word "spiritual." Perhaps this comes from the term "spiritual culture."

Paragraph #3.

A member of the Korean Alphabet Society complained that the architectural design of the Institute for Korean Studies resembles a Buddhist Temple and thus is not Korean. This is not so because Buddhism, though imported from India, is a Korean religion. Likewise Christianity is a Korean religion.

Paragraph #4.

Any attempt to label what is national and what is foreign fails.

Paragraph #5.

Perhaps too much emphasis on nationalism may do more harm than good.

Paragraph #6.

Instead of inspiring nationalism we should be appealing to universal reason and proper moral conduct. The civil spirit must take precedence over the national spirit.

Paragraph #7.

I am reminded of this when, changing trains at the subway, I witness the rush to occupy seats on route to the sports center where the Olympic Games are to be held. How do we enhance the nation's prestige through a sports event? As a teacher I am partly responsible for this situation.

Paragraph #8.

Spiritual poverty is best observed in a metropolitan area like Seoul. Why is our public transport system so multi-layered with standing buses at the bottom, then regular buses charging three times more than standing buses, and finally taxis which move constantly to catch more passengers?

Paragraph #9.

Once you catch a taxi you have to listen to the loud radio controlled by the driver.

Paragraph #10.

"Dear administrators, please do not talk about spiritual things unless you are interested in implementing concrete ethical conduct."

Thus, commencing with a search for a definition of "spiritual" by alluding to a government retraining program and the name of, and architectural style of, the building the program is to be held in, the main point, that civil spirit should take precedence over national spirit, is reached in paragraph #6. From a western English interpretation, loosely related examples of spiritual poverty are then given, including a description of the subway rush hour, a mention of the Olympic Games, a description of the transit system in the city, and finally a complaint about loud radios in taxis. The brief conclusion is an appeal not to think about spirituality until a level of ethical conduct is reached. The organization of the article appears to follow the indirect patterns shown in the previous paragraph examples. The main idea of the article is briefly stated halfway through the article and alluded to in the conclusion. There is no direct development of this theme, but rather from an English perspective, what is developed is a view of what the main idea is not.

Hinds (1982) has shown that one of the preferred rhetorical patterns of Japanese (*ki-shoo-ten-ketsu*) has its origin in classical Chinese poetry, where the first section (*ki*) begins the argument, the second section (*shoo*) develops the argument, the third section (*ten*), immediately after finishing the argument, abruptly changes the direction of the argument towards an indirectly connected sub-theme, and the fourth section (*ketsu*) reaches a conclusion. A Korean preferred rhetorical structure, *ki-sung-chon-kyul*, appears to follow the same pattern—a pattern which may be seen in Example 3 where paragraph #1 begins the argument; paragraphs #2, #3, #4, #5 loosely develop that argument, paragraph #6 states the main point of the argument; paragraphs #7, #8, #9 state concepts indirectly connected with the argument; and paragraph #10 concludes the main theme.

In contrast to American students who receive substantial instruction in structural rhetoric, Korean students are not exposed to formal instruction on writing styles. Models, such as the above mentioned *ki-sung-chon-kyul*, are given in discussions of literature, and students are asked to emulate them in their writing. In discussion between this researcher and a number of Korean students, mention was made by the Koreans that, if one wishes to write academic prose, one writes in the *ki-sung-chon-kyul* style, leaving out the *chon* (change) stage, thus creating a "beginning, development, end" pattern. Although this may bear some resemblance to the preferred English rhetorical pattern of "introduction, body, conclusion," the Korean interpretation of "beginning," "development," and "end" appears to be different from the American equivalents, as can be seen in Examples 1, 2, and 3. One can presume that Koreans would have little difficulty in gaining a clear understanding of the above texts and would not view them as being "out of focus" as native English speakers would. It appears that the discourse styles shown above constitute the preferred rhetorical pattern of Korean academic writing.

However, another rhetorical style is evident when one surveys Korean academic journals of the type written in Korean and English and especially when one concentrates on articles written by those authors who publish in both Korean and English and have earned academic degrees in English-speaking universities. The following example, translated from Korean, taken from a Korean-English journal published in Korea, written by a scholar who also contributes to the journal in English, and who has degrees from an American university, shows a linear, general-to-specific rhetorical pattern which, despite being slightly non-idiomatic, appears to be coherent and cohesive.

Example 4:

However the following problem is not solved by the [above] methodology. This problem is the fact that the effect of the "Saemaeul Movement" as well as any other effects, are part of natural changes of life. That is to say that this is a problem of history, and historical change. This means that the elevation of the standard of living on the farming and fishing communities is effected by the rapid progress of various economic fields, the construction of facilities and the improvement of international trade (Kim 1979:135).

It would appear that some Korean scholars who seem to be more proficient in English exhibit certain aspects of a linear structure in their Korean writing as seen in Example 4, while Korean scholars who are not proficient in English and who have not studied at English-speaking universities, exhibit the particular non-linear rhetorical patterns illustrated in Examples 1, 2, and 3.

A rather clear contrast between the more traditional rhetorical pattern and the apparently English-influenced pattern can be seen by examining any number of volumes on Korean-related studies containing contributions from Korean scholars. For the sake of the reader who may not be proficient in Korean, a brief examination of a journal containing articles written by Korean scholars which have either been written in English or translated into English is given below. The volume under examination (Sohn 1975) contains nine articles, eight written by Korean scholars and one by an American scholar. Six of the eight Korean scholars hold positions in American universities. Seven of the eight articles written by Korean scholars are structured in the organizational style typically found in most English academic journals, with an introduction containing a statement of the purpose of the paper and a thesis statement, a review of the literature, an examination of the subject, and a conclusion followed by a bibliography. Examination of these bibliographies shows a significant number of citations referencing English sources. One article, the eighth, however, has seven bibliographic citations all referencing Chinese or Korean sources; there are no references to English sources in the article. An examination of the article shows no statement of purpose; for the reader unfamiliar with Korean rhetorical patterns, there appears to be no thesis development, but rather a list of points revolving loosely around an unstated central theme. The brief conclusion of the article is as follows:

> In this paper I have raised a small problem in the structure of middle Korean, and I have tried to explain my own view on the structure of plosives of Middle Korean, particularly on the problems of doenshori (alpapranas) (Gim 1975:100).

This is the first time the reader is informed of the purpose of the paper. Obviously Gim is employing a different rhetorical pattern than the other seven Korean contributors to the journal. The fact that Gim references only Korean sources and that he is teaching in a Korean university may lead one to suspect that the rhetorical style he employs is one which has not been much influenced by English patterns; whereas the many English references cited by the other seven authors, as well as the fact that six of the seven are employed at American universities, would suggest that these scholars have been influenced by English rhetorical patterns.

It is interesting to note a finding by Clyne, who states, in his discussion of English/German rhetorical patterns, that:

> There appear to be some disciplines (e.g., mathematics, engineering) in which German scientists have adopted a basically linear discourse structure. This may be conditioned by the discipline or by leadership in the discipline of English speakers. In other fields of science (e.g., chemistry), the non-linear structure is quite common in German (1981:64).

Perhaps the academic rhetorical patterns of many languages of the world are adjusting to fit a linear style. Gonzalez notes, in a description of the languages of the Philippines, that a priest will commence his sermon in the local language, but "switches to English if the topic is academic and theological in nature, a function of the probability that the preacher did his studies primarily in English during his seminary days" (Gonzalez 1981:55).

If such a code switch is possible in oral discourse, it seems plausible that Korean scholars, for example, who have studied in the United States and who have been immersed in English for an extended period of time, have also been immersed in the written discourse features of English. Indeed most of the scholars' knowledge was gained, developed, discussed, argued, expounded, and defended in the rhetorical patterns of written English. Upon returning to Korea, these scholars may have been required to transfer knowledge gained in English into Korean. Obviously there would have been some difficulty, for Korean does not have the direct lexical equivalents of English. Another more subtle problem emerges, however. As previously indicated, English has rhetorical patterns different from Korean that may cause the writer either: (1) to adjust concepts developed in the preferred rhetorical style of English to fit the rhetorical patterns of Korean; (2) to translate the language from English to Korean, but retain the rhetorical patterns of English; (3) to develop some compromise between the rhetorical patterns of Korean and English. All three choices would seem to present impediments to effective communication. The previous discussion would indicate that many Korean scholars are (consciously or unconsciously) adopting the second of the choices; that is, writing in Korean while retaining the rhetorical structures of English. Thus, Koreans unfamiliar with English and its rhetorical patterns will find information presented in the English-preferred rhetorical patterns difficult to comprehend, even though that information is presented in written Korean.

The concept that differences in rhetorical patterns between writer and reader hinder optimal communication can be verified by reference to, for example, Clyne, who in a discussion of the English linear versus the German non-linear structure reports:

> The English translation of Norbert Dittmar's book, *Soziolinguistik,* a landmark in the development of sociolinguistics in West Germany, was described by Bills (1979) as "chaotic" and criticized for its "lack of focus and cohesiveness," "haphazardness of presentation," and "desultory organization." None of the four reviews of the original written by scholars from Central European universities (Rein 1974; Geye 1974; Leodolter 1974; Purcha 1974) make any criticism of this kind (Clyne 1981:64).

Obviously the translators of *Soziolinguistik* translated the language but not the discourse structure, and since one must presume that important information can be lost when one is reading "chaotic" material, the English speaking, non-German speaking, student must be missing vital information when reading the English version of *Soziolinguistik* because of the difference in rhetorical styles between these two languages. Thus, in many fields of German-English scholarship some breakdowns in communication must be caused by scholars trying to put English rhetorical patterns into German and German rhetorical patterns into English. If difficulties of this type exist between such linguistically related languages as German and English, one must presume that there will be significant difficulties between such linguistically more distant languages as English and Korean.

Krulee, Fairweather, and Berquist (1979) have supported the concept that optimal information transfer occurs when the organizational structure of a unit of written discourse agrees with the reader's preconceived notions of what that structure should be. These authors have shown that subjects are better able to comprehend and recall information when the discourse structure and the subject's personal organizational structure are compatible. Hinds (1983) has also demonstrated a similar finding cross-culturally. Japanese students and English-speaking American students were asked to read and then recall, immediately and then after a week, information contained in an essay written in one of the desired rhetorical patterns of Japanese. The essays were in the respective subject's native language. Results indicated that there is "a difference in the ability of Japanese and English readers to retain information in memory, depending on the organizational schema in which the information is presented" (1983:22). The Japanese readers were able to retain information better than the English readers because the Japanese readers were operating within a familiar rhetorical framework.

Such research is of importance when consideration is given to the huge amounts of information currently being transferred, not only cross-linguistically, but cross-culturally as well. Hinds (1983) verifies the position first taken by Kaplan (1966) that culturally influenced rhetorical patterns play an important role in effective communication through the written medium. It may be that, in the case of Korea, the English-influenced linear style some scholars prefer represents an impediment to effective communication between those scholars and other Korean scholars, as well as the general Korean public, who prefer the more traditional discourse patterns and who have had only limited exposure to the linear structures. In other words, do Koreans regard the linear structure of the type shown in Example 4 as being as unclear as English speakers would regard the non-linear structure shown in Examples 1, 2, and 3?

A preliminary investigation of this question was undertaken by collecting a corpus of eight samples of academic Korean writing. Four of the samples followed the preferred non-linear style of Korean while the remaining four followed the linear patterns of English. The eight samples dealt with public administration, political science, and linguistics, and were carefully selected to be comparable in content complexity. Fourteen Korean students who had all been in the United States for less than six months, and who had beginning ability in English, were asked to rank the samples from easiest to read to most difficult to read. If discourse structure had an effect on the ranking, it was predicted that the samples following the preferred Korean discourse pattern (sample numbers 1, 3, 4, and 6) would be judged easier to read than the sample which followed the English-influenced linear rhetorical pattern (sample numbers 2, 5, 7, and 8). The results indicated that samples 1, 3, 4, and 6 were ranked as being easier to read 71% of all the choices available, and samples, 2, 5, 7, and 8 were ranked as being more difficult to read 69% of all the available choices.

Thus, although it was recognized that the research technique was rather crude, the results stimulated further research in this area. Another study was conducted using the research design developed by Hinds (1983). The hypothesis of this study is that Korean speakers will be better able to reproduce information presented in the more traditional non-linear rhetorical framework than information presented in the linear rhetorical pattern frequently used by Korean scholars who have been influenced by the preferred rhetorical pattern of academic English.

Method

Subjects

Thirty-seven Korean adults newly arrived in the United States were asked to participate voluntarily in the study. Twenty-eight of the participants were college students in Korea and were planning to attend an American college once they had an acceptable English competency, while the remaining nine participants were more mature adults who planned to enter the workforce at the completion of an intensive English course. Ten of the subjects had been used in the pilot study.

Materials

Two paragraphs from separate articles in the October 1980 edition of the *Korean Journal of Public Administration* were selected. One of the paragraphs (Example 5) reflects the non-linear preferred rhetorical style of Korean written academic discourse. A simplified discourse analysis of the English translation of the paragraph is given below. The bracketed numbers are not part of the text and are included to identify sentences to assist in the discussion of the text.

Example 5:

[1] We intend to describe the general decision making process in Korean Government administrative offices in this report. [2] The term administrative organization means the housing, department, place and office structure of the office. [3] The purpose of this report is to

research the decision making process. [4] However the theory of office decisions is developed by involving formal and informal aspects. [5] Therefore this distinction is for convenient management. [6] Because the nature of office management is very complicated, my thinking, to help in understanding it, is to divide it into business, place, formal and informal parts (Cho 1980:248).

This paragraph begins with a statement of purpose in the first sentence. The second sentence is subordinated to the first by giving a definition regarding the administrative organization of an office. The third sentence runs parallel to the discussion of the purpose of the text begun in the first sentence and does not seem to have any linear relationship with the second sentence. The fourth sentence seems to be more related to the second sentence than to the third sentence by its reference to office procedures and the separation of that theme into formal and informal aspects. The fifth sentence is subordinated to the fourth sentence by giving an explanation of why the distinctions are made. The sixth and final sentence continues the divisions begun in the fourth sentence and seems to be an expansion of the fourth sentence and not related to the fifth sentence. The paragraph development appears to follow a two strand ordering, which may be graphically depicted as:

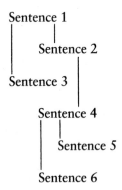

The other paragraph (Example 6) was written in a more linear style. The English translation of the text is given below. Once again the bracketed numbers identify sentences and are not part of the original text.

Example 6:

[1] In order to use the collective goods approach, it is necessary to characterize the cultural values of the social environment so that ramifications can be subdivided which enable individual preferences to be developed. [2] In general, "cultural values" may be regarded as a stock of institutionalized survival strategies written by present atti-

tudinal and behavioral rules. [3] Cultural values can be conceptualized in this way because all societies make forms of values and rules through the mutual reaction between the individual and the group. [4] If these values and rules are instituted, they have a tendency to continue under a neutral, or even a little hostile environment (Hoon 1980:15).

The first sentence explains the rationale of the following discussion. The second sentence is subordinated to the first by explaining in more specific detail the term "cultural values." The third sentence shows why "cultural values" can be explained in this particular way and appears to be coordinate to the second sentence. The fourth sentence is subordinated to the third by its expansion of the "values and rules" concept introduced in the third sentence. The organization of this paragraph follows a hierarchical subordinate-coordinate structure common in English academic writing (McDaniel 1980), and may be graphically represented as:

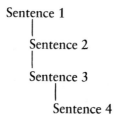

Sentence 1

Sentence 2

Sentence 3

Sentence 4

As previous research (Eggington 1983) has indicated, many Koreans have difficulty comprehending Chinese characters that are often inserted into Korean academic texts for no apparent communicative function. Since the ability to comprehend Chinese characters was not the purpose of this study, this distraction was removed and the subjects were given the paragraphs written only in Hangul (the indigenous Korean script). Thus, except for the replacement of the Chinese characters with Hangul, the paragraphs are natural in the sense that the words and the discourse elements remain exactly as they are in the original journal articles.

Procedure

The subjects were divided into two groups, one receiving the Korean version of Example 5, and the other receiving the Korean version of Example 6. The subjects were asked to read and study the paragraphs for two minutes and were told that they would be required to recall as much information from the paragraphs as they could. After two minutes the paragraphs were taken away; the subjects were given a blank piece of paper and were requested to write all that they remembered from the paragraph within eight minutes. At the conclusion of this task, the subjects were asked to return the following week for another test. Upon their return, the subjects were asked once again to reproduce as much as they could remember of the paragraph they had been exposed to the week before.

Scoring

A clausal analysis of the original paragraphs was conducted. It was found that, in Korean, Example 5 contained nine clauses, and Example 6 contained eleven clauses. The subjects' responses were also analyzed in the same fashion by three independent raters who were unfamiliar with the purposes of the research. Responses were scored on a five-point scale so that, if the information contained in a subject's clause agreed exactly with the original, then a score of 1 was assigned to the recalled clause; partial agreement resulted in a score of 2, 3, or 4 depending on the closeness of the information in the subject's clause to the original, while total disagreement, or no mention of the clause, resulted in a score of 5. Thus the higher the score, the less information was recalled. No penalty was given for any new information not found in the original, and the particular ordering of the recalled clauses had no effect on the scoring system.

Statistical Analysis

A standard two-tailed parametric T-test was used to test the reproduction differences between the traditional Korean text and the linear text in both immediate and delay conditions.

Results

Table 1 shows the mean of each group, the standard deviation from the mean, and the results of the T-tests. The null hypothesis of this study is that the means of the recalled scores of the traditional non-linear text will be statistically equal to their linear counterparts; i.e.,

$$X[nli] = X[li]$$

and

$$X[nld] = X[ld]$$

where

X = sample mean of the recalled averages
nli = the non-linear text in the immediate recall condition
li = the linear text in the immediate recall condition
nld = the non-linear text in the delayed recall condition
ld = the linear text in the delayed recall condition

Table 1

	nli	*li*	*nld*	*ld*
Mean	3.49	3.73	3.73	4.47
St. Dev.	0.50	0.52	0.48	0.31

Two-tailed T-test for immediate condition (i.e., *nli* and *li*) 1.22 (NS)
Two-tailed T-test for delayed condition (i.e., *nld* and *ld*) 4.80 (prob < .001)
df = 25 for both tests.

The T-test analysis revealed that in the immediate recall condition, the differences in the means of the groups were not sufficient to reject the null hypothesis. Thus, in the immediate condition the subjects were able to recall approximately the same amount of information from both the traditional text and the linear text. However, in the delayed condition there were significant differences (p < .001). Thus, in the delayed condition the null hypothesis is rejected, and the assumption can be made that Koreans do have more difficulty recalling information after a period of time when that information is presented in a linear rhetorical style.

Discussion

If reading is to be considered a "psycholinguistic guessing game," as Goodman (1970:93) has posited, then readers and writers have certain built-in expectations about the ordering of ideas in any stretch of discourse. In an optimal condition, the reader shares the same expectations of what is to follow what as does the writer. Breakdowns in communication between writer and reader occur when these expectations are violated (Martin 1980; Clyne 1980). Studies by Kintsch and Greene (1978), Meyer (1975b), and Thorndyke (1979) have shown the relationship between long-term memory recall and the particular organization through which information was presented. Over a delayed condition, information is retained far better when it is presented in a manner compatible with the reader's expectations. It would appear that this present study verifies these findings. Of more importance than the verifications, however, is the fact that the texts used in the study were written by Koreans for Korean consumption, and that the information contained within the texts has potential importance to the development of the Korean nation.

If, as this study indicates, a significant portion of Korean academic prose is written in a linear style, and if, as this study also indicates, significant segments of the Korean population, including college students, are unable to retain the information presented in this linear style as well as they can retain information presented in a more traditional non-linear style, then written academic communication in Korea must be suffering. Clearly, the size of the data base in this study is too small to permit any generalization, yet some preliminary recommendations will be attempted.

Implications and Recommendations

If the government of the Republic of South Korea wishes to continue its objective of modernizing the Korean society, then it must recognize that a key factor in this development is the creation of a highly efficient and openly available system of information storage and retrieval. Such a system does not come about through natural processes. The present system has the potential of creating an elite group of Korean academics who have had sufficient exposure to English education to enable them to acquire English as well as the preferred rhetorical patterns of English and thus be able to tap into the vast amount of current information available in English.

Another group of Korean scholars, numbering more than the preceding group, have not had the opportunity to acquire English, let alone the preferred rhetorical patterns of English, and thus must rely on their more fortunate colleagues to share that information with them. However, as the preceding study has shown, one group in this process of communication is using one written rhetorical pattern while the other group is using a different written rhetorical pattern—a situation which inhibits information recall and the optimal transfer of vital knowledge, as well as the optimal development of the nation.

It seems that a number of options are available to Korean educational authorities, should they desire to improve the present situation. At the present time there does not appear to be an academic written rhetorical component in the Korean educational system, but rather an informal system in which students in elementary and secondary schools are exposed to the rhetorics of classical literature and told that they should emulate these styles in their writing. Tertiary education places little importance on written style. What is needed, then, is the introduction of instruction in writing into the system. It would smack of linguistic imperialism if one were to advocate the preferred linear rhetorical pattern of academic English as the only rhetorical style to be taught in this curriculum. A better approach would be to teach both the traditional Korean styles and the English-influenced academic style. But it seems clear that the problem of differing rhetorical styles in Korean deserves serious attention.

Bibliography

Cho, S. C. 1980. Inter-agency decision process in the Korean government. *Korean journal of public administration*. 1.140–151.

Clyne, M. 1980. Writing, testing, and culture. *The secondary teacher*. 11.13–16.

———. 1981. Culture and discourse structure. *Journal of pragmatics.* 5.61–66.

Eggington, W. G. 1983. Impediments to effective communication in Korean academic writing. Unpublished paper. University of Southern California.

Gim, S. G. 1975. The phonological structure of middle Korean plosives. In H. M. Sohn (ed.) *The Korean language: Its structure and social projection.* Honolulu: The Center for Korean Studies. 91–102.

Gonzalez, A., FSC. 1981. Language policy and language-in-education policy in the Philippines. In R. B. Kaplan, et al. (eds.) *Annual review of applied linguistics, II.* Rowley, MA: Newbury House. 48–59.

Goodman, K. S. 1970. Reading: A psycholinguistic guessing game. In H. Singer and R. B. Ruddell (eds.) *Theoretical models and processes in reading.* Newark, DE: International Reading Association. 497–508.

Hinds, J. 1982. *Ellipsis in Japanese.* Edmonton: Linguistic Research, Inc.

———. 1983. Retention of information using a Japanese style of presentation. Paper presented at the Seventeenth Annual TESOL Convention, Toronto, March.

Hoon, Y. and D. S. Bark. 1980. An evaluation of the saemaul movement. *Korean journal of public administration.* 1.1–25.

Huh, W. 1972. Exclusive use of Hangul and Hanmun education. *Korea journal.* 4.45–48.

Kang, Y. H. and M. H. Kim. 1979. *Hankuko.* Seoul: Ihwa University Press.

Kaplan, R. B. 1966. Cultural thought patterns in intercultural education. *Language learning.* 16.1–20. (Reprinted in R. G. Bander. 1981. *American English rhetoric.* [Instructor's Manual] New York: Holt, Rinehart and Winston; also in H. B. Allen and R. N. Campbell (eds.) 1972. *Teaching English as a second language.* New York: McGraw-Hill; also in K. Croft (ed.) 1972. *Readings on English as a second language for teachers and teacher trainees.* Cambridge, MA: Winthrop. 2nd ed. 1980.)

———. 1972. *The anatomy of rhetoric: Prolegomena to a functional theory of rhetoric.* Philadelphia: Center for Curriculum Development. (Distributed by Heinle & Heinle.)

Kim, H. D. 1979. Q.L.I. of Korean rural populace: An individual approach to social indicators. *Korean journal of public administration.* 3.134–170.

Kintsch, W. and E. Greene. 1978. The role of culture-specific schemata in the comprehension and recall of stories. *Discourse processes.* 1.1–13.

Krulee, G. K., P. G. Fairweather, and S. R. Berquist. 1979. Organizing factors in the comprehension and recall of connected discourse. *Journal of psycholinguistic research.* 8.141–163.

Lee, P. K. 1973. *Hyuntae hankukoeo sangsong ununron.* Seoul: Seoul National University Press.

Martin, A. V. 1980. Proficiency of university level advanced ESL students and native speakers of English in processing hierarchical information in context. University of Southern California. Ph.D. diss.

McDaniel, B. A. 1980. Contrastive rhetoric: Diagnosing problems in coherence. *The English quarterly.* 13.3.65–75.

Meyer, B. J. F. 1975. *The organization of prose and its effects on memory.* Amsterdam: North-Holland Publishing Company.

Ong, W. J., S. J. 1979. Literacy and orality in our times. *Profession 79.* New York: Modern Language Association. 1–7.

Pae, Y. S. 1982. Thoughts of our times: What is spiritual? *The Korean times.* Seoul: The Korean Times Press.

Sohn, H. M. (ed.) 1975. *The Korean language: Its structure and social projection.* Honolulu: The Center for Korean Studies.

Thorndyke, P. 1979. Knowledge acquisition from newspaper stories. *Discourse processes.* 2.95–112.

Content Questions

1. How does the rhetorical style of written Korean discourse differ from the style used in written English discourse?

2. How has the rhetorical style of Korean scholars, even when writing in Korean, been affected by their having studied at English-speaking universities?

3. According to previous research, what correlation seems to exist between how closely a rhetorical pattern or style of a text matches a reader's expectations and that reader's comprehension and subsequent recall of the text?

4. What was Eggington's research designed to discover?

5. Describe the set-up of Eggington's test. How many subjects did he involve? What were they tested on? How were they scored? What kind of time element was involved?

6. Generally speaking, what did the results of his experiment show about the recall that Koreans would have of a linear and a nonlinear text, both immediately after reading those texts and later?

Questions for Analysis and Discussion

1. What is your reaction to the text given in Example #3? Does it feel disorganized to you? Explain.

2. How would Korean scholars who can effectively code switch between linear and nonlinear styles in their reading and writing have an advantage over Korean scholars who are unaware of such differences or who have trouble working with such differences?

3. How might Eggington's research be applicable to language policy and planning in Korea?

4. What implications do the results of Eggington's research have for a college or university teacher who is teaching composition to foreign students?

Ambiguity in College Writing
(To a College Freshman)

Norman C. Stageberg

The late Norman C. Stageberg was a linguist at the University of Northern Iowa. He is perhaps best known for his work in structural ambiguity and for the linguistic textbooks he authored or edited. In the following article, he explores some issues about ambiguity as it relates to composition. His article gives particular attention to structural ambiguities, especially syntactic ambiguities, and he identifies a number of linguistic situations in which these types of ambiguities are likely to occur. He also provides a set of strategies for removing ambiguities from writing. His insights should be valuable to writers interested in becoming better at recognizing and editing ambiguities from their own writing.

In college composition textbooks, ambiguity is given scant attention. Yet ambiguity is an ever-present peril to clearness of expression. If you are to read with discernment and write with exactness—and both skills are required for quality college work—you must become acquainted with the wily ways of ambiguity.

Ambiguity should not be confused with vagueness. A vague expression is merely indefinite. A diplomatic statement like "My government will take strong countermeasures . . ." is vague. Often the vague word is one expressing a quality that can exist in varying degrees, like strong. *An ambiguous expression, on the other hand, has two or more definite meanings. For example, in "The President rejected the Smith Appointment," Smith can be the one who appointed or the one who was appointed.*

Throughout your college years you will have much writing to do, from the pencil-gnawing labors of freshman composition to the painstaking preparation of senior reports. In all this writing the paramount literary quality that will be expected of you is clearness; for if your meaning is muddied, other writing virtues are of little use. Your instructors are accustomed to read with a sharp and critical mind. They want precision of statement: they expect you to say exactly what you mean, not approximately what you are muddling over. Thus, clearness should be your topmost writing goal.

Various enemies of clearness can beset you. A long disorderly sentence may misroute your reader as he wanders through a maze of phrases and clauses. A wrong word may baffle him. A careless comma may change your meaning, and a plethora of words may smother your thought. Each of these faults can fog over the lucidity you are striving for.

But the most insidious foe to clearness is ambiguity. Ambiguity means multiple meaning. A word or passage that can be understood in more than one sense is ambiguous. In isolation most words are ambiguous, because individual words have numerous meanings, as a glance in the dictionary will show. But in written discourse words are not isolated. Each is part of a larger whole, and this enveloping whole, this context, normally shuts out the unwanted meanings and permits only the one desired by the writer. For example, the entry *hand* in *Webster's New Collegiate Dictionary* is given eleven principal meanings; yet the meaning of the word is clear in each of the following sentences because of a short stretch of context:

> Let's play another *hand*.
> The *hand* of the clock pointed to twelve.
> Will you give me a *hand* with this tire?
> All *hands* on deck!
> This wool has a soft *hand*.
> I wish to ask for the *hand* of your daughter.

The next sentence, however, is ambiguous:

> 1. We breathlessly watched the *hand*.

Here the context is not restrictive enough to limit the meaning to a single sense. Thus it becomes evident that the careful control of context can help you to avoid ambiguity.

In college writing there are four types of ambiguity that it will be useful to examine.

The first type is **lexical ambiguity**. This occurs when two or more meanings of a single word are applicable in a given context, as is the case in the following sentence:

> 2. Buckley's salvos in defense of conservatism were fired first at Yale University.

The reader here does not know whether *at* means "against" or "in the location of." Lexical ambiguity often lurks in common words, as in this sentence:

> 3. For many purposes they used obsidian or volcanic rock.

Here *or* has two lexical meanings. It can express either an alternative, or an equivalence with the meaning of "that is." Some writers separate the two senses by punctuation, reserving commas for the meaning of equivalence, but this practice is not common enough to be a dependable key to meaning.

The other three types stem from the grammar of English, not from the semantic diversity of individual words, and are known collectively as structural ambiguity. We will take them up one by one.

The second type is **syntactic ambiguity.** This is occasioned by the arrangement of words. It can be illustrated by a story told about Governor Kirk of Florida. When a political opponent once called him

4. a fat ladies' man

the governor wittily retorted, "I like thin ladies too." Here it is the arrangement of /adjective + noun possessive + noun/ that makes the ambiguity possible. When this grammatical sequence occurs, the adjective can modify either the first or the second noun; but if the meaning of the adjective is compatible with that of each noun, the phrase will be ambiguous, unless, as always, the larger context channels the meaning to a single noun.

The third type, **class ambiguity,** occurs when the context allows a word to be interpreted as belonging to two different grammatical classes. A case in point is the tale of the Chinese philosopher who was addressing a class of American students one evening on the subject of Chinese thought. He had just asserted that much wisdom is embedded in old Chinese proverbs when the lights went out. Immediately he said to the class, "Will you please raise your hands?" A few seconds later the lights came on again, whereupon he remarked:

5. You see, many hands make light work.

Silly, of course, but it affords a nice illustration of class ambiguity, in this case an alternation between /adjective + noun/ and /noun + verb/.

The fourth type, **script ambiguity,** is that which occurs in writing (but not in speaking) because written words are not accompanied by the speaking voice. The voice, by variations in stress, pitch, pause, and length, can make countless distinctions in meaning that are not revealed in the written form of the spoken words.

As illustration, it will be instructive to read the opening sentence of a composition written by a sweet freshman girl who was very fond of camping and the out-of-doors:

6. I am an outdoor lover.

In her mind's ear she heard this sentence with high pitch and strong stress on the *-door* syllable, and the sentence expressed her meaning perfectly: I love the out-of-doors. But she failed to realize that the reader of an opening sentence, with no context to guide his interpretation, might put the stress-and-pitch emphasis on the *-love* syllable and get a startlingly different meaning.

To hear for yourself how the voice can make distinctions in meaning, try reading aloud each of these scriptally ambiguous sentences in two ways that will bring out two different senses. The key words are underlined.

7. Our milk has a <u>stable flavor</u> the year around.
8. Sandy enjoys <u>bathing girls</u>.
9. Nixon <u>swears in</u> his new cabinet.
10. The *Tribune* will take pictures of the Salvation Army <u>cooking students</u>.
11. He is going to <u>take over</u> a hundred pigs.
12. I suspect you are <u>right there</u>.
13. People who drink Old Fitzgerald don't know <u>any better</u>.

Script ambiguity is so ubiquitous in English that it would be impossible to list all the grammatical patterns in which it occurs. It will suffice to call your attention to its existence as a threat to clear writing and to present, as sample patterns, two simple grammatical situations in which it is often found.

Situation 1: Noun + noun head (= modified noun)
    14. giant killer

In cases like this the position of the heavier stress determines the meaning. *Giant kíller,* with stress on *killer,* means a killer which is a giant, like a large shark. But *giánt killer,* with stress on *giant,* is a killer of giants. Similarly we use stress to distinguish two meanings in

15. girl watcher
16. 18th century scholar
17. record sale

and many others.

Situation 2: /Adjective or noun/ + noun head
    18. patient counselor

This noun phrase consists of /adjective + noun head/ if we put the stress on *counselor,* and the meaning is "counselor who is patient." But it consists of /noun + noun head/ if the stress is given to *patient,* and the meaning becomes "counselor of patients." The next four examples behave the same way:

19. a French teacher
20. a mercenary chief
21. Boeing says it isn't seeking firm orders yet.
22. old-fashioned glasses

This concludes a quick glance at four general types of ambiguity that you should be aware of—lexical, syntactic, class, and script ambiguities. This classification is not watertight, and you will find that sometimes an actual case will fit into two categories. For instance, the lexical and class ambiguities are merged into a single one in the words of a sign on a seaside shop:

23. Buy your girl a bikini and watch her beam with delight.

Since *her beam* can be either /possessive adjective + noun/, or /object pronoun + verb/, this is a double class ambiguity. But the shift in the grammatical class of *beam* from noun to verb causes a change of meaning from "derrière" to "smile broadly." Thus it is also a lexical ambiguity.

In addition to genuine ambiguities, there is the pseudoambiguity that can mar your writing. Here is an example:

24. Joe Louis and Jack Dempsey moved around the small tables, each adorned with flowers and candles.

In this sentence we really know what the writer means. Nevertheless, the double entendre is momentarily distracting to the reader, and such distractions have no place in precise writing.

Of the four types of ambiguity that we have discussed, the one that is most amenable to specific and detailed explanation is syntactic ambiguity. So let us examine this type a little further. Syntactic ambiguity, you will recall, derives from the arrangement of words. By arrangement of words we mean syntactic structures. The question that arises here is this: Are there certain structures that are especially likely to be ambiguous? The answer is a firm yes. There are a great many structures in English that are potentially ambiguous, and some of these occur with high frequency. They constitute a semantic minefield for the writer. But if you learn the location of the mines, you can proceed with less danger. Therefore we shall now examine a few of the most hazardous structures, those that have blown up many sentences in student writing.

A considerable number of these can be subsumed under the label "Successive Modifiers." SUCCESSIVE MODIFIERS SHOULD ALWAYS BE CONSIDERED AN AUTOMATIC DANGER SIGNAL. And now, here is a series of such structures, grouped into two categories: (A) successive prenominal modifiers; (B) successive postnominal modifiers.

A.   Successive Prenominal Modifiers

Situation 3: Adjective + noun + noun head
    25. Oriental art expert

Here the adjective can modify either the first or the second noun. Our Oriental art expert can be an art expert who is Oriental or an expert in Oriental art. And more of the same:

    26. small business man
    27. old car law
    28. gray cat's eye

In the next four situations, the principle is the same as in Situation 3: The first item can modify either the second or the third. We must always remember, of course, that each example has been removed from its context and that a broader enclosing context could obviate the ambiguity.

Situation 4: Noun + noun + noun head
    29. student poetry discussion
    30. Maine lobster festival

Situation 5: "More" + adjective + noun head
    31. You get more modern service there.
    32. Use more colorful language.

This case can also be classified as a script ambiguity. If you will listen carefully to your own pronunciation of Example 32, you will perhaps notice that, when *more* modifies *language,* you lengthen it and give it a slightly stronger stress.

Situation 6: *-ing* particle + noun + noun head
    33. growing boy problem
    34. weeping woman's child

Situation 7: *-ed* participle + noun + noun head
    35. painted ladies room
    36. disturbed girls counselor

In each of the foregoing five situations there are two modifiers before the noun head. When three modifiers precede the noun head, the chances for ambiguity are increased; and it is not uncommon to find three readings for this type of pattern, as you will notice in Situations 8, 9, and 10 which follow.

Situation 8: Noun + noun + noun + noun head
   37. summer faculty research appointment
   38. English teacher training program

Situation 9: Adjective + noun + noun + noun head
   39. genuine gold coin purse
   40. old-fashioned teachers convention hotel

Situation 10: Adjective + noun + participle + noun head
   41. soft wool insulated bag
   42. solid steel cutting blade

B.   Successive Postnominal Modifiers

In our English system of modification, word-group modifiers follow the noun head. Word-group modifiers include these kinds: prepositional phrase (for example, *of a movie star*), relative clause (for example, *that the public sees*), noun phrase appositive (for example, the corporal, a *thickset man*), and participial phrase (for example, *located near the business district* and *weeping softly*). When two such modifiers of the noun head occur, there is the danger that the second may seem to refer to something other than the noun head. The next five situations, chosen out of many, will serve our purpose here.

Situation 11: Noun head + prep phrase + relative clause
   43. The life of a movie star that the public sees does look glamorous.

In this pattern the writer often intends the relative clause to modify the noun head; but when instead this clause appears to modify the last word of the prepositional phrase, the result is ambiguous.

   44. A test over a new subject which is hard and complex requires careful review.

Situation 12: Noun head + relative clause + prep phrase
   45. I was talking about the books that I had read in the library.

This pattern of modifiers is the reverse of the normal order, which is that of Situation 11, and presents great likelihood of ambiguity. In the preceding example, for instance, *in the library* could modify *had read* or *books* or *was talking,* giving three readings to a simple sentence.

46. Carlsen inspected the boat which Bob had bought at the landing.

Situation 13: Noun head + participial phrase + relative clause
47. There is a bronze statue standing near the fountain which many of the local populace admire.
48. He publishes books filled with color prints which are of excellent quality.

Situation 14: Noun head + relative clause + noun phrase appositive
49. The student who accused his roommate, a thief, dropped out of school.

Situation 15: Noun head + participial phrase + noun phrase appositive
50. The sergeant talking with the corporal, a thickset man, shook his head impatiently.

The thirteen situations above are samples of the hazards of ambiguity in the noun phrase; and if you read alertly you may notice many other ambiguous patterns of like nature. Remember that the general warning for all such patterns is: BE WARY OF TWO SUCCESSIVE MODIFIERS.

C. Postverbal Situations

Turning to the grammatical patterns that follow the verb, we find that the potentially ambiguous situations consist of complements and adverbials. There are at least nine situations involving complements alone, but these are really not common enough to warrant inclusion here. Of all the others, here are three—Situations 16 through 18—that will serve to show what can happen after the verb to perplex your reader.

Situation 16: Verb + noun object + adverb (or prep phrase)
51. Take the big bag upstairs.
52. This portable photocopier reproduces almost anything on white bond-weight paper.

Situation 17: Verb + prep phrase + prep phrase
53. The suspect had stolen away from the house in the darkness.
54. The teacher spoke to the boy with a smile.

Situation 18: Verb + noun object + infinitive phrase

55. The defendant was fined twenty rubles for selling his place in line to buy Czech woolen underwear. (The relevant verb is *selling*.)

We note here that the infinitive, *to buy Czech woolen underwear,* can go with either *place* or *selling*.

56. A California publisher created the CIA program to subsidize student, labor, and cultural groups.

The next four postverbal situations resemble one another in that the concluding adverbial has two verb forms to modify. The adverbial takes one of four forms: adverb, prepositional phrase, noun phrase, and adverbial clause. Each of these four forms will be illustrated.

Situation 19: Verb + infinitive (+ noun object) + adverbial

57. I promised to call at ten o'clock.
58. Nixon may act to combat racial discrimination decisively (or *with speed,* or *before Congress opens,* or *next week*).

Situation 20: Verb (+ noun object) + infinitive phrase + adverbial

59. The Lindbergs watched their grandson cross the platform proudly (or *with pride,* or *when the great hour arrived,* or *that morning*).

Situation 21: Verb (+ noun object) + "and" + verb + adverbial

60. He repaired the car and returned promptly.

Here *promptly* might refer to only *returned* or to both *repaired* and *returned*. (Let us digress a moment to point out that there are numerous cases in which a modifier on either side of an *and* is ambiguous in its reference. For instance, in the simple phrase "fellow teachers and administrators," the noun *fellow* might modify only *teachers* or both *teachers* and *administrators*.)

61. The guide fed the fire and waited until the sun arose.

Situation 22: Verb (+ noun object) + relative clause + adverbial

62. We might find something that we could do there.
63. I discovered the purse that was lost in my car.
64. They found the uranium that they were seeking when the rainy season was over.
65. The police saw the girl who had been kidnapped last night.

These twenty grammatical patterns are only a small fraction of the total number of syntactically ambiguous situations, but a study of these few should heighten your sensitivity to other traps of syntax where you might get caught in an equivoque.

When you have become sensitive to the possibilities of double meanings and have formed the habit of scrutinizing your own writing to locate intrusive and unintended meanings, you have won half the battle against ambiguity. The second half consists of eliminating them. This elimination will usually take place when you are revising and polishing your rough first draft. After you have spotted an offender, you face the question "How can I restate this clearly?" Although each case is a problem in itself, you have at your disposal eight methods of correcting ambiguous expressions. These methods, used singly or in combination, can be of help to you.

1. SYNONYMY.   As an example let us consider

66. The doctor made them well.

This sentence can be turned into two clear statements by synonymy: "The doctor made them skillfully" and "The doctor cured them."

2. EXPANSION.   Expanding by the addition of a word or two will sometimes remove an ambiguity.

67. He finished the race last Thursday.

This can be cleaned up with one word: "He finished the race last on Thursday" and "He finished the race on last Thursday."

3. REARRANGEMENT.   Rearrangement means using the same elements in a different order.

68. They are chewing tobacco and garlic.

Rearranging the elements, we can get two readings:"They are chewing garlic and tobacco" and "They are garlic and chewing tobacco."

4. CAPITALIZATION.   Capital letters are sometimes serviceable in making clear a sentence that would be orally ambiguous. Here is one instance: "You should call your Uncle George" and "You should call your uncle George."

5. PUNCTUATION.   Marks of punctuation are frequently the means of correcting or obviating written ambiguities. The next case is a good illustration.

69. The collection of funds has risen to the level of minimum need; thus much is needed to clothe the poor of the parish.

Thus much has two interpretations—"therefore, much ..." and "this much ..." A comma gives the first meaning and synonymy the second one. With the prenominal modifiers a hyphen is very useful. The next case

70. foreign study program

would be clear if written as either "foreign-study program" or "foreign study-program."

6. SPELLING.   The many homonyms in English that can be a source of ambiguity in speech are usually kept clear in writing by spelling, for example, "The governor went hunting bear last week." Rarely will spelling remove a written ambiguity.

7. ALTERATION OF CONTEXT.   Since, in clear writing, it is the context that restricts various meanings of words and structures to a single sense, it is obvious that an ambiguity can sometimes be remedied by making the context sufficiently restrictive. The following example will illustrate:

71. This fall the rich Winchester School District has been plagued with troubles between the teaching staff and the students. The investigator sent by the District School Board, after prolonged inquiry and many interviews, has recommended the hiring of a teacher counselor by the school.

The written words *teacher counselor,* by themselves, can mean "a teacher who counsels" or "one who counsels teachers," and the passage above does not restrict the meaning to either one of these. So let us alter the context: "This fall the rich Winchester School District has been plagued with troubles between the teaching staff and the students. The investigator sent by the District School Board, after prolonged inquiry and many interviews, has reported that the difficulties stem from unstable personalities among the teaching staff itself and has therefore recommended the hiring of a teacher counselor by the school." This new context now makes probable the interpretation of *teacher counselor* as "one who counsels teachers."

8. USE OF GRAMMATICAL SIGNALS. The English grammatical system provides us with a limited number of forms that can be used as signals in correcting ambiguity. Here are a few illustrations:

a. Gender signals (*his, her, its*)
   72. (ambiguous) The puppy by the girl with the contented look
      (clear) The puppy by the girl with (her/its) contented look
b. Person-thing signals (*who, which*)
   73. (ambiguous) The dog of the neighbor that bothered him
      (clear) The dog of the neighbor (who/which) bothered him
c. Number signals
   74. (ambiguous) One of the freshman girls who seemed downcast
      (clear) One of the freshman girls who (was/were) downcast
d. Coordination signals
   75. (ambiguous) A car which stood behind the garage that was in need of paint
      (clear) A car which stood behind the garage and which was in need of paint

Possibly no combination of these eight methods will seem to work for a particularly obstinate ambiguity you have created. For such cases there is a ninth method: Grit your teeth and rewrite the wretched thing in any way your reader will understand.

It is difficult to write clear prose; yet proficiency in this skill is mandatory for success in most professions that college graduates enter. If you learn to overcome ambiguity in writing, you will have taken one important step toward mastering this valuable skill.

Suggested Assignments

(Note to the instructor: The exercises below are designed to sharpen the students' perception of ambiguity. For the correction of ambiguities, it is perhaps best to work with those occurring in class themes.)

1. In each sentence the word that is lexically ambiguous is italicized. Show the two meanings of each.
   a. *How* will he find his dog when he returns?
   b. Going to the beach is like going to the attic: you are always surprised at what you find in *trunks.*
   c. For just $10 a year you can read *about* 3000 books a year. (advertisement)

    d. We must not disregard romantic visions *of* democracies and autocracies.

    e. He *rented* the house for $110 a month.

    f. I can do this *in* an hour.

    g. She *appealed* to him.

    h. The agents *collect* at the drug store.

2. Point out the class ambiguity in each sentence and indicate its meanings.

    a. Use indelible ink and varnish over it.

    b. You will forget tomorrow.

    c. The enormous gorilla back of Pedro swayed out through the door.

    d. We observed another sail.

    e. The bouncer turned out a drunkard.

    f. We were seated during the intermission.

    g. Fred looked over her bare shoulder.

    h. We decided on the boat.

    i. They stamped upstairs.

    j. They were both happy and excited.

3. These sentences contain prenominal modifier ambiguities, some of which follow patterns not taken up in the preceding essay. Point out the double or multiple meanings of each.

    a. Mabel took a novel course.

    b. Malcolm looked professional in his chef's cap.

    c. Nelson is a champion cow owner.

    d. Would you like a hot evening drink?

    e. Josephine is an Iowa farmer's wife.

    f. Imported gingham shirts were offered for sale.

    g. Where is the dark brown sugar bowl?

    h. Ferrari is the world's largest sports car maker.

    i. Write for free tape recorder and tape catalogue. (This advertisement really appeared.)

4. This is a group of script ambiguities. Read each item aloud in two ways to bring out two meanings.

    a. He was beaten up by the bridge.

    b. Do you have some metal screws?

    c. I consider these errors.

    d. The club will be open to members only from Monday through Friday.

    e. The proposal calls for charging an annual fee of $40 for all faculty parking on campus.

    f. Agatha is a designing teacher.

    g. This country needs a good roads official.

    h. I suspect you were right there.

    i. Smoking chief cause of fire deaths here (headline in the *New York Times*).

5. The varying uses of the present participle (-*ing* form of verb) involve it in several kinds of ambiguity. Point out the -*ing* ambiguities in these sentences.
   a. They are canning peas.
   b. My job was keeping him alive.
   c. The Greek government staged a crackdown on shortchanging employees.
   d. Moving vans, still in their civilian paint, carry guns.
   e. Testing ignorance involves private schools too.
   f. Easy chemistry for nursing students.
   g. His business is changing human behavior.
   h. MacLeish likes entertaining ladies.
   i. Eleanor enjoys growing roses.

6. The following sentences contain ambiguities of specific types not mentioned in your reading. Point out the meanings of each.
   a. She taught the group athletics.
   b. Investigators find makers of aircraft nuts. (headline)
   c. He found the mechanic a helper.
   d. Our spaniel made a good friend.
   e. They are ready to eat.
   f. At dress rehearsals she sang, danced, and tumbled very expertly.
   g. At her bedside were her husband, Captain Horace Brown, a physician, and two nurses.
   h. The seniors were told to stop demonstrating on campus.
   i. Few names are mentioned more often in discussions of students than that of Mikelson.
   j. His job is to post changes in address, telephone numbers, and performance ratings.

Further Readings

Black, Max. *Critical Thinking.* Englewood Cliffs, N.J.: Prentice-Hall, Inc., 1955. On ambiguity, see pp. 183–202; on context, see pp. 190–192.

Lee, Irving J. *Language Habits in Human Affairs.* New York: Harper & Row, 1941. An introduction to general semantics.

Ornstein, Jacob, and William W. Gage, *The ABC's of Language and Linguistics.* Philadelphia: Chilton Company—Book Division, 1964. On semantics, see pp. 103–119.

Payne, Stanley L. *The Art of Asking Questions.* Princeton, N.J.: Princeton University Press, 1951. On ambiguity, see pp. 158–176.

Philbrick, F. A. *Understanding English*. New York: Crowell-Collier and Macmillan, Inc., 1944. An engaging and lively introduction to semantics.

Stageberg, Norman C. "Structural Ambiguity: Some Sources." *English Journal*, May 1960.

———. "Structural Ambiguity for English Teachers." *Teaching the Teacher of English*. Champaign, Ill.: National Council of Teachers of English, 1968.

———. "Structural Ambiguity in the Noun Phrase." *TESOL Quarterly*, December 1969.

———. "Structural Ambiguities in English." *Encyclopedia of Education*. New York: Crowell-Collier and Macmillan, Inc. 1970.

Thouless, Robert H. *How to Think Straight*. New York: Simon and Schuster, Inc. 1950. On ambiguity and vagueness, see pp. 132–146.

Content Questions

1. What is the difference between ambiguity and vagueness?

2. How does structural ambiguity differ from lexical ambiguity?

3. What three major types of structural ambiguity does Stageberg identify? Describe what characterizes each type.

4. Based on his definition of a class ambiguity, why is Stageberg's example "many hands make light work" a class ambiguity? Which different grammatical classes are represented by the words *light* and *work* within the two different interpretations?

5. Why is writing particularly vulnerable to what Stageberg calls "script" ambiguities?

6. What does the author indicate "should always be considered an automatic danger signal"?

7. How does his cautionary advice relate to the numerous syntactic situations he identifies?

8. Identify the eight strategies listed by Stageberg for correcting ambiguities.

Questions for Analysis and Discussion

1. Select an ambiguity pattern identified by Stageberg and construct an ambiguity that occurs with that pattern. Identify which pattern it follows. Then describe how such an ambiguity could be corrected.

2. Writing teachers often caution students against misplaced modifiers. Explain the relationship that these might have with successive postnominal modifiers.

3. How might the identification and description of various types of ambiguities and their common environments help students as they proofread and revise their own writing?

A Linguistic Frame of Reference for Critiquing Chicano Compositions

Ricardo L. Garcia

Ricardo L. Garcia, who has researched various sociolinguistic issues related to bilingualism and composition, is the author of *Teaching in a Pluralistic Society: Concepts, Models, Strategies.* In the following essay he briefly discusses the role that linguistic interference can play in the kinds of nonstandard forms that Chicano English speakers might display in their writing. An understanding of such linguistic interference could be useful to some teachers as they critique the written work of their students.

When an English teacher critiques a composition written by a Chicano, strange expressions may appear, such as "on the forest" instead of "in the forest"; many of these expressions are superficial variations of English that the Chicano brings to the language that should not count against the Chicano's grade for the composition. Yet, because English teachers are generally unaware of the linguistic process of interference, they tend to rate such expressions as improper English. What follows is an attempt to explain the linguistic process of interference as it applies to the Mexican American student when he composes an essay. The term "Chicano" is used to define Mexican American, Spanish American, or Hispano students who are to some degree Spanish-English bilinguals.

Linguistic Interference and the Chicano

When the Chicano is producing speech in one of his languages, Spanish or English, phonemes and morphemes from the second language may intrude on the speech of the first, a natural mixing of linguistic components that occurs when languages come into contact with each other. Weinreich, one of the early scholars who attempted to describe the semantic systems of bilinguals, proposed that interference occurred in three areas: the phonic, the lexical, and the grammatical.[1] To a large extent, Weinreich's description of interference as it applies to the Chicano is accurate. While speaking his *caló*, or dialect of English, the Chicano thinks little of borrowing and mixing of Spanish and English phonic, lexical, and grammatical elements. For

---

[1] Uriel Weinreich, *Languages in Contact* (New York: Linguistic Circles of New York, 1953), chapter 1.

example, a Chicano will write the expression, "yeah, no?" meaning "this is true, isn't it?" which is a literal translation from the Spanish "Si, no?" The Spanish expression is natural; the English seems contradictory.

Linguistic interference is a natural phenomenon that occurs whenever two languages come into contact. Unfortunately, English teachers have treated the *caló* as serious defects in English, especially as the *caló* appears in compositions, an error that the teacher makes due to ignorance, bias, or linguistic insecurity.

Phonological Interference

Studies on the Chicano's English phonology have reported that the Chicano experiences phonic interferences with English phonemes that either do not exist in Spanish or are pronounced differently. As early as 1917, the Chicano's English phonology was described as a variant of his Spanish phonological system.[2] Espinosa attributed this to speech mixture in the Southwestern United States that occurred when the Chicano's Spanish and the Anglo's English phonetic systems came into contact. More recent studies have reported that the Chicano experiences interferences with vocalic, consonantal, and suprasegmental phonemes when he speaks English.[3] The Chicano's phonemic system filters the phonemes of English to the nearest equivalent phonemes in Spanish, which is to say that the Chicano substitutes Spanish phonemes for the English so that it is not uncommon to hear consonantal substitutions such as "hands" /hændz/ when "hangs" /hæŋz/ is meant, or vocalic substitutions such as "heat" /hit/ when "hit" is meant. Suprasegmental substitutions refer to the sing-songy rhythm attributed to the Chicano's English contour patterns.

Note the phonological interferences in an excerpt from a theme written by a Chicano:

> *This* pictures show Indians riding through the mountains. One Indian seems
> to be the leader. *Hes hans* are held up high, telling the others to follow.

The three italicized words are examples of phonological interference. "This" is pronounced as though it were "these" by the Chicano so that the Chicano is not committing a number error; he is spelling the word phoneti-

---

[2] A. M. Espinosa, "Speech Mixture in New Mexico: The Influence of English on New Mexico Spanish," *The Pacific Ocean in History,* ed. H. M. Stephens (New York: Macmillan, 1917), pp. 408–428.

[3] Gloria Jameson, *The Development of Phonemic Analysis Oral English Proficiency Tests for Spanish-Speaking School Beginners* (Austin: University of Texas Press, 1967), pp. 61–141. See also, Stanley Tsuzaki, *English Influence on Mexican Spanish in Detroit* (The Hague: Mouton, 1970); and Luriline Coltharp, *The Tongue of the Tirilones* (University City: University of Alabama Press, 1965), pp. 75–91.

cally according to his *caló*. Again, the English "his" is pronounced as "he's" by the Chicano so that "hes" is a phonetic rendering. In both the "this" and "hes" pronunciations, the Chicano is using the Spanish sound /i/ or "long e" in place of the English /ɪ/, because the /ɪ/ sound does not exist in his Spanish phonetic system. In neither vocalic variation is the Chicano making a grammatical error; he knows that "pictures" is plural and requires "these," and he knows that "he's" is a contraction of "he is," and indeed when he spells "hes" he is making a distinction between "he's" and "his." Consonantal substitutions occur when the Chicano writes "hans" for "hands," a substitution referred to earlier in this essay.

Essentially, phonic interferences are aural/oral discrimination difficulties which occur during the filtering process. They are quite easy to understand when one considers that there are only five Spanish vocalic phonemes, for example, as opposed to eleven English vocalic phonemes. The Chicano must learn the distinctions /iː/ /eɛæ/, /uu/, /aɑ/, and /ɔo/ on the basis of the five Spanish vocalic phonemes /i/, /e/, /a/, /u/, and /o/. Unless he is trained to hear and make the English distinctions, he will tend to substitute the Spanish phonemes.

Morphological Interference

Studies on the Chicano's morphology report that the Mexican American experiences lexical interference while speaking Spanish or English, thus tending to speak a portion of both languages simultaneously.[4] Essentially, the Chicano borrows words from both Spanish and English, regardless of which language he is speaking. He tends to anglicize Spanish words and hispanicize English words, as in the expression: "*Vamos pa la dance*," or "Your mother is *planching*." In the former expression, the English word "dance" has been hispanicized to conform to the Spanish; in the latter the word for "ironing," "*planchado*," has been anglicized to "planching" to conform to the English.

What occurs is a blending of two languages; hispanicized English words are altered to conform to the Spanish pattern of word structure, as the inflected ending of "*ganga*" for the English "gang." The Chicano is aware of such blendings and labels them *Anglicismos*, i.e., Anglicisms, and does not consider them unusual. Spanish words such as *mesa, plaza,* and *rodeo,* along with many other terms associated with ranching activities, have been mixed into standard English. English neologisms have been formed from the Spanish such as the popular "mustang" from the Spanish *mesteño* or "pinto" from the Spanish *pinto*. But even though this type of

---

[4] George C. Barker, *Pachuco: An American-Spanish Argot* (Tucson: University of Arizona Press, 1948), pp. 12–18. See also, Coltharp, *Tongue of the Tirilones*, pp. 75–91.

mixing is not unusual, the Mexican American's language mixing in the southwest is held in disrepute, being described by such pejoratives as "Tex-Mex" or "Poncho." [5]

Note the morphological interference that appears in the writing of a Chicano:

> This pictures show Indians riding through the mountains. One Indian seems to be the leader. Hes hans are held up high, telling the others to follow him. That's some *ganga,* this Indians. Probably, they will ride *on* those trees to the town where they will paint it *colorado.* They will drink a lot of *birria* and sing a lot of *songas,* but no one will give a care that they do this things.

"Ganga," "birria," and "songa" are hispanicized versions of "gang," "beer," and "songs." "Colorado" is a direct borrowing from the Spanish word meaning "red." "On those trees" means "in those trees" and is meant so by the Chicano. Because the preposition *"en"* in Spanish can be used either as "in" or "on," the Chicano uses only "on" in English, although he knows the difference between "in" and "on" as expressed in English. Other idiomatic interferences can occur, depending upon the Chicano's knowledge of Spanish.

The Chicano's morphology exhibits lexical interference in both Spanish and English. The Chicano borrows words and expressions from English or Spanish when he does not know or cannot immediately recall the equivalent in the language he is speaking. Generally, the Chicano's Spanish lacks the vocabulary refinement necessary to manage English neologisms. Isolated from the Latin cultures, and in many cases from the general American culture, the Chicano finds it necessary to hispanicize and anglicize neologisms that do not already exist in his lexicon. The purpose of the borrowing process is to extend the Chicano's vocabulary so that he can express himself in either the Spanish or English communities.

Interference and the language variations it causes are important only to the extent that they cause the Chicano negative language attitudinal problems. If latinized phonemes and anglicized morphemes do little to hamper the Chicano's cognitive activities in the school, then there is little need for concern. But, if teachers take the attitude that there is a single correct enunciation of particular phonemes and that any neologisms are an adulteration of the English language, then the significance of the Chicano's alterations is most serious. And to a large extent this has in fact been the attitude of educators who teach Chicano youth. Chicano English and Spanish have been described by teachers as "inferior" or "improper." [6] It is

---

[5] Thomas P. Carter, *Mexican Americans in Schools: A History of Educational Neglect* (New York: College Entrance Press, 1970), pp. 112–118.

[6] Carter, *Mexican Americans in Schools,* pp. 97–106.

significant to note that rarely is the Chicano taught in his own dialect of English or Spanish as is the middle class, monolingual student taught English. Only five and a half percent of all Chicano students receive some form of English as a Second Language (ESL) instruction. Less than two percent of all teachers of Chicanos are assigned to ESL programs, and most of these teachers have as little as six semester hours of training in ESL.[7]

Interference and Chicano Composition

Given interference on the phonological and morphological levels of structural analysis, one would suspect that interference would occur on the syntactic level; one would suspect that the Chicano would mix the syntactic patterns of Spanish and English. Yet, it is almost inconceivable that a Chicano would mix the syntactic patterns of the two languages if he is to speak coherently in either language. Spanish—a synthetic, highly inflected language—and English—an analytic, highly uninflected language—are almost opposite in syntactic structure. Research is not available to indicate that the Chicano inflects English as though it were Spanish, or that he excludes inflections from Spanish as though it were English. On the contrary, Peña's research indicates that Chicano first graders are capable of using basic syntactic patterns of both Spanish and English and that they have little difficulty handling fundamental transformations in either language.[8]

The writer conducted a comparative study on the syntactic patterns utilized by lower and middle class Chicanos and found that all of the Chicanos utilized the syntactic patterns that are basic to American English; they did not experience syntactic interference even though they were Spanish-English bilinguals.[9]

Understand that the Chicano exhibits a wide range of bilingualism; he may be bilingual only to the degree that he understands Spanish when it is spoken to him; obversely, he may be completely literate in Spanish and English, being able to speak, read, and write in both languages. Given this wide range of bilingualism in the Chicano student population, the English teacher should not assume that all Chicanos will experience interference when composing themes. Much depends upon the Chicano's linguistic community, where he may or may not hear and speak both Spanish and English. More importantly, the English teacher should consider phonological and morphological variations in Chicano compositions as natural

---

[7] U.S. Commission on Civil Rights, *The Excluded Student* (Washington: U.S. Government Printing Office, May 1972), pp. 21–49.

[8] Albar Peña, *A Comparative Study of Selected Syntactical Structures of Oral Language Status in Spanish and English First Grade Spanish-Speaking Children* (Austin: University of Texas Press, 1967).

[9] Ricardo Garcia, "Identification and Comparison of Oral English Syntactic Patterns of Spanish-English Speaking Adolescent Hispanos." Diss. University of Denver 1973, pp. 86–100.

manifestations of the language of the community. English teachers might best identify the variations and then utilize them in creative writing activities. Just as John Steinbeck had an ear for the *calós* of migrant Anglo peoples, and just as this talent is desirable in creative writing, the English teacher might do well to encourage the Chicano to develop an ear for the richness of his *caló*. Several Chicano poets, for example, are now experimenting with the Chicano *caló* as a viable medium for images that portray the Chicano experience in the United States.[10]

Also understand that this essay is not the final word on Chicano English as it appears in compositions. But hopefully it will provide the English teacher a frame of reference by which the Chicano's composition can be more equitably critiqued.

Content Questions

1. What is linguistic interference?

2. Why would the use of "this pictures" by someone who speaks Chicano English not necessarily indicate a lack of understanding about plurals? What might it indicate according to the article?

3. What kind of morphological interference might a Chicano English speaker have?

4. Why is it unlikely that a Chicano English speaker would blend the syntax of English and Spanish?

5. To what extent can it be assumed that a Chicano English speaker will experience the type of interference problems described in this article?

Questions for Analysis and Discussion

1. Do you think Garcia's point is that a writing teacher should never help correct a Chicano English speaker's nonstandard forms? Explain.

2. Describe the role that the difference in the vowel phonemic inventory between Spanish and English has in causing particular problems for a Spanish-speaking person or someone who speaks Chicano English to learn the standard English dialect.

3. If a composition teacher does seek to help a Chicano English speaker to remove the "*calós*" from essays or reports that must be in standard English, how might a more accurate view of what causes the interference help a teacher to address the issue?

---

[10] Victor Ochoa, *Nationchild Plumaroja* (San Diego: Toltecas en Aztlan Centro Cultural de la Raza, 1972).

Additional Activities and Paper Topics

1. Contrast the approach that Noguchi takes in addressing comma splices, run-on sentences, and fragments with the type of approach taken in a more traditional textbook or handbook that addresses itself to such mechanical and punctuation problems. Report on the differences you observe. (**Syntax**)

2. Stageberg's article shows how some structural ambiguities can be avoided in your writing, but there are contexts such as humor and advertising in which structural ambiguities are deliberately created. Using some of Stageberg's examples as models, generate some structural ambiguities of your own. Create examples illustrating a variety of types, label and categorize the various kinds that you have generated, and report on what distinguishes your examples from each other. (**Syntax**)

3. Locate some writing intended to be persuasive, such as a printed version of a campaign speech, a sales brochure, or an extended advertisement. Keeping in mind the discussion in Riley and Parker's article, identify some of the presuppositions in the text you have selected and discuss the structural devices that are involved in those presuppositions. (**Semantics and Pragmatics**)

4. There are many countries, such as India, Singapore, Korea, and various Arabic-speaking countries, where English, while not the dominant language, is still an important institutional language. Some of those countries produce an English version of the newspaper. Through the library or through the Internet, examine an English-speaking newspaper produced in a country for which English is not the official or dominant language. Compare and contrast a few articles in that newspaper with articles written on the same events in your local newspaper. Report on the differences you note in rhetorical style and organization between articles in the two newspapers. (**Language Varieties**)

Linguistics and
Literary Analysis

Linguistics shares a common tradition with literary study. Not so long ago, language and literature were studied together by philologists, who saw the study of both areas as mutually beneficial. Later developments and specialization in both fields have often produced scholars whose work does not cross over from one field to the other. But the potential for application of linguistics to literature remains and with further developments will arguably increase.

In its most fundamental application to literature, linguistics can examine the structure of various utterances within a literary work: the phonology, morphology, and syntax of particular phrases or clauses in that work. This chapter, however, includes articles that go beyond merely describing or noting linguistic structures in a given work. These articles suggest the interpretive significance of particular linguistic features in literary works or suggest ways that teachers can make language a meaningful focus in their teaching of literature.

The first reading in this chapter, "Understanding Poetic Speech Acts" by Michael Hancher, shows how an adjustment in perception about a particular speech act can greatly influence how a literary work is interpreted. The approach demonstrates an important linguistic perspective that literary critics can consider when examining literature.

In "Student Lexicographers and the Emily Dickinson Lexicon," Cynthia L. Hallen describes the apparent influence that Webster's 1844 Dictionary had on Dickinson's poetic composition. The historical connections between Webster and Dickinson have become more apparent through Hallen's *Emily Dickinson Lexicon*, which will be a valuable reference work for the interpretation of Dickinson's poetry. As part of Hallen's discussion, she explains how she involved students in research connected with the lexicon project.

Roger Fowler identifies and dismisses some of the mistaken notions and ideas that have caused some scholars to overlook the contributions linguistics can make to the analysis of literature. In his article, "Studying Literature as Language," Fowler discusses a passage from Faulkner's *The Sound and the Fury* and demonstrates how linguistics can illuminate the interpretation of literature.

Bruce Southard and Al Muller present a sociolinguistic approach in their article "Blame It on Twain: Reading American Dialects in *The Adventures of Huckleberry Finn*." After noting the disagreement that has existed about how accurately Twain represents dialects in his novel, they propose a different linguistic focus for teachers who discuss this novel in their classes. Southard and Muller suggest that teachers discuss specific language items that might interfere with students' comprehension of the dialogue. They also show how a discussion of some dialectal features can lead to a consideration and discussion of larger linguistic issues.

In his article "Some Psychodynamics of Orality," Walter J. Ong explains how the orientation and characteristics of orally based cultures relate to specific linguistic features in the literatures of these orally based cultures. Ong notes that these types of features are found in older works such as *Beowulf* or Homer's epics.

There are of course other areas of linguistic application to literary analysis or scholarship, which are not included in this reader. One of these involves "wordprint" analysis. Because each author has characteristic language patterns that distinguish his or her writings from other authors, an author's "wordprint" can be used to help resolve questions involving disputed authorship. This has happened, for example, with some of Shakespeare's work as well as with the *Federalist Papers*. In another type of application, there are many insights to be gained in older texts through learning more about the language at the time those particular works were produced.

Understanding Poetic Speech Acts

Michael Hancher

Understanding what someone has said involves more than understanding the content of what he or she has said. It also involves interpreting the intended function of the utterances. Knowing, for example, whether someone is making a promise or a threat makes a difference. Linguists and philosophers have given particular attention to the consideration of such "speech acts" in language. In the following article, which first appeared in *College English,* Michael Hancher of the University of Minnesota demonstrates the powerful insights that speech act theory can bring to literary criticism. Hancher illustrates how a consideration of the speech act in a poem can make a major difference in the interpretation of that poem.

The thesis of this paper[1] is simple, perhaps unexceptionable. I propose that in understanding "literary" or "poetic" discourse, as in understanding ordinary spoken or written discourse, we should and do regularly take into account what it is that the author or dramatic speaker is doing *in* the act of uttering a given piece of discourse.

Deliberate attention to such matters is common enough in ordinary speech. A mother says to her son, "It's time for you to clean up your room"; she may then go on to specify that in uttering those words she is *ordering* him to clean up his room (and not *suggesting* that he do so) by adding, "—that's an *order*." A diner says to a short-order cook, "This chili's hot"; the cook may ask, "Is that a *compliment* or a *complaint?*" When we (as speakers) do *not* deliberately specify the force of our utterances, nor (as hearers) raise such questions about the force of what we have just heard, it isn't because such niceties don't matter. We assume that they are patent and don't need to be specified.

What is true of ordinary discourse in this respect is true also of "literary" or "poetic" discourse—regardless of whether that discourse is as *bona fide* as ordinary discourse (as in the case of *Areopagitica*) or whether it merely mimics some of the rhetorical conventions of ordinary discourse ("My Last Duchess," for example). Some literary texts are evidently utterances of the author *in propria persona;* others are utterances not of the author but of a *dramatis persona:* in understanding both kinds of literary discourse the reader needs to register correctly what it is that the speaker is

---

[1] This paper has been improved—if not approved—by Paul Alkon, Thomas Clayton, Donald Ross, and Martin Steinmann.

doing in uttering the words he speaks. There is some uncertainty whether the first poem that I shall examine in this paper was meant to be taken as the utterance of the author, or as that of a dramatic *persona;* that uncertainty does not affect the point about it that I wish to make.[2] The poem is Shakespeare's Sonnet 19:

> Deuouring time blunt thou the Lyons pawes,
> And make the earth deuoure her owne sweet brood,
> Plucke the keene teeth from the fierce Tygers jawes,
> And burne the long liu'd Phænix in her blood,
> Make glad and sorry seasons as thou fleet'st,
> And do what ere thou wilt swift-footed time
> To the wide world and all her fading sweets:
> But I forbid thee one most hainous crime,
> O carue not with thy howers my loues faire brow,
> Nor draw noe lines there with thine antique pen,
> Him in they course vntainted doe allow,
> For beauties patterne to succeding men.
>   Yet doe thy worst ould Time dispight thy wrong,
>   My loue shall in my verse euer liue young.[3]

This startling poem seems not to have attracted much comment. What comment it has attracted is misleading in so far as it ignores what the speaker is doing at various points of the poem in uttering the words that he does.

In the middle of the last century Ignatius Donnelly remarked of the first four lines, "I know of no quatrain in Englis[h] poetry more heroic, more swelling, more original or more climactically finished."[4] Part of such an impression would stem from such powerful nouns as "Lyon," "Tiger," "teeth," "blood"; but much of the "heroism" might plausibly seem to lodge in the imperative verbs: "*blunt* thou the Lyons pawes," "*make* the earth deuoure ... ," "*Plucke* the keene teeth," "*burne* the long liu'd Phænix ...." This imperative syntax hammers on into the next quatrain: "*Make* ...," "*do* ...." Stephen Booth, noticing (I suppose) these features among others, characterizes the octave of Sonnet 19 as "affirmative," and therefore "set off against a third quatrain in which the verb is governed by

---

[2] For an account of the kinship of dramatic and non-dramatic texts, see Marcia Eaton, "Good and Correct Interpretations of Literature," *Journal of Aesthetics and Art Criticism,* 29 (1970), 227–233, esp. 231–232; and Michael Hancher, "Three Kinds of Intention," *Modern Language Notes,* 87 (1972), 827–851, esp. 847–848.

[3] William Shakespeare, *Sonnets, 1609: A Scolar Press Facsimile* (Menston, England: Scolar Press, 1970). I have adopted the standard emendation of "yawes" to "jawes" in line 3.

[4] Ignatius Donnelly, *The Sonnets of Shakespeare* (St. Paul: G. W. Moore, 1859), p. 14; cited in *A Variorum Edition of Shakespeare: The Sonnets,* ed. H. E. Rollins (Philadelphia: Lippincott, 1944), I, 53. A quarter-century later, Donnelly launched the notorious theory that there are Baconian ciphers embedded in the text of Shakespeare's plays.

not" ("O carue not with thy howers my loues faire brow").[5] But despite the bold diction and the even bolder grammar, it won't do to call either the first quatrain or the whole octave "heroic" or "affirmative" in any unqualified sense. If there is heroism here it is only of a special kind; and in a strict sense there is no affirmation in the octave at all.

For in uttering lines 1–8 the speaker does not *affirm;* nor, despite the boldly imperative verbs, does he *command;* rather, he *concedes.* His utterances are not *affirmations,* nor *commands,* but *concessions.* They bespeak not his strength and authority, but his weakness and incapacity.

Some part of this actual state of affairs should be clear from the start. The reader should early recognize that an apparent order issued to Time to exercise his power over the creation cannot be quite what it seems: that is, it cannot really be an *order.* For a mortal has no authority to issue genuine *orders* or *commands* to Time; and no *order* or *command* is genuine unless the speaker has the appropriate authority over the hearer.[6] (I cannot issue a *bona fide* order to the President of my university to dye his hair; for that matter, he cannot issue a *bona fide* order to me to cancel my subscription to *College English.* We may *advise* each other to do such things; but at present we each lack the appropriate authority to issue such an *order* to such an effect.) Furthermore, even if Shakespeare's speaker *did* have the social authority over Time that an authentic *command* would presuppose, he could not without anomaly pretend to *command* Time to do a thing that Time in any case could not help but do. (An absolute monarch may say to his slave, "Metabolize your blood sugar!"; but in so speaking he issues no genuine *order.*[7] Conversely, no parent can genuinely *order* his child to speak in Urdu unless he knows that that child *can* speak in Urdu.) Despite appearances, in addressing his many imperatives to Time the speaker is not *ordering* or *commanding* Time to do anything: we recognize this—or ought to—because we sense intuitively that these imperatives fail to satisfy at least two rules or preconditions that partly constitute the speech act of *ordering* or

---

[5] Stephen Booth, *An Essay on Shakespeare's Sonnets* (New Haven: Yale University Press, 1969), p. 43.

[6] The discussion here of speech-act anomalies assumes the prior interpretation and discounting of a more basic anomaly involved in addressing *any* remarks to a non-human entity ("time"—also printed as "Time"). Simply to talk to time at all is to violate what Noam Chomsky calls a selectional restriction rule of grammar (*Aspects of the Theory of Syntax* [Cambridge, Mass.: M. I. T. Press, 1965], p. 95). In this case the governing rule would be: the object of direct address must be human, or animate and human-like. To violate this rule by addressing an inanimate entity as if it were a person, is to invent an instance of personification—which is the figure of speech basic to Sonnet 19. That figure "explains away," as it were, the anomaly involved in talking-to-time *per se.* What remains to be explained, after one grants the personification, is the anomaly involved in *giving orders* to such a person or personification *without the proper authority.*

[7] This varies an example invented by Bruce Fraser, "On Accounting for Illocutionary Forces," *A Festschrift for Morris Halle,* ed. S. A. Anderson (New York: Holt, 1973); cited by Katherine Hammer, "Searle's Conditions and the Determination of Illocutionary Force," *Centrum,* 1:2 (1973), p. 146. The example of "This chili's hot," in my second paragraph, is adapted from Hammer's remarks on p. 137.

commanding. Despite their considerable syntactical power the speaker's many imperatives do not, as uttered, exert the power of *command.*

What the speaker *is* doing in uttering these imperatives is obvious in the last clause of the series: "... do what ere thou wilt ..." Despite the imperative grammar, the speaker of this utterance is not commanding Time to do anything, but rather is *conceding* to Time the power to neglect the speaker's wishes. So, in uttering all his imperative clauses, the speaker does not *command* Time, but *concedes* to Time certain powers that the speaker regrets but does not dispute.

As Donnelly and Booth suggest, there is great power in the octave of Sonnet 19. Much of that power takes the form of a tension between the dynamic, imperative grammar of what the speaker says, and the passive, concessive acts that the speaker performs in the saying.

The speaker's long introductory series of concessions ends abruptly with an utterance that is patently not a concession: "But I forbid thee one most hainous crime ...." The verb in this case makes explicit what the speaker would do in saying these words: in saying them he would *forbid,* he would *prohibit,* he would *enjoin.*

To find out *what* the speaker would forbid Time to do, the reader must go on to the next line:

> But I forbid thee one most hainous crime,
> O carue not with thy howers my loues faire brow ....

G. Wilson Knight comments on these two lines in a way that catches something of the force of the first, if not of the second: "He [the speaker] can even assume authority greater than death's." Knight then questions the sanity of such an assumption of authority: "Is this just rant? Or do we respond to anything deeper? Is there any point at all in talking like this? That is our problem."[8]

In a recent book on the *Sonnets* Philip Martin repeats Knight's question, "Is there any point at all in talking like this?"—and decides that there is no point: "For the command is plainly absurd, as the speaker himself must recognize...." (Martin goes on to reject the final couplet as "facile" and "unsatisfactory.")[9]

Knight's misgivings, and Martin's impatience, are both partly based on a misimpression—a misimpression shared by J. Dover Wilson, who paraphrases: "... the Poet ... boldly forbids the tyrant to lay a finger on his beloved's brow."[10] Knight, Martin, and Wilson all take line 9 as extending

---

[8] G. Wilson Knight, *The Mutual Flame* (London: Methuen, 1955), p. 76. Knight here identifies death with time.

[9] Philip Martin, *Shakespeare's Sonnets: Self, Love and Art* (Cambridge, England: Cambridge University Press, 1972), p. 160.

[10] John Dover Wilson, ed., *The Sonnets* (Cambridge, England: Cambridge University Press, 1969), p. 116.

and specifying the prohibition announced in line 8. But there is a difference between the two lines.

Though in uttering line 8 the speaker begins overtly to *forbid*, in line 9 he does not forbid at all; rather, he *pleads*, or *petitions*, or *entreats*. The force of line 9 as an *entreaty* is marked by the interjection "O"—a locution recorded by the *O. E. D.* A more explicit lexical marker would be the word "please": the speaker is in effect saying, "O *please* do not carve with thy hours my love's fair brow." The metrical reasons are obvious for doing without the word "please" here; and there is this additional reason: it is to the speaker's advantage not to make explicit the speech act of *pleading* or *entreating* that he carries out in uttering line 9. For if he were to make that act explicit it would clash impossibly with the act of *forbidding* that he has explicitly undertaken in the preceding line. Professor Martin's objection to lines 8 and 9—that the command is "plainly absurd, as the speaker himself must recognize"—nears the mark, but misses it. The command *is* absurd, and the speaker himself does sense that; but the command or prohibition occurs in line 8 only. By line 9 the speaker has already abandoned that kind of verbal enterprise as insupportable on its face.

The absurdity, the insupportability of *forbidding* Time to have his way with the speaker's love, is corollary to the absurdity and insupportability of *commanding* Time to have his way with other creatures: in both cases the speaker lacks authority over Time to issue such a prohibition or command, and in both cases Time lacks the requisite power to bind and loose. Line 8 begins boldly enough; the speaker is momentarily "heroic" and "affirmative"; but the bravado can't be sustained. Therefore in line 9 the speaker reduces his *prohibition* to a *plea*.

The speaker completes his adjustment of speech to reality at the start of the final couplet, with a massive concession: ". . . doe thy worst ould Time . . . ." This brings to a climax the concessions that began in a limited way in line 1; the speaker has now surrendered everything to Time, including his beloved. But he counterbalances all these concessions in uttering the final words: "Yet . . . dispight thy wrong, / My loue shall in my verse euer liue young." This last speech act engages the full affirmative power of Shakespeare's poem. It is not a *statement*, nor even a *prediction* or *prophecy*: it is a *boast*; and concentrated into it is the equal of all the power that the speaker has reluctantly *conceded* to Time. With this authoritative *boast* of his power as a poet to immortalize his beloved, the speaker all but reduces "deuouring time" to the impotent condition of a senile beast.[11]

---

[11] In the introduction to her edition of the *Sonnets* (New York: New York University Press, 1969), p. 29, Barbara Herrnstein Smith describes in passing the phrase, "Yet do thy worst, old Time," as a "challenge." Perhaps it is the combination of the *concession* in line 13 with the *boast* in line 14 that makes a *challenge* of the couplet as a whole. While this essay was in press I discovered Thomas Tyler's compact summary, which nicely coincides with the present account: "In this Sonnet

(An afterthought may be in order. I once thought, as in the general mode of Booth's *Essay on Shakespeare's Sonnets,*[12] that the reader of Sonnet 19 undergoes a shifting of perceptions while reading the poem roughly like the shift undertaken during the course of the speaker's speech acts. I still think that some such account is true of the second half of the poem, particularly of the shift from *prohibition* to *plea* in lines 8 and 9. But I doubt that the normal tendency to misread the early verbs by mistaking *concessions* for *commands* is in itself meant to be significant. That is, not too much should be made of the fact that the reader doesn't really know how to "take" the early lines until late in a first reading of the poem. If the initial misreadings were in some sense "required," and were meant to be meaningful, the reader would have to be thought slow to notice the speech-act rule violations that infect any supposed *order* issued to Time. Maybe competent readers and hearers *are* slow to register such phenomena; in that case attention to the reader's changing response might be justified. But that justification would hold only if Sonnet 19 were meant to be encountered exclusively in written or printed form. The confusions that beset the reader of a text are greater than any that beset the *listener* to a proper saying of the text aloud. The listener has more information available to help his understanding; the suprasegmental phonemes of live speech [stress, pitch, juncture] work to disambiguate speech-act performances, as well as aspects of syntax and semantics, which would seem unresolvably ambiguous in cold print. In the case of Sonnet 19, a rise in pitch in the articulation of such words as "blunt," "pawes," "make," and "broad," can make explicit what the speech-act conventions would otherwise suggest—i.e., that these opening lines are not *commands,* but *concessions.* Unless one holds that Sonnet 19 is meant to depend upon the spare ambiguities of the printed page only, it is safest to call the reader's misreadings of the early lines just that—misreadings.[13])

There is a brief poem by Robert Frost on page 532 that, like Sonnet 19, rewards close attention to its speech acts, for it is easily misunderstood unless the reader listens to what the speaker is doing in saying what he says.

Time is first *implored* to restrain his power; and then he is *defied"* (*Shakespeare's Sonnets,* ed. Thomas Tyler [London: David Nutt, 1890], p. 176; italics added).

[12] Cited in note 5. See also the program proposed by Stanley Fish in "Literature in the Reader: Affective Stylistics," *New Literary History: A Journal of Theory and Interpretation,* 2 (1970), 123–162; reprinted as an appendix to Fish's *Self-Consuming Artifacts* (Berkeley: University of California Press, 1973). Neither Booth nor Fish incorporates speech-act analysis into his critical method, but the possibility of doing so remains open.

[13] Those who hold that a poem is by definition "a structure in which ambiguity is a constitutive device," and who favor readings of poems that nurture ambiguity, may defend such "misreadings" along the lines of Samuel R. Levin's argument in "Suprasegmentals and the Performance of Poetry," *Quarterly Journal of Speech,* 48 (1962), 366–372; Booth's *Essay* offers another kind of support. (Levin's essay was published in 1962, and therefore does not go into the question of speech acts; but suprasegmentals can "flag" speech acts as well as syntactical constructions and lexical meaning.)

Spring Pools

These pools that, though in forests, still reflect
The total sky almost without defect,
And like the flowers beside them, chill and shiver,
Will like the flowers beside them soon be gone,
And yet not out by any brook or river,
But up by roots to bring dark foliage on.

The trees that have it in their pent-up buds
To darken nature and be summer woods—
Let them think twice before they use their powers
To blot out and drink up and sweep away
These flowery waters and these watery flowers
From snow that melted only yesterday.[14]

Discussion of this poem with students has shown that they often miss the point of the final stanza. They suppose the speaker to be merely expressing a private wish or desire that the trees might hold off a bit before they destroy the fragile and lovely spring pools. Such a reading pays little attention either to the emphatically accented word "snow" in the last line, or to the odd adverbial phrase that closes the poem. The last line is understood to have something to do with the spring pools, but not much to do with the trees.

Such readers take the final stanza as a *wish* (to give it the name of a speech act) probably because of the effect of the optative or subjunctive mood governing the phrase, "Let them think . . . ." ("Let" often introduces a *wish* or a *prayer*–"Let the garden flourish; let there be peace in the land.") Perhaps, too, readers expect to find wistfulness and sentimentality in Frost's poems. In any case, it helps to turn a reader's attention to the phrase "think twice," and to its ordinary uses. "You'd better think twice before going to New York"; "He should think twice before buying that house": such sentences are typically used to enact not an *order* or a *wish*, but a *threat* or a *warning*—whether directly (in the first or second persons), or obliquely (in the third person, as in "Spring Pools"). In saying what he says Frost's speaker does not *order* the trees to stop doing something, on the one hand, nor *wish* that they would stop, on the other; rather, he indirectly *warns* the trees about the consequences of their actions. He *warns* them that there will be a quick return of the snow and the season of death—from which they have escaped "only yesterday"—if they do not halt their destruction of the present moment and their mindless rush into the future. Frost varies this Wordsworthian topic in "Nothing Gold Can Stay," "The Oven Bird," "West-Running Brook," "Reluctance," and other

---

[14] From *The Poetry of Robert Frost*, edited by Edward Connery Lathem. Copyright 1956 by Robert Frost, copyright 1923, © 1969 by Henry Holt & Co., Inc. Reprinted by permission of Henry Holt & Co., Inc.

poems. If summer comes, can winter be far behind? The major irony of "Spring Pools" is the fact that the speaker knows that the trees are literally mindless and cannot act on his warning (which is one reason why the warning is oblique and not direct); like Shakespeare's Time, they cannot do otherwise than as they do.

I suggest that deliberate identification of speech acts, as in the examples given above, can be helpful in discussing some poetic texts—helpful, at least, in correcting misunderstandings like those cited. No doubt most texts don't need such an explicit analysis: for them we will have already grasped the force of the speech acts in the act of understanding the texts. That is because the conventions governing what we do in what we say are a natural part of language, as important as the conventions that govern syntax and semantics.[15] This aspect of language has engaged the attention of many linguists and philosophers of language, and several literary critics. Two comments will relate what I have said here to what has already been written on the subject.

First, the systematic study of speech acts undertaken recently by philosophers and linguists, preeminently J. L. Austin and John Searle, should prove useful in clarifying the interpretation of literary texts.[16] But I don't think that the projected audience for any such interpretation should be expected to master speech-act theory first. Successful analysis of language only codifies conventions that are already part of our knowledge of how to use and understand language. An instance of such a convention should be recognized as such by any competent speaker if it is pointed out to him. You don't have to be a philosopher of language to tell a *warning* from a *wish*. Nonetheless, explicitness and even jargon have their value, and I'd welcome, for practical purposes, any detailed and reliable taxonomy of what Austin calls "illocutionary acts"—the center of a cluster of verbal acts that Searle calls, collectively, "speech acts." (In this paper the acts referred to as "speech acts" have all in fact been, more narrowly, "illocutionary acts.")

Second, applications of speech-act theory to literary criticism have so far concentrated on either metacritical or stylistic concerns. The metacritical applications usually involve efforts to distinguish the concept of literature from that of ordinary discourse. The stylistic applications often involve characterizing an author's "style" in terms of the speech acts that he tends to engage in, and the presuppositions that lie behind those acts.[17] I

---

[15] For a recent explanation and application of this line of reasoning, see Martin Steinmann, "Figurative Language and the Two-Code Hypothesis," in Fasold, Ralph W. and Roger W. Shuy, eds., *Analyzing Variation in Language: Papers from the Second Colloquium on New Ways of Analyzing Variation* (Washington, D.C., Georgetown University Press, 1975), pp. 220–227.

[16] J. L. Austin, *How to Do Things with Words* (New York: Oxford University Press, 1965 [rpt. of 1962 ed.]); John R. Searle, *Speech Acts* (Cambridge, England: Cambridge University Press, 1969). Marcia Eaton's extensive checklist of publications in speech-act theory will appear in *Centrum* 2:2 (Fall 1974).

[17] Examples of metacritical applications are Monroe C. Beardsley's argument in *The Possibility of Criticism* (Detroit: Wayne State University Press, 1970), 49–61, revised in his essay "The Concept

think that a third, more narrowly interpretive kind of application, like that attempted in this paper, also holds promise. Understanding the meant meaning of any piece of discourse involves understanding what Austin calls its "illocutionary force" as well as its "locutionary meaning" (which involves "sense" and "reference"). The risk of misunderstanding illocutionary force is frequent enough in literature to require some precaution. Illocutionary ambiguity is as common in spoken and written language as are syntactical ambiguity and semantic ambiguity. Most sentences can be used to execute many different speech acts. Fortunately, the information contained in the context of a live utterance goes a long way towards disambiguating all three kinds of ambiguity. But, because the context available for understanding a *written* utterance is narrower, ambiguities can persist. In the normal course of events we may manage to muddle through such complexities without having to think about them. But there are times, in literature as in life, when we must deliberately study what it is that is being done *in* what is being said, or else run the risk of missing the illocutionay point altogether. Sonnet 19 and "Spring Pools" are two such occasions.

Content Questions

1. How have the imperatives in Shakespeare's Sonnet 19 traditionally been interpreted? How does Hancher's interpretation differ?

2. Certain preconditions must be satisfied in order for a particular utterance to qualify as a command. What two conditions does Hancher show were not satisfied with the imperatives in the sonnet?

3. For the last two lines of the sonnet, Hancher proposes a speech-act interpretation that varies from the speech act that others might propose for those lines. Explain the nature of the speech act that Hancher proposes.

4. How might an oral rather than a written presentation of the sonnet perhaps clarify the intended meaning of the speech acts in the poem? Explain.

5. What potential differences of speech-act interpretation in Frost's poem does Hancher point out?

of Literature," *Literary Theory and Structure,* ed. Frank Brady (New Haven: Yale University Press, 1973), 23–39; and Richard Ohmann's discussion in "Speech Acts and the Definition of Literature," *Philosophy and Rhetoric,* 4 (1971), 1–19. Stylistic applications are exemplified in Ohmann's two essays, "Speech, Action, and Style," *Literary Style: A Symposium,* ed. Seymour Chatman (New York: Oxford University Press, 1971), 241–254; and "Speech, Literature and the Space Between," *NLH,* 4 (1972), 47–63, esp. p. 54.

Questions for Analysis and Discussion

1. Comment on the degree to which grammatical form does not always match the illocutionary force of an utterance.

2. How could linguistic training help a person to more easily recognize a possible speech-act interpretation that differs from a more common interpretation attributed to a particular discourse? How could linguistic training help a person to explain and articulate that difference?

3. Do you think that a greater awareness of speech acts might help you to approach literary texts with an additional tool for interpretation? Explain.

Student Lexicographers and the Emily Dickinson Lexicon

Cynthia L. Hallen

Dictionaries are often considered to be useful only for looking up definitions or checking on spelling. But in the following article, which originally appeared in the journal *Dictionaries,* Cynthia L. Hallen, a philologist and lexicographer at Brigham Young University, reports on the literary insights that can be gained from examining the dictionary that Emily Dickinson appears to have used as she prepared her poetry. Hallen also reports on her involvement with students in the preparation of the *Emily Dickinson Lexicon.* This lexicon will constitute a valuable reference guide for those readers, scholars, and translators who wish to explore the lexical creativity and semantic intricacy of Emily Dickinson's work.

Emily Dickinson is an ideal subject for lexical studies because her diction derives in important respects from the lexicographical work of Noah Webster, the founding father of American philology and lexicography. Dickinson's poems are rich in synonyms, antonyms, metaphors, definitions, etymologies, allusions, and Americanisms. In P[oem] 48,[1] an allusion to the prophet Noah embedded in "Patriarch's bird" probably points toward Webster just as the allusion to Enoch in P 1342 points toward her deceased father, Edward Dickinson. The description of Noah's ark as a "floating casement" may allude to Webster's dictionary. And the allusion to Noah's dove in "Columbia" suggests the distinctive American or Columbian quality of Webster's lexicon:

> Once more, my now bewildered Dove
> Bestirs her puzzled wings
> Once more her mistress, on the deep
> Her troubled question flings—
>
> Thrice to the floating casement
> The Patriarch's bird returned,

---

[1] All references to and quotations from Dickinson's poems and letters are taken from the Johnson editions. Reprinted by permission of the publishers and the Trustees of Amherst College from *The Poems of Emily Dickinson,* Thomas H. Johnson, ed., Cambridge, Mass.: The Belknap Press of Harvard University Press, Copyright © 1951, 1955, 1979, 1983 by the President and Fellows of Harvard College.

Courage! My brave Columba!
There may yet be *Land!*

When Webster published his plan of "Dictionaries of the American Language" in 1800, William Dutton objected to the "Columbian dictionary, in which the vulgar provincialisms of uneducated Americans" would be quoted as language authorities (Warfel 1953, 289, 297). To express disapproval of Webster's American dictionary, Dutton proposed a title: "Let, then, the projected volume of foul and unclean things bear his own christian name and be called NOAH'S ARK" (Moss 1984, 99).[2]

Whether or not Dickinson was aware of the Noah's Ark epithet has not been established, but her familiarity with Noah Webster's dictionary is incontestable. She used Webster's 1844 *An American Dictionary of the English Language* (ADEL) as a source of poetic inspiration (Benvenuto 1983). In choosing the word *patriarch* for P 48, Dickinson probably noticed Webster's definition of *Noachian* 'relating to the time of Noah, the patriarch.' The "mistress" of the poem may be a poet, whose big dictionary is 'suggestive of the Ark in respect of size, shape, etc. esp. a large, cumbrous, or old-fashioned trunk or vehicle' (OED *Noah's Ark* 2). From a menagerie of words, the poet sends out a question into the unknown, hoping to find "land" like an ancient Noah,[3] or hoping to establish meaning like a Noah Webster.

Not only was Webster a "patriarch" or founding father of American lexicography (OED *patriarch* 4), he was also a venerable father in Emily Dickinson's hometown of Amherst, Massachusetts (OED *patriarch* 5). Not long before Dickinson's birth in 1830, Webster moved to Amherst to work on his 1828 dictionary (Leavitt 1947, 28). During a ten year residence, he helped establish Amherst Academy where Dickinson went to secondary school with Emily Ellsworth Fowler Ford, Webster's granddaughter and biographer (Sewall 1974, 369). Webster was also a co-founder of Amherst College with Samuel Fowler Dickinson, Emily's grandfather (King 1951, 82). Webster prepared and published the new 1841 edition of the ADEL before his death in 1843 (Miles 1991, 2), which was reissued in 1844 by the J. S. and C. Adams company of Amherst (Miles 1993). In 1844, Emily Dickinson's father Edward purchased, signed, and dated a copy of the 1844 reprint, which is now a part of the Dickinson family collection in Harvard's Houghton Library (Buckingham 1977). Austin Dickinson reports seeing Webster's big dictionary on the kitchen table where his sister would sometimes compose (Sewall 1965, 12). Dickinson never mentions Webster's dictionary by name, but she refers to lexicons and philology

---

[2] See the reference to "Noe" and the Ark in the 1911 *Punch* tribute to a new edition of Webster's dictionary (Ford 1912, 2. 490). Note also the title of Robert Leavitt's 1947 book, *Noah's Ark, New England Yankees, and the Endless Quest,* published by the Merriam company for the centennial of the 1847 edition of Webster's dictionary.

[3] In P 48, *brave Columba* and *Land* are also allusions to Columbus. See *brave Columbus* in P 3.

several times in her poems and letters (P 246, 728, 1126, 1342, 1651; L[etter] 2, 261).

Establishing meaning in a Dickinson poem is difficult for students and scholars alike because her lexis is so dense with polysemy and indefinite connections. Looking up the words in Webster's 1844 dictionary helps readers to better decipher the network of lexical ties in Dickinson's poetry. Unfortunately, the 1844 reprint is one of the rarest Webster editions (Miles 1993), and only a few copies of the 1841 edition are available for research through universities that allow interlibrary loans. Even if readers had easy access to a Webster's 1841 or 1844 dictionary, it would not be sufficient for a rigorous study of the poems. Further historical and linguistic insights can be found in the OED, which was emerging in Dickinson's lifetime, 1830–1886. But Dickinson's philology goes far beyond the expository information that a good dictionary can provide. Charles Anderson suggests that Dickinson made her own poetic "lexicon" of definitions because she found the dictionary to be inadequate (1990, 35). Given Dickinson's lexical creativity, her explorations in Webster's dictionary, and the semantic contexts documented in the OED, readers would benefit greatly from a lexicon such as the forthcoming Emily Dickinson Lexicon (EDL), which draws on these resources as a reference guide to the poems.

Lexicon Pilot Study

In the 1992–1993 academic year, I trained 137 university students to write entries for the EDL, a comprehensive dictionary of the words in Dickinson's poems. The training was a pilot program to initiate three years of collaborative research with Dickinson scholars and student apprentices, many of whom were new to lexicography.

I knew from the history of the OED that volunteers have played an important role in major dictionary projects, but I was astounded by the contribution of student lexicographers to the EDL. After I mentioned the proposed volume in a course on the history of the English language, Chad King, a student, was so interested that he volunteered to work for me. In spring 1992, he produced the first eighteen *A* word entries for the Dickinson lexicon as a sample. King's work helped us procure a publisher for the EDL (Greenwood Publishing Group, forthcoming ca. 1997) and became a model for trainees. He later formatted Dickinson's letters for a word-cruncher computer concordance that helps verify definitions in the poems. At the same time, English major Kasi Morris volunteered her services when she heard about the EDL project from one of my former students. From childhood Morris had been interested in Dickinson and dictionaries, so she was especially adept at finding the lexical connections between the "Lark," "Music," "Silver," and "Summer" in P 861.

Morris and King performed so well as volunteers that I decided to train all of my students as EDL lexicographers in the 1992–1993 school year. Students could choose a different project if they were not interested in the Dickinson lexicon, but only three people chose not to work on the EDL. The participants included 92 students in three sections of the History of the English Language class, 23 seniors in a seminar called "Emily Dickinson's Language," and 22 students in a graduate seminar on "Language and Literature."

Doing the work for credit did not dampen enthusiasm for volunteer service on the project. Nineteen students gave extra time to the EDL and seemed to have the natural affinity for lexicography that James A. H. Murray described in the introduction to the OED:

> While considerable training and experience are required by everyone, however well qualified, it is also true that the real dictionary worker is born and not made, and that no application or diligence will ever make up for the lack of natural aptitude for the work. (viii)

Even before I had formally presented the EDL as a term project in the fall of 1992, one of the students, Laura M. Harvey, decided to work on the lexicon as an Undergraduate Research Trainee funded by the Brigham Young University College of Education. I did not solicit participation beyond class requirements, but six other students asked to continue working on the EDL as volunteers at the end of the semester. In winter 1993, we started an alphabetical chart to keep track of all the words in the lexicon, and Harvey developed materials for training new volunteers in the tracking task.[4] Several students volunteered to work on the "EDL track" in addition to their lexicon assignments, because they enjoyed sorting the words by part of speech. Others volunteered at the end of the semester, and a former student from the seminar on Dickinson's language was hired as my graduate research assistant in spring 1993. Experienced volunteers went on to become "reviewers," preparing entries for external review by Dickinson scholars.

In classroom training, I took students through the definition process. They received additional instruction on an individual basis in my office. Each student was assigned a list of approximately 70 occurrences of headwords in the poems from the concordance. Depending on the number of times Dickinson used each individual word, some students had more headwords to define and some had fewer. Based on my experience as a lexicographer (handling about 17 occurrences per hour), I estimated that students might cover about 10 occurrences per hour, aiming at 8 to 10 hours of work per student for each allotment of 70 occurrences in Dickinson's

---

[4]In March 1993, Laura M. Harvey received an Undergraduate Research and Creativity Award from BYU for her work on the Emily Dickinson Lexicon.

Table 1   Hours Reported by Student Lexicographers, Fall 1992

HOURS PER STUDENT	NO. OF STUDENTS	TOTAL HOURS
5	1	5
6	1	6
7.5	1	7.5
8	2	16
8.5	1	8.5
9	6	54
9.5	1	9.5
10	6	60
10.5	3	31.5
11	8	88
12	11	132
12.5	3	37.5
13	2	26
14	2	28
15	3	45
16	3	48
16.5	1	16.5
17.5	2	35
18	1	18
20	3	60
25	1	25
30	1	30
40	2	80
	66 Students	867 Hours Contributed

Median: 12 hours per student
Mean: 12.2 hours per student

poems. Table 1 shows the hours reported by 66 student lexicographers in fall 1992. Most students had spent about 12 hours working on the project; the least amount of time taken was 5 hours and the most was 40.

The students followed four steps in the research process. First, they drafted definitions for assigned words after studying Dickinson's usage in the context of the poems. Then, they consulted Webster's etymologies and definitions. Next, they used the OED to verify etymologies and establish potential senses for each word. In the fourth step, students created a final draft of the entry for each headword, formatted the entries, and printed a hard copy. To complete the assignment, each student had to turn in the training materials, all of their notes and drafts, the final draft, a back-up copy on disk, and an evaluation of the project. Students received full credit if they did the work, whether they were born lexicographers or not.

As we worked together on the EDL, I warned my students that they were pioneers, that I had never trained groups of lexicographers, and that I could not anticipate all the problems and questions that they might encounter. In spite of the challenges, the majority of students who participated said that they thoroughly enjoyed lexicography. I would like to share the results of the Dickinson lexicon pilot project in three areas: (1) student responses, (2) student discoveries, and (3) ideas for further research.

Student Responses

For the project evaluation, I asked students to answer three questions: What did you like about the lexicon project? What problems did you have? What suggestions do you have? A summary of the answers of 93 student lexicographers to these questions may be found in Tables 2, 3, and 4. Table 2 shows positive responses to the project. The most frequent response,

Table 2   What Students Liked about the Lexicon Project

NO. OF STUDENTS/RESPONSE	
48	Helped me better understand Dickinson and her word usage.
29	Helped me better appreciate and understand the power of words.
16	Helped me appreciate lexicographers and dictionaries.
14	I liked/loved the project. It was something different (better than a research paper).
14	I liked finding the interconnections of Dickinson's poems, Webster's dictionary, and the OED.
11	I liked working on a project that is important, that will be published, and that is useful to others.
6	It allowed for personal interpretation/insight.
6	I would like to continue working on the project as a volunteer.
4	I learned a new way to read poetry.
3	The example definitions helped a lot.
2	I thought we were well-trained, plenty of examples.
2	A good way to learn English and the history of the English language.
2	Liked it when my draft definitions corresponded to Webster's.
2	I will use the lexicon project when I am a teacher.
1	I like having a limited number of sources—once I've copied the poems and dictionary entries, that's it.
1	It helped me understand parts of speech better.
1	Enjoyed formatting and organizing.
1	Liked comparing Webster's 1828 and the OED.
1	I appreciate your confidence in the undergraduate "minds."

Table 3 What Students Didn't Like about the Project

NO. OF STUDENTS/RESPONSE

24	I'm afraid I didn't do it right. I don't feel qualified. Dickinson is hard to understand.
19	Hard to get a hold of the dictionary (Webster's 1828) and/or the poems in the library.
14	Hard to decide what the words or poems meant.
11	Hard to choose between the many possible meanings of words.
7	Hard to figure out the parts of speech.
7	Hard to decide whether to lump or split definitions.
6	Hard to format onto an IBM/WordPerfect 5.1.
6	It took more time than estimated.
6	Hard to follow the format of the example definitions.
2	I didn't know how to handle differences in etymologies (OED vs. Webster).
2	I didn't like the project; I'm not a lexicographer.
1	Confused about how to indicate wordplay and figurative language.
1	It narrows possibilities for interpretation when you assign a definition.

Table 4 Student Suggestions for Improving the Project

NO. OF STUDENTS/RESPONSE

10	Have students start early. Doing the whole thing at once at the last minute can be too tedious or overwhelming. Tell students not to procrastinate.
8	Have students photocopy the pages from Webster's and the OED for their own convenience and have them turn in the copies so you can continue to use them in the project.
7	Have progress reports throughout the semester and have us turn in a preliminary draft of the project. Break up the project into parts and start due dates earlier.
4	Assign fewer words so we can spend more time on each word.
4	Do practice definitions as a class.
4	Have students buy the book of Dickinson's poems.
3	Have conferences with professor for questions, reassurance.
3	Give out a copy of a student's work as an example.
3	Ask students using library reference materials to stay in the vicinity and return them immediately after use.
3	Give more training on handling figurative language, parts of speech, headwords, and etymologies.
2	Provide copies of Webster's 1844 dictionary.
2	Tape all concordance slips on one sheet.
2	Make a check list.
1	Have students trade and edit each other's drafts.
1	Use a thesaurus—sometimes helps find more connections (with synonyms).

given by half of the students, was that the dictionary research had opened a door into Dickinson's style. One student wrote: "I always had problems with Emily Dickinson before because I didn't understand what she was talking about. But now I've learned that by looking up the meanings of the words . . . I can understand the poems a lot better." Another said that he gained a great respect for Dickinson "not only as a poet but as a lexicographer and a person who thought deeply." The consensus, expressed by one volunteer, was that "Emily Dickinson has a tremendous command of language."

About one third of the students felt that they had gained a greater appreciation of words and language in general. Some words, the students confessed, were more interesting than others:

> The first exciting word for me was "chimney-corner." I followed the directions by thinking about what the word means. And I figured out the "correct definition" as well as some of the connotations. That was really exciting for me.

Another student was equally enthusiastic:

> Who'd have known I could get so excited about "buttonhole"? Though many of my words needed to be taken at face value, some had intriguing links of symbolism and metaphor, and they are my lexicographical treasures. . . . Here is where I crossed the boundary of mere "lexicographer" to budding "philologist."

Members of the Dictionary Society of North America may be pleased to know that several students gained a greater respect for dictionaries and lexicographers. One person decided that she should use dictionaries more often in her reading: "I know a lot of words, but the words I know have many more meanings than I'm aware of." Another student said that she learned to view dictionaries as "something more than a mere spelling aid." Still another said that the project hardly seemed like work and that she was considering taking up lexicography as a profession. One student thanked me for trusting undergraduates with a challenging task. Another reported that because of her EDL experience she plans to teach high school students to explore words in context and then look them up in dictionaries.

Table 3 contains aspects of the lexicon project that were problematic for students. One-fifth of the students felt intimidated by the project or lacked confidence in their ability to do the work. Many were troubled by difficult language in the texts until I explained that well-known Dickinson scholars also struggle with her poems.

Students cited inaccessibility of reference materials as a problem. I had put two copies of Johnson's 1955 edition of Dickinson's poems on reserve in the library, but these volumes were hard to get, especially for people who procrastinated. To save time, some students bought a paperback copy of the collected poems. Others made photocopies of the poems they needed for the EDL research.

During the first semester, students had to use the 1828 Webster's dictionary, located in the Humanities Reference section of the library. If someone failed to return the dictionary to the reference shelf, other students experienced research delays for hours, even days. The problem was solved when we received an electroprint copy of the 1844 edition from Harvard, so I was able to provide students with photocopies from the very dictionary that Dickinson had used.

Another stumbling block for some students was the question of whether to put similar meanings together or to divide nuances into subcategories. I explained that most historical linguists tend to be either "lumpers" or "splitters" and asked students to balance these tensions so that EDL entries would be thorough but also concise.

One student resisted the whole project at first:

> I have to be extremely honest and say that I was not excited at all at the thought of lexicography. . . . However, as I progressed through it, I realized that lexicography is an essential part of language, and if I am majoring in English, I should have experience in all aspects of the language.

Two other students decided that they were not suited for lexicography, and one suggested that the act of defining is a violation of the text.

Student suggestions for improving the project are recorded in Table 4. From the beginning I urged students to start their work early. Those who started late advised future students not to procrastinate, because the slow starters discovered too late that they wanted to do much more with their words. One student admitted, "My biggest regret is that I didn't do more on my project sooner!"

Several students recommended that future EDL workers make photocopies of the Dickinson poems, Webster entries, and OED entries for each headword assigned to them. Many have done so and have donated the copies to the project, materials which have greatly facilitated the review process of entries in the lexicon.

Lexicography entails the practice of many language skills: alphabetizing, analyzing syntax, classifying, defining, determining grammatical function, establishing word histories, identifying figurative usage, interpreting text, selecting citations, and so on. Reading Dickinson's poems involves similar skills, including the challenge of dealing with sophisticated lexical puzzles. An EDL volunteer, Brett Storm, describes the challenge as an opportunity: "Dickinson's genius rests on the ability of others to repeatedly be illumined by the possibilities which derive from the ambiguity in her poetry."

Student Discoveries

Laura Harvey noticed one of the most dramatic instances of wordplay. In preparation for the Emily Dickinson International Society conference in October 1992, I had asked her to check Webster's 1844 dictionary to verify two senses of *minor* in P 1068:[5]

> Further in Summer than the Birds
> Pathetic from the Grass
> A minor Nation celebrates
> It's unobtrusive Mass.
>
> No Ordinance be seen
> So gradual the Grace
> A pensive Custom it becomes
> Enlarging Loneliness.
>
> Antiques felt at Noon
> When August burning low
> Arise this spectral Canticle
> Repose to typify
>
> Remit as yet no Grace
> No Furrow on the Glow
> Yet a Druidic Difference
> Enhances Nature now

Harvey noted that Webster's 1844 entry for the adjective *minor* confirmed the senses of smallness and of musicality:

1. Less; smaller; sometimes applied to the bulk or magnitude of a single object; more generally to amount, degree, or importance. . . .
2. In music, less or lower by a lesser semitone; as, a third minor.

Harvey also noticed a religious connotation in Webster's noun entry for *minor* 'a Minorite, a Franciscan friar.' The crickets in Dickinson's "minor Nation" are small friars or priests, singing their mass in a minor key. However, Webster's dictionary said nothing about the "pathetic" sense of *minor* or anything about the musical sense of *pathetic* (as in Beethoven's "Pathétique"), so Harvey turned to the OED. She found the connection between *pathetic* and *minor* under **minor** (definition 6), and discovered a remarkable

---

[5] For a fuller account of Dickinson's wordplay on "minor" in P 1068, see (Hallen and Harvey) "Translation and the Emily Dickinson Lexicon," in *The Emily Dickinson Journal* II, 2.

coincidence—Dickinson's mentor, Thomas W. Higginson, was the author of the first example listed under OED 6d:

> *minor* . . . **6. Mus** . . . **d.** Minor chords and keys, as compared with major, have usually a mournful or pathetic effect; hence various figurative allusions. 1869, T. H. [*sic*] Higginson Army Life 222. This minor-keyed pathos used to seem to me almost too sad to dwell upon.

Higginson, an abolitionist, had been the commander of a regiment of black soldiers during the Civil War, and his 1869 book *Army Life in a Black Regiment* had appeared earlier in the *Atlantic Monthly* as a series of essays. The use of *Pathetic, minor, mass,* and *low* in P 1068 mirrors Higginson's use of *mass, low,* and *minor-keyed pathos* in his 1867 essay "Negro Spirituals":

> A few youths . . . had learned some of the "Ethiopian Minstrel" ditties, imported from the North. These took no hold upon the mass; and, on the other hand, they sang reluctantly, even on Sunday, the long and short metres of the hymn-books, always gladly yielding to the more potent excitement of their own "spirituals." By these they could sing themselves, as had their fathers before them, out of the contemplation of their own low estate, into the sublime scenery of the Apocalypse. I remember that this minor-keyed pathos used to seem to me almost too sad to dwell upon, while slavery seemed destined to last for generations. . . . (172–73)

Dickinson sent P 1068 to Higginson in January 1866, a year before he wrote the essay, so it seems that he was influenced by her diction. Perhaps Dickinson should be listed as the first example for 6.d. in the OED definition of *minor.*

Not every word in a Dickinson poem has the intricate wordplay of *minor,* but many poems contain instances of "webplay," a term that I have coined to describe connections between an author's diction and the entries in a dictionary—specifically, the play between Dickinson's poems and Webster's 1844 dictionary. Some of the connections may be attributed to coincidence or to shared cultural context, but many Dickinson poems contain obvious lexical allusions to Webster's synonyms, etymologies, definitions, and citations.

Kristi Engelking Hollis found a connection between Webster's definition of *accidental* and Dickinson's use of "accidental Red" in P 1419:

> It was a quiet seeming Day—
> There was no harm in earth or sky—
> Till with the setting sun
> There strayed an accidental Red
> A Strolling Hue, one would have said
> To westward of the Town—

But when the Earth began to jar
And Houses vanished with a roar
And Human Nature hid
We comprehended by the Awe
As those that Dissolution saw
The Poppy in the Cloud

Webster defines *accidental colors* as 'those which depend upon the affections of the eye, in distinction from those which belong to the light itself' (def. 2). In Dickinson's poem, the eye sees more than red light; the eye sees red as the beginning of a sunset "casualty" (*accident* def. 1), whereas before there had been "no harm in earth or sky." Webster's etymology for *accident* includes 'falling' as a gloss, so Dickinson's *accidental Red* is synonymous with "the setting sun" in line three.

In the second stanza of P 966, Dickinson's use of *accounted* with *esteem* and *estimate* reflects Webster's synonymy:

Grace of Wealth, and Grace of Station
Less accounted than
An unknown Esteem possessing—
Estimate—Who can—

Definition 7 of *account,* n. in Webster says 'value; importance; estimation; that is, such a state of persons or things, as renders them worthy of more or less estimation; as, men of account.' Definition 8 includes 'a result or production worthy of estimation.' At *account,* v.t., we find 'to account of, to hold in esteem; to value' (def. 2).

Webster's etymology for *adjust,* v.t., includes the French cognate '*ajuster,* to fit or frame,' and definition 1 says 'to make exact; to fit.' Dickinson speaks of how we "fit our Vision to the Dark" and how "something in the sight / Adjusts itself to Midnight" in P 419. In another poem, she speaks of a deceased woman who is "adjusted like a Seed / In careful fitted Ground" (P 804).

Like "brave Columba" (P 48) or the "Tender Pioneer" (P 698), students who dared to venture into Dickinson's poems were pleased with the verbal fruitfulness of the lands they explored. As the EDL project continues, we will be able to catalog a complete list of web-play connections to determine the extent of Dickinson's mimetic word-crafting from Webster's entries.

Further Research

Two other areas of research have developed from the EDL project: (1) the differences between Webster's 1828 and 1844 editions, and (2) the accuracy and inaccuracy of Webster's etymologies. As mentioned above, Webster's 1844 dictionary was not available to students during the first semester of the pilot project, so they looked up each word in the 1828 edition. With the convenience of student photocopies, I have been able to analyze the revisions that Webster made for *A* words from the 1828 to the 1844 edition. Most of Webster's revisions are minor changes in capitalization, format, or punctuation. Content revisions are less frequent and most do not affect Dickinson's wordplay or webplay. Therefore, Webster's 1828 dictionary is suitable, though not preferable, for general studies of Dickinson's poems. However, some of Webster's 1844 entries do have new information that is relevant to interpreting Dickinson's poems. The 1828 entry for *abolition* has one general definition only: 'the act of abolishing; or the state of being abolished; an annulling; abrogation; utter destruction.' By 1844, an anti-slavery connotation had secured a place in the lexicon, so Webster adds definition 2: 'the putting an end to slavery; emancipation.' The metaphorical resonance of Webster's *emancipation* gives a transcendent slant to death in Dickinson's "Mortal Abolition" in P 306. A systematic study of the differences between the 1828 and 1844 editions may show further evidence in Dickinson's poems of Webster's influence.

Emily Ford records that her grandfather's "taste for the study of etymology became apparent as soon as he had learned to read" (Ford 1912, 1:48–49). Etymology was at the core of Webster's lexicography:

> If anyone had asked Webster upon what part of his dictionary he had expended the most time and now set the highest value, he would undoubtedly have answered at once the history and derivation of words. (Scudder 1881, 258)

Webster wanted to correct the erroneous and fanciful etymologies in Samuel Johnson's dictionary, but the earliest European works in comparative historical linguistics had not yet appeared, and scientific advances in philology were not well known in the Americas until about 1818 (Leavitt 1947, 26). The rule-governed comparative method of the Indo-European philologists did not come to Yale until 1839 (Shoemaker 1966, 234), so Webster had to rely on a more intuitive and less scientific comparative linguistics. Nevertheless, Robert Leavitt believes that Webster's comparative method was effective and that a great number of his etymologies were correct (1947, 32). In spite of shortcomings, "there can be no doubt that Webster's dictionary was more useful to the Americans who purchased it than any other available to them at the time" (Moss 1984, 107). Webster's lexicon gave Dickinson access to information about words and language that no other source could have matched until the complete OED was finally published in the early 20th-century.

As students prepare entries for the EDL project, they must determine whether Webster's etymology for a particular headword is accurate according to modern standards. If Webster's etymology is flawed, students will indicate the correct etymology without deleting material that Dickinson may have incorporated from Webster. The EDL research will enable us to thoroughly document Webster's etymological deficiencies and achievements.

Undergraduate Researchers

Three factors influenced my decision to include students in the EDL lexicon project: (1) the historical ties between lexicography and education, (2) the benefits of integrating research and teaching, and (3) student interest. According to the *American Heritage Dictionary of Indo-European Roots,* the words *teach* and *diction* share the IE root **deik-* 'show' or 'pronounce solemnly.' As Dickinson's poetry shows, a dictionary can teach the versatility of language in etymologies and definitions. Several scholars have recognized the complementary relationship between lexicography and education. Sidney Landau reminds us that "most of the early lexicographers were schoolmasters who compiled glossaries or dictionaries as teaching aids for their students" (1984, 39). Schoolmaster Noah Webster compiled the ADEL to remedy the inadequacy of language-teaching tools in 19th-century New England. Experience as a teacher prepared James A. H. Murray to serve as chief editor of the OED (Murray 1977, 33). Educators in the 20th-century have called for a restoration of philology (Becker 1984; Kent 1975, 155; Woods 1985, 16), and some are training their students as amateur etymologists and lexicographers (Pierson 1989, 57; Rossner 1985, 96).

Other educators have been discussing how research can coexist with teaching, especially in undergraduate programs (McCaughey 1992, A36). Some professors mention their research interests in class; some use students as research subjects; but some lead undergraduates to develop skills in significant research tasks. Research opportunities strengthen undergraduate education, and undergraduates "bring a level of dedication and enthusiasm to our research endeavor that is both refreshing and rewarding" (Walker 1991, 9). Since most of the EDL pilot lexicographers were undergraduates, I can confirm the value of actively merging research and teaching at the college level.

As EDL pioneers, the student lexicographers offered valuable suggestions and helpful hands in a weighty task; they gained hands-on training in a marketable skill. They enjoyed participating in a meaningful research endeavor. They experienced greater respect for dictionary makers and developed an appreciation of words and sensitivity to language, especially the language of Emily Dickinson.

References

The American Heritage Dictionary of Indo-European Roots. 1985. Ed. Calvert Watkins. Boston: Houghton Mifflin.

Anderson, Charles. 1990 [1959]. "The Conscious Self in Emily Dickinson's Poetry." In *On Dickinson: The Best from "American Literature."* Ed. Edwin H. Cady and Louis J. Budd, 33–51. Durham and London: Duke University Press.

Becker, Alton L. 1984. "Biography of a Burmese Proverb." In *Text, Play, and Proverb,* 135–55. Lancaster, PA: The American Ethnological Society.

Benvenuto, Richard. 1983. "Words Within Words: Dickinson's Use of the Dictionary." *ESQ* 29:46–55.

Buckingham, Willis J. 1977. "Emily Dickinson's Dictionary." *Harvard Library Bulletin* 25:489–92.

Dickinson, Emily. 1955. *The Poems of Emily Dickinson.* 3 vols. Ed. Thomas H. Johnson. Cambridge, MA: Belknap-Harvard University Press.

———. 1958. *The Letters of Emily Dickinson.* 3 vols. Ed. Thomas H. Johnson. Cambridge, MA: Belknap-Harvard University Press.

Ford, Emily Ellsworth Fowler. 1912. *Notes on the Life of Noah Webster.* 2 vols. Ed. Emily Ellsworth Fowler Skeel. New York: Private printing.

Hallen, Cynthia L. and Laura M. Harvey. 1993. "Translation and the Emily Dickinson Lexicon." *The Emily Dickinson Journal* II, 2:130–46.

Higginson, Thomas Wentworth. 1869 [1960]. *Army Life in a Black Regiment.* East Lansing: Michigan State University Press.

Kent, George W. 1975. "Why Teach 'Philology'?" *ETC: A Review of General Semantics* 32 (2):155–64.

King, Stanley. 1951. *"The Consecrated Eminence": The Story of the Campus and the Buildings of Amherst College.* Amherst, MA: Amherst College.

Landau, Sidney I. 1984. *Dictionaries: The Art and Craft of Lexicography.* New York: Charles Scribner's Sons.

Leavitt, Robert Keith. 1947. *Noah's Ark, New England Yankees, and the Endless Quest.* Springfield, MA: G & C Merriam.

McCaughey, Robert A. 1992. "Why Research and Teaching Can Coexist." *Chronicle of Higher Education,* Aug. 5, A36.

Miles, Edwin A. 1991. "William Allen and the Webster-Worcester Dictionary Wars." *Dictionaries* 13:1–15.

———. 1993. "Noah Webster's Last Dictionary, 1841." Paper presented at the meetings of the Dictionary Society of North America, Las Vegas.

Moss, Richard J. 1984. *Noah Webster.* Boston: Twayne Publishers.

Murray, K. M. E. 1977. *Caught in the Web of Words: James Murray and the Oxford English Dictionary.* Oxford: Oxford UP.

Oxford English Dictionary. 1933 [1961]. 12 vols. Oxford: Clarendon Press.

Pierson, Herbert D. 1989. "Using Etymology in the Classroom." *English Language Teaching Journal* 43 (1):57–63.

Rosenbaum, S. P., ed. 1964. *Concordance to the Poems of Emily Dickinson.* Ithaca: Cornell University Press.

Rossner, Richard. 1985. "The Learner as Lexicographer: Using Dictionaries in Second Language Learning." In *Dictionaries, Lexicography and Language Learning,* 95–102. Oxford: Pergamon.

Scudder, Horace E. 1881. *American Men of Letters: Noah Webster.* Boston: Houghton Mifflin.

Sewall, Richard. 1965. *The Lyman Letters: New Light on Emily Dickinson and Her Family.* Amherst: University of Massachusetts Press.

———. 1974. *The Life of Emily Dickinson.* 2 vols. New York: Farrar.

Shoemaker, Ervin C. 1966. *Noah Webster: Pioneer of Learning.* New York: AMS Press.

Walker, L. P. 1990. "Involving Undergraduates in Research." *New York's Food & Life Sciences Quarterly,* vol. 20.4:8–12.

Warfel, Henry R. 1953. *Letters of Noah Webster.* New York: Library Publishers.

Webster, Noah. 1828 [1967]. Reprint. *An American Dictionary of the English Language.* San Francisco: Foundation for American Christian Education.

———. 1841. *An American Dictionary of the English Language.* 2 vols. New Haven, CT.

———. 1844. *An American Dictionary of the English Language.* 2 vols. Amherst, MA: J. S. and C. Adams.

Woods, William F. 1985. "The Cultural Tradition of Nineteenth-Century 'Traditional' Grammar Teaching." ERIC Document 258267. Paper presented at the March 1985 Conference on College Composition and Communication.

Content Questions

1. What relationship seems to exist between Noah Webster's dictionary and Emily Dickinson's poetry?

2. What challenge will researchers who wish to study Webster's 1841 or 1844 dictionary encounter?

3. Describe the role that student volunteers have had in the development of the Dickinson Lexicon Project.

4. What do the terms *lumper* and *splitter* refer to in the context of this article?

5. What language skills does Hallen indicate are involved with lexicography?

6. How was one student's interpretation of a poem affected by her consulting of the word *minor* in Webster's 1844 dictionary and the *Oxford English Dictionary*?

7. What does Hallen mean by her use of the term *webplay*?

8. Describe the similarities in word use accompanying the word *accounted* in Poem 966 and the synonyms Webster provided in his dictionary for *account*.

9. What justifications does Hallen give for including student researchers in the Emily Dickinson Lexicon project?

Questions for Analysis and Discussion

1. What does the difference between the definition for *abolition* in Webster's 1828 and 1844 editions illustrate about the behavior of languages

through time? How would you characterize the semantic development of *abolition* between the two editions? Can you provide examples of other words that have undergone a similar development through time?

2. If some of the entries of Webster's 1844 edition are known to contain flawed etymologies, what value could there be in consulting those etymologies and still including them in the Emily Dickinson Lexicon?

3. Besides providing a greater understanding of Emily Dickinson's poetry, how could studying Dickinson's lexicon also be helpful to students studying the history of the English language?

4. How do you believe a person's interpretation of a literary text could be influenced by a greater awareness of sources actually used by the author?

Studying Literature as Language

Roger Fowler

Some literary critics have questioned the appropriateness or usefulness of applying linguistic analysis to literature. But in the following article, Roger Fowler, a scholar who has published extensively about language and literature, addresses some of the concerns among some literary critics about the relative importance of linguistics to literary study. Fowler shows the valuable insights that linguistic study can bring to literary interpretation, illustrating his point with a discussion of an excerpt from William Faulkner's *The Sound and the Fury.*

For the past twenty-five years or so, there has been a running dispute between literary critics and linguists on the question of whether it is appropriate to apply linguistic methods—that is to say, methods derived from the discipline of linguistics—to the study of literature. There has been almost universal confidence among the linguists that this activity is entirely justified; and almost universal resistance by the critics, who have regarded the exercise with almost moral indignation. In this unyielding dispute, the claims and denials on both sides have been voiced with great force and passion. Here is Roman Jakobson putting the linguist's case, in 1958:

> Poetics deals with problems of verbal structure, just as the analysis of painting is concerned with pictorial structure. Since linguistics is the global science of verbal structure, poetics may be regarded as an integral part of linguistics.[1]

But the critics will not have this. In a long, bitter controversy between the late F.W. Bateson and myself in 1967, the counter-argument against linguistics was based essentially on an allegation of unfitness. Linguistics is a science, claims Bateson, but literature has what he calls an "ineradicable subjective core" which is inaccessible to science. Again, linguistic processing is only a preliminary to literary response, so the linguist is incapable of taking us far enough in an account of literary form and experience.

Finally, here is a dismissive opposition formulated by David Lodge, which is really saying that never the twain shall meet:

---

[1] Roman Jakobson, "Concluding Statement: Linguistics and Poetics," T. A. Sebeok, ed., *Style in Language* (Cambridge, Mass.: MIT Press, 1960), p. 350.

One still feels obliged to assert that the discipline of linguistics will never *replace* literary criticism, or radically change the bases of its claims to be a useful and meaningful form of human inquiry. It is the essential characteristic of modern linguistics that it claims to be a science. It is the essential characteristic of literature that it concerns values. And values are not amenable to scientific method.[2]

The opposition between science and values is at the heart of the refusal to agree; it manifests itself in different specific forms in many distinct arguments among protagonists for the two cases. What I would like you to note in this contribution by Lodge is the way in which the key terms, "science" and "values," are felt to be self-explanatory and conclusive. Lodge, like most of the debaters on both sides, requires us to take the central terms on trust, to accept them in their commonsense meanings with their ordinary values presupposed. In effect, Lodge is perceiving the two disciplines in terms of stereotypes, rather than analyzing carefully the terms and concepts involved in the comparison. I do not say that Lodge is especially culpable, merely that this statement of his is characteristic of this habit, in the debate, of relying on undefined and stereotypical terms. Both sides are guilty of this.

I realised a long time ago that I must stop adding fuel to this dispute; since the confrontation was conducted in conditions of quite inadequate theorization, it was impossible to participate in it as a reasoned debate. Without getting involved in the controversy again, I would like to merely mention some common failures of theorization which render it impossible to deal sensibly with a question so naively formulated as "Can linguistics be applied to literature?"

1. A major difficulty, on both sides, is a completely uncritical understanding of what is meant by "linguistics." The literary critics make no allowance for the fact that there exist different linguistic theories with quite distinct characteristics. While it might be true of linguistic model "A" that it can or cannot carry out some particular function of criticism, the same might not be true of model "B" which has a different scope or different manner of proceeding. If the critics are not well enough informed to discriminate between models, the linguists do not acknowledge the distinctions; a linguist will work on literature in terms of the theory s/he happens to uphold as the "correct" theory. Such is the competitiveness of the schools of linguistics that a devotee of one theory will not acknowledge that a rival might have some advantages for the task in hand.

2. A second persistent fallacy about linguistics, again represented on both sides, concerns the analytic *modus operandi* of linguistic method. It will be clear from what I have just said that different models have quite diverse aims, and procedures towards those aims. One model may have the purpose of accounting for the structure of particular texts; another may fo-

---

[2] David Lodge, *Language of Fiction* (London: Routledge and Kegan Paul, 1966), p. 57.

cus on sociolinguistic variation; another may be concerned to increase our knowledge about linguistic universals; and so on.

But there is a common misconception that linguistics—any linguistics—is a kind of automatic analyzing device which, fed a text, will output a description without human intervention. (The critics of course regard this as a soullessly destructive process, a cruelty to poems, but that is simply an emotional over-reaction based on a misconception.) Now whatever differences there are between contemporary linguistic theories, I think they would all agree with Chomsky's insistence that linguistics is *not* a discovery procedure. Linguistic analysis works only in relation to what speakers know already, or what linguists hypothesize in advance. So the whole range of objections to linguistics on the grounds that it is merely a mechanical procedure can be dismissed; linguistic analysis is a flexible, directed operation completely under the control of its users, who can direct it towards any goals which are within the scope of the model being used. Complete human control is possible if you carefully theorize the nature of your objective, and the nature of the object you are studying.

Which leads me to mention a second set of deficiencies in the way linguistic criticism is theorized, and then to the more positive part of my argument.

Even if critics and linguists positively acknowledge that language is of fundamental importance to the structure of the literary text, there is no guarantee that they will present language in a realistic and illuminating way. There are three representations of language that I regard as particularly unhelpful, and I will briefly instance them by reference to the work of scholars whose commitment to language is undoubted and substantial.

1. The first problematic attitude is that which regards language in literature as an *object*. This position is implicit throughout the work of Roman Jakobson.[3] Jakobson's "poetic function" claims that the important thing about literature is the way in which structure is organised to foreground the substantive elements of text—in particular, phonology and syntax. The patterns of parallelism and equivalence which he finds in his poems, at these levels of language, bulk out the formal structure, e.g. metrical and stanzaic structure, so that the text is re-presented as if its main mode of existence were perceptible physical form. The cost of this imaginary process is minimization of what we might call communicative and interpersonal—in a word, *pragmatic*—functions of the text. As I shall show in a moment, it is exactly these pragmatic dimensions which give the richest significance for critical studies. It is a pity that this "objective" theory of language in literature should have been given currency by such a brilliant and influential linguist as Jakobson.

---

[3] See Roger Fowler, "Linguistics and, and versus, Poetics," *Journal of Literary Semantics,* 8 (1979), 3–21; "Preliminaries to a Sociolinguistic Theory of Literary Discourse," *Poetics,* 8 (1979), 531–56.

2. A second unhelpful attitude to language is that which treats it as a *medium* through which literature is transmitted. Here I quote David Lodge again: "The novelist's medium is language: whatever he does, *qua* novelist, he does in and through language."[4] Presumably language as a medium is analogous to paint, bronze or celluloid for other arts. But the metaphor easily comes to mean "*only* a medium": the real thing is the novel (or poem, etc.) which is conveyed "in and through" the medium. Thus the substance of literature is shifted into some obscure, undefined, sphere of existence which is somehow beyond language. But for linguistics, literature *is* language, to be theorized just like any other discourse; it makes no sense to degrade the language to a mere medium, since the meanings, themes, larger structures of a text, "literary" or not, are uniquely constructed by the text in its interrelation with social and other contexts.

This position is difficult for literary critics to swallow, because it appears to remove the claimed special status (and value) of literature, to reduce it to the level of the language of the marketplace. But this levelling is essential to linguistic criticism if the whole range of insights about language provided by linguistics is to be made available. We want to show that a novel or a poem is a complexly structured text; that its structural form, by social semiotic processes, constitutes a representation of a world, characterized by activities and states and values; that this text is a communicative interaction between its producer and its consumers, within relevant social and institutional contexts. Now these characteristics of the novel or poem are no more than what functional linguistics is looking for in studying, say, conversations or letters or official documents. Perhaps this is a richer and thus more acceptable characterization of the aims of linguistic analysis than literary critics usually expect. But for me at any rate, this is what theorization *as* language involves. No abstract literary properties "beyond" the medium need to be postulated, for the rhetorical and semiotic properties in question should appear within an ordinary linguistic characterization, unless linguistics is conceived in too restricted a way.

3. Implicit in what I have just said is my reluctance to accept one further assumption about language which is widespread in stylistics and criticism. This is the belief that there is a distinct difference between poetic or literary language on the one hand and ordinary language on the other. Critics generally take for granted some version of this distinction; and some linguists have attempted to demonstrate it: we find strong arguments to this effect in the writings of, for example, Jakobson and Mukařovský. But these arguments are not empirically legitimate, and they are a serious obstacle to a linguistic criticism which attempts to allow to literature the communicative fullness that is a common property of language.

I have given some reasons why the apparently simple question "Can linguistics be applied to literature?" is unlikely to be satisfactorily answered.

---

[4] Lodge, *op. cit.*, p. ix.

Because I believe that linguistics *can* very appropriately and revealingly be applied to literature, I want to reorient the issue, in different terms. The solution is, it seems to me, to simply theorize literature *as* language, and to do this using the richest and most suitable linguistic model.

To be adequate to this task, a linguistic model should possess the following broad characteristics. It should be *comprehensive* in accounting for the whole range of dimensions of linguistic structure, particularly pragmatic dimensions. It should be capable of providing an account of the *functions* of given linguistic constructions (in real texts), particularly the thought-shaping (Halliday's "ideational") function. It should acknowledge the *social* basis of the formation of meanings (Halliday's "social semiotic").[5]

The requisite linguistics for our purpose, unlike most other, artificially restricted, forms of linguistics, should aim to be comprehensive in offering a complete account of language structure and usage at all levels: semantics, the organization of meanings within a language; syntax, the processes and orderings which arrange signs into the sentences of a language; phonology and phonetics, respectively the classification and ordering, and the actual articulation, of the sounds of speech; text-grammar, the sequencing of sentences in coherent extended discourse; and pragmatics, the conventional relationships between linguistic constructions and the users and uses of language.

Pragmatics is a part of linguistics which is still very much subject to debate and development,[6] but it is clear that it includes roughly the following topics: the interpersonal and social acts that speakers perform by speaking and writing; thus, the structure of not only conversation but also of all other sorts of linguistic communication as *interaction;* the diverse relationships between language use and its different types of context; particularly the relationships with social contexts and their historical development; and fundamentally, the systems of shared knowledge within communities, and between speakers, which make communication possible—this is where pragmatics and semantics overlap. In various writings I have stressed the need in linguistic criticism to mend the neglect of the interactional facets of "literary" texts: the rhetorical relationships between addressor and addressee, the dynamics of construction of fictional characters, and the sociolinguistic relationships between the producers and consumers of literature.[7] The second strand of pragmatics, concerning linguistic structure and systems of knowledge, will enrich linguistic criticism even more, and bring it into positive collaboration with literary criticism.

A "functional" model of language works on the premise that linguistic structures are not arbitrary, nor, as Chomsky claims, broadly constrained

---

[5]For relevant selections from Halliday's writings see G.R. Kress, ed., *Halliday: System and Function in Language* (London: Oxford University Press, 1976); M. A. K. Halliday, *Language as Social Semiotic* (London: Edward Arnold, 1978).

[6]For a recent introduction, see G.N. Leech, *Principles of Pragmatics* (London: Longman, 1983).

[7]See Roger Fowler, *Literature as Social Discourse* (London: Batsford, 1981).

by universal properties of Mind. Rather, particular language structures assume the forms they do in response to the communicative uses to which they are put, within a speech community. Halliday proposes three categories of "function": ideational, interpersonal, and textual. The ideational function is a key concept in linguistic criticism. The experience of individuals, and, around them, their communities, is encoded in the language they use as sets of ideas; and the ideational will differ as the dominant ideas of speakers differ. A simple example would be the operational concepts of a science, coded for the relevant speakers in a technical terminology; for these speakers, the terminology is one part of the linguistic organization of their experience: though this is a specialized part of the ideational, a technical terminology is only an obvious instance of a general principle, namely that language structure, in its ideational function, is constitutive of a speaker's experience of reality.

And of a community's experience; this is what "social semiotic" means. Although, undoubtedly, some of the meanings encoded in language are natural in origin, reflecting the kind of organism we are (e.g. basic colour, shape and direction terms),[8] most meanings are social: the dominant preoccupations, theories or ideologies of a community are coded in its language, so that the semantic structure is a map of the community's knowledge and its organization. An important development of this principle follows from the fact that communities are ideologically diverse: the existence of complex and competing sets of ideas gives rise to diverse styles, registers or varieties carrying semiotically distinct versions of reality according to the distinct views of individuals and of subcommunities. For the critics, this is linguistic support for the traditional assumption (formulated by Leo Spitzer but implicit much more widely) that a style embodies a view of the world. The advance in Halliday's and my formulation is that the availability of a formal method of linguistic analysis facilitates the unpicking of relationships between style and the representation of experience.

I want now to look at a textual example; for economy of exposition, a very familiar passage. This will not "prove the theory," but it will suggest the directions in which this theory of language might take us. The extract is the opening of William Faulkner's *The Sound and the Fury,* a familiar but striking example of the way in which language structure gives form to a view of the world.

> Through the fence, between the curling flower spaces, I could see them hitting. They were coming towards where the flag was and I went along the fence. Luster was hunting in the grass by the flower tree. They took the flag out, and they were hitting. Then they put the flag back and they

---

[8]See H.H. Clark and E.V. Clark, *Psychology and Language* (New York: Harcourt, Brace Jovanovich, 1977), Ch. 14.

went to the table, and he hit and the other hit. Then they went on, and I went along the fence. Luster came away from the flower tree and we went along the fence and they stopped and we stopped and I looked through the fence while Luster was hunting in the grass.

"Here, caddie." He hit. They went across the pasture. I held to the fence and watched them going away.

"Listen at you, now," Luster said. "Ain't you something, thirty-three years old, going on that way. After I done went all the way to town to buy you that cake. Hush up that moaning. Ain't you going to help me find that quarter so I can go to the show tonight?"

They were hitting little, across the pasture. I went back along the fence to where the flag was. It flapped on the bright grass and trees.

The character from whose point of view this part of the narrative is told is Benjy, a 33-year-old man with the mind of a young child. It is obvious that Faulkner has designed this language to suggest the limitations of Benjy's grasp of the world around him. But how does the reader arrive at this almost instinctive realization? There are some linguistic clues, and these are very suggestive, but by themselves they do not answer the question of how we give the passage the interpretation I have assigned to it.

Starting with the language: although it is deviant, it is not disintegrated in a haphazard fashion, but systematically patterned in certain areas of structure. Two observations are relevant here. First, random deviance or self-consistent deviance were options for Faulkner; they could be considered different models of mental deficiency. Second, certain types of structure, through repetition, are "foregrounded" (a process well known to stylisticians): foregrounding implies perceptual salience for readers, a pointer to areas of significance.

Most striking is a consistent oddity in what linguists call *transitivity:* the linguistic structuring of actions and events. In this passage there are almost no transitive verbs; instead, a preponderance of intransitives ("coming," "went," "hunting," etc.) and one transitive ("hit") used repeatedly without an object, as if it were intransitive. It is implied that Benjy has little sense of actions and their effects on objects: a restricted notion of causation.

Second, Benjy has no names for certain concepts which are crucial to his understanding of what he is witnessing. In certain cases the word is suppressed entirely: notably, the word "golf"; in others he uses circumlocutions to designate objects for which he lacks a term: "the curling flower spaces," "where the flag was," "the flower tree." The implication of this is that he has command of only a part of his society's classification of objects.

Third, he uses personal pronouns in an odd way—look at the sequence "them . . . they . . . They . . . they . . . they . . . he . . . the other . . . ." He uses these pronouns without identifying who he is referring to and with little variation in the pronoun forms themselves. It is suggested by this that Benjy does not appreciate what is needed if one wishes to specify to another person an object which one knows about but the other person does not. This would obviously be a severe communicative handicap.

Fourth, there is a problem with Benjy's *deictic* terms: the words used to point to and orient objects and actions. There are plenty of these deictics in the passage: "Through . . . between . . . coming toward where . . . went along . . ." etc. But these words do not add up to a consistent and comprehensible picture of the positions and movements of Benjy himself, his companion Luster, and the golfers whom they are watching. Try drawing diagrams of the sequence of positions and movements. Benjy is literally disoriented, with little sense of his location and of others' relationships with him within a context. The deictic inconsistency produces, for the reader, a sense of incoherence in the narrating, a feeling of being in the presence of a storyteller whose perceptions are disjointed.

In each of the above four paragraphs, I have first noted a recurrent linguistic construction, and then added an interpretative comment. The question arises (or ought to) of what is the authority for these comments. Let us be clear that there are no mimetic considerations involved, and no question of objective criteria for fidelity of representation: what reader could say "I recognise this as an accurate rendering of the story-telling style of a person with such-and-such a cognitive disability"? and wouldn't this response anyway miss the point that language constructs fictions rather than models reality? But it might be argued, on the "fiction-constructing" premise, that what happens here is precisely that the specific language of this text somehow creates Benjy's consciousness *ab initio*. This kind of argument, common in literary criticism, has never seemed to me very plausible; since linguistic forms come to the writer already loaded with significances, it is unlikely that words and sentences could be used to create new meanings autonomously in a particular text. It is probable, then, that the significances here are conventional, but having said that, it is necessary to define more precisely what is going on in the interaction between text, reader, and culture. At this stage of research, I cannot be absolutely exact, but can indicate something of the complexity of the processes.

Functional grammar maintains that linguistic constructions are selected according to the communicative purposes that they serve. It can be assumed that the total linguistic resources available to a speaker have been cumulatively formed by the communicative practices of the society into which s/he is born, and then by the practices in which s/he participates during socialization. On this theory, an explanation of my phrase "loaded with significances" above would be that the linguistic units and structures available to an individual signify their associated functions: e.g. the word "photosynthesis," in addition to its dictionary meaning of a certain botanical life-process, has the association of a scientific register of language; "once upon a time" signifies narrative for children; and so on. If it were as simple as this, each individual would possess, in addition to his/her semantic and syntactic and phonological competence, a kind of "pragmatic dictionary" in which the communicative and social significances of forms were reliably stored. This would, of course, differ from individual to individual depending on their communicative roles within society, but with very substantial overlap.

The catch with this model is that linguistic forms may be pragmatically, as well as semantically, ambiguous. There is not an invariant relationship between form and function. So the linguistic critic, like the ordinary reader or hearer, cannot just recognise the linguistic structure and, consulting his pragmatic competence, assign a significance to it. A more realistic view of linguistic interaction is that we process text as *discourse*, that is, as a unified whole of text and context—rather than as structure with function attached. We approach the text with a hypothesis about a relevant context, based on our previous experiences of relevant discourse, and relevant contexts: this hypothesis helps us to point an interpretation, to assign significances, which are confirmed or disconfirmed or modified as the discourse proceeds. In the case of face-to-face interaction in conversation, feedback occurs to assist the refining of the hypothesis; with written texts, we are reliant on our existing familiarity with relevant modes of discourse and on our skill (developed in literary education and in other conscious studies of discourse, e.g. sociolinguistics) at bringing appropriate discourse models to bear. As critics know, the reader's realization of a literary text as discourse takes reading and re-reading, on the basis of the maximum possible previous experience of the canon of literature and of other relevant discourse; to assist this process and to firm up our hypotheses, discussion with other experienced readers of literature is invaluable.

I am not an expert on Faulkner, and can only suggest the direction in which the analysis might go. The features noted can be traced in other texts which characterize various limitations of cognitive ability or of experience. For example, similar peculiarities of transitivity have been noted by Halliday in the language which depicts the thought-processes of William Golding's Neanderthal Man Lok in his novel *The Inheritors,* and he has interpreted them, as I have done here, as suggestions of a weak grasp of causation.[9] Circumlocutions like Benjy's "the flower tree" are examples of a process called *underlexicalization* which is common in the characterization of naive, inexperienced people; cf. my comments on Kingsley Amis's treatment of his provincial heroine Jenny Bunn in *Take a Girl Like You.*[10] The use of personal pronouns without specifying their referents, according to the sociologist Basil Bernstein, is a sign of an excessive dependence on context characteristic of working-class speakers of "restricted code"; interestingly, this suggestion is based not on empirical evidence but on an example

---

[9] M. A. K. Halliday, "Linguistic Function and Literary Style: An Inquiry into the Language of William Golding's *The Inheritors*," in S. Chatman, ed., *Literary Style: A Symposium* (London and New York: Oxford University Press, 1971), pp. 330–65.

[10] Roger Fowler, *Linguistics and the Novel* (London: Methuen, 2nd edn 1983), pp. 101–103.

fabricated by a co-researcher: thus Bernstein is operating with an essentially fictional model.[11]

The fact that the three texts I have referred to all come many years *after* the publication of *The Sound and the Fury* is not especially damaging: I am not, in this paper, discussing sources and influences, direct historical influence of one specific text upon another. I could readily find earlier instances of all four constructions with comparable cognitive significances (in older Gothic, naïve poetry, diaries and letters of poorly educated people, etc.), but the point is to show that there exist for the modern reader established modes of discourse for the characterization of naïve consciousness and which guide her/him towards the interpretations which I have suggested. This is the only basis on which the contemporary critic can begin to read a text. Later stages of critical practice can, and perhaps ought to be, more strictly historical. Faulkner is building a specific model of idiocy, as in the other sections of the novel, he is constituting other types of consciousness. The moral relationships between these points of view are of course the central concern of the fiction: Faulkner is juxtaposing modes of discourse to involve readers in a practice of evaluation. What literary, psychological and sociological discourses went to mould and articulate his models of deviant personalities is a question in historical sociolinguistics and pragmatics which I am not competent to answer without a great deal of research. But the research would be a kind of historical criticism of discourse and values. Critics may find it comforting that such research is compatible with the present theory of language—though of course not with previous formalist conceptions of linguistic stylistics.

Let me add a brief pedagogical and methodological conclusion. The theory of literature as language as I have articulated it is congruent with the elementary observation that students' critical performance, ability to "read" in the sense of realizing text as significant discourse, is very much dependent on how much and what they have read. Because reading and criticism depend on knowledge of discourse, not ability to dissect text structurally, it should not be expected that teaching formal linguistic analysis to beginning literature students will in itself produce any great advance in critical aptitude. However, linguistics of the kind indicated in this paper, with sociolinguistics, discourse analysis and pragmatics, in the context of a literature course of decent length—in our case three years—is very effective. In this type of course students mature gradually in their command of modes of literary discourse, simultaneously gaining a theoretical knowledge of language and its use, and an analytic method and terminology with which to describe the relationships between linguistic structures and their functions

---

[11] B. Bernstein, *Class, Codes and Control*, Vol. I (London: Routledge and Kegan Paul, 1971), pp. 178–79.

in "literary" discourses. Finally, since knowledge is formed for the individual in *social* structure, this approach is best taught and discussed in seminar groups rather than lectures and tutorials: thus experience of discourse can be shared.

Underlying these comments on linguistic criticism in literary education are my answers to some basic methodological—or meta-methodological—questions which were implicit in my opening discussion. These have to do with whether linguistic criticism is *objective*. The linguistic description of structures in text is certainly objective, particularly at the levels of syntax and phonology (semantic description produces less agreement among linguists). But it is clear that the assignment of functions or significances is not an objective process, because of the noted lack of co-variation of form and function. This does not mean that interpretation is a purely subjective, individual practice (a desperate and anarchic position into which those critics who stress the primacy of individual experience argue themselves). Criticism is an *inter-subjective* practice. The significances which an individual critic assigns are the product of social constitution; cultural meanings coded in the discourses in which the critic is competent. It is understandable, then, that critical interpretation is a matter of public discussion and debate; linguistic description, allowing clear descriptions of structures and a theory of social semiotic, is of fundamental importance in ensuring a clear grasp of the objective and intersubjective elements of texts under discussion.

Content Questions

1. What arguments have some literary critics given for devaluing the potential contribution of linguistics to literary analysis?

2. Fowler refers to five "failures of theorization" that lead some to undervalue the contribution of linguistics to the study of literature. Briefly summarize these fallacies or "deficiencies in the way linguistic criticism is theorized."

3. What is a "functional" language model?

4. What are the four linguistic behaviors by which Faulkner's character Benjy demonstrates language deficiency? Explain what is unusual in the character's usage with each of these. What do they reveal about Benjy?

5. Are particular words or structures ever pragmatically associated with specific communicative functions? Explain.

6. Why is it still necessary to look at the whole discourse before attributing a specific function to a particular word or structure?

Questions for Analysis and Discussion

1. Fowler refers to Halliday's functional categories, one of which is the "ideational." Explain what this category refers to. How is it related to the interpretation of literary texts?

2. Fowler does not think "formal linguistic analysis" (phonology, morphology, and syntax) would be as helpful to an interpretation of literature by beginning students as sociolinguistics, discourse analysis, and pragmatics. Comment on why this might be true.

3. Does a study of sociolinguistics, discourse analysis, and pragmatics ever require an understanding of phonology, morphology, and syntax? Explain.

4. Comment on the insights that discourse analysis can provide to literary interpretation.

Blame It on Twain:
Reading American Dialects in
The Adventures of Huckleberry Finn

Bruce Southard and Al Muller

One application that linguistic study can make to the interpretation or discussion of literature comes in the examination of dialects represented in particular texts. One might consider, for example, the meaning of particular dialectal forms or how an author might be using particular speech forms to illustrate something about a given character. In the following article, which originally appeared in the *Journal of Reading,* Bruce Southard and Al Muller, both of East Carolina University, demonstrate how a linguistic analysis of the dialects in Mark Twain's novel facilitates its interpretation. They also show how a discussion of linguistic elements within the novel can introduce students to important concepts related to language change and variation.

The Adventures of Huckleberry Finn opens with Mark Twain's explanatory, and somewhat self-congratulatory, note on his literary efforts toward reproducing faithfully and objectively the spoken language of the region and era in which the novel is set:

> In this book a number of dialects are used, to wit: the Missouri Negro dialect; the extremist form of the backwoods Southwestern dialect; the ordinary "Pike County" dialect; and four modified varieties of this last.

The attention Twain's note directs toward his use of seven distinct dialects often creates within those preparing to teach the novel a sense of obligation to incorporate into the unit some aspect of language studies, for accessing the dialectal material may pose difficulties for even competent student readers. Developing an appropriate and effective approach to the language of *Huckleberry Finn,* however, is especially difficult, for the nuances of dialectal differences are complex and sometimes open to multiple interpretations. Accordingly, some teachers simply ignore the language, focusing instead on plot, character, theme, and structure (see Janeczko and Mathews, 1990, for example).

Those who do choose to examine the language of the novel, moreover, may take an oblique approach, presenting Twain's use of dialect from a literary rather than linguistic perspective. For example, Twain's introductory note provides a natural opportunity for a discussion about the expected role of language, specifically dialogue, in a realistic novel. The value of such a discussion is significant to the study of realistic literature in general, but is vital to the study of *Huckleberry Finn.*

It is imperative that students comprehend that Twain's attention to dialect was not motivated by an effort to establish as universal truths the attitudes, biases, and prejudices revealed in the language of his characters. Rather, students need to understand and accept that Twain's purpose was to record accurately and objectively the spoken language of his characters as is required in realistic literature and to use the spoken language to reveal the personalities of his characters as is required in dramatic characterization.

While this distinctly literary approach to the study of language in *Huckleberry Finn* is of indisputable value, the approach does not actually incorporate the study of language, specifically regional and social dialects, into the unit as an essential component of the task of reading the novel. And, unfortunately, teachers who look to published scholarship for assistance with Twain's use of dialect will discover that Twain's introductory note seems to have created a cottage industry for dialectologists (see Boland, 1968; Bryant, 1978; Buxbaum, 1927; Carkeet, 1979; Hoben, 1956; Lowenherz, 1963; McKay, 1974; Pederson, 1966; Rulon, 1967, 1971; Sewell, 1984, 1985; and Tidwell, 1942). These linguistic studies prove to be conflicting and even call into question the accuracy of Twain's own assertions.

Rulon (1971), for example, finds only two dialects represented (p. 219) and suggests that Twain was not "serious when he spoke of four modified varieties of Pike County speech" (p. 221). Carkeet (1979), on the other hand, identifies the speakers of the seven dialects Twain boasts of.

Complicating matters even more is the fact that linguistic geographers have not yet fully mapped out dialect distribution in the area where much of the action supposedly takes place: northeastern and southeastern Missouri, southern Illinois, southwestern Kentucky, and northern Arkansas. Moreover, a scholarly examination of dialect and geography would undoubtedly prove too esoteric and inconclusive for the secondary student. Consequently, teachers tend either to ignore the whole matter of dialect in *Huckleberry Finn* or, for the sake of satisfying their sense of obligation, deal with the topic by having students construct glossaries of distinct lexical items or particularly noteworthy expressions.

A Useful Alternative

There is, however, an alternative approach to the study of dialect in *Huckleberry Finn,* one which will not only assist the student in reading with comprehension the novel's dialectal differences, but one which will also lead the student to note the mechanisms of language change and to appreciate the social differences conveyed by language. This approach entails a close examination of recurring features of dialect appearing in the novel—features that students will encounter while reading and that they must decode or "translate" in order to understand the dialogue. While ignoring dialect study as a body of knowledge to be mastered, this approach attempts to familiarize students with those aspects of dialect that might pose an obstacle to the successful reading of the novel. Furthermore, the approach suggests the inherent possibilities of language study, creates or fosters an awareness of the varieties of language usage, and, perhaps, may even reinforce the conventions of contemporary standard usage identified in a grammar unit taught earlier in the year.

Dialect studies such as those conducted by Rulon and Carkeet can help identify the content for the approach suggested here. For example, Rulon (1971) identifies 12 minor dialect features that occur in *Huckleberry Finn* (p. 220). Some of these features can easily be converted into exercises that focus on Twain's neologisms or on nonstandard grammatical constructions that may prove a barrier to reading the novel. By learning the processes of word formation and by identifying the syntactic "rule" used in even nonstandard dialects, the student acquires new reading skills.

The exercises that follow are meant to illustrate the possibilities inherent in a language-oriented approach to reading *Huckleberry Finn;* specific examples are not comprehensive but merely suggest possibilities that teachers may wish to expand. The brief explanations that accompany specific exercises provide technical material that teachers may find useful.

Word Formation

As the popularity of "sniglets" and of recent slang demonstrate, students are often attracted to "new" words and expressions. They can learn to identify some of the general processes of word formation by examining Twain's neologisms, thereby becoming more aware of both derivational and inflectional morphology. The following exercises show how various endings can be added to create new words (derivational morphology), or how a limited set of inflectional endings can be used to create verbs from nouns.

1. **Formation of adjectives.** One of the ways by which English speakers make new adjectives is by attaching special derivational affixes to a particular part of speech. For example, *-y* added to a noun produces an adjective. Thus, from *hand* we get *handy*; from *spot* we get *spotty*. Twain uses this *-y* affix to create *rose-leafy* and *smothery*. Have the students look for other such creations as they read; then discuss the rule that Twain is apparently following. (Does he always attach *-y* to a noun, for example?)

2. **Formation of verbs.** Verbs in English have five forms; the uninflected or infinitive form (*eat*), and four inflected forms: the third person

singular present tense (*eats*), the past tense (*ate*), the present participle (*eating*), and the past participle (*eaten*). Should any part of speech be given these inflections, it can function as a verb. For example, the noun *spade* can be used as a verb when we write, "We are *spading* our garden" or "We *spaded* our garden." Twain creates new verbs in the following phrases; have students identify which of the five forms appears in each example.

    a. So Jim and me set to *majestying* him.
    b. But it warn't no time to be *sentimentering*.
    c. We *scrouched* down and laid still.

Word Formation and Pronunciation

Other of Rulon's examples may be used to examine the influence of pronunciation on the formation of words. For instance, an unstressed syllable tends to be "reduced" in English and may lose some of its consonants, or even disappear. Historically, this process has given the language *aboard* from *on board*, *ashore* from *on shore*, and so on. Twain presents the following words: *afire, a-purpose, a-horseback, anear, afront,* and *anigh*. Is Twain consistently using the same process of word formation? What governs his use of the hyphen?

Grammar

The language of *Huckleberry Finn* also provides activities to reinforce grammatical material that frequently poses problems for students. The following exercises focus on the use of past tense forms of irregular verbs, on the use of multiple negatives, and on pronominal apposition:

    3. **Past tense and past participle.** English "regular" verbs have identical forms for the past tense and past participle; thus, we write "I *walked*" and "I have *walked*." "Irregular" verbs, such as *eat*, have different forms: "I *ate*" and "I have *eaten*." In the following examples from *Huckleberry Finn*, Twain's characters use an inappropriate form; they may have added the "regular" -*ed* to an irregular verb or have used the past participle when the past tense form is required. Have students identify the standard form of each italicized verb.

    a. There was an inch of new snow on the ground, and I *seen* somebody's tracks.
    b. He watched out for me one day in the spring and *catched* me.
    c. When breakfast was ready we lolled on the grass and *eat* it smoking hot.

    d. The sun was up so high when I *waked* that I judged it was after
       eight o'clock.
    e. I left Miss Watson, Huck, I *run* off.

    4. Multiple negatives. Standard written English does not allow multiple negation, although informal spoken English throughout the U.S. may find multiple negation in use. Have students rewrite the following sentences to conform to standard written English:

    a. I didn't have no luck.
    b. I wouldn't want to be nowhere else but here.
    c. I hadn't no accidents and didn't see nobody.
    d. I ain't hungry no more.
    e. You ain't a-going to threaten nobody no more.

    5. Pronominal appositives. In some varieties of spoken English, a noun subject is immediately followed by a pronoun that renames the subject. Such "pronominal appositives" are considered unnecessary in standard written English and should be deleted. Have students delete the unnecessary pronouns in the following sentences from *Huckleberry Finn:*

    a. The Widow Douglas she took me for her son.
    b. Pap he hadn't been seen for more than a year.
    c. The door it slammed to.
    d. The widow she cried over me.
    e. Jim he grumbled a little.

Sociolinguistics

The previous two exercises may be used by the teacher to initiate a discussion of social dialects and of levels of language usage, or language "styles." Thus, while students themselves may use multiple negatives or pronominal appositives in informal speech, they should learn that such language is considered by many to be inappropriate for formal speech and in written English.

    While the previous two exercises contain language spoken by Huck Finn, examples may also be taken from other dialects presented by Twain. Carkeet (1979), for example, groups with Huck's speech, or the "ordinary 'Pike County' dialect," the language of Tom, Aunt Polly, Judith Loftus, and others; he identifies the "Arkansas Gossips" with the Southwestern dialect and Jim (and all other Black characters) with the Missouri Negro dialect; representing the "four modified varieties" are the speech of the thieves on the *Sir Walter Scott,* the king, the Bricksville Loafers, and Aunt Sally and Uncle Silas Phelps, respectively (p. 330).

Sewell (1985) contends that, to some extent, a character's speech indicates not only social position within a community, but also the moral and intellectual position that the character occupies (p. 202). Judge Thatcher's speech, for example, is free of any "nonstandard" characteristics. Dr. Robinson's speech in Chapter 25 closely resembles that of Judge Thatcher, but in Chapter 29, when the doctor's position has been accepted by the townfolk, his language "style" changes to that of his fellow citizens.

By examining such changes in style, students become more aware of their own styles of speech and of how all speakers modify their language to fit a particular occasion. The following exercise focuses on this change in style in the speech of Dr. Robinson.

6. **Language style.** Have students consider the following passages of Dr. Robinson's speech. What are the differences? Which represents the more formal style? Why does the doctor modify his language?

a. "I was your father's friend, and I'm your friend; and I warn you *as* a friend, and an honest one that wants to protect you and keep you out of harm and trouble, to turn your backs on that scoundrel and have nothing to do with him, the ignorant tramp, with his idiotic Greek and Hebrew, as he called it." (from Chapter 25)

b. "I don't wish to be too hard on these two men, but I think they're frauds, and they may have complices that we don't know nothing about. If they have, won't the complices get away with that bag of gold Peter Wilks left? It ain't unlikely. If these men ain't frauds, they won't object to sending for that money and letting us keep it will they prove they're all right—ain't that so?" (from Chapter 29).

A similar change in style occurs in the speech of Mary Jane Wilks after Huck tells her the truth about the duke and the king. Have students examine her speech to identify how it changes; discuss how Twain uses a character's speech to signify a moral position.

A final speech sample which teachers may want to examine is the language of Jim. While Black Vernacular English (BVE) has been the subject of considerable discussion and study since the mid 1960s, its use in the American public school system is still a matter of controversy. Of interest here is the fact that Jim's speech exhibits many of the characteristics associated with BVE. Thus, students can observe Jim's speech as a sample of language that follows its own logic and rules of pronunciation and syntax. BVE is not a recent development, but a continuation of a language that can be traced back hundreds of years. By studying Jim's speech, accordingly, students come to have a greater appreciation of the rules underlying BVE.

7. **Black Vernacular English.** Jim's speech exhibits a number of nonstandard spellings to indicate pronunciation features that distinguish it from other varieties of American English. Unfamiliar words can be made recognizable when the student learns the spelling rule that Twain has

adopted. One such rule involves the deletion of certain consonants. Have students consider the following words taken from Jim's speech and then formulate the rule that tells when a consonant is deleted:

a. Compare *mawnin'* (morning), *whah* (where), *heah* (here), *mo'* (more) with *struck, truck, right, raf'*. [An *r* is deleted when it follows a vowel.]

b. Compare *fas', las', lan', raf', en'* with *landed, 'fraid, quiet, wait*. [A final consonant is deleted when it is preceded by another consonant.]

Similar exercises could be constructed to have students identify other characteristics of Jim's speech: the substitution of *d* for the voiced *th* of English (*dey* for *they*), and of *f* for the voiceless *th* (*mouf* for *mouth*); the deletion of unstressed initial syllables (*'fraid, 'sturb, 'mongst*); and the use of "completive aspect" (*she done broke down*). Pederson (1966) provides additional features which teachers may choose to examine.

Conclusion

By adopting a language-centered approach to *The Adventures of Huckleberry Finn*, teachers will not only assist students in developing the tools necessary for reading the dialects presented in the novel, but will also foster an appreciation for language and its many social varieties. By scattering these suggested activities throughout the unit of study, teachers will also be able to show how Twain used language to emphasize those social, moral, and intellectual messages that have made *Huckleberry Finn* so popular for over a century.

References

Boland, S. (1968). The seven dialects in *Huckleberry Finn*. *North Dakota Quarterly, 36*(3), 30–40.

Bryant, K. (1978). The slavery of dialect exemplified in Mark Twain's works. *Mark Twain Journal, 19*(3), 5–8.

Buxbaum, K. (1927). Mark Twain and American dialect. *American Speech, 2*, 233–236.

Carkeet, D. (1979). The dialects in Huck Finn. *American Literature, 51*, 315–332.

Hoben, J. B. (1956). Mark Twain: On the writer's use of language. *American Speech, 31*, 163–171.

Janeczko, P. B., & Mathews, K. (1990). Don't chuck Huck: An individualized approach to the classics. *English Journal, 79*(4), 41–44.

Lowenherz, R. (1963). The beginning of "Huckleberry Finn." *American Speech, 38*, 196–201.

McKay, J. H. (1974). *A linguistic study of Mark Twain's style*. Doctoral dissertation, Princeton University, Princeton, NJ.

McKay, J. H. (1985). "An art so high": Style in *Adventures of Huckleberry Finn*. In L. J. Budd (Ed.), *New essays on Adventures of Huckleberry Finn* (pp. 61–81). Cambridge: Cambridge University Press.

Pederson, L. A. (1966). Negro speech in *The Adventures of Huckleberry Finn*. *Mark Twain Journal*, 12(1), 1–4.

Rulon, C. M. (1967). *The dialects in Huckleberry Finn*. Doctoral dissertation, University of Iowa, Ames, IA.

Rulon, C. M. (1971). Geographical delimitation of the dialect areas in *The Adventures of Huckleberry Finn*. In J. V. Williamson & V. M. Burke (Eds.), *A various language: Perspectives on American dialects* (pp. 215–221). New York: Holt, Rinehart & Winston.

Sewell, D. (1984). *Varieties of language in the works of Mark Twain*. Doctoral dissertation, University of California, San Diego.

Sewell, D. (1985). "We ain't all trying to talk alike": Varieties of language in *Huckleberry Finn*. In R. Sattelmeyer & J. D. Crowley (Eds.), *One hundred years of Huckleberry Finn: The boy, his book and American culture* (pp. 201–215). Columbia, MO: University of Missouri Press.

Tidwell, J. N. (1942). Mark Twain's representation of Negro speech. *American Speech*, 17, 174–176.

Content Questions

1. How many dialects (including the "modified varieties") did Mark Twain claim to have represented in *The Adventures of Huckleberry Finn*? Has subsequent dialectal research conclusively supported his claim? Explain.

2. What approach do Southard and Muller suggest that teachers can use as they talk about the language in the novel?

3. Which specific derivational suffix do Southard and Muller show is sometimes used in the novel to form adjectives from nouns? How does Twain use verb inflections to transform words from one part of speech to another?

4. Among the linguistic features within the grammar of the novel, which three specific features do Southard and Muller indicate could introduce class discussion or activities about differences in language varieties?

5. Consider the two contrasting examples of Dr. Robinson's speech style, which Southard and Muller provide from the novel. List the differences you notice. What do you think that Twain was trying to show by the differences in the speech styles?

6. Southard and Muller briefly mention some of the features of Black English that appear in Jim's speech. What are some of the examples they mention?

Questions for Analysis and Discussion

1. One scholar mentioned in the article explains that Twain uses differing varieties of speech not only to indicate differences in social standing but also differences in morality or intellect. Assuming that Twain tried to represent these notions through speech, do you believe that such a literary device corresponds with reality? Do you believe we can accurately judge people's morality or even intelligence through their speech forms? Explain.

2. How reliable do you think Twain was in representing genuine dialects of his time?

3. Contrast the kinds of linguistic analysis outlined in this article with the type of linguistic analysis that is shown in Hancher's article or in Fowler's article earlier in this chapter. Is any one of these approaches better than another? How does the nature of a literary work suggest which types of linguistic approaches might be most useful for examining that work?

Some Psychodynamics of Orality

Walter J. Ong

It is difficult for many of us today to imagine what it would be like to function in a culture that is primarily oral. In the article below, which first appeared in *Orality and Literacy*, Walter J. Ong, a former president of the Modern Language Association of America, identifies some of the features of an orally based culture and how these features manifest themselves in the literature produced in cultures that still retain a strong oral basis. The information in this article could be helpful in interpreting various features that appear in older literary texts.

Sounded Word as Power and Action

As a result of the work just reviewed, and of other work which will be cited, it is possible to generalize somewhat about the psychodynamics of primary oral cultures, that is, of oral cultures untouched by writing. For brevity, when the context keeps the meaning clear, I shall refer to primary oral cultures simply as oral cultures.

Fully literate persons can only with great difficulty imagine what a primary oral culture is like, that is, a culture with no knowledge whatsoever of writing or even of the possibility of writing. Try to imagine a culture where no one has ever "looked up" anything. In a primary oral culture, the expression "to look up something" is an empty phrase: it would have no conceivable meaning. Without writing, words as such have no visual presence, even when the objects they represent are visual. They are sounds. You might "call" them back—"recall" them. But there is nowhere to "look" for them. They have no focus and no trace (a visual metaphor, showing dependency on writing), not even a trajectory. They are occurrences, events.

To learn what a primary oral culture is and what the nature of our problem is regarding such a culture, it helps first to reflect on the nature of sound itself as sound (Ong 1967, pp. 111–38). All sensation takes place in time, but sound has a special relationship to time unlike that of the other fields that register in human sensation. Sound exists only when it is going out of existence. It is not simply perishable but essentially evanescent, and it is sensed as evanescent. When I pronounce the word "permanence," by the time I get to the "-nence," the "perma-" is gone, and has to be gone.

There is no way to stop sound and have sound. I can stop a moving picture camera and hold one frame fixed on the screen. If I stop the movement of sound, I have nothing—only silence, no sound at all. All sensation takes place in time, but no other sensory field totally resists a holding action, stabilization, in quite this way. Vision can register motion, but it can also register immobility. Indeed, it favors immobility, for to examine something closely by vision, we prefer to have it quiet. We often reduce motion to a series of still shots the better to see what motion is. There is no equivalent of a still shot for sound. An oscillogram is silent. It lies outside the sound world.

For anyone who has a sense of what words are in a primary oral culture, or a culture not far removed from primary orality, it is not surprising that the Hebrew term *dabar* means "word" and "event." Malinowski (1923, pp. 451, 470–81) has made the point that among "primitive" (oral) peoples generally language is a mode of action and not simply a countersign of thought, though he had trouble explaining what he was getting at (Sampson 1980, pp. 223–6), since understanding of the psychodynamics of orality was virtually nonexistent in 1923. Neither is it surprising that oral peoples commonly, and probably universally, consider words to have great power. Sound cannot be sounding without the use of power. A hunter can see a buffalo, smell, taste, and touch a buffalo when the buffalo is completely inert, even dead, but if he hears a buffalo, he had better watch out: something is going on. In this sense, all sound, and especially oral utterance, which comes from inside living organisms, is "dynamic."

The fact that oral peoples commonly and in all likelihood universally consider words to have magical potency is clearly tied in, at least unconsciously, with their sense of the word as necessarily spoken, sounded, and hence power-driven. Deeply typographic folk forget to think of words as primarily oral, as events, and hence as necessarily powered: for them, words tend rather to be assimilated to things, "out there" on a flat surface. Such "things" are not so readily associated with magic, for they are not actions, but are in a radical sense dead, though subject to dynamic resurrection (Ong 1977, pp. 230–71).

Oral peoples commonly think of names (one kind of words) as conveying power over things. Explanations of Adam's naming of the animals in Genesis 2:20 usually call condescending attention to this presumably quaint archaic belief. Such a belief is in fact far less quaint than it seems to unreflective chirographic and typographic folk. First of all, names do give human beings power over what they name: without learning a vast store of names, one is simply powerless to understand, for example, chemistry and to practice chemical engineering. And so with all other intellectual knowledge. Secondly, chirographic and typographic folk tend to think of names as labels, written or printed tags imaginatively affixed to an object named. Oral folk have no sense of a name as a tag, for they have no idea of a name as something that can be seen. Written or printed representations of words can be labels; real, spoken words cannot be.

You Know What You Can Recall: Mnemonics and Formulas

In an oral culture, restriction of words to sound determines not only modes of expression but also thought processes.

You know what you can recall. When we say we know Euclidean geometry, we mean not that we have in mind at the moment every one of its propositions and proofs but rather that we can bring them to mind readily. We can recall them. The theorem "You know what you can recall" applies also to an oral culture. But how do persons in an oral culture recall? The organized knowledge that literates today study so that they "know" it, that is, can recall it, has, with very few if any exceptions, been assembled and made available to them in writing. This is the case not only with Euclidean geometry but also with American Revolutionary history, or even baseball batting averages or traffic regulations.

An oral culture has no texts. How does it get together organized material for recall? This is the same as asking, "What does it or can it know in an organized fashion?"

Suppose a person in an oral culture would undertake to think through a particular complex problem and would finally manage to articulate a solution which itself is relatively complex, consisting, let us say, of a few hundred words. How does he or she retain for later recall the verbalization so painstakingly elaborated? In the total absence of any writing, there is nothing outside the thinker, no text, to enable him or her to produce the same line of thought again or even to verify whether he or she has done so or not. *Aides-mémoire* such as notched sticks or a series of carefully arranged objects will not of themselves retrieve a complicated series of assertions. How, in fact, could a lengthy, analytic solution ever be assembled in the first place? An interlocutor is virtually essential: it is hard to talk to yourself for hours on end. Sustained thought in an oral culture is tied to communication.

But even with a listener to stimulate and ground your thought, the bits and pieces of your thought cannot be preserved in jotted notes. How could you ever call back to mind what you had so laboriously worked out? The only answer is: Think memorable thoughts. In a primary oral culture, to solve effectively the problem of retaining and retrieving carefully articulated thought, you have to do your thinking in mnemonic patterns, shaped for ready oral recurrence. Your thought must come into being in heavily rhythmic, balanced patterns, in repetitions or antitheses, in alliterations and assonances, in epithetic and other formulary expressions, in standard thematic settings (the assembly, the meal, the duel, the hero's "helper," and so on), in proverbs which are constantly heard by everyone so that they come to mind readily and which themselves are patterned for retention and ready recall, or in other mnemonic form. Serious thought is intertwined with memory systems. Mnemonic needs determine even syntax (Havelock 1963, pp. 87–96, 131–2, 294–6).

Protracted orally based thought, even when not in formal verse, tends to be highly rhythmic, for rhythm aids recall, even physiologically. Jousse (1978) has shown the intimate linkage between rhythmic oral patterns, the breathing process, gesture, and the bilateral symmetry of the human body in ancient Aramaic and Hellenic targums, and thus also in ancient Hebrew. Among the ancient Greeks, Hesiod, who was intermediate between oral Homeric Greece and fully developed Greek literacy, delivered quasi-philosophic material in the formulaic verse forms that structured it into the oral culture from which he had emerged (Havelock 1963, pp. 97–8, 294–301).

Formulas help implement rhythmic discourse and also act as mnemonic aids in their own right, as set expressions circulating through the mouths and ears of all. "Red in the morning, the sailor's warning; red in the night, the sailor's delight." "Divide and conquer." "To err is human, to forgive is divine." "Sorrow is better than laughter, because when the face is sad the heart grows wiser" (Ecclesiastes 7:3). "The clinging vine." "The sturdy oak." "Chase off nature and she returns at a gallop." Fixed, often rhythmically balanced, expressions of this sort and of other sorts can be found occasionally in print, indeed can be "looked up" in books of sayings, but in oral cultures they are not occasional. They are incessant. They form the substance of thought itself. Thought in any extended form is impossible without them, for it consists in them.

The more sophisticated orally patterned thought is, the more it is likely to be marked by set expressions skillfully used. This is true of oral cultures generally from those of Homeric Greece to those of the present day across the globe. Havelock's *Preface to Plato* (1963) and fictional works such as Chinua Achebe's novel *No Longer at Ease* (1961), which draws directly on Ibo oral tradition in West Africa, alike provide abundant instances of thought patterns of orally educated characters who move in these oral, mnemonically tooled grooves, as the speakers reflect, with high intelligence and sophistication, on the situations in which they find themselves involved. The law itself in oral cultures is enshrined in formulaic sayings, proverbs, which are not mere jurisprudential decorations, but themselves constitute the law. A judge in an oral culture is often called on to articulate sets of relevant proverbs out of which he can produce equitable decisions in the cases under formal litigation before him (Ong 1978, p. 5).

In an oral culture, to think through something in non-formulaic, non-patterned, non-mnemonic terms, even if it were possible, would be a waste of time, for such thought, once worked through, could never be recovered with any effectiveness, as it could be with the aid of writing. It would not be abiding knowledge but simply a passing thought, however complex. Heavy patterning and communal fixed formulas in oral cultures serve some of the purposes of writing in chirographic cultures, but in doing so they of course determine the kind of thinking that can be done, the way experience is intellectually organized. In an oral culture, experience is intellectualized mnemonically. This is one reason why, for a St. Augustine of Hippo (A.D. 354–430), as for other savants living in a culture that knew some literacy but still carried an overwhelmingly massive oral residue, memory bulks so large when he treats of the powers of the mind.

Of course, all expression and all thought is to a degree formulaic in the sense that every word and every concept conveyed in a word is a kind of formula, a fixed way of processing the data of experience, determining the way experience and reflection are intellectually organized, and acting as a mnemonic device of sorts. Putting experience into any words (which means transforming it at least a little bit—not the same as falsifying it) can implement its recall. The formulas characterizing orality are more elaborate, however, than are individual words, though some may be relatively simple: the *Beowulf*-poet's "whale-road" is a formula (metaphorical) for the sea in a sense in which the term "sea" is not.

Further Characteristics of Orally Based Thought and Expression

Awareness of the mnemonic base of the thought and expression in primary oral cultures opens the way to understanding some further characteristics of orally based thought and expression in addition to its formulaic styling. The characteristics treated here are some of those which set off orally based thought and expression from chirographically and typographically based thought and expression, the characteristics, that is, which are most likely to strike those reared in writing and print cultures as surprising. This inventory of characteristics is not presented as exclusive or conclusive but as suggestive, for much more work and reflection is needed to deepen understanding of orally based thought (and thereby understanding of chirographically based, typographically based, and electronically based thought).

In a primary oral culture, thought and expression tend to be of the following sorts.

Additive Rather Than Subordinative

A familiar instance of additive oral style is the creation narrative in Genesis 1:1–5, which is indeed a text but one preserving recognizable oral patterning. The Douay version (1610), produced in a culture with a still massive oral residue, keeps close in many ways to the additive Hebrew original (as mediated through the Greek from which the Douay version was made):

In the beginning God created heaven and earth. And the earth was void and empty, and darkness was upon the face of the deep; and the spirit of God moved over the waters. And God said: Be light made. And light was made. And God saw the light that it was good; and he divided the light from the darkness. And he called the light Day, and the darkness Night; and there was evening and morning one day.

Nine introductory "ands." Adjusted to sensibilities shaped more by writing and print, the *New American Bible* (1970) translates:

In the beginning, when God created the heavens and the earth, the earth was a formless wasteland, and darkness covered the abyss, while a mighty wind swept over the waters. Then God said, "Let there be light," and there was light. God saw how good the light was. God then separated the light from the darkness. God called the light "day" and the darkness he called "night." Thus evening came, and morning followed—the first day.

Two introductory "ands," each submerged in a compound sentence. The Douay renders the Hebrew *we* or *wa* ("and") simply as "and." The New American renders it "and," "when," "then," "thus," or "while," to provide a flow of narration with the analytic, reasoned subordination that characterizes writing (Chafe 1982) and that appears more natural in twentieth-century texts. Oral structures often look to pragmatics (the convenience of the speaker—Sherzer, 1974, reports lengthy public oral performances among the Cuna incomprehensible to their hearers). Chirographic structures look more to syntactics (organization of the discourse itself), as Givón has suggested (1979). Written discourse develops more elaborate and fixed grammar than oral discourse does because to provide meaning it is more dependent simply upon linguistic structure, since it lacks the normal full existential contexts which surround oral discourse and help determine meaning in oral discourse somewhat independently of grammar.

It would be a mistake to think that the Douay is simply "closer" to the original today than the New American is. It is closer in that it renders *we* or *wa* always by the same word, but it strikes the present-day sensibility as remote, archaic, and even quaint. Peoples in oral cultures or cultures with high oral residue, including the culture that produced the Bible, do not savor this sort of expression as so archaic or quaint. It feels natural and normal to them somewhat as the New American version feels natural and normal to us.

Other instances of additive structure can be found across the world in primary oral narrative, of which we now have a massive supply on tape (see Foley, 1980, for listing of some tapes).

Aggregative Rather Than Analytic

This characteristic is closely tied to reliance on formulas to implement memory. The elements of orally based thought and expression tend to be not so much simple integers as clusters of integers, such as parallel terms or phrases or clauses, antithetical terms or phrases or clauses, epithets. Oral folk prefer, especially in formal discourse, not the soldier, but the brave soldier; not the princess, but the beautiful princess; not the oak, but the sturdy oak. Oral expression thus carries a load of epithets and other formulary baggage which high literacy rejects as cumbersome and tiresomely redundant because of its aggregative weight (Ong 1977, pp. 188–212).

The clichés in political denunciations in many low-technology, developing cultures—enemy of the people, capitalist war-mongers—that strike high literates as mindless are residual formulary essentials of oral thought processes. One of the many indications of a high, if subsiding, oral residue in the culture of the Soviet Union is (or was a few years ago, when I encountered it) the insistence on speaking there always of "the Glorious Revolution of October 26"—the epithetic formula here is obligatory stabilization, as were Homeric epithetic formulas "wise Nestor" or "clever Odysseus," or as "the glorious Fourth of July" used to be in the pockets of oral residue common even in the early twentieth-century United States. The Soviet Union still announces each year the official epithets for various *loci classici* in Soviet history.

An oral culture may well ask in a riddle why oaks are sturdy, but it does so to assure you that they are, to keep the aggregate intact, not really to question or cast doubt on the attribution. (For examples directly from the oral culture of the Luba in Zaire, see Faik-Nzuji 1970.) Traditional expressions in oral cultures must not be dismantled: it has been hard work getting them together over the generations, and there is nowhere outside the mind to store them. So soldiers are brave and princesses beautiful and oaks sturdy forever. This is not to say that there may not be other epithets for soldiers or princesses or oaks, even contrary epithets, but these are standard, too: the braggart soldier, the unhappy princess, can also be part of the equipment. What obtains for epithets obtains for other formulas. Once a formulary expression has crystallized, it had best be kept intact. Without a writing system, breaking up thought—that is, analysis—is a high-risk procedure. As Lévi-Strauss has well put it in a summary statement "the savage [i.e. oral] mind totalizes" (1966, p. 245).

Redundant or "Copious"

Thought requires some sort of continuity. Writing establishes in the text a "line" of continuity outside the mind. If distraction confuses or obliterates from the mind the context out of which emerges the material I am now reading, the context can be retrieved by glancing back over the text selectively. Backlooping can be entirely occasional, purely *ad hoc*. The mind concentrates its own energies on moving ahead because what it backloops into lies quiescent outside itself, always available piecemeal on the inscribed page. In oral discourse, the situation is different. There is nothing to backloop into outside the mind, for the oral utterance has vanished as soon as it is uttered. Hence the mind must move ahead more slowly, keeping close to the focus of attention much of what it has already dealt with. Redundancy, repetition of the just-said, keeps both speaker and hearer surely on the track.

Since redundancy characterizes oral thought and speech, it is in a profound sense more natural to thought and speech than is sparse linearity. Sparsely linear or analytic thought and speech is an artificial creation, structured by the technology of writing. Eliminating redundancy on a significant scale demands a time-obviating technology, writing, which imposes some kind of strain on the psyche in preventing expression from falling into its more natural patterns. The psyche can manage the strain in part because handwriting is physically such a slow process—typically about one-tenth of the speed of oral speech (Chafe 1982). With writing, the mind is forced into a slowed-down pattern that affords it the opportunity to interfere with and reorganize its more normal, redundant processes.

Redundancy is also favored by the physical conditions of oral expression before a large audience, where redundancy is in fact more marked than in most face-to-face conversation. Not everyone in a large audience understands every word a speaker utters, if only because of acoustical problems. It is advantageous for the speaker to say the same thing, or equivalently the same thing, two or three times. If you miss the "not only . . ." you can supply it by inference from the "but also . . . ." Until electronic amplification reduced acoustical problems to a minimum, public speakers as late as, for example, William Jennings Bryan (1860–1925) continued the old redundancy in their public addresses and by force of habit let them spill over into their writing. In some kinds of acoustic surrogates for oral verbal communication, redundancy reaches fantastic dimensions, as in African drum talk. It takes on the average around eight times as many words to say something on the drums as in the spoken language (Ong 1977, p. 101).

The public speaker's need to keep going while he is running through his mind what to say next also encourages redundancy. In oral delivery, though a pause may be effective, hesitation is always disabling. Hence it is better to repeat something, artfully if possible, rather than simply to stop speaking while fishing for the next idea. Oral cultures encourage fluency, fulsomeness, volubility. Rhetoricians were to call this *copia*. They continued to encourage it, by a kind of oversight, when they had modulated rhetoric from an art of public speaking to an art of writing. Early written texts, through the Middle Ages and the Renaissance, are often bloated with "amplification," annoyingly redundant by modern standards. Concern with *copia* remains intense in western culture so long as the culture sustains massive oral residue—which is roughly until the age of Romanticism or even beyond. Thomas Babington Macaulay (1800–59) is one of the many fulsome early Victorians whose pleonastic written compositions still read much as an exuberant, orally composed oration would sound, as do also, very often, the writings of Winston Churchill (1874–1965).

Conservative or Traditionalist

Since in a primary oral culture conceptualized knowledge that is not repeated aloud soon vanishes, oral societies must invest great energy in saying over and over again what has been learned arduously over the ages. This need establishes a highly traditionalist or conservative set of mind that with good reason inhibits intellectual experimentation. Knowledge is hard to come by and precious, and society regards highly those wise old men and women who specialize in conserving it, who know and can tell the stories of the days of old. By storing knowledge outside the mind, writing and, even more, print downgrade the figures of the wise old man and the wise old woman, repeaters of the past, in favor of younger discoverers of something new.

Writing is of course conservative in its own ways. Shortly after it first appeared, it served to freeze legal codes in early Sumeria (Oppenheim 1964, p. 232). But by taking conservative functions on itself, the text frees the mind of conservative tasks, that is, of its memory work, and thus enables the mind to turn itself to new speculation (Havelock 1963, pp. 254–305). Indeed, the residual orality of a given chirographic culture can be calculated to a degree from the mnemonic load it leaves on the mind, that is, from the amount of memorization the culture's educational procedures require (Goody 1968, pp. 13–14).

Of course oral cultures do not lack originality of their own kind. Narrative originality lodges not in making up new stories but in managing a particular interaction with this audience at this time—at every telling the story has to be introduced uniquely into a unique situation, for in oral cultures an audience must be brought to respond, often vigorously. But narrators also introduce new elements into old stories (Goody 1977, pp. 29–30). In oral tradition, there will be as many minor variants of a myth as there are repetitions of it, and the number of repetitions can be increased indefinitely. Praise poems of chiefs invite entrepreneurship, as the old formulas and themes have to be made to interact with new and often complicated political situations. But the formulas and themes are reshuffled rather than supplanted with new materials.

Religious practices, and with them cosmologies and deep-seated beliefs, also change in oral cultures. Disappointed with the practical results of the cult at a given shrine when cures there are infrequent, vigorous leaders—the "intellectuals" in oral society, Goody styles them (1977, p. 30)—

invent new shrines and with these new conceptual universes. Yet these new universes and the other changes that show a certain originality come into being in an essentially formulaic and thematic noetic economy. They are seldom if ever explicitly touted for their novelty but are presented as fitting the traditions of the ancestors.

Close to the Human Lifeworld

In the absence of elaborate analytic categories that depend on writing to structure knowledge at a distance from lived experience, oral cultures must conceptualize and verbalize all their knowledge with more or less close reference to the human lifeworld, assimilating the alien, objective world to the more immediate, familiar interaction of human beings. A chirographic (writing) culture and even more a typographic (print) culture can distance and in a way denature even the human, itemizing such things as the names of leaders and political divisions in an abstract, neutral list entirely devoid of a human action context. An oral culture has no vehicle so neutral as a list. In the latter half of the second book, the *Iliad* presents the famous catalogue of the ships—over four hundred lines—which compiles the names of Grecian leaders and the regions they ruled, but in a total context of human action: the names of persons and places occur as involved in doings (Havelock 1963, pp. 176–80). The normal and very likely the only place in Homeric Greece where this sort of political information could be found in verbalized form was in a narrative or a genealogy, which is not a neutral list but an account describing personal relations (cf. Goody and Watt 1968, p. 32). Oral cultures know few statistics or facts divorced from human or quasi-human activity.

An oral culture likewise has nothing corresponding to how-to-do-it manuals for the trades (such manuals in fact are extremely rare and always crude even in chirographic cultures, coming into effective existence only after print has been considerably interiorized—Ong 1967, pp. 28–9, 234, 258). Trades were learned by apprenticeship (as they still largely are even in high-technology cultures), which means from observation and practice with only minimal verbalized explanation. The maximum verbal articulation of such things as navigation procedures, which were crucial to Homeric culture, would have been encountered not in any abstract manual-style description at all but in such things as the following passage from the *Iliad* i. 141–4, where the abstract description is embedded in a narrative presenting specific commands for human action or accounts of specific acts:

> As for now a black ship let us draw to the great salt sea
> And therein oarsmen let us advisedly gather and thereupon a hecatomb
> Let us set and upon the deck Chryseis of fair cheeks
> Let us embark. And one man as captain, a man of counsel, there must be.

(quoted in Havelock 1963, p. 81; see also ibid., pp. 174–5). Primary oral culture is little concerned with preserving knowledge of skills as an abstract, self-subsistent corpus.

Agonistically Toned

Many, if not all, oral or residually oral cultures strike literates as extraordinarily agonistic in their verbal performance and indeed in their lifestyle. Writing fosters abstractions that disengage knowledge from the arena where human beings struggle with one another. It separates the knower from the known. By keeping knowledge embedded in the human lifeworld, orality situates knowledge within a context of struggle. Proverbs and riddles are not used simply to store knowledge but to engage others in verbal and intellectual combat: utterance of one proverb or riddle challenges hearers to top it with a more apposite or a contradictory one (Abrahams 1968; 1972). Bragging about one's own prowess and/or verbal tongue-lashings of an opponent figure regularly in encounters between characters in narrative: in the *Iliad,* in *Beowulf,* throughout medieval European romance, in *The Mwindo Epic* and countless other African stories (Okpewho 1979; Obiechina 1975), in the Bible, as between David and Goliath (1 Samuel 17:43–7). Standard in oral societies across the world, reciprocal name-calling has been fitted with a specific name in linguistics: flyting (or fliting). Growing up in a still dominantly oral culture, certain young black males in the United States, the Caribbean, and elsewhere, engage in what is known variously as the "dozens" or "joning" or "sounding" or by other names, in which one opponent tries to outdo the other in vilifying the other's mother. The dozens is not a real fight but an art form, as are the other stylized verbal tongue lashings in other cultures.

Not only in the use to which knowledge is put, but also in the celebration of physical behavior, oral cultures reveal themselves as agonistically programmed. Enthusiastic description of physical violence often marks oral narrative. In the *Iliad,* for example, Books viii and x would at least rival the most sensational television and cinema shows today in outright violence and far surpass them in exquisitely gory detail, which can be less revulsive when described verbally than when presented visually. Portrayal of gross physical violence, central to much oral epic and other oral genres and residual through much early literacy, gradually wanes or becomes peripheral in later literary narrative. It survives in medieval ballads but is already being spoofed by Thomas Nashe in *The Unfortunate Traveler* (1594). As literary narrative moves toward the serious novel, it eventually pulls the focus of action more and more to interior crises and away from purely exterior crises.

The common and persistent physical hardships of life in many early societies of course explain in part the high evidence of violence in early verbal art forms. Ignorance of physical causes of disease and disaster can also foster personal tensions. Since the disease or disaster is caused by something, in lieu of physical causes the personal malevolence of another human be-ing—a magician, a witch—can be assumed and personal hostilities thereby increased. But violence in oral art forms is also connected with the structure of orality itself. When all verbal communication must be by direct word of mouth, involved in the give-and-take dynamics of sound, interper-sonal relations are kept high—both attractions and, even more, antago-nisms.

The other side of agonistic name-calling or vituperation in oral or residually oral cultures is the fulsome expression of praise which is found everywhere in connection with orality. It is well known in the much-studied present-day African oral praise poems (Finnegan 1970; Opland 1975) as all through the residually oral western rhetorical tradition stretch-ing from classical antiquity through the eighteenth century. "I come to bury Caesar, not to praise him," Marcus Antonius cries in his funeral ora-tion in Shakespeare's *Julius Caesar* (v. ii. 79), and then proceeds to praise Caesar in rhetorical patterns of encomium which were drilled into the heads of all Renaissance schoolboys and which Erasmus used so wittily in his *Praise of Folly*. The fulsome praise in the old, residually oral, rhetoric tradition strikes persons from a high-literacy culture as insincere, flatulent, and comically pretentious. But praise goes with the highly polarized, ago-nistic, oral world of good and evil, virtue and vice, villains and heroes.

The agonistic dynamics of oral thought processes and expression have been central to the development of western culture, where they were insti-tutionalized by the "art" of rhetoric, and by the related dialectic of Socrates and Plato, which furnished agonistic oral verbalization with a sci-entific base worked out with the help of writing. More will be said about this later.

Empathetic and Participatory Rather Than Objectively Distanced

For an oral culture learning or knowing means achieving close, empa-thetic, communal identification with the known (Havelock 1963, pp. 145–6), "getting with it." Writing separates the knower from the known and thus sets up conditions for "objectivity," in the sense of personal dis-engagement or distancing. The "objectivity" which Homer and other oral performers do have is that enforced by formulaic expression: the indi-vidual's reaction is not expressed as simply individual or "subjective" but rather as encased in the communal reaction, the communal "soul." Under the influence of writing, despite his protest against it, Plato had rejected the poets from his Republic, for studying them was essentially learning to react with "soul," to feel oneself identified with Achilles or Odysseus (Havelock 1963, pp. 197–233). Treating another primary oral setting over two thousand years later, the editors of *The Mwindo Epic* (1971, p. 37) call attention to a similar strong identification of Candi Rureke, the performer of the epic, and through him of his listeners, with the hero Mwindo, an identification which actually affects the grammar of the narration, so that on occasion the narrator slips into the first person when describing the actions of the hero. So bound together are narrator, audience, and character that Rureke has the epic character Mwindo himself address the scribes taking down Rureke's performance: "Scribe, march!" or "O scribe you, you see that I am already going." In the sensibility of the narrator and his audience the hero of the oral performance assimilates into the oral world even the transcribers who are deoralizing it into text.

Homeostatic

By contrast with literate societies, oral societies can be characterized as homeostatic (Goody and Watt 1968, pp. 31–4). That is to say, oral societies live very much in a present which keeps itself in equilibrium or homeostasis by sloughing off memories which no longer have present relevance.

The forces governing homeostasis can be sensed by reflection on the condition of words in a primary oral setting. Print cultures have invented dictionaries in which the various meanings of a word as it occurs in datable texts can be recorded in formal definitions. Words thus are known to have layers of meaning, many of them quite irrelevant to ordinary present meanings. Dictionaries advertise semantic discrepancies.

Oral cultures of course have no dictionaries and few semantic discrepancies. The meaning of each word is controlled by what Goody and Watt (1968, p. 29) call "direct semantic ratification," that is, by the real-life situations in which the word is used here and now. The oral mind is uninterested in definitions (Luria 1976, pp. 48–99). Words acquire their meanings only from their always insistent actual habitat, which is not, as in a dictionary, simply other words, but includes also gestures, vocal inflections, facial expression, and the entire human, existential setting in which the real, spoken word always occurs. Word meanings come continuously out of the present, though past meanings of course have shaped the present meaning in many and varied ways, no longer recognized.

It is true that oral art forms, such as epic, retain some words in archaic forms and senses. But they retain such words, too, through current use—not the current use of ordinary village discourse but the current use of ordinary epic poets, who preserve archaic forms in their special vocabulary. These performances are part of ordinary social life and so the archaic forms are current, though limited to poetic activity. Memory of the old meaning of old terms thus has some durability, but not unlimited durability.

When generations pass and the object or institution referred to by the archaic word is no longer part of present, lived experience, though the word has been retained, its meaning is commonly altered or simply vanishes. African talking drums, as used for example among the Lokele in eastern Zaire, speak in elaborate formulas that preserve certain archaic words which the Lokele drummers can vocalize but whose meaning they no longer know (Carrington 1974, pp. 41–2; Ong 1977, pp. 94–5). Whatever these words referred to has dropped out of Lokele daily experience, and the term that remains has become empty. Rhymes and games transmitted orally from one generation of small children to the next even in high-technology culture have similar words which have lost their original referential meanings and are in effect nonsense syllables. Many instances of such survival of empty terms can be found in Opie and Opie (1952), who, as literates, of course manage to recover and report the original meanings of the terms lost to their present oral users.

Goody and Watt (1968, pp. 31–3) cite Laura Bohannan, Emrys Peters, and Godfrey and Monica Wilson for striking instances of the homeostasis of oral cultures in the handing on of genealogies. In recent years among the Tiv people of Nigeria the genealogies actually used orally in settling court disputes have been found to diverge considerably from the genealogies carefully recorded in writing by the British forty years earlier (because of their importance then, too, in court disputes). The later Tiv have maintained that they were using the same genealogies as forty years earlier and that the earlier written record was wrong. What had happened was that the later genealogies had been adjusted to the changed social relations among the Tiv: they were the same in that they functioned in the same way to regulate the real world. The integrity of the past was subordinate to the integrity of the present.

Goody and Watt (1968, p. 33) report an even more strikingly detailed case of "structural amnesia" among the Gonja in Ghana. Written records made by the British at the turn of the twentieth century show that Gonja oral tradition then presented Ndewura Jakpa, the founder of the state of Gonja, as having had seven sons, each of whom was ruler of one of the seven territorial divisions of the state. By the time sixty years later when the myths of state were again recorded, two of the seven divisions had disappeared, one by assimilation to another division and the other by reason of a boundary shift. In these later myths, Ndewura Jakpa had five sons, and no mention was made of the two extinct divisions. The Gonja were still in contact with their past, tenacious about this contact in their myths, but the part of the past with no immediately discernible relevance to the present had simply fallen away. The present imposed its own economy on past remembrances. Packard (1980, p. 157) has noted that Claude Lévi-Strauss, T. O. Beidelman, Edmund Leach and others have suggested that oral traditions reflect a society's present cultural values rather than idle curiosity about the past. He finds this is true of the Bashu, as Harms (1980, p. 178) finds it also true of the Bobangi.

The implications here for oral genealogies need to be noted. A West African griot or other oral genealogist will recite those genealogies which his hearers listen to. If he knows genealogies which are no longer called for, they drop from his repertoire and eventually disappear. The genealogies of political winners are of course more likely to survive than those of losers. Henige (1980, p. 255), reporting on Ganda and Myoro kinglists, notes that the "oral mode . . . allows for inconvenient parts of the past to be forgotten" because of "the exigencies of the continuing present." Moreover, skilled oral narrators deliberately vary their traditional narratives because part of their skill is their ability to adjust to new audiences and new situations or simply to be coquettish. A West African griot employed by a princely family (Okpewho 1979, pp. 25–6, 247, n. 33; p. 248, n. 36) will adjust his recitation to compliment his employers. Oral cultures encourage triumphalism, which in modern times has regularly tended somewhat to disappear as once-oral societies become more and more literate.

Situational Rather Than Abstract

All conceptual thinking is to a degree abstract. So "concrete" a term as "tree" does not refer simply to a singular "concrete" tree but is an abstraction, drawn out of, away from, individual, sensible actuality; it refers to a concept which is neither this tree nor that tree but can apply to any tree. Each individual object that we style a tree is truly "concrete," simply itself, not "abstract" at all, but the term we apply to the individual object is in itself abstract. Nevertheless, if all conceptual thinking is thus to some degree abstract, some uses of concepts are more abstract than other uses.

Oral cultures tend to use concepts in situational, operational frames of reference that are minimally abstract in the sense that they remain close to the living human lifeworld. There is a considerable literature bearing on this phenomenon. Havelock (1978) has shown that pre-Socratic Greeks thought of justice in operational rather than formally conceptualized ways and the late Anne Amory Parry (1973) made much the same point about the epithet *amymōn* applied by Homer to Aegisthus: the epithet means not "blameless," a tidy abstraction with which literates have translated the term, but "beautiful-in-the-way-a-warrior-ready-to-fight-is-beautiful."

The Interiority of Sound

In treating some psychodynamics of orality, we have thus far attended chiefly to one characteristic of sound itself, its evanescence, its relationship to time. Sound exists only when it is going out of existence. Other characteristics of sound also determine or influence oral psychodynamics. The principal one of these other characteristics is the unique relationship of sound to interiority when sound is compared to the rest of the senses. This relationship is important because of the interiority of human consciousness and of human communication itself. It can be discussed only summarily here. I have treated the matter in greater fullness and depth in *The Presence of the Word,* to which the interested reader is referred (1967).

To test the physical interior of an object as interior, no sense works so directly as sound. The human sense of sight is adapted best to light diffusely reflected from surfaces. (Diffuse reflection, as from a printed page or a landscape, contrasts with specular reflection, as from a mirror.) A source of light, such as a fire, may be intriguing but it is optically baffling: the eye cannot get a "fix" on anything within the fire. Similarly, a translucent object, such as alabaster, is intriguing because, although it is not a source of light, the eye cannot get a "fix" on it either. Depth can be perceived by the eye, but most satisfactorily as a series of surfaces: the trunks of trees in a grove, for example, or chairs in an auditorium. The eye does not perceive an interior strictly as an interior: inside a room, the walls it perceives are still surfaces, outsides.

Taste and smell are not much help in registering interiority or exteriority. Touch is. But touch partially destroys interiority in the process of perceiving it. If I wish to discover by touch whether a box is empty or full, I have to make a hole in the box to insert a hand or finger: this means that the box is to that extent open, to that extent less an interior.

Hearing can register interiority without violating it. I can rap a box to find whether it is empty or full or a wall to find whether it is hollow or solid inside. Or I can ring a coin to learn whether it is silver or lead.

Sounds all register the interior structures of whatever it is that produces them. A violin filled with concrete will not sound like a normal violin. A saxophone sounds differently from a flute: it is structured differently inside. And above all, the human voice comes from inside the human organism which provides the voice's resonances.

Sight isolates, sound incorporates. Whereas sight situates the observer outside what he views, at a distance, sound pours into the hearer. Vision dissects, as Merleau-Ponty has observed (1961). Vision comes to a human being from one direction at a time: to look at a room or a landscape, I must move my eyes around from one part to another. When I hear, however, I gather sound simultaneously from every direction at once: I am at the center of my auditory world, which envelopes me, establishing me at a kind of core of sensation and existence. This centering effect of sound is what high-fidelity sound reproduction exploits with intense sophistication. You can immerse yourself in hearing, in sound. There is no way to immerse yourself similarly in sight.

By contrast with vision, the dissecting sense, sound is thus a unifying sense. A typical visual ideal is clarity and distinctness, a taking apart (Descartes' campaigning for clarity and distinctness registered an intensification of vision in the human sensorium—Ong 1967, pp. 63, 221). The auditory ideal, by contrast, is harmony, a putting together.

Interiority and harmony are characteristics of human consciousness. The consciousness of each human person is totally interiorized, known to the person from the inside and inaccessible to any other person directly from the inside. Everyone who says "I" means something different by it from what every other person means. What is "I" to me is only "you" to you. And this "I" incorporates experience into itself by "getting it all together." Knowledge is ultimately not a fractioning but a unifying phenomenon, a striving for harmony. Without harmony, an interior condition, the psyche is in bad health.

It should be noted that the concepts interior and exterior are not mathematical concepts and cannot be differentiated mathematically. They are existentially grounded concepts, based on experience of one's own body, which is both inside me (I do not ask you to stop kicking my body but to stop kicking *me*) and outside me (I feel myself as in some sense inside my body). The body is a frontier between myself and everything else. What we mean by "interior" and "exterior" can be conveyed only by reference to experience of bodiliness. Attempted definitions of "interior" and "exterior" are inevitably tautological: "interior" is defined by "in," which is defined by "between," which is defined by "inside," and so on round and round the tautological circle. The same is true with "exterior." When we speak of interior and exterior, even in the case of physical objects, we are referring to our own sense of ourselves: I am *inside* here and everything else is *outside*. By interior and exterior we point to our own experience of bodiliness (Ong 1967, pp. 117–22, 176–9, 228, 231) and analyze other objects by reference to this experience.

In a primary oral culture, where the word has its existence only in sound, with no reference whatsoever to any visually perceptible text, and no awareness of even the possibility of such a text, the phenomenology of sound enters deeply into human beings' feel for existence, as processed by the spoken word. For the way in which the word is experienced is always momentous in psychic life. The centering action of sound (the field of sound is not spread out before me but is all around me) affects man's sense of the cosmos. For oral cultures, the cosmos is an ongoing event with man at its center. Man is the *umbilicus mundi*, the navel of the world (Eliade 1958, pp. 231–5, etc.). Only after print and the extensive experience with maps that print implemented would human beings, when they thought about the cosmos or universe or "world," think primarily of something laid out before their eyes, as in a modern printed atlas, a vast surface or assemblage of surfaces (vision presents surfaces) ready to be "explored." The ancient oral world knew few "explorers," though it did know many itinerants, travelers, voyagers, adventurers, and pilgrims.

It will be seen that most of the characteristics of orally based thought and expression discussed earlier in this chapter relate intimately to the unifying, centralizing, interiorizing economy of sound as perceived by human beings. A sound-dominated verbal economy is consonant with aggregative (harmonizing) tendencies rather than with analytic, dissecting tendencies (which would come with the inscribed, visualized word: vision is a dissecting sense). It is consonant also with the conservative holism (the homeostatic present that must be kept intact, the formulary expressions that must be kept intact), with situational thinking (again holistic, with human action at the center) rather than abstract thinking, with a certain humanistic organization of knowledge around the actions of human and anthromorphic beings, interiorized persons, rather than around impersonal things.

The denominators used here to describe the primary oral world will be useful again later to describe what happened to human consciousness when writing and print reduced the oral-aural world to a world of visualized pages.

Works Cited

Abrahams, Roger D. "Introductory Remarks to a Rhetorical Theory of Folklore." *Journal of American Folklore* 81 (1968): 143–58.

———. "The Training of the Man of Words in Talking Sweet." *Language in Society* 1 (1972): 15–29.

Achebe, Chinua. *No Longer at Ease.* New York: Ivan Obolensky, 1961.

Carrington, John F. *La Voix des tambours: comment comprendre le langage tambouriné d'Afrique.* Kinshasa: Centre Protestant d'Editions et de Diffusion, 1974.

Chafe, Wallace L. "Integration and Involvement in Speaking, Writing, and Oral Literature." *Spoken and Written Language: Exploring Orality and Literacy.* Ed. Deborah Tannen. Norwood, NJ: Ablex, 1982.

Eliade, Mircea. *Patterns in Comparative Religion.* Trans. Willard R. Trask. New York: Sheed & Ward, 1958.

Faik-Nzuji, Clémentine. *Enigmes Lubas-Nshinga: Étude structurale.* Kinshasa: Editions de l'Université Lovanium, 1970.

Finnegan, Ruth. *Oral Literature in Africa.* Oxford: Clarendon Press, 1970.

Foley, John Miles. "Oral Literature: Premises and Problems." *Choice* 18 (1980): 487–96.

Givón, Talmy. "From Discourse to Syntax: Grammar as a Processing Strategy." *Syntax and Semantics* 12 (1979): 81–112.

Goody, Jack. *The Domestication of the Savage Mind.* Cambridge: Cambridge University Press, 1977.

Goody, Jack, ed. *Literacy in Traditional Societies.* Cambridge: Cambridge University Press, 1968.

Goody, Jack, and Ian Watt. "The Consequences of Literacy." *Literacy in Traditional Societies.* Ed. Jack Goody. Cambridge: Cambridge University Press, 1968. 27–84.

Harms, Robert W. "Bobangi Oral Traditions: Indicators of Changing Perceptions." *The African Past Speaks.* Ed. Joseph C. Miller. London: Dawson; Hamden, CT: Archon, 1980. 178–200.

Havelock, Eric A. *The Greek Concept of Justice: From Its Shadow in Homer to Its Substance in Plato.* Cambridge: Harvard University Press, 1978.

———. *Preface to Plato.* Oxford: Basil Blackwell; Cambridge: Harvard University Press, 1963.

Henige, David. "'The Disease of Writing': Ganda and Nyoro Kinglists in a Newly Literate World." *The African Past Speaks.* Ed. Joseph C. Miller. London: Dawson; Hamden, CT: Archon, 1980. 240–61.

Jousse, Marcel. *Le parlant, la parole, et le souffle.* Paris: Gallimard, 1978.

Lévi-Strauss, Claude. *The Savage Mind.* 1962. Chicago: University of Chicago Press, 1966.

Luria, Aleksandr Romanovich. *Cognitive Development: Its Cultural and Social Foundations.* Trans. Martin Lopez-Morillas and Lynn Solotaroff. Ed. Michael Cole. Cambridge: Harvard University Press, 1976.

Malinowski, Bronislaw. "The Problem of Meaning in Primitive Languages." *The Meaning of Meaning: A Study of the Influence of Language upon Thought and of the Science of Symbolism.* Ed. C. K. Ogden and I. A. Richards. New York: Harcourt, Brace; London: Kegan Paul, Trench, Trubner, 1923. 451–510.

Merleau-Ponty, Maurice. "L'Oeil et l'esprit." *Les Temps modernes* 18 (1961): 184–85.

Obiechina, Emmanuel. *Culture, Tradition, and Society in the West African Novel.* Cambridge: Cambridge University Press, 1975.

Okpewho, Isidore. *The Epic in Africa: Toward a Poetics of the Oral Performance.* New York: Columbia University Press, 1979.

Ong, Walter J. *Interfaces of the Word.* Ithaca: Cornell University Press, 1977.

———."Literacy and Orality in Our Times." *ADE Bulletin* 58 (1978): 1–7.

———. *The Presence of the Word.* New Haven: Yale University Press, 1967; New York: Simon and Schuster, 1970.

Opie, Iona Archibald, and Peter Opie. *The Oxford Dictionary of Nursery Rhymes.* Oxford: Clarendon Press, 1952.

Opland, Jeff. "*Imbongi Nezibongo:* The Xhosa Tribal Poet and the Contemporary Poetic Tradition." *PMLA* 90 (1975): 185–208.

Oppenheim, A. Leo. *Ancient Mesopotamia.* Chicago: University of Chicago Press, 1964.

Packard, Randall M. "The Study of Historical Process in African Traditions of Genesis: The Bashu Myth of Muhiyi." *The African Past Speaks.* Ed. Joseph C. Miller. London: Dawson; Hamden, CT: Archon, 1980. 157–77.

Parry, Anne Amory. *Blameless Aegisthus: A Study of ἀμύμων and Other Homeric Epithets.* Mnemosyne: Bibliotheca Classica Batava, Supp. 26. Leyden: E. J. Brill, 1973.

Sampson, Geoffrey. *Schools of Linguistics.* Stanford: Stanford University Press, 1980.

Sherzer, Joel. "*Namakke, Sunmakke, Kormakke:* Three Types of Cuna Speech Event." *Explorations in the Ethnography of Speaking.* Ed. Richard Bauman and Joel Sherzer. Cambridge: Cambridge University Press, 1974. 263–82, 462–64, 489.

Content Questions

1. What does Ong mean by a "primary oral culture"?

2. How does sound differ from other sensations?

3. What kinds of oral devices are included under Ong's label of "mnemonics and formulas"? Explain why it is so important to "think memorable thoughts" in an orally based culture.

4. What are additive (in contrast with subordinate) structures? Which type is more commonly found in oral cultures?

5. How is an expression such as "the brave soldier" representative of how an oral culture uses language?

6. Why would redundancy be more important in an oral context than in a written one?

7. How does the introduction of writing into a society relate to the development of new and innovative thinking in that society?

8. What is flyting?

Questions for Analysis and Discussion

1. While Ong discusses linguistic features of oral cultures, he provides examples from written literary works. What relationship exists between works such as *Beowulf* or the *Iliad,* and oral cultures? Comment on how such works were first composed.

2. Ong mentions that oral cultures tend to be homeostatic. How does this feature manifest itself in the language? Discuss this feature also with regard to words in nursery rhymes and games.

3. Describe how a knowledge of the common characteristics of oral cultures could help you as you analyze and discuss literary features in older texts.

Additional Activities and Paper Topics

1. Some authors have created characters that engage in language play or that demonstrate some kind of distinctive pattern or abnormality in their pronunciation, morphology, or syntax. You might, for example, look at Sheridan's character Mrs. Malaprop, from his play *The Rivals,* or some of the characters in Lewis Carroll's works. Perform a linguistic analysis and report on the phonology, morphology, and/or syntax in the language of a character who displays such interesting or unusual features. (**Phonology, Morphology, or Syntax**)

2. Select a literary work with well-developed characters and passages of dialogue. Prepare a report that discusses the conversational behavior of one of the characters and how the author might be using particular discourse features to indicate something about that person. You might note, for example, the degree to which that character uses direct versus indirect speech acts and how that character's speech contrasts with other characters. (**Semantics, Pragmatics, and Discourse Analysis**)

3. Locate a literary text containing dialogue representative of a particular English dialect. Prepare a description of some of the distinctive features of this dialect based on patterns you observe in the speech of a particular character in the literary work you have selected. (**Language Varieties**)

4. Examine a text such as *Beowulf* that originated in an orally based culture. Using the list of oral culture characteristics, as identified in Ong's article, prepare a report that lists and discusses those features that appear in the literary work you have selected. (**Language Varieties**)

5. Consider a particular literary text from an earlier time period such as the Early Modern English period (the time of Shakespeare). Identify some of the words within the text whose meaning presents a problem to your understanding of the text. Look these words up in the *Oxford English Dictionary* to see what they may have meant at the time in which they were written; report on what you have found. (**Historical Linguistics**)

Linguistics and Translation

Translation is one skill widely associated with linguistics. Some people, however, mistakenly assume that knowing another language automatically equips someone to serve effectively as a translator. But translation involves numerous issues and complications. The articles in this chapter illustrate some important concerns for translators, showing how translators can apply linguistic knowledge in various ways.

The first article in this chapter is Susan Berk-Seligson's "The Role of Register in the Bilingual Courtroom: Evaluative Reactions to Interpreted Testimony." Anyone who knows another language well recognizes that there is more than one way to translate ideas from one language to another. But as Berk-Seligson shows, even when a person's meaning is translated accurately, the register in which it is translated—more specifically, the degree of formality—can have serious consequences. She demonstrates how a courtroom jury's assessment of the credibility of a witness can be affected by the type of register that a translator chooses to use.

Linguistics has a strong tradition in biblical translation. In fact, some of the twentieth century's most influential linguists have been involved in biblical translations. Of course, it is in the process of translating that one becomes even more aware of the substantial differences among languages. This is perhaps all the more true in the translation of a sacred text when a linguist might feel a particularly acute responsibility not to violate the integrity of the text. In "Communicating the Scriptures across Cultures," Philip A. Noss discusses some of the difficult choices translators have faced as they have tried to render accurate translations of the Bible into foreign languages. Noss considers issues such as the syntactic and lexical incompatibilities among languages; whether to translate according to dynamic or functional equivalence as opposed to a more literal translation; and the cultural differences among language communities that can interfere with the comprehensibility of a particular translation.

Linguistic study is usually applied to breaking down communication barriers among groups. But there are situations in which one group may not want another to understand them, such as when a group is trying to protect secrets. In such a case, linguists could help in identifying what sort of language or code could be most useful for that purpose, and conversely in cracking the code that another group may choose to adopt. In "The Unbreakable Language Code in the Pacific Theatre of World War II," M. Gyi recounts the vital role that Navajo code talkers served in the defense of the United States in World War II. The Navajo language was an effective military code in the Pacific military campaigns for a variety of reasons, which are discussed in this article.

Translation does not have to be limited to the human processing of language. Some linguists have, in fact, been working for a number of years in developing the capability of machines to process natural human languages. The field of natural language processing (NLP) involves working with computers on a variety of language-processing tasks. For example, this might involve programming a computer to translate a natural language into its own computerese, process the information, and then respond back in a natural spoken or written language that the human will understand. Or it might involve programming the computer to translate from one natural language to another. Most nonspecialists in natural language processing cannot imagine the linguistic complications that could be involved in programming a computer to translate languages. In his article, "Linguistics and Machine Translation," Victor Raskin explains some of the issues involved in this important field and how it can benefit greatly from linguistic research.

The Role of Register in the Bilingual Courtroom: Evaluative Reactions to Interpreted Testimony[1]

Susan Berk-Seligson

A translator must constantly make important choices when translating across languages. One choice involves how to represent the style and register of a speaker. In the following article, which originally appeared in the *International Journal of the Sociology of Language,* Susan Berk-Seligson, a professor at the University of Pittsburgh, shows how the choice of register by a courtroom interpreter can actually influence a jury's perception of the reliability of a particular witness. This research has significant implications for how translation is done in the courtroom.

Sociolinguists have long known that speech varies not only along the parameters of linguistic code, that is, language and dialect, but also along the dimensions of style and register. This article explores the significance of register in a Spanish–English bilingual legal setting. Using an experimental methodology, it will demonstrate that choice of register influences listener perceptions of speakers. In addition, it will show that linguistic intermediaries such as interpreters are influential in effectuating the changes that can make a difference between one register and another. This study forms part of a larger investigation in which the impact of politeness on Hispanic and non-Hispanic mock jurors has already been analyzed (Berk-Seligson 1988). The results of that analysis support the findings presented here on the impact of testimony style on mock jurors.

Register, defined as "a variety that is not typically identified with any particular speech community but is tied to the communicative occasion" (Bolinger 1975: 358), is generally conceived in terms of "formality levels." It is also alternatively referred to as "style" (Joos 1967) or "key" (Gleason 1965). For English, five registers have been delineated: (1) oratorical, or frozen; (2) deliberative, or formal; (3) consultative; (4) casual; and (5) intimate (Gleason 1965; Joos 1967).

[1]I owe the National Science Foundation much gratitude for funding this project (grant #RII-8516746), although the responsibility for the research is entirely my own. I also wish to thank the Department of Linguistics at Northwestern University, and its chairperson, Judy N. Levi, for hosting me. Thanks also go to the graduate students who helped me gather data: Vanessa McGreal; Parek McGreal; and Marisa Alicea.

The preceding classification makes no mention of one important speech style of particular significance to talk in the courtroom: hypercorrect speech. This speech style reflects the misapplication or overgeneralization of linguistic rules so as to produce nonstandard forms. Hypercorrection in grammar is exemplified by constructions such as, "He gave it to she and I." In lexical usage O'Barr's (1982) examples of hypercorrection in witness testimony include the use of "comatose" for "unconscious" and "not cognizant" for "unaware."

The present study departs from this conception of hypercorrectness, focusing on a register that will be called "hyperformal" style. This style does not use nonstandard grammatical or lexical forms, nor is it marked by a higher than expected use of prestigeful linguistic variants. Rather, it is a style that sounds bookish and stilted due to two principal speech characteristics: (1) the lack of ellipsis or syntactic deletions in surface syntax (for example, in answer to the question, "How old are you?" a hyperformal response would be "I am twenty-one years old," rather than the more typical reply "I'm twenty-one" or, simply, "Twenty-one"); and (2) the failure to contract linguistic elements that are frequently contracted in consultative style (for example, the copula "be" and the negative marker "not").

The Problem of Maintaining a Speaker's Register

Since the passage of the Federal Court Interpreters Act in 1978, the legislation of numerous state statutes, and the widespread implementation of state and municipal regulations, free court interpreting services are being provided to non-English-speaking and low-English proficient persons in all federal and in many state and municipal courts. These laws and regulations are based upon a recognition that linguistic minorities have the constitutional right to a fair trial, including the right to understand and confront witnesses testifying against them, and the right to effective communication with their attorney. The large number of monolingual Hispanics in the United States has created a need for Spanish–English interpreters in the courts.

The quality of court interpretation services varies widely. A previous investigation, based upon ethnographic observation in a number of courthouses (Berk-Seligson 1987), discovered that some court interpreters systematically render the Spanish testimony of witnesses in hyperformal style English, even though the original Spanish is given in consultative style.[2] The following excerpt, which exemplifies this problem, is taken from an actual case involving the transporting of undocumented persons across the United States/Mexico border into the United States. The witness who is tes-

---

[2] That study was supported by a National Science Foundation grant (#SES 8114617 and #SES 8341766), which provided baseline data on interpreted court proceedings.

tifying is an undocumented Mexican farmworker who was brought into the United States by a *coyote* "smuggler," the defendant in the case.

PROSECUTING ATTORNEY: And how old are you?
INTERPRETER: ¿Qué edad tiene usted?
WITNESS: Veinte años.
INTERPRETER: I am twenty years old.
PROSECUTING ATTORNEY: And what is your occupation?
INTERPRETER: ¿Y cuál es su oficio de usted?
WITNESS: Trabajar en el campo.
INTERPRETER: I am a laborer in the fields.
PROSECUTING ATTORNEY: Of what country are you a citizen?
INTERPRETER: ¿De qué país es usted ciudadano?
WITNESS: De Michoacán.
INTERPRETER: I am from the state of Michoacán.

In every case the Spanish-speaking witness answered in a register ranging between consultative and casual. The interpreter's rendition, however, is hyperformal. In striving for the goal of high fidelity verbatim interpreting, court interpreters are supposed to preserve the register in which the source language utterance emerged (Almeida and Zahler 1981: 11). The interpreting presented above fails to meet these expectations.

Given the systematic changes in register often made in the interpreting process, the research question was posed: do jurors form a different impression of the witness depending upon the register in which his or her testimony is interpreted? A review of the literature in this regard would lead us to expect an affirmative answer to this question.

Subjective Reactions to Speech Differences

It has been known for some time now that listeners react subjectively to numerous aspects of a person's speech, a notable one being dialect. Studies conducted in the United States have revealed the preference of both majority and minority group members for speakers of standard English over Black Vernacular English (Tucker and Lambert 1969), and over Mexican American accented English (Ryan and Carranza 1977). In Canada, it has been demonstrated that French Canadian listeners view speakers of European French more favourably than speakers of Canadian French (Lambert et al. 1960; d'Anglejan and Tucker 1973). Similar studies conducted in Great Britain demonstrate that persons speaking with a prestigious accent, in the case of Britain "received pronunciation," are evaluated more positively on semantic differential scales than are persons who speak with either regional, foreign, or lower class accents (see for example Giles 1971; Bourhis et al. 1975). A comparable study of attitudes toward nonstandard pronunciation and perception of personality indicates that Spanish speakers, too, judge personality from dialect (Berk-Seligson 1984).

The general finding that listeners make social/psychological judgments about speakers comes from numerous studies of speech communities where more than one language is spoken. For the case of Spanish and English alone, the evidence is overwhelming that listeners react subjectively both to the Spanish language and to Spanish-accented English (see for example de la Zerda and Hopper 1979; Ryan and Sebastian 1980).

Scholars interested in sociolegal questions, particularly the relationship between law and language, have begun to notice the relevance of the relationship between speech and perceived personality characteristics. A group of such scholars from Duke University has found a number of recurring testimony styles in the speech of witnesses, each style producing alternatively positive and negative reactions from listeners serving as mock jurors. Two of these styles were found to result in opposite evaluations: witnesses who testified in formal style were judged to be more convincing, competent, intelligent, and qualified than were witnesses who presented their testimony in hypercorrect style (O'Barr 1982:86).

It was hypothesized, therefore, that a witness whose Spanish testimony was interpreted in English in hyperformal style would be evaluated more negatively than one whose testimony was rendered in a consultative register. The hyperformal style is considered here to be a "marked" style, while the consultative style is thought of as "unmarked," or the expected norm for transactions between strangers.

Research Design

An experimental research design was devised to test whether the use of a marked speech style such as hyperformality in the English interpreted testimony of Spanish-speaking witnesses would leave a significant impact on persons playing the role of jurors. If such a differential impact could be found to exist, then it would show not only that speech register makes a difference, but that the interpreter is a crucial factor in the formation of juror impressions of non-English-speaking witnesses.

The experimental research design was that of verbal guise technique. Two audio recordings were made of a witness testifying in Spanish through an interpreter, the recordings being identical in every way except that in one version the interpreter faithfully interpreted every utterance of the witness in accordance with the speech style in which the witness gave his Spanish testimony, this being consultative style, and in the other version the interpreter inserted material that she felt was implicit in the Spanish answers and in addition refrained from using contracted forms.

It should be stressed that the text of the recordings was based on the transcription of an actual case of an undocumented Mexican recorded in a previous research project (Berk-Seligson forthcoming b). The actors who played the roles of witness, interpreter, and lawyer were in real life similar socially and occupationally to the persons whom they were portraying on the recordings: the witness was a Mexican immigrant living in a Chicago *barrio*, who knew very little English; the woman who played the interpreter was a Mexican American full-time court interpreter in a state level criminal court; and the lawyer was played by an Anglo male who had graduate level education.

Each participant in the study was given a standardized questionnaire, on which there appeared four lines representing four seven-point scales. At one end of each line appeared an adjective ("convincing," "competent," "intelligent," "trustworthy"). At the other extreme lay the polar opposite of the evaluative term. Everything written on the questionnaire, including general instructions, was written in Spanish as well as in English.

The Sample

A total of 551 persons participated in the study. A summary of some of their major demographic, socioeconomic, ethnic, and linguistic characteristics is presented in Table 1. A conscious effort was made to include in the sample as many persons as possible who were already in the work force or who had life experience beyond that found in educational settings. For this reason religious groups and adult education classes were included in the sample, as were community based vocational training classes and high school equivalency (G.E.D.) classes. Thus, the educational levels of the 551 subjects varied widely, 29 percent of the sample having no more than 12 years of schooling.

The ability to understand Spanish was deemed to be a crucial variable in the input that the subjects brought to the experiment. Since it was hypothesized that having access to the meaning of the witness's Spanish testimony would cancel out whatever effect the interpreter might have in creating in the minds of the mock jurors one sort of impression of the witness rather than another, it was necessary to determine the extent to which both the non-Hispanic and Hispanic population had understood the Spanish of the witness. For this reason, subjects were asked (1) if they had ever studied Spanish in school, (2) if they had, how many years they had studied it, and (3) if they had, how well they had understood the Spanish on the recording, on a 5-point scale ranging from "very well" to "hardly at all."

Findings

The major hypothesis of this study is that a difference in speech register in the testimony of a witness has an impact on the impression that jurors

Table 1. Selected Demographic, Socioeconomic, Ethnic, and Linguistic Characteristics of the Sample

SAMPLE N	551
Female	55.0%
Mean age	27.3
Mean years of schooling completed	13.7
Ethnic background	
Anglo-American	52.3%
Hispanic-American	39.4%
Afro-American	6.7%
Oriental-American	0.7%
Native American Indian	0.4%
Respondent's place of birth: United States	70.6%
Has been to court in the United States	51.5%
Has studied Spanish in school	64.1%
Hispanic subsample (self-report)	
Speaks Spanish better than English	50.2%
English better than Spanish	23.9%
Spanish and English about the same	24.9%
At home speaks Spanish most of the time	70.8%
speaks English most of the time	28.7%
speaks both languages about the same amount of time	0.5%
If does not speak Spanish, but understands it,	
Understands it very well/or well	80.8%
Understands it badly/or hardly at all	6.4%
Understood the English on the experimental tape recordings	
Very well/or well	79.9%
Badly/or hardly at all	5.9%

form of that witness. Given the findings of O'Barr and his colleagues regarding the negative impact of hypercorrect speech style upon mock jurors, it was expected that the interpretation of hyperformal speech in English by the court interpreter would cause mock jurors to evaluate the witness more negatively than when the interpreter did not interpret the witness's Spanish in a hyperformal style.

Table 2 summarizes the output of a difference in means test (t-test) of the answers of the entire sample of 551 subjects. The t-test was applied to the subject's impressions regarding the degree to which the witness seemed convincing, competent, intelligent, and trustworthy, comparing the mean answers of those who heard the "hyperformal version" of the English interpretation with the means of those who heard the consultative interpretation. The higher the number on the evaluations (numbers approaching 7),

Table 2. Difference of Means (t-test) for Entire Sample

ATTRIBUTE	N[a]	MEAN[b]	STD. DEV.	SIG.[c]
Convincingness				
consultative	286	3.7	1.7	NS
hyperformal	259	3.9	1.8	
Competence				
consultative	283	3.2	1.6	.004
hyperformal	256	3.7	1.7	
Intelligence				
consultative	283	2.6	1.6	.001
hyperformal	258	3.3	1.7	
Trustworthiness				
consultative	285	3.2	1.7	.009
hyperformal	258	3.6	1.8	

a. N varies because of non-response.
b. Scores for each attribute range between 1 and 7, 7 being the most positive evaluation and 1 being the most negative.
c. Values of .05 or less are considered to be statistically significant.

the more positive were the mock jurors; the lower the numbers (approaching 1), the more negative were the impressions. Looking down the column labeled "Mean" we see that in every case when the witness's testimony was not interpreted faithfully to the original (that is, where the interpretation was hyperformal rather than consultative), the means reflected a more positive evaluation on each of the four social/psychological attribute continua. More importantly, the difference between the means for the hyperformal version and those for the consultative version is statistically significant, for three of the four attributes: competence, intelligence, and trustworthiness. In other words, it is highly unlikely that the mock jurors reacted this way by chance.

Two substantive conclusions emerge from an examination of Table 2. First, even though the hyperformal English interpretation contrasts with the low socioeconomic status of the witness, and hence should have a negative impact on jurors, this study finds that just the opposite is true: hyperformality gives the witness an enhanced image. Second, what has made the difference between one version and another is the role played by the interpreter. The witness answered in Spanish in exactly the same consultative style in both versions of the experimental tapes. The interpreter's different rendition of the testimony was sufficient to cause mock jurors to evaluate the witness more negatively, demonstrating the pivotal role of the interpreter.

Table 2 represents the responses of Hispanic and non-Hispanic mock jurors alike. It does not reveal whether Hispanics, virtually all of whom reported understanding Spanish, are affected in any way by the interpreting process. It was hypothesized that Hispanics, capable of tuning into the original Spanish testimony of the witness, would not distinguish between the hyperformal version and the consultative version. This expectation is derived from the observation that bilinguals tune into both of their linguistic codes in other contexts. For example, many bilingual moviegoers read the subtitles even though they understand the language spoken by the actors. In the courtroom, however, jurors are regularly instructed by the judge to ignore the foreign testimony of the witness if they happen to understand the foreign language, and to pay attention solely to the English interpretation of the court interpreter.

To determine whether Hispanic mock jurors are affected in any way by the English interpretation of the witness's testimony, a t-test was computed on the responses of those Hispanics who had listened to the hyperformal version of the testimony, comparing them with those of Hispanics who had heard the consultative version. The results of the t-test are presented in Table 3.

Table 3 shows that for one of the social/psychological attributes, convincingness, there was no significant difference in the scores of those Hispanics who had heard the hyperformal interpretation and those who had heard the consultative version. It was expected that being able to understand the original language of the testimony would enable Hispanics to ignore the English rendition of the court interpreter. However, on three of the four social psychological attributes—competence, intelligence, and trust-

Table 3. Difference of Means (t-test) for Hispanic Sample

ATTRIBUTE	N[a]	MEAN[b]	STD. DEV.	SIG.[c]
Convincingness				
consultative	103	3.9	1.8	NS
hyperformal	108	4.1	1.9	
Competence				
consultative	100	2.9	1.8	.021
hyperformal	105	3.5	1.9	
Intelligence				
consultative	100	2.5	1.8	.010
hyperformal	107	3.2	1.9	
Trustworthiness				
consultative	102	3.3	1.9	.049
hyperformal	107	3.9	1.8	

a. N varies because of non-response.
b. Scores for each attribute range between 1 and 7, 7 being the most positive evaluation and 1 being the most negative.
c. Values of .05 or less are considered to be statistically significant.

worthiness—the English interpretation clearly had an impact on the formation of evaluations by the Hispanic mock jurors. On these three attributes there were statistically significant differences in the means of those who had heard the hyperformal version and those who had heard the consultative version. Once again, when the witness's Spanish testimony was interpreted in hyperformal style, the ratings he received on these three attribute scales were more positive than were the ones he received when his testimony was interpreted in consultative style.

Conclusion

This analysis has demonstrated that speech register is important to those evaluating witness testimony. Specifically, hyperformality is regarded positively by mock jurors, so much so that it improves the impression made by a witness testifying in Spanish: it makes him appear more competent, more intelligent, and more trustworthy than he does when his testimony is rendered in English in a less formal style.

This finding is contrary to expectation, since hypercorrection in the Labovian sense—which most closely parallels hyperformality—is poorly regarded by judges who are of the same socioeconomic status as is the hypercorrect speaker. Similarly, hypercorrection, in the traditional sense of the misapplication of linguistic rules on the part of the speaker in order to create a better impression, is likewise poorly received, according to the studies of O'Barr and his colleagues.

From the standpoint of a linguist-observer, it would seem that a hypercorrect rendition of this particular witness's testimony would be given a more unfavorable rating than would a less formal style rendition, for two reasons. First, a mismatch exists between the socioeconomic status of the witness and the excessively formal speaking style of his answers in English. We would tend to assume that a Mexican farmworker with less than a complete elementary education would not have a speech style associated with formal learning. What we know of the speaker and his social background does not correspond to the English utterances that are being attributed to him by the interpreter.

Second, O'Barr (1982) confirms in his ethnographic observation in the courts what the author has observed, that lawyers shift registers; their speaking style varies between formal and colloquial, including consultative as an intermediary style. The interpreter's rendition of the testimony of the witness in question, however, is carried out in an unvarying hyperformal style and thus stands in marked contrast to the style shifting of most lawyers.

It is puzzling, therefore, to find that mock jurors give a higher, more positive rating to a witness who sounds as if he were speaking in a homogeneously hyperformal style of English than they do to the same witness when he speaks in an unmarked speech style. The only conclusion that one can reach is that Americans, both Hispanic and non-Hispanic alike, consider hyperformal speech style to be appropriate to this particular setting and situation. A courtroom setting and the giving of testimony under oath apparently constitute an eminently formal speech context. To speak "appropriately" while being examined by an attorney on the witness stand is to speak bookishly.

What seems to be underlying this notion of communicative appropriateness in a legal setting is the notion of politeness. To speak hyperformally on the witness stand is to be polite to the examining attorney and to the court in general. By not shifting downward, one manifests deference to the interlocutor and to the listeners who are not direct addressees (that is, the judge and the jury). The very ability of lawyers to shift their styles in court is evidence of their sense of power and control over their interlocutors. It is akin to the greater sense of freedom of action that a host feels in his/her home, as opposed to the sense that a guest has of needing to maintain good manners throughout the visit. The courtroom is, ultimately, the lawyer's territory, and the testifying witness is merely a temporary guest whose length of stay on the lawyer's turf is beyond his or her control.

One additional explanation as to why hyperformal testimony is given more positive evaluations than is an unmarked speech style is that hyperformal utterances tend to be wordy. Longer answers, or "narrative-style" testimony, have been shown to evoke more positive social/psychological evaluation than do short, incisive answers, or "fragmented-style" testimony (O'Barr 1982: 80–81). What may have occurred in the present study is an interactive effect between utterance length and hyperformality, for hyperformality turns out to be manifested by wordier, more elaborate answers.

Finally, hyperformally worded answers convey a sense of certainty and definiteness, something which is absent from colloquial registers. The lack of contraction and the inclusion of linguistic material which otherwise could be interpreted as "being understood," or being implicit, in a short utterance, together produce answers that convey a sense of definiteness and deliberateness ("I am from the state of Michoacán" versus "From Michoacán").

An additional finding is that the interpreter is a powerful filter through which the speaker's intended meaning is mediated. In effect, the interpreter produced the hyperformal and consultative versions of testimony in this study. The witness's Spanish language testimony was a constant: identically consultative in both versions of the experimental tapes. The different reactions to the witness were due entirely to the role of the interpreter, who controlled the impressions that the listeners formed of the witness. For those mock jurors whose knowledge of Spanish was nil or quite limited, the interpreter's English rendition had to be relied on for comprehension of the testimony. Thus, the interpreter plays a pivotal role in how a jury perceives a non-English testifying witness.

It was expected that bilingual mock jurors would "tune in" to the Spanish testimony, and it was therefore assumed that the impact of the interpreter on these listeners would be minimal. In reality, the interpreter's addition of linguistic substance to the source testimony significantly affected the evaluations of bilingual mock jurors on three of the four social/psychological attributes examined: competence, intelligence, and trustworthiness. Thus, the lack of hyperformality in the interpreter's English rendition of the witness's testimony led Hispanic mock jurors to rate the witness more negatively on those three attributes than they did the witness whose interpreted testimony was realized in a hyperformal register.

This means that bilingual mock jurors do in fact pay attention to the English rendition of the court interpreter—as they are instructed to do by the presiding judge—and that in some social/psychological respects, the impact of the interpretation on them is the same as it is on non-Hispanics. On one trait, however, the hyperformal English rendition of the interpreter had no influence on Hispanic respondents: convincingness. There is no significant difference between their evaluations of the witness in the hyperformal experimental tape and their judgments of the same witness when his testimony was interpreted in consultative style. Although judges regularly warn jurors to ignore foreign language testimony, this admonition is extraordinarily difficult to accomplish—similar to the warning given to monolingual jurors to ignore testimony that has been objected to, when that objection has been sustained.

In conclusion, this study has shown that speech register is an influential variable for listeners who are assigned the task of evaluating witnesses. Apparently, one can never speak too formally on the witness stand, so long as one does not end up producing hypercorrections. Moreover, hyperformal testimony style in English is as highly regarded by Hispanic Americans as it is by Anglo Americans. Finally, the implication of these findings is that Spanish–English bilinguals are very much affected by the English interpretation of the court interpreter, despite having aural access to Spanish source language testimony. For bilingual and monolingual jurors alike, therefore, the court interpreter can be seen to be a crucial variable in the presentation of foreign-language testimony.

References

Almeida, F., and Zahler, S. (1981). *Los Angeles Superior Court Interpreters Manual.* Los Angeles: Los Angeles Superior Court.

Berk-Seligson, S. (1984). Subjective reactions to phonological variation in Costa Rican Spanish. *Journal of Psycholinguistic Research* 13, 415–442.

———(1987). The intersection of testimony styles in interpreted judicial proceedings: Pragmatic alterations in Spanish testimony. *Linguistics* 25, 1010–1047.

———(1988). The impact of politeness in witness testimony: the influence of the court interpreter. *Multilingua* 7(4), 411–439.

———(forthcoming b). Bilingual court proceedings: the role of the court interpreter. In J. N. Levi and A. G. Walker (eds.), *Language in the Judicial Process.* New York: Plenum.

Bolinger, D. (1975). *Aspects of Language.* New York: Harcourt, Brace, Jovanovich.

Bourhis, R. Y., Giles, H., and Lambert, W. E. (1975). Some consequences of accommodating one's style of speech: a cross-national investigation. *International Journal of the Sociology of Language* 6, 55–72.

D'Anglejan, A., and Tucker, G. R. (1973). Sociolinguistic correlates of speech style in Quebec. In *Language Attitudes: Trends and Prospects*, R. Shuy and R. Fasold (eds.). Washington, D.C.: Georgetown University Press.

de la Zerda, N., and Hopper, R. (1979). Employment interviewers' reactions to Mexican American speech. *Communication Monographs* 46, 126–134.

Giles, H. (1971). Ethnocentrism and the evaluation of accented speech. *British Journal of Social and Clinical Psychology* 10, 187–188.

Gleason, H.A. (1965). *Linguistics and English Grammar.* New York: Holt, Rinehart and Winston.

Joos, M. (1967). *The Five Clocks.* New York: Harcourt, Brace, Jovanovich.

Lambert, W. E., Hodgson, R. C., and Fillenbaum, S. (1960). Evaluational reactions to spoken language. *Journal of Abnormal and Social Psychology* 60, 44–51.

O'Barr, W. M. (1982). *Linguistic Evidence: Language, Power, and Strategy in the Courtroom.* New York: Academic Press.

Ryan, E. B., and Carranza, M. A. (1977). Ingroup and outgroup reactions toward Mexican American language and varieties. In *Language, Ethnicity and Intergroup Relations*, H. Giles (ed.). London: Academic Press.

———, and Sebastian, R. (1980). The effects of speech style and social class background on social judgments of speakers. *British Journal of Social and Clinical Psychology* 19, 229–233.

Tucker, G. R., and Lambert, W. E. (1969). White and Negro listeners' reactions to various American English dialects. *Social Forces* 47, 463–468.

Content Questions

1. What is register? According to this article, what are the five registers that have been identified in English?

2. In this study Berk-Seligson examines the use of "hyperformal" speech. What two characteristics does she associate with this speech style?

3. What have previous studies found about a speaker's use of nonstandard or nonprestigious forms and perceptions about that speaker?

4. What was hypothesized about the reactions jurors would have toward a witness using a hyperformal style? Was this hypothesis supported by the results of the study? Explain.

5. Describe the setup of the experiment.

6. In the case of mock jurors who spoke Spanish and thus were not solely reliant on the interpreter, to what extent did the interpreter's choice of register still affect the Spanish-speaking jurors' reactions?

7. The results of Berk-Seligson's work seem to be different from what would have been expected based on other studies that have been conducted. What does she indicate about how the setting and expectations people have about courtroom behavior might have influenced their judgments about appropriate speech?

Questions for Analysis and Discussion

1. Explain the difference between hyperformal and hypercorrect speech.

2. In light of Berk-Seligson's research, what responsibility do you think a court interpreter has besides merely translating the meaning of statements made by a witness?

3. If you were a courtroom attorney interested in the perceived reliability of one of your witnesses, how might a knowledge of such research influence the attention you give to what a courtroom interpreter is doing?

Communicating the Scriptures across Cultures

Philip A. Noss

Linguistics has a strong tradition in scriptural translation. In fact, many of the significant contributions that have been made to our understanding of various languages in the world have been made by linguists engaged in biblical translation projects. In this article from the *1986 Georgetown University Round Table on Languages and Linguistics*, Philip A. Noss explains some key issues that confront translators as they work between different languages and different cultures. Noss's descriptions of the linguistic issues involved in biblical translation should be of interest to people involved in cross-cultural translation whether or not they regard the Bible as a sacred work.

Introduction

One of humankind's oldest and most challenging tasks has been that of seeking to overcome the barrier of language which, in offering peoples distinct identities, separates them from each other. The barrier can only be breached by someone who knows more than one language and who engages in translation in one of its various forms.

According to biblical tradition, the barrier of language was imposed by God to thwart humankind's effort to challenge him by uniting their efforts in the building of a tower that would reach to heaven itself. Whether this is indeed the explanation of the origin of the world's more than 5,000 languages, the story does reflect the reality of language as a very powerful divisive element. The conflict is not resolved until the New Testament episode of speaking in tongues on Pentecost.

Within this biblical theme, there is the reality of the desire and need to communicate across existing language barriers, and the Old Testament offers several examples of translation in the proper sense of the word. The most notable instance occurs in Nehemiah 8:8, after the Israelites had returned to their homeland from 80 years of captivity in Babylon: "And Ezra read from the Law of God, translating and giving the sense, so that the people understood what was read" (JB).[1] Outside the land of Israel, it was

---

[1] Biblical quotations are taken from the Jerusalem Bible (JB), published by Doubleday and Company, Inc. (1966) and the Good News Bible (GNB), published by the Bible Societies (1965).

also recognized that communication needed to cross language barriers. In Esther 1:22 it is recorded that King Xerxes "sent letters to all the provinces of the kingdom, to each province in its own script and to each nation in its own language . . ." (JB).

In the book of Daniel, Kings Nebuchadnezzar and Darius issued decrees that were addressed to all the peoples, nations, and languages throughout the world. Translation necessarily accompanied the proclamation of the royal decrees. As evidenced by the Rosetta Stone, which has come to be a symbol of the unveiling of the unknown through translation, early efforts to cross language barriers were not limited to biblical times and places.

From ancient times to the present, translation has become increasingly important, whether in the realm of science and technology as at the Tower of Babel, in government administration and diplomacy as in the kingdoms of the Medes and Persians and Babylonians, or for religious activities as in the book of Acts. From the oral translation of Ezra and the written documents of King Xerxes, translation has moved to the era of headphones and simultaneous translation and now to machine translation with computers.

The elements that comprise translation—namely, word, message, communication, and language—are central to biblical thought, and within the context of the Great Commission of Matthew 28:19–20, it is not surprising that Scripture translation should be a major preoccupation of the Christian church. The first written Scripture translation of which we have record is that known as the Septuagint, which was done in Alexandria from Hebrew into Greek in about 295 B.C., during what Nida (1972:9–10) identifies as the first period of Bible translation. Jerome's translation into Latin in A.D. 405 also falls into the first period. The second period saw the translations of the Reformation—Tyndale into English (1525) and Martin Luther into German (1522–1534), among others.

Although tradition suggests that translation of Scripture into Coptic occurred as early as the third century A.D. and into Ethiopic, or Ge'ez, in the fourth or fifth century, translation into the languages of Africa did not begin on a large scale until the third period, which is that identified as the missionary era of the last century and the first half of this century. The earliest Bible to be published was that in Malagasy in 1835; the first on the continent itself was in Amharic five years later.[2] The modern era of Scripture translation has seen an ever increasing number of persons involved in the task, bringing to 286 the number of languages possessing Bibles as of the end of 1984 (United Bible Societies 1985:176). Of these, 109 are African languages, 90 are languages of Asia.

---

[2] The first ten Bibles published in Africa during the missionary era were the Malagasy (1835), Amharic (1840), Tswana (1857), Xhosa (1859), Gã (1866), Efik (1868), Twi (1871), Duala (1872), Sotho (1878), and Zulu (1883).

The earliest biblical example of mutual unintelligibility occurred at the Tower of Babel on the intraethnic level, following Yahweh's observation and decision: "So they are all a single people with a single language . . . Let us go down and mix up their language so that they will not understand each other" (Gen. 11:6,7 JB). The earliest examples of Scripture translation were also on the intraethnic level. The Hebrews who came back from captivity were no longer able to understand their own tradition as recorded in the Book of the Law and Ezra provided an interpretation. Likewise, the translation of the Septuagint was intracultural. It was done for the Jewish community of Alexandria, but instead of having as its purpose to bring the people back to their own heritage, Barthelemy (1974:31) argues that it may have been undertaken at the encouragement of the Ptolemies in order to Hellenize the Jewish community of Alexandria.

After the first period of Scripture translation, however, the majority of translations have been cross-cultural.[3] To use an image from the title of one of the early books of the Kenyan writer Ngugi wa Thiong'o (Ngugi 1965), the purpose of translation has been to cross "the river between." Bible translation aims less at bringing the reader or the listener into rapport with the original work (cf. Derive 1975:37, 235) than at communicating the message of that work.

The Nature of Scripture Translation

Translating the Bible is a daunting task for a number of reasons. In the first place, it is not one book but 66 or more, depending on which canon is selected. These are divided into two epochs, products of at least two civilizations, the Hebrew and the Greek. The total amount of time represented in the writing of the Bible is more than a thousand years, not to mention that it includes literary accounts of both the beginning and end of time. The two parts are written in different languages, the first in Hebrew and Aramaic (Semitic languages of the Afro-Asiatic language family), the second in Koine Greek (of the Indo-European family).[4]

The long time-span over which the Bible was written and its multiplicity of authors give it a complex literary nature with a variety of styles and forms. Certain of the books are of unknown authorship. Parts such as the creation stories of Genesis and the song of Miriam in Exodus reflect a clearly oral aspect, while others reflect diverse written forms from geneal-

---

[3] The Biakpan translation of south-western Nigeria is a modern-day exception in that the members of the Brotherhood of the Star and Cross believe their language to be the original language which they are offering to the world and into which they are now translating the Scriptures (cf. Ukpai 1985).

[4] The dependence of the New Testament upon the Old, or the influence of the Old upon the New, is so great that it may be argued that the New Testament is essentially a Hebrew document that was written in Greek words (Nida, Louw and Smith 1977:165).

ogy to narrative, riddle to proverb, parable to prophecy, vision to history, prayers to poetry, and letters to sermons.

The book, in all or in part, is sacred to Judaism and to all of Christendom. The translator does not normally translate it as an exercise or because he is interested in it as a literary masterpiece, but because of its significance in his religion. The Christian believes that he is acting under a divine mandate enjoined by Christ himself before his ascension, "Go, therefore, make disciples of all nations . . ." (Matt. 28:19 JB). He does not then necessarily translate into his own language. A Christian may travel to a people whose language he has never before heard spoken, in order to learn it and to translate into it. This new context will obviously be far removed from the history and geography of the Fertile Crescent, and it may also be very distant from the Semitic and Hellenic cultures of biblical times. The variety of cultures and languages into which the Bible is today being translated is global, from polar regions to tropical forest, from languages of worldwide scope to the speech of isolated ethnic communities in the back country of Australia or the highlands of New Guinea.

As the world grows smaller with more and more use of international trade languages, it might be assumed that the need for translations in additional languages would diminish, but the opposite seems rather to be true. The world is becoming increasingly multilingual as many nations, particularly in Africa, adopt international languages for national affairs, diplomacy, and business; national languages for internal politics and communication; regional languages for local administration and trade; with a fourth language sometimes being that of the home. Twenty-five years ago, a book was published with the title *Two Thousand Tongues to Go* (Wallis and Bennett 1959). In the most recent edition of *Ethnologue* published by The Wycliffe Bible Translators, the need for new translations is estimated to be as high as 3,186 (Grimes 1985:xv).

The difficulties faced by translators are always plentiful, but the translator of Scripture faces an additional factor. In the last chapter of the Bible he finds a warning that was first issued in Deuteronomy 4:2 in the form of a command. The reader (and by implication, the translator) is admonished neither to add to nor to cut anything out of the prophecies of the book lest the plagues cited therein be added to him or lest his share of the tree of life and of the holy city be cut off from him (Rev. 22:18–19). The translator faced with the task of communicating a divine message across barriers of language, culture, geography, and history sees himself working under the burden of achieving absolute accuracy.

Methods of Scripture Translation

The mode of the earliest translation mentioned in the Bible was oral, but whether it was sentence by sentence or by explanation over larger sections cannot be ascertained from the brief account given by Nehemiah. The text only records that the people understood and wept. According to tradition, the Septuagint used a team approach, with six men being selected from each of Israel's twelve tribes. Working in pairs, they produced 36 drafts which were all said to be identical. From this St. Augustine, instead of crediting the Muse for inspiration, argues for the divine inspiration of translators (Nida 1964:13).

The development of translation methodology is sometimes summarized as having progressed from being word-oriented to being sentence-oriented and finally to being discourse-oriented (Peacock 1981:6). However, this is an oversimplification. As early a translator as Jerome was aware of the difference between literal and semantic equivalence, for he says that his effort is "to render sense for sense and not word for word." However, he does not apply this method to translation of the Bible because in it, he says, "even the order of words is a mystery" (quoted in Arichea 1982:313).

Martin Luther felt none of the constraints under which Jerome labored, for in his translation into German he went beyond conveying the sense to adapting the culture itself. Bainton writes that Luther's Moses was "so German that no one would suspect he was a Jew." Furthermore, he adds, "Judea was transplanted to Saxony, and the road from Jericho to Jerusalem ran through the Thuringian forest" (Bainton 1955:255, 257; cf. Kasdorf 1978). A modern example of a cultural translation is Jordan's Cotton Patch Version (1969), where Jesus lives in the southern United States and is put to death by a lynch mob.

Although examples such as Luther's translation can be cited, they were the exception. Jerome's awe of Scripture and its effect on his approach to Bible translation tended to be the norm among translators (Prochazka 1942:93). Their fear of changing something in the text ensured that they endeavored to stay as close to the original as possible, even if this was at the expense of naturalness and intelligibility in the receiving language.

But as linguistics entered a new era following World War II, so also did Bible translation. The Scriptures began to be looked upon objectively as text, but text whose meaning was of prime importance. To render the text incomprehensible through slavish literalness came to be understood as unfaithfulness to the original and just as unacceptable as mistranslation of a word or phrase. Increasing emphasis was therefore placed upon an approach based on the principle of dynamic equivalence that stressed the importance of content over form (Nida and Taber 1974:12ff.; cf. Larson 1984). Emphasis was placed on seeking equivalent form and expression in the receptor language for conveying the sense of the original. More recent developments in sociolinguistics and semiotics have focused attention not only on the sense of the message but on its impact. Although the importance of emotive as well as cognitive content was implicit in dynamic equivalence, it was not always apparent. The focus in Scripture translation has therefore moved beyond equivalence in form for the communication of meaning to functional equivalence stressing the impact of the message on the new audience (cf. Peacock 1981:6).

Developments in dialectology, sociolinguistics, semiotics, and structuralism have all been found to offer insights for the translator. If he is to undertake a translation, into which dialect is it to be done? The choice cannot always be determined by features of geographic extension and mutual intelligibility alone, but must often be based on historical and prestige factors as well. Likewise, for whom is the translation intended and which level of language will be the most appropriate? Language use within the translation and stylistic features are also partly determined by sociolinguistic factors. For example, language appropriate for mixed audiences and expressions that must not be voiced in the presence of one's in-laws are considerations that are important for the ultimate acceptance of a translation. Signs and symbols in the receptor community as well as in the text must be given careful attention if the meaning of the original is to be communicated accurately with equivalent impact.

Problems in Scripture Translation

Any translator must begin with a text, and for the Bible translator, the problems begin at that level. Although there are numerous manuscripts of biblical text in existence, none, of course, is the original. The state of the source texts and our knowledge of the source language are such that the translator frequently finds himself confronted by textual problems that no one has been able to resolve. In the Good News Version of the Bible there are 22 footnotes in the book of Job stating that the Hebrew is unclear, 14 footnotes offering alternative translations, and 18 asserting the translation to be "probable" although the Hebrew manuscripts read differently.

There are also numerous exegetical problems where the meaning is unclear or ambiguous even though the text itself does not appear to be in doubt. The writers of the Translator's Handbook for the book of Job note that for the 13th verse of chapter 39, there were already in the 18th century 20 different interpretations that had been proposed. They observe that it may be because of the difficulty in translating them that verses 13 to 18 of this chapter were omitted from the Septuagint (Price and Reyburn n.d.:552).

In any translation there is inevitably the problem of form, both linguistic and literary. Lexical forms that had meaning in the original languages, whose etymologies and usages were understood by the early readers, must be explained in translation. The first names in the Bible, Adam and Eve, appear to be proper names, but the first also means "man" and resembles the Hebrew word *adamah* "ground, earth" from which Adam was formed, while Eve, or Hawwah in Hebrew, resembles the word "to live" *hayah*.

Biblical tradition frequently avoided the use of God's name. One method of accomplishing this in the New Testament is the use of the passive form of the verb. In many languages a passive form as such does not exist, and alternatives to the passive are not necessarily understood as being euphemistic. Where it does exist, it may have a different function than it has in biblical usage. In Thai, for example, the passive is used for referring to unpleasant experiences (Filbeck 1972).

The grammatical form of the new language may also create problems for the translator by requiring distinctions that do not exist in the original text. Fula of West Africa has two first person plural pronouns, the inclusive "all-of-us" and the exclusive "my-friends-and-I-but-not-you." In Mark 4:39, when the terror-stricken disciples awaken Jesus in the boat saying, "Master, do you not care? We are going down!" (JB), do they include him in their predicament?[5]

In the central African language Gbaya, as in French, courtesy requires that a superior be addressed in the second person plural form of pronoun. When Jesus is accosted by the Pharisses, do they use the familiar pronoun or the polite form? When he is before Pilate, who addresses whom in the polite form? In the Gbaya translation, the context of each meeting with the Pharisees and the tone of the meeting determined the level of courtesy marked by the pronouns. In the case of Pilate, the translators determined that Jesus and Pilate addressed each other in the familiar form on the grounds that both spoke from positions of authority and they would therefore both have used the familiar form implying equality. Obviously, in making judgments like this, aspects of language associated with sociolinguistics assume paramount importance.

An issue that has received increasing attention in Western translations has been the use of sexist language, but the question was faced by translators in Africa long before it assumed its present importance in the West. Where the Creator God is female and is referred to with feminine markers, how shall the God of the Old Testament be referred to (cf. Venberg 1971)?[6]

It is sometimes assumed that the most difficult items to find equivalents for must be those things which are unknown in the receiving society, but this is not necessarily the case. Animals that are not known can be described or compared to animals that are known. The same is true for trees, plants, herbs, and foods. Generic terms can be used for precise names, noun compounds can be constructed to depict the object denoted, words can even be borrowed as new products become known and adopted by the society.

---

[5] In Mark's account, the Fula translators used the inclusive "all-of-us are going down." In Luke 8:24, however, they used the exclusive form, thereby implying that they did not believe Jesus was in the same danger they were in; likewise in Matthew 8:25 where they say they, but not he, are dying.

[6] In the Peve language of western Chad, the name for God, *Ifray,* is feminine from the form *Yafray,* which means "mother" and "sky/heavens." In Scripture translation, the grammar of the language requires the use of feminine pronouns and modifiers in reference to God.

More problematic are philosophy and argument. Hebrews 11:1 as translated in the King James Version and in the Revised Standard Version is a definition of faith through the use of two words that are semantically related, "hope" and "expectation." Without restructuring this verse, translation may be very difficult in languages where the semantic cluster faith-confidence-hope-expectation is divided up differently and where these words may also include aspects of doubt, uncertainty, and even pessimism.

Less difficult but far more dangerous are expressions whose translation seems straightforward but conveys a wrong meaning. A translation team may become overly familiar with the biblical text, partly from study and extensive exposure, partly from working closely with the text while translating. Psalm 23:1 is a very simple statement, "The Lord is my Shepherd." In Gbaya the translation of this sentence posed no problem. A lexical equivalent may be found for each item and the grammatical structure is simple. The passage was translated, but when the translators re-read their draft several days later, they discovered the meaning of what they had written. Unlike English, where this construction has two possible meanings and everyone knows which one is meant here, the verse as it stood in Gbaya could only mean that the psalmist owned a flock of sheep and it was the Lord who looked after them.

If it is assumed that the translator should be as adept in the use of the receptor language as the original author was in the use of his language, it should follow that the linguistic and literary devices of that second language are used to the same extent as were those of the first language. If this is put into practice, African languages offer a feature that figures very prominently in traditional literary form. The item is known as the ideophone and includes onomatopoeic words as well as words that express any other sensation that the speaker might wish to denote (cf. Newman, 1968; Noss 1985).

In the parable of the two house-builders recorded by Matthew (7:24–28) and Luke (6:47–49), the writers use expressive grammatical constructions to describe in dramatic fashion the destruction of the foolish man's house. The Good News Bible translates Matthew's final line, "And what a terrible fall that was!" while Luke's final statement reads, "and what a terrible crash that was!" The Gbaya translation team observed that in Gbaya literary form the drama of this scene would be expressed by ideophones. Matthew's description therefore reads, "and the house broke to the ground *gete-gete,*" while Luke's reads, "and the house broke to the ground completely *mutu-mutu.*" The first ideophone *gete-gete* describes an object which is broken to smithereens, the second *mutu-mutu* describes something which is crushed and ground into little more than dust and debris.

Ideophones may be a particularly useful literary device in translating poetry, but they must be used with care. They are inherently focus items that draw attention to themselves and if selected without utmost precaution, inappropriate choices may be made. Instead of effectively communicating the message, they may detract and mislead by becoming the message themselves. Or they may introduce an element of comedy or irony that is quite out of place in the text.

The distance between the language and culture of the Bible and that of the people for whom the translation is being done is a frequent source of difficulty. When the book of Job ends with the statement that he died "at a very great age" (42:17 GNB), it may be taken as a curse rather than a blessing, for to live too long imposes hardship on the entire family. It is often impossible to transfer imagery from one culture and one literary tradition to another. When Satan is described as falling from heaven like lightning (Luke 10:18), the Gbaya understands perfectly, for is not lightning a result of sorcery and is not sorcery a thing of the devil? The image may even be understood to convey Satan's power as he descends with the force of a bolt of lightning.

Occasionally, however, an image may be transferred with meaning and even with telling effect. For instance, when Job is depicted as scratching himself with a potsherd (Job 2:8), the Chamba understands it as abject despair in the face of death, for a broken pot is placed on Chamba graves as a symbol of death. When a person dies far from home and cannot be brought back for burial, it is a broken neck and mouth of a pot that attests to his death and burial.

Problems in Methodology of Scripture Translation

It is inevitable that two different languages and cultures will not meet and mesh perfectly. However, methodology also imposes its guidelines on the translator and these will be the source of further problems. If the principle of dynamic equivalence is followed, the emphasis is less on duplicating the form than on communicating the meaning. For a culture very distant from the sociohistorical context of the New Testament, it is sometimes argued that implicit details understood by the original audience or readership must be supplied in explicit form in the translation. To be explicit for the sake of clarity is laudable, but not infrequently explicitness impoverishes the message. When the Apostle Paul uses the expression "in Christ" in 2 Corinthians 5:17, does he mean "joined to Christ" as it is translated in the Good News Bible or *uni au Christ* ("united with Christ") as rendered in the French equivalent of the Good News Bible? Translation and exegesis are here inseparable.

When the gospel writers use "kingdom of God" and "kingdom of heaven," it is commonly assumed that the two expressions are synonymous while being stylistically and perhaps culturally different. The reference to heaven reflects the Hebrew tradition of avoiding direct reference to God. To be true to New Testament thought, which is here reflective of Old Testament practice, the two expressions cannot be rendered by the same phrase. But there is a further problem. What is the meaning of the two expressions? Clearly, geographic territory is not intended, as would be conveyed in German if "kingdom" were rendered by *Reich*. However, for the German to use *Herrschaft* would imply an authoritarian rule which would be inappropriate to the biblical concept as well. In those traditions where there was no central kingship, the concept of kingdom may be difficult to convey. Should the biblical expression then be interpreted in each context according to whether it might refer to the imminence of God's rule, the completion of his work in establishing his rule, or the acceptance of his rule in personal submission by someone who will then enjoy the blessings of that rule (Kassühlke 1974:236–38)? Although the different renderings may capture the various meanings of the two phrases, the thematic unity and wholeness conveyed by the repeated use of the same two expressions in different contexts by the various New Testament writers is lost.

If the emphasis is to be on faithful rendering of the meaning, the translator may ask, meaning on which level? Jonah may be taken at many different levels, from a Marvellous Story to a narrative account to a parable. In addition, there may be deeper levels of meaning regarding a people's understanding of the mission of the prophet or of God's relationship to all humanity rather than to the chosen race alone. These different meanings must all be conveyed in the translation, or at least allowed by it, and that may be difficult. In a given tradition, the form of fiction and history may not be the same; the form of myth and parable may be mutually exclusive. Does the literary form of the receptor language then pose restrictions on the meaning of the translation as conveyed by its form? The answer is clearly yes.

Functional equivalence implies dynamic equivalence while shifting the focus from language to the receptor. The translation is intended to perform the same function as the original and to evoke in the audience or reader the same response as was evoked by the original text. The goal is a worthy one that may be very appropriate (cf. Prochazka 1942:95), but for numerous Scripture texts it poses problems. If the original author is not known, or the original readership, or even the date and context of authorship, how is it possible to determine what the function of the original text was and what impact it was intended to have? The Song of Songs may be taken as an example, or the book of Jonah.

Primary emphasis can be placed on the theological meaning of the text when translating the Bible, but the Bible is also a historical document and the factor of historicity may create a significant conflict for the translator. In attempting to render the message intelligible to the contemporary reader who is of another era and culture than the first readers, how far shall he go in putting dynamic principles into practice? Martin Luther presented Jesus as a German, but Jesus was not a German. Nor was he betrayed on Peach-Orchard Hill, he did not suffer under Governor Pilate of Georgia. The disciples did not live in this century; they are no more sons of the space age than they were sons of the stone age.

The implications of the conflict between history and contemporary communication extend to relatively insignificant details. Images have already been referred to. Those which convey no meaning in translation or the wrong meaning should be replaced by meaningful expressions in the receptor language. Where snow is unknown, another term may need to be found, but it is meaningless to devise some expression such as "your sins shall be white as hard water" (Isaiah 1:18). More meaningful might be an image such as "white as cotton," but cotton was not biblical. While this image, which is to a degree geography-specific, might convey the meaning of the original, it would be misleading in its historical implications. In cases such as this, it is preferable to use a historically neutral image or expression such as "pure white" or an ideophone depicting absolute whiteness.

Other images are very central to biblical thought. When adhering to the principles of equivalence, what is the translator to do when he finds no vine comparable to the biblical grape-vine (Isaiah 5:1–7; John 15:1–17)? Most cultures know vines, but the vines of the gallery forest are not very similar to those of the vineyard. The squash plant is a vine, but in Xhosa oral literature, it represents a destructive force which extends its tendrils to grasp other plants, smothering and suffocating them as it spreads throughout the garden. To adapt one's translation to local botany by using another locally well-known plant is not being faithful to the original and is unlikely to convey the same meaning or to have the same impact as the original vine did in Hebrew literature, where the vine enters the realm of theology.

Increasingly in this era of ecumenism, Protestant translators are moving toward their Roman Catholic counterparts in a reliance on glossaries to explain technical terms — "cherubim" and "seraphim," for instance — and footnotes to explain problems in the text or in the translation. Manuscript variants can be noted, alternate translations can be acknowledged, plays on words and etymologies of names can be explained, as well as the significance of certain cultural practices of biblical times and the meaning of major biblical themes. Unfortunately, not all new readers understand footnotes and glossaries.

In following the principles of dynamic and functional equivalence, there is a danger that must be guarded against. The frequency with which a translation falls short of conveying the full meaning of the original, or its failure to reproduce the literary qualities of the source, may be readily apparent, but there may also be instances where a translation goes beyond the original text (cf. Bassnett-McGuire 1980:30–31). If the emphasis on equivalence is not rigorously maintained, dynamism may be carried to the point where the style, for example, of the translation may be more dramatic than the original. Bainton writes about Luther that he "so lived his way into the Psalms that he improved upon them" (1955:262). The translator is constantly faced with the dilemma of creating something new while at the same time not creating something different.

Influence of Scripture Translation

If translation is a bridge, it extends in two directions. The contribution that the translation of the Bible into European languages has made in the development of those languages and their literatures is well known (Prochazka 1942:93; Steiner 1975:246). In the history of African languages and literatures, Scripture translation has also had significant influence.

Preparatory to translation is the study of language and of literary form. The earliest writings and studies of African languages and their literatures are the work of churchmen. The first Bantu publication of which there is record is the catechism prepared in kiKongo by the Portuguese Jesuit priest Mattheus Cardoso, printed in 1624 in Lisbon (Doke 1961:8). The first published grammar of a Bantu language is that of the Italian priest Hyacinthus Brussciottus, entitled *Regulae quaedam pro difficillimi Congensium idiomatis faciliori captu ad grammaticae normam reductae* ("Some rules for the more easy understanding of the most difficult idiom of the people of the Congo, brought into the form of a grammar"), published in Rome in 1659. Wilhelm Sigismund Koelle was sent to West Africa as a missionary by the Anglican Church in 1848 and in a period of five years he prepared three monographs on the Vai and Kanuri languages in addition to his well-known *Polyglotta Africana* (1854). In his book *African Native Literature, or Proverbs, Tales, Fables, and Historical Fragments in the Kanuri or Bornu Language, to which are added a translation of the above and a Kanuri-English Vocabulary* (1854), he includes 62 proverbs, 17 tales, and 9 narratives. The Nigerian Bishop Samuel Ajayi Crowther, who translated and supervised the translation of the Yoruba Bible, also published a grammar of Yoruba, a Yoruba primer for schools, and *A Vocabulary of the Yoruba Language* in which he recorded over 500 Yoruba proverbs (1852). If today there are translations of the Bible in more languages in Africa than on any other continent, and if "the oral repertoire of Africa is better known than that of any other area of the world" (Abrahams 1983:xiv), the two facts may be related.

The record goes beyond the analysis of grammar and the recording of oral literatures to the very foundations of writing. Since achieving independence, the younger nations of Africa have taken official and active interest in the development of national orthographies (cf. Tadadjeu and Sadembouo 1984), but prior to this development, it was missions and churches that laid the groundwork by establishing writing systems for the languages into which they wished to translate and by launching literacy campaigns to teach the new Christians to read the Holy Scriptures.

The fact that many early missions made reading a prerequisite for baptism, in addition to publishing the Scriptures in African languages, did much to foster the growth of literacy and of written African literature. The first printing press south of the Sahara Desert was set up in South Africa in 1823. It came to be known as Lovedale Press and played a major role in the development of Zulu and Xhosa literature in the last century and the first part of this century. Among early South African writers may be noted Tiyo Soga, one of the translators of the Xhosa Bible (1859), editor of the journal *Indaba* ("The News") and translator of *The Pilgrim's Progress*. Others whose names may be cited are William W. Gqoba, W. B. Rubasana, Benedict W. Vilakazi, D. D. T. Javabu, S. E. K. Mqhayi, and Thomas Mofolo. Perhaps in South Africa more than elsewhere in Africa, Scripture translation, as well as the translation of *The Pilgrim's Progress* into Xhosa, had a profound influence on the development of modern written literature. As stated by C. M. Doke (Doke and Cole 1961:125): "As was the case with the English Bible, so in Bantu lands, these various translations are tending to set the standard for the literary forms of the language." Similarly in Nigeria, the work of Bishop Crowther on Yoruba orthography and the style of his translation of the Bible continue to influence Yoruba writing up to the present day.

Conclusion

Today it is increasingly the mother-tongue speaker who through his choice of orthography and spelling, through his use of vocabulary and his adoption of new terminology, through his use of traditional literary form and its adaptation to the written page, develops and standardizes language and vocabulary and literary form. Above all, however, his effort is to communicate the message of the context of a new culture. Whether he is a son of the land or a stranger come to learn the new language, the translator's intent as he studies and analyzes and seeks ways to transfer meaning is "to translate without betraying" (Margot 1979). It is his hope and his prayer that he will be able to be faithful both to his text, which he believes to be the inspired Word of God to humankind, and at the same time to the receptor language and culture which is the gift of God to a particular group of people. Although he recognizes that translation must be a science as well as an art, for him it is also an act of faith.

References

Abrahams, Roker D. 1983. *African folktales.* New York: Pantheon Books.
Arichea, Daniel. 1982. Taking theology seriously. *The Bible Translator* 33: 3.309–16.

Bainton, Roland H. 1955. *Here I stand: The life of Martin Luther.* New York: Mentor Books.

Barthélemy, Dominique. 1974. Pourquoi la Torah a-t-elle été traduite en grec? In Black and Smalley (1974:23–42).

Bassnett-McGuire, Susan. 1980. *Translation studies.* London: Methuen.

Black, Matthew, and William A. Smalley, eds. 1974. *On language, culture, and religion: In honor of Eugene A. Nida.* The Hague: Mouton.

Brower, Reuben A. 1959. *On translation.* Cambridge, Mass.: Harvard University Press.

Cole, Roger W., ed. 1977. *Current issues in linguistic theory.* Bloomington: Indiana University Press.

Crowther, Samuel Ajayi. 1852. *A grammar and vocabulary of the Yoruba language.* London: Seeley, Service.

Derive, Jean. 1975. *Collecte et traduction des littératures orales.* Paris: Société d'Etudes Linguistiques et Anthropologiques de France.

Doke, C. M., and D. T. Cole. 1969. *Contributions to the history of Bantu linguistics.* Johannesburg: Witwatersrand University Press.

Filbeck, David. 1972. The passive, an unpleasant experience. *The Bible Translator* 23:3.331–36.

Garvin, Paul L., trans. 1964. *A Prague School reader on esthetics, literary structure, and style.* Washington, D.C.: Georgetown University Press.

Grimes, Barbara F., ed. 1984. *Ethnologue,* 10th ed. Dallas: Wycliffe Bible Translators.

Jordan, Clarence. 1969. *Cotton patch version of Luke and Acts.* New York: Association Press.

Kasdorf, Hans. 1978. Luther's Bible: A dynamic equivalence translation and germanizing force. *Missiology* 6:2.213–34.

Kassühlke, Rodolf. 1974. An attempt at a dynamic equivalent translation of *basileia tou theou. The Bible Translator* 25:2.236–38.

Koelle, Sigismund Wilhelm. 1854a. *African native literature; or proverbs, tales, fables, and historical fragments in the Kanuri or Bornu language, to which are added a translation of the above and a Kanuri-English vocabulary.* London: Church Missionary House.

Koelle, Sigismund Wilhelm. 1854b. *Polyglotta africana.* London: Church Missionary Society.

Larson, Mildred L. 1984. *Meaning-based translation: A guide to cross-language equivalence.* Lanham, Md.: University Press of America.

Margot, Jean-Claude. 1979. *Traduire sans trahir.* Lausanne: L'Age d'Homme.

Newman, Paul. 1968. Ideophones from a syntactic point of view. *Journal of West African Languages* 5:2.107–117.

Ngugi, James. 1965. *The river between.* London: Heinemann.

Nida, Eugene A. 1964. *Toward a science of translating.* Leiden: E. J. Brill.

Nida, Eugene, ed. 1972. *The book of a thousand tongues,* 2nd ed. London: United Bible Societies.

Nida, Eugene, and Charles R. Taber. 1974. *The theory and practice of translation.* Leiden: E. J. Brill.

Nida, Eugene, Johannes P. Louw, and Rondal B. Smith. 1977. *Semantic domains and componential analysis.* In Cole (1977:139–67).

Noss, Philip A. 1985. The ideophone in Bible translation. Child or stepchild. *The Bible Translator* 36:4.423–30.

Peacock, Heber F. 1981. Current trends in Scripture translation. In: *United Bible Societies* (1981:5–9).

Price, Brynmor, and William D. Reyburn. n.d. A translator's handbook on the book of Job. MS.

Procházka, Vladimír. 1942. Notes on translating technique. In Garvin (1964:93–112).

Steiner, George. 1975. *After Babel.* Oxford: Oxford University Press.

Tadadjeu, Maurice, and Etienne Sadembouo, eds. 1984. *Alphabet général des langues camerounaises.* Yaoundé: Université de Yaoundé.

Ukpai, E. K. 1985. *Biakpan: The new world language.* Calabar, Nigeria: Brotherhood of the Cross and Star.

United Bible Societies. 1981. Bulletin 124/125.

United Bible Societies. 1985. Bulletin 138/139.

Venberg, Rodney. 1971. The problem of a female deity in translation. *The Bible Translator* 22:2.68–70.

Wallis, E. E., and M. A. Bennett. 1959. *Two thousand tongues to go.* New York: Harper and Brothers.

Content Questions

1. What kinds of challenges are associated with biblical translation?

2. What is dynamic equivalence in translation? How does it differ from a literal translation?

3. What additional concern has led translators to work toward functional equivalence in their translations?

4. How can the passive present a problem for translation into different languages?

5. What is problematic about translating the first-person plural pronoun into Fula? What issue must be considered in translating the second-person pronoun into Gbaya?

6. Summarize some of the issues that Noss raises in his section on "problems in methodology of Scripture translation."

7. How have biblical translators contributed to our knowledge of other languages and cultures? How have the translators influenced those cultures?

Questions for Analysis and Discussion

1. What risks do translators run if they are unfamiliar with the culture they are translating into or translating from? Illustrate your answer with an example from the reading or from a language with which you are familiar.

2. Keeping in mind the translation issues raised in this article, comment on the kinds of differences that can exist among various Bible translations even within a single language such as English.

3. To what extent does a translation rely on an interpretation by the translator?

The Unbreakable Language Code in the Pacific Theatre of World War II

M. Gyi

The article below illustrates how linguistic knowledge about a particular language, in this case Navajo, became a critical factor in a decision that affected America's military success during World War II. Many people are unaware of the important role that Navajo code talkers played in American history. In the following article, from *ETC: A Review of General Semantics,* M. Gyi, a professor at Ohio University, explains what that important role was and why the Navajo language was such a good choice for a military code. This article represents an interesting perspective with regard to translation studies: the selection and use of a language for the purpose of incomprehensibility to all but a small group of people.

At the outbreak of the Second World War, the United States military and naval forces were spread over the two hemispheres. The secrecy of diplomatic and military communication was vital. An enciphered message speedily broken by the enemy could mean a major disaster for the U.S. forces.

Norbert Wiener, in his classic text, *The Human Use of Human Beings,* explained the importance of speed in decoding military messages:

> The matter of time is essential in all estimates of the value of information. A code or cipher, for example, which will cover any considerable amount of material at high-secrecy level is not only a lock which is hard to force, but also one which takes a considerable time to open legitimately.
>
> Tactical information which is useful in the combat of small units will almost certainly be obsolete in an hour or two. It is a matter of very little importance whether it can be broken in three hours; but it is of great importance that an officer receiving the message should be able to read it in something like two minutes. On the other hand, the larger plan of battle is too important a matter to entrust to this limited degree of security. Nevertheless, if it took a whole day for an officer receiving this plan to disentangle it, the delay might well be more serious than any leak.[1]

Throughout the war in Europe, North Africa, and Asia, the U.S. Army's Signal Intelligence Service and Naval Intelligence had to cope with

---

[1] Wiener, Norbert, *The Human Use of Human Beings* (New York: Avon Books, 1973), p. 168.

the European, with the Japanese, and with hundreds of other languages. In India alone there are over 250 different languages.[2] To those must be added all the languages of Southeast Asia, the Pacific Islands, Korea, Russia, the Middle East, Africa, and the many Chinese dialects.

The breaking of most modern diplomatic and military code and cipher systems generally depends upon the knowledge of the letter frequencies of the language in which the messages are encoded or enciphered. There are differences in the letter frequencies even in European languages. In the Japanese language, however, the U.S. code-breakers encountered the most difficult problems of all.[3] Written Japanese, as differentiated from the spoken language, is based on Chinese ideographs. In it, complexities developed in geometric proportions.

By 1937, the Japanese had developed a cipher machine called "97-Shiki O-bun In-ji-ki," meaning Alphabetical Typewriter 2597. This typewriter works on "Romanji," Roman letters, not Japanese Kata Kana.[4] In addition, this machine could scramble the 70 possible syllables into complex transposition and substitution systems. The Japanese Foreign Office was completely convinced of the impregnability of its cryptographic system which was extensively employed for secret diplomatic and military messages.

In 1939, the U.S. Naval Intelligence and the Signal Intelligence Service constructed a machine that could duplicate the action of the original Japanese Model A-T 2597.[5] By December of 1941, the U.S. Intelligence units were able to break the most sophisticated Japanese fleet signals dubbed "JN25 by OP-20-G."[6]

Early in World War II, the Japanese were also able to break the U.S. military signals with devastating results. Then in the spring of 1942, the staff of Tomumu Han (Special Communication Section) of the Imperial Japanese Navy was suddenly faced with new U.S. field radio signals. The Japanese cryptanalysts realized that the "strange sounds" that stymied them was the Navajo language transmitted by the Navajo Code Talkers of the U.S. Marine Corps.[7]

Allen Dulles, former Director of the U.S. Central Intelligence Agency, wrote:

> The United States military forces were able to resort to rather unusual "ready made" codes during World War I and during World War II in communication units in the field.

---

[2] "India," *The Encyclopedia Britannica*, 15th Edition, 1976.

[3] Smith, L. D., *Cryptography, The Science of Secret Writing* (New York: Dover Publication, Inc., 1971), p. 13.

[4] Way, Peter, *Codes and Ciphers* (New York: Crescent Books, 1977), p. 68.

[5] Kahn, David, *The Code-Breakers* (New York: The Macmillan Co., 1978), pp. 1–67.

[6] Way, *op. cit.*, pp. 68–70.

[7] Barnes, S., "The Navajo's Secret Weapon," *The American Legion*, Volume 104, No. 2, February 1978, p. 32.

These resources were our Native American Indian languages, chiefly Navajo language, which have no written forms and had never been closely studied by foreign scholars. Two members of the same tribe at either end of a field telephone could transmit messages which no listener except another Navajo could possibly understand. Needless to say, neither the Germans nor the Japanese had any Navajo.[8]

The practice of using Native Americans started when the American Expeditionary Force was bogged down in France in World War I and the U.S. radio signals were successfully intercepted by the Germans. Major A. W. Bloor, commanding officer of the 142nd Infantry wrote in his memo dated January 23, 1919:

The regiment possessed a company of Indians. They spoke 26 different languages or dialects, only four or five of which were ever written . . . There was hardly one chance in a million that the Germans would be able to translate these dialects, and the plans to have these Indians transmit telephone messages was adopted.[9]

With the help of Choctaw Indians of Company D, the regimental orders were transmitted by field telephone to the bewilderment of the German eavesdroppers.[10] Other Indian languages were also used. During preparation for World War II, the U.S. Intelligence Service and the Signal Corps tested Comanches and Indians from the Michigan and Wisconsin in numerous simulated battles and war games.[11] But most of the code-talkers selected for combat duties in the Pacific Theatre were Navajo.

Navajo Language

Navajo is the largest Indian tribe in the U.S., numbering close to 80,000 according to the estimates of the Bureau of Indian Affairs.[12] The Navajo reservations and the government allotted lands are located in the states of Arizona, New Mexico, and Utah. The Navajo speak a language closely related to Apache tongues and more distantly related to other Athapaskan languages.[13]

Anthropologists Kluckohn and Leighton described the articulation patterns of the Navajo:

---

[8] Dulles, Allen, *The Craft of Intelligence* (New York: Signet, 1965), p. 71.
[9] "Indians Were Code Talkers," *The Athens Messenger,* September 27, 1981.
[10] Kahn, *op. cit.,* p. 289.
[11] *Ibid.*
[12] *The Encyclopedia of Indians of the Americas* (E.I.A.) (Michigan: Scholarly Press, 1974), p. 339.
[13] *Ibid.*

Sounds (in Navajo) must be reproduced with pedantic neatness . . . almost as if a robot is talking. The talk of those who have learned Navajo as adults always has a flabby quality to the Navajo ear. They neglect a slight hesitation a fraction of a second before uttering the stem of the word.[14]

A glottal closure, which the speakers of European language rarely recognize, often differentiates Navajo words. Tsin means "stick," "log," or "tree," whereas ts'in (with glottal closure) means "bone." Similarly, bita' means "between," but bit'a' means "its wing." The Navajos also distinguish quite separate meanings on the basis of pronouncing their vowels in long, intermediate, or short manner. They also pay careful attention to the tones of vowels. Four separate tones consisting of low, high, rising, and falling can be differentiated.

The phonetic variations in the following words are quite imperceptible to the untrained listener.

bíni' = his mind	binii' = his face
bíníí' = his nostrils	bini = in it[15]
biníí' = his waist	

In the case of most nouns, as in the examples given above, meanings could be derived from context. But when Navajo verbs are examined, difference in pronunciation so slight as to pass unnoticed by speakers of Indo-European languages make for a bewildering set of variations, many of which would be equally suitable to an identical context. For example:

naash'á = I go around with the round object.
naash'aah = I am in the act of lowering the round object.
násh'ááh = I am in the act of turning the round object upside down (or over).
naash'áah = I am accustomed to lowering the round object.
násh'a = I am skinning it.[16]

The importance of these minute variations in Navajo cuts both ways in complicating the problems of communication between Navajos and non-Navajos. These variations make it difficult for Navajos to learn English phonetic patterns accurately, and they also make it difficult for English speakers to speak Navajo.

---

[14]Kluckhohn, Clyde, and Leighton, D., *The Navajo* (Cambridge, Mass.: Harvard University Press, 1946), pp. 186–187.
[15]*Ibid.,* p. 185.
[16]*Ibid.,* p. 187.

Navajo language has a very rich vocabulary. There are more than a thousand recorded names for plants, that the technical terms used in ceremonialism total at least five hundred, that every cultural specialization or occupation has its own special terminology. The language has shown itself flexible in its capacity for dealing with new objects and new experiences. But this has been done, for the most part, by making up new words in accord with old patterns rather than by taking over Spanish and English words and pronouncing them in Navajo fashion. For example:

"Tomato" is "red plant."
"An elephant" is "one that lassoes with his nose."
"Car" is "chuggi or chidí" which imitate the sound of a car.
"Gasoline" becomes chidi or chuggi bi to, "car's water." [17]

Because of its phonemic and syntactical complexities, the Navajo language became a desirable candidate to be employed as a secret military language code for the U.S. Marine Corps in the Pacific Theatre of war.

Platoon 382

In 1942, Sergeant Phillip Johnson, linguist and engineer, the son of Christian missionaries who had lived and worked with the Navajos for some 20 years, was assigned to direct the code training program of "platoon 382" made up of Navajo high school and college men.[18] Johnson and his platoon developed a code of some 200 characters and a vocabulary of 411 terms that could be memorized and used with speed. This Navajo secret signal code needed no ciphering or deciphering as it was in their own language.

Some of the examples of Navajo codes were, aircraft carrier = tsidi-ney-ye-hi = bird carrier, fighter plane = he-tih-hi = hummingbird, flare = wo-chi = light streak, and so forth.[19] The "platoon 382" was trained in sending and receiving messages from air to ground, ship to shore, tank to command post. Messages included mission and maneuvers, location and strength of the enemy, time and place of attack and other tactical orders. They thoroughly rehearsed and tested the accuracy and speed of the signals.

Lt. Colonel J. P. Berkeley, Commanding Officer of Code Training Program, reported:

The Navajo have no written language and there are many words in English that have no equivalent in Navajo, but it was demonstrated time and again when these teams were given complicated reports and instructions to transmit by voice over radio and wire that not a single mistake was

---

[17] *Ibid.*, p. 185.
[18] Barnes, *op. cit.*, p. 32.
[19] *Ibid.*

made, a fact that our regular communication men speaking in code could not match.[20]

The number of Navajo Code Talkers in the U.S. Marine Corps rose from 30 to 420 during the Pacific war. The Navajos were assigned in the regimental, divisional, or corps command posts, translating messages into a conglomeration of Navajo, American Slang, and military terminology.[21]

U.S. Marine Major Howard M. Conner of Iwo Jima Operation praised the success of the Navajo Code Talkers:

> Were it not for the Navajos, the Marines would never have taken Iwo Jima. The entire operation was directed by Navajo code. Our corps command posts were on a battleship from which orders were to the three division command posts on the beachheads and on down to the lower echelons.[22]

The Navajo Code Talkers efficiently relayed operational orders with great secrecy and speed that helped the U.S. Marines' successful advance from the Solomon Islands, Tarawa, Marianas Islands, Saipan, Tinian, Guam, Iwo Jima, Okinawa, and many other Marine operations in the Pacific war.

Success of Navajo Language Code

Throughout the war, the Japanese military and naval intelligence were unable to break the Navajo language code.

Six reasons could be credited for the success of this "unbreakable code."

1) There were only 28 non-Navajos who could speak the language. These few were linguists, anthropologists, and missionaries, and none of these were Germans or Japanese.[23]
2) Prior to World War II, German and Japanese linguists attempted to study the languages of American Indians to forestall the use of Indians as U.S. "Code Talkers" in warfare. But their attempt was foiled when war broke out.[24]
3) Navajo language is one of the most difficult languages to learn. Even if someone did learn it, it is nearly impossible to imitate or counterfeit its phonetic variations.
4) The Navajo tribe was large enough to furnish a sufficient number of trained code-talkers in numerous Marine operations.

---

[20] *Ibid.*
[21] Kahn, *op. cit.,* p. 580.
[22] Barnes, *op. cit.,* p. 32.
[23] *Athens Messenger,* September 27, 1981.
[24] *Ibid.*

5) Efficiency and thoroughness of the Marine Corps Code Training Program is clearly evidenced. Signal Officer S. Barnes of the 5th Marine Division described the accuracy and speed of the Navajo Code Talkers in one operation:

> During the 48 hours while we were landing and consolidating our shore positions I had six Navajo radio signal nets operating around the clock. In that period alone they sent and received 800 messages without a single error.[25]

6) The Japanese attempted to bribe some of the Navajos to defect with the promise of wealth so that they could assist in intercepting and decoding the U.S. Marine operational orders. None of the Navajo defected. They remained loyal to the U.S.[26]

Navajo Code Talkers Honored

During the Second World War more than 25,000 Native American Indian men and women of various tribes served in the U.S. Armed Forces,[27] and 3,600 were Navajo men and women.[28]

In 1945, the U.S. Native Indians were awarded 2 Congressional Medals of Honor, 34 Distinguished Flying Crosses, 47 Bronze Stars, 51 Silver Stars, and 71 Air Medals for courageous services during the war.[29]

Not until 1969 were the surviving Navajo Code Talkers awarded the long awaited recognition at the 4th Marine Division's 22nd annual reunion in Chicago. Each received a Bronze Medallion depicting Ira Hayes, Indian war hero of Iwo Jima operation. The Navajo organized their own reunion in 1970 and held their second in 1975 at the Navajo Tribal Museum in Window Rock, Arizona.[30] The third reunion was held in 1980 at the Navajo Nation Fair in Arizona.[31]

Recognizing the invaluable contributions of the Navajo Code Talkers in the Pacific Theatre of World War II, the U.S. Marine Corps did consider making the Navajo language code a permanent adjunct.[32] In June of 1981, an All Navajo Indian Platoon was reorganized at Camp Pendleton in California for the first time since the formation of Platoon 382 during the Second World War.[33]

---

[25] Barnes, *op. cit.,* pp. 32–33.
[26] Locke, R., *The Book of the Navajo* (Los Angeles, Calif.: Mankind Publishing Co., 1976), p. 449.
[27] *The Encyclopedia of Indians of the Americas,* p. 395.
[28] Locke, *op. cit.,* p. 449.
[29] *The Encyclopedia of Indians of the Americas,* p. 395.
[30] Interview, Staff at the Bureau of Indian Affairs, Washington, D.C., June 21, 1981.
[31] *The Evening Gazette,* Worcester, Mass., August 6, 1981.
[32] Barnes, *op. cit.,* p. 33.
[33] *The Evening Gazette.*

The military documents on "Navajo Code Talkers" were declassified recently by the U.S. National Security Agency and transferred to the National Archives in Washington, D.C.[34]

Are the Russians attempting to study Navajo, Comanche, Choctaw, and other Indian languages where the Germans and Japanese failed to do so prior to the war? The Soviet language training centers in Moscow, Leningrad, and other cities are quite secretive about their military language programs.

Content Questions

1. What linguistic aspect does Gyi indicate is often used to decipher codes?

2. When did the United States first begin using Native American languages as military codes?

3. Why is it unlikely that at the time of World War II any of our nation's enemies would have known the Navajo language?

4. What are some of the features of Navajo that Gyi indicates would be difficult for nonnative speakers to learn or understand?

5. Explain what the Navajo code talkers did with their language to ensure that their communications would be even more incomprehensible to the enemy.

6. What six factors contributed to the success of the Navajo code throughout the war?

Questions for Analysis and Discussion

1. Contrast the strategies and goals outlined in this article with the more usual characteristics of translation.

2. How would the fact that Navajo was primarily an oral language have served the interests of the military?

3. Many people are unaware of the Navajos' contribution to the war. To what extent do you think that the postwar delay in releasing information on the Navajo code talkers contributed to this?

4. How could a knowledge of the linguistic structure of languages, their historical roots, and their current distribution of speakers help in the selection of a language that is most likely to baffle outsiders who try to decipher it?

---

[34] *The Athens Messenger.*

Linguistics and Machine Translation

Victor Raskin

Victor Raskin is a linguistics professor at Purdue University who has done extensive work with natural language processing (NLP). Natural language processing is a field that involves computers in various language-related tasks, including machine translation (MT). In this updated article, which originally appeared in a book about machine translation, Raskin provides examples of some of the kinds of linguistic knowledge that a well-trained linguist could contribute to a machine translation project. Raskin also shows that linguists working on an MT team will be more useful to such a team if they can contribute information in a format that is more compatible with the goals of the project at hand.

Introduction

This chapter addresses the issue of cooperation between linguistics and machine translation (MT). Cooperation usually means mutual and reciprocal influence and help, and this bidirectionality does indeed apply to the relations between the two fields (see, for instance, Raskin and Nirenburg 1995: 21–29). But here, we focus on just one direction of such cooperation, namely applications of linguistics to MT, virtually ignoring any possible applications of MT to linguistics, which can range from providing computer-based research tools and aids to linguistics to implementing formal linguistic theories and verifying linguistic models.

Section 1 deals with the issue of MT and with the question why linguistics must be applied to it and what the consequences of not doing so are. Section 2 provides a counterpoint of sorts by discussing how linguistics should **not** be applied to MT and, by contrast and inference, how it should be. Section 3 narrows the discussion down to one promising approach to NLP, the sublanguage deal, and the interesting ways in which linguistics can be utilized within a limited sublanguage. Section 4 outlines ontological semantics, the most promising current approach to meaning in MT. Section 5 is devoted specifically to what linguistics can contribute to MT, and the Conclusion sums up the discussion by reemphasizing the importance of an applied theory of linguistics for MT and NLP. It also underscores the essential difference between human translation and MT.

1. What Is MT and Why Should Linguistics Be Applied to It?

Very early in the computer era, shortly after World War II, MT emerged as the earliest field, beyond numerical calculations (a.k.a. "number crunching"), in which computers could replace humans (see, for instance, Hutchins and Somers 1992: 5–9 for a brief history of MT). The idea of computer-executed translation from one language to another became, thus, one of the very first areas of what is now known as "artificial intelligence" (AI), and within AI, of natural language processing (NLP), which includes now such endeavors as intelligent searches and automatic abstracting, or summarization.

Both the desire to computerize translation and its timing were quite understandable. Throughout human history, as international contacts have increased, enormous and constantly growing armies of human translators have been paid to render texts from one language to another. While some of these people have been bilingual by accident of birth, most other, less fortunate individuals have had to spend years of learning on acquiring a foreign language, a process which is most time-consuming, often frustrating, and never straightforward. Both the preparation of interpreters and translators, i.e., verbal and written translators, and their upkeep has cost our societies a very significant part of their resources.

Obviously, no such expense would have been necessary if we all spoke the same language, but we do not. Whether one's explanation for this situation is the Tower of Babel accident or the historical divergence of languages from the same source or sources as various communities settled on vastly expanding territories and separated from each other, there are about 5,600 extant languages on this planet. Earlier in this century, massive proposals for an international language were made, Esperanto being just one, best known example, but this is not, apparently, how the problem of translation will be solved. For the last 50 years, English has made gigantic strides in becoming a de facto international language, but the need in translation is still there, and it will stay with us, at least for a while.

As the other contributions to this part of the volume show, translation from one language to another is a very complex process, and it requires more than just knowing both languages: typically, a bilingual person, untrained in translation, makes a poor interpreter or translator. The project of translating a Shakespeare sonnet or a Faulkner novel to another language is mind-boggling: one has to be able to match the mastery of the original, to know both cultures in their minute detail, to have a very well-developed literary and esthetic taste, and to be very lucky. The idea of computerizing all of that remains a very distant prospect even now, 50 or so years since the inception of MT, AI, and NLP.

The fact is, however, that most interpreters and translators are engaged in much simpler and more mundane practices, such as interpreting for politicians or translating specialized texts. It is much more realistic to computerize the latter endeavor, and the narrower the field of specialization, the more successful MT has proven to be.

The most naive approach to MT is word-for-word translation. What's the big deal, one may be tempted to ask, in putting the largest possible bilingual dictionary online and translating every sentence from, say, Russian into English by substituting each Russian word with its English equivalent? Some disasters, resulting from such a simplistic approach, are shown in (1) below:

    (1) (i)   Chelovek voshel v komnatu. ——→ Man came-in in room.
         (ii) Mne nravitsya gulat' po gorodu. ——→ Me pleases walk over city.
        (iii) Nado sbegat' za molokom. ——→ Needed run behind milk.

Obviously, no human translating at this level would be qualified to do the work. The problems range from the simple grammatical differences between the languages to more complicated meaning problems. Thus, in (1i), the English translation lacks the necessary articles because Russian does not have any. In (1ii), Russian uses an impersonal construction, in which the verb has no subject, but English cannot have a verb without a subject and, therefore, uses *I like* instead. A similar trap occurs in the third sentence, but also the wrong sense of the preposition *za* is chosen: a more appropriate one would be *for*.

Throughout the examples, there is the problem of choosing one of the many possible translations, virtually for every single word. Anybody who has ever used a bilingual dictionary knows that every word one looks up can be translated differently in different expressions or contexts. There are many other related and unrelated problems that word-for-word translation cannot begin to touch, and the key to all of them lies in the discipline that deals with language rules.

Linguistics is the discipline which is supposed to know about the organization of text. The primary goal of linguistics, according to an enlightened view, is to study the mental mechanisms underlying language. Since direct observation of these mechanisms is impossible, linguistics is trying to match, or model, the native speaker's language competence by observing the indirect consequences of his/her speech output and by discovering and presenting formally the rules governing this output. And this is precisely what MT needs from linguistics, the rules of the languages involved in the translation effort.

What the native speaker is competent about as far as language is concerned boils down to matching sounds and meanings. However, this is done not on a one-to-one basis but rather with the help of a heavily structured medium, consisting of quite a few interrelated levels of interrelated elements. These levels include phonetics and phonology, morphonology and morphology, syntax, semantics and pragmatics, and text linguistics/ discourse analysis.

At each level, linguistics tries to discover and/or postulate the basic units and rules of their functioning. Contemporary linguistics does things formally, which means utilizing one or more—and frequently all—of the various manifestations and/or interpretations of linguistic formality listed in (2).

(2) (i) formulating language rules as theorems and using mathematical notation for this purpose;

   (ii) relying entirely on the forms of the words and word combinations for establishing the applicability of each rule to a text element;

   (iii) adhering to the mechanical symbol manipulation device paradigm.

(2iii) is the strongest and most serious commitment to formality, having far-reaching consequences, free from concern for the pretty superficial and optional factors involved in (2i), and less constrained in its heuristics than (2ii). What the mechanical symbol manipulation device (MSMD) approach amounts to is a firm commitment to formulate all linguistic rules in such a way that they could be executed by a non-thinking device, capable only of recognizing strings of sounds or characters. Does that sound familiar? It should, because this description of the device fits the computer very well.

It might seem, and may have seemed for a while, that the MSMD format brings linguistics tantalizingly close to computer science and that the rules and sets of rules proposed by the former can be directly implemented by the latter for MT. It will be shown in Section 2 that "it ain't necessarily so," or rather that, while basically true, it is not quite as simple as it sounds: just take linguistic rules and implement them in a computer program. This, however, should not at all lead to the opposite reaction, displayed by quite a few NLP experts and groups in the past decades, that linguistics is practically totally useless for NLP—thinking so has proven to be a very costly mistake.

Everybody who has had some practical experience in MT knows that at a certain point one has to describe and to program morphological, syntactical, and semantic rules of a natural language. Not only does linguistics possess most, if not all, of the knowledge one would need in this situation, but much of it is already preformatted and preformalized, though hardly ever in the format required for computer implementation. The alternatives to tapping this resource are listed in (3).

(3) (i) using published grammatical descriptions, which are often imperfect and always inconvenient to use, especially for a non-expert;

(ii) resorting to monolingual dictionaries, which are nothing short of disaster in coverage, methodology, selection, and consistency (bilingual dictionaries are even worse);

(iii) doing introspection, i.e., using one's own (or an associate's) native competence, which invariably leads to the reinvention of the wheel, and quite often the wheel does not even come off quite round.

In many projects, ignoring linguistics and not employing active research linguists or defectors from linguistics, some combination of (3i–iii) used to be utilized, and a heavy price was paid for that in efficiency and quality. It is increasingly fair to say that every major MT project of the 1990s involves fully credentialled linguists, a situation which is quite different from that in the previous decades. In fact, the reverse of this description also holds true: if a project employs linguists, chances are it is a serious, major project.

Typical examples of linguistic wisdom, necessary for NLP and immediately available to a linguist but not easily accessible, though certainly known in principle, to the native speaker, are listed in (4)–(19), roughly according to the level of language structure. Almost all of the examples are related to ambiguity, easily the thorniest issue in MT and NLP in general.

Phonetics and phonology, the two linguistic disciplines concerned with sound, are important primarily for MT systems with voice recognition and synthesis, that is, systems which allow oral input and produce oral output; in other words, a sentence in one language is uttered by a speaker and its translation into another language is uttered by the computer. Such systems will definitely proliferate in the near future as the voice recognition technology is perfected and made more accessible and error-free.

The written correlate of phonetics and phonology, orthography, influences those MT systems which allow and, therefore, list permissible spelling variants, such as in (4i), a very reasonable functionality for an MT system to have. Another possibility of utilizing the linguistic knowledge at this level would be treating spelling as self-correcting codes and devising a robust program which would correct a misspelling to the nearest correctly spelled word in the lexicon (this functionality is already available as an option in the recent versions of most major word processors).

However, in most languages and certainly in English, there are too many pairs of words, such as in (4ii), the distance between which is 1, i.e., their spellings differ in just one character, and self-correcting may easily lead to the wrong results. Treating spelling as an error-detecting (but not self-correcting) code is more realistic if it is based on what might be termed "graphotactics," similarly to its known oral correlate, phonotactics. The latter deals with permissible sequences of sounds in a language; the former would deal with permissible sequences of letters (or other graphemes) in the orthography of a language. A simple program based on graphotactics would rule out strings like the ones in (4iii). However, this would be taken care of to some extent also by looking up—and not finding—a word in the system's lexicon if unfamiliar words are unlikely to occur. The problem with this approach, already implemented in the spell checkers of the major word processors is that many words not found by the checker are not misspelled but rather are words not (yet) included in the limited dictionary of the checker.

(4) (i)   fulfil : fulfill, antisemitic : anti-Semitic, stone wall : stonewall;
 (ii) read : lead : bead, lane : lake : lace, lace : lack, tie : tee, tie : tip
 (iii) *rbook, *tfa, *bkate, *stocm, *haa

Morphemes, the minimal language entities which have meaning, are, in fact, the lowest level of language structure which concerns all MT and NLP directly, simply because MT, like all NLP, is interested in what the processed text means. Morphonology and morphology are the two levels dealing with the morpheme. Morphonology knows that some morphemes have different spellings (and pronunciations) but remain identical otherwise—some obvious examples are listed in (5i). Morphology contains data and rules on the various exceptions from seemingly obvious rules, along with the rules themselves. Thus, while thousands of English nouns are pluralized by adding *-(e)s* to their singular form, quite a few are not—see some representative examples in (5ii). On the other hand, a noun having the standard plural form can, in fact, be in the singular and require the singular form of a verb to agree with it, e.g., in (5iii); then again, a noun may have the plural form and require the plural form of a verb, e.g., *are,* but still denote a single object (5iv).

The concept of the zero morpheme is not trivial either—in (5v), the lack of an additional form in the first word of each group is as meaningful as the italicized additional morphemes in the other words. The zero morpheme in the three listed cases means "noun, singular, nonpossessive," "verb, present, nonthird person singular," and "adjective, positive (noncomparative, nonsuperlative) degree," respectively. In other words, in these and numerous similar situations both in English and in most other languages is that the absence of an overt morpheme may be as meaningful as the presence of one.

One also needs to know that the same morpheme in a language can have multiple meanings, each determined by its position and function. Thus, in (5vi), the same English suffix *-s* means "verb, present, third person singular," "noun, plural, nonpossessive," and the apostrophe (present only in writing, not in pronunciation) has to be counted as a regular character in order to distinguish either of these two forms from the two possessive forms, plural and singular.

(5) (i)   cap*able* : cap*ability, serene : serenity, incredible : impolite;*
 (ii) many childre*n,* sheep, syllab*i,* formul*ae,* adden*da;*

(iii) news, linguistics, statistics;

(iv) scissors, trousers;

(v) boy, boys, boy's, boys'; walk, walks, walked, walking; white, whiter, whitest;

(vi) walks, books; student's, students'.

A linguist also knows, without having to figure it out in each individual case, that there are parts of speech, such as Noun, Verb, Adjective, etc., and that each of them has a typical paradigm of word forms, listed in (5v) for the three parts of speech in question. Somewhere on the border of morphology and syntax, another piece of wisdom, potentially of great interest for NLP, looms large, namely that the same morpheme in English can signify a different part of speech as in (6).

(6) (i) John saw a big *stone*.

(ii) In some countries they *stone* adulterous women to death.

(iii) This is a *stone* wall.

Only a syntactic analysis of each sentence or at least a part of it—and not a simple morphological characteristic in the lexicon—can determine whether the word in question is a noun, a verb, or an adjective.

In syntax, the available wisdom is even more varied and complex. A few less obvious examples are listed in (7). (7i)–(7iii) are typical cases of syntactic ambiguity, paraphrased as (8i), (8ii), (9i), (9ii), and (10i)–(10iii), respectively. (7iv) and (7v) are two sentences which have a different surface structure but the same (or very similar) deep structure. (7vi) and (7vii) are examples of the opposite—the surface structure is the same but the deep structures are different; (10iv) and (10v) illustrate the difference. (7viii)–(7x) contain a verb which must be used with maximum one noun phrase (the subject only), minimum two noun phrases (the subject and the direct object), and minimum three noun phrases (the subject, the direct object, and the indirect object), respectively.

(7) (i) flying planes can be dangerous;

(ii) old men and women;

(iii) time flies;

(iv) the dog bit the man;

(v) the man was bitten by the dog;

(vi) John is eager to please;

(vii) John is easy to please;

(viii) John snores;

(ix) John sees Mary;

(x) John reminds Mary of Bill.

(8) (i) It is possible that flying planes is dangerous.

(ii) It is possible that flying planes are dangerous.

(9) (i) old men and old women;
    (ii) old men and age-unspecified women.
(10) (i) One does not notice how much time has passed.
    (ii) You there, measure the performance of flies with regard to time.
    (iii) a breed of flies called "time."
    (iv) John pleases somebody.
    (v) Somebody pleases John.

In semantics, the most important item for NLP is the homonymy of words and ambiguity of sentences. Dealing with the written language, NLP has to be concerned not only with full homonyms (11i), which are spelled and pronounced the same way and have different and unrelated meanings, but also with homographs (11ii), whose pronunciations are different, and with polysemous words (11iii), whose meanings are different but related.

(11) (i) bear1 "give birth" : bear2 "tolerate" : bear3 "wild animal";
    (ii) lead "be the leader" : lead "heavy metal";
    (iii) bachelor "unmarried man; academic degree; subservient knight; young seal without a mate."

Homonyms, homographs, and polysemous words are the usual source of purely semantic ambiguity (12i), as opposed to the purely syntactic ambiguity in (7i–ii). (7iii), however, was an example of a mixed, syntactico-semantic ambiguity, which is very common, because both the syntactic structure of the phrase and the meanings of the two words are changeable (*time* is polysemous, and *flies* homonymous). Semantics is connected with syntax and morphology in other ways as well: thus, the animal meaning of *bear, bear3* in (11i), is excluded from consideration for (12i) because it is a noun, while the syntactic structure of the sentence determines the slot as a verb.

(12ii) exhibits a much more sophisticated kind of referential/attributive ambiguity, which tends to be overlooked by non-linguists almost universally and which is important for NLP, for instance, from the point of view of whether a token in the world of the system needs to be actualized or not—in other words, whether the object exists in reality or is a hypothetical concept. (13)–(14) paraphrase the ambiguous sentences of (12i) and (12ii), respectively.

(12) (i) She cannot bear children.
    (ii) John would like to marry a girl his parents would not approve of.
(13) (i) She cannot give birth.
    (ii) She cannot stand children.

(14) (i) There exists such a girl that John would like to marry and his parents would not approve of her (referential, "real" usage).

(ii) John would only like to marry such a girl that his parents would not approve of her (attributive, "hypothetical" usage).

While almost any sentence can be ambiguous, hardly any is intended as ambiguous in normal discourse. What it means is that disambiguating devices are available to the speaker and hearer. Some of them are in the text itself, others are in the extralinguistic context, and linguistics is supposed to know about both but, in fact, knows much more about the former. (15i) contains a well-known example of a sentence containing a homonymous word, *bill*, with at least three meanings, namely, "invoice," "legal," and bird-related, and in (15ii), it is disambiguated with the help of another word, *paid*, which corroborates only the invoice meaning.

(15) (i) The bill is large.

(ii) The bill is large but does not need to be paid.

Two words corroborate, or "prime," each other's meanings if they share one or more semantic features, and the concept of semantic feature is central to contemporary semantics. In various ways, it has been incorporated into a number of formal semantic theories and into quite a few NLP lexicons. Thus, *bill* and *paid* in (15ii) share the feature of "money related" or whatever else it might be called.

The processing of a text by the native speaker and, therefore, by the computer as well depends heavily on a number of even more complicated meaning-related items, which are studied by pragmatics, the youngest and least developed area of linguistics. It is known in pragmatics that the same sentence can play different roles in discourse (these roles are known as the "illocutionary forces," and each sentence with its specific illocutionary force constitutes a "speech act"—see Searle 1969), and pragmatics studies, among many other things, the factors which determine the occurrences of speech acts in given situations. Thus, (16) can be perceived as a speech act of promise, threat, or of neutral assertion, depending on whether the hearer would rather the speaker came home early, would rather the speaker did not come home early, or does not care when the speaker comes home.

(16) I will be back early.

(17) contains an example of a sophisticated and little explored speech-act ambiguity. The same sentence (17iii) in a dialog can signify agreement or disagreement, depending on whether it is uttered in response to (17i) or (17ii), respectively. The resulting polysemy of *no* is not obvious to most native speakers.

(17) (i)   The weather is not too nice over there.
    (ii)   The weather is nice over there.
    (iii) No, it isn't.

Pragmatics is also interested in situations in which sentences are not used in their literal meanings; such usages are known as the "implicatures"—see Grice (1975). Thus, (18i), which is phrased and structured as a question, is in fact, typically, a polite request. (18ii) may be used sarcastically about an idiot. (18iii), though ostensibly laudatory, may be a sexist putdown.

(18) (i)   Can you pass me the salt?
    (ii)   He is a real genius!
    (iii) She cooks well.

The examples in (17) involve two-sentence structures, (17i) followed by (17iii) or (17ii) followed by (17iii). The structure of such sequences of sentences, or of paragraphs, which are supposed to be logically organized sequences of sentences, and of whole texts, which are sequences of paragraphs, is the major concern of text linguistics/discourse analysis (with the second term, extremely homonymous in its use, often emphasizing the structure of dialogs, or conversational strategies). This discipline is somewhat older than linguistic pragmatics but even less definite about its facts or methods. Some of the simplest examples of sentential structures are such sequences as the enumeration in (19i), the temporal sequence in (19ii), and the causal one in (19iii)—the italicized words are the connectors, which provide explicit clues as to the type of the structure.

(19) (i)   The English verb paradigm contains four basic forms. *First,* there is the infinitive form, which doubles up as the nonthird person, nonsingular form of the present. *Secondly,* there is the third person, singular form of the present. *Thirdly,* there is the past form, which doubles up as the past participle form, with the regular verbs. *Fourthly and finally,* there is the gerund form, which doubles up as the present participle form.
    (ii)   In the morning, I get up at 6. *Then* I take a shower and have breakfast.
    (iii) I cannot fall asleep as easily as other people. *Because of that,* I try to avoid drinking strong tea or coffee after 6 P.M.

All of the examples listed in (4)–(19) and many similar pieces of linguistic knowledge are more or less immediately accessible to a linguist, though some do require more sophistication, e.g., (12ii) and (17–19). All of them are related to ambiguity and therefore (at least potentially) important for MT and NLP. One serious problem for NLP is that all of these facts cannot be found in any one published source and certainly not in any acceptable form, and the only way to obtain them all when they are needed is to have a linguist around on a permanent basis. Now, the reason the written sources do not exist is not because the linguists keep the knowledge to themselves so as to sell it—and themselves—to the highest bidder but rather because of serious theoretical problems, some of which are inherent only in linguistics while others are shared with the other human studies. It is essential, therefore, for any NLP project with some concern for adequacy and efficiency, to have a linguist on the staff—and, these days, almost all of them do. A much more serious problem for NLP is that having any linguist on the staff is not enough.

2. How Not to Apply Linguistics to NLP

A linguist on the staff of an NLP project should have an immediate and errorless access to all the linguistic facts of the kind listed in Section 1 and of potential or actual importance to the project. Now, much of this information comes packaged as part of a formal grammar, i.e., as a set of rules. The linguist should be smart enough to know that the packages are not ready for use in NLP. Much of the negative attitude to linguistics on the part of NLP researchers stems from their obtaining such a package by themselves and trying to implement it directly, without the benefit of a qualified linguist's advice, simply because it looked formal and even algorithmic enough.

Qualified linguists differ from regular linguists (even good ones) in that they know the rules of correct linguistic application. These consist of general rules of applying a theory to a problem and specific rules of linguistic application.

Generally, when a source field (e.g., linguistics) is applied to the target field (e.g., MT), it is essential that the problem(s) to be solved come entirely from the latter (i.e., from MT), while the concepts and terms, ideas and methods, and the research design as a whole may be borrowed from the former (i.e., from linguistics). If, instead, the problem comes from the source field, the application is not likely to yield any insight into the target area, nor will it be of much value to the source field either, because, in most cases, this source field does not need any additional proof that a certain method works.

Thus, it is clear that statistical methods can be applied to anything that can be counted. It may be perfectly possible to determine, with a great degree of reliability, which country in the world has the greatest number of Jewish-Gypsy couples, who have two or more children and an annual income over $21,999, and by how much, but unless this answers a real question in demography, ethnography, and/or economics, the research will be a reasonably trivial statistical exercise in futility.

Similarly, linguistics can, for instance, analyze any sentence syntactically and do it pretty well. It would be rather unwise, however, to hope to get a handle to poetry and to claim that linguistics is being applied to poetics if all one did was to analyze every sentence of a poem syntactically. On the other hand, if poetics comes up with a real question concerning the role of syntactic structure in achieving a certain kind of rhythm or effect, the same syntactic methods can be used fruitfully, and a correct application of linguistics to poetics will be taking place.

In other words, as far as linguistics as the source field and NLP as the target field are concerned, no purely linguistic problem should be imposed on NLP and substituted for a real NLP need. No linguistic method should be used or linguistic description attempted to be implemented unless this is necessary for the realization of the project. Now, all of this is different if the project is, in fact, about a research model in linguistics and the computer implementation aims entirely and deliberately at verifying a linguistic model or description or checking the linguistic formalism. This is the only situation in which a straightforward implementation of, for instance, Chomsky's transformational grammar would make any sense. It is quite possible that some useful results may be obtained in the course of this kind of work for regular, non-linguistic-research-model NLP, but these gains are likely to be indirect and almost tangential. The linguistic-research models will be ignored here for the rest of the chapter.

For a real-life, non-linguistic-research project in NLP, aiming at a working system, for instance, of MT, the typical dilemma is that a good linguistic description is needed but without the forbidding-looking, cumbersome, and inaccessible packaging it typically comes with. The weathered linguist should unwrap the package for his/her NLP colleagues, separate the gems of wisdom from the wrapping, which, at best, answers some purely linguistic needs, and let the group utilize the "real thing." In order not to perform that kind of operation from scratch and on an *ad hoc* basis every time it is needed, the NLP-related linguist should be able to rely on an applied linguistic theory, specially adapted for NLP. This is exactly what computational linguistics should be about, and this is what it has been in its most successful recent manifestations.

An applied linguistic theory for NLP contains "formulae of transition," as it were, from linguistic theories and models to models and descriptions practically digestible for NLP. It should be able to distinguish between elements of language substance that NLP needs, on the one hand, and the purely linguistic representation of them, not necessarily of much use for NLP, on the other. It should be able to take into consideration the state-of-the-art methods and tools of implementation in NLP and the convenience of implementing various kinds of linguistic information with their help. In other words, such a theory should have the beneficial effect of repackaging the linguistic goods NLP wants in the way which is most convenient for NLP to use.

As an example, Postal's classic and sophisticated treatment of the English verb *remind* (1970) can be compared with what NLP is likely to need to know about it. Focusing on just one meaning of the verb as used in (20i) and deliberately excluding the meaning in (20ii) from consideration, Postal comes up with a number of sharp, even if at times controversial observations about the verb, briefly summarized in (21). He then proceeds to propose a transformational treatment for the sentences containing the verb in the likeness meaning, again briefly summarized in (22). The sentences triggering and/or resulting from the transformational process are listed in (23).

(20) (i) Harry reminds me of Fred Astaire.
    (ii) Lucille reminded me of a party I was supposed to attend.
(21) (i) The verb *remind* must be used with exactly 3 NP's in one particular syntactic structure, viz., NP1 Verb NP2 *of* NP3;
    (ii) *remind* differs further syntactically from the very few other English verbs which can be used in this structure, for instance, as per (iii);
    (iii) *remind* is unique in that no two of its three NP's can be coreferential;
    (iv) sentences with *remind* in the likeness meaning are typically paraphrased as, for instance, (20i) or (23i).
(22) (i) The standard transformational generative processes are assumed to have generated a structure like that of (23a);
    (ii) a transformation, called "the psych movement," interchanges the subject and object of the higher sentence in the structure, yielding a structure like (23ii);
    (iii) a transformation, called "the *remind* formation," changes (23ii) into (20i).
(23) (i) I perceive that Harry is like Fred Astaire.
    (ii) Harry strikes me like Fred Astaire.
(24) Harry is like Fred Astaire.

Typically for the best transformational work and very elegantly, the choice of transformations is determined primarily by the unique feature of *remind* (21ii). It is demonstrated that each of the three non-coreferences involved is not unique and is, in fact, derived from one of the transformations applied to generate (20i). One non-coreference follows from presenting the sentence as a two-clause structure with (24) as the lower clause, with similarly non-coreferential NP's. Another follows from the "psych formation," motivated independently on other English material. And the last and most problematic non-coreference is shown to follow from the *remind* formation, which is, of course, postulated specially for the task and thus not independently motivated as a whole but, in its components, related to various other independently motivated rules.

The point of the description is that the verb *remind* is derived transformationally and therefore does not exist as a surface verb. That was supposed to prove that the claims of interpretive semantics concerning deep structure and lexical insertion were false.

NLP will ignore both the theoretical point of the previous paragraph and the entire contents of the one before it. What NLP, or the applied theory catering to it, should extract from the entire description and discussion can be briefly summarized as (25).

(25) (i) *remind* has (at least) two distinct meanings illustrated in (20);
     (ii) = (21i);
     (iii) = (21iv), elaborated as (iv);
     (iv) *NP1 reminds NP2 of NP3 = NP2 perceive(s) that NP1 is (are) like NP3 = it strikes NP2 that NP1 is (are) like NP3.*

The difference between what linguistics wants to know about the English verb *remind* and what NLP must know about it has a deep theoretical foundation. Linguistics and NLP have different goals, some of which are presented schematically on the chart in (26).

(26)

LINGUISTICS WANTS:	NLP NEEDS:
(i) to know all there is to know about the complex structure mediating the pairings of sounds (spellings) and meanings in natural language;	to use the shortest and most reliable way from the spellings to the meanings in the text(s) being processed;
(ii) to structure linguistic meaning and to relate it to context;	to understand the text and make all the necessary inferences;
(iii) to distinguish the various levels of linguistic structure, each with its own elements and relations;	to use all the linguistic information needed for processing the text(s) without much concern for its source;
(iv) to draw a boundary between linguistic and encyclopedic information to delimit the extent of linguistic competence and, therefore, the limits of the discipline;	to use encyclopedic information on a par with linguistic information, if necessary for processing the text(s);
(v) to present its findings formally, preferably as a set of rules in an axiomatic theory.	to implement the available information in a practically accessible and convenient way.

The situation is complicated by the fact that, in many cases, linguistics cannot offer a definite, complete, and conclusive knowledge of the facts. Thus, in spite of the enormous and concentrated effort in transformational grammar since the early 1960s, no complete transformational grammar of English or any other natural language has been written—a fact which often surprises and disgusts NLP researchers but should not, especially because linguistics has come much closer to this grandiose task than most disciplines to theirs.

If, for instance, linguistics had fulfilled (26ii), the processes of understanding in NLP could follow the resulting structure of meaning. In reality, NLP can only incorporate the abundant but fragmentary semantic findings as "ready-made" descriptions but the qualified linguist has to help to extrapolate those to the rest of the linguistic material that NLP needs to handle. This situation is, however, fast improving (see Section 4 below).

To ignore linguistics in this situation was perhaps simpler than to use it, but it was also extremely wasteful and self-defeating. One of the signs of true progress in NLP and especially in MT achieved in the late 1980s and 1990s is that no serious NLP effort can afford to be linguist-free anymore.

To apply linguistics fruitfully and correctly, one has to be both a well-trained and weathered linguist, with considerable descriptive skills and experience of working with language material, and an accomplished NLP-er. More realistically, a working tandem of a linguist, knowledgeable about NLP and willing to shed some of his/her theoretical arrogance, and a person in NLP, enlightened enough about linguistics to be respectful but firm enough to be demanding, has turned out to be a good approximation of the ideal and a good solution to the dilemma presented in this and the previous sections. It also helps enormously for such a tandem to understand where each of them is coming from and how their perspectives differ before they make a concerted effort to adjust mutually and to proceed in NLP together (see Nirenburg 1986 for a remarkably up-to-date discussion of this complex relationship).

3. Sublanguage

One significant difference between linguistics and NLP is that while the former is concerned with language in general, the latter deals with a(n often extremely) limited part of it. In fact, the difference is much less pronounced when one realizes that, on the one hand, in practice, a linguist also deals with the descriptions of very limited fragments or manifestations of language while, on the other hand, serious NLP research always aims at significant generalizations about the whole problem beyond a limited domain. The difference is more in the emphasis on what is typically done in either field.

If the linguist had to describe a particular language or its part every time he or she wanted to publish something, the problems would be at least partially very similar to the practical headaches and hard choices faced by NLP when working on a parser and a lexicon. If, on the other hand, an NLP researcher could get away with simply theorizing about the problem, he or she would probably move much closer to theoretical linguistics—in fact, those scholars who do, do.

Typically, an NLP project deals with a limited sublanguage of natural language, such as the language of an area of science or technology—one significant recent development, also facilitated by increasingly powerful computers, is that the size of these areas, or domains, has been growing in serious NLP projects. By doing that, NLP puts linguistics even further on the spot because to be useful, it would have to shed its most important, though for the most part unconscious idealization, namely that one native speaker's competence is identical to any other's, that is, that everybody speaks and writes English—or any other language—exactly the same way, which is, of course, blatantly untrue.

It is true that there are areas in linguistics, such as dialectology, sociolinguistics, and—most recently—linguistic pragmatics, which do not subscribe to the idealization. However, the bulk of linguistics ignores the obvious fact that, in a certain empirical sense, the Chinese, English, Spanish, Hindi, Swahili, Russian, etc., languages do not exist. What exist instead in reality are the 700 million or so Mandarin Chinese idiolects (individual languages), 400 million or so English and Spanish idiolects, etc. What follows is that the rules formulated for a language may not be true of many of its dialects and idiolects; the lexicon of the language is not utilized in its entirety by any of its native speakers; the syntactic inventory available in the language is used only partially in any dialect, and so on and so forth.

It is obvious, nevertheless, that the national language exists in some less empirical and more abstract way in spite of all that—it is something that makes all those bearers of different English idiolects understand each other more or less well. However, theoretically this situation is not easy to resolve, and linguistics has largely ignored it. Raskin (1971) seems to remain the only monograph on the subject, and even that effort was geared towards a computational aim. In more practical terms, some recent efforts in NLP are characterized by a growing realization of the predominantly if not exclusively sublanguage orientation in NLP (see, for instance, Kittredge and Lehrberger 1982, Grishman and Kittredge 1986) and of the need to take advantage of the situation without shooting oneself in the foot.

What happens practically when dealing with texts from a limited sublanguage is listed in part in (27).

(27) (i)   the lexicon of the sublanguage is often limited to just a few hundred words, which is a mere fraction of 500,000 or so words in the maximum dictionary of a full-fledged multiregister national language (see (28i));

     (ii) the amount of homonymy and polysemy is reduced drastically because many meanings of potentially troublesome words go beyond the sublanguage in question (see (28ii));

(iii) the amount of extralinguistic knowledge about the world described by the sublanguage is many orders of magnitude smaller than the global knowledge of the world (see (7iii));

(iv) the inventory of syntactic constructions available in the language is used only in small part in the sublanguage (see (28iv); see also Nirenburg and Raskin 1987 and Raskin *et al.* 1997 for further discussion).

Thus, none of the words in (28i) is likely to occur in textbooks or research papers on NLP, except perhaps in examples. The words in (28ii) will lose all of their numerous computer-unrelated meanings. The piece of common-sense knowledge in (28iii) will never be used. The syntactic structure in (28iv) is unlikely to occur in any text of the sublanguage.

(28) (i)   beige, whore, carburetor, serendipity;
     (ii) operate, data, user, insert, memory;
     (iii) a person considered good-looking is likely to attract sexually other persons, primarily of the opposite sex;
     (iv) that bad—what a shame—oh, all right, what can one do?

There are two undesirable extremes in dealing with sublanguages. The first one is to ignore their limitedness and deal with each as if it were the entire language. It would seem that nobody would be likely to do that, especially given the fact, mentioned at the end of the previous section, that linguistics typically does not furnish complete descriptions of the entire languages. It is surprising, therefore, to discover many traces of the (largely unconscious) language-as-a-whole approach, manifesting itself usually as worrying about phenomena which cannot occur.

The other extreme is much more widespread because it is tempting and, in the short run, efficient. Following it, one tends to describe only what is there in the texts being processed, in a highly *ad hoc* fashion, which makes it impossible to extrapolate the description beyond the sublanguage and which makes the system extremely vulnerable in case of the occurrence of any slightly nonstandard text or even individual sentence within the same sublanguage. Thus, it would be foolish to process the word *xerox* in a sublanguage entirely on the basis of its being the only word in the lexicon beginning with an x. More plausibly, it would be nearsighted, in the computer sublanguage of English, to take advantage not only of the fact that the verb *operate* has lost all of its computer-unrelated meanings, such as the surgery meaning, but also of the fact that its only direct object in the sublanguage is *computer*. A non-*ad hoc* solution would be to define it in this meaning as having something like MACHINE as its direct object and to make COMPUTER the only "child" of machine in the sublanguage ontology (see Section 4). Then, in case of an extrapolation, it may be easier to add children to the concept MACHINE than to redefine the verb. In general, an extrapolation is much simpler to bring about with the help of a mere addition than by restructuring the description.

A wise approach to sublanguage in NLP requires, therefore, not only that information elicited from linguistics be mapped onto NLP needs but also that it be reduced in size, as it were, to ensure an economical but non-*ad hoc* description of the linguistic material.

4. Ontological Semantics

One of the most significant developments in MT and NLP in the last 7–10 years has been the willingness of increasingly numerous NLP scholars to go into meaning. It is fair to say that until the late 1980s, NLP was dominated by computational syntax, and creating the best syntactic analyzer, a.k.a "parser," was the order of the day. It finally became clearer to a majority in the NLP community what very few of us had insisted on all the time, namely, that you cannot understand what a sentence is about even if you succeed in the finest syntactic analysis of this sentence. It is not really the case that the other had failed to understand that but rather that they had hoped that syntax would provide a close enough approximation to meaning, and the reason for that hope against hope was that semantics was so hard to do. But is (29i) a reasonable approximation of (29ii)? Certainly not in MT and hardly in any other complex area of NLP.

> (29) (i) Somebody engages in an action (or enters a state) which affects somebody else.
>   (ii) My lawyer loves your plumber.

What changed the syntactic-dominance scene in NLP is two major factors: first, NLP could no longer limit itself to the development of toy systems aimed at a realization of yet another parser but rather had to engage—or attempt to engage—in real-life tasks. Secondly, increasingly more members of the NLP community discovered the joy of lexical semantics (see, for instance, Pustejovsky 1995 and references there).

Lexical semantics is a constituent part of linguistic semantics, the study of meaning in natural language. Lexical semantics deals with word meaning, and it concerns itself especially with the design and practical acquisition of lexicons, something that the field of lexicography has traditionally concerned itself with—surprisingly without much contact with linguistic semantics. By the early 1980s, the concept of "frame," or "script" became prevalent in semantics.

A frame or a script is a structured chunk of semantic information about a word, linking it to other important words bordering in various ways on its meaning. Thus, (30) is a simple representation of a script for PHYSICIAN.

(30) PHYSICIAN

Agent:	+Human, +Adult		
Agent-of:	study medicine	see patients	cure disease
Time:	many years $t < 0$,	every day $t = 0$	every day, $t = 0$
Place:	medical school	office, hospital	office, hospital

(cf. Raskin 1985b: 85; see also Raskin 1986 and references there).

NLP's best answer to the concept of script-based semantics was semantic networks (see Raskin 1990 and Raskin *et al.* 1994a,b and references there), supported by ontology (see Hobbs 1986, Nirenburg *et al.* 1995, Mahesh and Nirenburg 1995).

In natural language, linguistic entities relate to concepts and other elements outside of language. The ontological approach to semantics captures this explicitly. For every domain covered by an NLP system, a "tangled hierarchy" of concepts is suggested. The basic hierarchical relation in the ontology is the "is-a" relationship, such as (31).

(31)

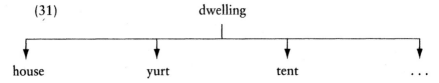

Thus, a house is a dwelling, a yurt is a dwelling, and a tent is a dwelling. Each of the words in (31) represents an ontological concept rather than an English word, and the concept can be designated by a word in any other language, a number, or an abstract symbol. Each concept is further characterized by a slotted frame, in which it is related to other concepts. Thus, HOUSE is related to LIVE-IN as a typical process affecting it, BUILD as its source, GROUND as its foundation, certain SIZES in the 3 dimensions, ROOM as its parts, etc. Similarly, a process concept, such as BUILD, has ANIMATE-OBJECT as its agent, ARTIFACT as its direct object or theme, HAMMER, NAIL, etc., as its instrument, BRICK, WOOD, etc., as its material.

Given a rich ontology of this sort, building a lexicon is much more feasible. Many nouns contain simple pointers to object concepts in the ontology: thus, one of the meanings of the English word *house* points to the concept HOUSE in (31); the other meanings of the word may contain pointers to different concepts. Similarly, many verbs point to process concepts, adjectives and adverbs to property concepts (see Raskin and Nirenburg 1995 for more examples).

In a more complex case, the lexical entry of a word combines a pointer to a concept with a constraint or a property, which may evoke other ontological concepts. Thus, the meaning of the English word *palace* points to the concept HOUSE and constrains it only to houses which are big in size, very expensive, and architecturally resplendent.

Besides helping to represent accurately the meanings of specific words, the ontology provides a language-independent foundation for the semantics of any natural language. Thus, the dwelling-related meaning of the corresponding word in any language may point to the same concept in (31).

The lexicon is only one component of NLP semantics. The other, much more complicated component combines the meanings of the words together in the sentence. This is done both on the basis of the syntax of the sentence and of the slotted frames in the concepts pointed at by the meanings of the words.

The result of this processing is the representation of the meaning of each sentence in an ontologically-based language-independent notation called the "text-meaning representation" (TMR). TMRs provide an obvious criterion for translation: if an English sentence and, say, a Russian sentence are represented as the same TMR, they are appropriate translations of each other.

This ontological-semantic approach has indeed proven to be the most promising direction in MT, and the largest resources for a non-toy MT system called MikroKosmos have been developed on this basis (see Onyshkevych and Nirenburg 1994 for a general description of the system).

5. Linguistics and Specific Issues in MT

So far, almost everything in this chapter has characterized the role of linguistics in NLP in general, and that, of course, includes MT. In the last paragraphs of the previous section, a promising approach to word and sentence meaning representation is presented as a sound basis for MT, but, by the same token, it is useful for any sophisticated NLP or AI task. In this section, we will focus specifically on those issues that arise in MT much more than in other areas of NLP.

Put somewhat differently, linguistics should be able to contribute to MT in two ways. First, within its general contribution to NLP as outlined above, since MT is primarily NLP, albeit with its own specific problems not necessarily shared by other areas of NLP. Secondly, MT should profit from an application of linguistics to a general theory of translation, no matter whether human or automatic. Only the latter aspect will be briefly commented upon in this section.

Unfortunately, linguistics has had rather little to say about translation. In fact, in the early literature on MT in the 1950s, those who claimed to be speaking for theoretical linguistics (or for the philosophy of language—see Quine 1960) argued against the feasibility of any MT and deplored any practical endeavors in this direction as impermissible short cuts, having nothing to do with the way language was. While they may have been right most of the time then, the unhelpful, standoffish attitude, resulting in virtually no attempt to look at the problem of translation from a serious linguistic perspective, was surprising. One explanation of that phenomenon could be the very limited constraints on linguistics at that time and the antisemantic attitude of the then dominant structural linguistics.

A much broader view of linguistics at present and the wealth of semantic and pragmatic wisdom accumulated in the last three decades or so, especially the spectacular progress in NLP semantics in the last decade, should have changed the situation, and it is true that these days, one notices more literature on translation appearing. However, most of the effort still comes not from linguists but rather from philosophers and philosophically minded literary scholars (especially, from the more formal schools of literary criticism) and practitioners. Much of the literature remains anecdotal, and the concerns expressed are often of a stylistic and/or aesthetic nature.

It is true that translation is not a linguistic problem *per se*—it is extraneous to the discipline. However, to the extent that translation involves the use of one or more natural languages, what linguistics knows both about language in general and about the involved language(s) cannot be ignored. Similarly to the reasoning in Section 2, the only chance for linguistics to contribute to translation is via an applied linguistic theory catering to the needs of the field, and the only chance for translation theory to succeed is to have such an applied linguistic theory at its disposal.

What is the main problem of translation theory? It can be presented as the ability to determine whether some two texts, each in a different language, are translations of each other. In order to be translations of each other, the texts should probably satisfy the following linguistic conditions (32):

(32)   Two texts in different languages are translations of each other if they have the same:
   (i)   meaning;
   (ii) illocutionary force and perlocutionary effect;
   (iii) inferences.

Obviously, (32i–iii) are interrelated, while focusing on general and specific facets of meaning. The term "perlocutionary" (see Austin 1962, and Searle 1969) is used here as an extension beyond linguistics of the notion "illocutionary," discussed in Section 2. The illocutionary force defines a sentence as a certain speech act, thus determining its role in discourse. The perlocutionary force takes this further, by dealing with the actual effects of the utterance on its audience. In other words, perlocution covers the extralinguistic effect of the text on the hearer and his/her resulting actions, moods, attitudes, etc. Perlocution is determined also by the additional factors in (33), but those go definitely even further beyond linguistics and into stylistics, rhetoric, and composition, respectively (to each of which linguistics can also be profitably applied, though again on a carefully limited basis—see, for instance, Raskin 1985a and Raskin and Weiser 1987).

(33)   Two texts in different languages are translations of each other if they have the same:
  (i) stylistic status (e.g., scholarly style);
  (ii) rhetorical effect (e.g., persuasive);
  (iii) aesthetic effect (e.g., well-written).

(It is interesting to note that the conditions in (32–33) are equally applicable to two texts in the same language, i.e., paraphrases of each other.)

Given the goal of linguistics to match the native speaker's competence, the applied linguistic theory of translation should aim at matching the bilingual native speaker's translation competence, which, of course, can only be done practically by observing and studying their performance. These observations will yield interesting results. It will become clear immediately that there is a many-to-many correspondence between texts in one language and their translations in the other. The differences between any two alternative translations will be primarily due to syntactical and semantical variations. The word-for-word translation is ruled out by morphological differences as well, and the more sophisticated morpheme-for-morpheme approach will not work out either. In decreasing degree of triviality (and increasing sophistication), (34) lists various deviations from the morpheme-for-morpheme approach in translation, and (35) illustrates them with English/Russian examples.

(34) (i)   there is no one-to-one correspondence between morphological forms in two different languages;
  (ii) syntactic structures cannot generally be copied from one language to another;
  (iii) due to differences in semantic articulation, the same word may be translated differently in two sentences;
  (iv) an element of meaning may have to be lost in translation;
  (v)   an element of meaning may have to be added in translation;
  (vi) significant changes in translation may be due to the necessity to control the "given-new," or "topic-focus" information;
  (vii) a significant rephrasing may be necessary for illocutionary reasons;
  (viii) additional information of a sophisticated pragmatic kind, e.g., the different systems of honorifics, i.e., forms of address depending on the speaker/hearer's (relative) status, may determine the outcome of translation.

(35) (i)   walk (V) = khodit', khozhu, khodish', khodim, khodite, khodyat; walk (N) = progulka, progulki, (o) progulke, progulku, progulkoy; he walked, had walked, was walking, had been walking = on gulyal;
  (ii) the train being late, he missed the meeting = poskol'ku poezd opozdal, on propustil zasedanie /because the train was late . . . /

(iii) they are romantically involved = oni neravnodushny drug k drugu /they are not indifferent to each other/;

The Soviet Union was heavily involved in Nicaragua = Sovetskiy Soyuz byl sil'no zameshan v delakh Nikaragua/ strongly mixed up in the affairs of . . . /;

(iv) I washed **my** hair—ya vymyl golovu /I washed head/;

(v) the sky was blue—nebo bylo goluboe /light blue/; are these shoes black or blue? = eti tufli chernye ili sinie? /**dark** blue/;

(vi) a man came into the room = v komnatu voshel chelovek /into room came man/;

the man came into the room = chelovek voshel v komnatu /man came into room/;

(vii) can you pass me the salt? = bud'te dobry, peredayte sol' /be (so) kind, pass salt/;

(viii) "I love you," Count X whispered to Princess Y = "Ya lyublyu Vas /polite, formal *you*/," prosheptal graf X print-zesse Y; "I love you," said Evdokim the shepherd to Agraphene the dairy maid = "Ya tebya /familiar **you**/ lyublyu," skazal pastukh Evdokim doyarke Agrafene.

The best contribution linguistics can make to translation, besides merely alerting translators to the factors in (34) and the other similar ones, is by providing, via the applied theory, the format for translation-oriented descriptions and by filling this format with information for each language.

Linguistic universals also play an important role in translation by facilitating it. Translating into a nonhuman language, i.e., an artificial or space alien language, is likely to be much harder. Thus, the English word *good* means different things when combined with different nouns: thus, in (36i–iii), *good* may mean (37i–iii), respectively,

(36) (i) good car;
      (ii) good soup;
      (iii) good book.
(37) (i) drives well;
      (ii) tastes good;
      (iii) interesting to read.

Figuring out what exactly the adjective means in each case and translating that meaning accurately into another language would be very hard. Fortunately, it is usually unnecessary because the target language is more than likely to have an equally vague adjective, designating a general positive attitude on the part of the speaker to something, and the translation possible at a superficial non-specified level (see Raskin and Nirenburg 1995:47–49 and references there).

The transition from a linguistic contribution to translation in general to a linguistic contribution to MT involves primarily the selection function. While many translations of the same text are possible, they are usually weighted on the scale from optimal to barely acceptable. The selection function assigning the weights is determined by the factors in (33) and other factors concerning, for instance, the special purpose of the text, e.g., to have a poetic effect. In MT, due to the limited nature of most projects, the selection function may often be allowed to stay strictly within the basic requirements in (32). It has been demonstrated in earlier work (Raskin 1971, 1974) that in addition to that, in limited sublanguages, some of the factors in (34) do not apply or at least not to the same extent. Thus, as far as (34ii) is concerned, all the permissible syntactical transformations of the same sentence—and in a limited sublanguage, the inventory is greatly reduced—can be treated as identical, and therefore, any variant will do, at least as long as (34vi) is not affected. (34iii) may be dropped altogether thanks to the limited lexicon. (34vii–viii) are extremely unlikely to play any significant role, either.

Conclusion

Linguistics can and must contribute a great deal to MT and NLP, and in the last decade, such a contribution has led to significant progress in these areas. The key to success is in a systematic, principled transfer of necessary information from linguistics into NLP, and this can be—and has been—achieved only within an applied theory of linguistics for NLP. The sublanguage and ontological-semantic approach offer a most promising direction in current and future research in MT and NLP. It is important to realize, however, that in both areas, and specifically in MT, evaluation criteria may have to be significantly relaxed and cruder, less subtle translations considered acceptable.

References

Austin, John L. 1962. *How to Do Things with Words*. New York–London: Oxford University Press.

Grice, H. Paul 1975. Logic and conversation. In: Peter Cole and Jerry L. Morgan (eds.), *Syntax and Semantics, Volume 3: Speech Acts*. New York: Academic Press, pp. 53–59.

Grishman, Ralph, and Richard Kittredge (eds.) 1986. *Analyzing Language in Restricted Domains*. Hillsdale, N.J.: Erlbaum.

Hobbs, Jerry R. 1986. Overview of the Tacitus project. *Computational Linguistics* 12:3, pp. 220–222.

Hutchins, W. John, and Harold L. Somers 1992. *An Introduction to Machine Translation*. London–New York: Academic Press.

Kittredge, Richard, and John Lehrberger (eds.) 1982. *Sublanguage: Studies of Language in Restricted Semantic Domains.* Berlin–New York: Walter de Gruyter.

Mahesh, Kavi, and Sergei Nirenburg 1995. A situated ontology for practical NLP. A paper presented at the IJCAI '95 Workshop on Basic Ontological Issues in Knowledge Sharing. Montreal.

Nirenburg, Sergei 1986. Linguistics and artificial intelligence. In: Peter C. Bjarkman and Victor Raskin (eds.), *The Real-World Linguist: Linguistic Applications in the 1980's.* Norwood, N.J.: Ablex, pp. 116–144.

Nirenburg, Sergei, and Victor Raskin 1987. The subworld concept lexicon and the lexicon management system. *Computational Linguistics* 13:3–4, pp. 276–289.

Nirenburg, Sergei, Victor Raskin, and Boyan Onyshkevych 1995. Apologiae ontologiae. In: Judith Klavans, Bran Boguraev, Lori Levin, and James Pustejovsky (eds.), *Representation and Acquisition of Lexical Knowledge: Polysemy, Ambiguity, and Generativity.* AAAI Spring Symposium Series. Stanford: Stanford University, pp. 95–107.

Onyshkevych, Boyan, and Sergei Nirenburg 1995. The Lexicon in the Scheme of KBMT Things. Memoranda in Computer and Cognitive Science MCCS-94–277. Las Cruces, N.M.: New Mexico State University. Reprinted in *Machine Translation* 10, 1995.

Postal, Paul M. 1970. On the surface verb *remind. Linguistic Inquiry* 1:1, pp. 20–37.

Pustejovsky, James 1995. *The Generative Lexicon.* Cambridge, MA: MIT Press.

Quine, Willard V. O. 1960. *Word and Object.* Cambridge, MA: MIT Press.

Raskin, Victor 1971. *K teorii yazykovykh podsistem/Towards a Theory of Linguistic Subsystems.* Moscow: Moscow State University Press.

Raskin, Victor 1974. On the feasibility of fully automatic high quality machine translation. *American Journal of Computational Linguistics* 11:3, Microfiche 9.

Raskin, Victor 1985a. On possible applications of script-based semantics. In: Peter C. Bjarkman and Victor Raskin (eds.), *The Real-World Linguist: Linguistic Applications in the 1980's.* Norwood, N.J.: Ablex, pp. 19–45.

Raskin, Victor 1985b. *Semantic Mechanisms of Humor.* Dordrecht–Boston: D. Reidel.

Raskin, Victor 1986. Script-based semantic theory. In: Donald G. Ellis and William A. Donohue (eds.), *Contemporary Issues in Language and Discourse Processes.* Hillsdale, N.J.: Erlbaum, pp. 23–62.

Raskin, Victor 1990. Ontology, sublanguage, and semantic networks in natural language processing. In: Martin C. Golumbic (ed.), *Advances in Artificial Intelligence: Natural Language and Knowledge-Based Systems.* New York–Berlin: Springer, pp. 114–128.

Raskin, Victor, Donalee H. Attardo, and Salvatore Attardo 1994a. The SMEARR semantic database: An intelligent and versatile resource for the humanities. In: Don Ross and Dan Brink (guest eds.), *Research In Humanities Computing 3.* Series ed. by Susan Hockey and Nancy Ide. Oxford: Clarendon Press, pp. 109–24.

Raskin, Victor, Salvatore Attardo, and Donalee H. Attardo 1994b. Augmenting formal semantic representation for NLP: The story of SMEARR. *Machine Translation* 9:2, pp. 81–98.

Raskin, Victor, and Sergei Nirenburg 1995. Lexical Semantics of Adjectives: A Microtheory of Adjectival Meaning. Memoranda in Computer and Cognitive Science MCCS-95–288. Las Cruces, N.M.: New Mexico State University.

Raskin, Victor, Sergei Nirenburg, and Svetlana Sheremetyeva 1997. *Sublanguages, Minitheories, and Case Studies*. Dordrecht–Boston: Kluwer (forthcoming).

Raskin, Victor, and Irwin Weiser 1987. *Language and Writing: Applications of Linguistics to Rhetoric and Composition*. Norwood, N.J.: Ablex.

Searle, John R. 1969. *Speech Acts*. Cambridge: Cambridge University Press.

Content Questions

1. Why can't machine translation be achieved by putting a bilingual dictionary on computer and having that computer just translate word for word between the two languages?

2. To what extent do machine translation projects now involve linguists?

3. Raskin provides a number of examples related to what he says is the "thorniest" issue in machine translation (MT) and natural language processing (NLP). What is that issue?

4. With regard to NLP and morphology, what kinds of problems surround the use of plurals in English? What other important morphological considerations for NLP does Raskin mention?

5. What are the three "typical" examples of syntactic ambiguity that Raskin provides?

6. A word such as *bill* can have more than one meaning. How does a word such as *paid* prime a particular meaning of *bill* in a sentence like "The bill is large but does not need to be paid"?

7. What kinds of interpretive problems can utterances such as "He is a real genius," or "Can you pass me the salt?" pose to natural language processing?

8. What is a sublanguage? Why would the translation of texts limited to a particular sublanguage reduce the potential for NLP problems related to homonymy, polysemy, "extralinguistic knowledge," and syntax?

9. Describe the relationship between semantic networks and NLP.

Questions for Analysis and Discussion

1. Consider the way in which a program utilizing graphotactics would identify misspelled words. Contrast this with how most computer programs approach the problem of spell checking.

2. Why could the illocutionary force of an utterance pose particular problems for machine translation?

3. What does Raskin say a linguist must be able to do in order to be useful to a natural language processing project? How does this relate to the metaphor Raskin uses of unwrapping a package?

4. What does the example with the word *remind* show about how a linguist in an NLP or MT project needs to be able to extract useful knowledge from linguistic research that is directed toward other goals?

5. How would a machine translation project benefit from having a knowledgeable linguist on the team?

6. How close is the field of NLP to the kinds of capabilities shown in science fiction films in which a computer can carry on a normal conversation with a human speaker?

Additional Activities and Paper Topics

1. Make a list of twenty idioms in English. Next interview a native or very fluent speaker of another language and compare how those idioms would be expressed in the other language. Provide the closest English approximation of how that idiom would be expressed in the other language. Then summarize some of your observations about the differences in the two languages. (**Morphology and Syntax**)

2. Assume that you have been able to input all of the English rules about pronunciation, morphology, vocabulary, and syntax into a computer to prepare it for natural language processing. Now prepare a report explaining what kinds of semantic, pragmatic, and discourse concerns remain and must be addressed in your work in order to help the computer to more closely resemble a human speaker's capacity for language. (**Semantics and Pragmatics**)

3. Interview someone who is bilingual or very fluent in another language. Ask him or her about what kinds of problems could result from a completely literal translation between English and the other language. Then prepare a small report on what some of the specific differences are in the two languages and how those differences could lead to problems if a translation is carried out by inexperienced translators.

4. Locate two different English translations of the same work. Discuss some of the types of differences that you notice between the two versions as the translators have chosen to render the text into English. You might refer back to some of the issues identified in Noss's article. Your analysis should go well beyond word choice and might consider such issues as register, style, syntactic complexity, and whether the translation appears to be literal or not.

5. Collect some jokes, bumper stickers, and advertisements. Then consider a non-English-speaking culture into which these items might be translated. Prepare a report that discusses how well you think that each of those items might be translated into the other culture's language. Comment on the kinds of factors that would make some of those items virtually impossible to translate with the same effect that they have in English. Remember also that some translation difficulties result more from cultural than linguistic differences.

Linguistics and Language Instruction

Much of the focus in linguistic research is directed toward language teaching and language acquisition. In fact, many people, including many linguists, have narrowed the scope of the term *applied linguistics* to the point of being synonymous with language teaching or its related concerns. Such a specialized use of the term reflects the importance of language teaching in linguistics. The articles in this chapter are primarily concerned with teaching English as a Second Language (ESL) or English as a Foreign Language (EFL), but the types of concerns or issues they address could be important to other language teachers as well.

Knowing a foreign language involves more than knowing proper pronunciation, vocabulary, and sentence formation. There are also important discourse functions that must be learned. In the first article of this chapter, "Compliments in Cross-Cultural Perspective," Nessa Wolfson notes the differences among cultures with regard to their expectations, use, and formation of compliments. She also reports on a collection of data that specifically shows how compliments are formed in American English. This study reveals some interesting patterns that indicate that compliment behavior in American English typically adheres to a restricted set of lexical and syntactic options. Wolfson describes these structures and indicates how this information could be useful to ESL or EFL students.

Current linguistic research related to language pedagogy emphasizes the importance of helping to develop communicative competence in students. This competence includes conversational skills that might be difficult for nonnative speakers to acquire without some instruction. In "Teaching Conversational Skills Intensively: Course Content and Rationale," Zoltán Dörnyei and Sarah Thurrell outline and discuss a number of discourse and conversational issues that English language teachers should address in their classroom curriculum. The information in this article provides some idea of the scope of material that should be considered by language teachers to help their students achieve greater fluency.

Marianne Celce-Murcia's article "Discourse Analysis and Grammar Instruction" considers the continued importance of grammar teaching, despite the increased emphasis among teachers on the functional aspects of language. She argues that, contrary to what some mistakenly believe about grammar, it is not merely a sentence-level phenomenon but maintains a significant relationship with larger discourse concerns.

In "Applied Linguistics: The Use of Linguistics in ESL," Christina Bratt Paulston examines the contributions of linguistics to language teaching, providing some conclusions based on a survey of some teachers of English about the aspects of their linguistic training they have found to be most useful. She also discusses some important linguistic research related to language teaching and briefly mentions some language teaching approaches and methods that have been applied in the classroom.

Extensive research has been done and continues to be done to answer questions about how people learn languages and what kinds of methods or approaches to language teaching would be the most effective. Some of the research investigates psycholinguistic concerns such as appropriate learning sequences or the validity of various theories of language learning. Other research examines cross-cultural or social factors related to language learning or acquisition. In addition, some research looks at how language is actually used by native speakers and tries to provide the most accurate and complete description of a language—a preliminary but necessary contribution toward the teaching of a language to nonnative speakers.

Compliments in Cross-Cultural Perspective

Nessa Wolfson

Speech acts vary widely across cultures, both in their structural forms as well as in the conventions regarding their usage. In this article, the late Nessa Wolfson of the University of Pennsylvania has reported on some of her research involving the specific speech act of complimenting in English. After illustrating how compliments differ across cultures, her article describes some of the lexical and structural characteristics of compliments in American English. Her research has some direct applications to English language teaching. This article originally appeared in the *TESOL Quarterly*, a journal that addresses itself primarily to professionals involved in the field of teaching English to nonnative speakers of the language.

It is well known that languages differ greatly from one another in their patterns and norms of interaction. Up to now, however, there has been very little systematic comparison of language from the points of view of speech acts and rules of speaking. The speech act of complimenting, as an example of the kind of sociolinguistic information needed in order to understand the problems of language learners, is here examined in some detail. The semantic and syntactic structure of compliments in American English is described and comparisons are made with complimenting behavior in other cultures.

Communicative competence is now widely recognized as an important goal of language teaching, and a good deal has been written concerning the necessity of making knowledge about sociolinguistic rules a part of classroom instruction in ESL or, indeed, in any second language (Hymes 1972b, Grimshaw 1973, Paulston 1974, Applegate 1975, Taylor and Wolfson 1978). At the same time, sociolinguistic studies, particularly those which take as their rhetorical framework the ethnography of speaking as proposed by Dell Hymes (1962), have made it clear that languages differ greatly in patterns and norms of interaction. Up to this point, however, there has been very little systematic comparison of languages from the point of view of speech acts and rules of speaking, and as a result, very little attention paid to describing the sorts of communicative interference[1] which may occur as people learn second languages.

---

[1]Communicative interference refers to misunderstandings which result from the transfer of rules of speaking from the speaker's L1 to the L2, parallel to interference on the phonological or syntactic levels. I owe this term to Dell Hymes (personal communication).

As an example of the sort of sociolinguistic information needed in order to understand the problems facing second language learners, it is useful to examine in some detail one speech act: complimenting. For the past three years, my colleague Joan Manes and I have been engaged in a thoroughgoing analysis of complimenting behavior in American English (Wolfson and Manes in press, Manes and Wolfson in press). For the purposes of comparison, we included in our corpus a small sample of compliments collected by non-native speakers of English interacting with members of their own speech communities, both in English and in their native languages.

Examination of these data makes it clear that a single speech act may vary greatly across speech communities. In particular, what counts as a compliment may differ very much from one society to another. Even allowing for problems of translation, some of the data which were collected by non-native speakers were totally unlike those gathered by native speakers of American English. Thus, an Indonesian student brought the following examples of compliments which he had heard in Indonesian and translated:

(1) s (HUSBAND): You must have been tired doing all the shopping.
    A (WIFE): Is it so? Now you can do the cooking.
(2) s (FRIEND): You have bought a sewing machine. How much does it cost?
    A: Oh, it is cheap. It's a used one. My wife needs it badly.
(3) s: You've saved a lot of money in your account, ha?
    A: Oh, no. Please don't tease me.

Of course, one could conclude from looking at these data that the non-native speaker had simply not understood the meaning of the term compliment in English. This hypothesis was unacceptable, however, since the Indonesian data, and indeed every set of data, included at least a few examples which were immediately recognizable to the English speaker as compliments:

(4) s (FRIEND): You have a nice one-room apartment.
    A: Yes. The rent is expensive. It is a burden.
(5) s (FRIEND INVITED TO DINNER): The food is delicious. I am full.
    A (HOSTESS): If you come again next time, I'll prepare the same food.

Compliments such as these which concern a nice apartment and good food are easy for English speakers to accept as falling within the category of compliments. It is much more difficult for us to understand why it is complimentary in Indonesian to mention that a friend has bought a sewing machine, saved money or done a lot of shopping. From conversations with one of the Indonesians who had collected data, it became clear that these remarks were given and interpreted as compliments because they implied approval of the addressee's accomplishments. Further discussion revealed that although a term for complimenting exists in Indonesian, native speakers feel that they occur relatively rarely and usually only among the educated who have been exposed to Western customs. Rural people, I was assured, rarely employ this speech act form.

In contrast with these Indonesian examples, the data collected and translated by native speakers of Japanese exhibit a great deal of resemblance to American English compliments:

> (6) s: The hat is really good. It suits you very well.
>   a: Oh, is that right? It's warm.
> (7) s: This is nice. Did you buy it in New York?
>   a: No, it's old. There's something wrong with the strap.
> (8) s: Oh, you have a nice dress on, Mrs. A.

That there is so much similarity between Japanese and American compliments must not lead us to assume that the realization of this speech act is identical in the two societies. As in the Indonesian data, some of the material collected as compliments in Japanese would certainly not be considered complimentary by a speaker of American English:

> (9) s: Your earrings are pure gold, aren't they?
>   a: Yes, they are. They must be pure gold when you put them on.
>   s: Money is a necessary condition to become attractive, indeed.
>   a: I think so too.

For speakers of American English it is difficult to accept the idea that it is considered complimentary to suggest that another's attractiveness depends on having money. When Japanese (or indeed any non-native) speakers produce compliments which conform to the rules of speaking for American English, the assumption is that they share these rules, and their deviations. Such deviations may therefore be more harshly interpreted than might rule-breaking from a speaker who clearly follows a very different system. Thus, the very fact that such similarities exist may lead to more serious misunderstandings than would otherwise occur.

Misunderstandings, of course, work in both directions. If we look at some data from American English, we can see that some of the comments that Americans regularly accept as compliments could easily seem very insulting to someone who understood the words but not the rules for interpreting them. For example, we have compliments by which the speaker, in saying that the addressee looks unusually well, implies that the reverse is usually the case. Thus, two men meet at an elevator and one says to the other:

> (10) s: Hey, what's the occasion? You look really nice today.

Or two friends meet and one greets the other by exclaiming:

> (11) s: Wow! Linda! What did you do to your hair? I almost didn't recognize you. It looks great.

Although Americans do not seem to take such remarks as anything but compliments, non-native speakers are often unsure of their meaning. Indeed, when a French speaker, living in this country while doing her graduate work and fully bilingual in English, received just such a compliment from a classmate, she assumed that an insult had been intended and was quite hurt.

Another noticeable contrast between American English compliments and those collected and translated by speakers of certain other languages is the difference in the use of proverbs and other precoded ritualized phrases. Compliments collected by Iranian and Arabic speakers exemplify this point particularly well. In a conversation between two Jordanian women, for instance, one says about still a third woman:

> (12) s: X is a nice girl and beautiful.

Her friend, in order to express the view that the speaker is even more beautiful, responds with a proverb:

> A: Where is the soil compared with the star?

In complimenting her friend's child, an Arabic speaker says:

> (13) s: She is like the moon and she has beautiful eyes.

And from an exchange between two Iranian friends, we have the following:

> (14) s: Your shoes are very nice.
> A: It is your eyes which can see them which are nice.

while an Iranian boy says to his mother:

> (15) s: It was delicious, Mom. I hope your hands never have pain.
> A: I'm glad you like it.

While it is true that Americans do not make use of such proverbs and set phrases in giving compliments, we do use a very restricted set of lexical and syntactic structures. And just as proverbs and ritualized phrases would have to be learned by anyone who wanted to communicate appropriately in Arabic or Farsi, so a learner of American English must become familiar with the appropriate syntactic structures and lexical items used in compliments in this society.

In order to make comparisons between the way compliments function in English and in other languages, or indeed even to begin to teach the rules of speaking for English, we must first have analyses of the patterns which govern the way English speakers use their language. In their study of complimenting behavior in American English, Manes and Wolfson (in press) discovered that one of the most striking features of compliments in American English is their almost total lack of originality.[2] An initial examination of a large corpus revealed surprising repetitiveness in both the object of the compliments and the lexical items used to describe them. On closer investigation, it was discovered that regularities exist on all levels and that compliments are in fact formulas.

It is obvious that since compliments are expressions of positive evaluation, each must include at least one term which carries positive semantic load. What is not obvious and could not have been predicted is that, notwithstanding the enormous number and variety of such positive terms in English, the overwhelming majority of compliments fall within a highly restricted set of adjectives and verbs.

We may categorize 80% of all compliments in the data as adjectival in that they depend on an adjective for their positive semantic value. In all, some seventy-two positive adjectives occur in the data and there is no doubt that if further data were collected, a great many more such adjectives would appear. What is striking, however, is that of these seventy-two adjectives only five (*nice, good, beautiful, pretty* and *great*) are used with any frequency. While most adjectives occur only once or twice in the data, these five adjectives occur with such frequency that of all adjectival compliments in the corpus two-thirds make use of only these five adjectives.

The two most common adjectives found in compliments are *nice* and *good,* occurring in 22.9% and 19.6% of the data, respectively. The fact that both these adjectives are semantically vague makes it possible for speakers to use them in connection with an almost unlimited variety of nouns:

(16) Your apartment's nice.
(17) Hey, that's a nice-looking bike.
(18) That's a nice piece of work.
(19) You have a very nice wife.
(20) That's a nice blouse.

and

(21) That's a good question.
(22) You're such a good cook.

---

[2] The data upon which this analysis is based consist of six hundred and eighty-six compliments gathered in a great variety of naturally occurring speech situations which the researchers observed or in which they participated. Careful attention was paid to recording information concerning the relationship between speakers and addressees, as well as their occupation, approximate age and sex.

(23) You sound good on tape.
(24) Mm. The chocolate sauce is good.

The other three most common adjectives, *beautiful, pretty* and *great,* appear in 9.7%, 9.2% and 6.2% of all adjectival compliments in the data. While *pretty* is somewhat more specific than the others, all may be seen to occur in conjunction with a great many different topics:

(25) You did a beautiful job of explaining that.
(26) You have such a beautiful baby.
(27) Your tie is really beautiful.
(28) Gosh, you have a beautiful living room.

and

(29) That was a really great meal.
(30) Your hair looks great that way.
(31) Your apartment looks great.
(32) You're doing a great job.

and

(33) You look pretty today.
(34) That suit is very pretty.
(35) Are those new glasses? They're pretty.

The extremely high frequency of these five adjectives in American English compliments may be very useful to language teachers and learners. The point is, of course, that learners may with perfect appropriateness make use of the members of this set to speak of very nearly any topic in a complimentary statement. What we have here is in effect a semantic formula and it would be well for learners to be made aware of it.

While 80% of all compliments in the corpus are of the adjectival type, compliments which make use of verbs to carry the positive semantic evaluation also occur:

(36) I like your bookcase.
(37) I really like your hair that way.
(38) I love your outfit.
(39) I really enjoyed your talk.

The only two verbs which occur with any frequency in compliments of this type are *like* and *love* and these occur in 86% of all compliments which contain a semantically positive verb. As with adjectives, most other positive verbs occur only once or twice in the data. Here again we find speakers of American English making use of what amounts to a semantic formula:

[like]
[love] NP

When we turn to syntactic patterns, we see that compliment structure is even more highly patterned here than on the semantic level. *To be precise, 53.6% of the compliments in the corpus make use of a single syntactic pattern:*

NP [is]
   [looks] (really) ADJ

(e.g. You look good, Your pin looks nice like that, This chicken is great, hon). In addition to this one major pattern, two others:

I (really) [like] NP
          [love]

(e.g. I like your shirt, I love your blouse)

and

PRO is (really) (a) ADJ NP

(e.g. That's a good system, That's a very nice briefcase) account for an additional 16.1% and 14.9% of the data, respectively. Thus, only three patterns are required to describe 85% of the compliments found. Indeed, only nine patterns occur with any regularity and these nine account for 97.2% of all the data in the corpus.

The fact that in a corpus of nearly seven hundred naturally occurring compliments in American English 85% of the data fall into only three syntactic patterns is information which can clearly be put to good use in ESL classrooms. Indeed, pilot lessons have already been taught at both intermediate and advanced levels with excellent results. When learners are given the three major syntactic patterns and the five most frequently found adjectives, they have little difficulty in producing compliments which conform to the patterns used by native speakers.

Unlike other formulaic expressions such as those for thanks and greetings, the formulaic compliment is not explicitly recognized by native speakers of American English. Indeed, it is for precisely this reason that the sort of systematic ethnographic study which underlies the analysis presented here is so important. The fact is that speech act patterns—or more generally, rules of speaking—are not only very different from culture to culture but are also largely unconscious. For this reason, native speakers who themselves follow all the rules are quite unlikely to recognize that such patterns exist. It is only through the collection and analysis of large amounts of naturally occurring speech (i.e. sociolinguistic analysis) that it is possible to uncover the patterns of speaking which exist in any society, including one's own.

Speech acts differ cross-culturally not only in the way they are realized but also in their distribution, their frequency of occurrence, and in the functions they serve. In American English, compliments occur in a very wide variety of situations. They are quite frequent and they serve to produce or to reinforce a feeling of solidarity between speakers, as Wolfson and Manes (in press) have shown. Compliments also serve other functions: they are used in greeting, thanking, and apologizing, or even as substitutes for them. They also serve as a way of opening a conversation. The frequency of compliments in American English is often remarked upon by foreigners. Comments are often heard from non-native speakers that Americans do an excessive amount of complimenting. People from cultures which are less open in expressions of approval are often extremely embarrassed by this.

Not only are there differences in frequency, but also distribution varies a great deal from culture to culture. Americans give compliments in situations where the compliment would be totally inappropriate in other cultures. A particularly interesting example of this came about recently when an American politician visiting France happened to compliment one of the members of the French government on the job he was doing. The French were very annoyed and articles appeared in the French press attributing all sorts of hidden implications to the act and condemning it as interference in French internal affairs. In reality, of course, the visiting American politician had done no more than the typical American would do when trying to be friendly to a stranger: give a compliment.

Thus we see that complimenting behavior varies cross-culturally along a number of dimensions. It may be extremely frequent, as in our own culture, or it may hardly exist at all, as among the Indonesians. It may be realized as a formula or even as a ritualized pre-coded phrase or a proverb. It may well be uninterpretable cross-culturally since the values and attitudes it expresses vary so much from one society to another.

The theoretical importance of recognizing this variation is that it points to the need for sociolinguistic descriptions of language in use. If true communication is to take place among people who come from differing cultural backgrounds, and if interference is to be minimized in second language learning, then we must have cross-cultural comparisons of rules of speaking. That is, contrastive analysis must be generalized to include not only the level of form but also the level of function.

References

Applegate, Richard B. 1975. The language teacher and rules of speaking. *TESOL Quarterly* 9:271–282.

Grimshaw, Allen D. 1973. Rules, social interaction, and language behavior. *TESOL Quarterly* 7:99–115.

Hymes, Dell. 1962. The ethnography of speaking. In *Anthropology and human behavior*. T. Gladwin and William C. Sturtevant (Eds.). Washington, D.C.: Anthropological Society of Washington.

Hymes, Dell. 1972b. On communicative competence. In J. B. Pride and Janet Holmes (Eds.), *Sociolinguistics*. Harmondsworth, England: Penguin Books: 269–293.

Manes, Joan, and Nessa Wolfson. In press. The compliment formula. To appear in F. Coulmas (Ed.) *Conversational Routines. Janua Linguarum.* Mouton.

Paulston, Christina Bratt. 1974. Developing communicative competence: goals, procedures and techniques. Paper delivered at the Lackland Air Force Base, English Language Branch, Defense Language Institute.

Taylor, Barry P. and Nessa Wolfson. 1978. Breaking down the free conversation myth. *TESOL Quarterly* 12:31–39.

Wolfson, Nessa. 1976. Speech events and natural speech: some implications for sociolinguistic methodology. *Language in Society* V, 2.

Wolfson, Nessa, and Joan Manes. In press. The compliment as a social strategy. To appear in *Papers in Linguistics*.

Content Questions

1. Consider the specific practices associated with speech acts. How universal are they?

2. In a cross-cultural exchange of compliments, why could there be even more potential for misunderstanding between two cultures that share many of the same practices than between two cultures that have few similarities?

3. What kind of compliment used among American English speakers does Wolfson indicate might be offensive to people from other cultures?

4. According to the study described in this article, which five adjectives do two-thirds of all adjectival compliments use?

5. Which two of those five adjectives were used the most in the study? What semantic characteristic in those two adjectives allows them to be used with many different kinds of nouns?

6. Compliments using "semantically positive" verbs are not as common as those with adjectives. But when they do occur, which two verbs account for 86 percent of that type in the study?

7. From a syntactic point of view, which three patterns account for 85 percent of all compliments in the study?

8. To what extent are native speakers consciously aware of the lexical and syntactic forms involved in their compliments?

9. How does the frequency of compliments differ from one culture to another? What about the situations in which they are used?

Questions for Analysis and Discussion

1. Native speakers have no trouble forming compliments. Why would they then benefit from learning about how they form compliments before they teach nonnative students of English?

2. Why is it significant for ESL teachers that many of the compliments used by American English speakers typically utilize a small number of adjective or verb forms?

3. What other kinds of speech acts do you think an ESL teacher might need to teach to students? What differences among other cultures are you aware of with these speech acts?

Teaching Conversational
Skills Intensively:
Course Content and Rationale

Zoltán Dörnyei and Sarah Thurrell

In the last two decades linguists have given much attention to the importance of communicative competence, including the discourse and conversational matters involved in this competence. Two scholars contributing
to the work in this area are Zoltán Dörnyei and Sarah Thurrell, both of
Eötvös Lorand University in Budapest, Hungary. In the following article,
which first appeared in the *English Language Teaching Journal,* they discuss important information to be considered and addressed in the curriculum of a course that seeks to help students learn conversational skills.
The article presents specific conversational strategies and structures, as
well as the social and cultural factors that a conversational course should
integrate.

*With the teaching of conversational skills a major objective of current com-
municative language teaching, conversation classes are becoming widespread. However, teachers are often unsure about which topic areas they
should focus on, with the result that many of their conversation classes
tend to be characterized by a random, intuition-based selection of general
communicative activities. Drawing on the results of oral discourse theory
and conversation analysis, this paper begins by providing a list of conversational teaching points to serve as a menu for teachers as they design a
syllabus for their classes. It goes on to discuss how these conversational issues can be taught in practice.*

Introduction

One of the biggest challenges to current language teaching methodology is
to find effective ways of preparing students for spontaneous communication. As one answer to this challenge, a new type of language lesson, the
conversation class, has appeared, whose main teaching objective is to improve the students' conversational skills.

In spite of the growing popularity of such conversation classes, they
are often not systematic enough, having been put together from a random
variety of communicative activities. The teachers running these courses can

hardly be blamed for this, because while communicative language teaching methodology has offered detailed guidelines for how to create genuine communicative situations in the language classroom, it has failed to specify which conversational skills and what kind of language input we should focus on. This paper addresses these issues by providing an overview of the relevant parts of oral discourse theory and conversation analysis, and then discusses how the selected conversational teaching points can be presented and practised in the language classroom.

Conversation and Conversational Skills

Many people believe that informal everyday conversation is random and unstructured. This is, in fact, far from true. Although conversation may take many forms and the speakers and situations vary widely, all conversation follows certain patterns. There are, for example, subtle rules determining who speaks and when, and for how long. By following these rules, people in conversation can take turns neatly, and avoid overlaps and simultaneous talk.

There are also rituals and set formulae for starting or closing a conversation and for changing the subject. There are conventions prescribing how to interrupt and how to hold the floor, and even determining which style is most appropriate in a given situation. These conventions are fairly strong and consistent within a given culture: when someone breaks them, people can tell immediately that something has gone wrong.

The analysis of the rules that govern conversation has been of great interest to linguists over the last two decades (for a detailed discussion see, for example, Brown and Yule, 1983; Cook, 1989; Richards, 1990). We now know that conversation is a highly organized activity which requires certain skills on the part of the speakers. This is why language learners who are familiar with the grammar of a language and know a vast amount of vocabulary may still "fail," that is, let themselves down in real conversation. They may need practice in the specialized skills that determine conversational fluency.

Two Approaches to Teaching Conversational Skills

The Indirect Approach

As Richards (1990:76) points out, there are currently two major approaches to teaching conversational skills. One is an indirect approach, "in which conversational competence is seen as the product of engaging learners in conversational interaction" such as situational role plays, problem-solving tasks, and information-gap exercises. This approach was typical of communicative language teaching in the 1980s.

The Direct Approach

The second, the direct approach, "involves planning a conversation programme around the specific microskills, strategies, and processes that are involved in fluent conversation" (ibid.:77). This approach therefore handles conversation more systematically than the indirect approach, and aims at fostering the students' awareness of conversational rules, strategies to use, and pitfalls to avoid, as well as increasing their sensitivity to the underlying processes.

The direct approach also involves providing the learners with specific language input. For example, there are many fixed expressions or conversational routines that crop up constantly in natural conversation. Polished conversationalists are in command of hundreds of such phrases and use them, for example, to break smoothly into a conversation, to hold the listener's interest, to change the subject, to react to what others say, and to step elegantly out of the conversation when they wish. Widdowson (1989:135) goes as far as to say that a great part of communicative competence is merely a matter of knowing how to use such conventionalized expressions, or as he terms them, "partially preassembled patterns" and "formulaic frameworks." These lend themselves ideally to explicit teaching, and can serve as important language input for conversation classes.

A Classification of Conversational Issues

In order to design the content of a conversation course, we must specify the relevant issues. We chose four topic areas as a result of reviewing research findings from linguistic fields such as discourse analysis, conversation analysis, communicative competence research, sociolinguistics, and pragmatics, and after considering them from a practical perspective. They are:

—conversational rules and structure

—conversational strategies

—functions and meaning in conversation

—social and cultural contexts.

We describe below the issues which fall under these four topic areas, many of which, as already stated, are realized in conversation by means of a specific set of typical conversational phrases and routines. We provide examples taken from *Conversation and Dialogues in Action* (Dörnyei and Thurrell, 1992), a language teacher's resource book that has been entirely based on this structure. Other publications that contain useful language input material for conversation courses are Keller and Townsend-Warner (1976, 1979, 1988), Jones (1981), Blundell, Higgens, and Middlemiss (1982), and Golebiowska (1990).

Conversational Rules and Structure

Conversational rules and structure have to do with how conversation is organized, and what prevents it from continually breaking down into a chaos of interruptions and simultaneous talk. The following points may be particularly relevant to a conversation course:

1. *Openings:* There are many ways of starting a conversation, and most of them are fairly ritualized as, for example, in different sequences of greetings and introductions (e.g. *How are you? / Fine thanks. And you?*). Other ways of initiating a chat include questions (*Excuse me, do you know ...?*), comments on something present (*That's a nice little dog ...*) or on the weather (*At last some sunshine!*), general complaints (*The traffic in this city is simply incredible ...*), social lines (*Great party, isn't it?*), etc. Students often don't know that they can turn a factual exchange (like buying something in a shop) into an informal conversation quite naturally by using some of these openings.

2. *Turn-taking:* How do people know when to speak in conversations so that they don't all talk at the same time? There are, in fact, some subtle rules and signals to determine who talks, when, and for how long, and these rules have been labelled "turn-taking mechanisms." The language classroom does not offer too many opportunities for students to develop their awareness of turn-taking rules or to practise turn-taking skills. This is unfortunate, since for many students— especially those from cultures whose turn-taking conventions are very different from those in the target language—turn-taking ability does not come automatically, and needs to be developed consciously through awareness-raising observation and listening tasks involving videoed and/or taped authentic conversation.

3. *Interrupting:* One special case in turn-taking is interrupting, which is a definite conversational blunder in many cultures. In English, a certain amount of interruption is tolerated (especially when the purpose is to sort out some problem of understanding), but too much, or in the wrong situation, appears rude. Interruptions are almost always introduced by set phrases (e.g. *Sorry to interrupt, but ...* or *Sorry, but did I hear you say ...?*), which, depending on how they are introduced into the conversation, provide polite and natural ways of performing this rather delicate task. Students should be familiar with such phrases.

4. *Topic-shift:* When we want to change the subject, either because we don't want to talk about a certain topic any longer or because we want to introduce a new topic, certain conversational routines such as *Oh, by the way ...* or *That reminds me of ...* come in very handy. Skimming over a considerable number of topics in a short

span of time is, in fact, a characteristic feature of informal conversation, and it is important that students know how to do it smoothly. They could also be taught phrases that help them *return to the subject*, e.g. *Going back to . . . , As I was saying . . .* , or *Yes, well, anyway . . .*

5. *Adjacency pairs:* There are some utterances (e.g. questions, invitations, requests, apologies, compliments, etc.) which require an immediate response or reaction from the communication partner; these utterances plus their responses (together) are known by linguists as adjacency pairs. One important feature of adjacency pairs is that after the first speaker's part (utterance), two different reactions are usually possible from the other speaker:

a. an expected, polite reaction (e.g. accepting an invitation or complying with a request), and

b. an unexpected, less common or more "difficult" reaction (e.g. turning down an invitation, or refusing to comply with a request).

The two types of reactions have been called *preferred* and *dispreferred answers* respectively. Just like native speakers, language learners typically find dispreferred answers much more difficult to produce. This is partly because they are more difficult language-wise, since in many cultures when you give a dispreferred answer, you must be tactful and indirect in order not to sound rude, and you may need to apologize or offer justifications. For language learners these skills require practice.

6. *Closings:* Unless we want to be deliberately rude, we cannot end a conversation by simply saying, "Well, that's all I want to say, bye," or, on the phone, just hang up abruptly without any notice. Instead, people typically apply a sequence of pre-closing and closing formulae to prepare the grounds for ending a conversation (e.g. *It's been nice talking to you . . . , Well, I don't want to keep you from your work . . . , We must get together sometime . . .*). Language learners can easily misunderstand closing signals in a foreign language, and they often lack a sufficient repertoire of such closing routines to be able to conclude and leave without sounding abrupt. It is therefore important to teach closing strategies explicitly, and to raise student awareness of the kind of phrases they might encounter in face-to-face conversation or on the telephone.

Conversational Strategies

Conversational strategies are an invaluable means of dealing with communication "trouble spots," such as not knowing a particular word, or misunderstanding the other speaker. They can also enhance fluency and add to the efficiency of communication. Knowing such strategies is particularly useful for language learners, who frequently experience such difficulties in conversation, because they provide them with a sense of security in the language by allowing extra time and room to manoeuvre (see Dörnyei and Thurrell, 1991). Research in the past two decades has identified more than two dozen conversational strategies, the most important of which are the following:

1. *Message adjustment or avoidance:* This involves tailoring your message to your competence, i.e. saying what you can rather than what you want to, or nothing at all. It can be done either by slightly altering or reducing the message, by going off the point, or even by avoiding the message completely. While this last is only to be used *in extremis,* the ability to evade answers when in trouble or to steer the conversation away from a topic to a new subject may considerably add to the learner's communicative confidence in general.

2. *Paraphrase:* Describing or exemplifying the object or action whose name you don't know: useful routines are structures like *something you can . . . with, a kind of . . . ,* etc.

3. *Approximation:* This means using an alternative term which expresses the meaning of the target word as closely as possible, e.g. *ship* for *sailing boat, vegetable* for *turnip,* or *buses* for *public transport.* A special type of approximation is the use of "all-purpose words," such as *stuff, thing, thingie, thingummajig, what-do-you-call-it,* etc.

4. *Appeal for help:* Eliciting the word you are looking for from your communication partner by asking questions like *What's the word for . . . ?* or *What do you call . . . ?*

5. *Asking for repetition* when you have not heard or understood something, e.g. *Pardon?* or *Sorry, what was the last word?*

6. *Asking for clarification* when something isn't clear, e.g. *What do you mean?, What are you saying/trying to say?*

7. *Interpretive summary:* This means reformulating the speaker's message to check that you understood correctly. Typical sentence beginnings are: *You mean . . . ?, If I've understood correctly . . .* or *So are you saying that . . . ?*

8. *Checking* whether the other person has *understood* what you have said e.g. *OK?, Is that clear?* or *Are you with me?;* or whether the other person is *paying attention* to what you are saying e.g. *Are you listening? Did you hear what I said?,* or over the phone, *Are you (still) there?*

9. *Use of fillers/hesitation devices* to fill pauses, to stall, and to gain time to think when in difficulty; e.g. *Well, Now let me see,* or *The thing is,* etc. Excessive and inappropriate use of fillers can be considered "bad" for native speakers and language learners alike, but in times of need, hesitation devices can be an invaluable aid to communication.

Functions and Meaning in Conversation

Functions and meaning in conversation concern the actual messages speakers convey and their purpose, that is, what meaning the speakers want to get through to their partners.

1. *Language functions:* Since the communicative approach to language teaching appeared in the mid-1970s, language functions (e.g. agreeing, asking for information, making suggestions, etc.) have played a very important role in the language classroom. A typical feature of language functions is that they involve a great number of set phrases and structures, and these are usually taught systematically through contemporary coursebooks. Conversation classes therefore need only to concentrate on those language functions which are particularly typical of conversation: asking and answering questions, expressing and agreeing with opinions, disagreeing politely, making requests and suggestions, and reacting in various ways to what a conversation partner is saying, for example by expressing happiness (*That's great!*), sympathy (*Oh dear!*), surprise (*Really?*), disbelief (*Surely not!*), or simply that you are listening (*I see, Uh-huh*).

2. *Indirect speech acts:* Speech acts are utterances which, rather than just conveying information, actually carry out an action or language function. For example, the question, *Could you open the window, please?* is not really a question but a way of getting the listener to open the window, and is therefore equivalent to a request.

   Some speech acts are direct and straightforward (e.g. *Put that gun down!*), but the majority in everyday conversation are indirect. For example, the sentence, *I wonder if you could post this letter for me* does not mean "I'm curious as to whether you are able to post this letter," but is rather an indirect way of making the listener post the letter.

   Language learners, especially at an early stage, can easily misunderstand indirect speech acts in English and take what has been said at its face value. This is not helped by the fact that indirect speech acts are rarely covered in foreign language teaching syllabuses. It is therefore very important to help learners early on to recognize indirect speech acts, and to encourage them as they become more advanced to use them naturally and with confidence in the way that native speakers do.

3. *Same meaning–different meaning:* It is not only with indirect speech acts that the literal meaning of a language form differs from the deeper meaning: utterances often have subconscious, semi-conscious, or quite intentional undertones. For example, a "compliment" like *What a nice car you have!* might mean "I didn't know you were so rich" or "I hope you'll let me borrow it next Saturday." It is well

worth students spending some time getting to grips with and analysing the possible differences between the "surface" and the "real" meaning of utterances. They could, for example, perform a dialogue in such a way that each sentence is followed by an "echo" which is an underlying hidden meaning of the message. Students should also be made aware that in some cases different language forms can have very similar meanings. A technique which tends to work well is to ask students to make alterations to every sentence of a dialogue while leaving the meaning intact.

Social and Cultural Contexts

Every conversation takes place in a social context within a particular culture. The participants may not realize it, but conversation is in many ways determined by these external contextual factors. In fact, a lack of awareness of social and cultural language rules can often be the source of much more trouble and embarrassment for language learners than gaps in their knowledge of grammar.

The fact that language is significantly determined by the context it is used in has been the topic of a great deal of research in linguistics, more specifically in sociolinguistics and pragmatics. The following sociolinguistic/pragmatic issues are among the most important for a conversation course:

1. *Participant variables—office and status:* A person's office is his or her job or profession, rank (military or other), and positions held (e.g. chairperson of the local council). Status refers to social standing or position in the social hierarchy and is determined by factors like age, education, family background, office, and wealth. Both office and status tend to determine how a person talks and is talked to in conversation. When someone does not follow the expected patterns of conversational behaviour in this matter, they might elicit comments like *I would never have thought she was a minister* or *He treated me like a VIP. What a laugh!*.

2. *The social situation:* Some social events require different behaviour from others. For example, a beach party is an entirely different social situation from a university degree ceremony, and as people are usually aware of such differences, they adjust their language accordingly. If they don't, they are likely to be on the receiving end of comments like *He behaved as though he was at a football match* or *You're not at home now, you know,* etc.

3. *The social norms of appropriate language use:* The two most important (and somewhat interrelated) dimensions of linguistic appropriacy are how formal or informal the style is, and what degree of politeness is present in the speech.

The *formal–informal continuum* is a measure of how much attention people pay to their speech. When they speak most naturally and casually, their style is informal, which is appropriate when the social setting is informal and the speakers are of more or less equal status. In contrast, the more carefully we attend to our speech production, the more formal it becomes, which is appropriate in formal contexts and between people of different status/office. The main features of the formal and informal speech styles can be summarized and taught to students directly.

The *degree of politeness* does not depend entirely on the degree of formality (informal speech, for example, is not necessarily impolite!); it refers to the extent people want to make the other person feel comfortable in conversation, either because, for example, they respect the person and his or her privacy, or because they would like something from him or her. There are several typical politeness strategies (for a practical overview, see van Ek and Trim, 1991; Dörnyei and Thurrell, 1992), and language learners can benefit a great deal from knowing and being able to use them.

4. *Cross-cultural differences:* Conversation is heavily loaded with cultural information, which becomes apparent when members of very different cultures meet. Language learners tend not to realize that a lack of cross-cultural awareness and sensitivity can cause more serious misunderstandings, and indeed communication breakdowns, than an incorrectly-used tense or wrong word order. In fact, there are so many culture-specific *do's* and *don'ts* that a language learner is constantly walking through a cultural minefield. Of course, students of different nationalities will find different cross-cultural aspects of conversation particularly difficult, and what teachers need to do is a sort of cultural needs analysis to select the relevant norms, conventions, and rules to be taught to their particular group of learners.

Teaching Conversational Issues Directly

The direct teaching of conversational skills does not differ radically from the indirect approach of communicative language teaching (CLT), but is rather an extension and further development of CLT methodology. Indeed, many of us who have used CLT techniques such as role-play activities, information-gap exercises, problem-solving tasks, discussions, and so on, will have found ourselves adding more and more conscious elements. Such elements might be part of the following three larger tendencies:

—adding specific language input

—increasing the role of consciousness raising

—sequencing communicative tasks systematically.

Adding Specific Language Input

As teachers we are beginning to realize that free communicative activities are potentially much more efficient, and are also appreciated more by the students, if specific language input, especially conversational routines and phrases, are included. One technique we have used a great deal is to give cue cards with some phrases written on them to each participant in a role-play activity, which the students have to incorporate in their parts a minimum of two or three times; the audience's task can be to spot these "person-specific" phrases. Another simple technique is to specify at the preparation stage the minimum number of different phrases the students are to include in their performance. This idea works even better if there is a competition between the various small groups on who can use the most phrases in their sketches.

Increasing the Role of Consciousness Raising

Consciousness-raising is based on the belief that making learners aware of structural regularities of the language will enable them to learn it faster (see Rutherford and Sharwood Smith, 1985). Consciousness-raising about grammar differs from traditional grammar teaching in that the new material is presented in a way that is compatible with the second language acquisition process in the learner. In a recent interview in *ELT Journal,* Ellis (1993) provided a very useful description of what this entails, distinguishing among three types of consciousness-raising activity:

   a. *Focused communicative activities*—producing a grammatical focus in the context of communicative activities.
   b. *Consciousness-raising activities*—helping the learners construct their own explicit grammar inductively.
   c. *Interpretation grammar activities*—providing learners with input that has been selected or manipulated to contain examples of the particular grammatical structures the teacher would like to focus on.

Although Ellis talks mainly about increasing grammatical awareness, the same approach can be followed to draw the learners' attention to the organizational principles of language use beyond the sentence level, including conversational strategies.

Sequencing Communicative Tasks Systematically

By giving communicative tasks a specific focus, it becomes possible to plan the sequence of communicative tasks in such a way that each activity introduces some new material while recycling material the students are already familiar with. The four larger areas of "conversational grammar" (structure, strategies, meaning, and sociocultural factors) are interrelated, and therefore a natural guideline for sequencing activities is to extend a task which concentrates on one area by adding a dimension from another. An example of this would be to start with a role-play task to practise disagreeing politely ("Functions and meanings in conversation"), and then add interruptions to the same conversation ("Conversational rules and structure"); the next step could involve the students in producing a formal and an informal version of their performance ("Social and cultural contexts"), and finally they could be asked to change the sketch into a telephone conversation where the line is so bad that the speakers have to constantly ask repetition and clarification questions ("Conversational strategies").

Conclusion

In this paper we have tried to outline a new approach to teaching conversation skills, based on a more explicit conceptualization of what such skills and subskills involve. The list of conversational focus areas presented is intended to serve a practical purpose; we believe that by drawing on such a list, it may be possible to introduce a firm and theory-based syllabus for conversation courses. Teachers should treat the list as a menu to choose topics from according to the need and level of their groups.

Although the focus of this paper has been on one area of language teaching, namely on conversation classes, the direct approach we advocate can be extended to the teaching of communicative competence in general. The interested reader could refer to Celce-Murcia *et al.* (1993), for a comprehensive and more theoretical discussion of this issue.

Acknowledgments

We would like to express our gratitude to Marianne Celce-Murcia and to Christopher Candlin for their valuable comments and advice on the structure we have presented in this paper.

References

Blundell, J., J. Higgens, and N. Middlemiss. 1982. *Function in English*. Oxford: Oxford University Press.

Brown, G. and G. Yule. 1983. *Teaching the Spoken Language*. Cambridge: Cambridge University Press.

Celce-Murcia, M., Z. Dörnyei, and S. Thurrell. 1993. "A pedagogical framework for communicative competence: content specifications and guidelines for communicative language teaching." Manuscript submitted for publication.

Cook, G. 1989. *Discourse*. Oxford: Oxford University Press.

Dörnyei, Z. and S. Thurrell. 1992. *Conversation and Dialogues in Action.* Hemel Hempstead: Prentice-Hall.

Ellis, R. 1993. "Talking shop: Second language acquisition research: how does it help teachers?" *ELT Journal* 47/1:3–11.

Golebiowska, A. 1990. *Getting Students to Talk.* Hemel Hempstead: Prentice-Hall.

Jones, L. 1981. *Functions of English.* Cambridge: Cambridge University Press.

Keller, E. and S. Townsend Warner. 1976, 1979. *Gambits: Conversational Tools. Vols. I–III.* Ottawa: Public Commission of Canada.

Keller, E. and S. Townsend Warner. 1988. *Conversation Gambits.* Hove: Language Teaching Publications.

Richards, J. C. 1990. "Conversationally speaking: approaches to the teaching of conversation" in Richards (ed.) *The Language Teaching Matrix.* Cambridge: Cambridge University Press.

Rutherford, W. E. and M. Sharwood Smith. 1985. "Consciousness-raising and Universal Grammar." *Applied Linguistics* 6/3:274–82.

van Ek, J. A. and J. L. M. Trim. 1991. *Threshold Level 1990.* Strasbourg: Council of Europe Press.

Widdowson, H. G. 1989. "Knowledge of language and ability for use." *Applied Linguistics* 10/2:128–37.

Content Questions

1. What kinds of strategies or routines do Dörnyei and Thurrell indicate might be taught when using the direct approach to teach students about conversation?

2. The authors identify four main areas to be included in the design of a conversation course. What are those areas?

3. What are some important issues related to turn taking? Why should this conversational feature be taught?

4. What are adjacency pairs? Which type of response within an adjacency pair requires more practice for nonnative speakers of a language?

5. Generally speaking, why is it important to teach students strategies such as message adjustment, appeal for help, and use of fillers?

6. What are indirect speech acts? Why would it be important to teach language students to recognize and use them?

7. What issues related to "social and cultural contexts" do the authors of the article discuss?

Questions for Analysis and Discussion

1. Much language instruction is limited to features within the phrase or sentence level. Comment on the level of analysis represented in this article.

2. Assume that you are a language teacher using a textbook that teaches only vocabulary, pronunciation, and grammar. Comment on the degree to which you should supplement that textbook. What kinds of additional information should you provide?

3. Consider a situation in which a nonnative speaker of English seems to have learned English well but appears to be rude. In light of what is discussed in the article, why might that be an inaccurate perception?

4. What does this article show about the value of linguistic research for the teaching of language?

Discourse Analysis and Grammar Instruction

Marianne Celce-Murcia

Marianne Celce-Murcia, a professor at UCLA, is well known in the field of ESL/EFL, her work often illustrating the practical application of linguistic research to language instruction. In the article below, which first appeared in the *Annual Review of Applied Linguistics,* she demonstrates that grammar is not a decontextualized or sentence-level phenomenon, but instead involves forms that are determined by discourse-related concerns. She also shows that such a perspective is important to counter the tendency of some ESL teachers, who in recognizing the importance of the functional uses of language have incorrectly devalued the teaching of grammatical knowledge.

Introduction

Only relatively recently has discourse analysis begun to have an impact on how English grammar (i.e., the rules of morphology and syntax) is taught to non-native speakers of English. In fact, a majority of teachers of English to speakers of other languages still conceive of grammar, and thus teach grammar, as a sentence-level phenomenon (if and when they teach it).[1] This state-of-affairs reflects a rather counterproductive view of grammar since, as Bolinger (1968; 1977) has long argued, there are relatively few rules of English grammar that are completely context-free.

The following grammar rules seem to be more or less context-free and thus exclusively sentence-level (perhaps the reader can add a few more):

- subject-verb agreement
- determiner-noun agreement
- gerund use after prepositions
- reflexive pronominalization

Even in this limited list there are qualitative differences among the rules. The first three rules are agreement rules and must apply whenever the appropriate morphosyntactic conditions are met. However, using a reflexive

---

[1]Language teachers are not alone in this respect; they are merely following the practices of generations of formal linguists, both structural (Bloomfield 1933) and transformational-generative (Chomsky 1965; 1982).

pronoun is partly a lexical matter (certain verbs are inherently reflexive, e.g., *to pride oneself on something*), partly a semantic matter (*John cut himself* vs. *John cut him/Bill*), and partly a pragmatic matter (factors motivating a speaker to choose between *He shaved* and *He shaved himself* to refer to the same activity).[2]

By far, the greater number of so-called grammar rules (i.e., grammatical choices that a speaker/writer makes) depend on conditions being met with respect to meaning, context, and/or discourse; they are thus not truly context-free. For example, I would consider all of the following rules or rule systems to be discourse-sensitive areas of grammar:

- passive voice
- indirect object alternation
- particle movement in phrasal verbs
- pronominalization (across independent clauses)
- article/determiner selection
- position of adverbials (phrases, clauses) in the sentence
- existential *there*
- tense-aspect-modality choice
- question formation (yes-no, alternative, wh-, tag)
- relative clauses
- complement selection (that-clause, infinitive, gerund)

In such cases, the learner's ability to produce the form or construction with linguistic accuracy is only part of the overall production task. One must also judge the situational and linguistic context in which the construction occurs to decide whether or not any given instance of language use is appropriate semantically and pragmatically as well as grammatically. For example, if the question *What did you give Jim?* (in its unmarked form) is asked of someone, an appropriate unmarked response (pragmatically) is *a/the tie* or *I gave him a/the tie,* but not *I gave a/the tie to Jim/him.*

There are also—not surprisingly—some areas where grammar and discourse overlap or interact. For example, there are certain rules for ordering prenominal adjectives, which appear to be arbitarily fixed or are syntactic in nature. For example,

size before color:
  a big red box (not, *a red big box*)
evaluation/opinion before size:
  a nice big house (not, *a big nice house*)

---

[2]To further complicate matters, reflexive pronouns are also used in semantically non-reflexive ways, e.g., as emphatic markers: *I talked to the man himself.*

Yet, there are other cases where two different orderings of prenominal adjectives are possible with subtle corresponding differences in meaning:

origin versus material (order varies)
>   *two Chinese wooden boxes* (two wooden boxes from China)
>   vs. *two wooden Chinese boxes* (two Chinese boxes made of wood)

In such cases, we must look for semantic and/or pragmatic rather than syntactic explanations; e.g., the more semantically peripheral of the two adjectives occurs first in the sequence, or farther away from the head noun.

Given the increasing influence of communicative language teaching over the last ten years (e.g., *Annual review of applied linguistics,* Vol. VIII), it is essential to understand the role of grammar in language use and its pervasive linkage with discourse and communication. In this review, grammar instruction can be reconceptualized as an integral aspect of communicative methodology, as it should be, rather than viewed as a vestige of traditional methods.

Connecting Grammar and Discourse

The Communicative approach to language teaching, which has been dominant is applied linguistics since the late 1970s (Littlewood 1981), also emphasizes the importance of meaning and context (especially situational pragmatics but also, to some extent, discourse-based pragmatics). However, some adherents of the communicative approach, in an effort to avoid giving context-free focus to any aspect of language, tended to neglect grammar altogether in favor of conversational interaction (Hatch 1978) or comprehensible input (Krashen 1981; 1982); then, as now, the prevailing view of grammar was that it operates exclusively at the sentence level without regard for meaning or context. For the language teacher to focus on grammar was viewed as being somehow incompatible with communicative language teaching.

One early work that demonstrated the extent to which grammar and discourse are in fact highly integrated levels of language was Halliday and Hasan's *Cohesion in English,* which appeared in 1976. It posited five kinds of cohesive ties in language—syntactic and semantic ties that cross sentence (or independent clause) boundaries and help create text:

1. Reference (pronouns, demonstratives, definite article, etc.); e.g.,
      Mark painted the picture. I like it.
   (where *it* and *the picture* are co-referential and form a cohesive tie).
2. Substitution (nominal *one(s)*, verbal *do*, clausal *so*); e.g.,
      A. I like the red car.
      B. I prefer the silver one.

(where *one* replaces *car* and forms a cohesive tie structurally and lexically but with no coreference).

3. Ellipsis (or substitution by zero); e.g.,
   A. Who's going to wash the car?
   B. Harry (is).
   (where *Harry (is)* functions elliptically to convey *Harry is going to wash the car*).

4. Conjunction (a word or expression that signals the type of link a sentence or clause has with the preceding sentence or text; from a broad semantic perspective, a conjunction expresses an additive, adversative, causal, or sequential tie); e.g.,
   James ate the ice cream and he liked it.
   vs. *James ate the ice cream because he liked it.*
   (where the difference is due to the semantic differences between *and* and *because*).

5. Lexical Cohesion (how words relate to each other semantically in various ways to form ties in a text); e.g.,
   He entered the *house;* then he closed the *door.*
   (where *door* forms a cohesive tie with *house* because *door* is an integral part of our concept of *house*).

The relationships among these five cohesive devices were reorganized in Halliday and Hasan (1989) and extended to include other discourse phenomena such as adjacency pairs (e.g., an offer followed by an acceptance), parallelism, theme-rheme development, and given-new information.

While several researchers have criticized various aspects of Halliday and Hasan's cohesion theory (e.g., Carrell 1982, Morgan and Sellner 1980), it has nonetheless had an impact on research in applied linguistics, especially research in the area of composition (e.g., Lindsay 1984, Scarcella 1984). The critics have pointed out that the 1976 version of Halliday and Hasan's cohesion theory does not account for all of discourse; it represents a bottom-up or microanalytic approach rather than a top-down or macroanalytic approach.[3] Both approaches, however, are needed to understand fully the interaction between grammar and discourse. If *Cohesion in English* is re-examined in light of the more interactive perspective being advocated here, its value as a pioneering effort in this area is undeniable.

In a top-down macroanalytic approach to discourse (e.g., Levinson 1983, Stubbs 1983), one begins by defining a written or oral genre such as narration or argumentation, or by defining a text type such as the scientific academic article. Then within the genre or the text type, one further defines specific divisions, episodes, or functions (e.g., rhetorical blocks, speech acts, steps) such as introduction, agreement, directive, spatial description,

---

[3]It is important, however, to note that the work of critics such as Carrell (1982) and Morgan and Sellner (1980) has also been criticized and called into question. See, for example, Eskey (1988).

past habitual events, and specific types of interactional transitions (e.g., topic shift, topic resumption). These divisions are some of the discourse units that have typically been the object of communicative language teaching. They are also some of the discourse units that turn out to have interesting language-specific grammatical correlates, as many of the examples cited and discussed below will illustrate.

Over the past ten to fifteen years functional grammarians (e.g., Givón 1979, Haiman and Thompson 1989, Halliday 1985) and discourse analysts (e.g., Chafe 1980, Schiffrin 1987, and Tannen 1989) have provided—both explicitly and incidentally—valuable grammatical information that has contributed to an understanding of the interaction of grammar and discourse, and which should influence the way both grammar and discourse are taught.

Research on Grammar and Discourse

In this section, research findings relevant to language instruction will be presented in five different areas: tense-aspect-modality, word order, subordination and complementation, special constructions, and topics and themes. The five areas demonstrate the myriad ways in which grammar and discourse interact. Yet all but the last of these five categories have traditionally been associated with sentence-level grammar rather than with discourse analysis.

Tense-Aspect-Modality[4]

The use of tense, aspect, and modality in discourse has become increasingly important in applied linguistics because of the pioneering work of sociolinguists like Wolfson (1979), who analyzed the systematic use of the historical present tense, and its variation with the simple past tense, in the oral narratives of native English speakers. The importance of such discourse constraints on tense choice is also explored in other research.

Matthiessen (1983), using Halliday's (1976) Systemic Grammar as his framework, examines the speaker/writer's choice of a primary tense and the consequences of this choice for tense sequence in discourse. With a similar objective, but by using the tense framework of Bull (1960) (which posits separate axes for present, past, and future time), Celce-Murcia and Larsen-Freeman (1983) explain tendencies toward certain tense sequences in discourse. Chafe (1972) has also made interesting observations on the sequence of tenses. In each case, discourse is shown to influence the appropriate tense choice in a number of contexts.

---

[4]Cook (1989) includes *sequence of tense* in his list of cohesive devices; if we accept Cook's account, this is an extension of Halliday and Hasan's (1976) five areas and even goes beyond their revisions in Halliday and Hasan (1989).

Some of the most interesting recent research in this area involves examining the patterns in which tense-aspect-modality forms are used within specific temporally organized episodes such as narratives dealing with the habitual past or with plans or predictions about the future. In both of these areas, Suh (1989a; 1989b), drawing on the rhetorical structure theory of Mann and Thompson (1988; forthcoming), has made important contributions. She has demonstrated that the periphrastic modal forms *used to* and *be going to* are employed to set up rhetorical frames for past habitual and future episodes; repeated instances of the modals *would ('d)* and *will ('ll)*, respectively, are then used to elaborate the discourse. The following texts are typical of the tokens Suh found in the course of carrying out her analysis:

(For Past Habitual Narrative)

The bad thing was they *used to* laugh at us, the Anglo kids. They *would* laugh because we'd bring tortillas and frijoles to lunch. They *would* have their nice little compact lunch boxes with cold milk in their thermos and they'*d* laugh at us because all we had was dried tortillas. Not only *would* they laugh at us, but the kids *would* pick fights.[5]

(For Future Planned Episodes)

They'*re going to* go in and have their gut slit open, their stomach exposed and have it stapled off so that there *will* be two pou-, an upper pouch in the stomach which *will* hold about two ounces of food, it's got a little hole right in the middle of that pouch where food when it's finally ground up *will* slowly go through.[6]

Interesting related research has also been carried out on the use of the progressive aspect and the perfective aspect in discourse. Schwarz (1988) looked at the frequency of use of the progressive aspect in her corpus and placed the many different data sources in her corpus on a register continuum going from informal/involved at one end to formal/detached at the other. She found that the relative frequency of the progressive aspect was highest in the informal/involved data sources and lowest in the formal/detached ones.

In a more linguistically oriented study, which included a variety of cross-linguistic discourse data, Andersen (1990) proposed that the English progressive is a type of imperfective marker because it depicts an event

---

[5]The source for this passage is Terkel (1977:32), who is quoting a bilingual Mexican-American reflecting on some of his school experiences.

[6]The source for this passage about the gastric restriction procedure is the UCLA oral corpus, a corpus informally put together at Fred Davidson's initiative while he was a graduate student at UCLA. The 140,000 word corpus is used by graduate students and faculty in Applied Linguistics for certain language analysis research. It is an in-house resource and not available for external dissemination.

from within and does not focus on its beginning or end. He shows how English speakers use the progressive to express iterative, continuous, or habitual events; however, he emphasizes that these are all derived by inference from the basic meaning of the progressive, which is temporary duration. Andersen emphasizes that these inferences can be made only if one considers the total context in which any given token of the progressive occurs. Any comprehensive discourse-based theory of the English progressive aspect will need to integrate Andersen's functional language analysis with Schwarz' sociolinguistic findings.

To date, the discourse function of the perfective aspect has received less attention than that of the progressive. However, Gunawardena (1989), in an interesting study using published articles in biology and biochemistry, suggested that in this genre the use of the present perfect relates in an interesting way to the rhetorical functions found in the introduction section of the journal articles. In these introductions, the writers use the present perfect specifically to refer to past experiments relevant to their present experiment; in more general instances, the writers also use the present perfect to signal that some past experience has current relevance. These specific and general functions are clearly related.

Word-Order Issues

Grammarians have long debated the difference between the two possible word orders in phrasal verb constructions such as:

Sharon turned off the light.
Sharon turned the light off.

Bolinger (1971) was among the first to suggest that the degree of newness or importance of the direct object was a factor in determining word order. The first version would be preferred in contexts where the direct object *the light* was truly new (or emphasized) information; the second order would be preferred in contexts where the direct object had already been mentioned but was not sufficiently recent or well established as old information to merit use of the pronoun, as in *Sharon turned it off.* Chen (1986), however, was the first to use discourse analysis to demonstrate this principle empirically and to elaborate on the fact that Bolinger's earlier insights reflected a valid generalization about English grammar and discourse.

Similarly, Thompson and Koide (1987) and Williams (1988) have carried out discourse-based studies of constructions exhibiting indirect object alternation such as the following:

Peter gave the book to Alice.
Peter gave Alice the book.

They concluded that indirect object alternation is, in most cases, determined at the discourse level by the relative degree of "given" or "new" information in the two object constituents.[7] In other words, when there are describable differences between the two noun objects on this dimension, the more established or "given" constituent tends to occur directly after the verb while the constituent expressing newer (or emphatic) information tends to occur later as the second object (i.e., as a direct object or the object of a preposition).

Subordination and Complementation

A study by Thompson (1985) examining where adverbial clauses of purpose are ordered with respect to the main clause (i.e., before or after) revealed that sentence-initial adverbial purpose clauses were important in organizing the overall discourse; sentence-final clauses, in contrast, were generally only local expansions of the main clause. Ford and Thompson (1986) came to a similar conclusion about the sentence-initial or sentence-final position of "if" conditional clauses in comparison with other adverbial clauses. Additionally, they observed that initial position is very strongly favored for "if" conditional clauses because if-clauses tend to play an important discourse-organizing role in establishing and maintaining topics.

In a study of nominal *that* clauses, Lisovsky (1988) examined a corpus to find out how English speakers make use of such constructions in discourse. More than 70% of the tokens he examined represented either reported thought or reported speech:

(Reported Thought)
    I feel that the first suggestion is the best one.

(Reported Speech)
    He said that he would come later.

He also identified four minor discourse functions for *that* clauses: reported facts, perceptual events, demonstrative events, and manipulative events.[8]

---

[7]This contradicts the account of formal syntacticians such as Akmajian and Heny (1975), Emonds (1976), and Ransom (1979), who propose that indirect object alternation is determined solely at the sentential level by the presence of morphological and semantic properties in the object noun constructions.

[8]Examples of Lisovsky's (1988) minor *that* clause functions are:
(reported fact)
    It is likely that more visitors will come.
(perceptual event)
    He saw that he was going to have to climb the fence.
(demonstrative event)
    The results of the study demonstrated that the benefits did not cover the costs.

The formal written portion of Lisovsky's corpus stood apart statistically from the other three data types (formal spoken, informal written, informal spoken) in that the formal written data had many more *that* clauses in subject position, more reported speech than reported thought (the reverse occurred elsewhere), frequent occurrence of demonstrative events (low frequency elsewhere), and few first person subjects of *that* clauses (high frequency elsewhere).

Special Constructions

Kim (1989) analyzed extensively the use of pseudo-clefts in English conversation by native speakers. He concluded that their general or overarching discourse function is to mark a disjunction from the preceding context which allows the speaker to go back to some utterance in the preceding context and address it. Within this general view of pseudo-clefts, Kim distinguished those pseudo-clefts that mark the gist of the talk (i.e., that establish, restate, or sum up the topic) from those that respond to a problem (a challenge from the interlocutor or a perceived misunderstanding/miscommunication). An example of the latter type of pseudo-cleft follows:

(Response to a Problem)
> A: An' I was wondering if you'd let me use your gun.
> B: My gun?
> A: Yeah.
> B: What gun.
> A: Don't you have a beebee gun?
> B: Yeah.
> A: Oh it's
> B: Oh I have a lot of guns.
> A: You do?
> B: Yeah. <u>What I meant was WHICH gun.</u>[9]

Another special construction, the relative clause, has traditionally been considered a sentence-level construction. However, this view of relative clauses is challenged by the work of Fox (1987) and Fox and Thompson (1990), who contend that the use of relative clause constructions in conversation is best explained with reference to the way the interlocutors attend to the flow of information. Fox and Thompson argue that the following pragmatic and semantic factors relate in important ways to information flow and thus to the function of relative clauses in English:

(manipulative event)
>   Tax reform requires that most businesses make their fiscal year conform to the calendar.

[9]This segment of conversation comes from data that Kim (1989) was able to use in his research courtesy of Professor E. Schegloff, who teaches seminars in conversation analysis at UCLA.

- degree of new/given information encoded in the head noun phrase and/or relativized noun phrase;
- grounding (locating a referent in conversational space by relating it to a referent whose relevance is established);
- humanness of the noun phrases concerned;
- degree of definiteness of the noun phrases concerned;
- discourse function of the relative clause (i.e., does it characterize or identify the referent?).

Fox and Thompson use data from English conversations to demonstrate that the information flow characteristic of this discourse genre can explain, for example, why non-human subject heads tend to occur with object relatives by a 4:1 ratio (e.g., *the only thing [you'll see] is the table*). In this construction type the object relative clause (*you'll see*) provides necessary grounding for the indefinite and nonspecific non-human subject head noun (*thing*).

Topics and Themes

In an analysis of sentences with non-referential *there* subjects in spoken American English, Sasaki (forthcoming) addressed the role that this construction plays with regard to topic continuity in discourse. For example, in the following sentence:

There are some special ways to cut the climbing roses.

Sasaki specifically looked at the discourse function of the logical subject and the postmodifying elements. In the example sentence provided, the logical subject is "(some special) ways" and the postmodifying element is "to cut the climbing roses." By applying modified definitions of "referential distance" and "decay," two terms from Givon (1984) that refer to how far back and how far forward respectively a topic persists in the discourse, Sasaki demonstrates that the sentences with non-referential *there* subjects in her corpus function in the following discourse-sensitive ways:

- The logical subjects tend to have low topic continuity; i.e., they tend to express new information (but they also tend to persist as the topic of subsequent clauses).
- The logical subjects tend to be entailed; i.e., they are a subcategory of something more general previously mentioned in the discourse.
- The elements that follow and modify the logical subjects have high topic continuity; i.e., their referents have been previously mentioned in the discourse.

In a similar vein, Lee (forthcoming) examined the discourse function of thematic sentence-initial adverbs (e.g., *perhaps, sometimes, obviously*) in oral and written English.[10] Two of her high frequency items in the study, *perhaps* and *maybe*, exhibited particularly striking behavior. Because many grammarians and dictionaries have treated these adverbs as synonyms of sorts, she examined their similarities and differences in some detail.

The first difference between *perhaps* and *maybe* that Lee noticed is the relative informality of *maybe* versus the more formal tone of *perhaps*. This is reflected in the fact that over 90% of her tokens of *maybe* come from speech or quoted speech, whereas over 60% of her tokens of *perhaps* occur in writing. Secondly, while almost one-fourth of the tokens of *maybe* could be associated with negation of some sort, fewer than one-tenth of the tokens of *perhaps* had this function. Indeed *perhaps* co-occurred most frequently with affirmative messages including strong superlative modifiers in more than 20% of the tokens (e.g., *Perhaps the best judgment comes from . . .*). These differences led Lee to hypothesize that one function of the speaker's use of *maybe* is to rule out previously stated possibilities and to move toward a more negative stance: ". . . maybe they had such faith in me as a person that they pulled off and then maybe there was no divinity in this whole thing at all. Maybe there was nothing except just the change of attitude on the part of the recipient. . . ."[11]

The above example also illustrates a third important difference between *perhaps* and *maybe;* tokens of *maybe* tend to cluster much more often than tokens of *perhaps*, suggesting that *maybe* is frequently used to offer multiple tentative possibilities while *perhaps* is typically used to offer one possibility that the speaker/writer puts forth with some degree of confidence.

ESL Grammar Textbooks

A recent examination made of several contemporary ESL grammar textbooks confirms the notion that most textbook authors—and most ESL teachers—view grammar as a sentence-level phenomenon and thus teach grammar at the sentence level. To exemplify the distinction between teaching grammar as a sentence phenomenon or discourse-based phenomenon, I reviewed the approach used in three textbooks for teaching the passive voice, one of the most important areas for analyzing and teaching the interaction of grammar and discourse. Two of the textbooks (Murphy with Altman 1989, and Azar 1989) typify the sentence-level approach while the third (Werner 1990) is more solidly discourse-based.

---

[10]This notion of "theme" or "thematic" comes from Halliday (1985), who proposes that the theme expresses the speaker/writer's point of departure for the clause as message. In English, the theme(s) will always be the initial constituent(s) in the clause or sentence.

[11]Lee took this token from the UCLA oral corpus. (See note 6 for a description of this corpus.)

Murphy with Altman (1989) offer eight pages (80–87) with explanation and practice exercises for the passive voice. Virtually each exercise is sentence-level and uses completion and rewriting formats to assist learners in producing passive forms and in rewriting active voice sentences as passives. A challenging variety of construction types is presented, often a new one in each exercise: passives with various tenses, passives with modals, sentences with *to be born,* gerundive passives after the verb *like* and after prepositions, passives with *get,* complex passives with anticipatory *it* or a raised subject, and passives with *be supposed to.*

Azar (1989) is even more thorough than Murphy with Altman (1989) and fills thirty pages (120–149) with charts, diagrams, and exercises on the passive voice covering most of the constructions in Murphy with Altman as well as a few other related ones (e.g., stative passives, passive-like adjectival use of past participles). Most, though not all, of Azar's exercises are sentence level. Some are mechanical in nature, yet others require analysis or judgment (e.g., change from active to passive if possible, retain *by*-phrase only if needed, explain why the passive is used in these sentences, create a sentence using the subject and verb provided). Three of the exercises involve the use of short multi-sentence texts/dialogues, and the final exercise involves error analysis. Yet, the overall sense that a teacher or learner gets from using the textbook is that the passive voice is a sentence-level phenomenon.

Werner (1990) teaches the passive voice in a unit on technology that is twenty-eight pages long (139–166). The unit consists of four cycles for presenting and practicing the passive: 1) simple tenses, 2) perfect tenses, 3) continuous tenses, and 4) modals. Each cycle begins with an extended text for reading comprehension and subsequent grammatical analysis (e.g., underline the subjects and the verb forms; identify active and passive voice; change the subject of certain sentences; and paraphrase the original sentence). The texts are followed by sentence-level exercises related to the passage and to the topic of the unit (i.e., Technology). The exercises are varied: fill in the verb form, change passive to active, change active to passive, generate sentences from contextualized cues, etc. These exercises in turn are followed by a long passage with 20 to 30 blanks where the learner must supply—as appropriate in the given context—either the active or passive form of the verb for each blank. At the end of each cycle there is an activity that encourages use of and discrimination in using the active and passive voice (e.g., say/write how some object or tool could be improved).

Of these three ESL grammar textbooks, Werner's is headed in the right direction as far as the integration of grammar and discourse is concerned. Teachers and textbook writers should be encouraged to examine carefully and to work at improving the approach and formats that are used in this last text; further elaboration and improvement of such a text-based approach would benefit all professionals who need to deal with grammar in language teaching.

Conclusion

This discussion of discourse and grammar instruction began with a re-statement of the Structuralist-Chomskyan view that grammar is sentence-based and context-free. Within applied linguistics, this narrow view has been broadened considerably due to a general acceptance of models of communicative competence (Canale and Swain 1980, Hymes 1972), whose proponents argue that grammatical competence is only one aspect of communicative competence—other at least equally important components being sociolinguistic competence, discourse competence, strategic competence, etc.

The incompatibility of context-free models of grammar with the communicative competence model has led some methodologists (e.g., Krashen 1981; 1982) and many language teachers to neglect all focus on grammar (i.e., all bottom-up aspects of language) in favor of teaching meanings and functions (top-down aspects of language). The assumption shared by such teachers and methodologists is that grammar—a low-level bottom-up phenomenon—would automatically take care of itself while the top-down aspects of language were being acquired.

However, as Schmidt (1990) aptly points out, language learners—especially those in EFL contexts—tend not to learn much indirectly (i.e., they tend to learn what they are taught and to not learn what they are not taught). Thus, if we teach grammar without reference to discourse, our students will fail to acquire the discourse competence so vital for developing effective reading and writing skills. Conversely, if we teach discourse (i.e., meanings and functions) without reference to grammar, our learners will produce discourse reminiscent of Kroll's (1990) college-level ESL composition students who exhibit the +rhetoric/-grammar syndrome; that is, they write logically organized and coherent texts but with such a high number of morphosyntactic errors that native speakers find it difficult, if not impossible, to read and understand their texts. What experience should teach us, then, is that we must work towards an interactive model of grammar and discourse, one that demonstrates the necessity and importance of both levels of language to the language learning process and to the attainment of communicative competence.[12]

Commenting on Rutherford and Sharwood Smith's (1988) call to incorporate grammatical consciousness raising into communicative language teaching, Swales (forthcoming) predicts that the nineties will be an era for consciousness raising about discourse and text-structure. I agree with Swales, but would argue that we now need to analyze vigorously the *interaction* of grammar and discourse, and then teach both discourse and grammar in appropriate ways to second-language learners. This is what we must

---

[12]This type of integration has already occurred in research on reading, for which Rumelhart (1977) and Perfetti (1985) have suggested the need for an interactive model (top down + bottom up).

do if we want students to become truly communicatively competent and if we want to present the English language to them in an integrated manner, acknowledging all its levels and all its complexities.

Annotated Bibliography

Bolinger, D. 1977. *Meaning and form.* New York: Longman.

> This volume contains many examples of Bolinger's early and constant challenging of the validity of context-free grammar, particularly of the transformational-generative variety. The topics he treats (e.g., pronominalization, existential *there,* reference, negation) are often relevant to discourse analysis being done today, although Bolinger himself did little or no corpus-based discourse analysis and generated most of his own examples.

Celce-Murcia, M. and D. Larsen-Freeman. 1983. *The grammar book: An ESL/EFL teacher's course.* New York: Newbury House.

> This pedagogical grammar for language teachers tried to make explicit the discourse functions of grammatical structures to the extent that this was possible in the early eighties.

Givón, T. 1979. *On understanding grammar.* New York: Academic Press.

> This volume presents grammar not as something that is autonomous and context-free but as a processing mechanism for constructing discourse. It is one of the first books dealing with the topic of grammar to argue explicitly for this perspective.

Halliday, M. A. K. 1985. *Introduction to functional grammar.* London: Edward Arnold.

> Halliday's most comprehensive and recent work in functional grammar indicates that he continues to be a major force in defining the interrelationship between grammar and discourse. He argues that discourse analysis must include grammatical analysis if it is to be more than mere text commentary.

Halliday, M. A. K. and R. Hasan. 1976. *Cohesion in English.* London: Longman.

> A pioneering volume outlining five microstructural cohesive devices used in discourse: reference, substitution, ellipsis, conjunction, and lexical cohesion. These are ties holding across sentences that speakers and writers use (along with other things) to achieve text.

Halliday, M. A. K. and R. Hasan. 1989. *Language, context, and text: Aspects of language in a social-semiotic perspective.* Oxford: Oxford University Press.

> This volume is, to a great extent, a revision and extension of *Cohesion in English.* Halliday contributes the theoretical framework in Part A, while Hasan explores more specific features of text structure in Part B, offering a redefinition of the notion "cohesive tie" in Chapter 5.

There are several influential edited volumes, not noted in the following bibliography, that have appeared during the past fifteen years, each of which contains several articles contributing to an understanding of the interaction of grammar and discourse; thus, these edited volumes are all recommended as potentially useful background reading.

Chafe, W. (ed.) 1980. *The pear stories.* Norwood, NJ: Ablex.
Cole, P. (ed.) 1981. *Radical pragmatics.* New York: Academic Press.
Givón, T. (ed.) 1979. *Discourse and syntax.* New York: Academic Press. [Syntax and Semantics. Vol. 12.]
Haiman, J. and S. A. Thompson (eds.) 1989. *Clause combining in grammar and discourse.* Amsterdam: John Benjamins.
Li, C. N. (ed.) 1976. *Subject and topic.* New York: Academic Press.

Unannotated Bibliography

Akmajian, A. and F. Heny. 1975. *An introduction to the principles of transformational syntax.* Cambridge, MA: MIT Press.
Andersen, R. 1990. Verbal virtuosity and speakers' purposes. In H. Burmeister and P. Rounds (eds.) *Proceedings of the tenth meeting of the Second Language Research Forum.* Eugene, OR: University of Oregon, Department of Linguistics and American English Institute. 1–14.
Azar, B.S. 1989. *Understanding and using English grammar.* 2nd Ed. Englewood Cliffs, NJ: Prentice-Hall Regents.
Bloomfield, L. 1933. *Language.* New York: Holt, Rinehart and Winston.
Bolinger, D. 1968. Entailment and the meaning of structures. *Glossa.* 2.2.119–127.
———— 1971. *The phrasal verb in English.* Cambridge, MA: Harvard University Press.
Bull, W. 1960. *Time, tense, and the verb.* Berkeley: University of California Press.
Canale, M. and M. Swain. 1980. Theoretical bases of communicative approaches to second language teaching and testing. *Applied linguistics.* 1.1.1–47.
Carrell, P. 1982. Cohesion is not coherence. *TESOL quarterly.* 16.4.479–488.
Chafe, W. 1972. Discourse structure and human knowledge. In J. Carroll and R. Freedle (eds.) *Language comprehension and the acquisition of knowledge.* Washington, DC: V.H. Winston and Sons. 41–69.
Chen, P. 1986. Discourse and particle movement in English. *Studies in language.* 10.1.79–95.
Chomsky, N. 1965. *Aspects of the theory of syntax.* Cambridge, MA: MIT Press.
———— 1982. *Lectures on government and binding.* Dordrecht: Foris.
Cook, G. 1989. *Discourse.* Oxford: Oxford University Press.
Emonds, J. 1976. *A transformational approach to syntax.* New York: Academic Press.
Eskey, D. 1988. Holding in the bottom: An interactive approach to the language problems of second language learners. In P. Carrell, J. Devine and D. Eskey (eds.) *Interactive approaches to second language reading.* New York: Cambridge University Press. 93–100.

Ford, C. and S. Thompson. 1986. Conditionals in discourse: A text-based study from English. In E. Traugott (ed.) *On Conditionals.* Cambridge: Cambridge University Press. 353–372.

Fox, B. 1987. The noun phrase accessibility hierarchy reinterpreted. *Language.* 63.4.856–870.

———— and S. Thompson. 1990. A discourse explanation of the grammar of relative clauses in English conversation. *Language.* 66.2.297–316.

Givón, T. 1984. Universals of discourse structure and second language acquisition. In W. Rutherford (ed.) *Language universals and second language acquisition.* Amsterdam: John Benjamins. 109–133.

Gunawardena, C.N. 1989. The present perfect in the rhetorical divisions of Biology and Biochemistry journal articles. *English for specific purposes.* 8.3.265–273.

Halliday, M. A. K. 1976. *System and function in language: Selected papers.* G. Kress (ed.) London: Oxford University Press.

Hatch, E. 1978. Introduction. In E. Hatch (ed.) *Second language acquisition: A book of readings.* Rowley, MA: Newbury House. 1–18.

Hymes, D. 1972. On communicative competence. In J.B. Pride and J. Holmes (eds.) *Sociolinguistics.* Harmondsworth, England: Penguin Books. 269–293.

Kim, K-H. 1989. Wh-clefts in English conversation: An interactional perspective. Los Angeles: UCLA. Mimeo. [Unpublished paper written for English 250K, dated Dec. 13, 1989].

Krashen, S. D. 1981. *Second language acquisition and second language learning.* Oxford: Pergamon Press.

———— 1982. *Principles and practice in second language acquisition.* Oxford: Pergamon Press.

Kroll, B. 1990. The rhetoric/syntax split: Designing a curriculum for ESL students. *Journal of basic writing.* 9.1.40–55.

Lee, D. Forthcoming. A discourse analysis of thematic sentential adverbs in oral and written American English. Los Angeles: UCLA. M.A. thesis.

Levinson, S. 1983. *Pragmatics.* Cambridge: Cambridge University Press.

Lindsay, D. B. 1984. Cohesion in the composition of ESL and English students. Los Angeles: UCLA. M.A. thesis.

Lisovsky, K. 1988. A discourse analysis of *that*-nominal clauses in English. Los Angeles: UCLA. M.A. thesis.

Littlewood, W. 1981. *Communicative language teaching.* Cambridge: Cambridge University Press.

Mann, W. and S. Thompson. 1988. Rhetorical structure theory. *Text.* 8.243–281.

———— Forthcoming. Rhetorical structure theory: A theory of text organization and its implications for clause combining. In L. Polanyi (ed.) *Discourse structure.* Norwood, NJ: Ablex.

Matthiessen, C. 1983. Choosing primary tense in English. *Studies in language.* 7.3.369–429.

Morgan, J. and M. Sellner. 1980. Discourse and linguistic theory. In R. Spiro, B. Bertram, and W. Brewer (eds.) *Theoretical issues in reading comprehension.* Hillsdale, NJ: Lawrence Erlbaum. 165–200.

Murphy, R. with R. Altman. 1989. *Grammar in use.* Cambridge: Cambridge University Press.

Perfetti, C.A. 1985. *Reading ability.* New York: Oxford University Press.

Ransom, E. 1979. Definiteness and animacy constraints on passive and double object constructions in English. *Glossa*. 13.2.215–240.

Rumelhart, D. E. 1977. Toward an interactive model of reading. In S. Dornic (ed.) *Attention and performance,* Vol VI. New York: Academic Press. 573–603.

Rutherford, W. and M. Sharwood Smith. (eds.) 1988. *Grammar and second language teaching.* New York: Newbury House.

Sasaki, M. Forthcoming. An analysis of sentences with nonreferential *there* in spoken American English. *Word.*

Scarcella, R. 1984. Cohesion in the writing development of native and non-native English speakers. Los Angeles: University of Southern California. Ph.D. diss.

Schiffrin, D. 1987. *Discourse markers.* Cambridge: Cambridge University Press.

Schmidt, R. 1990. Input, interaction, attention and awareness: The case for consciousness raising in second language teaching. Keynote address at the 10th annual ENPULI conference, Rio de Janiero, Brazil, July, 1990.

Schwarz, S. 1988. The progressive aspect in American English usage. Los Angeles: UCLA. M.A. thesis.

Stubbs, M. 1983. *Discourse analysis.* Oxford: Blackwell.

Suh, K-H. 1989a. A discourse analysis of past habitual forms: *used to, would,* and the simple past tense in spoken American English. Los Angeles: UCLA. M.A. thesis.

——— 1989b. A discourse analysis of *be going to* and *will* in spoken American English. Los Angeles: UCLA. Mimeo [Unpublished term project for English 250K, dated Dec. 13, 1989.]

Swales, J. Forthcoming. *Genre analysis and its applications.* Cambridge: Cambridge University Press.

Tannen, D. 1989. *Talking voices.* Cambridge: Cambridge University Press.

Terkel, S. 1977. *Working.* New York: Ballantine Books.

Thompson, S. 1985. Grammar and written discourse: Initial vs. final purposes clauses in English. *Text.* 5.1/2.56–84.

——— and Y. Koide. 1987. Iconicity and "indirect objects" in English. *Journal of pragmatics.* 11.399–406.

Werner, P. 1990. *Mosaic I: A context-based grammar.* 2nd Ed. New York: McGraw-Hill.

Williams, R. 1988. Indirect object alternation and topicworthiness. Los Angeles: UCLA. M.A. thesis.

Wolfson, N. 1979. The conversational historical present alternation. *Language.* 55.1.168–182.

Content Questions

1. To what extent are most grammar rules dependent on discourse or contextual features?

2. Which language teaching approach led some to devalue the role of grammar teaching?

3. Celce-Murcia refers to Halliday and Hasan's 1976 work that shows five types of cohesive devices that work beyond the sentence or clause level. Identify these devices.

4. Describe the discourse function that was found to exist with the perfective aspect as it occurs within introductions of scholarly articles dealing with biology and biochemistry.

5. What determines the word order involving a phrasal verb and a direct object? What about the word order involving an indirect object in a sentence? How are these word orders related to discourse considerations?

6. Generally speaking, what discourse purpose do pseudo-clefts serve?

7. Compare and contrast the uses of *maybe* and *perhaps*.

8. What does Celce-Murcia recommend about grammar instruction?

Questions for Analysis and Discussion

1. How does the author's treatment of grammar differ from traditional approaches that taught grammar rules in isolation?

2. After Halliday and Hasan's initial 1976 book about cohesion, they expanded their discussion to include other cohesive devices. One of these involved adjacency pairs. Explain why an adjacency pair would be an appropriate addition to the list of cohesive devices that work beyond the sentence level.

3. What weaknesses are there in considering grammar only at the sentence level?

4. Comment on the relationship between communicative competence and grammatical competence.

Applied Linguistics:
The Use of Linguistics in ESL

Christina Bratt Paulston

The contribution of linguistic training to the teaching of ESL or EFL, while significant, is not always immediately apparent. In this article, Christina Bratt Paulston of the University of Pittsburgh considers the opinion of a group of language teachers about which parts of their linguistic training seem to have been most helpful to them in the teaching of English. Paulston also briefly discusses some of the methods and approaches that have been used in teaching English to nonnative speakers. Paulston's chapter originally appeared some years ago and thus does not integrate some recent research, but it makes some important observations that are still relevant.

An exhaustive bibliography on the topic of this paper would fill pages, for linguists have written extensively on the subject. They have also disagreed extensively, from Newmark's (1970)

> the transformationist's analysis of verb phrase constructions, beginning with Chomsky's simple C(M) (have+en) (be+ing) V formula, brings startling simplicity and clarity to our understanding of the grammatical structure of a number of discontinuous and elliptical verb constructions; transformational grammar seems to offer suggestions neatly and precisely for what a program teaching English verb structure would have to include. (Newmark, 1970: 213)

to Chomsky's (1966) own

> frankly, I am rather sceptical about the significance, for the teaching of languages, of such insights and understanding as have been attained in linguistics or psychology. (Chomsky, 1966:43)

and he adds later

> It is the language teacher himself who must validate or refute any specific proposal. (Chomsky, 1966:45)

Who is right? In a sense, that is what this paper is about.

If by "applied linguistics," we mean the use linguists put their knowledge to in order to get things done in the real world, it is immediately clear that applied linguistics means a lot more than merely language teaching (Corder, 1975; Roulet, 1975; Spolsky, 1978). It is generally recognized that translation is one aspect of applied linguistics but in this context less frequently pointed out that translation existed centuries before linguistics, and, in fact, provided a powerful impetus for the development of the discipline of linguistics in the United States. Missionaries, in groups like the Wycliffe Bible Translators and the Summer Institute of Linguistics, were dedicated to spreading the Word of God by translating the gospels into primarily unwritten languages. They found that they made awkward mistakes. To give but one example: many languages have inclusive *we* ("all of us guys") and exclusive *we* ("my friend and I but not you guys"), and if you have never run into them before, the inclusive/exclusive feature of the first person plural pronoun is far from immediately apparent. So it is not surprising that the missionaries inadvertently translated "Our Father" with exclusive *we*, and subsequently discovered to their horror the Aymara Indians' interpretation of a God for white folk only, which notion was the last on earth they had intended. Accordingly, scholars like Kenneth Pike (1947) of the Summer Institute of Linguistics in his *Phonemics: A Technique for Reducing Languages to Writing*, Eugene Nida (1949) of the American Bible Society in his *Morphology: The Descriptive Analysis of Words*, and later H. A. Gleason (1955) of the Hartford Seminary Foundation in *An Introduction to Descriptive Linguistics* were genuinely concerned with what came to be known as "discovery procedures," the analysis of unknown and unwritten languages.

One result of the practical bent of anthropologists and missionaries was that it inadvertently developed techniques for language learning through the focus on discovery procedures, such as substitution drills. Partially, I suspect, the audio-lingual method, also known, albeit erroneously, as the linguistic method, was a historical accident, created in wartime by linguists who turned to their established procedures for getting things done. The point I am making here is that there is very much a two-way street between theory and application, between translation and linguistics and language learning and that problems in the real world do touch and test the development of theory. Linguistics as we know it today would never have existed if people had not tried to do things with language, all the way back to Panini. We clearly have to reject a model like that in Figure 1 as inaccurate and misleading, where the direction of influence is in one direction only.

There are two ways of answering the question of the significance of linguistics for language teaching. One is to argue from theory to speculative claims in a logico-deductive manner as Newmark does. The evidence for his "startling simplicity and clarity" claim is his own expert opinion. This is by far the most common approach, and the literature is replete with

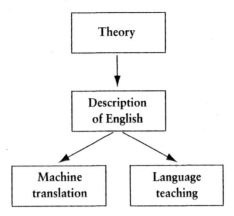

Figure 1   (*Source:* Roulet, 1975: 71.)

grand claims of what linguistics can achieve for the language learner. Furthermore, these claims cannot be dismissed on the grounds that there is no evidence to support them for they are made by men of stature and experience with language teaching, like Fries (1945), Lado (1957), Moulton (1970) and Allen & Corder (1975) to pick three classics and one more recent work.

The other way is of course to argue from data and to document the use of linguistic insights and knowledge in the classroom. We could ask the teachers of ESL what they find helpful from their training in linguistics and what they actually use in the classroom. Such data will share the weakness of all self-report data and should therefore be augmented by actual classroom observation, where the observer especially watches for any evidence of the use of linguistic knowledge. One can examine syllabi and textbooks for similar evidence as well as consider the claims in recent journal articles with a practical bent; the latter also a type of self-report data. One might consider examining the content of teacher training courses, but on second thought I think one will find merely that the director considered such content important but not whether the teachers in fact would ever use such knowledge.

I have attempted a rather cursory investigation of this kind. Our English Language Institute, modelled after the Michigan ELI, teaches English to some 200 students with some 25 instructors (the exact figures vary from term to term). Sixteen instructors returned questionnaire responses in which they (most of them are Teaching Assistants (TAs) in the Department of Linguistics) were asked to rate their course work on a scale 1–10 in usefulness for teaching purposes. I interviewed seven TAs who were students in a supervision seminar. I observed classes and immediately found an interesting research problem.

In none of the three grammar classes I observed was there any indication that the instructors had any linguistics training beyond a good public schools ninth grade class with Warriner (1973; now Warriner, Whitten & Griffith, 1975), any overt, clear, solid, unmistakeable evidence that the teacher was a linguist in the making. I confess that this fact surprised me. One of the instructors was a young man in the throes of his doctoral linguistic comprehensive exams, which is possibly the period in one's life of the most intense consciousness of matters linguistic. In an in-depth interview following my observation of his class, he made the following points:

1. He didn't use technical linguistics terms in the classroom (beyond "indirect/direct object focus in active/passive transformation") for the simple reason that the students would not understand it. (This attitude permeates the instructors' thinking in general.)
2. He found his knowledge of syntax very useful in selecting teaching points, i.e. what to teach and what to ignore about the passive construction as well as setting up and presenting the construction in model sentences on the board and in the explanations.
3. He thought the textbook exercises awful and that the best approach to teaching the passive is not through transformations of formal aspects of the active voice.

In essence, what we have here are cognitive and attitudinal influences of linguistics on the instructor which are not observable but nevertheless of extreme importance. It is a situation similar to documenting avoidance behavior in sociolinguistics, a very difficult problem. To compound the difficulty, we have an aspect of Labov's "observer's paradox." The young man had previously been admonished to beware of too much teacher talk by his regular supervisor, and we cannot exclude the possibility that he monitored carefully any linguistics jargon in my presence. Participant-observation is not a sufficient approach to data collection in problem areas which are so cognitively oriented as linguistics and teaching.

A third point should be made. It is surprising after 12 years of classroom observation in the ELI that I should be surprised. I take linguistics for granted and have just never looked for it, so to speak. The lack of its manifest presence,[1] when I was specifically looking, surprised me. This fact suggests a third way for answering our question about the significance of linguistics for language teaching, namely putting the two approaches together and using theory to guide our looking for supporting data, a common enough approach in experimental research. The model I propose using is that of Roulet's (1975), reproduced in Figure 2.

His major point, which others (Spolsky, 1969) have made before him, is that various fields besides theoretical linguistics contribute to language teaching and that one needs to understand the processes of their interrela-

---

[1]Had I gone to a pronunciation class, I would have found lots of evidence of phonetics.

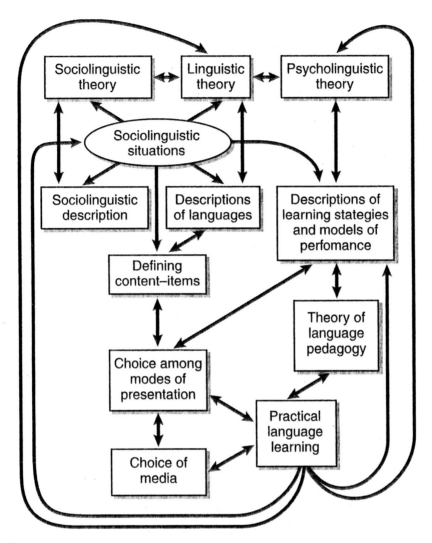

Figure 2 (*Source:* Roulet, 1975: 83.)

tionship as well. I propose to use Roulet's categories as a checklist for examining the possible contributions to language teaching we might find from linguistics in this broad sense of the word and then look for evidence that they occur somewhere in the teaching process.

Sociolinguistic Theory

This topic might usefully be divided into sociology of language and sociolinguistics. The sociology of language deals with language problems and

language treatments at the national level as problems arise within and between ethnic and national groups in contact and competition. Choice of
national language and of writing system, language standardization, bilingual education, language maintenance and shift efforts are all examples of
language problems. Naturally ESL is affected by the choice of teaching
Nigerian children to read in English, in choosing to teach Chicano children
to read in Spanish and in English, but it is more at a level of global understanding of contextual means and constraints than at a direct classroom
level of application.

Sociolinguistics refers to an approach to description of language which
takes into account the social features of a far from ideal hearer/speaker and
seeks to account for the rules of linguistic variability, be it social, regional,
cultural, gender, register or stylistic variation. (Labov has made the claim
that the term "sociolinguistics" is tautological since all linguistics need to
do this.) Sociolinguistics is probably the area which has most influenced
language teaching developments within the last ten years, especially
through its work with sociolinguistic description on speech acts, pragmatics, discourse analysis and cross-cultural communication. There is no one
sociolinguistic theory, and sociolinguists use notions and concepts from
several disciplines, primarily from anthropology, linguistics and sociology.
The work of Hymes, Labov and Bernstein may serve as representative examples. Hymes' notion of "communicative competence" which draws on
key concepts in ethnography has more than any other theoretical model influenced a new direction in language teaching (see below). Labov's (1969)
work on Black English helped legitimize this dialect with formal descriptions of its rule-governed behavior and dispel ideas of sloppy, lazy speech.
The interest in SESD (Standard English as a Second Dialect), as this special
interest group is known in TESOL, and the many resultant publications
(Baratz & Shuy, 1969; Dillard, 1972; Shuy & Fasold, 1970; Feigenbaum,
1970; Kochman, 1972; Mitchell-Kernan, 1971; Wolfram, 1969; Wolfram
& Clarke, 1971) peaked in the late 1960s and early 1970s and at present
form a less viable part of ESL. But the interest is bound to return because
the basic problems are still with us, and as the basic groundwork was done
in sociolinguistics, I am reasonably certain (I speak as a former SESD chair-
man) that ESL, or TESOL rather, will continue to be its spiritual and organizational home, an example of applied linguistics at its very best.

The attempts to explain, at a theoretical level, the educational failure
of lower-class and minority children have been many and varied from
Jensen's (1969) genetic model through cultural deprivation (Bereiter & Engelmann, 1966) to cultural differences (Abrahams & Troike, 1972; Burger,
1971; Cazden, John & Hymes, 1972; Saville-Troike, 1976; Spolsky, 1972;
Trueba & Barnett-Migrahi, 1979). Much of the linguistic work on Black
English was motivated exactly by the linguistic ignorance of the psychologists who wrote about the language of black children. Another series of
theory building which has marginally found its way into ESL but neverthe-

less has much influenced the thinking of sociolinguists is that of the British sociologist Basil Bernstein (1971, 1972, 1973). He posits the notions of restricted and elaborated code of which the latter is crucial for school success. Working-class children through their socialization in position oriented families have limited access to an elaborated code and so do poorly in school. This is an enormous simplification of his very elaborate argument but is nevertheless the gist of the matter. Bernstein has been widely misunderstood in the United States[2] where his work has been totally inappropriately applied to Black children.

We see then that the use of sociolinguistic theory tends to be problem oriented in its applications, frequently dealing with the language learning difficulties children from other than mainstream groups experience in our schools.

Sociolinguistic Situations

Sociolinguistic situations refer to the real world situation in which the students are going to use their English and so brings up the question of defining the objectives of language teaching in terms of the functions of these needs. "English for Special Purposes" and "English for Science and Technology" have been a major development during the last decade in ESL (Lackstrom, Selinker & Trimble, 1970; Richards, 1976; Selinker, Trimble & Vroman, 1972).

Sociolinguistic Description

This is the area where I think the most interesting work has been done in ESL during the last ten years, but then that may be a biased opinion. Still, my guess is that 20 years from now, when the Silent Way and Suggestopedia are gone, we will still use the sociolinguistic descriptions of speech acts, discourse, and cross-cultural communication which now surface in our journals.

Dell Hymes (1972a, 1972c, 1974), the anthropological linguist, has suggested that linguistic competence is not sufficient for an adequate description of language which must also take into account when, how and to whom it is appropriate to speak, that is a "communicative competence" or in Grimshaw's (1973:109) terms "the systemic sets of social interactional rules." More than any other single concept, the notion of communicative competence has influenced our thinking about teaching ESL. There are two major approaches within ESL at present, and one of them is a communicative approach to language teaching (Brumfit & Johnson, 1979; Canale &

---

[2]I understand from M. A. K. Halliday (personal communication, AILA conference, Greece 1990) that Bernstein is equally misunderstood in Britain. He is exceedingly difficult to read, but well worth the effort.

Swain, 1979; Candlin, 1975; Munby, 1978; Roulet & Holec, 1976; Widdowson, 1978; Wilkins, 1976). Such an approach argues that the focus of language teaching should be on language use rather than form, although most scholars consider linguistic competence to be part of communicative competence. The discrete units or teaching points of a lesson, syllabus, or textbook then cease being grammatical patterns, sequenced in an orderly manner, and instead become speech acts[3] or in Wilkins' terms notions and functions. Not that there is total agreement on this manner of organizing textbooks; in one of the latest issues of *Applied Linguistics* (1981, II, 1), both Brumfit and I argue against a purely functional approach in syllabus construction where the main argument is, I think, that language forms are generative while functions are not. One can, of course (and I would add should), combine form and function in one's teaching.

Johnson & Morrow's (1978) *Communicate* and (1979) *Approaches* were some of the first textbooks to adhere to a functional approach. Today it is a publisher's darling. A number of journal articles tackle the problem of speech act description (Borkin & Reinhart, 1978; Carrell & Konneker, 1981; Ervin-Tripp, 1976; Levinson, 1980; Rintell, 1979; Scarcella, 1979; Walters, 1979; Wolfson, 1981).

And interestingly enough sociolinguistics rated very high, right up with phonetics, on the questionnaire the ELI instructors had been asked to answer about the usefulness of linguistics for language teaching. All of them singled out speech act theory especially as helpful. I think this somewhat, to me at least, surprising response reflects the fact that although our cultural rules and ways of doing things permeate our life, we are rarely aware of those rules until they are broken. It is difficult to talk about and teach cultural rules without any training. Several instructors commented that such study had given them a way of systematically organizing the data and a meta-language—which they avoided using in the classroom—to think about such phenomena. One instructor added that such understanding also allowed her to know exactly what questions to ask in the classroom in order to bring out a kind of cultural contrastive analysis of speech acts. A compliment in Japanese is not necessarily one in English (Wolfson, 1981) and students need to be made aware of that.

Finally, ESL teachers are sensitive to their students as human beings. In the words of one instructor: "Sociolinguistics has helped me become aware of different cultural norms and *possible* differences, perhaps more importantly . . . It helps in dealing with the students on a personal level."

---

[3] Speech act is a difficult concept to define and Austin (1962) and Searle (1976) have written books to do so. Hymes (1972a:56) defines a speech act, like a joke, as the minimal term of the set speech event, a conversation, and speech situation, a party. Not that teaching speech acts is new. Kelley (1969) discusses the teaching of phrases of social life, like courting, social calls and quarreling, during the Renaissance. Shakespeare even satirized lessons from Florio. There is very little new in language teaching, except maybe the Silent Way.

Linguistic Theory and Descriptions of Languages

Back in 1969, Wardhaugh wrote a TESOL State of the Art paper in which he outlined the tenets of transformational-generative (TG) grammar and commented on the insights into language it gave. He concluded: "However, neither the grammar nor existing descriptions give teachers any way of teaching these insights nor do they provide any way of assigning a truth value to the insights on an absolute scale, apparent claims to the contrary notwithstanding" (Wardhaugh, 1969:12). I think Wardhaugh's remark still stands. The most intelligent statement of the value of TG grammar for language teaching was Robin Lakoff's (1969) "Transformational grammar and language teaching" and she has since (Lakoff, 1974) retracted her words, saying she was simply mistaken. Rutherford's (1968) *Modern English,* for which claims were made that it followed a TG approach, in its second edition reflects a change toward more traditional grammar. In fact, we tend to find the same absence of overt linguistics in textbooks as I found in classroom observation. Furey (1972) found in an analysis of the grammatical rules and explanations very little difference in textbooks of respectively audio-lingual, direct method, TG grammar and eclectic orientation. Presumably this is so, she says, because of the pedagogical necessity of simplifications of rules.

There are of course linguistic theories other than TG grammar, such as case grammar (Nilsen, 1971) and tagmemics (Paulston, 1970) which are used for ESL purposes. The trouble is that few ESL teachers today are trained in structural linguistics, which I maintain is much more suitable for pedagogical purposes. In fact, what happens is that the eclectic approach exemplified by Quirk & Greenbaum (1973) (and Quirk, Greenbaum, Leech & Svartvik, 1972) is the generally prevailing approach in language teaching.

My view that theoretical linguistics has lacked any influence on language teaching during the last decade needs to be modified. Chomsky undeniably changed the climate of linguistic thought in the United States. Chomsky's attack of language acquisition as habit formation has had enormous consequences on our thinking about language teaching. Language learning as a creative act is the basic foundation of most present-day ESL methods and one source for our interest in error analysis.

The way teachers deal with errors in the classroom is closely influenced by their linguistic knowledge. Experienced teachers tend to correct what they judge to be performance errors with a reference to the rule and so elicit the correction from the student himself while a competence error repeated by several students will bring on a modelling by the teacher of the grammatical pattern, sometimes in a contrast to other familiar patterns, and a grammatical explanation of its function. I saw this repeated several times in my class observations. Thinking on one's feet and being able to come up with good example sentences is in fact what one instructor cites as the major benefit of her syntax course. Most instructors agree that syntax, standard theory, is too abstract to be of much use in the classroom but they cite the insight into *patterns* of English, into knowing what is rule-governed behavior and what needs to be memorized, into what structures are similar and different, into knowing what goes together as very useful in their teaching. One of them writes: "Since I've studied linguistics I've become *more* convinced of the notion that language has a definite structure/ system, which means I now no longer feel quite so helpless about teaching grammar." The last point is important. It became very clear in the interviews that teachers dislike intensely to feel ignorant or uncertain about what they are teaching and that they worry about their explanations and presentation of teaching points. The study of linguistics brings them confidence and security, and they are very conscious about that relationship.

The instructors are unanimous in their opinion that phonetics is most useful; it is the only coursework that ranks higher than sociolinguistics. The reason is simple: "I understand how the sounds are articulated and can tell the students." It also develops their ear so they can hear and know what the students do wrong. It is hardly a recent development in linguistics; classic articulatory Eliza Doolittle period. They find basic concepts in phonemics useful but most reject generative phonology. Surprisingly, many also reject grammatical analysis, morphology, and field methods and less surprisingly, historical linguistics and Montague grammar. They all consider linguistic structures of English, in which they use Quirk & Greenbaum (1973), as basically boring but nevertheless essential.

We see then that even if I have doubt about the usefulness of present day linguistics for language teaching, our students do not. Even if they consider only two courses in linguistic theory—phonetics and English grammar—as core courses, they insist that the study of syntax brings them a *Weltanschauung*, a worldview of language which they find eminently useful.

Defining Content Items

By this term, Roulet means the selection and sequencing of language materials for the curriculum or textbook. Structural linguists gave a lot of thought and energy to the optimum selection and sequencing of language items, but these days this is an unfashionable topic. The occasional argument is rather whether one should teach function before form, and of course there is the notional-functional argument that syllabi should be organized on the basis of communicative functions rather than on grammatical patterns. As Canale & Swain (1979:58) point out, there are no empirical data on the relative effectiveness or ineffectiveness of either approach.

Psycholinguistic Theory

In 1969 Wardhaugh predicted that cognitive psychology would influence language teaching for many years to come and thus far his prediction holds. Ausubel (1968) is still frequently cited in footnotes, everyone insists language learning must be meaningful, the notion of language learning as habit formation is dismissed, and there seems to be a general consensus that grammatical rules and explanations are beneficial for adults.[4]

Besides cognitive psychology, psycholinguistics (Clark & Clark, 1977; Dato, 1975; Taylor, 1976; Slobin, 1971) and neurolinguistics (Albert & Obler, 1978; Lenneberg & Lenneberg, 1975; Rieber, 1976) are topics of recent interest. Especially in regard to neurolinguistics, caution is needed in drawing implications for the classroom. At this point I think it is safe to say that the evidence (from aphasia, split brain operations, dichotic listening tests, etc.) indicates that individuals have different ways of learning for which there may be a biological foundation. But that was known before. I find the readings in neurolinguistics the most interesting in the language-learning field today. But I worry about premature applications, and I react against the fads which claim to draw on neurolinguistics.

In psycholinguistics, there has been much L2 acquisition research during the last decade. Douglas Brown, in an editorial in *Language Learning* in 1974, comments on the "new wave" of research: "for perhaps the first time in history, L2 research is characterized by a rigorous empirical approach coupled with cautious rationalism" (D. Brown, 1974:v–vi) and goes on to claim that "the results of current L2 research will indeed have a great impact on shaping a new method" (D. Brown, 1974:v–vi). This hasn't happened, and it is still too early to see what the implications will be.

It is difficult to single out any specific studies, but the best place to begin is probably with Roger Brown's (1973) *A First Language*. Along with his basic finding that "there is an approximately invariant order to acquisition for the 14 morphemes we have studied, and behind this invariance lies not modeling frequency but semantic and grammatical complexity" (R. Brown, 1973:379) (a finding supported by the L2 studies), he also carefully investigates the psychological reality of TG transformational rules, a notion he is forced to reject as invalid. Instead he posits the concept of semantic saliency, a notion which may hold direct implications for language teaching.

Whatever the implications for language teaching which we will eventually draw from this "new wave" of L2 acquisition research, Brown is right

---

[4]This article was written before The Natural Approach (Krashen & Terrell, 1983). I would not want to mislead the reader that there is today general consensus on grammatical rules and explanations being beneficial. However, most scholars I know disagree with Krashen on the topic.

in pointing out a major significance, the turning to empirical evidence rather than unsubstantiated claims and counterclaims.

The greatest surprise of the questionnaire response was to be found in the TAs' reaction to psycholinguistic theory. They held it of marginal utility. I will quote one instructor at length.

> Nothing very directly applicable; but by increasing my knowledge of the mental processes involved in language use (well, at least of people's theories about them), it's increased my ... my what? I think this is a case where I have to resort to a general "the more I know about language learning, the better teacher I'll be." The most pertinent research (in reading, L1 acquisition, etc.) seems better at pointing out what variables are probably insignificant than at telling us which ones are important.

I think this attitude reflects the fact that we really don't know how people learn language.

Descriptions of Learning Strategies and Models of Performance

Theory of Language Pedagogy

A thorough exploration of these two topics would require a book or two to complete and take us too far afield for the purposes of this paper. The audio-lingual method drew heavily on linguistics in its development. Today that method has been discredited, maybe at times unfairly, as it is blamed for infelicities which Fries certainly never intended. A careful reading of his *Teaching and Learning English as a Foreign Language* (Fries, 1945) will reveal it as sensible a book today as the day it was written.

In today's thinking about language teaching, psychology seems to play a larger part than linguistics. Cognitive code (John Carroll's term) is recognized as a general trend, with its emphasis on meaningful learning and careful analysis of linguistic structures. The cognitive code approach can be considered a reaction against the audio-lingual, both from theoretical and practical viewpoints. The approach closely reflects the transformational-generative linguistic school of thought about the nature of language, and it is influenced by cognitive psychologists, critical of stimulus-reinforcement theory, such as Ausubel (1968). It holds that language is a rule-governed creative system of a universal nature. Language learning must be meaningful, rote-learning should be avoided, and the primary emphasis is on analysis and developing competence in Chomsky's sense of the word. We see the same nice fit between linguistic theory and psychological theory in cognitive code methodology as we once had in the audio-lingual method. The trouble with cognitive code is that I know of not one single textbook for beginning students which can be classified as strict cognitive code.

In practical fact, most language teaching specialists are eclectic and so are the textbooks they write. Carroll (1971) holds that there is nothing mutually exclusive in the theories of Skinner and of Lenneberg-Chomsky about language learning but rather that these theories are complementary. This opinion is reflected in the eclectic approach to methodology which is characteristic of most of the methods texts at the technique level. Most of the writers of these texts agree that all four skills—listening, speaking, reading and writing—should be introduced simultaneously, without undue postponement of any one. The importance of writing as a service activity for the other skills is generally recognized and there is considerable interest in controlled composition. No one talks any longer about memorizing long dialogues. Listening comprehension is still poorly understood on a theoretical level, but there is more emphasis on the teaching of that skill. The crucial importance of vocabulary, the ignoring of which was one of the worst faults of the audio-lingual approach, is increasingly gaining acceptance.

I think we agree with Chastain (1976) that "perhaps too much attention has been given to proper pronunciation," and we now tend to think that it is more important that the learner can communicate his ideas than that he can practice utterances with perfect pronunciation. The one thing that everyone is absolutely certain about is the necessity to use language for communicative purposes in the classroom. As early as 1968 Oller & Obrecht concluded from an experiment that communicative activity should be a central point of pattern drills from the very first stages of language learning. Savignon's (1971) widely cited dissertation confirmed that beyond doubt. Many bridle at pattern drills, but it is not very important because we agree on the basic principle of meaningful learning for the purpose of communication. And that basic principle is indicative of what may be the most significant trend: our increasing concentration on our students' learning rather than on our teaching (Oller & Richards, 1973).

In addition to the prevailing eclecticism, several new methods have gained visibility recently in the United States. In alphabetical order they are: Community Counseling Learning, Rapid Acquisition, the Silent Way, Suggestopedia, and Total Physical Response. The Monitor Model (Krashen, 1972) maybe should be mentioned here too, but at this point it is a theoretical model of language learning rather than a method for language teaching.

Community Counseling Learning or Community Language Learning (CLL) was developed by Charles A. Curran (1976) from his earlier work in affective psychology. In CLL the students sit in a circle with a tape recorder and talk about whatever interests them. The teacher whose role is seen as a counselor serves as a resource person rather than as a traditional "teacher." At the very beginning stages, the counselor also serves as translator for his clients: the students first utter in their native language, the teacher translates, and the students repeat their own utterances in the L2. The tape is played back, errors analyzed and the clients copy down whatever structures they need to work on. Adherents of this method tend to be ardent in their fervor as they point out that this method teaches "the whole person" within a supportive community which minimizes the risk-taking held necessary for language learning. Another value of this method lies in the motivational aspect in that students can talk about issues of concern to them (Stevick, 1976, 1980).

Rapid Acquisition is an approach developed by Winitz & Reeds (1973) called Rapid Acquisition of a Foreign Language by Avoidance of Speaking. The authors believe that there is a natural sequence (neurological) in language learning and stress listening comprehension until it is complete before students are allowed to speak. Length of utterance is limited, problem solving through the use of pictures are stressed, and the syllabus is limited to base structures and limited vocabulary.

The Silent Way was developed by Caleb Gattegno (1972) in 1963 but not published here until 1972. In the Silent Way, the teacher uses Cuisiniere rods, a color-coded wall chart for pronunciation, and speaks each new word only *once*; the responsibility for learning and talking is shifted to the students. Even correction is handled through gestures and mime by the teacher with no further modeling. Many teachers are enthusiastic about this method (Stevick, 1980), but I have also heard many anecdotes of student rebellion.

Suggestopedia, a method developed by Georgi Lozanov at the Institute of Suggestology in Sofia, Bulgaria (Lozanov, 1979; Bancroft, 1978) claims to reduce the stress of language learning. Listening and speaking are stressed with emphasis on vocabulary acquisition. The Suggestopedic Cycle begins with review of previously learned material in the target language, followed by introduction of new material. This is followed by a one-hour seance during which students listen to the new material against a background of baroque music. The students also do breathing exercises and yoga relaxation techniques which are said to increase concentration and tap the powers of the subconscious. There is also considerable role-play of real-life situations.

Total Physical Response, developed by James Asher (Asher, 1969; Asher & Adamski, 1977), also stresses listening comprehension as he believes that if listening and speaking are introduced simultaneously, listening comprehension is much delayed. Basically the method consists of having students listen to commands and then carry them out.

I refrain from commenting on these methods since it is not my opinion which is important but rather the teacher's. As long as teacher *and students* have confidence that they are in fact learning, and all are happy in the process, I don't think the methods make that much difference.

Conclusion

In conclusion, we can say that Newmark after all is more right than Chomsky about the significance of linguistics for the teaching of languages. But Chomsky is right too for that influence is not immediately apparent. Linguistics is like our proverbial bottom of the iceberg, mostly invisible, but massively giving shape and direction to the teaching. It took me several hours of reflection to realize that I had not heard any incorrect grammatical explanations, also an indication of linguistics at work.

Most of all linguistics becomes a worldview. It colors the approach to language, the recognition of problems and the attempts to solutions. Our TF's rejection of a formal approach to the passive, characteristic of a structural approach to linguistics, would once have been branded as mentalism, but reflects what may be the most important contribution of present day linguistics, a different attitude towards language.

References

Abrahams, R. and Troike, R. 1972, *Language and Culture Diversity in American Education.* Englewood Cliffs, NJ: Prentice-Hall.

Albert, M. L. and Obler, L. K. 1978, *The Bilingual Brain: Neuropsychological and Neurolinguistic Aspects of Bilingualism.* New York: Academic Press.

Allen, J. P. B. and Corder, S. P. (eds) 1975, *Papers in Applied Linguistics.* London: Oxford University Press.

Asher, J. 1969, The total physical response approach to second language learning. *Modern Language Learning* 53, 1, 3–17.

Asher, J. J. and Adamski, C. 1977, *Learning Another Language through Actions: The Complete Teacher's Guidebook.* Los Gatos, Calif.: Sky Oak Productions.

Austin, J. L. 1962, *How to Do Things with Words.* Cambridge: Harvard University Press.

Ausubel, D. P. 1968, *Educational Psychology: A Cognitive View.* New York: Holt, Rinehart and Winston.

Bancroft, W. J. 1978, The Lozanov Method and its American Adaptations. *Modern Language Journal* 62, 4, 167–74.

Baratz, J. and Shuy, R. 1969, *Teaching Black Children to Read.* Washington, DC: Center for Applied Linguistics.

Bereiter C. and Engelmann, S. 1966, *Teaching Disadvantaged Children in the Preschool.* Englewood Cliffs, NJ: Prentice-Hall.

Bernstein, B. 1971, *Class, Codes and Control* Vol. 1. London: Routledge and Kegan Paul.

——— 1972, A sociolinguistic approach to socialization; with some reference to educability. In J. Gumperz and D. Hymes (eds) *Directions in Sociolinguistics.* New York: Holt, Rinehart and Winston.

——— 1973, *Class, Codes and Control* Vol. 2. London: Routledge and Kegan Paul.

Borkin, A. and Reinhart, S. 1978, Excuse me and I'm sorry. *TESOL Quarterly* 12, 57–70.

Brown, D. 1974, Editorial, *Language Learning* 24, 2, v–vi.

Brown, R. A. 1973, *A First Language: The Early Stages.* Cambridge, Mass.: University Press.

Brumfit, C. 1981, Notional syllabuses revisited: a response. *Applied Linguistics* 2, 190–2.

Brumfit, C. and Johnson, K. (eds) 1979, *The Communicative Approach to Language Teaching.* Oxford: Oxford University Press.

Burger, H. 1971, *Ethno-Pedagogy: Cross-Cultural Teaching Techniques.* Albuquerque, NM: Southwestern Cooperative Educational Laboratory.

Canale, M. and Swain, M. 1979, *Communicative Approaches to Second Language Teaching and Testing.* Ontario: Ministry of Education.

Candlin, C. (ed.) 1975, *The Communicative Teaching of English.* London: Longman.

Carrell, P. and Konneker, B. 1981, Politeness: comparing native and nonnative judgments. *Language Learning* 31, 17–30.

Carroll, J. B. 1971, Current issues in psycholinguistics and second language teaching. *TESOL Quarterly* 5, 2, 101–17.

—— 1974, Learning theory for the classroom teacher. In G. A. Jarvis (ed.) *The Challenge of Communication.* Skokie, Ill.: National Textbook Company.

Cazden, C. B., John, V. P. and Hymes, D. (eds) 1972, *Functions of Language in the Classroom.* New York: Teachers College Press.

Chastain, K. 1976, *Developing Second-Language Skills: Theory to Practice* 2nd edn. Chicago: Rand, McNally.

Chomsky, N. 1966, Linguistic theory. *Language Teaching: Broader Contexts.* Northeast Conference on the Teaching of Foreign Languages.

Clark, H. E. and Clark, E. V. 1977, *Psychology and Language.* New York: Harcourt Brace Jovanovich.

Corder, S. P. 1973, *Introducing Applied Linguistics.* Baltimore: Penguin.

—— 1975, Applied linguistics and language teaching. In J. P. B. Allen and S. P. Corder (eds) *Papers in Applied Linguistics.* London: Oxford University Press.

Curran, C. A. 1976, *Counseling-Learning in Second Languages.* Apple River, Ill.: Apple River Press.

Dato, D. (ed.) 1975, *Developmental Psycholinguistics: Theory and Applications.* Georgetown University Round Table on Languages and Linguistics. Washington, DC: Georgetown University Press.

Dillard, J. L. 1972, *Black English: Its History and Usage in the United States.* New York: Vintage Books.

Ervin-Tripp, S. 1976, Is Sybil there? The structure of some American English directives. *Language in Society* 5, 25–66.

Feigenbaum, J. 1970, The use of nonstandard English in teaching standard: contrast and comparison. In R. W. Fasold and R. W. Shuy (eds) *Teaching Standard English in the Inner City.* Washington, DC: Center for Applied Linguistics.

Fries, C. C. 1945, *Teaching and Learning English as a Foreign Language.* Ann Arbor: University of Michigan Press.

Furey, P. 1972, Grammar explanations in foreign language teaching. Unpublished MA thesis, University of Pittsburgh.

Gattegno, C. 1972, *Teaching Foreign Languages in Schools the Silent Way* 2nd edn. New York: Educational Solutions.

Gleason, H. A. Jr, 1955, *An Introduction to Descriptive Linguistics*. New York: Holt, Rinehart and Winston.

Grimshaw, D. 1973, Rules, social interaction and language behavior. *TESOL Quarterly* 7, 2, 109.

Hymes, D. 1967, The anthropology of communication. In F. Dance (ed.) *Human Communication Theory*. New York: Holt, Rinehart and Winston.

———1972a, Models of the interaction of language and social life. In J. Gumperz and D. Hymes (eds) *Directions in Sociolinguistics*. New York: Holt, Rinehart and Winston.

———1972b, Introduction. In C. Cazden, V. John and D. Hymes (eds) *The Function of Language in the Classroom* (pp. xi–lviii). New York: Teachers College Press.

———1972c, On communicative competence. In J. B. Pride and J. Holmes (eds) *Sociolinguistics* (pp. 269–93). Harmondsworth, England: Penguin Books.

———1974, *Foundations in Sociolinguistics*. Philadelphia: University of Pennsylvania Press.

Jensen, A. 1969, How much can we boost IQ and scholastic achievement? *Harvard Educational Review* 39, 1.

Johnson, K. and Morrow, K. 1978, *Communicate*. Reading: University of Reading.

———1979, *Approaches*. Cambridge: Cambridge University Press.

Kelley, L. G. 1969, *25 Centuries of Language Teaching*. Rowley, Mass.: Newbury House.

Kochman, T. (ed.) 1972, *Rappin' and Stylin' Out: Communication in Urban Black America*. Chicago: University of Illinois Press.

Krashen, S. D. 1972, The Monitor Model for adult second language performance. In M. Burt, H. Dulay and M. Finocchiaro (eds) *Viewpoints on English Language as a Second Language* (pp. 152–61). New York: Regents.

Krashen, S. D. and Terrell, T. D. 1983, *The Natural Approach*. Hayward, CA: Alemany Press.

Labov, W. 1969, *The Study of Non-Standard English*. Washington, DC: ERIC, Center for Applied Linguistics.

Lackstrom, J., Selinker, L. and Trimble, L. 1970, Grammar and technical English. *English as a Second Language: Current Issues*. Chilton Press.

Lado, R. 1957, *Linguistics Across Cultures: Applied Linguistics for Teachers*. Ann Arbor: University of Michigan Press.

Lakoff, R. 1969, Transformational grammar and language teaching. *Language Learning* 19, 1 and 2, 117–40.

———1974, Linguistic theory and the real world. Paper presented at the TESOL Convention 1974, Denver, Colorado.

Larsen-Freeman, D. 1981, The 'what' of second language acquisition. In M. Hines and W. Rutherford (eds) *On TESOL '81*. Washington, DC: TESOL.

Lenneberg, E. H. and Lenneberg, E. (eds) 1975, *Foundations of Language Development*. New York: Academic Press.

Levinson, S. 1980, Speech act theory: the state of the art. *Language Teaching and Linguistic Abstracts* 13, 5–24.

Lozanov, G. 1979, *Suggestology and Outlines of Suggestopedy*. New York: Gordon and Breach.

Mitchell-Kernan, C. 1971, *Language Behavior in a Black Urban Community*. Monographs of the Language-Behavior Research Laboratory No. 2, University of California at Berkeley.

Moulton, W. G. 1961, Linguistics and language teaching in the United States, 1940–1960. In C. Mohemann, *et al.* (eds) *Trends in European and American Linguistics*. Utrecht: Spectrum.

———1970, *A Linguistic Guide to Language Learning* 2nd edn. New York: Modern Language Association.

Munby, J. 1978, *Communicative Syllabus Design*. Cambridge: Cambridge University Press.

Newmark, L. 1970, Grammatical theory and the teaching of English as a foreign language. In M. Lester (ed.) *Readings in Applied Transformational Grammar*. New York: Holt, Rinehart and Winston.

Nida, E. A. 1949, *Morphology: The Descriptive Analysis of Words*. Ann Arbor, Mich.:University of Michigan Press.

———1954, *Customs and Cultures*. New York: Harper.

Nilsen, D. L. F. 1971, The use of case grammar in teaching English as a foreign language. *TESOL Quarterly* 5, 4, 293–300.

Norris, W. 1972, *TESOL at the Beginning of the 70's: Trends, Topics, and Research Needs*. Pittsburgh, PA: University Center for International Studies.

Oller, J. and Obrecht, D. H. 1968, Pattern drill and communicative activity: a psycholinguistic experiment. *IRAL* 6, 2, 165–72.

Oller, J. W. Jr and Richards, J. C. (eds) 1973, *Focus on the Learner: Pragmatic Perspectives for the Language Teachers*. Rowley, Mass.: Newbury House.

Paulston, C. B. 1970, Teaching footnotes and bibliographical entries to foreign students: a tagmemic approach. *English Language Teaching* 34–3.

———1981, Notional syllabuses revisited: some comments. *Applied Linguistics* 2, 1, 93–5.

Pike, K. 1947, *Phonemics: A Technique for Reducing Languages to Writing*. Ann Arbor: University of Michigan Press.

Quirk, R. and Greenbaum, S. 1973, *A Concise Grammar of Contemporary English*. New York: Harcourt, Brace, Jovanovich.

Quirk, R., Greenbaum, S., Leech, G. and Svartvik, J. 1972, *A Grammar of Contemporary English*. New York: Seminar Press.

Richards, J. C. 1974, *Error Analysis: Perspectives on Second Language Acquisition*. London: Longman.

———(ed.) 1976, *Teaching English for Science and Technology*. Singapore: RELC.

Rieber, R. W. 1976, *The Neuropsychology of Language*. New York: Plenum Press.

Rintell, E. 1979, Getting your speech act together: The pragmatic ability of second language learners. *Working Papers on Bilingualism* 17, 97–106.

Roulet, E. 1975, *Linguistic Theory, Linguistic Description, and Language Teaching*. London: Longman.

Roulet, E. and Holec, H. 1976, *L'Enseignement de la compétence de communication en langues secondes*. Neuchatel: Université de Neuchatel.

Rutherford, W. 1968, *Modern English*. New York: Harcourt, Brace and World.

Savignon, S. 1971, Study of the effect of training in communicative skills as part of a beginning college French course on student attitude and achievement in linguistic and communicative competence. Ph.D. dissertation, University of Illinois at Urbana-Champaign.

Saville-Troike, M. 1976, *Foundations for Teaching English as a Second Language: Theory and Method for Multicultural Education.* Englewood Cliffs, NJ: Prentice-Hall.

Scarcella, R. 1979, On speaking politely in a second language. In C. Yorio, K. Perkins and J. Schacter (eds) *On TESOL '79.* Washington, DC: TESOL.

Schachter, J. 1974, An error in error analysis. *Language Learning* 24, 2, 205–14, 213.

Searle, J. 1976, A classification of illocutionary acts. *Language in Society* 5, 1–25.

Selinker, L., Trimble, L. and Vroman, R. 1972, *Working Papers in Scientific and Technical English.* University of Washington: Office of Engineering Research.

Shuy, R. and Fasold, R. 1970, *Teaching Standard English in the Inner City.* Washington, DC: Center for Applied Linguistics.

Slobin, D. I. 1971, *Psycholinguistics.* Glenview, Ill.: Scott, Foresman & Co.

Spolsky, B. 1969, Linguistics and language pedagogy—applications or implications? In *Georgetown University Round Table* 22, 143–55.

———(ed.) 1972, *The Education of Minority Children.* Rowley, Mass.: Newbury House.

———1978, *Educational Linguistics.* Rowley, Mass.: Newbury House.

Stevick, E. 1976, *Memory, Meaning and Method: Some Psychological Perspectives on Language Learning.* Rowley, Mass.: Newbury House.

———1980, *Teaching Languages: A Way and Ways.* Rowley, Mass.: Newbury House.

Taylor, I. 1976, *Introduction to Psycholinguistics.* New York: Holt, Rinehart and Winston.

Trueba, H. and Barnett-Migrahi, C. (eds) 1979, *Bilingual Multicultural Education and the Professional.* Rowley, Mass.: Newbury House.

Van Ek, J. A. 1978, *The Threshold Level of Modern Language Teaching in Schools.* Longmans.

Walters, J. 1979, Strategies for requesting in Spanish and English. *Language Learning* 29, 277–93.

Wardhaugh, R. 1969, Teaching English to speakers of other languages: the State of the Art. Washington, DC: ERIC Clearinghouse for Linguistics, Center for Applied Linguistics, ED 030119.

Warriner, J. E., Whitten, M. E. and Griffith, F. 1975, *English Grammar and Composition.* New York: Harcourt, Brace, Jovanovich.

Widdowson, H. 1978, *Teaching Language as Communication.* London: Oxford University Press.

Wilkins, D. A. 1976, *Notional Syllabuses.* Oxford: Oxford University Press.

Winitz, H. and Reeds, J. A. 1973, Rapid acquisition of a foreign language by avoidance of speaking. *IRAL* 11, 4, 295–317.

Wolfram, W. 1969, *A Sociolinguistic Description of Detroit Negro Speech.* Washington, DC: Center for Applied Linguistics.

Wolfram, W. and Clarke, N. 1971, *Black–White Speech Relationships.* Washington, DC: Center for Applied Linguistics.

Wolfson, N. 1981, Compliments in cross-cultural perspective. *TESOL Quarterly* 15, 2, 117–24.

Content Questions

1. What direction of influence does Paulston indicate occurs between linguistic theory and language learning?

2. What approach did Paulston use for identifying which aspects of linguistics might be most useful to ESL teachers?

3. Which branch of linguistics has in most recent years had the greatest effect on language teaching?

4. What is a functional approach in language teaching?

5. Besides sociolinguistics, what other branches of linguistics did ESL teachers report were useful to them?

6. Describe each of the language teaching methods summarized near the end of the article. Does Paulston prefer any one of these over the others? Explain.

Questions for Analysis and Discussion

1. Explain why learning a second language requires learning about the speech acts in that language.

2. Chomsky introduced an important distinction between language acquisition and language learning. The former occurs subconsciously, while the latter occurs through the conscious learning of rules. Comment on the teaching methods mentioned in this article and how they relate to notions about language learning versus language acquisition.

3. As far as language teaching is concerned, what kind of role does Paulston see for linguistics? How visible is that role?

Additional Activities and Paper Topics

1. Consider some of the kinds of choices a textbook designed to teach English to nonnative speakers must make about the pronunciation issues it addresses. For example, which variety of English should it represent (i.e. American, British, Indian, or Australian)? If it tries to represent American English pronunciation, which dialect of American English should it represent and why? How much variability in pronunciation even among American English speakers should it acknowledge? To what extent should it alert the learners to phonological processes such as assimilation that operate in the language? Notice, for example, how you might pronounce "What's your name?" or "Did you come?" quickly. How would the level of students or their communicative needs (whether primarily spoken, written, or both) affect the type of pronunciation that is taught? Which issues might someone without linguistic training not even consider or be aware of? Prepare a report discussing some of these types of issues. (**Phonetics and Phonology**)

2. Obtain writing samples that have been written by a nonnative speaker of English who is struggling with the language (one source may be your college or university's writing lab). Examine the linguistic features of the language that seem to be giving the student trouble. Then analyze and report on what you have observed. (**Morphology, Syntax, Semantics, and Pragmatics**)

3. Select one of the conversational rules or strategies mentioned in Dörnyei and Thurrell's article. Then observe how native speakers behave linguistically with regard to the item you have selected. Consult any linguistic research that you can find on that subject. Report on your findings. (**Semantics, Pragmatics, and Discourse Analysis**)

4. Consult textbooks that have been written to teach English speakers another language. Observe what kinds of material is presented in the text. Consider issues such as whether the text orders its material around grammatical structures or whether it does so according to functions such as apologies, requests, and the like. You might also note whether it shows how to use indirect speech acts. Write a paper describing what you have found.

5. Many methods and approaches have been used to teach language. These are based on different assumptions about the best way we learn or acquire languages. Some of these methods and approaches are briefly mentioned in Paulston's article such as the Silent Way, Suggestopedia, Rapid Acquisition, Community Language Learning, Total Physical Response, and the Natural Approach (see Paulston's note #4). Prepare a research paper discussing one of these methods or approaches.

Glossary

A

Ablaut A variation in vowels that indicates a change of grammatical function for a word; in English, the vowel sound in the verb *give* changes in the form *gave* to indicate the past tense.

Acoustic phonetics The study of the physical properties of speech sounds as they pass through the air in waves.

Acronym A word formed by combining the initial letters of a set of words, as in the word RADAR from *RA(dio) D(etecting) A(nd) R(anging)*.

Accusative The case (grammatical role) of a noun or noun phrase that in English acts as a direct object for a verb (see **Case**).

Adverbial A grammatical category of words, phrases, or clauses that function as verb modifiers, sentence modifiers, clause connectors, intensifiers, or negation particles; **adverbs** are adverbials that show manner, time, and place.

Affirmative A word or phrase expressing assent; *yes* is an affirmative marker in English.

Affix A bound morpheme that attaches to a root morpheme; in English, affixes are usually prefixes *(pre-, bi-)* or suffixes *(-hood, -ing)*; derivational affixes change the meaning of a word; inflectional affixes signal the grammatical or syntactical relationship of a word to other words.

Affricate A consonant sound articulated with a full closure (stop) followed by a fricative release of the air stream; the final consonant sounds in the English words *batch* and *badge* are affricates.

Alliteration The marked repetition of a consonant sound at the beginning of key words within a discourse unit, as in the tongue-twister *Peter Piper picked a peck of pickled peppers.*

Allophone Two or more predictable variants of a single phoneme; the [t] in *hit,* the [tʰ] in *time,* the [D] in *little,* and the glottal stop in *written* represent different allophones of the phoneme /t/ in English words.

Allusion A reference (or quotation) in a discourse to something well-known or familiar.

Alveolar A sound articulated with the tip or blade of the tongue near or on the alveolar ridge behind the upper front teeth. In English, /t/, /d/, /s/, /z/, /l/, and /n/ are alveolar consonants.

Alveolar ridge The bony edge of the gums behind the upper front teeth.

Ambiguity A language phenomenon which allows a word or structure to have more than one meaning or interpretation; for example, the phrase *large chairs and tables* may mean either *large chairs and [large] tables* or *tables and large chairs.*

Amelioration A semantic change toward a more positive connotation in the meaning of a word or morpheme; for example, the English word *nice,* which meant "foolish" in Middle English, has undergone amelioration.

American Sign Language (ASL) A visual-gestural language used by members of the Deaf community in the United States. ASL is not merely a hand-signaled representation of spoken English; rather it is a completely different language with its own morphology, syntax, lexicon, grammar, and pragmatics.

Antecedent A constituent that a pronoun refers to within a discourse unit; in the sentence *The table has papers on it,* the noun phrase *The table* is the antecedent to the pronoun *it.*

Antonyms Words that are related by complementary or opposite meanings; some pairs of antonyms are gradable, such as *dark/light,* and some are non-gradable, such as *male/female.*

Aphasia A group of language disorders resulting from injury to the brain; cortical damage may cause difficulty in writing, reading, or speaking skills.

Appositive A structure that renames another word or phrase at the same grammatical level; *the King of England* is an appositive for *George* in the phrase *George, the King of England.*

Argot Specialized vocabulary used by people sharing a common occupation or discipline; diction that is largely unknown to those outside a common group; jargon.

Article A kind of function word or determiner that can precede nouns in noun phrases; in English, the definite article *(the)* shows that a noun refers to something specified or understood, and the indefinite article *(a* or *an)* shows that a noun refers to something general or unidentified.

Articulator An element of the vocal tract that is used in the production of human speech, such as the lips, tongue, uvula, and velum.

Articulatory phonetics The branch of phonetics that studies how various speech sounds are articulated or produced in the vocal tract.

Artificial intelligence The approximation of human-like cognitive capabilities, such as experiential reasoning and language translation, by a computer.

Aspect A verb form indicating time notions such as duration of action, order of events, or habitual behavior; English has a perfect aspect *(has come)* and a progressive aspect *(is coming).*

Aspiration A marked release of air that sometimes accompanies a speech sound; in English, aspiration occurs with word-initial voiceless stops [pʰ], [tʰ], and [kʰ].

Assimilation The process by which one sound influences the articulation of a neighboring sound so that the sounds become similar or the same (see **Progressive assimilation** and **Regressive assimilation**).

Assonance The significant repetition of vowels sounds in key words within a discourse unit, as with the /aj/ sound in Isaiah 60:1, "Ar*i*se, sh*i*ne; for thy l*i*ght is come."

Attributive adjective In English, a modifying word that appears before the noun in a noun phrase; *blue* is an attributive adjective in the noun phrase *a blue car* (see **Predicative adjective**).

Audiolingual method A language-teaching method that emphasizes listening and speaking skills in the target language through dialogue memorization and practice drills.

Auxiliary verb A finite verb form that accompanies the main lexical verb in a verb phrase and carries tense, aspect, or modality; *has* in the sentence *John has seen her* is an auxiliary verb.

B

Backformation A new word produced by analogy when people remove a supposed affix from the perceived stem of a word; the verb *peddle* was created in English when people began removing the supposed affix *-ar* from the noun *peddlar.*

Back vowel A vowel produced when the top of the tongue is placed near the back of the oral cavity of the mouth; /u/ and /o/ are back vowels (see **Vowel**).

Bilabial A consonant sound that uses both lips as a point of articulation; the initial sounds in *pat, bat,* and *mat* are bilabials.

Black English A variety of English often spoken in African-American communities, sometimes referred to as African-American Vernacular English (AAVE).

Blending A word formation process in which parts of two different words are combined to create a new form; for example, *snirt* results from a blending of *snow* and *dirt.*

Borrowing The process by which a new word, pronunciation, phrase, or sense enters one language from another; for example, the loan word *raccoon* came into English from the Native American language Algonquin.

Bound morpheme A dependent morpheme that acts as part of a word but cannot stand by itself as a word, such as the prefix *re-* in the word *review.*

Broad phonemic symbols (or **Broad transcription**) A type of transcription that represents basic phonemes and ignores specific distinctions between allophones; broad transcription uses slanting brackets to record phonemes such as /p/; in contrast, narrow transcription uses full brackets to record phonetic forms such as aspirated [pʰ] or unaspirated [p] (see **Phonetic transcription**).

C

Caretaker speech A special variety of speech often used by adults, parents, or older siblings to young children. Caretaker speech may be characterized by simpler syntax, shorter utterances, higher pitch, clearer enunciation, and limited vocabulary.

Case The grammatical role that words play in a language. In English, the subject form of words is the nominative case (as in the pronoun *I*); the direct object form is the accusative case (as in the pronoun *me*); the indirect object form is the dative case (also *me*); and the possessive form is the genitive case (as in the adjective *my* and the pronoun *mine*).

Central vowel A vowel produced when the highest part of the tongue is placed in the center of the oral cavity of the mouth; the vowel sound in the English word *bug* is a mid central vowel (see **Vowel** and **Mid vowel**).

Chirography The study of handwriting or writing styles.

Circumlocution A more elaborate expression that replaces a word that a speaker wishes to embellish; the indirect statement of an idea that a speaker cannot retrieve; the process of talking around a word or expression that a speaker does not know.

Clause A syntactic unit that contains at least one subject noun phrase and a related verb phrase.

Clipping A word formation process that shortens an existing word to create a new word; the word *ad* from *advertisement* is an example of clipping in English.

Code switching The use of more than one dialect, register, or language by a speaker in a conversation; some speakers familiar with more than one language or language variety will mix lexical, syntactic, phonological, morphological, or grammatical features of the languages they know; English and Spanish are mixed in the sentence *Me gusta to speak Español* ("I like to speak Spanish").

Coherence The system of logical connections and rhetorical relations within a discourse or text; coherence depends on a careful development of ideas as well as factors such as shared knowledge between the person communicating and the audience.

Cohesion The lexical and grammatical connections between constituents in a discourse; for example, cohesion could involve the clear reference between a pronoun and its antecedent.

Coinage The formation of a new word or expression in a language; Eastman coined the word *Kodak* to name a new kind of camera film.

Comma splice A punctuation error resulting from the joining of two independent clauses with only a comma; *we like to read, knowledge is a treasure* is an example of a comma splice.

Communicative competence (see **Linguistic competence**)

Comparative A way of marking the degree of a quality in adjectives or adverbs; in English, the comparative degree involves either the inflection *-er* or the periphrastic modifier *more*, as in *friendlier* or *more friendly*.

Comparative historical linguistics The discipline that compares the features of genetically related languages and establishes the historical links between different languages; language reconstruction compares attested forms to establish historical relationships between languages in the past; language change explores the development of languages and dialects from the past to the present.

Complement A constituent that serves to complete the verb phrase.

Complementary distribution The mutually exclusive pattern of occurrence that exists between separate allophones of the same phoneme, such as [p] and [pʰ] in English; such sounds will never occur in the same phonetic environment in a language, but they are not separate phonemes that can create contrastive meanings between words (see **Minimal pair**).

Compound clause A sentence containing clauses that could function independently if they were not conjoined syntactically.

Compounding A process that forms words from two or more words; for example, *blackbird* is a compound of the words *black* and *bird*.

Concord The agreement of grammatical features (such as number, gender, case, and person) between elements in a sentence. The plural subject *We* is in concord with the plural verb *are* in the sentence *We are linguists*.

Conjunction A function word that connects phrases or clauses. In English, *and, or,* and *but* are coordinating conjunctions; *because, although,* and *if* are subordinating conjunctions.

Connotation An affective, peripheral, metaphoric, or extended meaning associated with a word or morpheme in addition to its central denotative meaning; the denotation of *uncle* is "brother of a parent"; a connotation of *uncle* is "an older male family member or friend" (see **Denotation**).

Consonant A sound produced when the airstream through the vocal tract is obstructed or significantly modified by an articulator; consonants are frequently classified according to their place of articulation, manner of articulation, and voicing.

Constituent Any member in the hierarchy of sentence elements, including individual heads, their modifiers, phrases, clauses, and full sentences; any subdivision of a larger syntactic unit.

Continuant A consonant sound that can be prolonged because its articulation does not completely obstruct the airstream; /f/, /m/, and /s/ are examples of continuants.

Conversational maxims Four principles of discourse that describe how participants in a conversation tend to construct and interpret utterances (see **Gricean maxims**).

Cooperative principle The expectation that speakers and listeners will observe certain principles in order to achieve as much understanding as possible between each other.

Coordinator (coordinating conjunction) A conjunction such as *and* or *but* that connects separate constituents at the same level in a syntactic hierarchy.

Copula A verb such as *be* or *seem* that introduces an equivalence relationship between a subject (noun phrase) and a complement (noun phrase or adjective phrase); a linking verb.

Creole A language that develops when a pidgin expands in complexity and becomes the native language of the next generation of children in a discourse community, such as the Gullah creole in the Carolina islands (see **Pidgin**).

D

Dative (see **Case**)

Declarative A sentence type used for conveying facts or making statements in the indicative mood, as opposed to sentences, for example, in the imperative mood (commands).

Deep structure The underlying basic mental structure of an utterance as described by phrase structure rules in Chomsky's early transformational model of language; a deep structure undergoes transformations to create the surface structure that a native speaker actually produces.

Definite article A determiner that indicates that a noun refers to something specific, unique, or understood; *the* is the definite article in English (see **Article**).

Deixis (Deictic) Words or expressions that index meaning by referring to more complete contexts of person, place, or time; in English, deictic terms include the pronouns *I/you*, the determiners *this/that*, and the adverbs *here/there* and *now/then*.

Deletion The omission of a phonological, morphological, or syntactic element from an utterance; the word *are* is deleted in the colloquial expression *Whatcha doin?*

Denotation The central meaning associated with a word or morpheme as opposed to its peripheral or extended connotative meanings; the denotation of *aunt* is "sister of a parent"; a connotation of *aunt* is "an older female family member or friend" (see **Connotation**).

Dental A consonant produced when the tip of the tongue makes contact with the teeth.

Derivational affix A bound morpheme which forms new words by altering meanings or changing the grammatical category of a base content morpheme; the prefix *in-* changes the meaning of *ability* to *inability*; the suffix *-ance* changes the verb *deliver* to the noun *deliverance*.

Determiner A syntactic category of function words (articles, demonstratives, possessive pronouns, quantifiers, and numerals) that can accompany and modify nouns in noun phrases.

Diachronic linguistics The study of language development through time and history, in contrast with the study of a language at a particular time (see **Synchronic linguistics**).

Dialect A particular variety of a language, which differentiates a group of speakers along regional, ethnic, historical, or social lines.

Diminutive An affix that attributes smallness, affection, or femininity to a person or thing; *sweetie* is the diminutive of *sweet*.

Diphthong A vowel combination created when the tongue starts in one vowel position and moves to another vowel position. English diphthongs consist of a stressed vowel followed by a lax vowel or glide; for example, [aj] and [aw] are diphthongs.

Directive A speech act used to motivate someone to do something, such as a request or a command.

Discourse analysis The linguistic study of spoken and written communication, including cohesion, coherence, role relationships, turn-taking, rhetorical figures, and speech acts.

Dissimilation The process by which a sound becomes less similar or more distinct from a neighboring sound; the second /r/ sound in the Greek word *porphura* became an /l/ sound in the English loan word *purple* because of dissimilation.

Do-support In English, the insertion of the auxiliary verb *do* to derive certain utterance types such as yes-no questions, as in *Do you speak Mandarin?*

E

EFL An acronym for English as a Foreign Language; the teaching of English to people who live in countries where English is not spoken as a native language.

Ellipsis The omission of a syntactic, morphological, or semantic structure that is recoverable from the rest of the discourse, text, or context. In the sentence *The summers are sunny, and the winters rainy,* the verb *are* is omitted from the second parallel clause.

Entailment A proposition that logically follows from information contained within an utterance; the sentence *Sue declined the offer* entails that *Sue received an offer.*

Epithet An adjective or concise appellation that describes the dominant characteristic of a person, place, or thing; *Great* is an epithet for Alfred in the phrase *Alfred the Great.*

ESL An acronym for English as a Second Language.

Ethnography A branch of anthropology that studies the distinctions between nations, kindreds, languages, peoples, customs, and cultures.

Etymology The history and origin of words and morphemes and the study thereof; the etymology of the English word *linguistics* is the Latin word *lingua*, meaning "tongue."

Euphemism A more positive word or less offensive expression used as a substitute for a taboo term to deal with unpleasant or sensitive topics; *sanitary engineer* is a euphemism for *garbage collector; passed away* is a euphemism for *died.*

Existential there The use of the word *there* as a substitute subject for an alternative sentence structure expressing location or being; for example, *There is a comet in the northwestern sky* instead of *A comet exists in the northwestern sky.*

F

False start An utterance that a speaker initiates one way and then interrupts to begin another way.

Finite verb A verb form that carries tense, or agrees with the subject in number and person; the present tense form *passes* is a finite verb in the sentence *Time passes swiftly.*

Formant The frequency bands and overtones of acoustical energy in a particular speech sound as can be measured and displayed by a spectrograph.

Free morpheme A lexical item that may stand independently as a word without needing to be attached to another morpheme.

Fricative A hissing consonant sound produced by moving articulators together to constrict but not completely stop the airstream through the vocal tract; /f/ and /s/ are fricatives.

Front vowel A vowel produced when the highest part of the tongue is placed near the front of the oral cavity of the mouth; /i/ and /e/ are front vowels (see **Vowel**).

Full stop A punctuation mark that is used to indicate closure, normally a period.

Functionalism A linguistic approach that emphasizes the uses of language forms in real-life discourse and contexts.

G

Generalization In language change, an extension in the meaning of a word to include wider applications and connotations; the word *holiday* initially referred only to religious days but has broadened to include other festive days.

Genitive A grammatical case, often corresponding with the possessive use of a noun or pronoun; in English, *his* is the genitive case form of the pronoun *he,* while *cat's* (or *cats'*) is the genitive case form of *cat* (see **Case**).

Glide A semi-vowel sound that can serve as a diphthong component; /j/ is a glide which occurs in the English diphthong /aj/ (see **Diphthong** and **Semi-vowel**).

Glottal A sound produced at the glottis with a constriction in the vocal folds; the center consonant in the word *button* is often produced as a glottal stop.

Grammar In transformational theory, the mental knowledge of linguistic structures acquired naturally by native speakers of a language (see **Usage**).

Grammatical (1) Characteristic of a structure that a native speaker would regard as well-formed or standard in a language; (2) Having to do with the syntax in a language in a narrow sense; (3) Having to do with all structural disciplines such as phonology, morphology, syntax, and semantics in a broader sense.

Great Vowel Shift A set of sound changes in the transition from Middle English to Early Modern English that affected long vowels. Mid and low vowels moved higher; for example, the pronunciation of the word *sweet* changed from [swe:t] to [swit]. High vowels became diphthongs; for example, the pronunciation of the word *house* changed from [hu:s] to [haws].

Gricean maxims (or **Gricean implicatures**) Cooperative behaviors between speakers in their conversations; these behaviors, identified by H. P. Grice, relate to quantity (how much information we share), manner (how that information is presented), relation (the relevancy of the information), and quality (the truthfulness of the information).

Grimm's Law A series of systematic consonant changes that distinguished Germanic languages from other branches of the Indo-European language family; the patterns were first described by Rasmus Rask and then publicized by Jakob Grimm. As part of the Germanic consonant shift, voiceless stops became fricatives; thus, the /k/ sound in the Indo-European root **kerd-* became an /h/ in the English word *heart;* compare the word *cardiac* from Greek, which did not undergo Grimm's Law.

H

Head The principal part of a constituent phrase; in the noun phrase *the blue boy,* the noun *boy* is the head.

Hedging Equivocation; the use of imprecise language to avoid precise statements that could be contradicted.

High vowel A vowel produced when the body of the tongue is placed near the top of the roof of the mouth; /i/ and /u/ are high vowels (see **Vowel**).

Historical linguistics The study of language change and historical relationships that exist among various languages (see **Comparative historical linguistics**).

Holophrastic speech Discourse that is characterized by one-word sentences in child language acquisition.

Homograph A word that has the same written form as another word but differs in meaning and/or pronunciation; *lead* the verb ("guide") and *lead* the noun ("heavy metal") are homographs; the present tense form *read* and the past tense form *read* are homographs.

Homophone A word that has the same pronunciation as another word but differs in written form and meaning; *pear* ("fruit"), *pair* ("two of a kind"), and *pare* ("peel") are homophones.

Homonym A word that has the same written form and pronunciation as another word but differs in meaning; *bear* the verb ("carry") and *bear* the noun ("large mammal") are homonyms.

Hypercorrection A linguistic overcompensation used by a speaker to avoid a form that is mistakenly assumed to be incorrect; the use of the nominative *I* instead of the objective *me* in the sentence *He wrote to Sally and I* is a hypercorrection.

I

Iconic Characteristic of symbols and gestures that resemble in some way the intended meaning.

Ideograph An iconic symbol representing a word or concept. Many Chinese characters are ideographs; in English, the use of a smiley-face symbol to mean "like" or "enjoy" is an ideograph.

Ideophone A sound representing a word or concept; a spoken expression rather than a written symbol.

Idiolect The variety of a language spoken by a single individual, which may have certain unique features.

Idiom A set expression whose meaning is not the literal sum of its parts; a syntactic collocation that functions as a semantic unit; as an idiom, *to kick the bucket* means "to die," not "to boot a pail."

Illocutionary force The communicative function such as an apology or command that an utterance conveys (see **Speech act**).

Imperative A verb form used to issue commands or directives; in English, the imperative form uses an infinitive and typically drops the second person subject; for example, *Listen to me!*

Indefinite article A determiner that indicates that a noun refers to something general or yet unspecified; *a* is the indefinite article for English words that begin with a consonant sound; *an* is the indefinite article for English words that begin with a vowel sound (see **Article**).

Independent clause (or **sentence**) A clause that may stand by itself as a complete idea; a clause that consists of at least one noun phrase and a finite verb phrase.

Indirect speech act A communicative purpose conveyed through an alternate type of expression; *Can you pass the salt?* has the form of a question but is actually an indirect request to pass the salt.

Indo-European languages A family of languages found in India, Iran, and most of Europe, that linguists have traced back to a reconstructed ancestor language now called Proto-Indo-European; English, German, Spanish, Russian, Welsh, Greek, Lithuanian, Sanskrit, Armenian, and Avestan are all Indo-European languages.

Infelicitous Characteristic of an utterance that disregards important semantic or contextual concerns.

Infinitive A basic verb form that has not been inflected for tense, aspect, mood, number, or person; in English, the infinitive form of a verb often includes the word *to,* for example *to read.*

Inflection An affix or form change that indicates grammatical relationships without changing the basic meaning or "part of speech" category of a word; English has eight inflectional suffixes that mark functions such as number, person, aspect, and verb tense; for example, the inflection *-ing* marks the present participle forms of verbs in English.

Informant A person who gives language data to a linguist who is researching a particular language.

Initialism (see **Acronym**)

Intensifier An adverbial word that emphasizes the semantic content of a verb, adverb, or adjective; *slowly* is an adverb and *very* is an intensifier in the sentence *They walked very slowly.*

Interdental A consonant produced by placing the tip of the tongue between the upper and lower front teeth; [θ] and [ð] are interdental sounds.

Interrogative pronoun A pronoun used for eliciting information in questions; *who,* *what,* and *which* are some of the interrogative pronouns in English.

Intervocalic Refers to a consonant that occurs between two vowels; the /d/ sound in the word *coda* is intervocalic.

Intonation The contrasts and contours that occur in the pitch of words or phrases in spoken discourse.

Inverted commas Quotation marks.

IPA transcription An abbreviation for the International Phonetic Alphabet, which is used for transcribing speech sounds; a phonetic transcription using the symbols that have been adopted by the International Phonetic Association.

J

Jargon Technical vocabulary (see **Argot**).

K

Kinesis Physical movement accompanying speech; paralinguistic body language and facial expressions.

L

L2 An abbreviation of the term "second language," meaning a language other than the native language of a speaker.

Labial A consonant sound produced with one or both lips (see **bilabial** and **labiodental**).

Labiodental A consonant produced by contact with the upper teeth on the lower lip; /f/ and /v/ are labiodental sounds in English.

Language academy A committee or institution officially designated to make pronouncements about the acceptability of various linguistic forms or structures within a particular language; the English language has never had a language academy.

Larynx The voice-box in the trachea containing the vocal folds that stretch and vibrate in the production of various speech sounds.

Lateral A consonant produced by placing the tongue on the alveolar ridge and allowing air to escape on either side of the tongue; /l/ is a lateral sound in English.

Lax A vowel quality produced when the tongue muscle is relatively relaxed rather than tense; in English, the vowels in the words *lit, get,* and *book* are lax (see **Vowel**).

Lexeme A basic word form; a root for which other inflected forms are regarded as merely variants; *walks, walked,* and *walking* are variants of the lexeme *walk.*

Lexical Relating to the meaning of a word or the vocabulary of a language.

Lexical shift A change in the meaning of a word; the word *thatch* meant "roof" in Old English, but now it refers to a type of roofing material.

Lexicon A specialized dictionary of words and their meanings; the vocabulary of a speaker; the storehouse of words, morphemes, their meanings, and their grammatical functions in a language.

Lingua Franca An already existing language chosen as a medium of communication by people who would otherwise not share a common language; French has been a *lingua Franca* for several countries in Africa.

Linguistic competence The underlying mental knowledge of language that enables individuals to produce an infinite number of sentences, to understand unique expressions from others, to recognize ungrammatical utterances, and to recognize ambiguities in a particular language (see **Linguistic performance**).

Linguistic determinism The idea that language shapes the thoughts and determines the perceptions of people (see **Sapir-Whorf hypothesis**).

Linguistic performance The linguistic output of an individual; what someone actually does with the language. A person's linguistic performance may not always match their linguistic competence, being subject to varying factors such as fatigue, fear, or mind-altering substances (see **Linguistic competence**).

Liquid A consonant sound such as [l] or [r] that is produced without friction at the point of articulation.

Low vowel A vowel produced when the body of the tongue is placed toward the bottom of the mouth; /a/ is a low vowel (see **Vowel**).

M

Manner of articulation A modification of the airstream that can occur to produce consonant sounds; English uses various manners of articulation such as stops, fricatives, nasals, affricates, and liquids.

Marked A linguistic utterance that contrasts with a more frequent, more basic, more central form of that utterance; when asking about age (*How old are you?*), the use of *young* instead of *old* would be marked.

Middle English The variety of English that existed from approximately A.D. 1100–1500, in which the Germanic base of Old English was modified by French vocabulary, grammar, and phonology.

Mid vowel A vowel produced when the body of the tongue is placed midway between the top and the bottom of the oral cavity; the vowel in the word *but* is a mid central vowel in English (see **Central vowel**).

Minimal pair A pair of words that share the same phonetic characteristics except for one sound; minimal pairs are used to determine whether two sounds are distinct phonemes or whether they are allophones of a single phoneme. In English, the minimal pair *lice* and *rice* shows that /l/ and /r/ are separate phonemes (/l/ and /r/ create a difference in meaning between the two words); in Japanese, the use of /l/ and /r/ would not result in a meaning change since they are allophones of the same phoneme.

Modal An auxiliary verb that shows notions such as permission, possibility, obligation, or probability; *may, might, can, could, shall, should, will, would,* and *must* are modals in English. Modals are followed by an uninflected verb form, as in *She can learn.*

Modifier A word, phrase, or clause that serves to particularize the meaning of something; in the sentence "The tall man saw the girl with the hat," the adjective *tall* and the prepositional phrase *with the hat* are modifying expressions.

Monophthongization The development of a single simple vowel from a diphthong.

Morpheme A minimal unit of meaning, function, or structure within a word, such as *re-* and *write* in the word *rewrite.*

Morphology The study of the minimal units of meaning and function in a language; the study of word structure, morpheme combination, and word formation rules (see *Morpheme*).

N

Narrow allophonic transcription A transcription that is detailed and specific enough to show differences between allophones such as aspirated [pʰ] and unaspirated [p] in English (see **Broad phonemic symbols**).

Narrowing A semantic change in which the meaning of a word or morpheme moves from general to more specific, from a broad meaning to a more restricted application. In English, the word *meat* used to mean "food," but has since changed to mean a particular type of food.

Nasal A consonant sound which is produced by allowing the airstream to be released through the nose while speaking, rather than through the mouth, such as /m/, /n/, /ŋ/ or /ñ/; vowels may also be nasalized.

Native speaker A speaker who acquires a particular language as a first language in childhood.

Natural language A language that people can acquire as native speakers in a discourse community, as opposed to artificial languages, such as Esperanto, that have been consciously invented.

Negative A word such as *no* or *not* that expresses denial, disagreement, disparity, prohibition, refutation, opposition, contrast, or contradiction.

Neologism A newly coined term or expression; a new word that fills a lexical gap or conceptual gap in a language. The word *quark* was created to describe a newly discovered sub-nuclear particle.

Neurolinguistics The study of the chemical, electrical, and physical processes of the human brain in language production and perception.

Nominal A noun, pronoun, or other constituent that functions like or occurs in the same environments characteristic of a noun.

Nominative The subject form of a noun phrase; in English, *she* is the nominative case form of the third person singular female pronoun (see **Case**).

Null hypothesis A research strategy that sets up a formulation in terms of disproving that formulation in scientific experimentation; in linguistics, a Null hypothesis could posit that language is not rule-governed but a random set of features and characteristics.

Number In English, the grammatical category indicating whether an entity is singular or plural; *child* is singular in number while *children* is plural.

O

Object A noun phrase that is a constituent part of a transitive verb phrase (direct or indirect object) or of a prepositional phrase (object of a preposition); the direct object typically "receives" the action of a verb. *The bus* is the direct object of the verb *painted* in the sentence *They painted the bus.*

Obstruent A class of consonant sounds that includes some measure of obstruction of the airstream; stops, fricatives, and affricates are obstruents (see **Sonorant**).

Onomatopoeia A word such as *swish* or *buzz* that is imitative of actual, natural sounds; an utterance that sounds like what it means.

Orthography The spelling system of a language; a systematic writing system for a language.

P

Palatal A speech sound produced when the top of the tongue is on or near the hard palate; the initial glide in the English word *yes* is a palatal sound.

Palate The bony structure on the roof of the mouth behind the alveolar ridge and the teeth; the soft palate is behind the hard palate in the back of the mouth.

Participle A verb form that lacks tense but is used in verb constructions that express aspect. English verbs have a "present" participle and a "past" participle form; *-ing* marks the "present participle" verb form; *-ed* frequently marks the "past participle" verb form (sometimes an equivalent form is used, such as the vowel-stem change in *sung* or the *-en* in *taken*).

Particle A free function morpheme that acts as an adjunct to a verb in English; for example, *up* is a particle in the sentence *They will set up the chairs.*

Passive A construction in which the logical direct object is expressed as the subject and the logical subject is either left out or included in a prepositional phrase as part of the verb phrase. The passive counterpart of the active sentence *We saw them* is *They were seen (by us).*

Pejoration A semantic change in a word or morpheme toward a more negative connotation; the English word *silly* ("foolish") used to mean "holy" or "blessed" in Old English.

Perfect A verb construction that involves a present or past time aspect; *has come* is a present perfect verb construction in English; *had come* is a past perfect verb construction (see **Aspect**).

Perlocutionary force The resultant effect of an utterance on an individual.

Person The grammatical notion indicating whether an entity is self (first person), an other that is present (second person), or an other that is not present (third person); *I* and *we* are first person pronoun forms in English.

Personal pronoun A nominal that substitutes for a noun phrase and identifies people (or things) as self, present other, or absent other; *I, we, thou, you, she, he, it,* and *they* are nominative personal pronouns in English.

Philology The study of language in context with particular regard to history, comparative linguistics, written texts, rhetoric, poetry, literature, anthropology, and etymology.

Phoneme A basic unit of sound that distinguishes meanings in a language; /s/ and /z/ are phonemes in English because they allow speakers to recognize a difference between the words *sip* and *zip.*

Phonemic inventory A set of all of the meaning-distinguishing sounds used in a particular language.

Phonemic merger The loss of a distinction between phonemes due to sound change.

Phonetic transcription A detailed representation of spoken sounds or utterances through the use of a systematic set of symbols; phonetic transcription helps linguists avoid the inconsistencies found in some alphabetic writing systems (see **Broad phonemic symbols**).

Phonetics The branch of linguistics that deals with the articulatory, acoustic, and auditory description of sounds in a language.

Phonology The study of sound systems in human language, including sets of sounds, distinctive features of sounds, rules governing sound combinations, and types of sound changes.

Phonotactic constraint A restriction on the permissible sequence of sounds, which is observed by native speakers in a language; English no longer permits the phonotactic combination of /gn/ or /kn/ at the beginning of words, though such combinations may continue in spelling.

Phrase structure rule A rule that describes the ordering and possible combination of syntactic constituents in a language; one phrase structure rule shows that $S = NP + VP$, meaning that a sentence consists of a noun phrase and a verb phrase.

Pidgin A language variety that develops between groups not speaking a common language; pidgins typically utilize basic vocabulary from a "dominant" language and lack many grammatical features found in fully-developed languages (see **Creole**).

Place of articulation A position in the vocal tract where the sound is modified through contact with speech articulators; the hard palate, the alveolar ridge, and the lips are some places of articulation for English consonants.

Plosive A type of stop consonant produced by complete obstruction of the airstream in the oral cavity followed by an abrupt release of the built-up air; in the phonemic inventory of Aymará (South America), /p/ is a stop, /pʰ/ is an aspirated stop, and /p'/ is a plosive stop (see **stop**).

Pluperfect A verb construction that expresses a time before a past point in time; for example, *had (already) plowed* is in the pluperfect in the sentence *When she came, Farmer Brown had already plowed the field.*

Polysemy The capacity of a word to have multiple but related meanings; the English word *foot* has a central meaning (body part), a peripheral meaning (bottom part of something), and an extended meaning (unit of measurement).

Pragmatics The branch of linguistics which deals with language use and language structure in communicative contexts.

Predicate The verb phrase part of a sentence that expresses an action performed by the noun phrase subject or a state characterizing the subject; in the sentence *The monkey played the piano well,* the predicate is *played the piano well.*

Predicative adjective A modifying word that occurs after a "be" verb or "linking" verb as a complement to the subject of a sentence; *blue* is a predicative adjective in the sentence *The car is blue* (see **Attributive adjective**).

Prefix A morpheme that attaches prior to the root in a word; *in-* and *de-* are prefixes in the word *indescribable*.

Prescriptive grammar A language approach that stresses the acquisition of socially correct or academically proper linguistic forms in order to make speech and writing habits conform to a standard.

Presupposition Information that is presumed to be true before and up to the time of an utterance; the utterance *How long did they work?* presupposes that *they worked*.

Preterite The past tense form of a verb that expresses completed action in past time; the preterite form of *thank* is *thanked*.

Progressive A verb construction that gives a present or past time aspect to a verb phrase; *is coming* is a present progressive verb construction in English; *was coming* is a past progressive verb construction (see **Aspect**).

Progressive assimilation A process in which a preceding sound causes a following sound to change; the voiced /g/ consonant in the word *bags* causes the plural suffix *-s* to be pronounced as the voiced sound /z/.

Proposition The fundamental meaning expressed by an utterance.

Prosody The suprasegmental features of speech, such as pitch, stress, volume, timing, and intonation.

Pro-verb A verb such as *do* that takes the place of a verb phrase as a pronoun stands for a noun phrase; *do* is a pro-verb in the sentence *They eat candy, and we do too* because *do* represents the verb phrase *eat candy*.

Q

Qualifier A word modifying another word; an adverb or adjective.

Quantifier A word indicating number or amount, such as *many, much,* or *some.*

R

Reflexive pronoun A direct object pronoun or indirect object pronoun that is coreferential with the subject; *myself* is a reflexive pronoun in the sentence *I saw myself.*

Register A level of style or formality within a language, such as oratorical, formal, normal, casual, or colloquial.

Regressive assimilation A process in which a following sound causes a preceding sound to change; the /n/ sound in the word *sunbeam* often assimilates to a bilabial /m/ sound because of the bilabial /b/ sound that follows it.

Relative clause A clause that modifies a noun in a noun phrase; the relative pronouns *who* and *which* often introduce a relative clause, as in *the team who made history.*

Root Base morpheme; stem; the most basic semantic element of a word to which other affixes may be joined or other words may be compounded; *nation* is the root of *international; bird* is the root of *bluebird.*

Rounded vowel A vowel produced when the lips are drawn together in a circular shape; /o/ and /u/ are rounded vowels (see **Vowel**).

Run-on A written utterance that joins independent sentences without any punctuation to indicate separate thoughts; the sentence *Philology is the study of language in context some modern linguists prefer context-free analyses* is a run-on sentence.

S

Sapir-Whorf hypothesis (also **Whorfian hypothesis**) A theory attributed to Edward Sapir and Benjamin Lee Whorf to explain the relationship between language and thought; the hypothesis indicates that language shapes the way people perceive the world (see **Linguistic determinism**).

Schwa (sometimes **shwa**) A mid-central vowel produced when the tongue is in a neutral position between the top and bottom and between the front and back of the mouth [ə]; in English unstressed syllables, the schwa sound often works as the reduced form of another vowel, as in the first syllable of the word *acquire.*

Script The frames of reference that are related to a particular situation; a person's knowledge of the associations, contexts, events, and language expectations involved in a particular circumstance.

Semantics The branch of linguistics that studies meaning, reference, truth values, and lexicon in a language.

Semiotics The theory of the properties of signs; the study of the relationships between symbols and their meanings in communication systems.

Semi-vowel A sound that has both vowel and consonant properties, such as /j/ and /w/ in English (see **Glide**).

Sibilant A class of consonant sounds that involve the hissing release of a constricted airstream; fricatives and affricates are sibilant sounds.

Silent Way A language-teaching method involving very little oral production or modeling by the teacher but extensive use of props, charts, and gestures.

Slang A type of informal, nonstandard, or innovational expression that does not enjoy full acceptance by educated speakers of a standard language variety.

Sociolinguistics The branch of linguistics that studies the relationship between language and social factors such as age, gender, education, socio-economic status, multilingualism, and national language policies.

Sonorant A class of voiced sounds produced with relatively free air flow, including nasals, laterals, glides, vowels, and liquids (see **Obstruent**).

Sound symbolism The semantic associations that sounds may raise in the minds of speakers of a language; for example, several English words that begin with /sl/ have negative connotations, as in *slash, slay,* and *sleazy;* sound symbolism shows that the relationship between language sounds and meanings is not always completely arbitrary.

Spectrogram A visual representation of the acoustical features of speech as displayed by a spectrograph, a sensitive electronic instrument that plots the intensity and duration of sounds.

Speech act A type of utterance that includes special intentions, functions, or relations; promises, requests, apologies, questions, and directives are speech acts.

Speech community A group of speakers who share a language system, with common social conventions and cultural contexts.

Speech pathology The study, diagnosis, and treatment of language disorders, such as stuttering.

Standard The dominant variety of a language that is taught in schools, spoken by most educated speakers, and used for economic advancement in a nation or society; the so-called "correct" form of a language.

Stative A verb or adjective that indicates a continuing state or enduring characteristic rather than a dynamic or changing action.

Stop A consonant sound that is produced with complete obstruction in the oral cavity and then subsequent release of the airstream as with sounds such as /p/ or /g/.

Strong verb A verb form that relies on vowel mutation to express the past tense, often called an "irregular verb" form in modern English; for example, present tense *give* and past tense *gave.*

Structuralism A linguistic approach that emphasizes the classification and interpretation of utterances with a special examination of linguistic forms.

Subject In English, the noun phrase that determines the form of the main verb of a clause or sentence; it is frequently the first noun phrase in a clause or sentence.

Subjunctive A grammatical mood that manifests itself in its own set of verb forms and expresses such notions as wishes, desires, or concepts that are contrary to fact; this mood has largely been lost in Modern English but may still be seen in expressions such as "Long **live** the queen" or "If I **were** you. . . ."

Subordinate clause A clause that cannot stand by itself in a sentence.

Suffix A morpheme that attaches after the root.

Suggestopedia A language teaching method that uses relaxation techniques to enhance second language acquisition.

Superlative A grammatical construction used for showing an absolute relationship among items or people being compared, involving the inflection -**est** or the modifier **most.**

Suprasegmental A characteristic such as tone, pitch, or stress (see **Prosody**).

Surface structure In Chomsky's Transformational Grammar, the surface structure most closely approximates the utterance that results from the operation of a transformation.

Syllabic A consonant sound that can function on its own as a syllable.

Synchronic linguistics A study of language that looks at a language within a given time period.

Synonym A word that shares the same meaning with another word.

Syntactic Relating to syntax.

Syntax The order and possible combinations of words and structures in a language.

T

T-test A test that compares the mean scores of two groups and assesses their difference for statistical significance.

Taboo Words or terms that are marked, restricted, or forbidden except in specific contexts.

Tag question A question attached onto the end of a statement and which is typically used to ask for verification of that statement as in "Dogs are animals, aren't they?"

Tautology A variation of the same word, phrase, or idea in the same utterance; for example, *he dreamed a dream.*

Telegraphic speech Discourse that is characterized mainly by content words (and a lack of most function words), resembling the language of a telegram.

Tense The feature of time (past, present, future) marked on a verb; verb tense is frequently manifested by inflections on the basic form of the verb.

Tense vowel A vowel quality produced when the root of the tongue is slightly advanced rather than relaxed; the vowel sounds in the words *bean, gate,* and *bone* are tense in English (see **Vowel**).

TESOL An acronym for Teachers of English to Speakers of Other Languages.

Tone In writing, the stylistic feature that indicates a writer's attitude toward a subject. In speech, the pitch level involved with an utterance.

Transformation An operation performed on a basic sentence type or structure to derive a new form; the change from an active sentence such as "We saw the car" to a passive one such as "The car was seen (by us)" involves a transformation.

Transformational grammar A grammatical model devised by Noam Chomsky, which outlines rules for the formation of basic constituents and sentence structure and identifies transformations for deriving new resulting forms.

Transitive verb A verb that requires a following direct object.

Turn-taking A characteristic of conversation in which the contribution of each participant is regulated through understood behaviors and strategies.

U

Universal grammar The set of rules that are non-specific to a particular language. Some linguists believe that these universals in language are related in important ways to children's acquisition of their native language.

Unrounded vowel A vowel produced when the lips are more relaxed or open rather than close together; /i/ and /e/ are unrounded vowels in English (see **Vowel**).

Usage (1) Language as it is used; (2) the study of prescriptive forms.

V

Velar A consonant produced at the velum or soft palate.

Velum The tissue ridge at the back of the roof of the mouth (also referred to as the soft palate).

Vernacular The variety of a language that is spoken in less formal circumstances, such as in the home.

Vocal cords The bands of muscle that stretch over the larynx, their vibration provides the voicing for sounds.

Voiced A term used to describe a consonant made while the vocal folds (larynx) are vibrating; in English all vowels are voiced.

Voiceless A term used to describe a consonant that is made without the vibration of the vocal folds (larynx).

Voice onset time The time when the vocal folds actually start to vibrate.

Voice Print The acoustical output that is characteristic of a particular speaker.

Vowel A sound produced through the vibration of vocal cords and without significant obstruction of the airstream in the oral cavity. Vowels can be altered and thus labeled according to the varying positions of the tongue in the mouth as a vowel is produced. Such labels refer to the height of the tongue (high, mid, or low), the placement of the highest part of the tongue in relation to the front of the mouth (front, central, or back), the relative tenseness of the tongue muscle (tense or lax), and whether the person's lips are rounding themselves in the production of the vowel (rounded or unrounded).

W–Z

Weak verb A verb such as jump or sleep whose past tense is formed by adding the inflection -ed (or -d or -t).

Zero morpheme An "invisible" morpheme; in the sentence "they walk," the verb walk is said to have a zero morpheme since the absence of any particular inflectional morpheme actually tells us the verb is not the 3rd person singular present tense, *she walks.*

Acknowledgments

Berk-Seligson, Susan. "The Role of Register in the Bilingual Courtroom: Evaluative Reactions to Interpreted Testimony." Originally appeared in the *International Journal of the Sociology of Language,* Vol. 79. Copyright © 1989 Mouton de Gruyter. Reprinted with permission.

Card, William, Raven I. McDavid, Jr., and Virginia McDavid. "Dimensions of Usage and Dictionary Labeling." From the *Journal of English Linguistics,* Vol. 17 (pp. 57–74). Copyright © 1984 by the *Journal of English Linguistics.* Reprinted by permission of Sage Publications, Inc.

Celce-Murcia, Marianne. "Discourse Analysis and Grammar Instruction." Originally appeared in *Annual Review of Applied Linguistics,* Vol. 11 (pp. 135–151). Copyright © 1991 Cambridge University Press. Reprinted with the permission of Cambridge University Press.

Cohen, Bob. "There's More to a Name." Reproduced from Vol. 63, No. 3 of the *Stanford Business School Magazine.* Copyright 1995 by the Board of Trustees of the Leland Stanford Junior University. All rights reserved.

Cushing, Steven. "Fatal Words: Communication Clashes and Aircraft Crashes." Originally appeared in *Bostonia* (Summer 1994). Reprinted by permission of *Bostonia.*

Diaz-Duque, Ozzie F. "Communication Barriers in Medical Settings: Hispanics in the United States." Originally appeared in the *International Journal of the Sociology of Language,* Vol. 79, Copyright © 1989. Reprinted by permission of Mouton de Gruyter.

Dickinson, Emily. (Selected Poems and excerpts within Cynthia L. Hallen's article.) Reprinted by permission of the publishers and the Trustees of Amherst College from THE POEMS OF EMILY DICKINSON, Thomas H. Johnson, ed., Cambridge, Mass.: The Belknap Press of Harvard University Press. Copyright © 1951, 1955, 1979, 1983 by the President and Fellows of Harvard College.

———. Poem #966 excerpt from *The Complete Poems of Emily Dickinson,* edited by Thomas H. Johnson. Copyright 1929 by Martha Dickinson Bianchi; copyright © renewed 1957 by Mary L. Hampson. By permission of Little, Brown and Company (Inc.).

Dörnyei, Zoltán and Sarah Thurrell. "Teaching Conversational Skills Intensively: Course Content and Rationale." Originally appeared in *ELT Journal,* Vol. 48, No. 1. Copyright © 1994 Oxford University Press. Reprinted by permission of Oxford University Press.

Eagleson, Robert. "Forensic Analysis of Personal Written Texts: A Case Study." From *Language and the Law,* edited by John Gibbons. Copyright © 1994. Reprinted by permission of Addison Wesley Longman Ltd.

Eggington, William G. "Written Academic Discourse in Korean: Implications for Effective Communication." From *Writing Across Languages: Analysis of L2 Text,* edited by Ulla Connor and Robert B. Kaplan. Consulting editor Sandra Savignon. Copyright © 1987 Addison-Wesley Publishing Company, Inc. Reprinted by permission.

Fisher, Sue. "Doctor Talk/Patient Talk: How Treatment Decisions Are Negotiated in Doctor-Patient Communication." From *The Social Organization of Doctor-Patient Communication,* edited by Sue Fisher and Alexandra Dundas Todd. Copyright © 1983. Reprinted by permission of the Center for Applied Linguistics.

Fowler, Roger. "Studying Literature as Language." From *Linguistics and the Study of Literature,* edited by Theo D'haen. Copyright © 1986 Rodopi. Reprinted with permission.

Frost, Robert. "Spring Pools." From THE POETRY OF ROBERT FROST, edited by Edward Connery Lathem. Copyright 1956 by Robert Frost, copyright 1923, © 1969 by Henry Holt & Co., Inc. Reprinted by permission of Henry Holt & Co., Inc.

Garcia, Ricardo L. "A Linguistic Frame of Reference for Critiquing Chicano Compositions." Originally appeared in *College English,* Vol. 37, No. 2. Copyright 1975 by the National Council of Teachers of English. Reprinted with permission.

Gyi, M. "The Unbreakable Language Code in the Pacific Theatre of World War II." Reprinted from *ETC: A Review of General Semantics,* Vol. 39, No. 1 (1982). Reprinted with permission of The International Society for General Semantics, Concord, California.

Hallen, Cynthia L. "Student Lexicographers and the Emily Dickinson Lexicon." Originally appeared in *Dictionaries,* Vol. 15. Copyright 1994 Dictionary Society of North America. Reprinted with permission.

Hancher, Michael. "Understanding Poetic Speech Acts." Originally appeared in *College English,* Vol. 36, No. 6. Copyright 1975 by the National Council of Teachers of English. Reprinted with permission.

Heath, Shirley Brice. "Teacher Talk: Language in the Classroom." From *Language in Education: Theory and Practice.* Copyright © 1978 Center for Applied Linguistics. Reprinted by permission of the Center for Applied Linguistics.

Kaplan, Robert B. "Applied Linguistics and Language Policy and Planning." From *Introduction to Applied Linguistics,* edited by William Grabe and Robert B. Kaplan. Copyright © 1992 Addison-Wesley Publishing Company, Inc. Reprinted by permission.

Khosroshahi, Fatemeh. "Penguins Don't Care, but Women Do: A Social Identity Analysis of a Whorfian Problem." Originally appeared in *Language in Society.* Vol. 18 (pp. 505–25). Copyright © 1989 Cambridge University Press. Reprinted with the permission of Cambridge University Press.

Labov, William. "The Judicial Testing of Linguistic Theory." From *Linguistics in Context: Connecting Observation and Understanding,* edited by Deborah Tannen. Copyright © 1988 Ablex Publishing Corporation. Reprinted by permission.

Labov, William. "Recognizing Black English in the Classroom." From *Black English: Educational Equity and the Law,* edited by John W. Chambers, Jr. Copyright © 1983 Karoma Publishers, Inc. Reprinted by permission.

Lentine, Genine and Roger W. Shuy. "*Mc-*: Meaning in the Marketplace." From *American Speech: A Quarterly of Linguistic Usage* (65:4). Copyright © 1990 The University of Alabama Press. Reprinted by permission of the publisher.

Leonard, Laurence B. and Marc E. Fey. "Facilitating Grammatical Development: The Contribution of Pragmatics." Reprinted with permission by Singular Publishing Group, Inc. From *Pragmatics of Language: Clinical Practice Issues,* edited by Tanya M. Gallagher. San Diego: Singular Publishing Group, Inc. Copyright 1991.

Loftus, Elizabeth F. "Language and Memories in the Judicial System." From *Language Use and the Uses of Language,* edited by Roger W. Shuy and Anna Shnukal. Copyright 1980 Georgetown University. Reprinted by permission.

Luthy, Melvin J. "A Place for Phonetics in High Technology." Reprinted by permission of the author.

Martin, Laura. "'Eskimo Words for Snow': A Case Study in the Genesis and Decay of an Anthropological Example." Reproduced by permission of the American Anthropological Association from *American Anthropologist* 88:2, June 1986. Not for further reproduction.

Moskowitz, Breyne. "The Acquisition of Language." Originally appeared in *Scientific American,* Vol. 239, No. 5. (Nov. 1978). Reprinted with permission. Copyright © 1978 by Scientific American, Inc. All rights reserved.

Noguchi, Rei R. "Transformational-Generative Syntax and the Teaching of Sentence Mechanics." Originally appeared in the *Journal of Basic Writing,* Vol. 6, No. 2. Copyright © 1987 by the *Journal of Basic Writing,* Instructional Resource Center, Office of Academic Affairs, The City University of New York. Reprinted by permission.

Noss, Philip A. "Communicating the Scriptures Across Cultures." From *Georgetown University Round Table on Languages and Linguistics 1986,* edited by Simon P. X. Battestini. Copyright 1987 Georgetown University Press. Reprinted with permission.

Nunberg, Geoffrey. "Testimony before the State Legislature on California Proposition 63." From *Perspectives on Official English: The Campaign for English as the Official Language of the USA,* edited by Karen L. Adams and Daniel T. Brink. Copyright © 1990 Walter de Gruyter & Co. Reprinted by permission.

Okrand, Marc. "Nouns." From *The Klingon Dictionary.* Copyright © 1985 by Paramount Pictures. Addendum copyright © 1992 by Paramount Pictures. Reprinted with permission of Paramount Pictures. All rights reserved.

Ong, Walter J. "Some Psychodynamics of Orality." From *Orality and Literacy* by Walter J. Ong. Copyright 1982 Methuen. Reprinted by permission of Routledge Ltd.

Paulston, Christina Bratt. "Applied Linguistics: The Use of Linguistics in ESL" from *English as a Second Language: Dimensions and Directions,* edited by Irwin Feigenbaum, 1984, is republished here by permission of the Summer Institute of Linguistics.

Raidt, Edith H. "The Role of Women in Linguistic Change." From *Historical Linguistics 1989,* edited by Henk Aertsen and Robert J. Jeffers. John Benjamins Publishing Company, Amsterdam/Philadelphia, 1993. Reprinted by permission of John Benjamins Publishing Company.

Raskin, Victor. "Linguistics and Machine Translation." A new article using parts of "Linguistics and Natural Language Processing," which originally appeared in *Machine Translation,* edited by Sergei Nirenburg. Copyright © 1987 Cambridge University Press. Reprinted with the permission of Cambridge University Press. This article was published by permission of Victor Raskin.

Riley, Kathryn and Frank Parker. "Tone as a Function of Presupposition in Technical and Business Writing." *Journal of Technical Writing and Communication,* Vol, 18, No. 4 (pp. 325–343), Baywood Publishing Company, Inc. 1988. Reprinted by permission.

Romaine, Suzanne. "Pidgin English Advertising." From *The State of the Language,* edited by Christopher Ricks and Leonard Michaels. Berkeley: University of California Press, 1990. Reprinted by permission of The Regents of the University of California. Copyright © 1989.

Romich, Janet Amundson. "Understanding Basic Medical Terminology." Originally appeared in *Veterinary Technician,* August 1993. Reprinted by permission of Veterinary Learning Systems. Copyright 1993.

Shuy, Roger W. "Language Evidence in Distinguishing Pilot Error from Product Liability." Originally appeared in the *International Journal of the Sociology of Language,* Vol. 100/101. Copyright © 1993. Reprinted by permission of Mouton de Gruyter.

Southard, Bruce and Al Muller. "Blame It on Twain: Reading American Dialects in *The Adventures of Huckleberry Finn.*" Originally appeared in the *Journal of Reading,* Vol. 36, No. 8. Copyright © 1993 International Reading Association. Reprinted with permission.

Spector, Janet E. "Phonemic Awareness Training: Application of Principles of Direct Instruction." From *Reading & Writing Quarterly,* Vol. 11 (pp. 37–51). Published by Taylor & Francis. Copyright 1995. Reproduced with permission. All rights reserved.

Stageberg, Norman C. "Ambiguity in College Writing (To a College Freshman)." From *Introductory Readings on Language,* 4th ed, edited by Wallace L. Anderson and Norman C. Stageberg. Copyright © 1975 Norman C. Stageberg. Reprinted by permission of June S. Stageberg.

Tannen, Deborah. "The Power of Talk: Who Gets Heard and Why." From the *Harvard Business Review* (Sept.–Oct. 1995). Reprinted by permission of *Harvard Business Review.* Copyright © 1995 by the President and Fellows of Harvard College. All rights reserved.

Thieme, Paul. "The Indo-European Language." Originally appeared in *Scientific American,* Vol. 199, No. 4. (Oct. 1958). Reprinted with permission. Copyright © 1958 by Scientific American, Inc. All rights reserved.

Wolfram, Walt. "Beyond Black English: Implications of the Ann Arbor Decision for Other Non-Mainstream Varieties." From *Reactions to Ann Arbor: Vernacular Black English and Education,* edited by Marcia Farr Whiteman. Copyright © 1980 Center for Applied Linguistics. Reprinted by permission.

Wolfson, Nessa. "Compliments in Cross-Cultural Perspective." 1981, *TESOL Quarterly,* Vol. 15 (pp. 117–124). Copyright 1981 by Teachers of English to Speakers of Other Languages. Reprinted with permission.

Wolkomir, Richard. "American Sign Language: 'It's Not Mouth Stuff—It's Brain Stuff.'" Reprinted from *Smithsonian,* July 1992. Copyright © 1992 Richard Wolkomir. Reprinted by permission of the author.

Index

DATE DUE